Long Time
No See
Magic Hour

SUSAN ISAACS

Grafton

HarperCollins*Publishers*
77–85 Fulham Palace Road
Hammersmith, London W6 8JB

This omnibus edition published in 2004
by HarperCollins*Publishers*

Long Time No See
Copyright © Susan Isaacs 1991

Magic Hour
Copyright © Susan Isaacs 1991

A catalogue record for this book
is available from the British Library

ISBN 0 007 71197 2

Typeset in Bembo by Palimpsest Book Production Limited,
Polmont, Stirlingshire

Printed and bound in Great Britain by
Mackays of Chatham plc, Chatham, Kent

Long Time
No See

To Larry Ashmead,
my editor and my friend, with love.

———

Acknowledgments

I sought advice and information from the people listed below. All of them gave it freely and cheerfully. I am grateful for their generosity and hope they will understand that on the occasions when their facts did not fit the needs of my fiction, I gave the facts the heave-ho: Michael Adler, Jennifer Stern Bernbaum, Paul Blackman, Kevin Caslin, Mona Castro, Gerard Catanese, Cesar Collier, Jr., Teena Deocales, Jonathan Dolger, Frank Guidice, Lawrence Iason, Robert M. Kaye, Robert W. Kenny, Erica Johanson, Edward M. Lane, Susan Lawton, Chris McCandless, Alice T. McGillion, Robert McGuire, Robert G. Morvillo, Marcia Riklis, John Royster, Cynthia Scott, Lisa Bochner Sims, Greg Suridis, William Wald, Roger Widmann, Jay Zises, and Susan Zises.

As always, I am grateful to the staff of the Port Washington (N.Y.) Public Library.

Owen Laster has represented me for more than fifteen years. He is a splendid agent and a great man.

My editor, Larry Ashmead, is a legend. He is revered for his instinct, admired for his ability, and adored for his humanity by everyone in publishing. What a guy! What a mensch!

The following people made generous contributions to charities. Their prize (I hope they will find it so) was to have a character in this novel named for them: Susan Viniar, Cecile Rabiea, Andrea Leeds, and Dana Friedman for her mother, Zelda Friedman. Beth Cope became a character because she was exuberant, goodhearted, and got me to the train on time.

Elizabeth J. Carroll's research for this novel is a book in itself, and a well-written one at that. Liz is not only marvelously smart, she is creative, tenacious, and patient.

My assistant, Michelle E. Goldberg, is a blessing in my life. A list of laudatory adjectives to describe her would run pages, so let me briefly say that she is kind, intelligent, intuitive, cheerful, thorough, indefatigable, and diplomatic. She is also great fun.

My children and their spouses give me love, warmth, support, humor, and editorial advice. An infinity-infinity's worth of gratitude to Leslie Stern and Andrew Abramowitz and Elizabeth and Robert Stoll. Thanks also to my grandson, Nathan Henry Abramowitz, for pure joy.

Lastly, my love and appreciation to my first reader and my one and only, Elkan Abramowitz. He is still the best person in the world.

SUSAN ISAACS is the author of nine novels, including *Red, White and Blue* and *Compromising Positions*. She lives on Long Island, New York, with her husband.

Chapter One

On an unseasonably warm Halloween night, while I was reading a snappy treatise on Wendell Willkie's support of FDR's war policies and handing out the occasional bag of M&M's to a trick-or-treater, the fair-haired and dimpled Courtney Logan, age thirty-four, *magna cum laude* graduate of Princeton, erstwhile investment banker at Patton Giddings, wife of darkly handsome Greg, mother of five-year-old Morgan and eighteen-month-old Travis, canner of peach salsa, collector of vintage petit point, and ex-president of Citizens for a More Beautiful Shorehaven vanished from Long Island into thin air.

Odd. Upper-middle-class suburban women with Rolexes and biweekly lip-waxing appointments tend not to disappear. Though I had never met her, Courtney sounded especially solid. Less than a year before, there had been a page one feature in the local paper about her new business. StarBaby produced videos of baby's first year. 'I thought it would succeed because I knew in my heart of hearts there were thousands just like me!' Courtney was quoted as saying. 'It all started when Greg and I were watching a video we'd made of Morgan, our oldest. Fifteen minutes of Morgan staring at the mobile

in her crib! A beautiful, intelligent stare, but still ...
After that, another fifteen of her sucking her thumb!
Not much else. Suddenly it hit me that we'd never
taken out the videocam for Travis, our second, until
he was six months old!' (I've never been able to understand this generation's infatuation for using last names as
first names. Admittedly it's a certain kind of name: you
don't see little Greenberg Johnsons gadding about in sailor
suits.) Anyhow, Courtney went on: 'I was so sad. And
guilty! Look what we'd missed! That's when I thought,
it would be so great if a professional filmmaker could
have shown up once a month and made a movie starring
my son!'

Though not unmindful of the *Shorehaven Beacon*'s
aggressively perky style, I sensed Courtney Bryce Logan
was responsible for at least half those exclamation points.
Clearly, she was one of those incorrigibly upbeat women
I have never been able to comprehend, much less be.
She'd left a thrilling, high-powered job in Manhattan.
She'd traded in her brainy and hip investment-banking
colleagues for two tiny people bent on exploring the
wonders inside their nostrils. And? Did even a single
tear of regret slide down her cheek as she watched her
children watching *Sesame Street*? Was there the slightest
lump in her throat as the 8:11, packed with her Dana
Buchman-suited contemporaries, chugged off to the city?
Nope. Apparently, for can-do dames like Courtney, being
a full-time mom was full-time bliss. Ambivalence? Please!
Retirement was merely a segue into a new career, motherhood, another chance to strut their stuff.

However, what I liked about her was that she spoke

about Shorehaven not just with affection but with appreciation, with familiarity with its history. Well, all right, with its myths. She mentioned to the reporter that one of the scenic backgrounds StarBaby used was our town dock. She said: 'Walt Whitman actually wrote his two-line poem "To You" right there!' In truth, Courtney was just perpetuating a particularly dopey local folktale, but I felt grateful to her for having considered our town (and our Island-born poet) important.

I think I even said to myself, Gee, I should get to know her. Well, I'm a historian. I have inordinate warmth for anyone who invokes the past in public. My working hours are spent at St Elizabeth's College, mostly squandered in history department shriek-fests. I am an adjunct professor at this alleged institution of higher learning, a formerly all-female, formerly nun-run, formerly first-rate school across the county border in the New York City borough of Queens. Anyhow, for two and a half seconds I considered giving Courtney a call and saying hi. Or even Hi! My name is Judith Singer and let's have lunch. But like most of those assertive notions, it was gone by the end of the next heartbeat.

Speaking of heartbeats . . . Before I get into Courtney Logan's stunning disappearance and the criminal doings surrounding it, I suppose a few words about my situation wouldn't hurt. I am what the French call *une femme d'un certain âge*. In my case, the *âge* is fifty-four, a fact that usually fills me with disbelief, to say nothing of outrage. Nonetheless, although I still have the smooth olive skin, dark hair, and almond-shaped eyes of a mature extra in a Fellini movie, my dewy days are over. My children are in their twenties. Kate is a lawyer, an associate in the corporate department of Johnson, Bonadies and Eagle, a Wall Street firm whose founding partners drafted the boilerplate of the restrictive covenants designed to keep my grandparents out of their neighborhoods. Joey works in the kitchen of an upscale Italian deli in Greenwich Village making overpriced mozzarella cheese; he is also film critic for a surprisingly intelligent, near-insolvent Web 'zine called *night*.

As for me, I have been a widow for two years. My husband, Bob, the king of crudités, flat of belly and firm of thigh, a man given to barely suppressed sighs of disappointment whenever he saw me accepting a dessert menu from a waiter (which, okay, I admit I never declined), died at age fifty-five, one-half day after triumphantly finishing the New York Marathon in four hours and twelve minutes. One minute he was squeezing my hand in the emergency room, a reassuring pressure, but I could see the fear in his eyes. As I squeezed back, he slipped away. Just like that. Gone, before I could say, Don't worry, Bob, you'll be fine. Or, I love you, Bob.

Except when the love of your life actually isn't the love of your life, the loss still winds up being devastating. Golden memories? No, only vague recollections of passionate graduate-school discussions and newlywed love-making fierce enough to pull the fitted sheet off the bed. Except those times had blurred in direct proportion to the length of the marriage, and after more than a quarter century together, Bob and I had wound up with sporadic pleasant chats and twice-a-month sex that fit neatly between the weather forecast and the opening credits of *Nightline*.

4

But back to Courtney Logan. 'Something's very, very wrong with this disappearance business,' I announced to my friend Nancy Miller a few days later. We were strolling around Gatsby Plaza, an upscale shopping center named, without a trace of irony, for Fitzgerald's nouveau riche character. It was one of those places that offers the woman who longs to spend two thousand dollars for a handbag a myriad of venues; it also provides the setting in which passersby, with one discerning blink, can acknowledge not just handbag owner's status, but her worth.

Anyway, the evening was lovely, clear, although too balmy for early November. The early stars were outshone only by the twinkly lights wrapped around the trunks and branches of the slim, pampered trees that sparkled Christmasly all year round. The air, heavy with the pungent autumnal scent of designer chrysanthemums, felt thick and humid, as though it had been shipped from the greenhouse along with the mums. Supposedly, we were on our way to a restaurant. For me, six-thirty is dinnertime. For Nancy, it's late lunch. Naturally, we were nowhere near a grilled salmon.

She'd halted in front of a store window, transfixed by a dress, a clingy, tubular thing in white cashmere with a hood. It was displayed on one of those chichi mannequins. This one had a barbed-wire head and Ping-Pong-ball-sized breasts that, for some reason, had nipples so prominent they looked like a pair of teeny Uzis.

'You like that dress?' I demanded.

'I more than like it,' she replied. Her response came out something like 'Ah mo thun lak it.' Although Nancy had rarely been back to her native Georgia in thirty years, she'd clung to its syrupy accent, convinced, correctly, that it added to her charm. 'I *love* it.'

'It's a white cylinder.'

'That is the point,' she replied, too patiently.

'It probably costs a fortune,' I warned.

'Of course it costs a fortune!'

'With that hood, you'll look like one of your white trash Klan relatives.'

She gave one of her sighs of Christian forbearance. 'You have several areas of competence, Judith. Haute couture is not among them.'

'What *do* you think about Courtney Logan just vanishing?' I persisted as she was pulling open the heavy door to the shop. It was the Thursday after the disappearance, a night the stores stayed open until nine.

'She probably had some kind of secret life,' Nancy said offhandedly. 'That white dress in the window,' she murmured to a saleswoman who, naturally, had walked straight to her after passing right by me, as though my wearing a not-genuine camel's-hair coat had rendered me invisible. The woman took Nancy's measure in a single flutter of her eye-lashes, each one of which appeared to be individually mascaraed, after which she rested her chin on the pad of her index finger. Her long, squared-off nails were the color of prunes. (I, for one, find fingernails with right angles strangely disturbing.) A true size eight, the saleswoman intoned. Nancy, who had never been able to exorcise completely her inner Southern Belle, said nothing, merely lowering her eyes with sweeter-than-molasses-pie modesty: I concur. The woman left on her mission.

'What the hell is a "true" size eight?' I inquired. 'As

opposed to what? A false size eight? Do sixes and tens try to pass?'

'I thought you wanted to discuss that Courtney woman.'

'I do,' I quickly answered.

'There's nothing to discuss.'

'Your arteries are hardening.'

'You do loathe reality, don't you?' Nancy observed. 'Not that I blame you. Reality is hardly ever amusing. But my guess as to what happened is, Courtney Logan, woman of mystery, ran off with her kitchen contractor.' She shook her head. 'So fucking tedious. All these broads searching for meaning with anything that has eight inches.'

'First of all, there's no indication that Courtney had anyone –'

'How do you know she didn't?' Nancy challenged.

'I don't. But women like her don't just disappear into the night. If she wanted to leave, she'd confide in a friend, talk to a matrimonial lawyer . . . tell her husband directly, for God's sake. She was hardly some passive-aggressive wimpette. She'd been an investment banker. Even if she were going to run off, would she just bring her little girl home from trick or treating, drop her off, and leave without a word?'

'What should she do, take the kid along?' Nancy crossed her slender arms over her true size eight chest, clearly miffed I was not anticipating the arrival of The Dress with sufficient enthusiasm.

'Nancy, focus: I've read everything about this and seen whatever they have on TV.'

'For me,' she declared, 'this case is mildly interesting. For you, it's unhealthy. I don't like seeing you –'

'Relax. I'm fine! Listen, this is what seems to have happened: Courtney brings the little girl home. She says to the au pair: "I forgot something. I just have to run to Grand Union for a minute." Then she *doesn't come back.*' I chewed my lip for a moment. 'Have you heard any gossip or about anything the paper *hasn't* printed?'

Several years earlier Nancy had given up freelance writing to become first an assistant, then an associate editor of 'Viewpoints,' *Newsday*'s op-ed pages. Before she could even tell me she was too overwhelmed with work to listen to reporters' gossip, a blatant lie, the saleswoman returned. She carried the hanger aloft. The white dress wafted in the breeze she created. Together, she and Nancy fingered the hem reverently, in the manner Catholics might touch the Shroud of Turin. Then off they strode toward the dressing room.

Halfheartedly, I leafed through a rack of gray clothes which appeared designed to fit a Giacometti sculpture and thought about Courtney. According to both *Newsday* and Channel 12, the Long Island all-news cable station, no one had seen her at the supermarket or in its parking lot. That was not in the least remarkable, as the market was about a mile and a half from her house, and her car, a 1998 Land Rover, was later found right where it usually was, in the garage. Not one neighbor had seen or heard anything unusual. That was no big deal either. In that part of town, Shorehaven Farms, the houses stood at least an acre apart.

The following day, an announcement was made in the middle school and high school's homeroom classes requesting anyone who had been trick or treating in Shorehaven Farms between five and six P.M. – the time the au pair believed Courtney left for the supermarket – to please come to the main office ASAP. A few minutes before three, after a proffer of full immunity was broadcast over the PA, six juniors who had spent a productive night toppling mailboxes finally came forward. All swore they had seen nothing of Courtney.

Nancy returned from the dressing room, gray-green eyes shining, cheeks aglow. It was clear the dress had done for her precisely what she'd hoped, an event that has not yet occurred in my life. But then, Nancy is one of those natural . . . Well, not quite beauties. One of those women in their fifties who remain natural lovelies, all peaches-and-cream skin and long legs and auburn hair and huge eyes and wasp-waistedness, although the last had been facilitated by Jason J. Mittelman, M.D., F.A.C.S., Long Island's premier plastic surgeon, and his gluttonous liposuction machine. 'The husband,' Nancy postulated.

'Feh.'

'What do you mean, "feh"?'

'Too obvious,' I told her.

'You're clearly not as bright as you think you are. It happens to be a thesis that's so obvious it's actually subtle.'

'Wrong,' I informed her. 'If there's a shred of proof they would have arrested him.' Then I mused: 'I wonder what they actually have, if anything.'

'Judith, you're not going to –'

'Please! Of course not. I'm just wondering. It's a sign of intellectual curiosity, not that you would know. Now what about the husband?'

9

'Somebody Logan.'

'Greg Logan,' I said encouragingly.

'Well, you asked if I'd heard any gossip,' Nancy went on, tossing her head back so her hair flopped prettily, the southern belle gesture that accompanies any reaction from mildly pissed off to utterly hysterical. 'I did hear one thing. He did not come into this world as Gregory Logan. He changed his name from – Are you ready?' I nodded. 'Greg *Lowenstein*.' She began to spell it for me.

'Don't waste your breath,' I interrupted. 'So big deal. People anglicize their names. Three generations ago half the Eastern Europeans and a quarter of the Italians who came through Ellis Island –'

'Greg's father is Fancy Phil Lowenstein. The gangster. The one who wears all that jewelry. He's the guy who brokered the truce between the Italian mob and Russian Mafia and he's this close' – she held up her index and middle fingers so they looked glued together – to the Gambellos.'

I switched from chewing my lip to gnawing my knuckle for a while. 'So what are you getting at?' I was finally inquiring just as the saleswoman came into view. A garment bag with Nancy's KKK robe was hooked over her index finger; her other hand held the sales receipt and charge card. As she seemed to be advancing at the pace of a bride coming down the aisle, I kept going. 'Are you saying some two-bit hood with an asinine nickname was dispatched to throttle Courtney Logan, the mother of Fancy Phil Lowenstein's grandchildren, and dump her body in Long Island Sound?'

'In Fancy Phil's circle,' she replied, 'that's a quickie divorce.'

What Nancy did not reply, but which I learned when I picked up the papers from the driveway the next morning, was that *Newsday* was going with Greg Logan's pedigree as their front page, along with a photograph of Greg carrying his small son and holding his daughter's hand, heading toward a BMW in the driveway. The picture might have been taken with a telephoto lens because Greg did not look intruded upon and outraged. Merely sad. Possibly exhausted. Good-looking, though not conventionally; his face was more valentine-shaped than standard rectilinear Wheaties box. Still, with his high cheekbones and thick, dark, upslanting eyebrows, he seemed intriguing in a slightly Genghis Khan way, even though the perpetually off newspaper color gave his skin that odd tone which makes people look as if they belong to a race with mauve skin.

Fancy Phil's picture — a black-and-white mug shot — was inset. He did not look like a Calvin Klein model. The headline made a semi-clever reference to 'family,' which anyone more worldly than Travis the Toddler would know was intended to mean not only a group of people related by ancestry, marriage, or adoption but also the old *la famiglia* so beloved by Mafia genre movies — dialogue inevitably accompanied by glasses of Chianti held high by men with inordinately hairy arms.

The *New York Times*, naturally, buried the story in the depths of the Metro section, allotting it three short, untitillating paragraphs. The *Shorehaven Beacon*, which was tossed onto driveways on its customary Friday, said nothing new about the Lowenstein connection, only that a 'spokesperson for the Logan family' asked for the community to pray that Courtney would turn up '"alive and well."' What the *Beacon* did print was the photo of Courtney they'd run earlier with their original feature on StarBaby. It was captioned: 'WHERE IS SHE?'

In the picture, Courtney, wearing slacks and a sweater set and an open, friendly smile, leans against a tree in front of what seemed to be a pretty nifty Georgian-style colonial. It was hard to tell precisely what she looked like because the *Beacon* is printed on such tissuey stock – the sort used for toilet paper in Second World countries – that the ink was always smudgy. Her nose and eyes, scrunched up in the act of smiling, offered too much nostril and too little eye; it was hard to read her expression. But her dimples were so deep that, even under the sad circumstances, I found myself smiling back. Her blond, shoulder-length hair was surprisingly full and wavy, more Grand Ole Opry than Princeton, although perhaps it had just been the humidity.

'Where is she?' took over the town. In the bakery, a neighbor gazed covetously at a cheesecake while proclaiming Courtney the victim of a serial killer. Leaning against the Shorehaven Triplex's popcorn machine – not cleaned since the Carter Administration – the kid behind the counter held a monster cup of Sprite and opined that Courtney Logan was an FBI agent, undercover to get evidence on the Logan-Lowensteins, and, at that precise moment, was probably being debriefed in Washington. Or maybe dead. In my book group the favorite theory held that Courtney's body was in the trunk of some hood's Lincoln Continental, courtesy of Fancy Phil, who wanted his son to marry some other Jewish gangster's daughter from Scarsdale, thus creating an unstoppable

Long Island–Westchester organized crime axis. (This was no more idiotic than their interpretation of *Mrs Dalloway*.) At work, the perpetually overwrought history department secretary suggested in her usual choked voice that maybe the au pair had buried Courtney alive in a graveyard, *where nobody would think to look for her.*

For the next few weeks, with increasing desperation, I read the papers and listened to the news hoping for a driblet of information about the Courtney Logan case. But Courtney had disappeared from the media as completely as she had from Shorehaven. People who'd only wanted to gossip nonstop about the Logans went back to warring over the 'No Right Turn on Red' sign on Main Street and Harborview Road: Neighbors shook fists at neighbors at Town Hall meetings over whether the sign was a prudent traffic control measure or an edict that violated the due process clause of the U.S. constitution. Who else could I carry on with about the mystery? My children were busy being adults. Nancy suddenly had even less free time than usual, having tumbled for her new Jaguar mechanic. My other friends were involved with their own less interesting, less adulterous affairs.

I was so hard up for someone with whom to analyze the Courtney case that I actually wound up trying to discuss it with Smarmy Sam, aka Samuel P.B. Braddock III, the department chair. As always, because he thought of himself as a patrician and me as his inferior, the Smarm had simply pushed open my office door without knocking and stuck in his head. With his limp-lidded eyes and awesome overbite, this was no treat. He looked as if a couple of crocodile genes had glommed onto his double helix. 'I'd liiiike an answer,' he was saying. Well, he'd come to my office to again try to persuade me that teaching an additional two classes of America from Reconstruction to the Cold War in the spring was not just good for the commonweal, but for me as well.

'Before we get to that,' I said with unseemly animation, 'did you happen to hear that a woman from my town vanished into thin air?' Before Sam could get a word in edgewise, I offered a synopsis of what had been reported.

Sam understood that before he had a chance at my jumping at his offer, he'd have to let me jabber. 'Is this Greg Loooogan a suspect?' He spoke more in a honk than a voice, that lockjaw Long Island accent still extant among polo players, random debutantes, and fakers. 'By the by, is this Logan related to the Logans of Oyster Bay?' Sam inquired.

'No. He's related to Fancy Phil Lowenstein, a mob guy. Actually, Fancy Phil's his father.'

'Oh.' The Smarm, predictably, was doing his best to hide that he was appalled by the likes of me. His best, as usual, was not good enough. He was a man who not only taught American history, but believed he owned it. An ambulatory anachronism in our age of diversity, Sam was an East Coast WASP who not only thought he and his ilk were better than, say, me and my ilk – or anybody's ilk – but also believed we needed constant reminders of what our place was, for our own good. Was his accent the real thing? Was he genuinely wellborn? None of us had a clue. Well, he did keep his pens in a mug with a St Paul's insignia and he managed to work the phrase 'preparing at Sint Pol's' into a sentence at least once a week. Naturally,

14

the entire department was on continuous Sint Pol's alert, all sworn to report an occurrence the second it passed the two-dimensional lines that were his lips.

'Caaaan we return to the business at hand?' Sam asked. 'Your class load, or, if I may be so bold, your lack of it?'

So my need to talk about Courtney and what had happened to her was, yet again, frustrated. After the Smarm left, I told myself it was better he wasn't interested. Many mysteries in life remain unsolved. No matter how much I yearned, it would not be productive for me to try to insert myself into a situation that was none of my concern, even though every fiber of my being, and I had a fair number of fibers, cried out to do precisely that.

A few words of explanation might be appropriate here. Here they are: I am passionate about whodunits. The fictional kind. Hand me a Robert Parker novel, a John Dickson Carr locked-room mystery, even one I've read three times before, and you'll be giving me the gift of pleasure. But I love real-life whodunits more. About twenty years ago, as I was passing over to the bleak side of thirty-five, at a time when my now-lawyer daughter and film-critic son were little more than tykes, a local periodontist, M. Bruce Fleckstein, was murdered. I recall hearing about it on the radio and thinking: Who could have done such a thing? Before I knew it, I was investigating, and feeling thrillingly alive.

I am not sure why. Maybe it had to do with my sense of fair play − trying to bring the scales of justice back into balance. Murder is an attack on the body politic as well as on a particular body, and perhaps I felt the need to set things aright in my home town. Maybe I liked solving the puzzle,

15

or maybe I was simply drawn to the dark side of the street. Believe it or not, I actually was instrumental in determining just who the killer was. But in the course of my detective work, I came into contact with a real homicide detective, Lieutenant Nelson Sharpe of the Nassau County Police Department.

To make a long story short, I had an affair with him. That was it. Six months of faithlessness in a twenty-eight-year marriage. Even for a historian like me, aware of the persistence of the past, it should have been ancient history – except I fell in love with Nelson. And he with me. For a time we even talked about leaving our spouses, getting married. We simply couldn't bear being without each other. Not just for the erotic joy, and there was plenty of that, but for the great fun we had together. But even more than my secret belief that a marriage that rises from the ashes of two other marriages is doomed from the start was our mutual, acknowledged awareness of what our leaving would do to our children. At the time Kate was six and Joey four. Nelson had three kids of his own. So he stayed with his wife June and I remained with Bob Singer. Nelson and I never saw or spoke to each other. For almost twenty years.

And then, less than a year before, we'd caught a glimpse of each other. For barely an instant. Unplanned. Nelson looked even more shocked than I felt. All he could manage was a brief nod as he kept walking. The next morning at eight-thirty – the time he used to call me knowing Bob would be on his way to the city – my phone rang.

However, the three seconds of seeing him and that very short phone conversation proved, for me, three seconds

16

too long and one talk too many. After Bob's death, I wasn't exactly going to win any mental health awards. It took me months to get over that fleeting encounter with Nelson. I lifted the phone to call him a couple of thousand times. The only reason I hung up before the connection was actually made was that he was a cop and could no doubt trace any call. Naturally I couldn't sleep. Some internal motor kept racing. Some inner voice wouldn't stop screaming Fight or Flight; all that held me back from fighting or fleeing was a cloud of despondency so thick I couldn't see my way through it. Since I was already the Zoloft Queen, I tried to cure my ills with more therapy. Relaxation cassettes. Self-help books. A yoga video. Ben & Jerry's Chunky Monkey. Finally, what helped was time. So no more detecting for me. I'd vowed as much to Nancy. The previous week, when I discovered my Jeep straying onto Bluebay Lane, the street on which the Logans lived, I made a U-turn and drove straight home.

With Smarmy Sam gone, I turned back to my computer screen. There were the same three paragraphs of what was supposed to be a seven-hundred-fifty-word review of a book about the Glass-Steagall Act I'd promised to email two weeks earlier. Yet instead of a fourth paragraph, I typed an outline of what I knew from the papers, radio, and TV:

GREG . . . SHOULD HE BE SUSPECT IN COURTNEY DISAPPEARANCE?
1. Spouse usually 1st suspect.
2. Greg owns small chain of take-out places called Soup Salad Sandwiches.

One in Huntington. Rest on the
South Shore.

A. Smart. Graduated from Brown, MBA from
Columbia.

B. Got into food business when father, Fancy
Phil, gave him 2 fast food franchise stores in
N.J. called Mr Yummy's. Sold them for the
$$$ to start own business from scratch.

3. SSS: Stores sell 3 varieties of soups, salads, and
sandwiches daily. Big on quality ingredients.
Stores in upper-middle-income towns.

4. An au pair living with Logans. University
student. Depending on which account, from
Austria or Germany. She was one Courtney
told, 'I forgot something. I just have to run
to Grand Union for a minute.' Any funny
business with au pair and Greg??????

I also noted all the information I could recall about
Courtney and her company, StarBaby. The following
morning, on my way to work, I became one of those
pitiful sensation sniffers and drove (shamefully slowly)
down Bluebay Lane. It was the day before Thanksgiving.
I should have spent those extra minutes at home with an
orange so I could toss a few dozen strands of zest along with
a tablespoon of Grand Marnier into the canned cranberry
sauce – an old family recipe. Instead I found myself
scrutinizing Greg and Courtney's red-brick colonial.

The house was set well back from the street on a velvet
carpet of lawn. On each side of the dark green front door,
three white columns stood tall and proud. The shutters

were painted that same old-money green. Nevertheless, despite its classic Georgian features, the scale of the house was slightly off. It was set back on an acre, and though the builder had wisely not hacked down the property's impressive old trees, the Logans' place seemed overly large for a single family. It looked more like the Romance-languages department at a New England college.

In mysteries, it always annoys me when houses in which strange doings have occurred are described as 'strangely still.' What are they supposed to do? Cha-cha? Nevertheless, there was absolutely no sign of life in what the *Post*, obviously hoping to prevail in some tabloid alliteration competition, was calling the 'lush Lowenstein-Logan Long Island estate.' It really was strangely still. No BMW in the driveway today, no tricycle left out overnight. The curtains were drawn. A stubby flagpole over the door, the kind that displays those flags mail-order catalogs have managed to palm off on the public, was not flying the national colors of Pumpkinland or United States of Pilgrim Hats or whatever hideous banner suburbanites run up for Thanksgiving. However, if the *Post* could be trusted, Greg Logan was still in residence, having been 'advised by Nassau County police authorities to remain in the community.' Well, with Courtney having been missing for almost a month now, that advisement was no surprise.

The only surprise was that I had sunk so low that instead of going straight home after work to prepare what my kids referred to as Mom's Secret Sweet Potato Recipe (which, even with its optional canned crushed pineapple, was no different from the thirty million casseroles of marshmallow-covered golden glop that grace the tables of American households every fourth Thursday of November), I drove straight to the house of Mary Alice Mahoney Schlesinger Goldfarb. Nancy and I had known Malice since our college days at the University of Wisconsin, so I guess she was something between a longtime, unwelcome acquaintance to Nancy and a semifriend to me.

Mary Alice talked more than anybody in Greater New York and said the least. Was she annoying? Usually. Vacuous? Indubitably. Stupid? Probably. However, somehow her pea-brain was optimally structured for the absorption and retention of every item of Shorehaven gossip that flitted through the air, no matter how vague.

'Who's catering you?' Mary Alice inquired as we stood in her dining room. Her gold-and-white outfit, with its skintight pants and embroidered bolero jacket, would have looked better on a matador. I sensed it was the work of one of those avant-garde designers she had, sadly, grown to favor. Naturally, she was not cooking, but, as her third husband, Lance Goldfarb, urologist to the North Shore's best and brightest, was suburbane enough to understand, only first wives cooked.

Mary Alice, however, was preparing for the next day's feast. She leaned over her table (gleaming black wood with red and yellow glints, made from what was doubtless an endangered species in the Amazon rain forest), her long, thin fingers rearranging squashes, purple grapes that I guess were supposed to look slightly moldy, sprays of bittersweet, and some ruby-petaled flowers that looked like a cross section of female genitalia. The arrangement overflowed a sterling silver tureen the size of a footbath. Mary Alice's engaged-to-Goldfarb ring, a diamond dazzler, sparkled in the genteel light of a Venetian chandelier.

'No one's catering for me,' I responded. 'I'm cooking.'

A saddened 'Oh' popped out from between her high-gloss lips, but she quickly put her index finger against them, as if she were a kindergartner who'd just been signaled to shush. For a woman halfway into her fifties, Malice had an astonishing repertoire of little-girl mannerisms. I knew what she was thinking: Bob had left me practically in the poorhouse, i.e., unable to afford a caterer who could bring in baby squabs stuffed with wild mushroom polenta which would be touted, by the caterer's Manhattan-actor-waiters, as much more authentically Native American than any turkey. However, poverty was not an issue for me. Bob had grown into the sort of man who could never resist a frolicsome lunch with an insurance actuary. He'd planned for everything except his own early death and had left me, though not rich, well fixed enough to spring for a squab or two.

But I repressed a powerful urge to babble a defensive: I *like* cooking my own food. Instead I asked: 'What's new?' Then, before she could utter her first word in what would be an exquisitely detailed description of how she was having her chinchilla jacket relined, I immediately tossed in a 'Oh, Mary Alice, I keep forgetting to ask . . . Has anyone seen Greg Logan around town?'

'Not that I've heard about,' she replied, pulling out one of her Empire dining-room chairs (from Husband Mahoney) and sitting. I did likewise, although the large Napoleonic bee design on the center of the burgundy damask of each seat had always seemed slightly menacing. 'But you know who *has* been seen around town?' She waited, patient. I was, too, so finally she pronounced: 'The

21

au pair! In the patisserie. Buying rye bread.' I noticed Mary Alice was still rolling her *R*s intermittently, so 'rye bread' came out vaguely Gallic; she'd recently returned from a weeklong urethra conference in Lyons with Husband Goldfarb. 'She was wearing what everyone was positive was an Hermès scarf.' She gave a humorless, monosyllabic laugh. 'You know what *that* means.' She rested her left arm on the table and, with her right fingertips, caressed the gold threads of what was either a leaf or a duckling embroidered on the jacket's sleeve.

'She knows how to accessorize?' I suggested.

'No. Most people were saying, Well, *we* know who's dipping into Courtney Logan's scarf drawer.'

She waited for me to respond, so I said 'Wow.' Actually, I was impressed with the notion of an entire drawer dedicated to scarves. Mine were kept in two Hefty One-Zips that resided with my nightgowns and a lifetime's collection of half-slips I couldn't bring myself to throw out.

'But then I heard, no, she isn't stealing. It was one of many, many, many *gifts.*' To make sure I understood, she added: 'From Greg Logan.'

'So people are saying he's taken up with the au pair?'

'Not now. *Before.*' Malice took a deep breath to compose herself after imparting this electrifying news. As for me, I'd already said Wow, and a gasp would have been extravagant, so I just sat quietly. 'Before Courtney disappeared,' Mary Alice explained. 'They say what happened is that Courtney came home with their little girl Morgan from trick or treating. One guess what she walked in on?'

'Greg Logan and the au pair?' She gave a knowing nod. I was still trying to get used to the notion that

'Morgan' had become more than a financial institution or a surname. It was what former investment bankers named their daughters. Then I asked, 'Where was their little boy during this liaison?' Mary Alice shrugged. 'And wasn't Greg at a business dinner in the city that night?' I went on, 'That's what I've been reading, that when Courtney didn't come back, the au pair made no attempt to call him. She just put the kids to bed and waited until he got home. Then she told him she didn't know where Courtney had gone.'

'Not according to my sources.'

'Who are your sources, Mary Alice?'

'Everybody.' She adjusted one of Husband Schlesinger's three-carat diamond-stud earrings. 'Everybody knows about them, Judith.'

'Well, let's say Courtney did walk in on that kind of a thing,' I conceded. 'What is she supposed to have done? Or what was done to her?'

'Ha!'

'They're saying Greg and the au pair murdered Courtney?'

'That's the number one theory. They did it, maybe to keep her from screaming or something and —'

'Where did they stash the little girl with a bagful of candy while they were murdering Courtney Logan?'

'I don't know.' Trying to appear blasé, she pretended to be absorbed in a cuticle, although knowing Malice, she could have been genuinely engrossed.

'And then?' I demanded.

'Well, it could be they buried the body someplace. Everyone said the police had a dog and they looked in the wooded area in back between the Logans' and — I think it's the Lanes' house, Judy and Ed. He's the ear, nose, and —'

'But they didn't find anything.'

'The other theory,' she said, recovering quickly, 'is that Greg's father, Mr Big, did something with the body. I mean, that's his meat and potatoes.' Mary Alice had the gift of unfortunate metaphor. 'Or . . . But not too many people believe this one.'

'What?'

'It's a psychoanalytic theory. You'll probably laugh.'

'Tell me, Mary Alice.'

'That Courtney was, you know, traumatized. She just ran off when she saw them together. And it was *so* traumatic she got amnesia. She could be anyplace, not knowing who she is. You've got to admit, that's better than being beaten to death or knifed or strangled or something by your own husband and a foreign au pair, for God's sakes, who then gets free range to your scarf drawer. And everything else, if you get what I mean.'

'How about this: Maybe Courtney went outside and met up with someone weird. Halloween's the one night of the year you have lots of people – a lot of them in masks – roaming around, even in the quietest neighborhoods.'

'But *everyone* says in this kind of thing, it's usually the husband. Isn't it?' Mary Alice reached over to her Thanksgiving centerpiece and tapped a sprig of bittersweet forward an eighth of an inch. '*Isn't it?*'

Isn't it? Sleeping with a homicide cop for six months does not qualify one as an expert on criminal detection. Neither does reading Maj Sjöwall/Per Wahlöö and Ed McBain police procedurals. Not even once having helped solve a murder. Still, if I hadn't distracted the ever-distractable Mary Alice Mahoney Schlesinger Goldfarb by inquiring what, as Thanksgiving hostess, she was going to wear (and then listening to her pleat by pleat description of an Issey Miyake skirt), I would have had to say yes, absolutely, it usually is the husband they suspect when the wife suddenly and inexplicably disappears.

Throughout that winter, I heard whispers and mutterings that Greg Logan's arrest was imminent. None of the rumors panned out. It wasn't that I forgot about Courtney. One bitter night, when the snow on the spruce outside my bedroom window grew so heavy that my light sleep was broken with the ominous crack of a limb about to crash, I lay in bed knowing in my heart that she hadn't been grabbed by some monstrous Halloween deviate and was being held against her will, but that she was lying in some shallow, icy, suburban grave. I'd think about her children: One day they'd had a mother who adored them. The next day she was no more. Were these poor kids told Mommy will be back, or Gosh, honey, we don't know where Mommy is but we hope she'll call? Were they told anything?

But because it seemed there would be no conclusion to the Courtney case, it was easier to push it from my mind. I threw myself into work and lived for the times I'd see Kate and Joey or my friends. When I was by myself, mostly I thought about Bob. True, he and I hadn't had a fairy-tale marriage. Still, even when all that's left is polite conversation and low-wattage marital sex, you have to remember (I'd told myself during those years we were together) that once upon a time it *must* have been a love story. I guess I always half expected the plot would get moving again: Some incident will touch off a great conflict in our relationship. Then, lo and behold, not only will the air between us finally clear, but there'd be romance in it! The two of us will walk hand in hand into a sunset, happily ever after – or until one of us went gently into the night in our eighth or ninth decade. Imagine my surprise when he died before my eyes in the ER of North Shore Hospital.

So not only no husband. No prospect of another one. Not one more blind date, that was for sure, not after the two geriatric wonder boys Nancy had dubbed Old and Older. After Christmas break, I began to go out occasionally with Geoff, a postmodernist from the English department at St Elizabeth's. I rarely understood what he was talking about, his clothes smelled as if he patronized a discount dry cleaner, and unfortunately he had a healthy sex drive. No one else was knocking at my door.

I had long before disciplined myself not to think about Nelson Sharpe. And to dwell on the Courtney Logan case would be to invoke him: What would he make of all this? Would he be putting pressure on the husband? Would he be investigating other leads?

I didn't want to jeopardize again the life I'd fashioned for myself because, whatever it was, it worked. I had kids, friends, library and Blockbuster cards. I had a job that evoked remarks like, Gee, or Ooh, how intellectually stimulating. The truth was, my work occasionally had my mind. Never my heart.

So winter warmed into spring and early one evening in the middle of May I came home from St Elizabeth's and raced straight to the garden to cut lilacs. When I came back inside, in the way of so many people who live alone, I reflexively turned on the radio for company. My face was buried in my armful of lavender, purple, and white blooms and I was getting dopey on those first ecstatic sniffs. So it took a few seconds before I actually tuned into the sandpaper voice of Mack Dooley, the Logans' pool man. He was telling WCBS radio: 'Like, this morning, about eleven, I'm taking off the Logans' pool cover with this kid who works for me – you know, pump it out, acid-wash it, get it ready and –' The reporter did attempt a question but Dooley kept going. 'So listen. The cover's fine, tied down real tight like I left it in the middle of September when I closed them up. The kid and I are kind of rolling it back and I see something. I say, Holy – You know how big raccoons can get? Except for the life of me I can't figure out how even a raccoon could work its way under that cover. Well, that second I see, you know, it's . . . It's a body! Jeez. Believe it or not I'm still shaking.'

Chapter Two

The news about the body in Greg Logan's swimming pool consumed local TV and radio, a tristate info-blob engulfing any news about Al Gore's plummeting poll numbers or the raging wildfires in Los Alamos. Everyone was broadcasting: I heard about it at teeth-grinding length from my next-door neighbor, Chic Cheryl, in her skintight silver racewalking getup that highlighted each buttock as if it were a separate trophy. Mary Alice Mahoney Schlesinger Goldfarb left three breathless messages on my answering machine, during which I sent up three prayers of thanks for the invention of Caller ID.

I also heard from two of my colleagues at St Elizabeth's, from my doctoral adviser at NYU, and from Bob's college roommate, Claymore Katz, a criminal lawyer. Needless to say, postmodernist Geoff called; he wanted to know (a) Was it not beyond irony that the paradigmatic suburbanite was found dead in a backyard swimming pool, and (b) Did I want to see a revival of *Krapp's Last Tape*. I called his voice mail and retorted (a) I wasn't sure what lay beyond irony, and (b) No thanks. Nancy phoned from *Newsday*, but that was to verify I was actually home, not skulking about in Holmesian drag in a pathetic attempt to attract

28

the attention of a certain member of the Nassau County PD. Not one of them could add a single factlet to what I'd initially learned on the radio, although that didn't stop them (or me) from discussing it.

Late the following morning I was at my kitchen table grading my classes' final exams, determined to dismiss all thoughts of murder, mostly because I felt obliged to give my students a fair shake. The majority were either good kids or hardworking get-a-college-education retirees. None were born scholars. (The most elementary of my four essay questions, 'Describe the programs Franklin D. Roosevelt's first administration put forth to help "the forgotten man at the bottom of the economic pyramid,"' evoked answers as exhaustive as Darci Lundgren's 'FDR's Brain Trust' and Seymour Myron Bleiberman's 'emerg. banking bill + hire men for govt relief projects + helping farmers.') In the interest of full disclosure, I have to admit that once I achieved my goal, teaching history on the college level, I discovered a disturbing truth about myself: I didn't like to teach. What I wanted was to read history, or talk history, preferably with someone who knew more than I did.

After an hour I gave myself a coffee break, hopped onto the Web, and discovered that the Nassau County medical examiner had already completed the autopsy. He had determined (no doubt employing a procedure so revolting I wouldn't even begin to contemplate it) that the woman in the Logans' pool had died from a bullet in the head. The condition of the body indicated that death could have occurred around the time Courtney disappeared on Halloween night. Furthermore, his examination of dental records confirmed what all of us would have been glad to tell him: The body was indeed that of Courtney Logan. Then, thank God, the phone rang.

'Hey!' My son had such an astounding basso voice that, on hearing it, you half expected him to burst into 'Some Enchanted Evening.' Clearly this wasn't to be. Joey was not a Rodgers and Hammerstein kind of guy. 'Mom, did you hear? They found that woman. She was in her own pool, over in Shorehaven Farms!' For a cinéaste and ironist who never wore a color inappropriate for a state funeral, he sounded remarkably cheery. 'Did you know her?'

'No,' I said regretfully. 'I don't think I ever even saw her.' I set down my red pen atop a blue book on which I'd written a large *C*. Then – what the hell – I picked up the pen and added a conspicuous plus sign after the *C*. 'Isn't there some movie that begins with a body in a pool?' I mused.

'*Sunset Boulevard*,' he suggested in an overly gentle manner.

'It's just mild senility.' I chuckled but received not even a polite heh-heh in response. 'With . . . You know who I mean. William what's-his-name.'

'Holden.' An offspring's sigh of tedium is inaudible to all human ears except a parent's. Boring your child who, at one point in his or her life, found you unspeakably delightful is humbling. 'So what do you think?' Joey asked, slickly changing the subject before I could blurt out that the director was William Wyler instead of Billy Wilder and further humiliate myself. 'I mean, about the woman they found.'

'Her name was Courtney Logan,' I said.

'Who did it? The husband?'

'Only if he's a total moron.' Chewing the top of the pen for a moment, I debated whether to self-censor all talk of murder. I would probably become excessively enthused and knew from experience that giddiness in the postmenopausal was generally less than appealing to the recently postpubescent. Nevertheless, I found myself bubbling, 'Listen, kiddo, the *minute* a wife is missing, there's speculation about the husband's guilt. But let's assume for the sake of argument that Greg Logan, Brown graduate, is not self-destructive. And that he's smarter than Fred MacMurray in *Double Indemnity*. Okay? And let's also assume he plans a murder.'

'Okay,' Joey said in bright anticipation, the way he had when he was ten and I'd allowed him to see *Return of the Jedi* yet again.

'Now, I don't mean Greg actually sat down and plotted anything. Let's say it was a spur-of-the-moment crime of passion. But tell me, why would he stash his wife's body in the one spot where – *guaranteed* – she would be found the following May, if not earlier? And on his own property? Why not simply let her stay missing? Even if everyone assumed she was dead, no one would have the foggiest notion where she was.'

'So if there wasn't any body . . .' Joey thought aloud.

'Where's the physical evidence a murder was committed? Nowhere, that's where. All there'd be is a *belief* Courtney was dead. Everything I've ever read says it's very hard to get a conviction without a corpus delecti. But now her death – her *murder* – is a fact.'

'Except maybe this Greg guy *is* a total jerk,' Joey mused.

'Or some kind of psycho. Or okay, maybe it was temporary insanity but then he panicked and just wanted to get rid of her. Except once he calmed down, he couldn't figure out a way to fish her out of the pool.'

'Maybe,' I submitted, 'he didn't do it.'

'Maybe,' he countered, 'he did do it because it was part of some scheme.'

'Are you giving me an Oliver Stone conspiracy theory?'

'No. Listen, Mom. Maybe he was willing to take a huge risk, because he needed the body to get insurance money – except he needed a few months to make sure he'd covered up all his tracks. Or maybe it wasn't the husband. Maybe it was his old man, Gangster Guy, who ordered the hit.'

'Why? Because Courtney forgot to send him a birthday card? Joey, even if Fancy Phil Lowenstein wanted his daughter-in-law dead, is he going to deep-six her in the one place sure to incriminate his son?'

'Maybe Fancy Phil has issues with Greg.'

'Still, would he stash her where, God forbid, his grandchildren could conceivably see their mother's body?'

'You're talking as if Fancy is a normal human being. What if he's an animal? Do you think he'd care about his grandkids' mental health?'

A few minutes later, after tossing a few more theories back and forth and discussing whether the plot of *The Big Sleep* made any sense and agreeing that it probably didn't, we said our good-byes. I must have flaked out for a minute because when I glanced down, I noticed that pen was still in hand. Mine. And it had jotted:

1. Greg Logan?
2. au pair?
3. did Courtney have boyfriend???
4. enemy from Courtney's investment banking days?? or earlier??
5. Greg girlfriend??? + was she jealous???
6. stalker/psycho???
7. mob hit by Fancy Phil/Fancy Phil's enemies???

It was only then that I realized I'd been scribbling on an exam booklet of one Amanda Gerrity, a whispery, milk-white young woman with a distressing number of body parts pierced by studs and hoops. I ripped off the cover with my notes, transferred the C+, jotted an apology about spilled coffee. Trying not to think about the process of getting a silver ball embedded in one's tongue, I studied my list of possible perps. Back to work, I finally commanded myself. Crumpling Amanda's bluebook cover, I strode purposefully across the kitchen and lobbed it into the garbage.

Three hours later, by the time my daughter Kate called, I had lunched on suspicious three-day-old deli tuna salad and survived, and graded seven more exams.

'Mom,' Kate began efficiently. The law firm for which she worked billed two hundred and sixty dollars an hour for their second-year associates; as she'd always been an honorable child, she dispensed with gratuitous words like 'hi' when calling on office time.

'Hi, sweetheart!'

'I cannot believe you haven't called me,' she said.

'About what?'

'About who done it.' Kate sounded playful, a quality I was sometimes afraid she would lose practicing corporate law; Johnson, Bonadies and Eagle's clients did not sound like a pack of merry madcaps. Stretching the telephone cord until its curlicues became an almost straight line, I retrieved the red-penned list from the garbage. It smelled, not surprisingly, like suspicious three-day-old deli tuna salad. Holding it as far from my nose as I could, I read off the possibilities. 'What do your detective instincts tell you?' my daughter inquired.

'Hard to say. I have no sense of what the husband's like. Do you have time to talk now?'

'No problem,' she said, indulgent, generous.

'Well, there's an au pair, German or Austrian. Maybe she's gorgeous. Maybe she's Voof-voof the Dog-faced Girl. Who knows? But people are definitely gossiping about her and the husband. So far, though, no one's described her in any way except to say she's twenty-two.'

'Not a capital offense in New York,' Kate suggested leisurely, as though the debt restructuring of Southeast Pulp and Paper she'd been slaving over fourteen hours a day including weekends was a trivial detail she could attend to at her leisure.

I was about to continue down my list of possible perps when I had one of those belated 'aha!' moments. It was no coincidence, my children calling on the same day, wanting only to chat about Courtney Logan's murder. They'd had a conference, Kate and Joey, and had obviously concluded that with semester's end at St Elizabeth's imminent, there was nothing to keep me amused. Amused? More likely, the last time they'd seen me, a few days before on Mother's Day, they'd intuited the limitations of psychopharmacology. So here they were, my two good kids, demonstrating a way for me to get some life back in my life: get revved up about a murder. A few minutes later I gave my firstborn what I hoped was a reassuringly upbeat good-bye. Then I went searching for the Yellow Pages.

Two days later, Mack Dooley of Pools, Etc. was standing in my backyard, a very short man with a very long tape measure. 'I hope you're talking gunite, Mrs Singer.' As he spoke, he kept flapping back his hand again and again, ordering his assistant, a blond, buzz-cut, blank-eyed kid to move farther back with the tape measure to give me an idea of the length of the pool.

'Well, Mr Dooley –'

'Call me Mack,' he said cheerfully. For such a short man, he had remarkably long arms. Except for the lack of hair, he resembled those jolly chimpanzees in baseball caps who are perpetually being trotted onto TV by anthropologists to prove that human beings aren't the only primate with language and tool-making skills.

'As I told you on the phone,' I told him, 'I'm only *considering* a pool right now. I'm not ready to commit to –'

'Sure, sure, but with a place like yours –' Mack Dooley glanced back at the house. It's a Tudor-style of brick and stone with a fine mullioned bay window. It's not imposing, but solid, the sort of house Henry VII's favorite furrier might own. '– how could you go with vinyl?' He was not entirely successful in suppressing a shudder at that thought. 'Now, you're probably talking a lap pool, about four feet deep, right?' I nodded. 'And fifty feet long, although you could do sixty here easy and in the end you'd say, "Mack, thanks for pushing me to sixty."'

'Maybe you can give me estimates for both,' I suggested. I pulled back my head and eyed him. 'Were . . . Were you the one I saw on TV?' He nodded modestly, although his light eyes, bright against his tanned-to-leather skin, sparkled at the recognition. 'God, it must have been terrible for you, finding her like that.'

'Yeah, well, it was no treat. I mean, every couple of years, you open a pool and there's somebody's ex-cat. But trust me, nothing like this.'

'Were you able to see who it was?'

Mack Dooley shook his head. 'She was like floating – you okay, hearing this kind of thing?' I nodded encouragingly. 'Except what I saw was her back. At first I thought, This is some kind of big animal, a raccoon, or one of those eight-hundred-dollar big dogs – I forget what you call them – that drop dead when they're seven years old. But then I see, Sweet Jesus, it's a *person*. I could make out the back of her neck and a little of her ear. So I say to John –' he pointed with his chin at his assistant at the other end of the tape measure. '"Get out of here." Then I threw him my cell phone and I told him, "Get 911." You don't want a kid like him having to see something like that.'

'Was the body badly decomposed?'

'What can I tell you? She was facedown. But what I seen of her, you wouldn't call her composed.' Mack didn't appear to resent the questions. After three days of interrogation, not just from cops but from reporters and neighbors, he seemed to be resigned to the attention that comes with celebrity.

'Was she clothed?' I asked.

'Yeah, but what she was wearing didn't look so good either.'

'What was she wearing?'

He looped his thumbs over the waistband of his light-weight gray sweatpants, pursed his lips, and moved them left, right, left as he thought; this was a question no one seemed to have posed. 'Looked like some kind of jacket. My best guess? One of those blazers.'

'What color?'

'Hard to say. Probably used to be dark, but it was kind of faded. I guess from the chlorine. All I could see was the shape at first. The back. That's how come I thought: Raccoon? I didn't see the rest of her. You know how they say "dead man's float" when you're learning to swim?'

'Right.'

'Well, for some reason it wasn't like that with Mrs Logan. I couldn't see her arms and legs. They must have been hanging down in the water, and after – what is it? – all those months, the water isn't what they call crystal clear. Now don't think that's a problem for you, poolwise, Mrs Singer. All pools get algae and stuff over the winter no matter how much chemicals we dump in the fall. One acid-wash in May – takes hardly no time – and you'll have perfect water all summer.'

I had to admit, the notion of a pool was sounding not so ridiculous. Laps in the morning before work, laps in the evening. I could have unimaginably firm upper arms and be one of those women who wear sleeveless turtlenecks. I could have friends over for a swim and a barbecue, or drift alone on a float with a plastic cup of Chardonnay and watch

37

the sun set. My head began making up-and-down motions as if I were already saying yes to Mack Dooley. 'Did you know her?' I asked quickly, to divert attention from my bobbling head. 'Courtney Logan, I mean.'

'Yeah,' he said, 'because she was the one I had to deal with, putting in the pool. She signed us up for the maintenance, too.'

'What was she like?' I paused. 'I guess you've been asked that too many times.'

'I don't mind,' Mack replied graciously. 'She was really nice. But businesslike. Know what I mean? A lady. Hello, how are you, did you have a good weekend – that kind of stuff. Not snotty or snooty or whatever you call it, like some of them – I hope you'll pardon me, but you're not one of them ... The younger ones. The yuppie ladies. They leave the business world to raise their kids, but you know what? They still gotta show you what big shots they are. They're so ... tough. Not Mrs Logan. She was just nice to deal with.'

'Was she a hard bargainer? Did she accept your first price?' He seemed to hesitate. 'Don't worry,' I reassured him. 'If I decide on a pool, you'll make a profit. I'm not such a good negotiator.' He pressed a button and the tape measure whizzed back into its receptacle. The blond kid moseyed back to the truck.

Mack Dooley smiled again, a pleasant, crooked-toothed smile in an orthodonticized universe. 'She had one shrewd business brain, I'll tell you that. Every time the husband was ready to sign on the dotted line, she'd say to him, "Greg, let's sleep on this." But in the nicest way. She handled herself so nice you couldn't resent her.'

I thought back to the photograph the *Beacon* had published: Courtney *had* looked genuinely nice. 'Did the husband seem brow-beaten by her?'

He shook his head. 'I don't think so. I kind of assumed he was more the easygoing type.'

'Did the police want to know all about him.'

'Did they ever!'

'Like what?'

'Did he have a temper. Did I ever see them fight. How they got along.'

'How did they get along?'

'As far as I could see, good.' He rubbed his chin thoughtfully. His beard made a sandpaper sound. 'What else? Oh, did I notice anything between him and the foreign girl who watched their kids.' I raised my eyebrows in what I hoped was a subtle query. 'I saw her a few times, with the little girl, by the pool. Quiet type. Not what they call a looker. With the hair that kind of separates into strings. Like a mop just before it dries. Except – I don't know – maybe it's how girls' hair is supposed to be these days and it's really pretty.'

'What did you tell the police when they asked you about this au pair and Greg Logan?'

'The truth. I didn't see nothing. If I was Logan, I guarantee you, I wouldn't be tempted with such a nice wife, blond hair, dimples. Except the girl didn't have a bad shape. And listen, how the heck can you tell what's doing in some other guy's heart? Right?'

Right. And three days later on a gloomy Sunday afternoon, with the sky a ceiling of gray steel, I said zero to Nancy about hearts or about Mack Dooley. I didn't want to listen to another lecture on what she'd decided was my fixation not on solving a puzzle – figuring out who–dunit – but on Nelson Sharpe. Instead I politely inquired: 'Besides looking at it, does anyone actually *use* a gazebo?' We were making our way through the acre and a half of woods on the side of her house, taking minuscule elflike leaps to avoid the poison ivy and nettles that were already choking to death the spring wildflowers. 'Besides, if it's stuck all the way out here, you wouldn't see it from the house.' We turned to look behind us. Only a dark shingled edge of the roof of the Millers' sprawling Victorian was visible through the newly leafed trees. 'I guess you could bring a book out here. But would you want to read on a wooden bench or one of those wrought iron garden chairs that make your ass numb? Plus –' I glanced up at the lofty oaks, maples, and other assorted trees – 'in this light, what could you read? The first two lines of an eye chart?'

'I need *someplace*.' Nancy sounded less huffy than desperate. 'Larry's going to trash the house again.' Every five or six years her husband, an architect, would be gripped by a new artistic vision: *This* is what the world should look like. Then the grand old house's guts would be ripped out and replaced – with all white walls, floors, and furniture. Or with a single, immense terra–cotta–tiled space that was kitchen–dining–room–living–room–den–library. Or with such rococo moldings and fixtures that even the downstairs guest bathroom looked as if a Bourbon king could be in there signing an entente.

'Well,' I said, stopping to admire a miniature forest of knee-high ferns, 'better Larry finds a new aesthetic when he gets bored than a new wife.'

Nancy shrugged. 'I am no longer certain that is true. What do I need him for?'

'You love him.'

'You are an incorrigible romantic, Judith.' She shook her head, saddened by my foolishness. 'Of course, being a romantic is a cinch once you don't have a husband. Tell me, how can I love someone who wants his creative legacy to be a Gothic media room? Do you know what he confided to me last night, *post* the usual *coitus nauseus*?: "Nancy, the Gothic style is the only morally correct form of building." Any moment he'll get a tonsure and a hair shirt.' She shrugged. 'The man is fifty-eight years old. This is probably the beginning of dementia. I'll be changing his diapers soon.'

'Would it blight this day even more if I reminded you that the age difference between you and Larry is three years, not thirty-three? But so what? For a woman in her mid-fifties, you look fabulous. You even look fabulous for a woman in her forties. Why get hung up on age –'

Setting her hands on the slim hips of her tight, low-slung jeans, Nancy snapped, 'Hush!'

'You know what my new motto is?' I asked her.

'Regurgitate every syllable of psychobabble I hear on *Oprah*?'

'No,' I said. '"Never be afraid of the truth."'

'The truth is, it's Viagra three nights a week. The only thing *not* limp about Larry is his dick. His very essence is limp. And speaking of limp, it's high time you reconsidered your adolescent fantasy about that cop. If you don't think he has to put a splint on it these days you are seriously deluded. You're deluded anyhow. A

41

few months' fling twenty years ago and he's the love of your life?'

I slammed my hands onto my hips. 'I did not bring him up.'

'He's in the air. I can sense his continual presence in your head.'

'You're way off base,' I lied.

'You wonder why you're not meeting any decent men –'

'No. I don't wonder. You do.'

'He's married, Judith.'

'Not to the same one.'

Nancy stopped short before a copse of bamboo. 'No. You're right. To a new one.'

'It's not working.'

'How do you know? You ran into him a year ago for a couple of seconds.'

'But then he called,' I protested feebly.

'And you had a four-second conversation.'

'It lasted a few minutes. I could hear it in his voice: He wasn't happy. Anyhow, he's not in Homicide anymore. He's head of some other unit, Special Investigations. Something like that. But if you're thinking I'm obsessed, it so happens *I* was the one who said "Nice talking to you again" and got off the phone.'

'Sure. So you could faint.'

'I don't faint.' I hated fighting with her. It was one thing to be assertive professionally, to tell a history department chair you will not teach four sections of America from Jamestown to Appomattox the following fall, especially if he's going to stick forty students in each section. It's another thing to go head-to-head with your dearest friend. But Nancy possessed what I guessed was a journalist's ability to withstand unpleasantness and keep going. In fact, confrontation seemed to refresh her. So I turned away and got busy studying her house. All that was visible was the roof and what I was pretty sure (but not a hundred percent) was the top of a linden tree. I didn't really want to ask if it was, because it would clue her in that I wanted desperately to change the subject. Naturally, Nancy would know if it was a linden. It has always been my belief that Protestants, born with innate knowledge of the names of all things botanical, cannot help but think less of you if you have to ask.

'In three-quarters of an hour,' she observed, 'I haven't heard one word about Courtney Logan from you. Why? To prove to me you're really not interested in a murder, i.e., not interested in *him*.'

Precisely. So I snapped, 'No. I've been listening to you nattering on about gazebos.' I decided not to add: and couldn't get a word in edgewise.

'I was expecting you to ask me to hit up our reporters for unpublished tidbits about the head wounds.'

'*Wounds*?' I demanded. 'I heard about *a* bullet.' Nancy made a big show of casualness, taking off her sweater and tying it around her waist. It was a peach-color wisp of a thing, made from some suddenly chic fluff I think was shaved off the gonads of Indonesian goats, the must-have knit now that cashmere had become a bore and pashmina a cliché. 'Wounds?' I repeated. 'Did I hear a plural?'

'I heard something about there being two bullets in her

43

head. The first shot killed her. The second one was . . . I don't know. Maybe insurance.'

'Do they have any idea what the weapon was?' I demanded.

'The medical examiner may. I don't.'

'Are you sure both shots were from the same gun?'

'No.'

'Can you find out?'

'No, Judith. I don't do crime. I assign and edit op-ed pieces – other people's diatribes about health care. Or bilingual education. Friday I cut a thousand-word paean to desalinization to seven hundred.' She shook her head. Her expertly cut auburn hair swung gracefully a quarter inch above her shoulders. 'It still sucked the big one.'

'You could ask the reporter who's covering the Courtney –'

'Listen to me. You know how you think my drinking is bad for me? That's what I think this detective business is for you. Okay, fine, twenty years ago you had some fun figuring who did it to that dirty dentist. It showed you there was a world that extended beyond your car pool. And you got laid. Maybe even made love to. Fine. I do it all the time.' In Nancy's mind, Mount Sinai was the place God had given Moses the Nine Commandments. In her thirty-one years of marriage, at least fourscore lovers had come – and gone. 'Gives you a glow that beats a paraffin wrap. But you're not me. You take fucking seriously.' Somewhere in the deepest south there is a finishing school that teaches young ladies a thousand and one wiles – from the moist-lips-slightly-parted-as-if-anticipating-fellatio-while-hanging-on-every-word trick to cunningly contrived cleavage displays. Only when belles have mastered all thousand and one stratagems are they given carte blanche to say anything that comes into their heads, any place, any time, no matter how obscene or shocking, along with a guarantee they will be deemed far more enchanting than conventional eyelash-batting magnolia blossoms who mind their tongues. 'There's nothing *wrong* with taking fucking seriously, even though it's a tiresome way of looking at the world.'

'It's not,' I told her, although I was just keeping up my end of the argument. For all I knew, Nancy was right, and I'd pissed away my juicy decades. Now all I could ever hope to attract was someone like post-modernist Geoff with his ear hair. 'But if you think there's no advantage to doing it because it would be tedious or because Nelson would need a derrick to get it up, then what would be so terrible if he and I were to get together – which I swear I'm not planning.'

'Because you're emotionally vulnerable now.'

'I'm much better.'

'Do I have to hum "The Merry Widow Waltz" to remind you?' She picked up a dead branch and, with a final glance toward her house, staked it in the dirt: Ground Zero for her gazebo. 'You lost a husband. You lost him to death, not to a twenty-something with perky tits and a law degree from Harvard. So you can't hate him for leaving without feeling guilty, which being Jewish you have a genius for anyway. And you lost him –' She snapped her fingers – 'like that. Whatever you felt for him, you're still getting over the loss. It would be one thing if you took up with a cute guy with a wad in his jeans to offer you a little temporary comfort. But not this cop. All he can offer you is *Sturm und Drang* and *maybe* middle-aged fucking and champagne for one on New Year's Eve – none of which you need.' She pulled the branch out of the ground and started walking again. 'So no cop.'

'No cop,' I said quietly.

'And no murder.'

'Fine.' Thirty hours later I knocked on Greg Logan's front door.

Chapter Three

'I'm Judith Singer.' I'd rehearsed what I would say to Greg as I was putting on eyeliner. Not bad, I thought: both the makeup and the introduction. As far as the makeup went, for once both eyes came out as if they belonged to the same person. As for the second, I thought the simple intro sounded pleasant, self-assured. Not pert. Pert was the last thing a guy needed one week after his late wife was found in his backyard pool.

Except as I introduced myself, I went hoarse either from nerves or the cheapo estrogen my HMO was foisting on me. My 'Judith Singer' sounded like Marlon Brando's Don Corleone – not a plus at the front door of the Son of Fancy Phil. I cleared my throat and offered Greg Logan a small, sad smile. He stood in the doorway, gazing at something beyond me, so I glanced back.

Nothing. Although technically night, after eight, a band of sky just above the horizon was still pearly with light from the just-set sun. In the deep twilight, the front walk, a path of blue-black stones, appeared to be pools of water. No floodlights were on, but probably none were needed. People weren't dropping by this house. It was only me and Greg.

I waited for him to ask What can I do for you? or return my mini-smile. But he said nothing. His face was blank. So I said hello. It was so quiet I could hear the jets of a distant plane heading for La Guardia, then the *pop!* of an automatic sprinkler head emerging from the grass. After that, silence again. Not a bird, not a car, not a rustle of a leaf: silence so intense it felt as if life had stopped. My gut started poking me in the ribs: Get going! My mind was soothing: Relax. What's he going to do? Put a gun to your head?

The widower Greg, in olive shirt with a crossed golf club insignia over his heart stood before me in khaki slacks and bare feet. He was centered in the green door frame against a background of the celadon-on-celadon wallpaper in his front hall. I'd been wanting him to look at me? Oh God, now he was staring into my eyes. Unblinking, unless he and I were having simultaneous blinkage again and again and again.

Trying to find the humanity behind those eyes, I looked deeper. All I saw was more nothing. No intelligence, no dullness, no compassion, no belligerence, no bereavement. Merely two eyes of that ho-hum hue between blue and gray. True, they were those thick-lashed, perpetually moist eyes that, with some men, evoke bedroom thoughts. Except any intimation that Greg was hot stuff in the whoop-de-doo department would have been instantly nullified not just by his silence but – I cleared my throat – by his hair. Potentially, it was gorgeous hair, the blackest brown, that lustrous, heavy hair a gigolo would wear long and gelled back. Greg Logan, however, wore it clipped so close on the sides and in the back he looked less like a lover boy and more like the congressman from Raleigh-Durham on his way to a prayer breakfast. Few sights are less erotic than pallid scalp with brown birthmark viewed through sheared sideburn.

Besides, Greg was too intriguing looking to be conventionally handsome. His eyes and cheekbones slanted upward, and his nose had a slight northerly tilt that gave him the delicate quality I'd spotted on the front page of *Newsday*. In the illumination of a brass chandelier, all that kept his heart-shaped face from being downright girly was his end-of-day stubble and his eyebrows – the crazed, curly kind that look like a pair of invertebrates creeping across a forehead.

I tried to look at him without appearing to stare. Despite Greg Logan's valentine of a face, the word 'effeminate' did not come to mind: The delicacy of his features was more than countered by a tough-guy physique. He had a thug's thick neck, barrel chest, legs like two giant sequoias. He looked like a man who had to work out double-time to transform the family flab to muscle, and who only seemed to be managing time-and-a-half. His heft made him a presence you had to look up to. Not that I actually had to look up all that far; he wasn't more than five-nine or ten.

The encounter was moving from uncomfortable to disturbing. I swallowed hard. Whatever gland pumps adrenaline was working overtime; a wave of nausea was accompanied by tingling skin and a spike of heat that sent perspiration washing down my cleavage.

The silence was broken at last by the deafening tinging of a wind chime. Immediately after, I heard Greg Logan's breathing, noisy, rapid. I vaguely remember praying, Oh please let this be his adenoids and not some prelude to frenzy, a mere awkward silence with both of us mute from the paralyzing dread that we'll start blithering at the same instant. But his nonresponse was lasting too long. If I hadn't been frozen by his stare I would have squeaked Whoops, wrong house and made a break for my Jeep. How the hell could I not have rehearsed anything beyond 'I'm Judith Singer'?

At last, thankfully, Greg took a deeper, quieter breath. A flicker of hope: Maybe the deadness in his face was because he was so taken aback by having a visitor that he was in shock. Social shock. He was, after all, the prime suspect. After Courtney's disappearance on Halloween, through winter and early spring until this very instant in the month of May, I doubted that few, if any, Shorehavenites had stood on his doorstep offering kind words or homemade gingersnaps. Those who had rung his chimes most likely had been more bad news – cops, journalists, crackpots.

But that instant, Greg Logan showed me that no matter if he was murderer or victim, he was still clearheaded enough to recall the suburban motto: Congeniality now, congeniality forever. Even at this moment, just one week after the discovery of his wife's body, he was able to flash me a mechanical and inordinately white smile. Once more, time could march on.

Exhaling so loudly with relief I almost whinnied, I decided this was not the moment to get distracted figuring out whether Greg's teeth were capped or bleached. I forced up the corners of my mouth and declared brightly: 'I'm on the board of the Shorehaven Public Library.' This was true.

'Oh,' he replied. He opened the door wider and stepped back into the house, letting me come in.

The house smelled of macaroni and cheese which some-one had sought to mask with room spray – not the sort that spritzes fake strawberries but the expensive kind that has the scent of genuine apricots. Greg Logan and I stood two squares apart on the dark-green-and-white marble checker-board floor of the entrance hall beneath the chandelier. I glanced up, beyond his face. Each flame-shaped bulb at the ends of the chandelier's brass arms had its own miniature celadon lampshade, which in turn was edged with a deeper green trim – sort of like rickrack, except instead of zigzags it was scalloped, so it seemed an unending chain of teeny-weeny smiles.

'Is there anything I can help you with?' Greg inquired, too politely. He was plainly expecting me to ask for a donation. Or to make some grotesque pronouncement: Your wife borrowed *The Lively Art of Pumpkin Carving* in October and it's seven months overdue.

'I'm sorry to be dropping in like this, Mr Logan. I know you've had a family tragedy – and still must be going through a terrible time.' I waited for him to say Thank you for your concern, or something. But all I got from him was a bigger dose of nothing. I managed to say: 'I'd like to talk to you for a few minutes.'

I stared boldly at him once more. This didn't seem to bother him, but once again, the lifelessness in those eyes unnerved me. I averted my glance and peered down, until I got nervous he would think I was staring either at his personals (which I wasn't, not that you could see anything with those baggy khakis) or at the swirls of hair on top of his feet that looked unnaturally plopped down, like two tiny toupees. Then, ever hopeful, I looked up again. I shouldn't have. His stare was still as dead as Courtney.

I quickly glanced over at four gilt-framed botanical prints hanging from satin ribbons just to have something other than eyes and foot hair to concentrate on. Was Greg thinking I was some kind of nut? That silent voice inside me started screeching again: Get out, you jerk! *He's* the nut! A smiley, Ivy League psycho whose dead eyes are going to be sparkling with merriment as he squishes your hacked-up body parts into his compost bin. At which point my intellect's sweet voice of reason inquired: Judith, is there any need to make yourself crazier than you already are?

Greg gave me a quick once-over. I'd gotten dressed to look more stereotypical library board member than casual neighbor: a navy skirt, a powder blue cotton sweater, a complementary blue silk scarf with butterflies, and only enough makeup so as not to look gruesome. My blue trustworthy look was evidently working because at last Greg said, 'Please come inside.'

He led me down the long center hall into a living room so expansive it had four seating areas, like the lobby of a Ritz-Carlton. The house, with its grand rooms and soaring ceilings, seemed precisely the sort of place that would be built by the upwardly mobile too young to remember the 1973 Arab oil embargo. He switched on a lamp or two and offered me a seat on a long, fat-armed couch covered in green, cream, and yellow striped silk – that heavy, nubby stuff. Unfortunately, the couch was heaped with so many throw pillows that despite its vast length, there was only room for a couple of anorexics to sit. I wound up with a giant, overstuffed yellow square on my lap. Each of its four corners had a big tassel, the kind strippers twirl from their nipples (a talent, like playing the xylophone, I've always vaguely wished I possessed). Another pillow, a thickly fringed rectangle with a petit-pointed yellow dog, competed for space with my right hip.

'Professionally, I teach history at St Elizabeth's College. I was thinking that an oral history from you –' In that instant, Greg Logan froze, his backside inches from the dark green wing chair cater-cornered to the couch. 'I understand my being here may seem an intrusion, but I was hoping you might have something important to tell the community about how the criminal justice system operates – or fails to operate.'

He did sit, but his bushy, dark eyebrows were now raised so skeptically high they came close to being curly bangs. 'I don't understand,' he replied, still courteous. Or at least not discourteous.

From the depths of my shoulder bag I pulled out a copy of my curriculum vitae in a clear plastic sleeve – along with a bonus, a petrified wad of Trident wrapped in an ancient shopping list. As I slipped the gum gob back into my bag and handed over my CV, I answered his unasked question. 'It seems to me you've been the victim of leaks to the press, of knee-jerk assumptions that have more to do with prejudice than reality.'

Greg's eyes didn't mist in gratitude, as I suppose – subconsciously, arrogantly – I'd hoped they would. Instead, he responded to my proposal pretty much as he'd been responding from the instant he opened the door. You could say it was the way you'd expect a guy with an

53

MBA to respond – with polite neutrality that really was no response at all. Or else you could say it was the behavior of a well-mannered psychopath. He glanced down at the CV. He was less tentative now, more the businessman. His eyes darted back and forth at an astounding rate. I hoped he wasn't one of those entrepreneurs who take up speed-reading because they have time for nothing. Obviously he was: In seven seconds he knew what I had to offer and didn't want it. 'This is all very nice, Ms, Dr Singer.'

'I don't use the "Doctor,"' I told him. 'And please, call me Judith.'

He didn't call me either: 'A Ph.D. in history from NYU. I'm sincerely impressed.' He was neither sincere nor impressed. I felt so letdown. He was talking like a well-programmed android: 'And I appreciate your sympathy. Although I don't really understand what an oral history would do.' He gave what was supposedly an apologetic shrug, which was nothing more than a brief, robotic shoulder lift.

'It might elicit some understanding of what you're going through. Maybe even some empathy that could translate into community support.' I kept waiting for him to start nodding in comprehension. But he sat unmoving, neck frozen, arms bonded to the arms of the wing chair, so I went on. 'It seems to me you've gotten a raw deal. You've been convicted without even being tried.' He did nod then, but barely, merely to indicate he was listening as he tried to figure out the real reason why I was there, and who'd sent me. 'I'm also here because I don't believe you had anything to do with your wife's murder.' As I said the word 'murder,' his right hand slid across his lap to his left and he began to twist his wedding band around slowly. My mouth went dry. My tongue stuck to my palate, which made my next words sound gluey. I managed to say: 'You're too smart to have done it so stupidly.'

'I'm sorry,' he snapped. At last he had an expression. Disdainful. His nostrils flared in impatience, as if I had come to his door peddling a frivolous product. 'I don't have time for this.' With each word of the sentence, his voice grew louder and more contemptuous. His fingers curved until his hands turned into fists.

'Don't you see?' I pleaded. 'The police have only been focusing on you. And while they are, they're not looking for the person who *did* commit the crime. Also – please hear me out – I'm a first-rate researcher. If you'd like I can look into it, see if I can find anything that might lead to someone else.'

Now he was shaking his head. No. A definitive no. Worse, he was standing. 'My lawyer has hired a private investigator.' I could hear the contempt behind his words.

'Please, give me one more minute,' I pleaded, looking up at him. 'When I say look into it, I'm not talking about canvassing the neighborhood and asking who saw what on Halloween. Or what, if anything, your neighbors told the police. That's a legitimate job for your private detective. What I can do is go deeper, follow a paper trail, search into people's pasts. Also, I have some small experience investigating homicide and –'

It's so mortifying, to watch someone who's been trying to dope you out finally conclude *Shit! A wacko!* So I stood as well. I was on the verge of grabbing him by his golf shirt, shaking him and shouting, Please believe me. *I am not a wacko!* Which probably would have been as convincing as Nixon announcing he was not a crook.

We were saved from whatever – maybe only another agonizing silence – by the *clomp-squeak, clomp-squeak* of heavy rubber soles, through the dining room, across the center hall, *clomp-squeak, clomp-squeak* until their noise was hushed by the lush wool of the Persian rug. For an instant he and I glanced at each other, embarrassed, as if we'd been caught doing something illicit.

A tall, rawboned woman crossed the living room and stood before Greg. She looked like Janet Reno in a henna-rinsed pixie cut. Her tan shoes, laced up, had inch-thick, orange rubber crepe soles. Her slacks and matching T-shirt were the hue of canned salmon. The phrase 'older woman' sprang to mind, along with the word 'polyester,' until I realized she was not that much older than I, albeit dressed in some unnatural fabric that did not reflect kindly on her.

'Mr Logan, sir?' A bizarre speech impediment? A heavy Scottish burr?

'Yes, Miss MacGowan?' Burr. He made no attempt to introduce us.

'The little ones are asleep.' She offered a professional nanny's benevolent smile, which didn't last long. So, I mused, the au pair did not seem to be part of the Logan household anymore. What had made her leave? Had she been fired? Could the au pair and Greg actually have been lovers and were now playing it cool? Or had her departure been due to something else – like fear of Greg Logan? Was I nuts to keep dismissing my own fear of him? I'd watched enough TV news to know: The most dangerous people weren't maniacs with eyes that swirled like pinwheels. They were the guys who looked virtuous enough that you would invite them over for dinner. 'I thought I might drive to Dairy Barn,' the nanny was saying, 'and buy those berry pops Morgan's been asking for.'

'Great!' Greg declared. His eyes were no longer dead; they were sparkling at her. His manner was vigorous. It was as if Greg Logan had vanished and instantly been replaced by an extroverted identical twin. 'Excellent! Thank you very much.' Miss MacGowan pursed her lips, a gesture that might have been Scottish for 'you're welcome.' Then, with barely a glance at me, she hurried off. The only sound was the *clomp-squeak* of her shoes.

In those few seconds of silence, my eye drifted to the table beside the chair in which Greg had been sitting. On it was an artful juxtaposition of a pile of antique leather-bound books beside a bottom-heavy onyx vase. Their dark browns and greens glowed in the gold light spilling from a lamp fashioned from a porcelain urn festooned with dragons. On the other side of the lamp, in an old tortoiseshell picture frame (the shell probably yanked off the back of some luckless Edwardian-era tortoise) was a photo of Greg and Courtney Logan. They wore tennis whites. Their arms were around each other, pulling each other close so there was no space between. Her blond head, bound in a terrycloth headband, rested against the chest of his cable-knit sweater. His darkness was a pleasing contrast to her pastel prettiness. They weren't merely smiling for the camera, they were laughing: two people made for each other, like pieces of jigsaw puzzle that formed a picture of marital happiness. God, what a sickening loss he'd sustained.

Suddenly Greg switched off the lamp and said, 'I have a great deal to do, Ms –'

'I wish you'd call me Judith,' I urged. But Greg Logan didn't say anything. The light from the front hallway was more than enough for me to see that he was shaking his head. No.

And good-bye.

. I passed that night squirming in my dark bedroom, feeling my face flame again and again as I cringed over my visit to Greg's. Over and over I asked myself *What in hell possessed you to try such an idiot move? Forget humiliating yourself. He's Fancy Phil's boy. Daddy could arrange to have someone dispatched to take care of Singer, J., 63 Oaktree Street. Your address right there for all to see in the Shorehaven Nynex Community Directory.* And even if he were to turn out to be a sweetie, the world's most benevolent man, he obviously thinks you're a major creep, to say nothing of a loser. You've blown the whole damn investigation.

I tried not to tune into house sounds: the clunk as the refrigerator switched off downstairs, the creak of absolutely nothing on a floor-board. I hated being alone at night. In bed. In life, come to think of it. I didn't feel so bad when I was working, or out with my kids or a friend. But dating, at least with the major and minor drips I'd met, only made my loneliness feel not just painful, but pathetic. Postmodernist Geoff wasn't even a nice guy; he was merely the least dreadful. He had asked me to go to the English Lake District with him in June ('Naturally we'll share expenses,' had been his second sentence). But I'd said no. Having made out with him on Long Island, I knew there was no point in taking the show – this time with three complete acts – on the road to Windermere.

The truth was, yes, sure, I was a person in my own right. Historian. Mother. Friend. Reader. C-SPAN junkie. Movie lover. Library board member. Nassau County Coalition Against Domestic Violence volunteer. But what I yearned to be was a wife again, to hear Bob's sleepy voice murmuring 'G'night' as he turned over, to sense the warmth of a man's body across a few inches of bed, to inhale the homey bouquet of the fabric softener on his pajamas, to know we'd have boring sex every other week. Of course, if I'd left Bob and married Nelson, I thought, he and I would still be in a state of postcoital ecstasy, sitting up in bed discussing the Courtney Logan case and – Stop!

Over the years I'd become my own tough cop, policing myself from crossing the line from the occasional loving or lustful memory of Nelson to hurtful fantasy: What is he doing this minute? Is he happy? Would it be *so* terrible to call him and offhandedly say, You just popped into my head the other day and I was wondering how you . . . Stop! An hour later I finally managed to lull myself to sleep by thinking about who could have killed Courtney Logan.

The next morning, I had some business to attend to: detective business. I hunkered down at the end of my driveway pretending to be preoccupied by the fate of a dwarf juniper or malnourished baby yew to which I actually had very little emotional attachment. Look, I was desperate for some kind of lead and knew this was the time for Chic Cheryl, my next-door neighbor, to come careening home

59

after driving Spike (husband) to the 8:11. Sure enough, her Mercedes wagon, capacious enough to transport a *Schutzstaffel* battalion, was roaring down the street. Chic Cheryl had to race home in order to have quality time with TJ and Skip (children) and Danny, Colleen, and Bridget (Irish water spaniels) before she had to floor it to get to her nine A.M. golf lesson on time.

Her brakes didn't squeal as much as give a squawk of panic as she slammed them on when she was a foot away from me. 'Ju!' she blared. Then, modulating her usual roar, she shouted at me: 'How *are* you?'

'Fine,' I told her. She nodded sadly, secure in the fact I was no such thing. I couldn't say exactly why Chic Cheryl always condescended to me. It may have been that I was a woman without a man, although more likely it was that I drove an American sports utility vehicle. I knew better than to ask her about the Logans, since she'd conveyed the only unique piece of information she had months before (while simultaneously pointing out to me the features of the soles of her new Nike Streak Vengeances), which was the riveting news that she'd heard Courtney Logan had cooked on a La Cornue range with a built-in simmer plate. 'Cheryl,' I said, 'do you happen to know anyone who used StarBaby, Courtney Logan's –'

'Not me!' she thundered, shaking her head so vigorously that the morning sunbeams caught each of the Merlot highlights she went to Manhattan for every six weeks; Cheryl had patiently explained, without my ever asking, that truly first-rate highlighting was unobtainable anywhere east of Madison Avenue until France. 'I mean, don't you think it looks' – Her voice grew even louder – 'T-A-C-K-Y to show a video of your kids that looks *professional*?' I was never sure about Chic Cheryl, if she talked so loudly to me because she thought hearty voices were the cat's meow or if for some reason she'd decided that, at fifty-four, I was so old I ought to be deaf. 'Can you imagine? "A StarBaby Production" *right up there*? I mean, God, does that spell Long Island *or what*?'

'Right. Did you know anybody who ever used . . . ?'

And so the next day I paid a visit on Jill Badinowski.

Chez Badinowski was what those shelter magazines – the ones that feature homes of couples so rich you know they don't sleep together – would call 'a small jewel.' It had been the gatehouse on some late-nineteenth-century robber baron's estate, but now the mansion (Greenbough) and the baron (Jeremiah Eccles Stumpf) were history, and the Badinowskis' mini Norman villa stood in the shadow of eighteenth-century trees a respectable fifty yards inside the border that separated patrician (i.e., cost more than anyplace else) Shorehaven Estates from the rest of our town.

I'd prepared an explanation about why I was interested in StarBaby and Courtney Logan that would have satisfied anyone not prone to analytical thought, but the minute Jill Badinowski saw me on her doorstep and heard 'Shorehaven Public Library Board,' I was welcomed inside without having to say another word.

Jill was in her early thirties, although her prominent freckles, wide-spaced eyes, and fair number of extra pounds gave her the sweet, goofy look of those excessively adorable cartoon kids on greeting cards. By the time I got finished telling her I was trying to get some information on StarBaby

61

and Courtney, I was seated at a big, round, rough, made-to-look-worn wood farm table in her granite-countered, oak-floored dream of a kitchen watching her grind beans for a fresh pot of coffee. This last was no mean feat, as a chunky toddler who was either a short-haired girl or a long-haired boy clung to her leg and shrieked 'Chips! Chips!' no matter how many times Jill gently responded with 'No more chips!' (I, of course, would have given in and handed over a king-size bag of whatever high sodium, additive-suffused carbohydrate would stop that nerve-grinding duet of gasping sobs and hiccups. Jill, however, was obviously one of those mothers so placid they can remain sympathetic but unmoved by screaming, breath holding, and even turning blue.)

'Were you friendly with Courtney?' I called out over the din. 'Was that how come you had the video made?'

Jill's response was a loud single-syllable laugh of the you've-got-to-be-kidding variety. 'No,' she boomed back. 'I mean, could you see someone like Courtney Logan and someone like me being friends? Not that she wasn't nice.'

The toddler's screeching subsided, so I was able to ask: 'Why wouldn't the two of you be friendly?'

'Let me tell you,' Jill said slowly. 'In every town there are two kinds of women home with their kids. Typical women like me who can't imagine *not* being home. Then, you know, the high-powered ones. The ones who were executives or journalists or high-finance types like Courtney.' Cautiously, as if concerned the machine might spit back the coffee, she sifted in the ground beans. 'Their motto is' – she made the sort of half-amused, half-sneery sound that, charitably, might be called a chuckle – '"achieve,

achieve, achieve." Which, if their husbands are raking it in, becomes "buy, buy, buy" once they're full-time moms. Not that they do much mothering. Maids. Sitters. Nannies. Au pairs. Believe me, with these two types, never the twain shall meet, if *they* have anything to say about it.'

'But aren't all of you mothers now?'

'Yes,' she said, slowing down even more. Maybe this was her pensive mode. You could practically take a nap between each word. 'But giving birth and staying home doesn't . . . you know, kill the "achieve, achieve, achieve" bug, does it?'

I gave what I hoped was a knowing laugh and quickly changed the subject. 'How long have you lived on Long Island?'

'We're pretty new.' Jill seemed to think she still owed me something more, so while she straightened the curled-up elastic waistband of her bright yellow shorts, she added kindly: 'We really like it here.'

'Where are you from?'

'You mean a thousand years ago? From Indianapolis. But Pete – my husband – is with Delta.' Then she added: 'The adhesives – not the airline, not the faucet. We've moved seven different times.' She tossed off the Delta business in the overly affable manner of someone who had grown weary of explaining a thousand explanations ago. 'We started in Houston, then Pittsburgh, Chicago . . .' One of the subsequent cities was either so abominable or so dull all that came out was a sigh. 'That's why I needed StarBaby, because Luke – this little guy here' – the kid's shrieks for chips had modulated to whimpers and now became mere whines – 'was five months old and we couldn't even find our videocam. It's probably in one of the cartons we never got around to unpacking in Denver. That's where we were before Long Island.'

'How did you hear about StarBaby?'

Jill turned to pour water into a well in the great coffee machine. Even from the back she would have looked like a pudgy cartoon kid except for her varicose veins. 'Half a second,' she murmured. She appeared befuddled until she found which button to press to start the thing; it was one of those oversize shiny contraptions with so many valves, buttons, and spouts it looked capable of playing the Italian national anthem. 'It's new,' she explained, although that seemed to be the case of everything but the house itself, and even that was suffused with the smell of freshly hung wallpaper. 'Oh, StarBaby, right. I saw the ad for it in one of those giveaway papers. My husband – Pete – and I talked it over. Then I called.'

Unfortunately, the Saga of Jill Badinowski, from Delta Adhesives to her StarBaby connection, was still emerging with unbearable slowness. A yeast dough could rise in the time it took her to move from sentence to sentence. I couldn't tell if this was just her midwestern style (unlike New York talk, in which natives tend to shove out each phrase in their hysteria to get to the next, even more brilliant one) or if she was so lonely she wanted to keep me around longer. My longing to snap, Spit it out! grew in direct proportion to the length of her narrative.

'She came here the next day. Courtney Logan, I mean,' Jill went on. Then she shuddered, probably recalling the murder, although it might have been the house's overenthusiastic central air-conditioning, unwarranted on such an exquisite May morning. She was wearing a yellow-and-white striped tank top that matched her shorts and the skin on her rounded upper arms was dotted with pink goose bumps. 'Are you writing up something about her for the library?'

'No. I happen to be a historian. I'd like to try some sort of oral history.' She nodded, impressed. 'But before I start taking down the history,' I went on, 'I just want to get a sense of all different aspects of Courtney's life. I was looking for someone who had used StarBaby. My neighbor Cheryl mentioned you.'

'Cheryl's little girl TJ is in my daughter Emily's class. First grade.' A brief, soft smile made her face glow. Since it would be impossible to achieve that look of tenderness thinking of Chic Cheryl, I read it as the expression of someone who not only liked the idea of having children, but who actually enjoyed their company. Absentmindedly, Jill stroked Luke's head.

'You have two children?' I asked because I sensed she expected me to.

'No. We also have twin boys, Michael and Matthew. They're nine. Oh, they're all in the video! The StarBaby video. Do you want to see it?' She seemed so desperate for me to say yes I found myself nodding with maniacal eagerness, if only to prove to her that we Long Islanders are decent folk.

I sat on a new-smelling brass-studded leather couch in a wood-paneled TV room that had once been a small library. Shelves that had been built for hundreds of volumes were now filled with family photos, athletic trophies, and arrangements of silk flowers; everlasting ivy and wisteria drooped from shelf to shelf, obscuring the spines of the Clancys, Jude Deverauxes, and diet and parenting books that constituted their library. Together, Jill and I watched sixty minutes of Luke and family.

I was a movie buff, not an expert on film. But from what I could see on the TV room's giant screen, StarBaby's efforts were the work of a pro, giving genuine value for the year's worth of videotaping. Of course, whether that one cassette was worth the three thousand dollars Jill told me it had cost was another story. There were slick opening credits: A logo of a five-pointed star rocked cradlelike on a crescent of film. Seconds later the word 'StarBaby' in chubby pink-and-blue letters appeared beneath it. Then the star dissolved into a shot of baby Luke Badinowski's toothless grinning and the video began.

Throughout winter, spring, summer, fall, there were relatively few of the predictable home movie scenes most parents show to tolerant relatives and friends: no baby waving bye-bye, no toddler cautiously touching baby goat at a petting zoo, no tyke gnawing on a new Christmas or Hanukkah toy. Instead, Luke and family walked along the Shorehaven waterfront and checked out the progress of a horseshoe crab, ate swirls of frozen yogurt and watched sailboats from the town dock, visited the pediatrician's for a checkup, and explored every room of their house. The Badinowskis' seven moves had paid off, I guessed; Pete's last promotion must have been a big one, because the furniture, rugs, and window treatments in each of the rooms were not just newly acquired, but expensive.

'Did Courtney do the filming herself?' I asked. For an instant Jill looked startled, as if I started blabbing in a movie theater, unnerving her, taking her out of the mesmerizing story up on the screen. She shook her head no. It was clear she wanted to keep watching the video, and almost as clear that she was hoping an outsider would revel in her family with her. Seven cities, I thought. If you have to say good-bye to friend after friend, there must come a point when you finally cannot allow yourself friendship. I could hardly imagine a life in which I had to ask a stranger to watch my home movies.

So I turned back to view Luke peering up at *Blue's Clues*, pulling up a carrot from the family vegetable patch, playing a baby version of football with his two brothers, being taught how to climb up a playground slide by his sister. Watching wasn't that great a sacrifice. The Badinowskis seemed a good-hearted clan, although crew-cut Pete of Delta Adhesives carried himself as if he'd gotten an M-16 up his ass in some marine boot camp.

StarBaby had done not merely a professional job, but an intelligent one. Throughout the video, someone offscreen must have been asking specific questions, because every-one – from the pediatrician to siblings to the mailman to shoulders-back, chin-up Pete – spoke of Luke affec-tionately and occasionally articulately, with none of the predictable, awkward Hi! It's me and I just want to say, uh, hello to, uh, the big boy on his birthday.

When it was over, I offered my praise of Luke, who was sitting on the floor taking apart a red-and-yellow plastic truck which I assumed was meant to be taken apart. Then I asked Jill: 'Did you spend much time with Courtney?'

'Oh sure,' she replied. With her midwesterner's passion for Rs, her sarcastic response emerged as Eww shrrrr.

'Actually, she came with a sample video and talked to me about what I wanted. She was probably here for less than an hour.'

'What was she like?'

'I can't honestly say. I guess . . . We must be, must have been, around the same age. But I felt like she was a lot older.' Jill pulled at a loose thread on the hem of her shorts, causing a giant pucker. 'She was so sophisticated. She wore slacks and a plain white blouse. It had to be silk. And a gold watch but no other jewelry. Except her wedding and engagement rings. She just looked . . . perfect. Not like in *Vogue*. But you know that quiet good taste people in the East have? And she was so self-confident I couldn't imagine *not* signing up for the video.'

'Well, it looked great to me.'

Jill offered me a sunny smile. 'To me, too.'

'You called her sophisticated. Is that Indianapolis for cold?'

She flushed and cocked her head to one side to consider my question, and I had enough time to notice that if you played connect the dots with the darker freckles on her left cheek you got a snowman with one arm. 'Not cold,' she finally replied. 'She was nice. I didn't feel like she was looking down on me or anything. But then again, she wasn't judging me as a potential friend. I guess you could call her charming. But it was strictly business charm. I knew not to take it personally. She wouldn't be interested in me.' She glanced down at Luke. 'Well, why should she be? Even though Pete's chief operating officer of Delta now, my job hasn't changed. *My* motto isn't "Achieve, achieve, achieve." Why should I interest someone like her?' Jill may have been waiting for me to protest, but I took too long. She continued: 'Not that I'm finding fault with Courtney. She was a type. And a businesswoman. She didn't come here to be my friend.'

'But her business was kids,' I suggested. 'That's kind of a warm and friendly way to make a living.'

'Warm and friendly is what sells these days,' Jill snapped, so sharply that I was still sitting frozen on the leather couch recovering from her tone while she was bending over to disengage Luke from the pieces of red-and-yellow truck he'd started to heave at the blank TV screen. 'That's what Courtney Logan was here for. Selling something. Making money on a product. Babies. But her business could have been making cookie cutters.' Then she added in her amiable, middle-America way: 'Or poison gas.'

Jill's poison gas floated over my head all day as I read an article – a revisionist analysis of Harry Hopkins's administration of the lend-lease program by a Tulane University historian besotted by his own audacity – and planted my lettuce and arugula. It stayed with me, too, as I pushed my cart up and down the supermarket aisles, looking over a recipe for 'French cutlets' on the tofu container, knowing in my heart – wishing it could be otherwise – they would not turn out *délicieux*. Everywhere I'd turned in Shorehaven, all I had heard about Courtney was 'smart' and 'nice.' Very nice. Really, really nice. Genuinely nice. Jill's was the first not-nice. I didn't have to open the can of Vanilla Almond tea leaves in my cart to read the animosity behind 'poison gas.'

It was nearly seven when I set my bag of groceries in the back of my Jeep. Too much time studying frozen cheesecakes, scrutinizing sponge mops. Living alone, I'd noticed a tendency to check and recheck the unit price on Ultra Charmin and to squeeze far too many nectarines in order to put off going back to an empty house. So, I mused as I drove back up Main Street and down Beacon Road, was Jill simply reacting to a real or imagined condescension to a housewife on Courtney's part? Or had she, even subliminally, picked up on a ruthlessness that everyone else, gasping or tsk-tsking over Courtney's murder, had been eager to overlook?

What an evening it was, sugary with the mingled scents of flowering crabapple, dogwood, cherry, and apple trees. Except I kept thinking about poison gas. For me, better than nice. Because, I told myself as I pressed the garage-door opener, nice women do indeed get murdered, but nice cuts way down on motives:

Q: What did Courtney Logan ever do to you?
A: Nothing. She was incredibly nice.

But a cold woman, a ruthless woman, a poison gas woman might give me something to work with.

I drove the car into the garage, got out, and opened the rear gate of the Jeep thinking, Hmm, Boston lettuce with sliced mushrooms and how could I get leads to the investment bankers who'd worked with Courtney, and oh, to her close friends, too, and –

'You Judith?' a rough voice demanded. And, from a cobwebbed and shadowed corner in the back of my garage, out stepped Fancy Phil Lowenstein.

Chapter Four

In a voice that had the delicacy of sulfuric acid, Fancy Phil Lowenstein demanded, 'You Judith Singer?' Simultaneously, he put an arm around my shoulders that weighed enough to compress the disks between each vertebra. I thought of all those movies in which the heroine plunges her hand into her pocket-book and retrieves one of those femme items, like a metal nail file, that can be instantly converted into a weapon. But the notion, Aha! I'll poke my Jeep key into his eyeball to distract him, did not occur to me. My brain, fear-frozen into suspended animation, did not instruct my hand to unzip my shoulder bag, plunge in, and retrieve my house keys – with the nifty little panic button for the alarm system I kept on my key ring. In fact, all I could think to do was nod, like one of those dopey dolls whose heads bop up and down on a spring: That's me, uh-huh, yes, right, I'm Judith Singer.

Fancy Phil muttered: 'I'm asking . . .' His voice trailed off as his eyes peered upward, at the motor of the garage-door opener. Then they scanned the rear wall, at the rake, snow shovel, and mysterious–object–left–by–children–that–might–have–pumped–up–basketballs–or–served–as–hookah–or–bong–or–whatever–they–call–it that dangled from the

Peg-Board. Apparently, he suspected my garage was bugged because he murmured: '. . . because of that research stuff you mentioned to . . .' His eyebrows lifted in a gesture I suspected was Felonese for 'my son.'

With that, I found myself being transported toward the door that led from the garage into the house. I wasn't being shoved or dragged so much as simply having my location altered by an elemental force. 'You know who I am?' Fancy Phil inquired as his fingers grasped my upper arm. It was like being held by five bionic bratwursts, the smallest of which sported a ring with a diamond the size of one of Jupiter's lesser moons.

I stood before the entrance to the kitchen, my heart banging against my chest like some desperate creature pounding on a door, begging to be let out. In, actually, was the place I wanted to go. Nevertheless, I knew there was no real sanctuary: Garage, kitchen, this guy could kill me anywhere. I stood paralyzed, my face inches from the door, my handbag gripped under my free arm. My car keys were clenched so tight their metal teeth bit into the flesh of my palm. I didn't realize I was hugging my grocery bag with such passion until I heard a dull *bloop!* of splitting plastic and immediately inhaled a whiff of vanilla yogurt. Finally some words emerged. 'You're Mr Lowenstein,' I replied.

'Yeah. Phil Lowenstein. And you know whose father I am.' I nodded. I'm pretty sure I didn't actually turn to look at him, although I vaguely recall allowing my eyes to drift sideways. Fancy Phil's head had been plopped midway between his shoulders without benefit of neck, so his second chin rested against the heavy gold neck chain exposed by the open collar of his shirt. He'd put

72

on quite a few pounds since his last mug shot. 'Call me Phil.' He released my arm and wiped his forehead. His skin, glazed with perspiration, was flushed an ominous red that, as I watched, was darkening to purple. 'Hot in here,' he observed. A flash of gold caught my eye. A snake bracelet entwined around his meaty wrist, the mouth and tail separated by an inch of over tanned skin and graying arm hair.

'I know it's hot,' I acknowledged. 'And you having to stand in a garage, waiting for me, with the door shut and no air circulating –'

'Lemme help you with that bag.'

'No. No thanks,' I chirped much too quickly. 'Really, I can manage!' I sounded revoltingly hearty.

'So you can get to your key.' Obviously Fancy Phil was perceiving a smidgen of unease on my part because he took a step back – although he remained within easy stabbing/strangling/stomping distance. 'We could sit down inside, where it's cooler. You don't have to be scared of me. I want to talk business.'

'Business?'

'Yeah. I'm here on business. You *are* the history lady? Right?' His 'his-tor-y' was three deliberate syllables. No uncouth 'histry' for Fancy Phil. My guess was he picked up the pronunciation from watching Public Television against his will during his last stopover at the Elmira Correctional Facility. Two and a half years, according to the news. For aggravated assault on the person of one Ivan 'Chicky' Itzkowitz during a contretemps over certain funds obtained by withholding gasoline sales tax from the state of New York. 'You're a history professor.'

'That's right.'

He smelled clean but insanely citrusy. This was one badass lime cologne, a scent for capos and rappers. 'A doctor of history. Now listen, Doc. Don't worry about Gregory, about him saying he wasn't interested.'

Who knows what happened in that instant? It could have been I recognized that Fancy Phil had indeed bothered to put on aftershave, or made the effort to grant 'history' its three syllables. But suddenly I sensed that if I wasn't safe, at least he had no intention of murdering me right away, although I was not unaware that he might delegate the job to some discount contract killer who hung out on the fringes of the Mafia or the Russian mob. My throat made a swallowing movement even though all my saliva was still sloshing in that secret reservoir to which bodily juices flow in times of terror.

'Maybe I overstepped my bounds,' I began to apologize. 'Going to his house –'

He cut me off: 'It don't matter Gregory wasn't interested. I'm interested.'

And then we were inside. Fancy Phil offered to help me unpack the groceries, but seemed relieved when I said no thank you. I sat him at the kitchen table, an overly long, narrow, rickety quasi-antique of dark wood that was more appropriate for a Castilian monastery than a Long Island Tudor. But I'd bought it (along with a Swedish wood-burning stove and a frightening Art Nouveau umbrella stand) in the year I'd taken leave of my senses, after Bob died.

Anyhow, I opened the back door, muttering something inane about loving the evening smells this time of year, although both of us knew I needed to see a way out. The air outside the screen door was cooling down fast: Summer was still a month away. I glanced around the kitchen. Being too nervous to think of a novel hors d'oeuvre to please the discriminating criminal palate, I microwaved a bag of popcorn and poured it in a salad bowl shaped like a deformed daisy – one of those hideous, indestructible wedding presents that lasts longer than the marriage. For a millisecond Fancy Phil's boulder of a head wobbled on his shoulders, which I took to mean 'Thank you.' He also accepted the only kind of beer I had in the refrigerator, some microbrew of Joey's, one of those concoctions that have the hue and aroma of rancid pumpkin pie.

'Essentially,' I said, at last feeling capable of uttering a simple declarative sentence, 'your son didn't want my services. He said he'd hired a detective.'

After a couple of glugs of beer, Fancy Phil's chubby cheeks and domed forehead were no longer that alarming aubergine, as if he were on the verge of a cardiovascular incident. His color subsided to a rosy flush – almost an exact match for the bright pink in the gingham of his short-sleeved shirt, an odd choice of fabric, but perhaps one of his chums had hijacked the wrong truck. His slacks were a white linen that picked up on the white checks in the gingham and matched the white loafers. As did his white patent-leather belt. I decided it was not politic to mention one does not wear such attire until after Memorial Day or, ideally, ever.

'Gregory's lawyer's got some detective she works with,' Fancy Phil continued. 'His lawyer's a she. Anyhow, she says her guy – this ex-cop – knows his ass from his elbow.

75

Pardon my French. But listen, an ex-cop . . . What can I tell you? You know how the world works.'

'I have a general idea,' I conceded.

'What I mean is, you're no kid.' Wearily, I nodded. 'I meant that as a serious compliment.' With what I guessed was his suave gesture, Fancy Phil smoothed back his hair with the heels of his hands. The top had thinned, but the sides and back were thick and profoundly dark, a black that does not occur in nature. It was held in position by a mousse that apparently hardened into Plexiglas upon application. 'Like, for instance,' he went on, 'you didn't scream when you saw me in the garage, which, to tell you the truth, I was a little worried you'd do. Not that I'd blame you. I mean, here I am, some guy you never met before. Except I figured, Hey, if she knows enough to think she should get hired, she probably saw my picture on TV or in the paper, with all the publicity about the thing with—' He looked away from me, past his snake bracelet, down into the jumble of popcorn, and in a mournful tone added: 'Courtney.'

For a moment after he uttered her name he seemed mesmerized by the yellow-white puffs, no two alike. Then he began playing knock hockey with one of the few unpopped amber kernels. At long last he shrugged and went on as if no time at all had passed: 'So I figured about you, she's not gonna think I'm some dangerous lunatic in her garage. Sorry if I scared you. But it wouldn't be a good idea for me to sit outside in my car. You know how people are.' He shook his head, disheartened by man's distrust of his fellowman. 'One of your neighbors could dial 911.'

'Where did you put your car?'

'I had a friend of mine drop me off. I don't want trouble with cops. Know what I mean?'

'I do.' The popcorn, I was relieved to see, was a success, though some diet guru or woman in Fancy Phil's life had clearly coached him to eat only one puff at a time, not a handful. But his arm kept moving so swiftly between bowl and mouth it was almost a blur.

I fetched a Diet Coke and joined him at the kitchen table. 'Anyway,' he went on, 'you not being a kid, you being someone who's a doctor of history, you probably could dig up stuff from a library or computer or whatever that this ex-cop won't even think of.'

'I was trying to explain my research capabilities to your son,' I said. 'Also, I know the mores of this community. Your son's neighbors might offer me information they wouldn't confide in an ex-cop.'

'"The Moreys,"' he repeated. I saw he was trying to recall if the Moreys were a Shorehaven couple Greg had mentioned. Not that Fancy Phil was stupid. On the contrary. Even in the garage I sensed he was not just observing me, but was using my every word, my every action to add to his sum of knowledge. Moment by moment, he recalculated more precisely who and what I was.

'Mores,' I said offhandedly. 'Local customs. Also, I've had a little experience investigating –'

'Yeah, I know. The dead dentist. Dr Dirty. I remember seeing your picture in the paper.' I must have looked surprised, because Fancy Phil gave me a smile, a surprisingly likable flash of teeth and popcorn. 'I got an incredible memory,' he explained, in the modest manner of a man stating the simplest fact about himself. 'I said to myself, way back then, "Hey, that's one smart cookie." So, Doctor, I want you on the case. You want to work for me?'

'You mean, for your son.'

'No. When I say me I mean me. He don't want no part of you.' Then, realizing he may have been a tad less than gallant, Fancy Phil offered an apologetic lift of his eyebrows. 'Kids. Do I have to tell you?'

'Did he think I was one of the local crazies, coming out of nowhere, knocking on his door?'

'They grow up and what can you do with them?' A Kissinger-like response, I thought. 'So, Dr Singer, you charge by the hour or by the job?'

'Please, call me Judith. For you' – I looked straight into his dark eyes. They absorbed the light in the room, yet gave off none – 'there's no charge.'

'What are you not charging for? You still scared of me?'

'Less than I was in the garage.' He nodded slowly – head down, head up – to show me he understood and that he was still listening. 'I think it's best for me not to be your employee. But I really would love to do the work.'

'Why would you work for nothing?'

'Intellectual curiosity.'

The side of Fancy Phil's mouth began to twist, but the expression vanished before it could become a smirk. 'Okay. I can understand curiosity. But you should know something. I'm retired. Not dealing with my former associates.' He crossed his arms over his stomach, which was so rotund that his arms made their X right above his wrists. 'I got grandchildren. You got any?'

'Not yet,' I said.

'Well, when you do, your whole life changes. You don't want them thinking, Hey, because of Poppy Phil, I didn't get invited to some little kid's birthday party. So I had to stop being what I was. Know what I mean?'

'Sure.' I was not sure this was a genuine change of heart. In fact, I wasn't sure if it was a change at all or simply the sort of line gangsters give girls with doctorates. I didn't have time to reflect, because he was waiting for me to say more. 'Wise decision,' I added. Not enough. 'I bet it was a tough thing to do, not just to give up a way of life, but some of the friendships that go with it.'

Fancy Phil thrust out his lower lip and gave me a slow nod of acknowledgment, a silent You get it. 'So go ahead. Ask me anything.'

'Well, as I told your son, the cops think they have their man. They're not looking to clear Greg.' I stood to get him another beer. 'So beside the fact that he's the husband, which automatically puts him under suspicion . . .' I handed him the bottle and the opener, sat, and leaned forward so I could look him straight in the eye. 'Tell me, Phil. How come the cops are so damn sure it's your son?'

'Some money business.' He offered this complete explanation proudly, then pressed the cold bottle against his forehead with a soft 'Whew,' just to let me know that such candor was enervating.

'That's it?'

'That's it. Money business.' He got busy studying the label, perhaps to find out what in God's name the brewmeisters in the Bronx could be putting in their beer.

'The more information you give me,' I told him, 'the

deeper I can dig. The less you give me, the longer it will take and the less effective I'll be. You know that.'

'It's like this.' Fancy Phil was one of those men with the dexterity to uncap a bottle of beer with one hand. 'Halloween was on a Sunday, right? So the Monday before the Monday before Halloween ... The cops found out Gregory transferred some money that day.' He sat back, took a swig of beer, and appeared happier, relaxed, as if he'd finally told the whole truth and nothing but.

'Transferred whose money from where to where?'

'Most of what was in their joint money market account.'

'To?'

'He transferred it to an account in just his name.'

'How much?' I inquired.

Fancy Phil emitted a minor snort, which I assumed was to show me he was amused, not irritated, by my persistence. 'Forty and change,' he finally said.

'Forty thousand? Greg took forty thousand out of his and Courtney's joint account?'

He nodded. The sun had set. The patio and lawn beyond the open kitchen door lay black in darkness, but the window over the sink was still a rectangle of indigo. 'The cops think that's suspicious,' he sniffed.

'How did he account for moving the money?'

'He told them the truth.' I waited. 'Look, honey, Doc, what can I tell you? He's got a business.'

'Soup Salad Sandwiches,' I said.

'Right. But he's got a problem.'

'What?'

'Me.' Fancy Phil fiddled with the medallion on the buckle of his belt, a circle about the size of the average grapefruit. 'I'm not what a CPA would call an asset. That's why I made Gregory change his name to Logan before he went to college. He went to Brown, in the Ivy League. Just like Harvard, only in Rhode Island. Anyway, Gregory's a straight kid. I swear to God. And smart. All he wants is to keep his business on the up-and-up. But if I'm the problem, here's the catch: Courtney.'

'How was she the catch?'

Wearily, he shook his head. 'StarBaby. You know about that?'

'Her company,' I said. 'Videos of baby's first year.'

'Right. So here's my kid, who's dealing with bankers who are totally legit. If he wants to grow legit, expand his business, the bankers gotta lend him money. Understand?'

'I'm with you.'

'So when they lend money, they gotta see all his business records. Plus his personal stuff. It's called net worth.'

'I know what net worth means. Go on.'

'He has to prove he's a solid citizen. Like, he has to be substantial enough so he's not gonna loot Soup Salad Sandwiches to, whatever, pay his liquor bill – not like he drinks, maybe a couple of glasses of wine. None of that single-malt yuppie crap.'

'What did StarBaby have to do with Soup Salad Sandwiches?'

'Courtney thought "joint account" meant "Take me. I'm yours." Two or three times she dipped into their money market account. She helped herself from their brokerage account, too: She sold stock from their Smith Barney thing that was also joint. One time she put it back. The other times . . . And the thing of it was, she didn't say,

Hey, Gregory, I'm borrowing from the brokerage thing because I need to buy thousands of dollars' worth of' – for an instant Fancy Phil's generous-lipped mouth contracted into a bitter slit – 'camera junk to take pictures of babies and to advertise. She just took it. Like it was all hers. She kept pouring big bucks into that *fershtunkiner* StarBaby. Gregory told me about that afterwards, after she was missing. He's never been, you know, a crybaby. Whatever was going on, he kept it between man and wife.'

'What did he think was going on?'

'He said all he thought at the time was that Courtney was a little out of control businesswise.'

'How come she didn't go to one of those legitimate bankers for a loan?'

'Trust me, honey, she did. And they said, Hey, not one thin dime more until you start doing serious business.'

'Was StarBaby failing?'

'No. But she wasn't breaking her back carrying sacks of money to the bank vault either. She was doing so-so.' Speaking about his daughter-in-law, Fancy Phil's face didn't harden into anything resembling hatred, but it didn't get warm and fuzzy either.

'Maybe she would have built the business up in time.'

'Maybe. And in time maybe the bank would have given her a big loan. But meanwhile, she couldn't believe the real reason the business was slow: because it was a *stupnagel* moneymaking idea. No, Courtney was positive all she needed was capital. Capital, capital. She wouldn't shut up about having to capitalize.'

'And Greg?'

'Gregory was scared she'd go through everything they

had together without telling him. Then the banker would check his net worth figures and say, Hey, Logan, you're full of it. You don't got no fifty-five thousand in the money market account and eighty in stocks.'

I must have blinked: a young couple in their thirties with so much. Even though Bob had done well, there were years we had to choose, especially early on, and the choice hadn't been between a BMW or a Mercedes; it was a new roof or a new septic tank. But the Logans had it all, along with money in the bank. 'How much did Greg say Courtney took without telling him?'

'Fifteen from the money market. Twenty total from Smith Barney. So she took thirty-five. But she put back . . . I forget. I think ten. So they were down a total of twenty-five big ones for the cameras and for ads.'

'When did this happen?'

'Around this time last year,' Fancy Phil replied.

'Let me be clear about this.' I stood, got my shopping-list pad and pen from near the telephone, and came back to the table to do the arithmetic and make a few notes. 'Courtney's fiddling with their money happened about a year ago. But about two weeks before she disappeared – and was murdered – Greg transferred forty thousand dollars from a jointly held money market account into an account that was in his name only.'

'Yeah. A coincidence. I mean, him moving the money and then Courtney getting killed. He needed another loan from his bank in October.'

'Let's go over the math. If she'd helped herself to fifteen out of the money market account, that meant originally they had fifty-five thousand.'

'Yeah.'

'And how much was in their Smith Barney brokerage account?'

'Eighty minus twenty. Plus the ten she put back.' He watched patiently until I wrote *70,000, Smith B.* 'You don't got a doctor in arithmetic, do you?'

'No. So tell me, Phil, do you sense Greg was very angry about Courtney's money manipulations?'

Fancy Phil shook his head vehemently, as if the words 'Greg' and 'angry' could not occur in the same sentence. 'Nah. Upset. Like he knew Courtney was going through a tough time, being home with the kids, trying to get used to going from being on the fast track to being a mother. And a businesswoman, but not in the city. What she couldn't get through her head was that now Gregory was the breadwinner. He couldn't let her keep sticking her hand in the till for a business that was – I hate to say it of the dead – stupid. Every young married couple has one of those video cameras. All they *do* is take pictures, like they invented babies and they've gotta show the world. Little Buster in the high chair. Little Buster out of the high chair. Little Buster in the grocery store. They take their babies out at night, for God's sake, to restaurants, so everybody can share their joy. So there's Little Buster screaming and puking that milky lumpy stuff all over the polenta and making everybody else crazy, and they're *still* taking pictures. "That's Little Buster *breching* in Mario's."'

'But you think Greg and Courtney's marriage was basically sound? They were just going through a rough time?'

'Yeah.'

'You're sure? No serious trouble?' Fancy Phil raised his right hand as if taking an oath. His palm was oily from the popcorn. 'What about the au pair?'

'What about her?' he snapped. 'A hundred different languages in the world and they pick a girl who speaks German. Teaching the kids: "*Auf Wiedersehen, Grossvater.*" And she had a face that could stop a clock and probably did.'

'Maybe. And maybe she had a great figure or a sweet vulnerability that attracted your son. I don't know. The police and half of Shorehaven obviously believe there was something between her and Greg.'

'Well, there wasn't. Cross it off your list. Gregory loved Courtney. He didn't step out.'

Fancy Phil's nostrils dilated. I sensed this was not a sign of pleasure. So I decided to skip any more questions about the au pair. Still, considering I was alone in a house with a gangster convicted of aggravated assault, I felt remarkably comfortable. There he was, my first client, sitting at the head of my narrow kitchen table. Fancy Phil was clearly a man who expected respect, or at least not condescension, much less a hard time. Still, even if I gave him an argument, I sensed I probably wouldn't wind up bloated, bobbing in the East River, a New York moment for the folks from Toronto on a Circle Line tour. But I felt I had to say: 'Phil, from time to time I may ask you questions you don't like.'

'That's okay.'

'Good. I don't want to have to be concerned you'll hold a grudge.'

'What are you worrying about?'

'I wouldn't say worrying. It's just those two and a half

years you spent upstate because of an aggravated assault on a fellow –'

'Chicky Itzkowitz?' He snorted a dismissive laugh. 'That's what *I* call history. Plus I told you, I retired. A new man. Anyway, with Chicky it was a business matter.'

'Well, you and I are doing business even if I'm not taking money.'

'Hey, Dr Judith.'

'What?'

'You got nothing to worry about.'

He did look relatively benevolent, a hoodlum Buddha. So I asked: 'What did you think of Courtney?'

'Me, personally?' I nodded. He thought for a minute, then shook his head sadly. '*Lukshen*. You know what that is?'

'Noodles?'

'Yeah, but the thing is, *lukshen* without butter, without salt and pepper . . . What's the word? Blah. A *b* word.'

'Bland?'

'Yeah! Bland.' He put his elbows on the table and rested his chins on the heels of his hands. 'You send your kid to an Ivy League college because you want him to be better than you. But he winds up bringing home a bowl of *lukshen* from the West Coast with blond hair and blue eyes who went to another Ivy League college and is an investment banker and plays tennis and is even cute looking if you like cute looking. Looks like a great package. But then you look for a personality and it's not there.'

'There is a kind of West Coast low-key style.' Well, I wasn't about to interject that his son wasn't exactly a live wire either, although in fairness, I had met Greg under strained circumstances during a terrible period in his life.

'Excuse me, Doc,' Fancy Phil said, 'but bullshit. Low-key, laid-back, loafers without socks – that's how they are. But people from the West Coast still have a personality.'

'Was she a good mother to the kids?'

'Yeah. Fine. I mean, she could talk your ear off about Travis's teething. She was always saying to Morgan, "I need a huggy-buggy," and Morgan would go running to her.' With his thumb and index finger he massaged the bridge of his nose. An altered nose, the broad-bridged, slightly upturned schnozz many got in the fifties and early sixties, in the era of frantic assimilation, a nose which made thousands of second- and third-generation American Jews look as if they'd descended from Porky Pig. 'And she was good to Gregory, too, except for putting her hand in the till. Always calling him "sweetie" or "honey" or "Greggy," but listen, she was a good wife. You saw their house?'

'It was lovely.'

'She fixed it up herself. No interior decorator or nothing.'

'On the other hand . . .' I prompted.

'On the other hand,' Fancy Phil went on, 'if she's quitting her job to stay home with the kids, how come she's not staying home with the kids? She's out all the time. Call the house and you got that kraut. "Mizzus Logan is at her exercise class,"' he mimicked in what I assumed he believed to be a German accent. 'A class? What kind of crap is that? Someone's gotta teach you to touch your toes? Or she's at a meeting, or having lunch with her girlfriends, or taking a run, or in her office –'

'Did she have an office outside the house?'

'Nah. She took over a bedroom. Anyway, she's in her office doing business and cannot be disturbed.'

'Did you meet Courtney's family?'

'Yeah. They're what you'd expect. *Lukshen* comes from *lukshen.*'

'Where do they come from?'

'Washington. The state. Olympia. It's somewhere, but I don't know where.'

'Are both parents alive?'

Fancy Phil gave an exaggerated sigh of boredom. 'You want to call that alive, then they're alive. The old man's a comptroller of some two-bit lumber company. The old lady designs flowers. Puts them in bowls or something.'

'Did they come east to the funeral?' He nodded. Not one of his fleshy features moved, yet I sensed a change in his expression. 'How did they act?' He shrugged. 'Phil, I'd like to get a sense of the people Courtney came from. Was the finding of the body a shock to them? Or do you think they had a sense she was dead in the months before, when she was missing?'

'They think it had something to do with me,' Fancy Phil said, his tone so flat it might have been one of those computer-generated voices. 'At the funeral. Episcopal. But I go over to the mother and try to hug her.' He lowered his arms so they were rigid against his sides. 'She goes like this. It was like hugging a little block of cement. She's short, like Courtney. And neither of them – her or the husband – would look in my direction. And not one word.'

'What made them think you had something to do with it?'

'Just – you know, what I was supposed to be.'

'You never had any arguments with Courtney? Or with Greg about Courtney?'

'No!'

'Did they think Greg had anything to do with it?'

'I don't know. At least they talked to him.'

A night breeze blew through the open kitchen door and gave me a chill. One of my neighbors' dogs began that hysterical staccato bark you hear from nutsy dogs or from dogs with nutsy owners. Fancy Phil glanced at his beer bottle and seemed surprised to find it empty. 'Did they put up any kind of a fuss about Greg having custody of the children?'

'What are you talking about?' he asked, annoyed. Then he answered his own question: 'You mean, if they thought Gregory did it, they would want to get the kids away from him. No. They didn't say a peep about custody.'

'Right. Okay, the first few days after Courtney disappeared: Did the cops ask Greg to see if anything of hers was missing?'

'Yeah, and as far as he could tell, nothing was. The only money that was touched was the money Gregory took out of their joint account two weeks before. The sapphire earrings he got her for her thirtieth birthday were where she kept them, in a little safe they have in a closet. Some other jewelry. Her mink was in the closet.'

'Did she have an engagement ring?'

'Yeah, sure. She was wearing it, you know, when they found her. And her Rolex, too.'

'So all that was missing was the twenty-five thousand

she'd taken from the money market and stock brokerage accounts months before she disappeared?'

'Right,' he agreed.

'So now what I've got to do is find out if she paid out twenty-five thousand dollars for video equipment and advertisements.'

'And if she didn't?'

'Then I'll need to figure out what was going on in Courtney's life right before her death.'

Chapter Five

StarBaby's videographer, Zee Friedman, bent over the railing on the landing outside her fifth-floor walk-up. 'Just one more flight!' she called out encouragingly. She lived in a run-down neighborhood just north of the grand, high-ceilinged apartments around Columbia University and south of the renovated brownstones of Harlem's latest renaissance. The stairwell of her building exuded that Old New York smell which has nothing to do with Henry James and lavender; for nearly a hundred years, the yellow-brown walls had soaked up garlic and onion vapors from the various ethnic groups that had used the place as their first step up from New York's bleakest tenements. Now optimistic twenty-somethings and disillusioned thirty-somethings paid nearly a thousand bucks a month rent for each room.

Zee graciously ignored the mewling sounds that came from my throat with each breath as I made my way up the fourth flight of ridiculously steep stairs that seemed designed for a longer-legged species than *Homo sapiens*. In her leaning over, cascades of her black hair fell forward, forming a curtain around her face. It wasn't until I finally clomped up to her landing that I got a good look at her. Zee definitely outclassed her surroundings. She had the pudgy apple cheeks of one of those Victorian bisque dolls, except instead of the expected vacant blues, her eyes were alert, sparkling black. 'Hi!' Her handshake was like a stevedore's, although she wasn't much more than five feet tall.

'Hi,' I gasped.

'Half Chinese, half Jewish,' she replied to my unasked question as she led me into her studio apartment. I nodded, not yet trusting myself to speak two consecutive words without snorting. 'Twenty-four. Years old, I mean. The Zee's for Zelda. After Zelda Fitzgerald. Why, you may ask, did my parents think it was a good idea to name me after some poor demented woman who burned to death in a mental hospital? The answer is: I don't know.'

Her not-very-large studio was divided into three areas: a kitchen that was simply some shelves above a sink and a two-burner stove; what I assumed was the bedroom, although it was hidden behind a curtain that looked fashioned from hula skirts; a five-by-five square that was the living room. Zee escorted me in and gestured toward a Baby Bear-size club chair. It was covered in one of those sage green, one-size-fits-all slipcovers that are better in catalogs than in life, although on her chair it had the schleppy charm of a child playing dress-up in her mother's clothes. She sat across from me on a love seat draped with three or four flowered fringed shawls, the ones you see on pianos and fortune-tellers. None of the floral prints matched.

Obviously Zee Friedman possessed that gift I'd always longed for, flair, the intuitive sense of when less is less and when less is more. Her outfit, plain black cotton pants cut off mid-shin and an ordinary white T-shirt, was stylishly minimalist. I, on the other hand, was in navy slacks, my perpetual blue sweater with butterfly scarf, and gold button earrings. Hopefully she'd think my retro look was intentional.

I'd spent the two previous days doing research and making calls. At last, through a friend of a friend of a neighbor of Jill Badinowski, I came up with another StarBaby client who had taken down Zee's phone number. 'Sorry to bother you on Memorial Day weekend,' I told her.

'No problem,' Zee assured me. She had the voice of a more imposing woman, the contralto the Statue of Liberty would have if she could speak. She pulled her feet up on the cushion of the love seat so her heels touched her backside. She hugged her knees. Her toenails were the pale blue of bleached denim. 'Are you a detective?' she asked hopefully.

'Let's just say I've been hired to see what I could find out about Courtney.' Zee gave me an enthusiastic nod. Her dark hair bounced cheerfully, as if eager to know more. 'Do you have any idea how many other people she employed?'

'At least one other guy, but I can't say for sure if there were any more. I worked for her freelance, on weekends.' Between us was her coffee table, an old wood toy chest with peeling decals of the Little Misses Muffet and Bo-Peep.

'Only on weekends?' I asked.

'Well, that's when both parents are home. You want the two of them interacting with the baby, since the video's at least partly to prove to the kid how great his parents were,

93

no matter what he remembers. Anyway, I work full-time, so Saturday and Sunday were it for me.'

'What do you do?'

'I'm a production assistant for Crabapple Films.'

I nodded respectfully, as if to say, Oh, but of course, Crabapple, though I'd never heard of it and prayed they didn't make movies about adolescent girls being chainsawed. 'What do you do there?'

'The stuff nobody else wants to do,' Zee replied, smiling happily. She seemed inordinately content, one of those people miraculously missing the resentful gene. Not only was her voice big, her smile was also: overwide, the grin you'd see in a nursery school drawing. 'Like I get permits from the mayor's office, copy and file stuff, run back and forth to the set. That's how I got onto Courtney. One of the guys on the set was filming for her and he moved to L.A. He passed the job on to me.'

'Do you want to be a cinematographer?' I was tempted to drop the fact that my son was a movie critic, but decided it sounded undetective-ish. Also, just in case her cheeriness was a sham and she'd pumped two bullets into Courtney, the less she knew about me the better.

Zee shook her head definitively. 'Actually, I enjoy the managerial stuff a lot more – knowing where the money's going, making sure a seventy-foot crane is at Grand Army Plaza in Brooklyn Tuesday at six A.M.' She had managed to get her legs into a knot so complex all but one pale blue toenail was hidden. Her arms, meanwhile, were stretched out along the back of the love seat, as if about to embrace two invisible friends. 'As far as Courtney goes – eeesh, sorry . . . As far as Courtney went, I was surprised she stuck with me. I'm just another Columbia film major whose parents got her a digital camera for graduation.'

'Did Courtney ever talk about her background with you?'

'No. After you called I started thinking. I realized how much I don't know about her. Except like obvious things. Married, two kids. She'd been an investment banker. I mean, we talked a little. Like how much we'd loved college and hated high school. But who loved high school? Maybe one dumb jock and an Epsilon semimoron Most Popular. Anyone who still has a clear memory knows how awful it was.'

'Why did Courtney hate it?'

'I think ... The usual. You're either skinny or fat or puny or a giant and you don't have a boyfriend. And you like to read. Courtney was sawed off and scrawny, although she said she filled out by college. But most of the time she was all business with me.'

'Was she good at her business?'

'She definitely didn't have a cinematic eye – which was why she decided I was a good videographer. She seemed nice, I guess.'

'What do you mean, "I guess"?'

Zee pursed her glossed lips and gave it several seconds of thoughts. 'It's terrible to sound New Age-y,' she said slowly, 'especially when you have tendencies. But some people emit niceness rays. You know?'

'Did Courtney emit not-niceness rays?'

Zee shook her head. 'No. Not at all. But at the beginning I thought, Wow, what a woman! I mean, this bundle of energy. She'd talk about StarBaby and make it sound like

I was joining her on some kind of crusade: *Courtney and Zee's Excellent Adventure*. That StarBaby would really *do* something. People would be able to see themselves as they were, as their parents and siblings were. Maybe an idealized version, because they were being filmed, but at least not filtered through fantasy or an imperfect memory. Courtney was going to franchise it all over the country. And probably the world – though she didn't say that.'

'Did she have a plan?' I asked.

'I remember she showed me a list of all the zip codes and what the per capita income was for each one plus lots of other demographic boring stuff. She was so optimistic, so *positive*. I could almost see her on the cover of *Time*.' Zee put her feet up on the seat again, wrapped her arms around her legs, then rested her chin on her knees, a feat of elasticity I found impressive. 'At first anyway.'

'She changed at some point?'

'Yeah, I guess last summer, probably in July. She'd said something a few months before then that summer might be a little slow for business because parents were around more, kids could do more outdoors and all that. I'd have thought that was a good time for filming, except I had this feeling that if I liked my job, I shouldn't contradict her. But business didn't pick up after school began again.' Before I could ask she added: 'It didn't slow down either. Courtney just seemed kind of bummed to me, although that was strictly me and my ESP. For all I know I could have been reading her totally wrong. Because she wasn't all that readable. She never made small talk. And she had zero curiosity.'

'What do you mean?'

'Like when people meet me and hear "Friedman," they tend to squinch up their eyes because they're thinking: Asian and adopted? Half-and-half? Or because of the film-major business, they're curious about what my favorite movie is. But with Courtney, zilch. She read my résumé, checked out the first two minutes of my student film, and told me what the pay was. I was less a human being and more the mechanism that operated the camera. She was Total Business Person.'

'She was cold?'

'Not what most people would call cold. With a truly cold person, you're always wondering, Shit, what did I do wrong? But she never made me feel inadequate. In fact, I could tell she liked the way I worked. She'd even say Good work! and sound as though she meant it. So I felt she had her code of privacy or sense of boundaries and it wasn't anything personal.'

'Did she stay so dispirited about the way the business was going?' I asked.

'Not really. By the time mid-September came she . . . I honestly don't know. She did what she had to do – go over what each family was looking for, how much to shoot. But she acted disengaged, like her mind was someplace else. Before that, even when she was going through her bummed phase, she'd always brainstorm ideas on where to film, or think of ways to get the parents to ask for more time, which equaled money, but essentially she said to me, Whatever.'

'I'm trying to get a handle on her,' I explained to Zee. 'She doesn't sound as if she was the world's warmest person,' I mused.

'Except that's really not right because with her kids she *was* Mrs Warmth. Mrs Mom. I mean, Travis, the little boy, came into the room once. She put her arms out for him and her face got this blissed-out expression. Madonna and child – the Virgin Mary, not the singer. And from the way her house was fixed up, she was really into that Mrs Homebody role. She had no eye in terms of film, but she did have . . . I guess you'd call it Rich Suburban Lady good taste.' An uh-oh expression came over Zee's big-cheeked face.

'Don't worry,' I reassured her. 'I'm not rich. And if left to my own devices – although fortunately my friends restrain me – I'd probably put up purple plaid wallpaper. But I know what you mean. Nothing offensive.'

'Right. But nothing imaginative. Nothing personal. Everything *done*. I mean, you couldn't pee there without good taste. Sorry. My mom hates it when I say "pee." Anyhow, you'd go to the bathroom – the guest bathroom, downstairs. She had a pile of guest towels – the kind you're afraid to use because they have to be ironed, but then you've got to because you're scared she'll think you didn't wash your hands. And then on the sink counter – pink marble – she had this basket with eensy-weensy Tylenol and Motrin tins and a teeny sewing kit. Tampaxes with a pink bow around each one. I swear to God!' She shook her head and added: 'Courtney lined the bottom of the wastebasket with a paper doily.'

Zee Friedman's breezy manner was actually not that distant from my own children's more sardonic Long Island style: Both were true to the Generation X credo that when one is profoundly cool, life can hold no surprises, and thus, there is never any reason to act excited. 'You couldn't go into that house without feeling awe,' Zee went on, sounding noticeably unawed. 'It was the apotheosis of its kind. Did you get that? "Apotheosis"? That's four years at Columbia. Anyhow, her house is to upper-middle-class suburban houses what the Parthenon is to Doric architecture.'

I nodded, recollecting the miniature decorated lampshades over each candelabra bulb in the chandelier in the front hall, the impeccable arrangement of photograph, lamp, and leather-bound books on a small antique table in the living room. How Courtney must have loved what she created. Then I said: 'I saw the StarBaby video you made of Luke Badinowski.' Zee simultaneously grinned and pressed her fingertips against her temples, as if Luke or his parents had been a headache. 'Your work looked professional to me.'

She shook her head. 'Thanks, but it's just competent. I've got an editor friend with super-rich parents. She's got a monsterly expensive piece of computer editing equipment, an Avid. Trust me: If you used one, your videos would totally look Kar-Wai Wong.'

'What kind of equipment did Courtney Logan have?'

Zee ran her fingers through her hair, pulling it back from her face and shoulders, then twisting it into a bun. 'Not that much. Lights for indoor shots. No big, expensive deal. I forget what they're called – the things those guys who make wedding videos use. Maybe eight, nine hundred bucks' worth of lights.'

I thought about the fifteen thousand bucks Fancy Phil had claimed came out of the Logans' joint money market account plus the ten thousand Courtney had ultimately kept from the Smith Barney brokerage account. Fancy

Phil had said that sum, twenty-five thousand dollars, was spent for 'camera crap' and promoting the company. 'What about cameras?'

'I used my own,' Zee replied. She let her hair fall back to her shoulders.

'Any other equipment?'

'No. The other guy she had filming kept the StarBaby equipment in his house. He went to Wesleyan.'

'Did you ever meet him?'

'No. Typical Courtney. She said practically zero about him. I got the impression she didn't want us to get to talking, which probably meant she was paying one of us more than the other. Anyway, she expected I'd use my own equipment. I did rent a mike because the one on my camera makes everybody sound like King Kong.'

'Did she spent a bundle on ads or publicity?' I asked.

'That I don't know. If she did, I couldn't see any serious results. The whole time I worked for her, the level of business seemed about the same.'

'Did she ever talk shop with you?'

Zee leaned her head against the back of the love seat and gazed up at the carved molding at the top of her wall. The decoration could have been a series of grapes or rosettes, but obscured by a century's worth of paint, it was just evenly spaced bumps. 'One time. She said businesses fail for two reasons. Lack of capital and one other thing. Patience or a plan or something.' She looked apologetic. 'I'm interested in production, but what she was going on about was more like a business school rant. I tuned out.'

'What made her chatty about business all of a sudden?'

'It must have been when I asked her if she had any more

work, around July, when she started to act bummed. I'd been hoping she'd give me more to do. But she sort of intimated that she wanted to spread whatever work there was around, not to have to rely on one person.'

'Did that make sense to you?'

'If you believe the clichés about film people – that we're undependable and narcissistic – it did, even though the truth is making movies is a highly organized operation. If people aren't reliable they don't work again. But to me her talk about patience and stuff sounded defensive. I couldn't see that she was on any road to franchising.'

'How often did you work for her?'

'Two or three weekends a month.'

'What did you think of StarBaby?' I asked. 'As someone interested in the producing end of making movies.'

'I guess it's not a bad idea for wealthy communities, where people have a lot of disposable income and not that much time. Probably there are, like, rich dot-com couples with babies who buy videocams but then are too busy to read the instruction book. Except unless Courtney could get the price down, StarBaby wasn't going to become the McDonald's of kiddie video. I mean, she'd been talking about wanting to trademark everything with the word "star" in it: StarChild, StarKid, StarGirl, StarBoy. And before the summer, she'd been looking into all sorts of other stuff. She'd gotten two pediatricians to let their exams be photographed, which had to have been a brilliant con job on her part because of doctors' malpracticephobia. And she was thinking about renting or buying some cuddly dog – a beagle or a collie – the kids could snuggle up to if the family didn't have its own dog. But she said there was a liability problem, like if lovable dog decided StarBaby was lunch.'

'What about her husband?'

'I only met him once – the last time I saw her. He came in after golf. The way she looked at him you'd think he was this combo of – I don't know – Gary Cooper and Jude Law. You mentioned warmth: She acted pretty warm with him, as if he was really, really hot. To me, he was a majorly boring golf guy with good facial planes.'

'Do you think the hot stuff was an act on her part?'

Zee cocked her head to one side for a moment of introspection. Finally she said: 'I never had enough of a sense of the real Courtney to know if there was a false Courtney. For all I could tell, she was deep and unknowable. Or shallow and what you saw was all there was.'

'But with you she was just businesslike?'

'Right, but . . . In the last couple of months, she did seem kind of detached. I mean, not upset or sad it wasn't doing better. Indifferent. Distant. Her mind was someplace else.'

'Where?'

Zee offered an I-don't-know shrug. 'I couldn't begin to guess. But Courtney went from trying to inhale for me – which was a real pain, I'm very organized – to basically letting me wing it.'

'Could she have been depressed?'

'Well, she always acted so peppy. It was hard to see beyond that. She'd say hi and it would come out "Hi-ee!" with this cute little squeak at the end. I'd say she was pretty low in July, but she was still squeaking. And by September she was squeaking Hi-ee, except her head was someplace else that wasn't StarBaby country.'

'Did she seem afraid of anything? Nervous in any way?'

'Not that I could see, but then again, how much was she going to let me see?'

'Could she have been in love? Having an affair?' Zee offered me an I-don't-know shrug. 'Did you ever see her emotional about anything?'

Zee shook her head slowly, though I could see she was still mulling over my question. While she mulled, I concluded she wasn't a homicidal psychopath and would be terrific for Joey. 'It was weird,' she said finally. 'One time she got a phone call. We were in her office, which was an upstairs bedroom she'd converted. Cool. She used a beaten-up table that *had* to be an antique for her desk. There were tons of real flowers in vases. The room was done to a tee, like everything in the house. Anyhow, she put whoever was calling on hold and then went someplace else. But she must have stayed on the second floor, maybe her bedroom, because I could hear her, although a lot of it was muffled. She seemed pretty upset: "Why can't you . . ." And what else? Oh. "You *promised* . . ." That was all I heard, but boy, did she sound hassled. Almost desperate. I don't know, I could be reading too much into it.'

'Could you tell if she was talking to a man or woman?' Zee shook her head. 'Do you happen to remember when it was?'

'Late afternoon, when she was making out my check. That's why I was in her office. It must have been my last check – which would have made it a Sunday. The Sunday before Halloween. The Sunday before she disappeared.'

'Was that before or after you met her husband that afternoon?'

'After. Definitely after.'

From Zee's I drove from Manhattan over the Williamsburg Bridge – a structure that does not inspire confidence in the profession of civil engineering – into Brooklyn to keep a lunch date I'd made with Joey two weeks earlier. Ever since Bob died, I had to force myself out of the house to live something that vaguely resembled a life.

Except whenever I was out, all I wanted to do was get home. It wasn't so bad the days I was teaching at St Elizabeth's, because my classes were all in the morning. I could be safely home by twelve-thirty. But for the first few months after his death, when I had days off, and I'd be doing volunteer work or running errands, I found myself scurrying to my car and rushing back to the house at lunchtime. And once I got there, my face damp from the tension, my breathing harsh . . . What? What was I expecting? Bob calling really long distance?

So for the last eighteen months or so I'd pushed myself back into the world, making lunch and dinner dates weeks in advance. Some nights I went to meetings, lectures, concerts. I was in an adult-ed class for beginning conversational Spanish. Or I let Nancy drag me into the city, to the galleries or the theater. When I was alone I buried myself in piles of term papers or exams. Or I'd reread a favorite book – nothing new, nothing unexpected for me. I played endless, numbing games of computer solitaire. Or I'd watch my favorite old movies until I'd become so enervated by Rosalind Russell's pluck that I'd fall asleep.

Maybe Socrates was right and the unexamined life was not worth living, but I was giving it my best shot. Weekends were harder. Everybody else knocked themselves out with leisure. But unless Nancy or one of the kids was free, or I had a date, I'd have no answer for the universal Monday-morning-at-work question: What did you do this weekend? For a while I made elaborate to-do lists in eighteen-point boldface and taped them up on the refrigerator. However, by Sunday night the only crossed-out item would be something like 'Find Jane Fonda low-impact video,' which, instead of inserting into the VCR as I'd pledged to myself, I'd inserted into the garbage can. All I seemed able to do was clean house. Along with the cassette I'd toss out stuff I'd previously been unable to part with: a bag of potting soil from around the time of the Reagan-Carter-Anderson race, five thousand pounds of *Gourmet* magazines, Bob's collar stays.

Anyhow, Joey took me to a new, hot restaurant near his apartment. The waiters, in white, short-sleeved shirts, black slacks, and skinny black ties, looked like funeral directors from Tuscaloosa. The food, however, was not southern but a trendy fusion, Californian and Cuban, which seemed to mean vertical stacks of rare fish, greens, and assorted legumes over *al dente* rice. Joey had not only heard about Crabapple Films but had actually given their latest release, a film set on Staten Island but based on *As You Like It*, four and a half out of his five stars. But he said no, I could not call and ask Zee if she was interested in being fixed up with him. And no, movie critics do not casually saunter into production offices and ask half-Chinese, half-Jewish PA's for information on their latest projects.

When I got home, I weeded my flower beds and vegetable patch until it was too dark to find weeds. It wasn't only the loss of Bob, the change of my status from wife to widow, that made weekends so tough. It was the other loss in my life – Nelson Sharpe. For twenty years I'd spent too many Saturdays and Sundays in a reflective fog, summoning up every episode of our relationship – and there were plenty of episodes. Worse, the previous year when I'd accidentally bumped into him for a total of three seconds: I compulsively replayed that scene again and again, choosing it hands down over anything the present had to offer.

Okay, the scene: It had been almost twenty years since Nelson and I had last laid eyes on each other. Suddenly there he was, walking right past me. The truth? He looked semilousy. His salt-and-pepper hair had hardly any pepper left. His face was the chalky, indoor color of a life-long civil servant, though later I tried to tell myself he'd simply gone pale with shock at seeing me. While I had neither the time nor the presence of mind to give him the once-over, his body still looked fine. His eyes, still beautiful, large, and velvety brown, were wide open – with amazement or horror. For those three seconds they did not leave my face.

It's amazing how long three seconds can last. Naturally, I immediately thought there was some ghastly flaw he'd spotted, one of those hideous imperfections of middle age I'd missed because my eyesight had gone to hell – a giant hair growing out of my chin, an entire cheek covered by a rampaging liver spot. I held my arms tight to my sides so as not to reach up and feel for what was wrong. But then I reassured myself that for someone who, in her youth, had assumed that by her mid-fifties she'd resemble Albert Einstein, I was still fairly attractive. However, before I could think of something unmortifying to say, or offer him a serene nod, he had passed me by.

When I reported the encounter (in encyclopedic, adolescent detail) to Nancy, she made me swear not to do anything crazy like call him. I swore. Nevertheless, she insinuated I'd try some cute trick to get around my oath – like faxing him Bob's obituary – so I slammed down the phone.

Actually, it was Nelson who called me the next morning. He explained he hadn't meant to be rude, but was so shocked to see me he couldn't think of anything to say. We talked for just a few minutes. He told me there was a new political regime in the department. He was out of Homicide and head of a unit called Special Investigations. He also said he and June had gotten divorced fifteen years before. He'd been married for three years to a woman named Nicole, a high-school guidance counselor. Naturally, being the Compleat Schnook, I asked how old she was. Thirty-nine, which technically made him old enough to be her father and untechnically made me speechless with something pretty close to despair. He filled the silence by asking what I was doing, so I told him I'd gotten my doctorate and was teaching college. I didn't say a word about Bob. Nelson said, Maybe one of these days we could get together, have a cup of coffee. I said no, I didn't think that was a good idea.

And that was it. End of conversation. Later I was positive that when he spoke of his new wife his voice hadn't had a lilt, but Nancy declared I was *non compos mentis* or, alternatively, engaged in the most pathetic sort of wishful thinking. So I demanded, Then how come he wants to have coffee with me? She replied he's probably an old lech who reflexively whips out his wonker for an airing every time a woman passes by. He's not *that* old,

I chimed in, and he was never a lech. Drop this, Nancy warned. Whatever it was you had together, it never meant to him what it meant to you.

But back to the Courtney Logan case. Since it was Memorial Day, I had the leisure on that Monday morning to attempt to come up with a reasonable suspect for the murder who could take the place of Greg. However, I soon realized I didn't know anywhere near enough about Courtney's friends and associates to begin. Since I couldn't interrogate Greg, I did the next best thing and called my client, Fancy Phil Lowenstein. He said he'd meet me that night in a new restaurant. In Port Washington. La Luna Toscana. Eight o'clock. You get there before me, you tell Antonio, Listen, I'm the doctor of history who's here for Phil. He'll take care of you till I get there.

But Fancy Phil had arrived before I did, and was seated at a corner table. He faced the room, his back toward a mural of a moonlit olive grove that for some reason was overrun by a herd of cross-eyed sheep. At first all I could see of Phil's outfit was a giant red napkin over his chest. Then I saw it was tucked into the neck of a black sports shirt that had a minuscule pattern of what appeared to be chartreuse boom-erangs. He wore a gold link bracelet and a gold watch with twelve diamonds instead of numerals. Maybe to go with the watch, he had on his doozy of a diamond pinkie ring.

Before Fancy Phil was so much antipasto that what must have been the large oval platter beneath it all was completely camouflaged. Cheese vied with peppers for air. Artichoke hearts tried their best to squeeze in between the bresaola and pepperoni. His pudgy fingers were busy rolling up slices of prosciutto and provolone into a cigar shape. He

108

stuffed the entire cylinder into his mouth, chewed once, swallowed with a big bounce of his Adam's apple, and commanded: 'Sit down, sweetheart. I ordered some stuff. If you don't like it, Antonio'll have the chef make whatever you want. So, you come up with any, uh, theories?'

'I'm working on it,' I answered as he poured me a glass of red wine.

He held my glass up to the light. 'Rosso di Montalcino.' His accent would make an Italian shriek with laughter. Not to his face, of course. Someone might have the nerve to laugh with Fancy Phil, but never at him. 'It comes from Tuscany. That's what "Toscana" means. Tuscany. It don't mean parrot.'

I decided not to inquire why anyone might think such a thing. 'I need to speak to more people who knew Courtney,' I told him. 'I've got feelers out trying to get the names of her close friends, but I could get going quicker if you could help me.'

'No problem.' He picked up a dark olive so huge it looked like a major organ from a small mammal. He popped it into his mouth and it disappeared. He did not seem to know or care if it had a pit.

'When do you think you could come up with some kind of a list?'

'Now,' he said.

'You have it all written down?'

'Not written. I know stuff from Gregory. I spoke to him and then I went there after you called me.'

Iron sconces on the wall held flickering bulbs that were supposed to approximate the gleam of candles, but instead of a soothing glow, the continual sputter of light made you wonder if your retina was detaching. La Luna Toscana. For some reason I never could explain, whenever a new culinary trend got under way in Manhattan, like Tuscan cuisine, it spread to the other four boroughs, then went west, straight out to Kansas City – with a side trip to Emporia – before it could manage to cover the twenty-six miles east to the north shore of Long Island.

'Greg gave you specific names?' I asked, pondering a chunk of white cheese that felt hard enough to break a tooth. I set it on the side of my plate and picked up a bread stick. 'For you to give to me?'

Wearily, Fancy Phil shook his head. Naturally, not a single jet black hair changed position. 'Nah. I asked him what he told the lawyer. One of the things he told her were the names of Courtney's friends, her business people. Then when I was upstairs with Morgan playing Candyland, I walked out for a few minutes and went into her office.' He paused. 'This is strictly between you and me.'

'Sure.'

'So I'm in her office. I don't know about computers, but I look at the fat leather book she had, with a calendar and addresses and other crap. A map of the Underground in London.'

'It's called a Filofax. It's made in England.'

'Bully for England.'

'So you took notes of what was in her Filofax?'

'No, no, no. I didn't need to take no notes. I never forget nothing.' He snapped a celery stick in two and shook one of the pieces at me the way a teacher would shake a pointer at a deliberately dense student. 'You should remember that, Doc.'

110

'Is that a veiled threat that's supposed to make me feel chilled to the bone?'

Fancy Phil laughed a deep, big-bellied laugh, said 'Nah,' and recommended the Tuscan pot roast.

The next morning was one of those exquisite end-of-May days, the air sweet with the fragrance of new-mown grass and so clear that from the highest hill in Shorehaven you could see the Manhattan skyline shining gold in the sunlight. But I was in a carrel at the library. The unending creak of the elevator transporting books was my background music while I studied Fancy Phil's list of names. Unlike him, I'd had to write things down. I was awed by his ability not only to remember the spelling of each name, but to spew out the phone numbers and addresses that he'd cribbed from Courtney's Filofax.

I didn't know where to begin, so before I took on Courtney's friends, women who might also tie their tampons with ribbons, I flipped a quarter. Heads meant that Steffi Deissenburger, the Logans' former au pair, was German. Tails she was Austrian. She'd been reported in news accounts as being from both places. Austria won. I got out my cell phone and called the consulate in Manhattan and – *Mein Gott!* – finally got connected to a man who clearly knew who she was.

Nevertheless, Herr Toasty – which was the best I could make of his name, since his speech was exceedingly clipped – told me, in a huffy manner that all but said *Dummkopf*, that it was the United States embassy in Vienna that issued visas to Austrian citizens, not the Austrian consulate in New York. So I addressed him, in an even huffier tone: Excuse me, Herr Toasty, but it's one thing for an Austrian national to be an innocent victim of our overeager media, and it's quite another (I raised my voice) FOR FOREIGNERS TO USE OUR LIBRARIES AND THEN RUN OFF WITH BOOKS THAT ARE PROPERTY OF A PUBLIC INSTITUTION! After some mutual, guttural harrumphing, Herr Toasty agreed that if he could *possibly* find someone who *might* know Fräulein Deissenburger's whereabouts, which was *highly* unlikely, he would mention my name, the Shorehaven Public Library, and overdue books in the same sentence.

Naturally, I considered all the reasons why I should not have used the name of the Shorehaven Public Library in vain not before I'd hung up with Herr Toasty, but after. Like if Steffi Deissenburger actually had taken out *Madeline and the Bad Hat* to read to little Morgan but had borrowed it on Courtney's card and ergo knew that the library having her name in its records was fishier than last week's flounder. Like if Steffi (or worse, her lawyer) did call but, instead of calling me at school, decided to call the library and demanded to speak with the head of the library, thereby getting me kicked off the board and well on my way to becoming a town scandal. And then of course there was the little question I'd been avoiding answering: Was I nuts? Nuts to think I could set myself up in the detecting business, nuts to risk chasing down a murderer, and even more nuts to take on a client like Fancy Phil Lowenstein.

For most people, this sort of anxiety leads them to say: I'm so upset I can't eat a thing. Usually for me, it's: I'm so upset I need a grilled-cheese-and-tomato sandwich and a glass of milk and multiple Fig Newtons. So by the time I went out to dinner with a historian who taught at Queens College, I could only gaze into the brown depths of the Spicy Chicken Soong feeling something between existential nausea and plain pukey. However, that awful feeling evaporated as we wound up comparing and contrasting Watergate and the Whitewater/Lewinsky debacle, alternately howling with laughter and nodding sagely with the usual wild abandon of two historians sharing a half bottle of Chardonnay.

So if I wasn't singing 'Life Is Just a Bowl of Cherries' by the time I got back, I was in a pretty decent mood. No messages at home. I listened expectantly to the one that was on my voice mail at the college, hoping to hear Steffi Deissenburger's girlish Teutonic tones advising me she had no library books and leaving a phone number, but it was only Commodore Patrick Daley, USN, Ret., one of my oldest students, telling me he had recovered still more memories of Admiral Hyman Rickover and the development of the *Nautilus* and would I consider writing his memoirs with him?

I was thinking semideep thoughts about how so many older students at St Elizabeth's would find excuses to come to my office and then not talk about the course, but their own personal histories. I wasn't simply because they were lonely. They needed the solace of knowing that their lives had meant something. So when the doorbell rang I didn't think, Gee, it's nine forty-five and people don't just drop in at this hour. I sauntered over to the front door and peered through the peephole I'd had put in after Bob died, along with an alarm system and an overzealous motion detector that warned me of any squirrels humping within a five-mile radius. At first all I saw was an eye squinting back at me. And then I realized it was Nelson Sharpe.

113

Chapter Six

Nelson Sharpe.

Faced with the precise scenario I'd been dreaming of for twenty years, I was, of course, completely unprepared. My entire body, from my scalp to the soles of my feet, was jolted by an electric *Yikes!* With each beat, my heart slammed harder until my entire chest filled with what felt like life-threatening hammering. Except it wasn't my heart, but the geyser of blood erupting in my head that made me sure my imminent death certificate would read 'cerebral accident' instead of 'myocardial infarction.'

After a couple of seconds, relieved to find myself alive, I managed to put the chain on the door and open it its three inches. Nelson looked significantly better than he had the year before, when I'd bumped into him for that instant. Casual now, his sports jacket (a houndstooth check patterned after a hound who needed orthodontia) was open, displaying an admirable section of broad, white-shirted chest, bisected by a yellow knit tie, and what appeared to be a still-flat belly. His coloring was no longer the civil-service parchment I'd been shocked by a year earlier. Actually it was now a fairly furious red. 'Come on, Judith, open the damn door!'

Never a girl who could play hard to get, I eased off the chain, grateful I was still wearing slacks and a silk blouse and hadn't changed into one of my tantalizing bits of lingerie, like an oversize T-shirt and stringy terrycloth robe, neither of which disguised the fact that my breasts were no longer looking up. Anyhow, the instant the chain came off, Nelson used his suburban variation on the old TV cop routine, though instead of slamming his body against the door, he used a discreet combo of knee and shoulder that pushed the door open far enough that I could not change my mind about letting him inside.

Like I would change my mind. Except his first words in the front hall as he stood beside the umbrella stand were not: 'Ah, Judith, eternally my beloved,' but 'What the hell were you doing last night?' Well, I thought, at least he wasn't shouting. In fact, his volume control was turned down suspiciously low.

'What are you talking about?' I whispered back. Not a particularly scintillating response, but I was so flustered being with him, alone in the house, that it was a small miracle that five consecutive words emerged. I couldn't really listen for his answer, being too busy focusing all my energy on breathing slowly so he wouldn't think I was panting with desire – or wheezing with the über-hysteria of postmenopausal women in Freud's lesser case studies. Also, with the exhilaration of Nelson's presence, I couldn't think straight enough to recall what I had done the previous evening. Plus, my cognitive processes weren't helped by his sports jacket. A thought flitted through my head: If you're dressing to drop by at your former lover's house, even if you don't have an iota of feeling left, you spiff up.

What could have possessed him to wear a sports jacket that belonged in a smutty vaudeville act?

So for an interminable time that probably lasted four seconds, we stared into each other's eyes and I think were mutually embarrassed to discover that, despite twenty years' worth of crow's-feet and hideous houndstooth, the old flame was still blazing.

I got busy clearing my throat while Nelson recovered from the moment's awkwardness by acting like a detective, i.e., glancing over at my mail that was strewn over a small, skinny-legged half-an-oval table across from the umbrella stand. Since all that was in sight was a Long Island Power Authority electric bill, a thank-you note from Human Rights Watch for the contribution, the June issue of the *Journal of American History*, and a Williams-Sonoma catalog, he turned back to me and snapped: 'Last night.' His snap, however, was still pretty damn sotto voce. What was with him? In the old days he'd never been a sotto voce kind of guy when in snappish mode. Not that he was a screamer, but boy, could he be loud.

Then it dawned on me that the reason for his self-control was his conviction that I was not alone, that Bob must be upstairs. In our briefest of brief phone conversation the previous year, he'd told me about his new wife. I hadn't mentioned my late husband. However, since my hands were now on my hips (my acutely pissed-off position) with my unringed ring finger clearly visible, I concluded his deductive skills might have dimmed a tad.

'Okay,' I said, 'I give up. What about last night?'

'You were seen in the company of a certain Philip Joseph Lowenstein.'

'A certain Philip Joseph Lowenstein? You mean out of all the Philip Joseph Lowensteins in Nassau County –'

'Fancy Phil Lowenstein, damn it!' He made a fist, but before he could smash it against the wall for emphasis, which, as I recalled, was one of his Top 10 Intimidating Cop Tricks, he thrust his hand into his pocket. 'Look,' he said more calmly, 'I know what you like to do.' Then quickly, abashed, he added: 'Are you involved in looking into his daughter-in-law's murder? Or are you . . . Is Phil Lowenstein some kind of an acquaintance, or a business associate?'

'How about my paramour?'

'Come on, Judith.'

'How come you're asking me about Courtney's murder? Didn't you tell me you weren't in Homicide anymore?'

'I'm heading up the unit called Special Investigations.'

'Which does what? Investigate with whom your ex, uh, lady friends are dining?'

'It deals with organized crime. And so does Fancy Phil.'

'Let's see . . . What happened?' I asked. 'You have a tail on him and . . . Give me a minute to think this through. You or someone in your unit saw him coming out of La Luna Toscana with me. Being a gentleman, Fancy Phil walked me to my car –'

Peeved that I wasn't awestruck by his unit's investigatory prowess, he cut me off: 'Yeah, right. And my guy ran your license plate. And there was your name and address on my desk this morning.' He permitted himself a small smile: 'The report had you down as "an alleged history professor."'

'That's what they say where I teach, too. Listen, do you want to come inside and sit down so you can grill me more comfortably?'

'I don't want to grill you,' he was saying as he followed me into the kitchen. We sat across from each other at the table, which sounds proper, but being a narrow refectory kind of thing, it brought us close enough together that I could sense the heat radiating from his knees. Every few seconds his eyes would dart around the room, maybe searching for some familiar landmark still there after twenty years. But the white-flecked beige Formica counters had turned to blue-black granite and the GE refrigerator with the kids' artwork had been replaced by a Sub Zero the size of a small kitchen. Or maybe he was checking to see if Bob was shuffling about in slippers and robe. I offered, but he declined anything to eat or drink. I flipped open the tab of a can of Dr Brown's Diet Cream and took a sip. 'Do you know who Phil Lowenstein is?' he continued. 'I mean, beyond whatever it is you read in the paper?'

'I have no doubt you'll fill me in.' The next second I panicked that he'd think what I'd said was a double entendre, so with enormous nonchalance I took another sip of soda, which naturally was too ambitious. I leaped up for a napkin sensing it less than suave to wipe my dripping chin on the shoulder of my turquoise silk blouse.

'He's got high-level ties to both the Italian Cosa Nostra *and* the Russian Organizatsiya,' Nelson said as I sat back down. 'He's done everything dirty – dealt in stolen checks, diamonds, stock manipulation, bootleg gasoline, all sorts of stuff. Phil Lowenstein stinks to high heaven.'

118

'Some might call him the personification of the American entrepreneurial spirit.'

'Don't blow this off, Judith. Look, he took a vacation for aggravated assault, but we think he's been behind at least half-a-dozen hits.'

'Are you saying Fancy Phil himself pulled the trigger?'

'Fancy Phil makes bad things happen.'

'When?' I demanded. 'Recently?'

'Over the years,' he responded coolly. He rubbed his lower lip. I warned myself: Don't start picturing what it would be like to kiss him there. So naturally I got a graphic mental image of kissing his finger, then brushing it aside and kissing the very place he'd been touching.

'How come you haven't arrested him?' I asked.

'Grow up.'

'I have. And I know if you'd had any real evidence, he'd have been convicted of murder. But the truth is, all Fancy Phil was convicted of was aggravated assault. One conviction. Fine, I'm the first to concede it's not nice to hit people.'

'Especially not in the face with a brick,' Nelson remarked.

'But Phil paid his debt to society. Now he's a grand-father, and he wants to play it straight for the children's sake.'

'I can't believe you fell for that.'

'And also for the sake of his son, especially since sus-picion's fallen on Greg for Courtney's murder. I think Phil feels if it weren't for the way he's lived his life, the authorities would be doing what they should be doing – investigating who killed Courtney Logan – and not harassing Greg.'

119

Nelson leaned back so the chair rested on its two rear legs and crossed his arms over his chest. 'Tell me you aren't that naive,' he said quietly.

'I'm not naive at all,' I said to the cream soda. I was thinking it was actually a plus that the light over the table was strong enough to show him I hadn't become a shriveled-up crone when, all of a sudden, looking down at his big hands resting at the edge of the table, I got a flash of the past, how Nelson used to undress me as we made love, how so many times I'd looked down at those hands unbuttoning my shirt.

'Phil Lowenstein is an animal,' he said harshly. 'Don't pretend you don't know that.'

'Phil Lowenstein is a human being.'

'Don't start shoveling the liberal bullshit, Judith. I don't like seeing you getting involved with –'

'I can take care of myself.' He shook his head: No, you can't. 'Is Phil a suspect in the Courtney business or is it just Greg?'

'What's your involvement in this?' he demanded.

'I'm curious. You didn't answer my question.'

'I'm not in Homicide anymore.'

'That's not an answer.'

'Your "I'm curious" isn't an answer either.' He shifted forward so the chair again rested on all four legs and stood. 'Listen, I know better than almost anyone that you've got brains and guts. So if you want to pursue your detective thing, fine. Personally and legally I would warn you to stay out of it, but if that's what you gotta do, you gotta do it.' Reluctantly, I got up, too. 'Except find yourself another case,' he went on. 'Dealing with this guy: Listen to me.

There are top-level mob guys too scared of Fancy Phil to go near him. You should be, too.' He turned and walked to the door that led back to the hallway. When we reached the front door, he took a deep breath and said: 'Someone like you, a person of your station in life, shouldn't have her name in the folder that comes to my desk every morning. And I want you to hear me on this . . .'

'Go ahead,' I told him.

'If you step over the line in his company, don't count on any favors for old times' sake.' Having said that, he at least had the decency to look embarrassed. On the other hand, he didn't take it back.

Since I couldn't think of any response, clever or insipid, I simply reached around him and pulled open the front door. 'Does your husband know you're involved in this?' he asked as he stepped out into the balmy May night.

'I very much doubt it,' I replied. Quickly, before there could be that instant of awkwardness followed by something he might regret and I might not, I closed the door behind him.

Naturally I didn't sleep much, being busy playing over the scene with Nelson a few hundred times, coming up with all sorts of reasons for his dropping by, from strictly business to he-wants-to-be-completely-certain-before-he-leaves-his-wife-for-me. Much of the time I substituted sparkling repartee for what I'd actually said. Nevertheless, when my alarm rang at seven, I didn't go back to sleep, perchance to dream of Nelson. Instead, I called my voice mail at St Elizabeth's.

To my amazement, Herr Toasty of the Austrian consulate had actually come through! Steffi Deissenburger, in a minimal German accent — the sort that makes the speaker sound like an American who just needs a little time with a speech therapist — said she was certain she had returned all her books to the Shorehaven Library, but to call her. She left a number with a Connecticut area code. Two hours later, when I called, I explained that Herr Toasty might have misunderstood: I was a historian who happened to be on the library board. I'd been asked to write a historical overview of crimes against the wealthy on Long Island for an academic journal. Could I have just a few minutes of her time to get some background on Courtney Logan?

Well, Steffi thought aloud, her employer, Ms Leeds, would be taking the twins to a breeder to look at puppies. That would be at one o'clock. Therefore, Steffi would be free from one until two. Although she wasn't supposed to have visitors at the house. But then again, the brakes on her car were being relined, so she couldn't get out. If I was prompt . . .

I drove about an hour and a half northwest, up to one of the farthest of Manhattan's bedroom communities. Whitsbury was a town of flawless lawns sheared to velvet, patrician trees, and houses so stately they could con their owners into believing they were to the manor born. From the roots of the English ivy to the tops of the stone chimneys, homes and grounds were unrelievedly refined, as if exuberance had been banned by local ordinance. This was stiff-upper-lip country. No new waves of immigrants reinterpreting the American dream the way we do on Long Island. No Tudor with a skylight to outrage the neighbors; no Dutch colonial resurfaced in ersatz fieldstone. Not even a château with a hot tub: Whitsbury was orthodox Anglo-Saxon.

I tooled up a cobblestone driveway to a red-brick house so splendidly solid it made the Logans' impressive Georgian look like something made from Lego pieces. Steffi Deissenburger stood at the front door, watching with apprehension as I narrowly missed scrunching half a flower bed under my right front tire. As I exited the Jeep, I gave her an all's-well wave that must have been a little too hearty because she inched backward into the house, perhaps fearing I'd do something embarrassingly Long Island, like bear-hug her or screech Hey, fancy-schmancy!

'Hello,' she said cautiously.

'Hello,' I said genteely, though with extra warmth, in my be-nice-to-German-speaking-people-so-they-don't-think-you-think-they're-all-Nazis manner. From everything I'd heard, I'd assumed Steffi would be plain, and in khaki slacks, a white shirt, and sneakers, she definitely wasn't fashion's fool. Still, she would never be mistaken for an understated lady of the manor. Instead of the au naturel Connecticut horsey set's no-makeup look, in which a woman strives for a family resemblance to her mare, Steffi was cosmeticized to the nth degree. What looked to be ivory skin was agleam with a heavy coat of that shiny, slimy foundation and cheek color that I guess is supposed to make the young look dewy but winds up making most of them look like hookers who need astringent. Too bad: She had a classic oval face with placid gray eyes touching in their gentleness. Her nose, unfortunately, was ice-cream-cone-shaped and stuck a bit too close to her mouth. But if she wasn't actually pretty,

123

at least she was better than advertised, projecting an aura of calm and kindness.

She was working as an au pair for an advertising-agency owner and his wife who had twin three-year-old girls. 'Gwendolyn and Gwyneth,' she informed me as she led me through the house, stopping to hand me a silver-framed photograph as we tippy-toed through a living room that was so vast it needed three different Oriental rugs to cover its dark wood floor. She waited eagerly for a reaction, as if wanting to make sure she had communicated her fondness for her charges.

'Very sweet,' I replied. Gwen and Gwyn were fat-faced and red-cheeked, with identical puckers above their noses; to me, they looked more like anxiety-prone Munchkins than preschoolers. I handed back the picture. Reflexively, Steffi buffed the frame with her shirttail before leading me into the glassed-in porch she referred to as a conservatory.

A white wicker couch and chairs were covered in a chintz of tulips, hyacinths, and daffodils that practically sang 'Spring Is Here.' Expensive picture books on flowers and glossy gardening magazines were fanned across a marble table resting on a short Neoclassical pedestal. Leaves and flowers cascaded down a high, graceful steplike structure like chorus girls in a Busby Berkeley movie. I wouldn't have minded taking the room back with me to Long Island. 'Do you miss Travis and Morgan?'

'Of course,' she said quickly. 'Now, you're here because you wish to get a sense of what Courtney was like?'

'That's right. As background for my project.' Steffi, like Gwen and Gwyn, seemed older than her years. Her brown hair had frosty platinum and copper streaks, the sort of color job a woman my age, desperate for top down, hair-wild-in-the-wind youth, might inflict on herself. Sunlight shone on her hair and gave the dyed streaks a green, phosphorescent gleam. 'As I told you on the phone,' I continued, 'this chat can be off-the-record. It's for my benefit, so I can be better prepared when I begin to write.'

'Yes. Okay.'

'Good. Then we'll get on to Courtney.'

'Yes, well, you see I am calling her Courtney as well because she asked me not to call her Ms or Mrs Logan. She was so kind.' Steffi pursed her thin, scarlet lips, meticulously outlined in darker red pencil, while she pondered what Courtney was like. Meanwhile, her index finger was busy tracing the outline of a large, pink hyacinth on the creamy chintz on the arm of her chair. 'She was not at all formal. But neither was she . . . friendly. No, that is not the word I want.' Though she was taking her sweet time thinking about adjectives, she didn't strike me as pedantic as much as concerned about being precise. '"Accessible" is what I mean,' she finally said. 'Most people in the U.S. are very free with information about themselves. Courtney was not. She was, I would say, a lady.'

'Can you give me an example?'

Steffi massaged her forehead with her thumb and index finger. In an American, I would have called the gesture full of baloney, but for all I knew it could have been a common posture for thinking Austrians. 'I am sorry but . . . It was not that she did not talk. Sometimes she could talk a great deal. She would ask me about my country and would speak of how it was here.' Her massaging left two dull lines in the sheen of her makeup. 'But I learned little of her from all her talk, if you understand me. She spoke of government or economics or about the children, of course. So for instance, I did not know she came from the state of Washington until, you know, I read it in the newspaper when she was missing. I think I knew about her only that she went to Princeton College and worked as an investment banker.'

'Was she specific about what she wanted or didn't want with the kids, or your duties around the house?'

'Oh yes. Very specific. Only fruit snacks. One hour of television a day. She must approve all videos and play dates. For the children, I mean. She asked me please not to let them see me eating sweets. Or watching television. I had a television in my room, so I could watch programs after they were asleep. But she was so kind. She said, "I hope this won't put you out, Steffi," and I said, "No, of course not, Courtney."'

'What about Gregory Logan?' I asked.

'I saw less of him.' Under the layer or two of makeup, I thought I saw Steffi flush. I couldn't tell if it was because of some sexual memory, or a crush on her employer, or simply from chagrin at having been whispered about in connection with him. 'He worked late many times. When he was home, naturally he was with the children or Courtney.'

'Did you call him Greg or Mr Logan?'

'Neither.' Her violet-lidded eyes gave a single blink. 'He never asked me to call him by his Christian name, but as Courtney had invited me to do so with her, I never knew what to say.' She shrugged. Just for an instant she looked flustered, like the postadolescent she actually was. 'I didn't call him anything.'

126

'What happened on the night Courtney disappeared?' I asked softly, praying she would find this an appropriate question for a historian to ask.

'She came home from tricking and treating with Morgan and went to the kitchen. She said we had no more organic apples. She did not wish the children to eat too many sweets, you see, from Halloween. So she said to give them an apple for dessert, then one sweet. After the apple they would not be so hungry and ask for extra sweets. I told her: I will go to the Grand Union and buy the apples. No, she said, because it was the one night of the year children run around the streets, tricking and treating. They wear masks, so they could not see properly. She would prefer to drive. You see? Always thoughtful.'

'What time was that?'

'Between five-thirty and six.'

'Did you hear her car? Or actually see her drive away?'

'Yes.' Steffi came across as one of those naturally tranquil people, with her gentle eyes and low-pitched, calm voice. Until you looked at her hands. They would not stay still; they traveled down to her khakis and rubbed her knees. 'We always saw her go, because in the beginning, Travis used to cry when she would leave the house. Courtney said we should, you know, make a game of Mommy going bye-bye. Morgan would climb onto the window seat in the family room and look out the window where, you know, you could see the car leaving the garage. I would pick up Travis. We would all wave and say: "Bye-bye, Mommy. See you soon."'

'And on Halloween night, as she left to go for the

apples . . . Did Courtney seem preoccupied or fearful or in any way not herself?'

Steffi's hands slid back from her knees and began to knead her thighs. 'No. I am certain. I have thought about this many, many times. She played Mommy going bye-bye with us in the same way. She waved good-bye. She smiled.'

'What happened next?'

'Nothing. I waited. It was seven o'clock. Then seven-thirty. I couldn't understand, but I gave the children each a small Snickers bar – from the bag I bought to have for trickers and treaters, not the sweets from Morgan's bag because I knew Courtney would not want them eating candy from other people. I put them to bed.'

'Where was Greg Logan then?'

Steffi's hands came together as if in prayer. She rested her chin on top of her middle fingers. 'In Manhattan. A dinner for business.'

'Did you try to call him there?'

She shook her head, wearily. Clearly, she had repeated this account over and over to the police. 'No. I did not call him.'

'How come?' I tried for that look of benevolent curiosity women friends have in laxative commercials.

Her scarlet lips formed a tight fish mouth. 'I was afraid that Courtney would become – what is the word? – upset with me.'

'For bothering her husband?'

'No, no. For letting him know she was not at home. One time early that month he called. I told him I did not know where Courtney had gone. It was about four in the afternoon. He called back several times. When she did come home, at seven o'clock, she was angry with me. Angry in a quiet way. That was her way of being angry.' Steffi hugged herself in consolation, as though still shaken. 'It was my fault. I had forgotten what she had instructed me.'

'What was that?'

'That when I did not know where she was, I should say she was shopping so her husband would not worry.' I probably lifted an eyebrow or two skeptically. 'Courtney worried that *he* worried,' she explained. 'She said to me, "My husband has enough on his plate."'

'What did she mean by that?'

'That he had much to think about. As they say, "pressured."'

'Did he seem that way to you? A pressured business-man?'

'No.'

'What was he like?'

'Quiet.'

'Nice to you?'

Steffi nodded, but I thought I caught her swallowing hard. Was Greg not nice? Had there been something between her and her employer, either before or after Courtney's disappearance? Did she simply have a lonely young woman's crush on her boss? Or was it about those rumors floating around Shorehaven? Could there be some darker reason for that swallow? 'Yes. Nice. Very polite.'

'He's an interesting-looking man.'

'Yes, interesting. Somewhat Asian in the upper part of his face, I think, but his manner is very American.'

'How were he and Courtney together? I'm asking because in preliminary interviews, I heard several different accounts. You have the advantage of being in the house.'

'They were fine. They were in love.' Steffi's eyes left mine and gazed out the glass wall of the conservatory at the high stands of pink rhododendron on the far side of what was either a huge puddle or a small fishpond. 'Her face – when he walked through the door she would become . . . like a bride on her wedding day. So happy. He would always kiss the top of her head and ask her, "How is my Courtney?"'

'Any sign of violence or threat of violence? Did he ever hit her or threaten –'

She jerked back her head, startled at the suggestion. 'Oh no!'

'Was she out of the house often – I mean, where you didn't know where she was?'

'No.' Reluctantly, she brought her eyes back to mine. 'Well, more so in the week or two before Halloween. Three or four times, I think. Mr Logan did not come home until eight, so she could be out until then.'

'How did she dress those times she went off?'

'I don't understand.'

'Was she dressed in casual clothes, as if she were staying in Shorehaven? Or dressier.'

She took a deep breath and exhaled slowly. 'I think . . . She was in – yes – a suit and high-heeled shoes.'

I recalled Jill Badinowski reporting how simply and elegantly Courtney had dressed, in slacks and a silk blouse. 'The sort of outfit she would wear when she visited couples to tell them about StarBaby? Or dressier?'

'As though she was going to something important. I would say in Manhattan, but I do not know, of course.'

'A sexy suit?'

'No, no. Business, I think. A beautiful suit. Although she put on makeup and once put her hair up on her head. But she wore a blouse. Not sexy. You could not see her, you know, her breasts.'

'Let's get back to Greg Logan. He came home around eight during the week?' Steffi nodded. 'Every night?'

'Yes. His business was food, take-out food. People bought their dinners in his stores, so he had to be in his office, above the commissary where the food was prepared if something was not correct. And these times she was away so long, she would be gone from after breakfast to seven or once even seven-thirty. If he called, I had her beeper number and was to call her right away. But he had her cell phone number, of course, so I am sure he could always speak to her.'

'But most of the time?'

'She was home. In her office. Courtney spent many, many hours there. She worked so hard.'

'What time did Greg Logan come home the night she disappeared? He wasn't working, was he? Halloween was a Sunday.'

'He was meeting a Chicago man in the city. I believe for an early dinner. He came home about fifteen minutes past eight o'clock.' Steffi's voice was flat, as if she'd recited this story so many times that the words were without meaning.

'Did he look the way he always did?'

'His face, yes.' I waited. 'He usually wore what is called

131

a sports shirt to his office. But that night he wore a suit and tie.'

'How was he behaving? Same as always?'

'Yes.'

'Not excited or upset? His clothes not messed up?' I was looking to find the truth and, hopefully, clear Greg. But I also wanted to find out what Steffi had told the cops.

'No. He acted' – she clasped her hands in her lap like a schoolgirl – 'as always. Appeared as always.'

'Which was . . . ?'

'Neat. Very neat. Pleasant. And, you know, a little tired.'

'Was he worried when you told him Courtney had gone out for apples – How long before was it?'

'She left between five-thirty and six o'clock.'

'So was he worried that she'd been gone so long?'

'Not at first. But as it got closer to nine I would say he was maybe concerned. He said she might have met some friends.'

'And then?'

'He went upstairs. The children were asleep. I think he stayed upstairs in his bedroom.'

'His bedroom? Did he share a bedroom with Courtney?'

'Oh yes. I meant *their* bedroom.'

'Do the windows up there overlook the swimming pool?'

Steffi closed her eyes and put back her head to think. There was a U of beige glossy makeup around the white skin on the underside of her chin. 'No. Their bedroom windows are in front and on the side of the house. The pool is in back.'

'Did Greg come downstairs again?'

'Yes. About nine-thirty or nine forty-five. He looked worried. He said he'd called the police, but there were no auto accidents, so I need not worry. She might have gone to a friend's and forgotten to tell him is what he said.'

'He'd tried her beeper and cell phone?'

'Yes, he said he did that. She did not call back. He left a message on the voice mail of her cell phone, but she did not call.' She lowered her head until she appeared to be gazing at the hands in her lap. 'He stayed downstairs after that. Walking from room to room. I did not know what to do. He kept looking at his watch. I thought I should get out of his way. I went upstairs –'

'About what time?' I inquired gently.

'About ten o'clock. From my room I can hear the garage door open, but I heard nothing.'

'Did your windows overlook the pool?'

'No.'

'Okay. Please go on.'

'I came downstairs at about ten-thirty. I asked him if he thought he might call the police to say she was missing. He said no, not yet, that Courtney might be out to dinner or a movie with some friend and be angry if he called the police. He seemed, you know, calm. But then he started going from room to room looking for a note she might have left. More than one time he asked me: "Are you *sure* you didn't throw away a piece of paper?" I tell him I am sure, but a few minutes later I go into the kitchen because I thought I hear sound from there and he is going through the garbage pail.'

'Did he call his father?'

'I don't know. He used the telephone, but I do not know who he was talking with. I just see the telephone line light up again and again. And then I went upstairs because I thought, if Courtney comes in, it is not my place to be there when he greets her. Just before midnight there is a knock on my door. It is Mr Logan and he tells me, "None of Courtney's friends know where she is. I called the police. They are coming."'

Chapter Seven

'Sounds like a bullshit case to me,' remarked Claymore Katz, criminal lawyer and bon vivant, as he stroked his luxuriant mustache.

Clay resembled Theodore Roosevelt or a walrus, depending on whether or not he was wearing his glasses. He had been Bob's roommate at Columbia College. As long as Bob lived, they'd had lunch every six months or so to talk business, politics, and relive the 1955 World Series. There had also been an annual dinner in Manhattan with me and the girlfriend or missus of the moment, during which – usually seconds before the entrée was served – Clay would lean over for his sincere moment with me: Tell me, Judith, how are the kids doing?

Clay stirred his martini with his index finger. Two tiny white cocktail onions chased each other madly around an ice cube as if trying to conjoin, breed, and form a string of odoriferous pearls. 'Then again,' he was saying. I pulled my eyes away from the glass. 'I've seen one or two guys like this Greg Logan go up the river on nothing more than dumb-ass circumstantial evidence.' He tore off the end of a sourdough-fennel roll and popped it into his mouth.

'*Totally* true,' Heather Peters-Katz, the latest wife, said as she reached across the table and solicitously brushed several crumbs off the husbandly mustache. Heather should know. She'd been an assistant United States attorney, a federal prosecutor. Now, evidently, she was Clay's junior partner, not only in his firm, but also in his life. Giving no sign he'd heard his wife speak, the barrister cleared his throat to go on.

The Katzes of East Sixty-eighth Street and East Hampton had such an active social schedule that I hadn't anticipated getting an actual dinner with them. I'd called Clay to invite him to lunch and pretty much expected a damn-I'm-all-booked-up-how-about-Wednesday-at-3:07-in-my-office. My guess about his dinner invitation? He felt guilty for having called only a couple of times to find out how I was doing sans Bob in the more than two years since the shiva. Or else he had visions of me sliding my hand over his generous thigh in a midday paroxysm of widowy lust while he was halfway through his broiled-without-butter arctic char. His hearty courtroom voice had boomed over the telephone: Judith, Heather would never forgive me if I kept you all to myself. She's dying (having let 'dying' slip out, Clay was too cosmopolitan to falter, though I did sense a millisecond's pause) to see you. The restaurant he'd chosen was one of those new chic wonders with a one-word name – Esplanade or Thyme or Gala – with bare ecru walls and so many candles that you feel you're not getting enough oxygen, the way you do on a long flight.

'The police seem to think the husband did it,' I said in a sprightly voice. I'd brought up the Logan case as if it were a lively bit of suburban lore to amuse these city slickers, not as though it were a crime I was investigating. 'Everyone says they've stopped looking for the killer and are bent on making a case against this Greg Logan.'

'Another Boulder.' Clay sighed, taking his final forkful of a salad composed largely of beets and kidney beans. Clearly, we were living in what would become known as the Year of Maroon Food.

'Boulder as in the JonBenet Ramsey case?' I inquired.

'In the sense of the cops not wanting to do the work, going for the obvious solution. 'Though to me it seemed likely that Boulder had been an inside job, I kept my own counsel.

'What's the *evidence*?' Heather demanded. Clay, his lower lip thrust out in vague annoyance, peered around the restaurant as if someone at another table had been talking too loudly. I began to ache for Heather. Her husband's generic female companion was thirty-two and bosomy, and Heather looked on the verge of receiving those birthday cards of dubious hilarity, the sort with 'Look out! Here comes the big 4-0!' on the front.

'The evidence?' I responded. 'Well, Greg took over forty thousand dollars out of their joint account and put it under his own name. His explanation is that Courtney was withdrawing money for her business and he needed to keep a certain amount of cash on hand to keep his bankers happy. Evidently the cops aren't buying his story. Oh, and her body was found in the family pool.'

'Was *he* having an *affaire de coeur*?' Heather inquired.

'Well, there were the usual rumors around town, about his taking up with the au pair either before or after the murder. But I doubt that happened.'

'Why not? It's been *known* to happen.' Heather Peters-Katz was one of those people who italicize at least one word per sentence, making everything she said sound sarcastic, which I didn't sense was her intention. Actually, she was polite enough, if not truly benevolent.

In looks, she was the picture of good-natured simplicity, reminding me of the Strawberry Shortcake doll my daughter Kate used to have, with that toy's pinchable, fat cheeks and ridiculously red hair. Unlike Ms Shortcake, however, Ms Peters-Katz was built like a brick shithouse. She generously exhibited her endowments by means of an out-of-court pea-green silk dress so clingy it gave evidence she had cleavage both front and rear.

Seated beside her, alas, I'd noted that with lackluster eyes and nostrils the diameter of the average garden hose, she wasn't particularly pretty. Clay, I suspected, like many presbyopic middle-aged men, probably didn't know precisely what his new wives actually looked like except for the more obvious features: breast projection, ankle thickness, hair color.

'Well, I can only give you my impression of the case,' I replied, throwing in an 'uh' and an 'um' to show I'd only just begun to think about the Logan murder. 'I don't know what the cops really have on Greg. But the au pair is working up in Connecticut now. People tell me she still speaks of him respectfully, as a former employer – not as a lover or an old lech or anything. I'm sure she told the cops the same thing.' Husband and wife propped their chins on their fists and waited for my next question, which I addressed to a neutral sliver of space halfway between them: 'You're both defense lawyers. If you were representing Gregory Logan, how would you handle the case?'

'I would —' Heather began.

But Clay was already mid-sentence: 'I'd make the DA and the cops sweat. Why the hell should it be easy for them? I'd dig into this Courtney's background.' Instead of looking peeved at being beaten to the punch, Heather's head bobbed up and down, agreeing with her husband's every sentence as if to say: That's *precisely* what I would have said. It was as though Betty Friedan had never lived. 'Any men in her life?' Clay demanded. 'Unsavory characters? Criminal associations?' I told him about Fancy Phil. 'Ah,' he sighed. With evident fondness, he smoothed his hair with the tips of his fingers. Both his hair and mustache were dark brown, but with that mysterious orange Ronald Reagan tinge that occurs when men hit the dye bottle. 'Okay, so he set aside that forty thou. Now how much did she take from their account?'

'Between their money market and brokerage accounts I hear the total she actually wound up with was twenty-five thousand. She told Greg it was for StarBaby, her business, for camera equipment and I guess what you'd call promotion — ads and stuff.'

'*Well?*' Heather asked, twirling the stem of her wineglass impatiently between her thumb and index finger. 'Has anyone *seen* a twenty-five-thousand-dollar camera or a full-page ad in the *Times*?'

'Not that I know of,' I responded.

'That's my point!' Clay trumpeted, banging his empty martini glass on the table for emphasis. 'Too many unanswered questions.' You're telling me, I said to myself.

'There's been a rush to judgment,' he continued. 'I'd have private detectives and forensic accountants all over the place looking for stuff on this woman, following the money, finding out who her friends were. Of course, with Logan's old man, Lowenstein, there could be some organized crime angle and Courtney could be pure as the driven snow. But I'd buy time demanding a lot of forensic tests. And I'd look for anyone who might have a reason to want her dead.' The waiter, probably an actor whose career was already kaput because he looked like Leonardo DiCaprio's older, less handsome brother, slid our entrées in front of us and faded out.

'Who had reason to want her out of the picture?' Clay demanded. His hands gripped the edge of the table. Leaning forward, he jutted his head toward me as if he were Queen's Counsel in some British courtroom drama and I an accessory to murder standing in the witness box. 'Who?' he repeated.

'As far as I can tell,' I answered, 'no one. I mean, who'd want to kill a woman out to buy organic apples for her kids? On the other hand, there is the inescapable fact that she was shot in the head twice.'

'Does the husband *at least* have a decent alibi?' Heather interjected. Clay had fallen momentarily silent during the Sniff, Swish, Swallow, Cerebrate, and Nod Ceremony over the Burgundy he and the sommelier had earlier conferred about exhaustively. When I took a sip, it tasted like Manischewitz without the blessing of sugar.

'Greg had an early dinner meeting that night,' I told her. 'Unfortunately, he was still driving to it around the time Courtney drove to Grand Union – or wherever she went

140

– between five-thirty and six.' I'd heard that from Steffi, who had seemed observant enough. 'He got home about eight-fifteen –' I would have gone on, but all of a sudden a man about my age was standing behind the fourth chair at our table, the empty one. He sighed and shook his head: 'Just got in from D.C. All the flights were delayed.'

I waited for Clay to suggest to the man that he was at the wrong table. Instead, he leaped up, vigorously pumped the man's hand, and announced to me: 'This is Dan . . .' I didn't get the last name because Heather was cooing 'Dan!' and springing from her seat, leaning forward to offer her cheek to his cheek. They briefly smooched the air then switched cheeks only to peck once more to conclude their Euro-kiss. Immediately after that Clay and Heather began a battle of words: 'Judith, this is our *dear* friend –'

'Dan Steiner,' Clay cut in. 'He retired last year from running his own – and may I add – very, very successful hedge fund –' Dan Steiner was approaching six feet, although he hadn't gotten there. Still, he was inches taller than Clay, who, unsettled being so near a man of greater height and vaster wealth, began to stroke his already smooth tie uneasily.

'But the *real* point is Dan is going for a Ph.D. in Russian history *at Yale* –' Heather, I thought, was being excessively delightful. I surmised her sparkle was not evoked by his academic credentials. Dan the Man himself did not appear the sort to inspire such enthusiasm. Although he fairly could be described as slim, or at least trim, he had developed one of those mush faces that are visited upon many in their fifties; it had lost not just color, but definition, so precisely from the point the jaw rose out of the chin he resembled an overkneaded oblong of dough topped with thin gray hair. The chin itself, however, a hard-edged rectangle, protruded out of his face as though it were an appendage donated by another species; it was so long I kept marveling he hadn't grown a beard to camouflage it, especially now that he was one with Academe.

'He drives up to New Haven every week to take –'

'Dan – I hope Clay told you – Judith *has* a Ph.D. in American history and teaches at a *very prestigious* small Catholic college –'

Since the three of them were standing, I decided it might appear surly to remain seated. But just as I was about to rise, Dan reached across the table and gave my hand the limp shake of a man who's never gotten over the notion that women are the weaker sex. His eyes looked past me, or nearly so; an observer would have thought he was saying Nice to meet you to my earlobe. Then he took his chair. Now that Heather and Clay had only each other to look at, they, too, quickly sat. Within two seconds Dan was asking about one of Clay's SEC cases and Clay immediately began simultaneously declaiming and violating the Canon of Ethics: 'The guy's in a sweat. He's leveraged beyond belief.' Dan intoned: 'You know, when you get that kind of leverage, certain moves in the market are magnified and –'

Not that I cared that they were (a) boring and (b) rude. Okay, I did care. But also, I was so agitated by being half of what I gathered was a blind date that all I could do was stare at my Tender Young Chicken in a Rosemary-Mustard Marinade Grilled over Apple Wood and try to calm down. What was as galling as the presumption of fixing me up without asking me if I'd be interested was the fact that Dan appeared utterly uninterested. He was spouting to Clay about unlearned lessons of the Long-term Capital Management scandal while disregarding me with such intense concentration that I could tell he'd been strong-armed into the dinner and wanted to be either at home with a tome about the terribleness of Ivan IV or on the town with whatever his definition of a hot number was.

Heather leaned so far over to me her left breast brushed across the fruit salsa atop her halibut, leaving a small dark stain and a fleck of what I guessed was peach but could have been some new fruit I'd never heard of. 'Judith,' she whispered, unaware of the to-do on her left nipple. 'We didn't tell you about Dan because we didn't want you to get your hopes up.' As I was literally dumbstruck she filled in the blank: 'In case he didn't show.' Then she sat back, waiting for me to attempt to entice Dan.

Except as I sat there, watching two middle-aged male hotshots vying to say something so insightful it would stun the other into silence, watching the exquisitely cleavaged Heather, this litigator who confronted for a living, say 'Um' three times in an attempt to join the conversation only to have her husband and Dan reflexively raise their voices so her 'Um' could be ignored without blatant discourtesy, I realized there was nothing I could say or do that would entice Dan Steiner.

Someone might ask: Why the hell would I even be tempted to entice a guy I wouldn't want even if he exhibited the politesse of a Lord Chesterfield and a schlong that went from here to Cleveland? Well, because he was a prime catch, what someone like me ought to go gaga for. Smart enough to get into Yale, or so astoundingly rich he could buy his way in. Definitely rich enough – from the sheen of perspiration on Clay's forehead to the gleam in Heather's insignificant hazel eyes – to be the sort of magnate revered for his cool instead of being blown off as the cold fish he was.

What saddened me most was that in his snazzy pale gray pinstripe of exquisite summer-weight wool so painstakingly cut it (almost) concealed the mini-love handles no exercise or diet could expunge, Dan was precisely the man my late husband had always yearned to be.

The worst of the worst was, a sweetie pie smile kept trying to take over my face in a pitiful attempt to win the favor of the man who was ignoring me. Two more seconds and I'd be batting my lashes, complying with Article Two of the Girl Constitution: If he rejects you, try harder. I actually had to command myself: Wipe off that sycophantic smile. 'Excuse me,' I said to Dan in an Elizabeth Cady Stanton voice. 'There was a murder in my town on Long Island. I was asking Clay and Heather about how they would defend the chief suspect.'

'A murder?' he echoed. There followed an instant of silence during which we could hear the clink of fork against plate as a waiter deboned a fish at a nearby table. Dan seemed to recognize another sentence was required of him, which he evidently found vexing. For him, this was a dismal evening after a rough day in Washington. His cheeks inflated, prelude to a petulant exhalation. Clearly he knew intuitively (as well as from studying the Houses of Rurik and Romanov) that, as a rich and powerful person, he had an absolute right to behave badly. Finally, however, he exhaled his pissed-off sigh through his nose and in a resigned voice inquired: 'Who was killed?'

So while the waiter dashed off to get him a Salad of Baby Greens with Four Variations on Duck, nothing else, thanks, which was no doubt how Dan the Man kept himself slim to trim, I offered a précis of the Courtney Logan case. 'Clay told me the lawyer for Greg, the husband, should be hiring a forensic accountant. The goal seems to be to follow the money.'

'No one knows where the twenty-five thousand she took went to?' Dan asked. His suit was one of those trendy, three-button numbers that expose shirt and tie only to mid-sternum. It had the effect of making him look straitjacketed, and the impression was underscored by his stiff bearing and the way he held his upper arms close to his sides, even when he reached for his water glass and took a sip. It was not the posture of a guy who could, in any way that counted, be fun.

'From what I've heard, all Courtney said was that she needed the money for her business,' I replied.

'If she didn't hide it really well, that should be easy enough to find out,' Clay interjected. 'I mean, for the husband's lawyer.'

What I was thinking was: No one had actually seen any expensive cameras, had they? Zee Friedman had told me she'd used her own stuff: Could the equipment Courtney told Zee was at the Wesleyan graduate's house be a fiction? If so, then what could she have used the money for? Why would she lie about it? 'Just out of curiosity,' I inquired, 'what would a woman in her position need thousands and thousands for if not the business?' I halted for what I hoped was a meaningful pause, although it was probably a little overdramatic. 'Blackmail?' I proposed. No one said no. On the other hand, I didn't hear any resounding yeses.

'Face-lift,' Heather offered to break the silence. 'Seriously, the works can *easily* be around thirty-five thou. Or could she have had a jewelry habit?'

'She didn't seem the type.' Could the Wesleyan student himself be a fiction?

'Drugs?' Clay was asking.

'Courtney seemed to function very well – at everything,' I told them.

All I wanted to do was ransom my Jeep from the overpriced Manhattan garage, tool back to Long Island, and again read over my notes on the case. Maybe this time they would tell me something. Yet I kept talking to Dan, trying to get something out of him, at least some snippet of financial expertise that might shed some light on the Courtney Logan case. 'You were a businessman before you became a scholar?' He nodded, a single nod, clearly not being profligate in the nod department. Still, he seemed gratified enough by the word 'scholar' that I half regretted using it. (The other half, sad to report, was preening that I'd finally done something to please him.) I went on: 'Let's forget what the murder victim needed the money for. Let's just say she needed it, ostensibly for the business. If she'd been turned down for a loan by the banks but still needed more money, where would she get it?'

'Family money?' Dan suggested. I shook my head, which seemed to disconcert him. He rubbed his shovel of a chin

146

and, after a few seconds, 'Money in the market?' emerged from his pale lips.

'There was some. I think eighty thousand in one particular account.' Dan blinked, probably in shock at such a chicken-feed number. 'She took out twenty, but put ten back. Her husband wouldn't let her get at the rest.'

'Well, maybe she only needed a small amount,' he replied in a rather hushed tone. 'She did have a small business.' He appeared slightly dazed to find himself in a discussion whose subject he hadn't set.

'But she had big ambitions for it,' I explained. 'Franchising, stuff like that.'

'Maybe a loan shark?' Clay ventured. 'Someone whose name she heard bandied about by her father-in-law?'

'She'd been an investment banker at Patton Giddings,' I explained to Dan.

'Could she have used the money for on-line trading?' Heather chimed in. 'Or for day-trading?'

'Possible,' Dan replied, 'but only barely. Most of these people, even the so-called sophisticates . . . Cocksure of themselves. They wind up losing it far easier than they run it up. She'd have had to be very, very good just to break even over the long term. Day-traders are addicts, no better than the blue-collar guy who squanders his salary on offtrack betting week after week.'

'But with her background in finance?' I reminded him.

'Please,' he said, in the overly patient manner of someone who is trying to appear open-minded rather than supercilious. He pointed his fork straight at me. I pulled my eyes away from the drippy leaf of baby spinach woven between the tines and looked right at him. His lips were compressed into a hyphen. Despite his mush face, the flesh above and below his lips was protuberant, well muscled, evidence that his disdain for me was almost nothing personal, that Dan's native expression was one of scorn. 'Ask yourself,' he said. 'If she were really first-rate, would she have quit Patton Giddings? To live in the *suburbs*? To be a *mommy*?'

Dan was so odious I actually skipped dessert. The worst thing about the evening was that it would be too late to call Nancy and recount it, thus giving her the chance, in her role as official best friend, to rage against Claymore Katz's ill breeding and sexism in fixing me up without asking my consent, to orate on Heather's self-victimization, and to offer a diatribe about Dan Steiner's boorishness, ego-tism, pomposity plus, naturally, several scathing, southernly accented sentences about how teeny his penis must be – that being the universal and official female put-down. Alas, I've always felt it a form of vengeance (while not without its immediate satisfactions) that is sadly impotent.

Driving home on the Long Island Expressway, I put Dan out of my mind, tried not to devote even one neuron to Nelson, and didn't waste a microsecond on post-modernist Geoff. Musing over murder most foul, I decided, was far more comforting than contemplating the unholy trinity of me, men, and my future. Except I found little comfort. I was beginning to feel uneasy about the case. The more I learned, it seemed, the less I knew, not the sort of progress I wanted to report to a client like Fancy Phil.

What could I tell him? That I'd spent the day at the library searching databases for all variations on Courtney Bryce Logan, Courtney Bryce, StarBaby, Courtney AND

Princeton, and Courtney AND 'Patton Giddings.' All that popped up was a wedding announcement, the fact that Courtney had been treasurer of Princeton's Class of '86 Fund, and an article from *The Olympian* in Washington state, Courtney's hometown paper, reporting her murder with quotations from a few of her Summit High classmates, one of whom had used the adjective 'shrewd' where 'smart' might have been more seemly.

And when I'd gotten home from the library in the late afternoon, there had been a message on my voice mail: 'The clock's ticking. You got anything yet?' No name of course, but there was no doubt it was Fancy Phil. With more than a hint of strained patience in a gravelly baritone unaccustomed to expressing forbearance. '*You got anything yet?*'

Did my client simply and sincerely want to discover the truth? Or had he wound me up and sent me searching to find out all that was find-outable, that is, to see if there was any evidence the average detective might miss that could lead back to Fancy Phil himself, or to Greg, evidence he could then destroy – along with the historian who'd dug it up?

Nelson Sharpe hadn't warned me about Phil Lowenstein just so I could swoon and throw myself into his arms. Basically, Nelson was saying: This guy doesn't just have a nasty temper. This guy can order a murder, although if he likes you, he'd probably ask one of his associates just to maim. What kind of lunacy or presumptuousness had led me first to knock on Greg Logan's door, then after that let me think I could handle his old man?

So the next morning, feeling a little shaky, I phoned

Mary Alice Mahoney Schlesinger Goldfarb and my next-door neighbor, Chic Cheryl, to try to track down some of Courtney's friends. Mary Alice said she knew 'tons' of them, but, under not very rigorous cross-examination, was unable to come up with any names. On the other hand, Chic Cheryl blared out not only names, but net worth and country-club memberships. Also, according to CC, the explication I'd gotten from Jill Badinowski of the social stratification among younger, stay-at-home mothers was in error: They formed cliques not based on the status of their occupations in their former lives — cosmeticians vs. bankruptcy lawyers — but on the wealth of their husbands, a notion that would have desolated me for weeks had I not been so eager to gather enough information that I could get to Fancy Phil before he decided to get to me.

After writing down Chic Cheryl's candidate for best friend, Kellye Ryan, I must have had some 'When Irish Eyes are Smiling' stereotype in the back of my head, because the tall, tan, slender, long-limbed near-beauty who rang my doorbell that Friday afternoon was a surprise.

'Hey,' she greeted me.

'I appreciate your coming over,' I told her.

'No prob.' Kellye didn't seem to notice the missing 'lem.' 'Nice house. Hey, I'm glad you're doing something to — what's that word? — whatever, to honor Court.' Although she did appear to be vocabularily challenged, she was alert and self-confident. I led her through the house, out the back door, and offered her a seat on an old cedar bench. Unobtrusively, she flicked off what might have been an atom or two of pollen before executing that deft bent-knee, ass-to-seat maneuver that indiscernibly transforms the naturally graceful from a standing to a sitting position. 'So much publicity. Yuck. It's nice someone wants to hear nice things about her.'

'I do want to hear nice things,' I assured her. 'But if I'm going to write about it, or turn it into an oral history, it's my obligation to ask all sorts of questions. My job isn't to commemorate Courtney Logan, even though I'm sure she deserves it.'

'Gotcha,' she replied. Kellye Ryan did not look like the average Shorehaven mommy, in a T-shirt and khakis with just enough forgiving Lycra to get her through dinner at Burger King without having to open her zipper. Instead, she wore one of those dresses of palest peach silk and lace that is barely distinguishable from a full-length slip. As she was at least five feet ten, it ended mid-thigh, which in her case was not a problem.

With the dark hair pulled back into a bun at the nape of her neck and her almost black eyes, Kellye looked like a beautiful flamenco dancer. That is, until she smiled. Then she looked like a flamenco dancer from Transylvania. Dracula teeth: Her upper canines were so elongated they appeared to pierce her lower gums. I had to stop myself from lowering my chin to protect my neck.

'Tell me a little about yourself,' I prompted. 'What's your background?'

'You know.' Sensing this might not be quite enough, she went on. 'College, Bard. After, Bill Blass.'

'Were you a model?'

'Uh-uh,' she said, while giving me a modest little shrug to acknowledge the compliment. Then she got busy aligning the two spaghetti straps on her slip-dress.

'What did you do there?'

'Marketing.'

I sensed a little more small talk was needed before I started asking her about her murdered friend. 'Did you like working in the fashion industry?'

'I mean, to work for Bill Blass? Total, total dream job.'

'Uh-huh,' I found myself saying.

'The whole line. Quality. Down to the seams. Beautifully finished. You *never* have to be ashamed to take off your jacket.'

'Right. And now?'

'Married, two kids.' Her smile slowly faded and a sorrowful expression elongated her face. 'Same as Court.'

'How did you meet her?'

'Tennis tournament. Rolling Hills.'

'That's a country club?'

She nodded. 'Yeah. They paired us. Doubles team. I mean, Mutt and Jeff. Short and tall. But we were great. Together. We started playing singles. A powerhouse, that girl! Fridays. Strategy, strategy. And a killer serve.'

'And you became close friends?'

'Right.'

'What was she like?' I asked.

As Kellye considered she scraped some invisible lipstick or crumbs from the corners of her mouth with the tips of her pearl-colored pinkie nails. 'Court? Smart. Adorable. I used to kid her. Call her Miss Perfect,' she said, smiling sadly. 'But she was. Always there for you. Great friend. Totally, totally in love with her kids.'

'And what about her husband?'

'In love with him, too,' she said quickly, although I

noticed the 'totally, totally' was dropped. 'She was cute looking, too. But smart enough not to wear ruffles, you know? Princeton, and it's not easy to shake that boring, Ivy style, so she was a little too safe fashionwise. But who's going to argue with Armani?'

'Not me,' I said.

'And always . . . *doing*. StarBaby. Before that Citizens for a More Beautiful Shorehaven, president one time. Volunteer, Island Hospital. Something else with cancer. Tennis, running, learning golf. And doing for Trav and Morgie? Like the day she . . .' Kellye, suddenly breathless, pressed her hand against her chest and paused to compose herself. 'The day Court was missing. Got killed probably, but who knew that then? She made a Halloween pumpkin cake. You wouldn't believe it! Two cakes in bundt pans. Put them together, one on top of the other – you know, bottom to bottom, with frosting for glue. It honestly did look like a pumpkin. Orange frosting, black frosting eyes, and she smushed together green gumdrop thingies for the stem. I said, "Court, you don't have enough to do?" and she said, "Yes, but wait till the kids see this. They'll be" . . . Some word like "so happy."' Kellye's eyes grew moist. A tear rolled out onto her black lower lashes. She carefully dabbed it off with the side of her index finger to avoid smudging her mascara.

'I'm sorry,' I told her.

''Sokay.' Her tears kept flowing. Kellye Ryan might have been deficient in language, but perhaps not in intelligence and definitely not in feeling. I found a tired Kleenex in my back pocket and handed it to her. 'When she was missing,' she finally went on, 'I couldn't stop thinking.

Sicko people out there, you know? Like the guy who killed Versace. Except not gay. And creepier. So I was petrified. Like what could be happening to her? I didn't want to think about all the things that could be – oh, Jesus! – done to her. But I couldn't help it. And then when they found her body . . . I just pray whoever shot her in the head just did it, not later after doing like sex things or torture things.' She folded the tissue and inserted it under her lashes, holding it at one eye, then the other until the tears finally stopped. 'Sorry.'

'Don't be sorry,' I replied. Kellye closed her eyes for a moment to regain her composure. Then she nodded – I'm okay now – patted around her nostrils with the tissue, and swallowed hard. She crossed her legs at the ankle, and swung them over to the left, in that uncomfortable posture women's magazines urge upon you to look ladylike and/or to prevent onlookers from having an I-Thou relationship with your pudendum. 'Did Courtney ever talk about her past?' Kellye shook her head. 'Old boyfriends?'

'Uh . . . Some guy at Princeton. Chip? Chuck? One of those names.'

'Any last name?' I asked.

'Uh-uh.'

'Did she ever talk about her family?'

'Uh-huh. Only child. Crazy about gymnastics, but even though she was skinny then . . . You know how they say: "You can't be too thin."'

'Anything else?'

'Her mother was born-again for a little while. She talked about Jesus *really* loud at Taco Bell or one of those places. Courtney said she was so mortified she wanted to die.'

I waited. Kellye got busy twirling a silvery bangle around her wrist. I said: 'I'd like to ask you a painfully direct question.'

'Okay.'

'You're describing a terrific person. So who in the world would want to hurt Courtney, or get her out of the way? I'm trying to get a handle on her for this history and I can't seem to get past that question.'

'I can't either. I guess . . . maybe . . . one of those serial killers.'

'Is that what you told the police when they questioned you?'

Kellye shook her head and her white-gold or platinum earrings made a tiny tinkling sound. 'They didn't question me.'

'Did they call you or –?'

'No. Nothing. I was surprised. Best friends. They called a couple of the others. But not me. I asked Denny, my husband, should I call them? I was at Court's the day she was missing. Or killed. But early, when she put the cake together. My Dexter is seven and her Morgan is five, so . . . What you'd expect. Boy, girl, age difference. Would they trick-or-treat together? Of course not. So Denny, my husband, said: "Do you have something to tell the cops? Something that would help them?" So I said: "No." So he said: "Then don't get involved, babe." Denny's a lawyer. Tax, but . . . hey, they know. Right?'

'Right. Did Courtney herself seem to change in any way over those last few months, before she disappeared?'

Kellye bit her lip while she thought, a youthful gesture that might have been endearing except for her fangs:

'Yes and no,' she finally responded. I waited. 'Like I said about her being perfect.' Kellye bit again. 'But you know when a friend is just going through the motions. Court was doing that for weeks. Toward the end. Maybe months. At tennis she'd call out "Good shot," but I could tell. She wasn't *in* it. And she kept canceling. Her mind was someplace else. And Halloween, with the cake. She couldn't *not* bake – I mean, Veterans Day cake, Chinese New Year cupcakes, and like, is she Chinese? Every holiday. But she was, you know, at least fifty percent flaked. For like a month, maybe two or three, before.'

'Did you ask her if anything was wrong?'

'Sure.'

'And what did she say?'

'That she was – what do you call it? – preoccupied with StarBaby. But it was starting to take off. Everything was fine.'

'The marriage?'

Kellye shrugged her exquisitely tanned shoulders. 'She said it was. I mean, she would have liked it if Greg had, whatever. Bigger ideas. She wanted him to open up on the West Coast. New York was okay, but it's, like, ethnic and they want dinner to be a dinner. Not soup, salad, or a sandwich. Even *and* a sandwich. But California is spelled L-I-T-E. Except Greg said no.'

'Why?'

'Capital.'

'Is that what Courtney told you?'

'Uh-huh.'

'But other than that?'

'They were fine.' She nodded, satisfied with her account. But a second later she was shaking her head.

'What made you think it wasn't fine?' I asked.

'ESP.' I offered what I hoped was a nod more encouraging than her own had been. 'And ask yourself: Why do people get flaked?'

'Did you think she was frightened?' I asked. 'Or under pressure of some sort?'

'Not *that* kind of flaked.'

'You mean Courtney might have been interested in someone else?'

'I hate to say this, but I did kind of think: Some guy? I mean, what could make Court go, like, through the motions. Not have her heart in her pumpkin cake. And she *bought* Morgan's costume. Queen Amidala.' I was trying to think of a way to ask Kellye who that might be when she added: 'If you said to me, Hey, here's a billion dollars. Who could Court possibly get hot for, even though she was always hinting Greg was the hottest guy ever.' At this thought, Kellye covered the front of her neck with both hands, then stuck out her tongue as if she were choking. Then, in case I didn't get it, she added: 'Gag, double-gag.'

'What's wrong with Greg?'

'Q-U-I-T-E.'

'What?'

'He's too quiet. It's creepy. Denny, my husband, says it's because his father is a Jewish Mafia guy. Greg's father. Not Denny's. Denny's father has an air-conditioning company in Glen Cove. And not Jewish. Half Irish, half Polish, or something else foreign. I think. Whatever. But Greg

157

wants everyone to think he's got class, not that he's like a gangster. That means low-key. So when he's with you he acts so low-key it's like he's not there. So you won't think he's – what's that word? For always pushing people around and stuff?'

'Pushy? Aggressive?'

Kellye gave me a grateful Bride of Dracula smile. 'Right! But maybe Courtney didn't know better.'

'About?'

'About what was hot. But maybe he really was. Is. Do I know? Except I don't think so, and I swear to God, I have radar. All my friends say so. They say, Kellye, is so-and-so hot, and I say –'

'So if your theory's right and Courtney was involved with someone else –'

'But who? Except even for a billion,' Kellye said, shaking her head sadly, 'I couldn't tell you who it could be.'

Chapter Eight

Here I was again, shuffling down the road that I was less and less sure would lead me to the killer. Everyone around Courtney was so pleasantly nonhomicidal. Who in God's name could murder a woman who cut bunny stencils for Year of the Rabbit cupcakes? Even the Lowenstein-Logan boys, my top two candidates (if Fancy Phil hadn't been my client) seemed incapable of such an atrocity.

Yet two bullets in the head didn't appear on any list of Common Household Accidents. Someone had pulled the trigger – twice – and I had to find out who. So here I was, sitting in another kitchen with yet another of what the politicians and media now, universally and nauseatingly, call a 'mom.' At some point, I suppose, it was decided 'mother' sounded too old-fashioned. Or too prim. Or maybe in the minds of the boomers it was forever linguistically tainted by its linkage to 'fucker.'

Anyhow, the mom in question, Susan Viniar, sat at the head of her table. I, by default the guest of honor, sat at her right hand. My own hands were nearly frozen onto an iced beer stein into which she'd poured the thick, freezing drink she'd blended for me.

'It's a Lime Refresher,' she explained, her firm chin high with self-assurance.

I had to give her credit. I, for one, wouldn't have been that confident. The bright green stuff in the mug, with flecks of frost dispersed throughout, looked like mad-scientist poison in 1950s horror movies. Still, feeling I was getting noplace fast on the Courtney front, I couldn't be too fussy. So I waited till Susan sipped, then I did, too. It tasted like a blend of green Chuckles, Gatorade, and crushed ice. That sounds fairly revolting, except to my relief, not only didn't I die, I found the Refresher, well, refreshing.

'How close were you and Courtney?' I asked.

Unlike Kellye Ryan, Susan had no tears for her friend. Then again, she explained, she and Courtney hadn't actually been friends. 'My son Justin and Travis Logan are in the same play group.' She shrugged, apologetic she couldn't be of more help. As she did, the deltoids under the straps of her chartreuse-piped-with-apple-green tank top gleamed darkly. I decided I wouldn't want to be on the opposite side of a school bond fight with this dame. Her muscular, unspeakably firm upper arms were bisected by the sleeves of a coordinating apple-green sweater with chartreuse trim that was fashionably tied around her shoulders. Though slender, Susan Viniar looked weight-trained beyond buff: She could probably bench-press Fancy Phil.

Outside her kitchen window, a bolt of lightning ignited the low-hanging sky. Instead of startling at the flash, as I did, my hostess seemed to be silently counting the seconds until the rumble of thunder began. Then her head bobbed a single bounce, as if to let God know she was satisfied with His performance.

The Viniars' pine kitchen table was tucked into an alcove with a bay window and framed by the pale and dark leaves of hanging plants. Outside, beyond a brick patio, we could see the drenched velvet carpet of backyard lawn going on forever. Its perfection was interrupted only by a picket-fenced lap pool and a dark green swing set elaborate enough for Justin to train for the 2016 Olympics. Gorgeous greenness. Even the thick gray storm clouds at second glance seemed to have taken on an olive-drab tinge. In my red pinstripe shirt, I felt like an interloper in Emerald City.

'One time we did have a conversation about signing the boys up for Pre-Swimbees,' Susan was saying, obviously believing she owed me another sentence or two. 'But it was part of a larger conversation with a bunch of mothers of one- and two-year-olds.'

'Oh,' I said, feeling I'd taken her Lime Refresher under false pretenses. 'Someone told me you were a good friend of hers.'

Susan shrugged again, her deltoids rising, to say nothing of her triceps and biceps brachii. She was such a perfect specimen that, except for the covering of her dark brown skin, she might be the model for one of those charts of striated muscle the teacher pulls down in high-school biology. 'I guess it's understandable, someone thinking we were friends. I mean, we run with the same crowd.'

'What crowd is that?'

With her thumb, she wiped a spatter of Lime Refresher off the rim of her stein. 'Maybe "crowd" isn't the right word. That makes it sound as if we're the fast country-club set in a John O'Hara novel. What I'm talking about is seven or eight women. We're mostly in our thirties, with preschoolers Travis and Justin's age.'

'Better a crowd than going through it alone,' I remarked.

'I guess so. A United We Stand, Divided We Fall mentality.' For about two seconds the teacher in me overcame the detective; I gave her a *Very good!* smile of commendation for her historical reference. Except the last thing I wanted was for Susan Viniar to decide she'd invited a grinning madwoman into her house, the way Greg Logan had. So I tried converting my smile into a genial I'm-all-ears expression.

'But you're not really close with these women?'

'In the group? I have one good friend. But it's like this.' She spoke to the sky as it darkened even more. 'If you go the mommy route' – her eyes came back to me – 'even if you love your kids more than anything, there's still only so much gratification you can get from hearing them saying "coo-kie."' Not only did I recall that time, I found myself nodding so empathetically I nearly lost an earring. Susan didn't need more incentive to go on. Clearly she'd been thinking about this for a long time. She gestured to the panorama beyond the glass, to the acre of lawn, its color deepened to June lushness from the ethereal green of spring, although that more intense hue might just have been shadows of storm clouds. 'Living here, you feel so disconnected. You keep asking yourself: Where's all the suburban kaffeeklatsch stuff, the sisterhood that's supposed to be coming my way?'

I swallowed my mouthful of Lime Refresher. 'I remember. Until I met the woman who's still my dearest friend, I was so damn ... I guess the word is isolated. No. Lonely.'

'I think a lot of us are,' Susan agreed. 'Especially if you worked in a big office the way I did. You go from all that collegiality to pureeing peas in a food mill by yourself. And there's no one except your husband to discuss all the other things you care about besides children. He becomes your only connection to the world beyond Pampers.' I was about to ask her: What did you used to be? But then I worried that Susan would conclude the question assumed her present identity was less than satisfactory. Meantime she was saying: 'You start to ask yourself: Oh my God, what have I done to myself, quitting work, sentencing myself to life in the suburbs? So we travel in packs, taking the kids to all their activities.'

'And Courtney Logan was part of your pack?' Susan nodded and her ponytail bounced. She had the silky black hair of African-American women with six-figure incomes. 'But she wasn't a friend?'

'No.'

'As far as you know, did the police question any members of your circle about Courtney's habits, connections?'

'They spoke to a couple of the women.'

'And?'

'And what could anyone say? That Courtney loved her family. That she was smart. That StarBaby was not just a great idea, but that she actually brought it to fruition, so maybe she was more focused than the rest of us. And she was a nice person.'

'So how come you and Courtney weren't really friends?'

'No particular reason.' I waited. 'We weren't on the same wavelength.'

'What was her wavelength?'

'This is some project for the library? You mentioned you were on the board.' Susan posed the question with the cool of someone who already knew the answer, so I didn't play it cute.

'No, more for me. I can't seem to get a handle on Courtney Logan. I suppose I shouldn't be . . .'

Susan Viniar didn't immediately leap up to proclaim, No problem, your asking me questions about personal matters that are none of your business. For a moment that felt uncomfortably long to me but obviously not to her, she gazed at the vapor from the air-conditioning register as it misted up the bay window and considered what I'd asked. 'Moms,' like Susan and her crowd, I decided, had remained out in the world a lot longer than we mothers had. They'd worked longer, married later, had children later. They seemed cooler cookies than my contemporaries. These younger women mulled, they pondered, they deliberated. They seemed less desperate, or at least slower, to please.

Finally, as my Lime Refresher began to separate into its somewhat grotesque-looking components, Susan seemed to conclude that: a) I could be trusted, b) it couldn't hurt for her to be accommodating and for me to owe her a favor; and c) it might be pleasantly kaffeeklatsch-like to talk about Courtney. I sensed she had the self-possession of a diplomat. Not a Talleyrand. Her flawlessly plucked arched eyebrows and bittersweet-chocolate-brown eyes were far too expressive for her to hammer out a strategic-arms-limitation treaty with, say, the foreign minister of Ukraine. However, I sensed that for someone like Susan, negotiating a trade agreement with a petulant neutral power would be a snap.

'There was nothing *wrong* with Courtney,' she began diplomatically. 'In fact, who could be righter? Good school, glamorous Wall Street job. Then came the nice husband, two adorable children, mommyhood. What else? Her house – Lord, when we went there for play group! It was so complete, so decorated, but in that undecorated old-money way. It looked as though there'd been Logans in it for centuries. And I guess you know that with all her volunteer work, she was highly thought of in the community. Plus she had a new business that could go through the roof. She was a decent athlete, too, and pretty – if your idea of pretty is the blond rah-rah type. As far as I could see, the only fly in her ointment was the father-in-law.'

'In what way? Did he interfere in their lives?'

'No. Not that I know of. I'm talking about the simple fact of him. He's a . . . whatever, a gangster. That's not a social asset in most circles. But I liked the way Courtney dealt with it. Directly. She actually referred to him as Fancy Phil Lowenstein and – I'll bet not in front of Greg – mimicked him.' Susan cleared her throat, then pitched her voice to a low bad-guy growl: '"Hey, sweetheart, how're t'ings?"'

'She sounds like fun,' I remarked.

Susan tilted her head to one side to consider. 'Actually, no. I mean, you never had to hold your sides to keep them from splitting. But Courtney was definitely an upbeat person.'

'So if there was nothing wrong with her, what wasn't right?'

She turned from me and looked outside, and for a moment seemed lost contemplating the masses of green curled around the grape arbor that formed the portal to her backyard. For all I knew, it might actually have been a genuine grapevine. Finally she turned back. 'Did you ever see the movie *The Invasion of the Body Snatchers*?' she asked sheepishly.

'Sure!' I decided that since she seemed convinced of my sanity I'd better not mention that I'd seen all three versions, the Donald Sutherland one twice. 'So what are you saying? That there was a pod person inside Courtney?'

Susan's index finger slowly traced the whorls of a knothole in her pine table. 'I guess what I'm saying is that the Courtney I came into contact with didn't feel totally real.' She shook her head, dissatisfied with her answer. 'It wasn't that she was phony. But there was something . . . unusual about her. I sensed she had some other, inner life that the pod person was running – a pod person who had researched the culture of the north shore of Long Island but who'd only gotten an A-minus on the term paper. Almost perfect, but not quite. Or if there wasn't a pod person, maybe part of Courtney Logan was missing and that's why she didn't feel real.'

'Like what?' I inquired.

'The part that makes us *not* unique, but like everybody else.' Another brutal slash of lightning. The lights flickered, then stayed on, although across the kitchen the digital clocks on the wall oven and microwave began flashing in a crazed bid for attention. Susan didn't notice. 'That part that gives us the sense that a stranger is okay, that he or she shares our humanity and isn't off in some way, or empty inside, or a threat.' She set her glass down on her napkin, then crossed her powerful arms and turned so she was facing me directly. 'Saying this straight out, it sounds asinine.'

'No, it doesn't sound asinine.' It was easy to sound reassuring because, aside from her evident devotion to her own musculature, so much about Susan – her impressions of suburban motherhood, her historical and movie allusions, her recognition of her own isolation, her introspection – reminded me of me at her age. 'It sounds as if there's good communication between your intellect and your gut. You know, the longer I'm around, the more I believe that if your gut says something's going on here, something usually is.' Then I added: 'Just one question. Couldn't it be a less cosmic explanation? Like Courtney's mind might have been someplace else? Business reverses? Maybe she was having a fling?'

Susan tried to come up with an answer, but in the end all she could come up with was another shrug of her impressive shoulders. 'It's hard to say, because I really didn't know her. I never had a sustained one-on-one discussion with her. She could have had some secret problem weighing on her. But as far as an affair? That gut of mine you think I should trust? It says: No way.'

'Why not?'

'That thing that makes us feel real to each other?' She paused for a moment to organize her thoughts, then spoke carefully. 'Sexuality is an aspect of it, the sexuality we sense in other people as part of their he's-normal, she's-normal package. You know, the fact that a person *has* sexuality. Forget whether somebody's hot or cold or into bizarre practices. Real people give off subliminal signals that some aspect of sex – wanting it, not wanting it, being able to do it only when wearing spike heels – has some value in their lives. Pod people don't.'

'And with Courtney?'

'God rest her soul and all, but she was the chirpiest, least sexual human being I'd ever met.'

It wasn't just muscles that gave Susan Viniar her air of authority. Unlike the pontificators and the boasters who aim to wow you, she spoke with quiet simplicity, as though her words came from both her heart and head, such a decent heart and a good head that they had to be right. Then again, I reflected, she could be one of those people so bedazzled by their own fantasies that they truly believe their fabrications are truer than truth.

'Okay,' I said, 'so if we assume no lover, but a husband who adored her, neighbors who thought highly of her, friends who liked her, or at least saw her as a decent person, then it comes down to: What kind of person would want to kill her?'

Susan's arms crossed even tighter, as if she were beginning a set of isometrics or warding off a chill. 'Based on what I saw? What I knew Courtney to be?' I nodded encouragingly. 'Absolutely no one,' she declared.

So no one had anything against Courtney Logan. I thought: Then how come she won't be making a strawberry, blueberry, banana Flag Day cake this year?

That night, the storm finally exhausted itself around ten-thirty, leaving behind it the intoxicating smell of ozone and wet grass. A soft breeze blew through my open bedroom window and touched me gently, as if aware I needed special handling. I pressed the eject button and a tape I'd made years earlier of *Old Acquaintance* slid out of the VCR. I probably sighed, an audible *hommage* to Bette Davis, Miriam Hopkins, and female friendship, and with another flick of the finger turned off the TV.

It was one of those rare, lovely nights that I wasn't feeling at least a little depressed-lonely or frightened-lonely. Depressed, that I'd wind up alone in an assisted-living facility rife with denture-clacking, Trotskyite bridge players and Lucky Strike-smoking, anti-Semitic Republicans. Or frightened, that I'd have an anaphylactic reaction to the sting of a bee which had slipped through the quarter-inch rip in my bedroom window screen: I'd be discovered a week later, the phone receiver clutched in one decomposing hand, the other having had only enough life left to dial 9–1 . . .

But this night was good. I lay at ease in bed, my pillow perfectly fluffed, my blanket just the right weight, enjoying the sweetness of almost-summer in a dreamy way that carried me back and gently set me down in the backyard of my Brooklyn childhood. As far as I can recall, I wasn't even thinking about who killed Courtney Logan, though I might have subconsciously weighed Acquaintance Susan Viniar's No Possible Extramarital Funny Stuff theory against Good Friend Kellye Ryan's Courtney Was Having a Fling hypothesis. I turned onto my side, flipped over the pillow so it was cool against my cheek and closed my eyes.

Ahhh. So naturally when the phone rang, the sound shot through me the way current zaps a convict in the electric chair. My legs kicked and I made one of those Nyah! noises and answered the phone with a croaky 'hello.'

'Hi,' he said.

'Hi.' Even had I been more composed, I don't think I would have pretended I didn't know it was Nelson Sharpe.

'How's it going?' he asked.

'Not bad.'

'Good. Is it too late?' He wasn't actually slurring his words, but he was inordinately slow. He'd had a touch too much of something. 'Can you talk now?'

'Sure.'

'How've you been?'

'All right,' I told him. I pictured him leaning against the dark-paneled wall of a smoky Irish bar, talking into a pay phone. Except he wasn't Irish. He was a WASP, a Methodist, but I couldn't conjure up a Methodist bar. Or else he was sitting at his desk in the Special Investigations bureau, his bottom drawer with its half-drunk bottle of whiskey still open. Then I realized I was thinking in black-and-white, which no doubt came from watching more noir movies than were healthy for me. So I opened my eyes to the reality of my dark room and asked: 'How have you been, Nelson?'

'Good. Hey, listen. I was out, talking with a couple of guys.'

'Uh-huh,' I said encouragingly.

'Couple of buddies from Homicide. That Courtney, the one who's Fancy Phil's daughter-in-law. She had this car, a Land Rover.'

He seemed to be waiting for something from me, so I said: 'Right.'

'You didn't hear this from me, but the mother's helper who was working for them reported she saw Courtney drive away in it. But then later that night, when the husband called and the precinct cops went over, there it was, in the garage – the garage in their house.'

'Right,' I said again. My heart was beating faster than it should, though it was less the fact of Nelson calling me than that he was calling me about the Logan case. I think. Anyhow, I reached up and switched on the lamp to kill any fanciful thoughts. 'So do they have any idea who brought the car back? The murderer with Courtney dead? Courtney alive and the murder was done at the house?'

'The only physical evidence in the car was evidence of Courtney – and the husband and the au pair. Lots of kids' fingerprints in the back.'

'Husbands drive their wives' cars,' I told him. 'It's not a felony in New York.'

'Right. Sure. But there wasn't a sign that any other adult had been in it besides the two of them and the au pair.'

'But anyone else who would have planned for even two seconds to kill her would have worn gloves,' I protested. 'And the fact that Greg Logan's prints were on it might have meant he took her car out to get his lawn mower blade sharpened or something.'

'The guys from Homicide said it was warm that day.' He'd pretty much dropped the *d* sound from 'Homicide' and 'said,' as though lifting his tongue to the front of his palate was too great an effort. 'Warm for Halloween. Anyone wearing gloves would get looked at funny.'

'Maybe it was someone wearing a Halloween costume,'
I suggested.

I waited for the Nelson I knew to give me an argument.
But all I heard was breathing so slowly I thought he might
have fallen asleep. Then he surprised me. 'For all I know,
you may be right,' he said. 'Not about the costume. You
probably read all those idiot serial-killer books.'

'I do not.'

'But there is enough talk on TV these days about DNA
that, okay, if it wasn't a spur-of-the-moment thing, even
a dope would have taken precautions, like wearing a hat
so hair doesn't get on anything. Maybe gloves, too, and
he'd stick his hands in his pockets or something so no one
would ask questions.'

'Or her hands.' All I got was silence. I had a sense
Nelson was waiting for me to continue, since he was just
pie-eyed enough to have forgotten that it was he who'd
made the phone call. 'So the car was in the garage,' I
prompted. I wasn't about to shout hosannas of gratitude
since the detail that the Land Rover was back in the
garage was in practically every news account I'd come
across. 'Anything else?'

'About what?' he demanded, annoyed, as though I was
trying to pump him for police secrets. 'Oh, she'd had the
car serviced on October fourteenth.'

'Right. And she disappeared on the thirty-first.'

'And between those two times, do you know how many
miles she put on the car?'

'How many?' I asked, probably too eagerly.

'Seven hundred sixty-two,' he replied coolly.

'Wow. That would be a lot of car pools.'

'Yeah, Judith. A lot of car pools.' And before I could ask him anything else, or even say thank you, he hung up.

And that should have been that. The next morning, a Saturday, I put hot rollers in my hair so I'd look sleek at the New-York Historical Society's exhibit on female allegories of America. With luck, and enough hair spray to increase the hole in the ozone layer, I could get to my daughter's apartment in an unfrizzled state so that she and her boyfriend could serve me a dinner of shockingly expensive, oddly mated foreign dishes – bouillabaisse, tandoori chicken, and gnocchi the size of softballs had been their last offering – from their local gourmet take-out joint.

Kate's boyfriend, Adam, was a slender young man who worked in MTV's legal department. He dressed in slacks so baggy that it looked as though he were carrying a load in his diaper. He wore only black shirts, like Il Duce's thugs. Never a tie. What kind of thirty-year-old guy (who spoke as if he'd spent his youth in a Watts rap group instead of being what he was, Mr White Boy at Palos Verdes Peninsula High School) would be that susceptible to fashion that he would actually don a zoot suit? Could someone like him be man enough for my beautiful and brilliant Kate? Every time I visited them (for he and his wardrobe of fascist shirts had moved in with her), I worked myself into a fair case of melancholia, to say nothing of indigestion.

Except at ten o'clock, Kate called and said she had to cancel, that she'd been called into the office to work on a hostile tender offer. I refrained from demanding what I wanted to demand, which was What the hell is so important about a tender offer that it can't wait till Monday? And I emitted not a single guilt-inducing sigh of resignation:

Women without husbands are dependent on the kindness of children. So I told her I was looking forward to seeing her as soon as the pressure let up. Then I trudged into the bathroom, removed the hot rollers, ran my fingers through my hair until, regarding myself in the mirror, I was pleased to discover I didn't look like Mike Myers playing Linda Richman. Rather, I looked sensuous, albeit slightly world-weary, a combination of Anna Magnani and Simone Signoret – though admittedly I had the advantage of having forgotten to turn on the light.

Then I clomped downstairs, determined not to wimp out of going to the Historical Society simply because it held no prospect of human contact. However, I gave myself permission to take a later train. So when the doorbell rang a little after ten-thirty, I'd had just enough time to get sweaty and crabby from unsuccessfully trying to get my new Palm Pilot to form a relationship with my computer.

Of course as I called out 'Who is it?' in nauseatingly mellifluous tones, I was picturing Nelson at the door: Having found my voice on the phone so Siren-like the night before, he'd been compelled to come over. So when I looked through the peephole and saw him, then heard 'Nelson Sharpe,' I stood rather stupidly for a moment, astounded that it actually was he. Quickly, I patted my damp forehead with the hem of my skirt, stretched out the neck of my T-shirt to blow two blasts of cool air under my arms, and opened the door.

'I, uh . . .' he said. This time there was no houndstooth sports jacket to make me think twice. Evidently, this was dress-down Saturday for the Special Investigations unit, and he looked so good in a plaid shirt and jeans I temporarily forgot about the gold ring on his left hand.

'Would you like to come in?'

'I don't want to disturb anybody.' I knew him well enough to know he was simply double-checking. Nelson was nothing if not thorough. He'd probably already driven past the house a few times, staked it out for a while, then looked in the garage, where he'd seen only one car – mine, the car registered in my name whose license plate the cops in his unit had called in the night of my dinner with Fancy Phil. No doubt he'd concluded Bob was, in all likelihood, in the city, clearing off his desk on a Saturday morning.

Okay, it did surprise me that Nelson hadn't considered that my husband's MO might have changed sometime during the last twenty years. On the other hand, had Bob been alive, without a doubt he would have been at his office.

Nelson's wedding band flashed its cold light at me a minute later, when we were sitting four feet apart on the living-room couch. 'Listen,' he said, 'last night . . .'

'You're not sure what you said to me. You're afraid you might have whispered sweet nothings in my ear. Don't worry. You didn't embarrass yourself.'

'No, no,' he countered, with an isn't-that-ridiculous chuckle. Then he applied his detective skills to checking out the weave of the upholstery on the arm of the couch. 'I'm concerned I might have repeated some, uh, casual conversation about the Courtney Logan case I heard from a couple of guys.'

'Guys in Homicide.'

'Guys in Homicide,' he repeated quietly.

'Well, you didn't blab any state secrets – Stop pulling at that thread. You'll unravel the whole couch.'

'I wasn't pulling on it.'

'What were you doing? Investigating it?'

He shifted so his body was facing mine. His legs parted and I found myself staring into his eyes to hypnotize myself so I wouldn't even take a quick peek at the bulge in his jeans. It's bad enough when you're simply attracted to a guy; it's much worse when you already know what the prize inside is. What had I expected, that it would retract when he hit his fifties?

The problem was gazing into his eyes, which were big and a beautiful satiny brown. Soft, like cow eyes, except that implies a bovine quality, and his were, as they had been, intelligent, aware. And sexual. Women know: Some guys have the heat that makes their eyes almost feverish when they're looking at someone they want. Nelson had probably had those eyes at age ten. He'd definitely had them when he and I had been lovers, in his late thirties. I knew he'd have them for the rest of his life. 'Look, Judith, can we have an honest talk?'

I quit looking into his eyes. 'No.'

'No?' He acted shocked, as if I'd said something that would scandalize any decent human being.

'Unless you want to have an honest talk about the Courtney Logan case,' I added.

'Listen, don't you think . . . when we happened to run into each other last year, don't you think that was meant to be?' Nelson's voice was low enough to be bedroomy.

'"Meant to be"? What's happened to you? Are you buying CDs of pounding surf and wind chimes? The answer is no, it was not meant to be. You and I had an accidental meeting because of a shared interest.' His eyes had narrowed, which meant he was probably burning over my associating him and wind chime recordings, so I quickly added: '"Shared interest" being homicide.'

'I'm out of Homicide. I told you that.'

'Why did you leave?' He didn't answer. 'Did you jump, Nelson? Or were you pushed?'

'Pushed,' he said quietly to his knees.

'What happened?'

'Nothing important.' He seemed to be waiting for me to say something. When I didn't he added: 'Department politics. They said it wasn't fair, me being there so long and so many guys wanting in and wouldn't it be a great opportunity to establish my own unit which would be elite and all that shit.'

'What's the real translation?'

'Take this or take nothing.'

'Did you think about leaving, collecting a pension, and doing something else?'

'Homicide is the top of the game. What could I do if I took my pension? Be chief of security at some mall and bag a teenage girl shoplifting lipstick?'

'Do you like what you're doing now?'

He was already shaking his head as I began formulating a sentence about how Special Investigations could be interesting, important work. 'It's more baby-sitting than investigation,' he said. 'Wiretaps, tails, following a paper trail of fraudulent financial schemes that bore the hell out of me. These days a guy like your boyfriend Fancy Phil is mostly doing stuff like on-line trading with the

Russian mob, so the FBI gets it, not us. Of course, if he wants a skull cracked, Phil doesn't do it himself. He hires a guy who hires a guy who hires some dumb kid to do it.'

'Is that why you were having him tailed? You think he ordered a hit?'

'You know I can't tell you that.'

'Don't you think that the work you're doing is still important? You're going after the bad guys.'

His mouth expanded into what I guess he thought was a cynical smile. 'At least I'm not in uniform saying, "Hi boys and girls, and welcome to Safety Town."'

Even after a break of twenty years, it's amazing how fast two former lovers can fuse and become a couple again. Rules have long ago been agreed upon, parameters are still in place. Aside from the good news and bad news of getting older – the self-confidence Band-Aids we've managed with time to put over the wounds of childhood versus the decline of our bodies and our dreams – those same old cues still set us off.

As Nelson's hand was reaching across the cushion of couch that separated us, mine was ready to offer a concerned squeeze, eager to be enveloped in his hand's familiar size and warmth. Unfortunately, the hand he was extending was his left, the one with the ring from his new wife. I clasped my hands in my lap and said: 'I sense there's more than one thing going on in your life that you're not thrilled with.'

'I was so *right* in Homicide. When they created the new unit for me, it was like getting tossed out of the Garden of Eden. I kept telling myself, "Well, at least I still have one

thing to make me happy. I'm Adam and I still have Eve."
Actually, her name's Nicole. But then one night we were
watching TV and I looked at her – and she wasn't. Eve, I
mean. When we talked, I kept thinking, Who the hell is
this woman and –'

'I can't help you.'

'And the worst of it is, I think she feels the same
way but –'

'I don't want to hear about your marriage – either one
of them.'

'Judith, trust me. You're not cool enough for the
I-don't-want-to get-involved stuff.'

'As I'm sure you know, I was involved with you.
Maybe I still am, or could be. And if that's the case,
most likely it'll always be that way. When we agreed
never to see each other again, it wasn't because we'd
gotten bored or had grown to detest each other. We
were still in love. So even though there's been a hell
of a lot of water under both our bridges, it's tempting
to think we can start up where we left off, or at least
begin something new. Maybe I shouldn't be saying this.
Maybe all you're looking for is a friendly pat on the head
and my thinking you want something more is hideously
uncomfortable for you because your tastes now run to
nubile nineteen-year-olds.'

'Cut the crap.'

'So let me explain why this isn't going to happen.'

He gave a sigh of boredom, as if he already knew what
I was going to say. 'You found you really love Bob and
even though there's still whatever, a mental and physical
attraction, it doesn't justify blah, blah, blah.'

'The blah, blah, blah is that Bob died two years ago, suddenly.' For an instant incomprehension turned his intelligent face slack and stupid. Then he lowered his head. I couldn't see his expression, but the flush on his cheek was spreading to his ear, so I knew he was embarrassed about the blah, blah, blah business. 'I'm less of a mess than I was,' I went on, 'but I can't afford to get involved with a married man who has a sad story.' I expected him to give me the sad story of his marriage anyway – since a fair number of men believe that women cannot fight their natures, which is to nurture everything from baby goldfish to depressed, middle-aged cops.

Instead he said, 'I'm sorry for your loss. Really sorry.' He stood and so did I.

'Thank you.'

'I won't bother you again.'

This last bit of business nearly had its intended effect: having me sniffle, then sob, then rush into his arms for comfort. But I couldn't let myself. Since junior high, I'd always been one of those girls/women who would lose all reason in the face of love. I'd allow a guy to so inhabit my head that every act, from dicing celery to offering the defense of my doctoral dissertation, could not be executed without three-quarters of my brain occupied by thoughts of him. This was one time I wasn't going to let that happen. 'I appreciate that, Nelson.'

Wearily, like two explorers retreating after having failed to reach the Pole, we trudged back to the front door. 'Oh,' he said. 'I forgot to tell you what I came over to tell you.' I gave him a go-ahead nod. 'It's not much. I should be keeping my mouth shut, but it's not so terrible if I don't.

It's this: The guys have pretty much given up looking for the gun that killed Courtney.'

'What kind of gun was it?'

'Probably a Walther PPK/S. Do you know what that is?'

'I can look it up. Why have they given up? Where have they looked for it?'

'I don't know. I guess in and all around her house and grounds, the parking lot at the grocery store where she was supposed to have gone.'

'Were there any groceries in her car?'

'Not that I heard of.'

Which I sensed was a no. 'I get the feeling,' I told him, 'that either you're obsessed with the goings-on in Homicide or you know more about this case than the head of the organized crime unit normally would.'

'Well, you're involved in it. And with Greg Logan's father being Fancy Phil Lowenstein, I have a reason to be interested.' The cuffs of his plaid shirt had been rolled up, and now he began smoothing them out and rolling them up again.

'Do you think they should still be looking for the murder weapon?'

'I can't comment.'

'Nelson, I'm not a reporter shoving a microphone in your face. I'm –' He shook his head: No comment. 'Well, let me talk, then. It seems to me that whoever is running this investigation, Lieutenant Somebody, I have the name inside, is not very thorough. Maybe he should look a little harder.'

'Why do you say that?' he asked, finally satisfied with his cuffs.

'If you were handling the case, wouldn't it have occurred to you that if some pillar of the community, a wife and mother, is suddenly missing and you can't find her, you might consider taking a peep under the cover of the pool in her backyard, even if it looks tied down tight. Or am I misguided?' No answer, though his nostrils flared in a manner that I knew something was bothering him. 'If you'd been in charge, wouldn't you have thought, What the hell, I'll just take a quick look to see if maybe there's a body? Or a weapon?'

'It's been a sloppy investigation,' Nelson said, so softly I could barely hear him.

'Did they ask the neighbors if they saw anyone suspicious in the neighborhood that evening?'

'You don't ask it like that. Very often, the perpetrator belongs in the neighborhood. You ask: What did you see?' And before I could ask anything more, he turned the knob, stepped out into the sunny day, and closed the front door quietly behind him.

The next day, Sunday, was less boring than usual since Nancy's husband Larry was out of town. His newest client, a dot-com near billionaire who had probably played too many games of Dungeons and Dragons in his youth, was consulting with Larry on the design of a forty-thousand-square-foot-Gothic castle in Virginia hunt country. After I rejected tennis and Nancy vetoed my sport, porch-sitting, we wound up walking along the beach of Shorehaven Bay, an inlet of Long Island Sound that, at low tide, offered a flat path of wet, compacted sand, glossy seaweed, and paving of the blue-black shells of the mussels that had been lunch for the gulls.

'It doesn't matter that the cops are sloppy,' Nancy was saying. 'What bothers me is that you're avoiding the truth like it was some mangy old coon dog with hydrophobia.'

'Shush! You sound like Strom Thurmond.'

'You're missing my point.'

'Which is?' I asked.

'That even if Homicide is as lame as Lieutenant Cutie Pie says they are —'

'He's a captain now.'

'Even if Captain Cutie Pie is right about their sloppy methods, the Homicide guys are probably also right about Greg Logan killing Courtney. Why do they have to take off pool covers and ask a bunch of vexatious questions to half of Shorehaven? They knew damn well who done it.' For a few seconds I enjoyed silence as we cautiously clambered over some boulders slick with seaweed. The afternoon June sun had turned from warm yellow to white-hot and beat down on us with the savagery of an August dog day. It evaporated the tiny pools of water in the empty mussel shells, perfuming the beach with the heady scent of dead fish. I turned away from the lethargic waves lapping against the shore to look up to a house of cantilevered white rectangles perched on a bluff above the beach. 'Stop checking out real estate and avoiding what you have to do,' Nancy commanded.

'Which is?'

'Call Fancy Phil and tell him straight out: "Honey, looks to me like it's sonny boy that done the deed."'

'You know,' I told her, 'even if you're wrong, you're right. Because except for Greg, I've probably spoken to most of the same people the cops spoke to. And so far

I haven't been able to figure out why they're so in love with the idea of Greg having done it that they haven't looked elsewhere. They may be sloppy, Nancy, but they're not stupid.'

'You say that with the confidence of someone not intimately acquainted with Nassau County's criminal justice system. Or at least, not intimately connected anymore.'

'I can pretty well guess why they're onto Greg, besides his being the husband of the victim. Someone told the cops something they didn't tell me, something that made Homicide think, Hey, it's definitely gotta be the husband.'

Nancy exhaled impatiently. 'They're cops, for crissake! Genuine authority figures. Nothing personal, toots, but why would you expect people to be as open with some history lady as with the Nassau County police?'

'First of all, I'm not *just* some history lady. I'm a good interviewer, an empathetic human being. Why would any of them lie to me?'

'Maybe it wasn't a sin of commission. Maybe it was a sin of omission.'

'Nancy, it was hold–nothing–back time. Well, at least they all talked to me. And do you know what I learned Courtney was like? Nice, perky. And cold, emotionally deficient. The sensual woman, the compleat asexual. Madly in love with her husband or maybe having an affair.'

'You can do both, easy,' Nancy assured me cheerfully.

'Now listen, after all those interviews – including a couple of people the cops never got to, like her best friend – and all that snooping, what I can't get is who Courtney Bryce Logan really was. But even so, whether she was a cipher, an angel, or a bitch on wheels, who could possibly have gained with her death? No one.'

'Except if Greg had a reason to want her dead. He did take the "theirs" money and made it "his."'

'But that was in response to her sneaking money out of their accounts. And it was forty thousand dollars he took. Major bucks to some people, but not to him.' Nancy was eyeing the ruins of an old seawall in the distance and looked as though she might consider climbing it, with me. So I sat on the sand and kept talking. 'Unless, you're going to say, the murder wasn't about money. Maybe he was having an affair and wanted his freedom. But then you could say, if that were the case, he'd get a good divorce lawyer. Unless . . . well, it might be better to have her dead than squealing Fancy Phil's secrets, things she overheard in the house.'

'As long as you're having this scintillating dialogue with me without my participation,' Nancy remarked, 'I'm going over and check out that old wall.'

I shook my head and patted the beach beside me. Reluctantly, correctly thinking it one of my ploys to avoid walking the extra mile, she sat beside me, took out the tortoiseshell banana clip that held up her hair, and rearranged it into a distant relative of a French twist. 'I don't think Courtney Logan from Olympia, Washington, knew gangster secrets. Listen, Nancy, Fancy Phil's main thrust, you should pardon the expression, was to keep his son out of the world of mafiosi and Russian hoods and all the other scum. He's proud Greg went to Brown. He's proud that Greg was borrowing for his business from a legitimate bank. He's proud of his grandchildren.'

'Maybe Fancy Phil was having a thing with Courtney and whispered secrets in her shell-pink ear,' Nancy suggested. 'So she had to die.'

'No. He would never betray his son.'

'Why not? It was in that movie we saw. The father-in-law and the daughter-in-law. With Jeremy Irons and a one-word title. And the actress with the lips.' Nancy, who could never sit completely still, began to stretch her fingertips down toward her toes. 'Well, maybe Courtney was putting too much pressure on Greg. Get rich, buy me a pied-à-terre in the city or a Louis Quinze desk.'

I recalled what Kellye Ryan had said about Courtney wanting Greg to open some Soup Salad Sandwiches stores on the West Coast, but that hardly sounded like enough pressure to drive a man to murder his wife. 'You know, the cops didn't even talk to all of Courtney's friends. They felt – they feel they have the killer and the motive.'

'Face it. Greg *is* the killer,' Nancy said. 'Although with that result, it's not likely Fancy Phil will write you a letter of recommendation.'

For all I knew, she could be right. But I asked myself out loud: 'Who *did* the cops talk to? Neighbors. Greg. Fancy Phil. And who else? Who could cast a shadow over Greg?' Nancy didn't reply, although she did grunt in triumph when the tip of her middle finger finally made it down her stretched-out leg and touched a toe. 'I'll tell you who. Steffi, the au pair.'

'But you talked to her, too, and said she only had nice things to say –'

'I guess that was only our first talk,' I replied.

Chapter Nine

I can't say I raced to Connecticut, because that would imply eighty miles per hour up I-95 in a Porsche. Forget the Porsche: Besides the forty thousand dollars over the price of my Jeep, my delusion of myself as suburban sex goddess was more easily sustained climbing down from an SUV than heaving myself out of something low-slung, penis-shaped, and racing green. But after my hike on the beach with Nancy, I jumped into the shower, dressed, and was driving past an excessively quaint sign that said ENTERING WHITSBURY (in the colonial-style lettering that rendered Whitsbury as Whitfbury), when I realized two things. I hadn't called Steffi Deissenburger to ask if I could speak with her again and that four-thirty on a Sunday afternoon was not a swell time to pop in anywhere. So I gave myself an assertiveness lecture recycled from one of those Women Who Loathe Themselves/Women Who Love Themselves books I wind up ordering on the Web because I'm embarrassed to ask for it at the Dolphin Bookshop in town.

The next thing I knew, I was telling Steffi's employer, Andrea Leeds, that my name was Judith Singer – right, just like sewing machine – and she was telling me that Sunday was Steffi's day off and that she'd gone (parallel paths of foreboding formed between her brows) to Manhattan.

'I'm sorry to stop by without calling, Ms Leeds, but I was visiting friends in New Canaan and forgot my little phone book.' Three lies in one sentence. I wasn't sorry to stop by without calling, I knew absolutely no one in New Canaan, and having spent a wild Saturday night getting the Palm Pilot and the Dell to make peace with each other, I had transmogrified into an e-babe with no little phone book. 'I'm on the board of the Shorehaven Library. That's how I know Steffi. She was always there with the Logan children.'

'Please, come in.' She was dressed in a yellow polo shirt and a short yellow skirt with green frogs all over it, so I assumed she'd just come home from the golf course. Andrea Leeds would probably be called rangy, being a head taller than I. She was definitely angular, almost bony, with knobs for elbows and knees. Though her face was technically an oval, with a broad forehead and Balkan cheekbones, it was more like an oval balanced on its side: Thus, with an impeccable pageboy curving under precisely at her wide jawline, she gave the impression of a woman who displaced far more space than she actually did. 'Call me Andy, by the way.' She led me along a hallway, taking such long strides I had to double-time it to keep up. The walls were covered with nursery school scribble drawings, matted and framed. 'I'm spending quality time' – she smiled to signal I-know-it's-a-cliché, so I gave her an I-get-it smile in return – 'with my girls.'

She led me into a room I hadn't seen on my last visit. The library. Perfect. Tall windows and French doors welcomed the late afternoon sun. The light burnished the pale wood paneling so it shone gold. The cordovan leather couch had been so well used it looked as if the Invisible Man were lounging on its tastefully crackled cushions. On the shelves were books – genuine books – with those little bulges mid-spine to indicate they'd been read, or at least opened. With a single sniff you'd know these weren't the mildewed tomes homeowners buy by the yard to give the illusion of literacy. I had the sense that had Courtney seen the Leedses' library, she'd have understood in an instant that for all her botanical pictures on ribbons, and doilies in the bottom of wastebaskets, Andy Leeds, with her roomful of books (at a glance, a good but unsurprising white-guys-writing-in-English collection), was the one who'd gotten it right.

'Gwendolyn, Gwyneth, this is Mrs Singer.'

Together, the identical twins cheeped a happy hello as well as something that sounded as if it could be 'Mrs Singer,' the sort of gracious greeting my children couldn't manage until they were in their early twenties. Then, side by side in a club chair, the children went back to studying *Horton Hatches the Egg*. Gwen and Gwyn not only had their mother's wide Slavic features, pale brown hair, and long limbs, they were wearing the same yellow getup avec frogs. Since I doubted that three-year-olds golfed, even in Whitfbury, I decided the mother-daughter froggy business was a fashion statement that, by the grace of God, would not survive a voyage across Long Island Sound to Shorehaven.

After I complimented Andy Leeds on the girls' deport-ment – deportment being one of those words I figured

189

would go over big – and she did her 'Say thank you to Mrs Singer, Gwendolyn and Gwyneth' bit, all of which seemed to take a half hour, she offered me a seat at a small table, probably an antique she and Mr Leeds used whilst they played whist of an evening.

'I'm so relieved Steffi's found such a fine family to work for,' I told her.

'We think the world of her.' Beneath Andy's upper-class civility, I sensed authentic civility. However, I also detected an unuttered question mark. Any parent who leaves her children in the hands of a relative stranger, even one with a solid résumé and enthusiastic references, looks for additional reassurance, and all the more so when the young woman in question comes from a house in which a murder had been committed. 'She seems like a lovely young woman,' was all I would say, since I wasn't handing out endorsements for anyone connected to Courtney Logan.

'What a dreadful time she went through!' My hostess shuddered. The frogs on her skirt quivered sympathetically.

'To see someone just drive away like that' – I tsked-tsked – 'and never . . .'

'Would you like some lemonade?' Andy Leeds asked meaningfully, glancing at her daughters. We left behind the gold glow of the library and the twins – who apparently could be trusted not to bean each other with Trollope and Updike novels they'd yanked off the shelves – and repaired to the kitchen.

Another mom, another kitchen. Yet another elaborate stove with six burners and several strange little ovens, as though all these suburban women were vying for three Michelin stars. Andy Leeds took a pitcher out of the refrigerator and poured the lemonade over crystalline ice cubes in a slender glass. 'They still suspect the husband?' she inquired.

'From everything I hear.'

'He sounds . . .' She hesitated. I nodded, as if I already knew what she would say. Yet my heart speeded up as if to outrace the dread starting to come over me: I was about to get news that Fancy Phil wouldn't want to hear. I was right. 'To put it bluntly,' Andy said definitively, 'this Mr Logan sounds horrid.' Well, I decided, Fancy Phil would have to cope, although I wasn't looking forward to witnessing his anger-management strategies. Nevertheless, if I had/have any personal philosophical view, any slogan I'd want to put on a T-shirt, it's this: Never be afraid of the truth. 'Perfectly horrid,' she was kind enough to reiterate.

So the prime witness in the case, the Logans' au pair, Steffi Deissenburger, was saying Greg was horrid? Okay, not a plus. Had Steffi confided Greg's horridness only to Andy Leeds? Or to Nassau County Homicide as well? That would be a major minus. However, better to know the truth and deal with it. So I pretended to take 'horrid' well. I even nodded – How horrid that Greg Logan was horrid! – then sighed with what I hoped sounded like commiseration. I felt Andy Leeds was bothered and on the verge of forgetting that gentlefolk are reticent. My biggest contribution would be keeping my lip zipped.

I received a thank-you-for-understanding sigh. Finally, before I had to come up with a you're-welcome exhalation, she went on. 'What I can't understand is, how can it be a coincidence that his wife is missing just three or four days and he . . . you know, with Steffi?' I swallowed hard. And waited. 'I mean, unless he had his eye on the girl all along and was just marking time until his wife quote disappeared unquote. I get ice-cold every time I think of it.'

'It's amazing Steffi still managed to stay on there,' I murmured. No wonder the cops weren't looking elsewhere for Courtney's killer.

'She was so devoted to those children. I suppose she felt a moral obligation.'

'I suppose so,' I said.

'Doesn't it break your heart when you think of them, their mother just vanishing and then . . . ?'

I nodded. It did. 'But then Steffi did leave,' I prodded.

'How could she not?' Andy Leeds responded. I sipped the lemonade wishing she'd come up with a cookie to go along with it. 'The anonymous phone calls. The police knocking on the door there three, four nights a week to question him.'

'I know,' I said. 'And once Steffi admitted to the police that Gregory Logan had been, you know . . .'

'Forward,' my hostess politely suggested.

'Forward. Right.' So Steffi had told the cops about Greg. Was he so obtuse or so utterly devoid of ethics that days after his wife was reported missing he decided to make whoopie with the au pair? 'After his being forward,' I continued, 'it probably seemed suspicious to the authorities that Steffi *hadn't* picked up and left immediately.'

'She told you about how he behaved?' Andy asked. I didn't lie and say yes. On the other hand, I concede that my head might have wobbled in an up-and-down direction.

'The . . . the awfulness!' I heard a tremor in her voice and she didn't seem like the tremulous type, but Steffi's story about Greg clearly had shaken her. I gazed at the lemon circle resting on some ice cubes in the bottom of my empty glass. 'Steffi's a strong girl,' she went on, 'but she broke down when she told me. Being in a strange country, going through this lovely woman being missing – and Steffi the last person to see her. And then having a detective try to make her say she had been . . . involved with the husband *before* the wife disappeared. Devotion or no devotion to those children, Steffi *had* to get out fast – before the police began to wonder what was keeping her there.'

'Before they began suspecting her,' I added.

'Absolutely!' said Andy Leeds.

About three minutes later, as I turned left out of the driveway, I asked myself whether I ought to stake out the intersection of Old Farm Road and West Pequot Drive to await Steffi's return from Manhattan. That way, I could confront her about what she'd told her new employer and the cops about Greg (lecherous slimeball) versus what she'd told me (quiet, nice, very polite).

A stakeout would definitely make me feel very sleuthish. On the other hand, it would probably be boring. And, without the requisite stakeout accoutrements that I'd gleaned from noir movies and novels – powdered doughnuts, cardboard container of coffee, a jar for relieving myself, which, not being a man, would no doubt result in a revolting mess involving me, the driver's seat, and a bag of Dunkin' Donuts – I'd probably be longing to get out of there within fifteen minutes. Besides, if Steffi had been duplicitous the first time I'd interviewed her, would she suddenly open up to me if I leaped from my car into the middle of West Pequot and forced her to slam on her brakes?

So I headed home. While waiting to pull out a week's worth of laundry before it could get scorched by my pyromaniacal dryer, I took a can of Diet Coke onto the patio and reread my notes on all the interviews I'd done. I was mulling over what my next step would be when Nancy called.

'How was Little Liebchen?' Uh-oh. Nancy's sloooow talk. 'Did she fess up about Greg?' Generally, when Nancy drew out her syllables so long it seemed she'd never part with them, it was not Flower of Southern Womanhood Hour. It meant she'd had a vodka or two. Or three.

'Are you coherent?' I asked, nibbling on a no-fat cracker that tasted, predictably, like salted Styrofoam.

'Of course I'm coherent. Would you lay off about my drinking.' The last sentence was more command than request.

'Why not stick a straw into a bottle of Absolut and just glug away?' I advised. 'Save all that tedious pouring.'

'Why don't you put a cork in it?'

With a sigh I hoped was sufficiently passive-aggressive to induce guilt, I went back to the subject at hand. 'Steffi wasn't there. I spoke to the lady of the house, who had green froggies on her skirt. She told me Steffi had broken down and wept while telling her how Greg made a pass at her a few days after Courtney was missing.'

'He must be très stupide. To say nothing of très tacky.'

'I don't get it. Greg's not stupid. Not tacky either. And

he didn't strike me as the type who would be swept away.' Then jokingly, I added, 'But what do I know about passion?'

'Not much,' Nancy snapped. When she drank she tended to get a bit testy. 'To tell you the truth,' she conceded, 'I don't know everything either. Do you want a for-instance?'

'I'm going to get one, so yes, I want a for-instance.'

'For instance, I don't understand all these women you're speaking to – Courtney's friends, the Connecticut froggy woman. What do they *do*? They're all thirty-five, forty tops. Whatever happened to jobs? Remember jobs, Judith? Remember all those asshole husbands in 1972, yours and mine included, who said "*My* wife isn't going to work," and how we stood up to them and that idiot mentality. *So what are all these women doing home?*'

'What are you talking about?' I asked. 'They're raising their children.'

'I see. And may I inquire precisely why we went through a revolution in women's rights, why we bothered to have our consciences raised? So our daughters could sit on a bench in a playground and talk about whether Pampers or Huggies hold poopy better. That's how they talk: Cross my heart, hope to die. Poopy and peepee. Four years of higher education, graduate school – a whole world of possibility open to them – and they elect to sit on a park bench and talk shit.'

'We fought so our daughters could choose –'

'We fought so our daughters would be allowed to do the work for which they were suited. Now what happens? They go to law school, medical school, business school and become lawyers or doctors or number crunchers for how long? Three or four years. But the minute they see they're just another cruncher or whatever, that they're not having *fun*, whatever that means, that they're flying to Milwaukee with their knees squished and will never get near the corporate jet, what do they do? They up and quit.'

'Who's supposed to raise their children?' I inquired. 'An illegal immigrant who doesn't speak English, who they underpay and overwork? Take a woman like Courtney Logan –'

'Courtney Logan!' Nancy huffed. 'Give me a break.'

'She had a business,' I argued.

'She had a business that was going noplace fast,' Nancy replied. 'StarBaby was no star and Courtney was no business genius. On her best day she was third rate. I bet you she wasn't humping anywhere near the top of the totem pole at her old investment bank.'

'Not everyone's a winner, Nancy. I'm not exactly a tenured professor at Harvard.'

'But you *work*. Nobody's begging me to be executive editor of *The New York Times* either, but BFD, big fucking deal: I work.'

'But I raised my kids, before I even finished my dissertation. And if you can remember that far back, you were freelancing, not working full-time.'

'But we didn't have a path to follow. They do. Because we cleared it.'

'Maybe they don't like the path.'

'Maybe in a few years men will be saying: "Hey, how come they're letting all these women like Courtney Logan into law school and medical school and into the hot jobs on Wall Street when all they do is work three years and quit? That's not fair. Why can't those places go to men who will stay the course?" And they'll be right.'

'Women like Courtney are better, more involved mothers than we are,' I told her.

'Women like Courtney quit good jobs and wind up banging tambourines on their heads in Mommy and Me class and fucking their golf pros and doing anything to avoid real work. Women like Courtney are up a goddamn creek without a paddle. What was she planning on doing when she turned forty-five? Fifty? Better someone shot her and put her out of her misery.'

After delivering herself of that magnanimous insight, Nancy announced she had to wash her hair, although from the clunk of ice cubes against glass, not muffled by any liquid, I surmised she wanted to get downstairs to pour herself another drink. She was less than appreciative when I asked her what was the first letter of the alphabet, then suggested she double it and find the nearest meeting.

After wasting a half hour folding underwear and towels so meticulously they could be displayed at an *American Washday* exhibit at the Smithsonian, I broke down and called Fancy Phil and gave him the gist of what Steffi had told the cops. I expected a gangster-ish outburst: thunderous Fucks! and fists breaking plaster. But after a long silence, he merely asked what he should do. So I told him.

Around eleven that night my bell chimed. Fancy Phil. Not that he woke me; I'd gotten absorbed finishing an article by a Korean War veteran turned historian on the

Second Infantry Division's role in the fighting at Heart-break Ridge. (And, big surprise, thinking about Nelson.)

The night was cool, in the low sixties, and Phil was wearing a sweatshirt. Brown University. The 'vers' stretched across his gut looked larger than all the other letters. I assumed he'd borrowed it from his son, although the gold Egyptian amulet on a thick herringbone chain was clearly his. 'I talked to Gregory,' Fancy Phil announced in a voice loud enough to broadcast that he knew I lived alone. I didn't want to think about how he knew. I invited him in. 'You got time now?' he asked, but by then he was in the living room, on the couch, gazing at a bowl of potpourri on the coffee table, ruefully concluding it wasn't a snack.

'You asked Greg about Steffi Deissenburger?' I inquired.

'Yeah. You know, you hate like hell to ask your kid the one thing he doesn't want to talk about. But like I told him, "Listen, Gregory, I know you got more'n you can handle. But you gotta stop shittin' me – pardon me for saying that – because I swear to God I'm keeping out of this. Except my friends – high-class friends – hear things, you know. And what I'm hearing is the cops think something was going on with you and that German girl that was watching the kids. And that's how come they think you . . . you know, did it to Courtney."'

With sad but hopeful eyes, he glanced away from me and down at the potpourri again, so I excused myself, went into the kitchen, and brought back a plate with a bunch of red grapes and a couple of plums. 'What did Greg have to say?' I asked.

'It took a while.' He started on the grapes. 'Men don't

like to talk about . . . things they don't want to talk about. Know what I mean?'

'Emotional stuff,' I suggested.

'Right. So I said to him, I said, "Gregory, I'm your old man. There's nothing you ever done that I didn't do maybe a hundred times." So finally he tells me. A few days after Courtney's missing, he's sitting with the German girl and she's showing him a list. So she can go shopping. Probably still buying those pukey-tasting health cereals Courtney made the kids eat. But anyways, all of a sudden, in the middle of reading over the shopping list, Gregory breaks down. Crying. Sobbing his head off because it's like all of a sudden he's beginning to get it, that Courtney might never get found. So the German girl pats his hand' – Fancy Phil motioned for my hand and offered a couple of demonstration pats I doubted would leave bruises – 'like that. And so Gregory starts to cry even harder.' Fancy Phil shook his head. 'Can you picture what it was like for him to have to tell me this, even though I'm his own flesh and blood? I mean, about the crying and stuff. But I told him, "Hey, kid, listen, I've sobbed my head off, too, and I didn't have no wife disappear on me." I didn't say "unfortunately" because my first ex is his mother. So anyways, Gregory puts his head on the girl's shoulder to cry. Like they say, "A shoulder to cry on," you know?' Fancy Phil leaned back, resting his head atop the couch cushion. He pulled a few grapes off the branchlets with his teeth. 'All of a sudden,' he went on, 'the girl pulls back! Like Gregory's grabbed her. Whatever. So Gregory pulls back, too, and they finish the list like nothing happened. And then the girl went shopping.'

'And?' I asked.

'And he swears that was it. *Nothing*, not one thing else, happened. He didn't lay a finger on her. It was that he just broke down for a minute and laid his head on her shoulder.'

'Phil.'

'What?'

'Do you believe him?'

'It's funny.' He spoke more cautiously than usual, but that might have been because he had a mouthful of grapes. 'If anybody else told me that story I'd be thinking: Big bull. But I'm his old man. I know my kid. I even know how my kid lies. All kids do. He doesn't now. But when Gregory was a kid, he'd get three words of a lie out and his ears would turn bright red. I'd give him a smack and say, "Don't lie to me, you little pisspot!" My ex used to say, "Philly, stop with the pisspot, for crissakes!"'

'And you think Greg's telling the truth now?'

'I think someone should get hold of this German girl –' I shook my head. 'I didn't mean hurt her,' Fancy Phil explained. 'I meant to help her try –'

'No,' I said softly.

'You don't have to whisper with me, you know. I'm not some nut who's gonna blow your head off that you gotta get to calm down.'

'I wasn't whispering,' I replied. 'I was talking softly. You know Theodore Roosevelt? He said, "Speak softly and carry a big stick; you will go far."'

'You trying to teach me history?' Fancy Phil shook his head, the way people do when dealing with a hopeless case.

'It couldn't hurt.'

'Fine. History.' He put his hands on his knees and, with a weary grunt, pushed himself up from the couch. 'It so happens I know history. Theodore Roosevelt was before Franklin Roosevelt.'

'That's right.'

'So listen, call me right away if you hear something.' I said I would, and yes, of course he could take the rest of the grapes and the plums with him.

It was nearly eleven-thirty. Too late to call anyone and I didn't have the energy to start the new book I'd taken out of the library. I'd already seen the AMC movie *The Sundowners* at least three times, so TV was out. It was hit the Ben & Jerry's or give myself a pedicure. As I was twirling a tissue to separate my toes, I realized: Hey, it's not even eight-thirty on the West Coast – in Courtney Bryce Logan's hometown. Not too late.

So I riffled through my clippings, found the one I'd printed out from the *Olympian* Web site, and within a minute was on the phone with one Lacey Braun, the high-school classmate of Courtney's who'd been quoted as saying Courtney was 'shrewd.' A curious adjective. Okay, maybe not all that curious, but I had no other ideas.

Lacey hemmed and hawed for a minute or two but finally admitted it was because of an incident that had occurred in her senior year of high school, something that had happened between her best friend Ingrid and Courtney. No, she didn't want to talk about it. Hem, haw again, and then a third time, but at last she gave me a name, Ingrid Farrell, as well as a phone number.

· '"Shrewd,"' Ingrid repeated. 'Well, Lacey's right. That's what Courtney was.' I heard two puffs and a slurp. 'Ow, hot! Sorry, I just made myself a camomile-clove tea a second before the phone rang.'

'Could I ask you a couple of questions about Courtney, Ingrid?'

'I never saw her again after high school.'

'But you may know something that could be helpful,' I urged.

Ingrid emitted a dubious 'uuuuuuh.' Finally, four actual words emerged: 'What is this for?' she finally asked.

'I've been hired to check out Courtney's background. Just to make sure the wrong person isn't . . .' My voice trailed off more because dealing with Lacey and then Ingrid felt like too much expenditure for too little return. 'The wrong person could be accused of her murder and . . .' I was suddenly too sleepy to offer her an image of an innocent being gassed or fried or whatever they did in the state of Washington.

'You're not a reporter?'

'No.'

'It's not nice to say anything bad about the dead,' Ingrid informed me. I thought I heard a regretful note.

'I guess not – except if it can help the living.'

'I mean, it was a high-school thing.'

'What was?'

'See, Courtney Bryce was always doing stuff. You know?' She took a long, noisy sip of tea. 'President of every club. Helping out teachers. Courtney Bryce was the smartest, best, nicest girl in the whole school.'

'Right.' I stifled a yawn.

'Everyone always said, "Oh, Courtney, she's wonderful."' I waited. 'Well, it's like this: She was running the Crunch-Munch sale. Fund-raising. Candy bars. It was chocolate then. I think now it's energy bars made from rainforest nuts and stuff. That's what seniors do every year to raise money for a sit-down dinner on Prom Night.'

'Uh-huh,' I said. My back and shoulders began to ache for bed. I massaged the back of my neck.

'Courtney stole eight hundred dollars in cash from the Crunch-Munch sale. And got away with it.'

'*What?*'

'We had all this cash. I was treasurer. So I had to put it in a sealed envelope and give it to Mr Cooper, the principal. And I did. Courtney was with me when we went to Mr C's office. And he opened the safe. It was late Thursday afternoon, like almost four o'clock, so he said he'd deposit it first thing Friday.'

'A wall safe?'

'No. This big heavy thing on the floor. And so his phone rang and he picked it up and Courtney and me were just standing there and I went to check out pictures of old graduating classes to see if I could find my dad. Courtney was looking at all of Mr Cooper's books. My back was turned to her. So was his. Anyhow, then he got off the phone and shut the safe. The next morning it wasn't there. The cash.'

'Is it possible the principal took it?'

'Of course not! I mean, he did this every year, holding the money for the seniors because a lot of kids get it in late. He called Courtney and me down separately. Guess who got blamed?'

'That's an awful story!' I said.

For a long moment, Ingrid was silent. Then she said: 'Do you know what the worst of it was? He called Courtney down first. By the time I got there, he was totally, totally convinced she never would have done it. That I did it. No, the worst of it was, ninety-nine percent of the kids thought it was me, too, except Lacey and one other girl. Everyone else believed Courtney. The school made my parents pay it back and even my parents . . . Water under the bridge, right? But my name was totally mud. And that kind of thing stays with you forever. I mean, I've never been invited to one class reunion. And I was volunteering at the county animal shelter. Well, one day I walked in – this was two or three years ago – and nobody said a word, but I knew somehow someone had heard the story. And then told it to everybody, and everybody *believed* it, people who'd always thought I was a good person. A story, a lie, from way back in high school!'

'Did Courtney avoid you the rest of your senior year?' I asked.

'Well, we never hung out. But whenever there were other kids around, she went out of her way to be sweet to me, like she was full of pity for my being such a bad person. Everyone thought, wasn't it great of Courtney to be so fantastically nice to Ingrid after the terrible thing Ingrid tried to do – and almost got away with.'

Chapter Ten

A giant brown eye stared back at me from a magnifying mirror as I plucked my eyebrow. Cautiously. A few months after Bob died, I'd decided it was time to start looking like a human being again. I dug out my old tweezer. Alas. When I finished, one brow was so much higher than the other that for several weeks I looked inappropriately ironic. Soon after, I'd bought the mirror.

So there I was, bright-eyed at six A.M., hell-bent on an hour's worth of self-improvement. What had wakened me? Rambunctious bird business outside my window, or maybe CourtneyLoganangst. In any case, I showered and exfoliated enough to go down a dress size. Then, so intently was I concentrating on my eyebrow's image in the magnifying glass, that when I lifted the portable phone from the edge of the sink, I didn't catch the opening words of Steffi Deissenburger's early morning conniption fit. However, it wasn't necessary. Each time I tried to butt in she squawked: 'How, *how*, how could you visit the Leedses' house on my day off? *How?*' again and again, turning up the volume with every 'how.'

I recalled Nelson telling me, a couple of decades earlier, of something he'd heard at a cop seminar: a technique for dealing with people who'd gone over the edge – something like Calming a Psychotic Who Has an Assault Rifle in One Hand and a Fistful of Plastique in the Other. The idea was not to be confrontational and say something like: What's your problem, dipshit? It was to ignore the madness and pursue pleasant discourse. As in: Gee, you like the Uzi nine millimeter, too!

So I enthused: 'Steffi! I'm glad you called. Too bad I missed you yesterday afternoon.' Only then did it occur to me that Steffi wasn't behaving irrationally, that she had a right to be steaming. Plus that Nelson had muttered something about the congeniality tactic probably having only a thirty percent chance of working, and if it didn't, you were dead (albeit good-natured) meat.

Just as I was about to beg her pardon and offer extravagant apologies, Steffi replied: 'It would have been better if you telephoned.' Stress still vibrated her voice. Her German accent was heavier – 'would have been' became 'vut hof bean' – as if her last year in America had not happened. Nevertheless, she was no longer squawking.

'You're right,' I said quickly, 'Forgive me for not calling ahead. It's just that I happened to be in Connecticut and thought I'd pop in and say hi.' In the mirror, my humongous eyelid flickered at this lie. 'You know, I was wondering about something you said about Courtney.'

'Perhaps I did not explain when I spoke.' Steffi was now sounding only mildly snippy. 'Courtney was my employer. I did not know her well.'

'You lived in the same house.'

'Yes, that is true. But when she was at home she was in her office nearly all the time. For hours. I was with the children. She was at the computer or on the phone. Her door was closed.'

'Just out of curiosity . . .' I said (turning from the mirror so I didn't have to see my crow's-feet in the early-morning sun, which, magnified, looked deep as pterodactyl tracks). 'How did you know Courtney was on the computer so much?'

'The light of the phone line.'

'She couldn't have been talking to someone?'

'She could have been.' Her reply was still somewhat testy. Still, Steffi did not seem to have the heart to hold a grudge. An explanation quickly followed of how her boyfriend Stefan was studying economics in Dusseldorf and how they emailed each other several times a day and how difficult it was for her to get his letters with Courtney being on-line so long – How could she only be talking for hours and hours? Yet she insisted Steffi keep the other line free for incoming calls. Stefan looked a little like Dave Grohl. The drummer from Foo Fighters.

'He sounds wonderful.' I put my hand over the mouthpiece so she wouldn't hear my yawn. And Steffi kept going. I was finally able to cut her off while she was still at the beginning of confiding Stefan's carefully laid career plans. Nevertheless, her obvious loneliness, living in a foreign country on eight or so acres with a husband, wife, and two three-year-olds, saddened me. On the other hand, perhaps when she was on Long Island, her solitude had inspired fantasies about Greg Logan. Enough to make her want to murder Courtney Logan? That would be a nifty solution. Fancy Phil would be happy. The only problem was I didn't think I could buy it. 'Steffi and Stefan sounds like a great team,' I added cheerfully.

'Thank you.'

Now that we were pals again, I inquired: 'By the way, Steffi, did Courtney work all day, every day? Didn't she ever go out with friends or have friends over?'

'Yes. Now and again. Women friends.'

'Do you happen to know any of their names?'

'There was Kellye Ryan. She was a visitor many times. Have you seen her? Tall, thin, like a supermodel. Very beautiful. fine, fine clothes. And nice. Very kind.'

'Anybody else?'

'Yes, three or four. I can't remember their names. I saw them. They always said hello – they were nice women, although not so friendly to me like Kellye – but often Courtney would ask me to take the children someplace out of the house so with her friend, she could have a quiet talk.'

'I see. Oh, by the way, remember we spoke about Gregory Logan?' Steffi's answer was silence. 'That Courtney had said if he called while she was out to say she was shopping. Because she didn't want him worrying about her: He had too much on his plate.'

'Yes.' Wary. She was stretching out the monosyllable as long as she could.

Phone to my ear, I stepped from the cold tile of the bathroom onto the comforting softness of the bedroom carpet. 'Did you find Greg like that, under pressure?'

I waited. Well, I told myself, she sure doesn't talk off the top of her head. I sat cross-legged on the bed, reaching behind me to prop up a couple of pillows against the headboard. I felt around my night table for a pen, came up with a long-lost lip-liner, and jotted a few notes about what Steffi was saying on a milk-mustache ad in *Entertainment Weekly*. At last Steffi spoke: 'No. Mr Logan seemed – I do not know exactly how to say it – like anyone else. Of course, I do not know American men very well, you understand. After Courtney disappeared, he was what you would call a man under pressure. Very, very unhappy. The police were visiting. Often he would call his father. You know about his father?'

'I think so,' I mealymouthed. 'He's supposed to be a gangster, right? Fancy Somebody.'

'Yes. Fancy Phil Lowenstein. A man with many jewels. Very friendly. Informal, I should say. He said to me, "Call me Phil." He himself often called me "honey," but I believe that was because he could not remember my name.'

'Did Greg Logan speak with anyone besides his father after Courtney disappeared?'

'His mother, I think. His sister. A friend from college. His lawyer of course.'

'Did he pay attention to the children during that time?'

'Oh yes. He was very nice with them. Always. Before and after.'

The early, pre-car-pool silence beyond my open bedroom window was broken by the screech of a jay, a stupid-sounding *Waaa?*, as if the bird couldn't figure out what was obvious to every other creature. 'You know, Steffi, from what I hear around Shorehaven, the police believe Greg had – well, a romantic interest in you.' She didn't chuckle at the foolishness of such a notion, so I plunged ahead. 'I suppose it's one of the reasons why they suspect him.' Still no response. 'You know, I have two kids not much older than you are. I can hardly imagine . . . It must have been a terrible situation for you.'

'Yes.'

'I give you credit, staying there as long as you did.'

'They were good children,' Steffi explained. 'With their mother missing . . . It was very sad.'

'You were so devoted to them. It must have been tense in the house, I mean after Greg Logan . . .'

'Yes. He was . . . He watched me all the time. When I read to the children, or watched television with them – he allowed them to watch television. Courtney would not be approving of that.'

'But you knew his eyes were always on you.'

'Yes.'

'Awful. Did he ever actually touch you?' When she didn't reply, I said: 'I'm sorry, Steffi. It's just that I feel protective. As if you were one of my kids.'

'He was crying one afternoon, about Courtney. I touched his hand, with pity, you understand, a light touch. He put his arms around me. He pulled me to him.'

'My God! What did you do?'

'I tried to pull away, but he would not allow me to. He kept saying, "I need . . . I need" . . . but he was breathing too hard. I could feel his tears or maybe – *Schweiss* in English – yes, his sweat. I could feel wet on my neck. I told him, "You must stop this!" but he did not. I said it louder, so loud I was afraid the children would hear, but I had to get away.'

'Of course! You did the right thing. And then did he let you go?'

'Yes.'

'But he kept looking at you.'

'He never stopped.'

I led her back to talking about Stefan. Within a minute she was cheery again, telling me of the hobby they shared, collecting Monty Python memorabilia. Beguiling though her tale was of Stefan's pursuit of a *Life of Brian* T-shirt, I managed to get myself off the phone.

Downstairs in the kitchen, quartering an orange, I felt almost certain Steffi did not have it in her to shoot Courtney Logan twice in the head, then deep-six the body in the swimming pool. And as far as the he said/she said versions of Crying Greg, I didn't see much in Fancy Phil and Steffi's accounts that was inconsistent. Maybe Greg had put his arms around her, maybe not. Perhaps he·was looking for solace, perhaps nooky (though my vote was for solace). In any case, the awkward moment had lasted less than sixty seconds. Were his eyes always on her after that? If so, it was impossible for me to know if the cause was lust or mortification.

When I noticed myself arranging orange pits in a row, I perceived my mind had meandered. I'd been going over the Zee Friedman timetable on Courtney. From what Zee had said, business hadn't seemed up or down in July, yet she claimed Courtney had been 'bummed.' But by early fall, she'd noted, Courtney was detached; her mind, according to Zee, was someplace other than StarBaby. She'd gone from trying to breathe for Zee to letting her wing it. I sauntered over to the refrigerator and retrieved a still-unopened container of no-fat pineapple cottage cheese I'd successfully avoided. I checked: seventy-two hours past its freshness date. Lacking courage to break the seal and confront what could be going on inside, I chucked it into the garbage.

Now that I thought about it, Zee's assessment of Courtney's September and October detachment had been backed up by Kellye Ryan: By September, Courtney's mind was no longer on StarBaby. So what had it been on? Monkey business? Money business? Was she phasing out Greg, in love or lust with somebody else? Or had she simply moved on to some new, more sophisticated investment bankerish interest than StarBaby?

Since becoming a widow, I'd tried hard not to indulge in the lonely person's Happy Hour: talking to oneself. About a year earlier, in the drugstore, I found myself befuddled, dithering between a condom rack and a display of batteries and was startled when I heard my own loud voice demanding: 'Why am I here?' But now I gave in and had a chat with me.

That was because my kind of thinking never turned out to be pure reason. Instead, my thought processes were a mishmash of random ideas, intuition, and untoward meddling by my subconscious. What I wanted was logic, so I inquired aloud: 'Is there any way to determine whether it was sex, money . . . or absolutely nothing preoccupying Courtney?' One of the orange quarters smiled up at me. I ate it, then answered myself: 'What have I learned about Courtney? That she was different things to different people. She was nice, very nice, really nice, having an affair, was asexual, was a poison-gas person. Oh, right, and a perfect human being. In death, she's a Rorschach test. Was she that much of a cipher in life?'

I finished the orange and chomped on a petrified oat-bran pretzel while waiting for the coffee to drip. As I could not talk and chew at the same time I reverted to thinking. How had people reacted emotionally to Courtney? Steffi, who'd worked for her and lived in her house, appeared not just to like her but to revere her. Greg had either loved her (or liked her enough to stay in the marriage) or downright hated her enough to kill her. Not only was it easier for me to believe the love stuff, what with Fancy Phil having hired me to clear his son, it also was more comforting to picture the single parent of two young, traumatized children as another innocent victim of Courtney's murder rather than as the monster who could execute such a crime.

My client, Fancy Phil himself, hadn't liked his daughter-in-law. Yet he hadn't seemed to hate her. He'd compared her personality to *lukshen* – the Yiddish word for noodles, i.e., something limp, bland, and tasteless – a description that could in no way be construed as a compliment. On the other hand, blahness did not seem enough of an affront to get a person on a mobster's hit list.

Or on anybody's hit list. So had Courtney Logan been truly blah, truly nice, truly the supermom and diligent young entrepreneur? Or had she hidden some aspect of her life from those who supposedly knew her best? Had her detachment meant a preoccupation with love or money, something that had led to another person wanting or needing to wipe her off the face of the earth? Or had she been heading for a quickie with her inamorato on Halloween night? Had he (or she, positing a jealous wife of said inamorato, or an inamorata of Courtney's) murdered her? And if so, how come her body wound up in her own swimming pool? Had some meandering maniac decided trick instead of treat? 'Beats the hell out of me,' I announced, and poured myself a mug of coffee.

But wouldn't the killer have been taking a sickening risk? To transport a dead body back from wherever to the Logan house on Bluebay Lane, across a lawn, through the gate of a high, wrought-iron fence onto the deck around the pool? Or had the deed been done at or right near the Logan house? Wouldn't two shots to the head in the garage or backyard, even with a silencer, have made some noise? And unfastening the tied-down-tight pool cover to shove the body into the water couldn't have been easy. Okay, maybe it made sense to stow her there. Algae-killing chemicals in the water might prevent a god-awful smell, whereas burying a body in the wooded area beyond the backyard was the quickest way to make a Nassau County Police Department beagle look good. But think of the danger! Greg might have come home early. A trick-or-treater could have cut through the backyard. Steffi or Morgan or little Travis might have peeked out a window.

Okay, let's say the killer had been lurking outside the house waiting for Courtney to return. She put the car in the garage and . . . *whammo!* Except if she'd just come home from Grand Union, where were the apples she'd gone out for? Though it was certainly possible, I had trouble picturing a gunman shoving a gun back into one pocket, then four organic Winesaps into another.

Another thought. Another mug of coffee. One percent milk. Half an Equal. I sat back down at the kitchen table. Had Courtney's body been put in the pool in order to implicate Greg in the killing? If so, why had the killer refastened the cover so tightly? I recalled when I'd first heard Mack Dooley, the Logans' pool man, on the radio in May. He'd said something about the cover looking fine: 'tied down real tight' the way he'd left it in the middle of September when he closed it up.

Did the killer want people to believe Courtney was simply missing? If that was the case, why risk putting her body in the pool? No murderer would rely on incompetence from the Nassau County PD's Homicide unit – that they would *not* look under the pool cover. Because the department had a good reputation. Obviously there might be the predictable politically connected losers or lazy guys, like the guy in charge of the Logan case. Still, most of the detectives were thought of as well qualified. Or terrific, the way Nelson had been.

I put on a pair of gray slacks (which delighted me by buttoning without my having to inhale) and a white shirt, then tied a yellow cashmere cardigan around my shoulders in that trendy, capelike style that made adult females look as if they were playing some communal game of Wonder Woman. Slipping into a pair of Gucci loafers I'd bought in Rome in 1985, I was so *comme il faut* I looked like a chic distant relative of myself. So I dropped by both Susan Viniar and Kellye Ryan's houses. And all just after nine o'clock.

Susan's housekeeper led me upstairs into a home gym with floor-to-ceiling mirrors. I found her straddling a menacing-looking machine, pulling down a bar that resembled a deformed wishbone; the bar was attached by pulleys to – I squinted. Yikes! – ninety pounds of iron plates. The weight did not seem to faze her in the least.

At Kellye's, after I rang the bell and called out my name,

she herself reluctantly opened her own door. No live-in housekeeper. Not quite in supermodel gear yet: Her black hair was wrapped around giant foam cylinders. Strips of parchmentlike paper were glued to her nose, forehead, and chin – a beauty treatment, not rampant weirdness. Whatever she was doing to the rest of her was doubtless even less inviting, because she kept gripping the neck of an ankle-length cotton robe to make sure not an inch of skin was showing. 'A North Shore Child and Family Guidance luncheon,' she explained. 'I'd love to invite you in for a cup of coffee, but like, you know . . .' We chatted at the door for about ten minutes.

Afterward, I drove to Starbucks and sat in the parking lot with a container of iced decaf. Okay, what had I just learned? Not much. Neither woman had altered her view: Susan was still convinced Courtney was sexless; best friend Kellye sensed Courtney was preoccupied, the way a woman with a lover might be – and, Kellye added, clutching the sky-blue robe even tighter to make sure whatever glop she had on her neck was invisible, Courtney had 'that glow, if you know what I mean.'

Well, at least between the two of them I came up with a list of ten other women who might know Courtney well. So I spent most of the day and early evening visiting and phoning upwardly mobile thirty-somethings.

After dinner, around seven-thirty, I phoned my daughter the lawyer. What could Courtney have been doing? Was it possible she'd made a mint doing on-line trading – hundreds of thousands? millions? – and someone learned of it and wanted to get their hands on the money?

Like Dreadful Dan Steiner, Kate thought it was unlikely

although conceivable. 'Mom, even in a bull market, I don't think it's easy to be a genius for more than a month or two. I don't know. Maybe she had a special knack for it and picked the right Internet stocks. I mean, you hear amazing stories about fortunes being made, but my guess is most of them are probably myths.'

My response, I regret to say, was one of those vocal maternal sighs designed to make offspring feel they owe you something. Anyway, Kate offered me another minute despite the predictable lunacy (senior partners pounding on conference tables, clients screeching) of whatever merger or acquisition that she was working on. 'Listen, Mom, if this Courtney was on-line for hours on end, she could have been reading tech reports on particular securities or on certain industries. Or watching a tape of stock prices. Maybe she wasn't investing. Just interested or trying to learn. Or she could have been investing small time. From what I hear, even that can get addictive. Or maybe it was something having zero to do with trading. Like hanging out in chat rooms, talking to friends she'd made. Or looking at porn sites, having cybersex, or bidding on baseball cards. There are a million things she could have been doing.' Kate paused for a breath. 'Hey, how about trading on insider information from one of her old colleagues?'

How about it? One thing I knew: That whole day, no one said anything to make me leap up and shout *Aha!* On the other hand, though I was wide awake, my mind was tired. Like soap bubbles, shimmery ideas of who-done-it or how-done-it rose and gleamed for an instant, then popped into thin air. So around eight-thirty, just as the sun was setting, I tooled over to Nancy's. For a while we just sat silently in her office gazing out at the pink-and-orange June sky – luscious pastels, what you'd see at an Estée Lauder counter.

'Pretty,' she observed. The colors of the sky glowed on her cheeks and forehead, giving her the complexion of a flamingo.

For someone who found looking in mirrors a pleasant experience, who paid a fortune for clothes, who planned what earrings she'd wear a week in advance, Nancy's office was remarkably unpretty. In fact, it was a mess of a space, with an old rocking chair with a splintery rush seat, a sagging daybed, piles of books serving as endtables, and two dusty afghans left over from the few months in the early seventies when Nancy had gone through an Earth Mother phase and bought a used loom. Nevertheless, the office was the only room in the house that had survived her husband Larry's latest renovation. No pointed arches, not one gargoyle.

Nancy's only decoration was on one wall, where she'd taped up some of her early freelance writing efforts: 'Bubble, Bubble, Soil and Trouble: What You Need to Know About Phosphate Detergents' and 'One Hundred Ways to Say "No" to a Man' (a notion, alas, that had never occurred to Nancy). Now the articles were yellowed and dry, held up by Scotch tape so old it had turned bronze. Flakes of desiccated paper crumbled from the curling edges of the pages and adhered to the baseboard and rug.

'So?' she inquired, sipping a little water or a lot of vodka.

'I spent the day talking to young mothers,' I reported.

'Did you get anything? Besides bored?'

'Were you boring when you stayed home with your kids? Was I?'

'I wasn't. You were.'

'Shush. I want to talk about Courtney.'

She nodded. In an instant her expression transmuted from snide to solemn. In the grand tradition of best friends, Nancy resembled one of those exquisitely calibrated instruments that sense the first rumbling of a quake a thousand miles away. Unlike a mere good friend or a pal or a chum who might proclaim, Hey, let me know if you need anything/I'm always here for you/If you feel like company just call, Nancy, in a split second, would sense the slightest shift in my seismic activity and respond accordingly. 'I'm all ears,' she said.

'A couple of the people I interviewed thought there'd been a change in Courtney this fall. She seemed kind of depressed over the summer, maybe about the business, maybe about something else.'

'Something male?' Nancy inquired.

'Possibly. In any case, she was still working to make a go of StarBaby. But come September, she acted detached from it. The last couple of weeks before Halloween, there were a few times she got all dolled up and was away for the entire day. Her husband doesn't get home till around eight. And she told the au pair to tell him she'd gone shopping. Most of the time, though, she stayed in the office for hours on end, maybe on-line, maybe talking. Zee, her videographer, says she was just going through the motions, businesswise, with StarBaby. Her best friend sensed something else was occupying her – a guy. Courtney supposedly had "that glow." On the other hand, a woman in her group who really wasn't close to Courtney told me she thought Courtney was utterly asexual.'

'How did she have her children? By budding?'

'Now, the best friend is superfashionable. Very attractive, too, except for inordinately long canine teeth.' I did my Bela Lugosi imitation for a few seconds, until Nancy closed her eyes. 'She seems to have a good heart. But I think the other woman in the group is infinitely brighter. She picked up on something about Courtney that I'd picked up on after talking to a whole bunch of people: She was . . . incomplete. The woman, Susan, told me Courtney reminded her of the pod people in *Invasion of the Body Snatchers*.'

'Excellent,' Nancy said. 'Another evening of high culture. I can always count on you to elevate any discussion.'

'I really understand what she meant by pod people. Courtney had all the qualities of a winner – fine education, good job after college, decent-to-terrific husband, money, lovely children.'

'Except she wasn't a winner? Something was wrong with her?'

'Not wrong. It was that something wasn't quite right. Listen, some people liked her or thought she was a decent sort. The au pair looked up to her. But except for the best friend, no one had a single tear for her. No one seemed to have the wind knocked out of them by the awfulness of murder.'

'Well, it's been a while since they found the body.'

'It's three weeks today,' I told her.

'But she's been gone since October thirty-first. After a few days, people must have assumed some kind of foul play. So finding her body wasn't a shock.'

'Listen, imagine if the same thing happened to someone we were peripherally friendly with, say Mary Alice. She certainly is a peripheral friend. But wouldn't you still be stunned?'

'No. I'd be dancing in the streets,' Nancy said.

'You would not.'

'Doing the tango up Northern Boulevard.'

'No. You'd be stunned.'

'Fine. Whatever you say.'

We were quiet for a minute, Nancy studying the quotes on a paperback she'd bought, me combing the fringe of a brown-and-gold afghan. 'I keep thinking about something you said,' I told her. She set aside the book. 'About Courtney being third-rate and StarBaby not being a star. Was that something you heard at *Newsday*?'

She flung back her head in a southern-belle-taking-umbrage gesture and muttered a weary 'Mah Gawd!' When my only response was to keep combing afghan fringe, she added: 'No, you turkey. It's something I heard my inner voice say. Courtney Logan quits her job when she has her first kid. Have you heard one tiny little word about her having been dying to get back to Wall Street or wherever she'd been? Or missing it?'

'No.'

'She was running one of those cute home-office businesses that seemed to be going noplace fast.' Before I could challenge her, she added: 'I swear I'm not being snotty. If the company had potential, she wasn't the one who could take it there. Ambition's fine, but you also need what we used to call in Georgia stick-to-it-iveness.'

'Because no one down there ever heard the word "tenacity."'

'Do you want my opinion or not?' she demanded.

'Go ahead.'

'Courtney strikes me as one of those people . . . They

have all the right credentials but they end up going through life appalled that instead of being, say, CEO of J. Walter Thompson, they're running the second biggest ad agency in Florence, Alabama. I mean, look at her. Cute as a button. Must have won a Little Miss Dimples contest back home. Smart. Princeton, *magna cum laude*. With an Ivy League, MBA husband. Worked at that big investment banking firm.'

'Patton Giddings,' I said quietly. 'Listen, Nance, I think it's time for me to go farther.'

'Which means what?' she inquired, somewhere between huffy and belligerent. 'Seeing your cop?'

'No! Literally going farther. If there was a guy in Courtney's life, the way her best friend says, no one in town has a clue as to who he is. Or at least no one I've come up with. If there was some big fight or a business deal here in Shorehaven that blew up and made someone want to kill her, I haven't heard a peep about anything that could lead to me finding out about it. And I haven't sensed anyone trying to hide anything either. Frankly, for someone so active locally, she doesn't seem to have made more than a superficial impression on people.'

'Thus your pod–person thesis.'

'Listen, Nancy, she just could have been a plain old nebbish. Or maybe she was hiding something dark and dirty. But I think sooner or later I have to go into the city because I'm coming close to the end of my rope here.'

'What's at the end of your rope?' Nancy asked.

'Don't ask.'

'I'm asking.'

'Fancy Phil.'

Chapter Eleven

'What's wrong?' Fancy Phil Lowenstein peered across the yellowed laminate of our table in a booth in Coffee Heaven. A half step up from greasy spoon, the place stood in grubby contrast to the recently renovated, excessively quaint white clapboard railroad station across the street, about eight miles up the track from the Shorehaven stop.

A few leisurely commuters, dressed down in chinos or suited up in seersucker, atilt from attaché cases and tote bags, let their eyes drift in our direction to check if . . . Yes! The Long Island Bad Guy himself was at his usual table. Uh-huh, today he was wearing – Je-*sus* – a giant sun medallion on a rope of gold and a belly-hugging sports shirt, gray, with wide, horizontal bands of red. The shirt was so tight it broadcast the news nobody really had to know, that his navel was an outie. Before he could catch them ogling, they turned to check the day's special: OJ 2 POCHED EGGS ON TOAST COFFEE $2.20.

Still, these suburbanites, basking in the shine of Fancy Phil's celebrity, suddenly seemed to be living more fully. Like drooping plants brought into the sun, they were revitalized by his light. Shoulders rose from their slumps. Eyes sparkled. 'Two eggs over easy, *very* crisp bacon!' was ordered in a cocksure manner, as if being a mere few feet from the source of power had transformed men and women alike into wise guys. Mornings couldn't get much better than this unless a genuinely more transcendent celebrity, a Dick Cavett, say, or a Madeleine Albright, would pop into Coffee Heaven for a bagel and cream cheese.

'You don't like your breakfast, Doc?' my client inquired. My half-eaten egg white omelette lay on the plate like an exhausted invertebrate.

I myself was feeling fairly jaunty. 'No, the omelette was fine,' I replied.

'Because if you want, I can get Monte to make you a waffle. Or a real omelette, with the yellow in it.' Phil himself had finished off a breakfast of scrambled eggs and all the accoutrements. Not a shred of hash-brown potatoes was left, nor a crust from the tower of toast he'd been served. Miniature foil containers of grape jelly and strawberry preserves, now empty, as well as a minor mess of small paper rectangles Phil had ripped off pats of butter, were strewn across the table. 'Maybe some pancakes?' He grabbed a few napkins from the dispenser and dabbed the already clean corners of his mouth. 'They got hot oatmeal. The kind that still's got a little crunch in it, not the mushy kind.'

'No thanks, Phil. Look, I want to talk about money.' His poker face was impressive, though the almost imperceptible slosh of black coffee in his cup showed me something had registered. 'No, no,' I came back quickly. 'Not money for me. I'm in this as a volunteer, just as I said I'd be. I mean Courtney's money. I need to ask you some questions about her, and please understand I don't mean to be disrespectful –'

'What are you talking? Respect? You think I'm some godfather where you gotta kiss my ring?'

'No, because I have no intentions of kissing anything of yours. So, let's move along. If your daughter-in-law had a strong guiding force in her life, what would you say it was? Love – including sex – or money?'

Fancy Phil didn't even bother with a token 'Hmm.' 'Money.'

'How come you're so sure?'

He gave himself time to mull this over by calling out to the man behind the counter. 'Hey, Monte, what's a guy gotta do around here to get more toast?' Monte smiled, undoubtedly knowing his role in this game, and gave a snappy, yes-sir! salute. Fancy Phil, knowing his role also, graciously inclined his head. Then he turned back to me. 'It's like this.' He massaged the first of his chins. 'Picture a business thing, okay? You meet some guy. He looks right, says all the right words. Except you pick up little things. Let's say you're talking about a deal. But all of a sudden a girl walks by and he's checking her out. Then he turns back to you; he says, "What were you just saying?" Now, the guy only lost his concentration for maybe half a second, but you know, hey, he don't have the . . . the focus for you to want to do a deal with him. A girl's a girl, but a deal's a deal. Like with Courtney. Focus. You talk about business stuff, and even though she was a good wife and mother, always googly-eyeing Gregory and calling the kids "Sweetie," in my heart of hearts –' Fancy Phil whacked the northwest corner of his paunch to show me where his heart was – 'she'd drop the sugarplum shit – pardon me – if somebody three blocks away whispered "spreadsheet."'

'What did she like more about business?' I pumped him. 'The wheeling and dealing? Or the money?'

'Well, she knew how to spend all right. Clothes. That house, the cars, the vacations. Bali the last time. Making Gregory go halfway around the world to go to the beach? Antiques, too. Let me tell you, for two kids playing it straight –'

'By straight you mean legal?' I cut in.

'Yeah. Legal. Legit. For two kids keeping their nose clean, Courtney and Gregory were doing nice. Living nice. Too nice, because Courtney was always spending. Getting plans drawn up for a greenhouse one time. Pressuring him to buy the house next door when it went up for sale. So's they could knock it down and have more land. Land. They already got two acres. Who the hell was she, Miss Scarlett O'Hara?'

I finished cleaning off the tops of the salt and pepper shakers with my napkin and willed myself not even to glance at the ketchup-encrusted seam between the table's top and sides. Instead I inquired: 'So it was more money – what money could buy – than wheeling and dealing that interested Courtney?'

'Nah, that's not right either. Because you couldn't shut her up about business when she started StarBaby. Blab, blab, blab. And when she finally said everything twice, she'd talk about other people's businesses, too. Like telling you *Wall Street Journal* stories. Boring corporate crap: "Schmuckola, Incorporated's quarterly profits exceeded all forecasts." Like I really give a you-know-what about Schmuckola. But after a while, when StarBaby wasn't raking it in, she didn't have nothing to say about anybody's business. So put it this way: Courtney liked wheeling and dealing only if she was in the plus column.'

'That money she took from her and Greg's brokerage and bank accounts,' I said. 'We've gone over how she put some of it back. But in the end, she wound up keeping for herself twenty-five thousand dollars of what used to be joint money.'

'Yeah,' Fancy Phil said. 'That's right. She needed it for StarBaby.'

'Can you remember when all that taking out and putting back on her part happened?'

'Lemme think. Gregory told me about it . . . I guess the second week of November, two weeks after she was missing, when the cops began asking him about that forty thou he took out from their joint account and put in his own name.'

'That was the money that was supposed to make his bankers feel comfortable, right?'

'Right. You're running a legit business, you need an open line of credit, you don't want no uncomfortable bankers.' He paused, then bunched up his lips and spat out – fortunately not in my direction – as if he'd just tasted something revolting. 'Except those dummy putzes, those Homicide cops! They took Gregory's putting forty thou aside to make Soup Salad Sandwiches secure to mean *he* was the reason Courtney was missing, if you get me.'

'You mean, the cops' theory is that Greg wanted to get his hands on the family money, and maybe he and Courtney fought. So he killed her.'

'You ever hear such crap? Anyways, Gregory told me

something like he had a talk with Courtney on Mother's Day, whenever that is.'

'Mid-May.'

'So a talk in mid-May, about her pulling money out of their joint accounts for that stupid StarBaby. Then later they had words again; I guess in the summer. That's when she dipped in and helped herself the second time. Can you believe such chutzpah? But he told me she calmed down moneywise around the time Morgan started kindergarten. So that's around Labor Day or a little after. Courtney said she was sorry and Gregory said *he* was sorry but he had to keep a certain cash balance to make his bankers happy. He told me everything was lovey-dovey after that.'

I took a deep breath and asked: 'How sure are you that your son is telling the truth?'

Fancy Phil answered 'As sure as I can get' so quickly and so calmly I decided to believe him.

'From what I've heard . . .' I was interrupted as Monte came from behind the counter with what looked like an entire loaf of bread, toasted, as well as a bowlful of jelly containers and butter pats. When at last he stopped smiling and moved back behind the counter, I continued: 'Courtney's usual pattern seemed to change in September. She lost interest in StarBaby. According to both her best friend and the young woman who worked for her part-time, her mind was elsewhere. It all jibes with what you're saying.'

'Want a piece?' He held out a triangle of toast.

'No thanks. Listen, Phil, you're a smart businessman. What does it tell you if someone who is really interested in money and business starts neglecting the very business she'd thought would be the key to her making it big?'

'It could tell me a couple of things,' he said carefully.

'Like?'

'Like with a woman? She could've had a boyfriend. But I don't think so. Not Courtney. She could've been, you know, having depression or something – a nervous breakdown. Or maybe she was getting born again, the Jesus stuff they do. But I don't think that either. If I had to guess, I'd say she found some other business that was more, you know, interesting than the one she had.'

'Could she have gotten involved with something messy? Wound up paying blackmail? Or did she have it in her to possibly be blackmailing someone else?'

Fancy Phil shook his head as if I'd suggested something beyond idiocy. 'When someone's in trouble, there's like . . . an invisible black cloud over them. They can go ha-ha a million times a day, but some-one like me – you know, someone who knows what trouble really means – can sniff it out. And Courtney didn't have no black cloud like she was scared or in a jam or trying to pull a racket that wasn't going right.'

'What about the opposite? Could she have found some other business interest more lucrative than StarBaby?'

'"Lucrative."' He chuckled without any discernible humor. 'I know what "lucrative" means.'

'I'm sure you do. That's why I used it. I don't talk down to you, Phil. We're both too smart for that.'

'Yeah, I know, Doctor. Anyhow, if you're right, and I say *if*, then yeah, some other lucrative business thing makes more sense to me than a boyfriend or blackmail. But that's

229

The Big If. You could be going on a wild-goose chase. Mark my words.'

'But there's a time you've got to trust your instincts, isn't there?'

'There's a time,' he agreed.

'So regarding the love versus money approach,' I went on. 'If I believed it was love that drove her, I'd keep looking in Shorehaven. But as far as money goes, I need to follow Courtney's finance contacts. So what I'd like you to do is see if you can get something from Greg –'

Fancy Phil was squeezing the contents of a container of strawberry jam onto the corner of his thickly buttered toast. The jam looked like a clot of blood. 'Done,' he declared.

'But you don't know what I want yet.'

'Whatever you want,' he said, carefully seeing that the jelly covered every crevice of his toast, 'I can do.'

What I wanted was names of Courtney's colleagues. True to his word, Fancy Phil delivered, calling me just before noon with a list of names and telephone numbers. My Caller ID indicated he was phoning from a Shorehaven number. I figured it was safe to assume that he'd gone to the Logan house while his son was at work and made himself comfortable – perhaps in Courtney's home office – by Greg's invitation. Or more likely not. Fancy Phil probably considered his own need invitation enough.

I almost couldn't believe it was me acting so fast, but by four that afternoon there I was, marching up a downtown Manhattan street two blocks from Wall even though the blood supply to my little toe was being choked off by a patent-leather shoe. I felt sort of choked off, too. Even though this was the heart of High Finance City, it was a creepy neighborhood. The sidewalk lay in the perpetual dimness of shadows cast by office buildings that seemed to be leaning toward each other, tall, dank, and dreary, on either side of the narrow thoroughfare. Number twenty-two's gray masonry gave off a moldy odor as if it had been decaying since – I eyed the cornerstone – the second decade of the twentieth century. Once past the almost immovable revolving brass-and-glass door, I found myself confronted by a long-lashed security guard who reminded me of one of the teenage rapists in *A Clockwork Orange*. He gave me a slit-eyed gaze, even after Cecile Rabiea, vice-president of Patton Giddings, whom he phoned, told him it was fine to send Ms Singer up to the thirty-fourth floor.

Patton Giddings was one of those institutions venerable enough to gain even more respect from looking seedy. The rug in the reception area was worn down to the mesh in spots, and what was left looked as if it hadn't been shampooed since FDR beat Hoover in '32. A secretary came and led me down darkly lighted halls. I wasn't quite sure what to expect in an investment bank. Certainly there were no shirt-sleeved hysterics screaming 'Buy!' or 'Sell!' Most doors were closed. The hallway was carpeted and I couldn't even hear my own footsteps.

Besides my tight shoes, I was wearing my several-years-old almost-Armani black pant suit, an austere, cream-color silk T-shirt, and the gold watch Bob had bought me for my fiftieth. If I wasn't exactly dressed for success, I felt fairly confident no one in the financial community would break out in scornful laughter upon seeing me. However, when I was ushered into the brave new world of Cecile Rabiea's ultramodern office, I immediately knew that the shoulder pads of my suit jacket (which could have replaced first and second bases at Shea) were clearly not of the twenty-first century.

Cecile, of course, was. First of all, she was probably six feet. I sensed she'd never been one of those tall and gawky twentieth-century girls who had wished themselves diminutive and adorable. No, as she stood to shake my hand, her bearing asserted: I'm glad I was born to be tall! She appeared to be in her mid-thirties, around Courtney's age, although she had lineless, pulled-tight-over-her-features skin and a chin-length helmet of dark brown shiny hair that, sooner or later, would have people referring to her as 'ageless.' On her right cheek was a mole precisely where a Madame de Pompadour might have pasted on a beauty spot.

'Thanks for seeing me, Ms Rabiea.'

In charcoal slacks with a matching, high-collared, zippered tunic, she was strictly contemporary. She looked appropriately got up to lead a hostile takeover of Briny Deep Fish Sticks or to captain a NASA voyage to Uranus. The only jewelry she wore was a plain, thin platinum wedding ring so understated that suddenly I had an overwhelming urge to take off my watch.

'Please call me Cecile,' she requested, gesturing for me to take a seat in a chair that resembled a squared-off, leather toilet, although it was probably some incredibly brilliant design by one of those gaunt Milanese designers with black-framed glasses you always see in the *Times*'s Style section.

'Judith,' I responded. 'As I mentioned on the phone, I'm

working on behalf of the family. So far, the police haven't made much progress.'

'Are you a detective?' Cecile asked. Frankly, I could have done without the way her eyebrows started rising, ready to signal disbelief if I said yes.

'No. By training, I'm a historian. What the family wants me to do is a research project.' Her eyebrows looked as if they were about to go up again, so I added: 'Historical research often means trying to extract meaning from the past, so in that sense it's a form of detection.' No gales of derisive laughter, no snort of incredulity, so I kept going. 'I want to see if there's anything in Courtney Bryce Logan's past that might have played a part in her disappearance and murder.'

Instead of more eyebrow theater, Cecile gave me an encouraging nod. 'That makes sense,' she said. 'I vaguely remember a saying about "Study the past . . ."'

'"Study the past, if you would divine the future,"' I quoted. 'Confucius said it.'

'When was Confucius again?'

'Somewhere around the fifth century B.C.'

Either I sounded authoritative or I was right, because whatever the test was, I passed. Cecile asked: 'What do you want to know about Courtney?'

'How well did you know her?'

'We weren't friends, if that's what you mean,' Cecile said, leaning back in her high-backed starship *Enterprise* black suede chair. 'Look, investment banking can be a cutthroat field. Who'd want to have a close friend who knows your innermost thoughts, your vulnerabilities, when you might get into a competitive situation with her? On the

233

other hand, neither of us felt any hostility toward the other – at least I'm sure I didn't. We were business-friendly, but not friends.'

'How would you assess her capabilities?' I asked.

'Hard to say,' she said cautiously. 'We graduated college and came to Patton around the same time. If you come in without an MBA, the way we did, you're put in a two-year analyst program. It's really a kind of boot camp. You spend a hellish amount of time crunching numbers, doing computer models of businesses, and so forth. But you work alone, or with associates and partners, twelve, fourteen, sixteen hours a day, all-nighters – whatever it takes.' Cecile was clearly not the sort who would try to be engaging, yet her manner was so forthright and low-key that the word 'agreeable' came to mind and stood alongside 'formidable.' 'So I never got to know her all that well,' she went on. 'I'd have known her even less if she hadn't been a woman. Thirteen years ago, when we started here at Patton, women were already more than a novelty. But we weren't an established fact yet. Every once in a while a small group of us would meet for dinner or drinks for mutual morale raising.'

'What was Courtney like?'

'Like all of us. Focused on career. Ambitious. At the beginning, though, we were all pretty useless. I believe Courtney was a psych major and I majored in math, but – I can only speak for myself – I came here knowing next to nothing about investment banking.'

'Did Courtney seem to know more than you did? Less?'

'I have no idea. The game in this business is to act as

if you know what's going on as you try to grab onto the next rung of the ladder. Or at least not to look as panicked as you feel. Naturally, you have to scramble up the ladder pretty fast, or someone will throw it over.'

'If you'd been in different fields, if say, she'd been a lawyer, could you have been close to Courtney Logan?'

Cecile Rabiea had obviously been conceived without nervous mannerisms. She simply sat motionless in her grand suede chair. Finally she said: 'I don't think so. She was a bit too rah-rah for my taste. Happy, happy, Patton, Patton, go team go. I mean, she was perfectly fine. It's simply a matter of personal style.'

'I understand.' I peered around her spare but expensive office. 'You seem to have done pretty well.' She wasn't a person given to modest shrugs or self-effacing You've-got-to-be-kiddings. 'Was Courtney as successful as you before she retired to become a full-time mother?'

'No.' I counted one-banana, two-banana to give her whatever time she wanted. Cecile would say only what she wished to say. I sensed my pressing her or prattling to cover the silence would be counterproductive. Anyhow, by the time I got to the fourth banana, she went on: 'The first two years she did as well as I did. Most of the others got a thank-you for having been with us, Godspeed, and have a nice life, but the two of us were asked to stay on. But then . . .'

She swiveled back and forth, which I sensed was a prelude to standing and saying Nice meeting you. So I leaned forward and said: 'Listen, you have my word that anything you tell me won't have your name attached. You're one of five names and I'm only going to report what was said, not who said it.'

When her nod finally came, it said, Okay, I believe you. 'What a lot of people don't understand is that everyone on Wall Street is really smart,' she began. 'I didn't get where I did by having the highest IQ, because I don't. I'm only as smart as the next guy. You get ahead in this business by being persistent. I think that's the point Courtney couldn't comprehend. There's no magic. You do first-rate work. Courtney did, from what I heard. But after that, you've got to be tenacious. When they finally let you get near a client or potential client, you offer him your information and your insights. *Then* you call to wish him happy birthday. You ask him all about his fly-fishing trip. You help him get more office space. You give him hot news on one of his competitor's earnings-per-dollar sales. You take him out to dinner with his wife and your husband. Pretty soon, you're an established fact in his life. When he needs an investment banker, who does he turn to? To you. Except Courtney apparently felt her work alone could speak for itself.'

'Didn't anyone tell her it wasn't enough?'

'I'm sure something was said. But if you don't have a good sense of people, if you can't read the subtext beneath their words, then you're not going to get it. And you definitely won't be able to fulfill a client's needs, needs maybe even he hasn't identified yet.'

'So she had something of a tin ear for' – I paused – 'the human stuff?'

'I wouldn't put it that strongly. She just lacked a little something, it always seemed to me. Maybe depth. Maybe sensitivity. Not that she wasn't nice.'

'But she didn't have the right stuff?' I asked.

'If you're a professional cheerleader, or a wife and

mother, nice and pretty and bright is more than enough. But not if you're an investment banker. Clients expect commitment. Solidity. Now subtract from that the fact that once the research and the spreadsheets were done, the reports written and the meetings held, Courtney believed she'd done enough. To win the client. To earn the big money.' Cecile got up from her big chair. I rose from mine. 'She never comprehended that at that point her work was only half finished.' She walked me to the door. 'Courtney wasn't capable of going the full mile. She could only make it halfway. I'm sure at some level she understood she didn't have it. I remember feeling sad for her, but I knew her leaving was inevitable. And sure enough, once she had the baby, she didn't even try to get back into this world.'

So I checked off the first name on Fancy Phil's list. Then I spent the next day and the one after that traveling into Manhattan, speaking with Courtney's former colleagues – an investment banker here, a real-estate mini-mogul there, as well as the chief operating officer of some mammoth conglomerate that apparently couldn't stop itself from buying anything that had the word 'broadband' attached to it. Actually, I was surprised all these hotshots were willing to see me without due diligence, or at least a few probing questions. My guess was they all considered themselves, to one degree or other, traffickers in information – gossip as well as the financial stuff – and they wanted to be inside the Courtney Logan learning curve.

So I wound up sitting in some nifty leather chairs and drinking Diet Cokes in crystal tumblers proffered by private secretaries, all of whom had soothing mommy voices. But in the end all these custom-tailored VIPs could offer were similar recollections, that Courtney had been bright, ambitious, and friendly, although not quite top drawer professionally. That is, until I visited Joshua Kincaid.

'Hey, call me Josh!' he'd insisted before I could get to the second syllable of 'mister.' A smiley man, he wore a dark blue loose-weave shirt that looked like a screen door at dusk, tucked into black silk slacks. He was the least investment bankerish of the people on Fancy Phil's list. No wonder: He'd gotten an invitation to go elsewhere after one year at Patton Giddings and had wound up in his family's business. Now he was president of Kincaid, Kincaid & Kincaid, Mortgages.

We sat on a couch in his midtown office and worked on a plate of zucchini and celery sticks his secretary brought in. 'Keeps my mouth busy when you're talking,' he explained, 'otherwise I'd never shut up. Bad habit, talking. This works, except by late afternoon . . . Do I have to tell you?' Apparently he thought he did. 'Gas. Detroit could use me as an alternative energy source.'

'Right,' I managed to get in.

'That's why I walk home every night.' Josh was sandy-haired and fair, with pipe-cleaner arms and legs that looked even longer and thinner because he was so lanky. The more he chattered the more it seemed as if he'd had a successful personality transplant from some short, Falstaffian donor. 'So – let me think a second – I guess the last time I heard from Courtney was like about a year ago. May, June, I forget.'

'What did she –'

'She wanted financing. For her company. Whatever it was called.' I didn't even try to slide the word 'StarBaby' in edgewise. 'So I said to her, "Courtney, if you want a jumbo mortgage, I'm the man. But we're not in the banking business." Naturally, that took around fifteen, twenty minutes for all the back-and-forth I-think-the-world-of-you-but-I'm-giving-you-the-bottom-line. To tell the truth, if the baby-video thingie had sounded good, I might have put some of my own dinero into it, but it sounded like she was no way near getting it off the ground, much less fly, much less stay up. Because we aren't talking seed money. Uh-uh. Courtney wanted heavy bucks and she was nowhere near ready for such a big step and anyone with an IQ higher than cheesecake would have known it. You know what was really pathetic?'

'Wh –' I think I managed to say.

'That the Courtney I knew at Patton Giddings would have turned her own proposition down in two seconds flat. Maybe one. And I think she knew that. It's soooo weird. Everyone always said what a bubbly personality she had, and she did. But this time when we talked, her bubbles had bubbles. She went so over-the-top on the baby idea that I knew at some level – Christ, I *hate* myself when I say "at some level" – Courtney had to know she wasn't going to make it. But she was desperately trying anyhow, and I give her credit for that. Except she really wasn't all that skillful at hiding her desperation, and someone who's really good, someone I'd want to back, would be. Good at hiding desperation, I mean. And you know what's even weirder?'

'What?' I asked, realizing that by the time his next sentence was finished I would have missed my chance of catching the 4:43 to Shorehaven.

'Right after Courtney was missing, guess what? *Another* woman – a banker in New Jersey. She disappeared without a trace, too!'

Talk about weird: my reaction. Not one shiver of Dear God! passed through me. Not one gasp. I can only guess it was because I have neither the temperament nor the cheekbones for high drama. I was tempted to say, Yeah, Josh, right, weird. Or maybe I was suppressing my excitement because I didn't want false hopes. In any case, if the notion of some connection did zip through either my conscious or subconscious mind, even for a second, I didn't seriously consider the possibility of danger. Like, Egad, a serial killer targeting smart women in greater New York. Or, some heinous plot by evil masterminds is afoot that I must steer clear of. If I had been the least bit fearful, unlike all those plucky protagonists in movies, I would have walked away from the Courtney Logan case, hopped the 5:03 back to Long Island, and taken guitar lessons. Or Chinese cooking lessons. Or had a face-lift and spent the rest of my years looking like Cindy Crawford's Semitic aunt.

But at that moment all I was aware of was that I'd spent two days of interviewing people in custom-made haberdashery and all I'd gotten was that Courtney was cheerful, smart, but not quite top-drawer professionally. Thus, when Josh's secretary followed up the zucchini and celery sticks with iced tea with an actual sprig of mint along with a plate of Oreos, I decided this might be a lead worth pursuing.

'Wow,' was how I responded. '*Another* missing woman. Did you know her?'

'I met her once. We did the home mortgage for some major client of Red Oak – the Red Oak National Bank, little dippy three-branch operation – and Emily was there for Red Oak to make sure his feathers didn't get ruffled, not that we were out to do that.'

'What was her name?'

'Emily something. Hispanic. Or Latino. I'm not sure: Is there a difference? I'm always afraid I'll use the wrong one and insult them. Or it could have been Italian. Anyhow, she was okay. Not a major deal at the bank, I don't think. But she seemed to have done a lot of work for this client and he seemed very comfortable with her.'

'Do you remember who the client was?'

'A guy with English teeth. You know, two hundred teeth in one small mouth, like they have. Except he wasn't English. Probably New England. Or super preppy. I remember he kept saying "cahn't" instead of "can't." Except they never say "cahn" for "can," do they? So you know they're full of it.'

'Do you remember his name?'

Josh sucked on an ice cube while he ruminated. Then he crunched it and offered: 'Richard Gray? Gray Richards? He inherited like fifty-one percent of the shares of a company that manufactures containers for the pharmaceutical industry. His sister has the other forty-nine. Heavy, heavy money. Dumb, dumb guy.'

'And this Emily was his personal banker, his contact at this Red Oak place?' Josh nodded, but before he could start talking again I asked: 'Why didn't the bank give him his mortgage if he was such an important client?'

'The government won't let you lend more than fifteen

241

percent of capital to any one borrowing entity, so with a small operation like Red Oak ... probably has two hundred million in assets, well' – he chuckled – 'you can do the math.' If I had a day and a half and a calculator.

'Tell me what happened with her disappearance,' I went on.

'I don't know. Like one day she was there and she went on vacation and she never came back and no one knew where she was.'

'How old a woman was she?'

'Early thirties. At least that's the impression I got. I could be wrong, ha-ha. Come to think of it, I vaguely remember her introducing herself as an assistant branch manager and she was hand-holding an important client like Pharmaceutical Container Man and I thought, like, "*Assistant* branch manager?" and guess what I thought next? "Glass ceiling." Just so you know I'm a sensitive guy.'

'Did they check to see if she had embezzled any –'

'Of course,' he said, managing not to snicker at my too obvious question, although barely. 'She didn't. So what else can I tell you? This Emily was zero-point-zero-zero percent like Courtney. I think whoever called to tell me about her said she was single and ultraserious and from what I can remember not good-looking and didn't have a personality because I *can't* remember. You know what I mean? Like a total blank. Not *totally* total. I get' – he closed his eyes and swayed his head like a fortune-teller – 'an aura of dorkiness. If I'm thinking of the right person. Actually, no. Not dorky. A loser.'

'Could her path have crossed Courtney's?'

'Anything's possible,' Josh replied, pulling an Oreo apart

and scraping off the filling with his top front teeth. 'Is it likely? Statistically, I'd say like two shots out of a hundred. Red Oak is way down in South Jersey, and whoever was telling me about her disappearing mentioned – I think, but I wouldn't swear on a stack of Bibles – that she also lived somewhere around Cherry Hill. And Courtney had been out of it for years, for however old her oldest kid is. Also, I doubt if a diddly little bank like Red Oak had much business with Patton Giddings, although anything's possible, and, like Patton Giddings told me, basically, I don't know shit about investment banking. So for all I know maybe Emily and Courtney were best friends.'

'Did they ever find any trace of her? Or her body?' I asked.

'I'm hardly on the A-list of calls to make when the cops or whoever trip over Emily something's body,' Josh replied. 'But I never heard anything else.'

It was only when the train from Manhattan came up out of the tunnel that I allowed myself to tingle with anticipation. How many young women in New York and New Jersey who are somehow involved in finance could vanish into thin air or, in Courtney's case, into the family swimming pool? Sure, it was possible that the answer was forty-seven. But I had a gut feeling that somehow there was a connection between Courtney Logan and – I went straight from the Shorehaven station to my computer – Emily Chavarria.

Bingo? Maybe. According to the *Courier-Post*, Emily Chavarria, age thirty-one, a graduate of the Wharton School of the University of Pennsylvania, an assistant branch manager at an office of the Red Oak National

Bank in Cherry Hill, New Jersey, left for a three-week trip to New Zealand and Australia on Friday, October 22. A week and two days before Courtney's disappearance. She was never seen again. On Monday, November 15, the president of the bank, concerned that Emily had not only missed the eleven A.M. trust department meeting but hadn't called in — two occurrences utterly at odds with her perfect-attendance, perfect-person record — had his secretary drive the fifteen minutes to Emily's place not far from Cherry Hill. When there was no answer at the door, the secretary called the police and, getting a key from the apartment complex's property manager, she and two cops entered the premises. No sign of disturbance. No sign of luggage. No sign of Emily Chavarria. Not then. Not since.

Chapter Twelve

Bless the World Wide Web. The articles from the local New Jersey newspapers I came up with mentioned Emily Chavarria belonging to two groups: an organization of New Jersey bankers and the South Jersey chapter of a national group called FIFE – Females in Financial Enterprises – which I guessed was preferable to WIFE.

I called Fancy Phil and gave him the assignment of finding out if Courtney had been a member of FIFE. Again he muttered about a wild-goose chase, I muttered back that if it was a wild-goose chase, I was doing it on my dime, not his. He grumbled, I'll get back to you. I was relieved it did sound as though he meant I'll get back *to* you rather than *at* you, a concern I would likely not have had if my first client had been a podiatrist. Anyhow, I went back to the articles. Emily came from a small town, Leesford, Oklahoma. I checked out Leesford on the Yahoo white pages: Only one Chavarria was listed. I called Chavarria, Pete, and got his wife on the phone. 'Mzzz. Chavarria,' I began, to avoid the Ms/Mrs quandary which, for all I knew, might not have been completely resolved in Oklahoma, 'my name is Judith Singer. I'm an investigator on Long Island. I've been looking into a case that has some similarities to your daughter's disappearance.'

'Uh-huh,' she replied.

'I hate to bother you during what must be an upsetting time for you —'

'We don't . . . know where . . . she is,' she cut in, pausing between every two words. She didn't sound obviously broken up, but more like someone not inclined toward conversation, though whether that was out of taciturnity or grief I couldn't tell.

'I understand that. I'd just like to ask you a few questions, maybe come up with some parallels between the woman who is missing on Long Island and Emily.' She didn't say anything, so I went on: 'I know she was scheduled to make a trip to Australia and New Zealand. Did you hear from her, or get any postcards or anything?'

'No.'

'I see.'

'The police in New Jersey. They said . . . it didn't look like Emily went.'

I decided not to ask how they knew, because her answer might exhaust her willingness to talk. So I made a guess that the Jersey cops had found she didn't board her plane — or something like that — and instead asked: 'Does Emily have any close friends on the East Coast?'

'I guess. I wouldn't know their names.' Ms or Mrs Chavarria had what I guessed was an Oklahoma twang, the sort of accent that makes most people sound open and uncomplicated. Not her. Yet even though I assumed she must be going through hell, there was something about her — or maybe about me — that did not automatically evoke sympathy, which made me feel both guilty and wary. I sensed my reaction might mean something, because even though Greg Logan had been a cold fish the night I'd gone to speak to him, I still had felt terrible about his loss. 'I *told* the police that,' she added.

'Right. Do you know if Emily had a boyfriend?'

'I don't know. She came home for Christmas, but she only stayed two days.'

'So maybe she didn't get a chance to keep you up to date.'

'Maybe,' Ms or Mrs Chavarria replied.

'Was she going someplace else?'

'No. Christmas and New Year's is busy at the bank.'

'Do you know if Emily ever went up to New York City, or to Long Island?'

'No.'

'Did she ever mention a friend named Courtney? Courtney Logan.'

'No.'

'Her maiden name' – I almost slipped and said 'was,' but caught myself in time to keep it in the present tense – 'is Courtney Bryce.'

'No.'

'Can I ask: When was the last time you heard from Emily?'

'A couple of days before she went on her trip. Except the police say she didn't go. She called to say good-bye.' There was no break in her voice at the word 'good-bye.' Not a flicker of emotion.

'Did she sound as if she were upset about anything?'

'No.'

'Was she excited about her trip?'

'I guess.'

'Did she say she was looking forward to it?'

'No.'

Finding myself winding the telephone cord around my finger, I made myself stop when I noticed the upper joint turning cerise from strangulation. 'Did the police from New Jersey ask you anything I haven't?' I finally asked.

It took a very, very long minute, but finally Ms or Mrs Chavarria answered: 'They wanted to know where she kept her money.'

'And did you know?'

'No.'

'Did they say why they were asking?'

'Because she took her money out of the bank.'

'All her money?'

'That's what they said. And out of her stocks and bonds.'

After I gave her my number and asked her to call collect if anything else occurred to her, I hung up and stared at the phone as if I could see through the wires and circuitry. If only I could call Nelson was my first thought and Stop it! was my second. And my third was that years earlier he'd told me how most investigative work was supposed to be boring, following A to B to C and so on, in mind-numbing, skip-nothing sequence. However, he'd found the thoroughness of it comforting. Even if you were ninety-nine percent sure of knowing what G was, you still had to go through D, E, and F. For some mysterious reason, that time-consuming process sometimes led to bright, new ideas and almost always made for a stronger case.

Easy to be meticulous, I thought, if you're a cop and you have access to A, B, C, D, and so on. Go through missing people's houses, get to their bank or brokerage accounts, flash a badge, and ask your questions. I had no subpoena, no license, not even a business card.

However, I did have Fancy Phil, and he was turning out to be a not-bad gumshoe. Courtney had been a member of the Wall Street chapter of FIFE, he reported back, though in the past few years, what with living on Long Island, having two young children, and running StarBaby, Greg doubted she'd gotten to any meetings. I closed my eyes, trying to envision a joint tea/meeting/cocktail hour between the downtown Manhattan FIFEers and the South New Jerseyites, but I couldn't get a picture. I probably exhaled a careworn sigh, because Fancy Phil demanded: Whatsa matter? Nothing, I replied. But do you think you can go back and ask Greg if Courtney was ever active in the association, or if she'd gone to any event where she might have met members from other chapters? There's a FIFE member from New Jersey who's been missing since November. What would stop me from asking him? he asked, sounding cranky. Well, I replied, for starters he might think it curious, your asking such a specific type of question. Curious? Fancy Phil declared. I'm his old man. If Gregory can't trust me, he can't trust no one. If you think he don't know that then you're not thinking.

I decided I needed to stop worrying the Courtney-Emily connection to death. Unfortunately, I couldn't call Nancy, who would instruct me not to be an utter ass. She and her husband had gone to a dinner party at some *Newsday* executive's house where she was convinced Larry would jabber on about Gothic architecture, mock her political observations, spill red wine, laugh his raucous donkey laugh, and cost her her job. So I meandered into the sunroom, channel surfed, and came across *Stagecoach* with John Wayne and Claire Trevor as the whore with the heart of gold – one of my favorite westerns. I settled in for a night on the couch, a squishy throw pillow perfectly supporting the back of my neck and my head. Except I couldn't concentrate because I couldn't stop brooding over what connection there could be between Courtney and Emily.

My first reaction was to consider more carefully Fancy Phil's suggestion that I was on a wild-goose chase. The two women had been in separate chapters of FIFE, which was probably a good-sized organization. What were the odds against them knowing each other? As I'd always been queen of the SAT verbals and among the deeply pathetic in math, I couldn't begin to calculate what the chances were against two highly intelligent, reasonably successful and responsible women around the same age winding up murdered or missing. Thus, unencumbered by fact, I kissed off the wild-goose-chase hypothesis.

My next guess was that some third person – a nutcase, an icy, methodical killer – had done them both in. Whoever it was might have been cruel beyond belief – besides being homicidal – because he/she had stashed Courtney in her family's swimming pool. Or maybe he/she had just been pressed for time: trick or treaters out and about, people inside the Logan house. Or he/she had to get rid of the body fast because he/she needed a day, a week, or, as it turned out, months, to get out of town? But when had he/she done the deed? Steffi and the children had seen

Courtney driving away. Was it when she arrived back home with the mysterious missing apples? Could she have been murdered in the Grand Union parking lot and driven home in her own car? If so, how come there were no traces of blood from the head wounds? Or was she kidnapped, held, and killed a day or a week later? After all that time in the pool, how precise could the medical examiner be?

I turned off the TV, strolled into the kitchen, took out a bag of those pygmy peeled carrots, and started to chew. There was a big difference between the two dead/missing women, if indeed there was a Courtney-Emily link. Courtney's sapphire earrings that Greg had given her for her thirtieth birthday were where they were always kept, in the safety-deposit box. Other than the twenty-five thousand she'd helped herself to from around Mother's Day to Labor Day, her money was where it belonged, in joint bank and brokerage accounts and in her StarBaby business account. And possibly most important, there were no signs of planning; Courtney had actually said: 'I forgot something. I just have to run to Grand Union for a minute.'

Emily Chavarria, on the other hand, she of never missing a day's work, had been discovered missing only after the three weeks' vacation she was supposedly taking, when she didn't return to the Red Oak Bank. The New Jersey police had asked her parents about her money – specifically, where was it. How much had it been? Five hundred, five thousand, fifty thousand dollars? Five hundred thousand? Who knew? After all, Emily had been graduated from one of the best business schools in the country. She could have been a canny investor. On the other hand, maybe she'd lost a bundle guessing on the wrong dot-com stock.

I took another carrot, despite my chronic worry that I'd chew too fast, choke, not be able to do the Heimlich maneuver on myself, and would die not only needlessly but still sixteen pounds above the 'large-boned' group on the height/weight tables. Anyhow, the difference between the two women was that there seemed to have been planning behind Emily's disappearance and, perhaps, murder. If she'd vanished or been killed after her last day of work, no one would look for her for three weeks. She'd left for her trip on a Friday, more than a week before Courtney disappeared. Just like someone with a perfect attendance record to finish up the complete week, I mused. Just like someone that meticulous to have a plan.

I was telling myself to stop imagining and start digging, that the guilty party, the person with the nefarious plan, had most likely been a third person. Or, I mulled, going back to the Fancy Phil-wild-goose-chase theory, maybe there'd been no plan at all: Emily Chavarria's disappearance and Courtney Logan's murder had nothing to do with each other. The phone rang. I risked my life swallowing a not-quite-chewed bite of carrot so instead of saying hello, I coughed.

'You okay?' Fancy Phil asked.

I coughed again and said, 'Fine.'

'Gregory thinks she could have gone to some meeting of that FIFE a while ago. Probably before she got pregnant with Morgan. Or maybe when she was pregnant but before she decided to stay home and be a mother. But it could have been some other group. He's not sure.'

'Morgan's five years old, right?'

'Yeah,' he replied. 'He thinks she went to Baltimore, but it could have been Washington, D.C. What's this all about? That girl from New Jersey who's missing? You really don't think –'

'Phil, it could be a wild-goose chase. I don't know.' It occurred to me I might be sounding crabby, but – I looked at the clock – it was almost eleven and I was too tired to care. 'But don't you want me to check on this Emily Chavarria so I can rule out the possibility?'

'Do whatever the hell you want,' Fancy Phil answered. A microsecond later he hung up the phone.

As I was getting into bed, I gave myself a figurative pat on the back: You've got guts, I told myself, not being fazed by Fancy Phil's pique or anger or fury, whatever the slamming down the phone had meant. Naturally, about twenty minutes later, just as I was floating in that brainless state between wakefulness and sleep, I sat up wildly alert, panting with fear. From outside the house, I'd heard the change of hum a car engine makes as it slows down. It was just past the house. Whoever was in the car could have been admiring the contrast between my purple pansies and the violet ones planted around my mailbox. Except it was too dark for that. Or perhaps the driver had merely shifted gears, although not being one of those manual-transmission kind of dames, I couldn't be sure. On the other hand, I didn't know Fancy Phil's precise address, but twenty minutes would be a reasonable estimate as to how long it would take from his town to mine. By the time I got up, locked the bedroom door, then pulled back an edge of curtain to peek out the window, all I could see was a pair of red taillights disintegrating in the blackness of the night.

Two days later, though, Phil and I were pals again, although not chummy enough that I could expect an honest answer to the question: Did you drive past my house after eleven Thursday night? So I didn't bother asking it. Instead, I nodded respectfully as he related: 'So I told Gregory,' Fancy Phil was explaining, '"Hey, Gregory, it'd be nice to take Morgan and Travis and that ugly nanny to a matinee of that *Sesame Street* show." You wouldn't believe what that rat-bastard scalper charged me, but it's worth it. We won't get bothered.' A weighty gold link bracelet on his right wrist and what looked like a cabochon emerald set in a braid of gold on his pinkie made no sound against the leather-covered steering wheel, but they sparkled in the sunlight.

At that moment his yacht of a car pulled into the Logans' driveway, right up to the front. Fancy Phil opened the old-money-green door with a key, punched four numbers into the alarm pad, and stood back, the compleat gentleman, to let me precede him inside. Well, with a compleat gentleman, one doesn't fret about being shot in the back or whomped on the head with brass knuckles. On the other hand, he seemed content just to follow me around.

'Who did the cooking?' I asked as we headed toward the kitchen. 'The au pair, or Courtney?'

'Courtney. I gotta give her credit. She made an excellent meat loaf.' As he tsked for a moment – probably more over loss of meat loaf than loss of daughter-in-law – I glanced around. Expensive. A floor of terra-cotta tiles of a hundred subtly different shades, that virtually announced:

Not machine-made! Dark granite counters that gave off a blue sheen. Wood cabinets with glass doors that displayed blue-and-white dishes, some from a set of one of those classic Royal Copenhagen patterns, some that were likely antique pieces. There was every sort of drinking glass, from juice tumblers to brandy snifters. An elaborate stove. A double refrigerator with glass doors to display the Logan mustard collection and the family's preferences in yogurt. A floor-to-ceiling collection of cookbooks, from *Apples, Apples and More Apples!* to *The Elegant Vegetarian.*

I whipped out a pair of the translucent plastic gloves they sell in boxes (which I used to change the litter box whenever I baby-sat for Kate's loathsome, allergen-laden Persian cat Flakey). I wasn't quite sure why I felt compelled to bother with the glove business, but it had a hard-boiled detective-ish quality that appealed to me, and seeing Fancy Phil nodding appreciatively as if he approved of my cunning, I realized at the least it was a good marketing move.

Drawer by drawer, cabinet by cabinet, appliance by appliance, I went through the kitchen, but all I found was a small mound of black, hardened glop on the bottom of the oven, which I decided was more likely blueberry drippings than a clue, and an impressive accumulation of twist ties for plastic bags kept in its very own plastic bag. Finally, Fancy Phil and I leafed through every cookbook, then shook each one hard, a task he seemed to enjoy. Nothing fell out: no old grocery store receipts, no premortem shopping lists, no 'call so-and-so' notes.

By that time I was beginning to get that sluggish feeling of overload that comes with seeing an overambitious museum retrospective, so I passed on the rest of the downstairs. With Fancy Phil following me, I went upstairs and into Courtney's office. Pretty, done up in raspberry and pale green, feminine but not frivolous. Costly, no doubt. The trimming on the valance over the curtains had its own dainty fringe. I turned on her computer, an extravagant-looking IBM with one of those giant, flat monitors I'd never actually seen in person. The Windows clouds looked spectacular. Even better, no password was required. Five seconds later, of course, when I got to her financial program, QuickBooks, there was a blank box. I typed in 'Courtney,' 'Court,' 'Gregory,' 'Greg,' 'Logan,' 'Bryce,' 'Lowenstein,' 'Olympia,' 'Princeton,' and so forth, the way they do in movies, but gave up after her birth date and the kids' names failed.

'Was there any pet name Courtney or Greg called each other?' I asked.

From where he was sitting, on a window seat that overlooked the backyard and pool, Fancy Phil said wearily: 'Beats the hell out of me. You done yet?'

'No. Listen, do you want to go downstairs and read' – from his curdled expression I gathered he did not find this suggestion appealing – 'or watch TV?'

'Nah. I'll watch you.' Oddly, the remark sounded more flirtatious than threatening, so I ignored it and double-clicked on Courtney's calendar database. No password! I studied her calendar pages from May through December, past the thirty-first of October when she disappeared. Play dates, Mommy and Me classes, weekly nail and monthly hair appointments, Saturday-night dates with people who had local numbers. Ditto with the dates that said 'Filming' and 'Meeting 1' and 'Meeting 2.' The contacts were all suburbanites with phone numbers from Shorehaven and the surrounding towns of Port Washington, Manhasset, Great Neck, and Roslyn. Zee Friedman's name was there for the weekends she worked. However, I found no sign of the name of the other assistant, the Wesleyan guy, who supposedly was holding Courtney's video equipment.

Steffi Deissenburger had told me that in the weeks before Courtney disappeared, she had gone out, dressed in suit and heels, very pretty, very business looking. She'd stayed away all day, returning shortly before Greg was due home. She'd warned Steffi that if Greg called to tell him she was shopping, an activity which he'd have no trouble in believing his wife capable. Nowhere were there any indications of these appointments, assignations, shopping expeditions, or whatever they were.

'Done yet?' Fancy Phil inquired, reasonably patient.

'No,' I said, or possibly grouched. My hands were clammy under the plastic gloves.

I went back to two years before Morgan was born, when Courtney was still at Patton Giddings. This was easier because there were more blank days; whatever calendar she'd kept for business appointments did not seem to be on this computer. What was there, however, in 1994, on April 8, 9, and 10, the weekend after Easter, was FIFE EAST–BALTIMORE.

'Hot shit!' Fancy Phil exclaimed. I turned on the printer and copied that month as well as all of 1999, when Courtney disappeared in October, until May 2000, when she was found. 'Good work.'

'Thanks, but it's not good work until I find out if Emily Chavarria was at that meeting also.'

'How do you find that out?' he asked.

'Beats me. I'll figure something out.'

'Wanna go out for a drink, Doc?' he asked.

'No thanks. I want to check out their bedroom. Her chest of drawers or whatever and her closet. You can go down and make yourself a drink. Trust me: I'm not going to heist her panty hose.'

'Nah. I'll keep you company,' Fancy Phil said.

To make an hour-and-a-half-long story short, I went through every drawer built into her walk-in closet, every handbag in the handbag cubbyholes – many Kate Spades and something that had cost a navy-blue alligator its life. I searched every pocket of every garment and I felt inside each size-six shoe on her rows of slanted shoe shelves, five pair of which were Manolo Blahnik, a label whose price I once inquired about upon seeing a pair of brown-and-black spectators with a flawless little bow and was told a dollar amount that actually caused me to gasp.

Deciding against using Fancy Phil as my stenographer, I wrote down from which article of clothing and which handbag I found the stuff I laughingly decided to call evidence: a fold-up hairbrush, two Clinique lipsticks in Copper Rose, a Clinique compact, a wad of purple bubble gum I assumed was Morgan's and not Courtney's wrapped in a sales receipt, a Montblanc pen, and a sales slip from Barneys in Manhasset for an eighty-five-dollar candle and a fourteen-dollar lip balm. There was also a twenty-dollar bill in a pair of gray wool slacks. In other words, unlike the half ton of junk that could be salvaged from my closet and dresser, Courtney Logan had left little behind; she'd been neater and more organized than I, though not quite obsessively orderly.

'Wanna go for cocktails?' Fancy Phil inquired, pausing an instant before 'cocktails' as if seeking a word refined enough for a lady.

I couldn't understand his sudden desire for my company, but I figured I ought to do better than my earlier No thanks. 'I wish I could, Phil, but I have a date and I have to do all the girl things to get ready.'

Refinement no longer required, he wiped his nose with the back of his hand. 'Who's your boyfriend?'

'An English professor at the college where I teach.'

'A *professor?*' he said, obviously controlling an over-whelming urge to shudder at the horror of such a union or perhaps at the notion of a man teaching English. I couldn't really tell. 'You gonna marry him?'

When, slightly aghast, I said, 'God, I hope not,' he gave a genuine if monosyllabic chuckle. Then he said, 'You're a good kid, Doc.'

Actually, I had no Saturday-night plans. Postmodernist Geoff had found someone else willing to share expenses and was safely in England. With any luck, I was rid of him at least for the summer, if not forever. I'd spotted him during exam week walking across the quad (and brushing arms in a significant manner) with Promiscuous Patti of the music department and suspected she might be his companion in the Lake District. Anybody I actually wanted to see was being otherwise amused and I didn't have the patience to listen to any of my après-Bob single-women acquaintances recounting all-men-are-louses/all-men-are-little-boys/all-men-only-want-one-thing sagas.

On the other hand, I was too steamed up about Courtney-Emily possibilities to watch a movie or read a mystery. Instead, since Nancy wasn't around to stop me, I called Nelson Sharpe and spoke to his voice mail. He called back less than a half hour later.

By seven P.M. we were sitting across from each other at a table out on the gray wood deck of Fisherman's Folly, breathing in the salt air of Long Island Sound and whiffs of gasoline from the boats at the marina next door. 'This isn't a social meeting,' I said to Nelson after a waiter with a shaved head and a tiny, curly pigtail so unkempt I wouldn't have been surprised if he oinked set down Nelson's gin and tonic and my Campari and soda.

'You said that on the phone,' he snapped. 'You don't have to repeat yourself.' He set his wedge of lime on the side of his cocktail napkin.

When we'd been lovers, we'd met during the day, when my kids were in school, so I'd only seen him in a jacket and tie or on the way to getting naked. Now, in a red plaid short-sleeved shirt and khaki slacks, he looked as if he'd embarked on an entirely different line of work – construction foreman or phys-ed teacher. His forearms were more thickly muscled than they had been. I tried not to imagine the second wife running her hands over his arms while they made love. I decided not to think that he was pumping iron to impress her, but as his accommodation to some new department fitness regulation. 'I appreciate your seeing me on such short notice,' I said congenially.

'Cut the crap, Judith.' We smiled at each other and

sipped our drinks. I didn't inquire: What did you say to your wife to get out on a Saturday night? He glanced at my ringless ring finger, then looked into my eyes and asked, 'What do you want to know?'

'Have you heard anything more about the Courtney Logan case? I mean, there hasn't been anything in the papers or on TV for a while now. Are the Homicide guys just going through the motions because they think it's the husband?' Before he had a chance to talk, I added: 'I'm not asking you to betray your oath or tell me classified police secrets.'

'You're really smooth at this,' he remarked.

'Thank you.'

His eyes were still on mine. Over the years since we'd parted, I'd recalled so many details about Nelson, but this I'd forgotten, his ability to win any staring contest in the world. Never actually a contest: Nelson didn't appear to be holding your eyes to confront, the way an animal does to establish dominance. At least it had never seemed that way then. His velvet-brown eyes seemed always gentle and a little sad. I remembered long ago thinking he gazed the way he did because he was searching for something he desperately needed. Sitting there, listening to the soft lap of surf against the wood pilings of the deck, I told myself such romantic notions ought to have been tossed out right after my early adolescence, along with the stuffed animals and the pressed corsages. I pulled my eyes from his and turned my attention to my own lime wedge, squeezing it into the red bubbles of my Campari and soda. Naturally, I'd forgotten what I'd asked him.

Fortunately, he remembered. 'I hear about the case every now and then.'

'Have you heard anything about a missing woman in the south part of New Jersey in relation to it?'

Nelson shook his head. 'Who is she?'

'She's a banker. She was scheduled to go on a three-week vacation to Australia and New Zealand. She left a little over a week before Halloween, when Courtney Logan went off to buy apples and never came back.'

'It might mean nothing.'

'I know. But it might mean something.'

He took out a business card from his ID case and said: 'What's her name?'

A little too late it dawned on me that if I gave Emily's name, the Nassau County cops would either be on the Turnpike in two seconds flat to interview Emily's neighbors and colleagues or request the Jersey cops to do it. I'd never get a shot. So I looked Nelson right in the eyes and lied: 'I don't know.'

'You're lying.'

'That's not very nice.' Possibly I dilated my nostrils to illustrate how offensive his accusation was.

'You're a lousy liar, Judith.'

'I am not. You just know me too well.' We finished our drinks and ordered dinner while I filled him in on what I'd learned about FIFE and Emily, without giving her name. However, I did offer up the name of the Red Oak Bank in the spirit of fellowship.

If I wasn't ebullient, sitting out on that deck in the pink-and-blue light of an early evening in June, at least I was as happy as I'd been in years. I didn't want to count how many years. Looking at the menu, I told myself it was because I was actually getting a chance to talk about what truly enthralled me, and with a pro, no less. But by the time I decided on a small Caesar salad, without anchovies, and grilled halibut, I realized that most of my pleasure was being with Nelson. I still loved looking at him, hearing his voice again, being in his company. My sex drive, which I long assumed I'd misplaced somewhere in my late forties, was definitely in working order.

'How did you find out about this woman's existence?' Nelson asked.

'I was speaking with a former colleague of Courtney's who'd stayed vaguely in touch with her. He didn't strike me as a genius. He'd gone from investment banking to joining his family's company, giving mortgages or something. Anyhow, he'd met this New Jersey woman once doing some mortgage deal. Later someone told him about her disappearance. All he was saying was something like "Weird, two women just vanishing like that."'

'What was his name?'

'What do I get in return?' I asked.

'My regards. Tell me his name.'

'What do you think, this guy killed both of them?' Nelson said nothing. 'Trust me, he's not a murderer. A little blabby for my taste. Immature.'

'Thank you for the psychological profile,' he remarked.

'For the record, even though Courtney had been in finance and this woman was, too, he wasn't able to come up with any connection between them.' Still, I gave him Joshua Kincaid's name because I couldn't come up with any reason not to. I felt pretty confident that since Nelson wasn't in Homicide any longer, the name wouldn't get to them at least until Monday morning. Which gave me Sunday. 'What does it mean, when someone vanishes into thin air? Do you assume they've been murdered and go looking for a killer?'

'If they're like your two women, leading a seemingly normal life? Even if it's not some psycho raping and killing, it's still pretty often homicide. Most of the time the perpetrator turns out to be the boyfriend or husband. If this Courtney or the other one was leading a wild life, with a mountain of debt or some clear sign of irresponsibility, then we'd think in terms of them skipping and trying a new life under a new identity. Those types usually screw up just because they are so careless. It's not easy to disappear.' Nelson fell silent for a moment. Too many intelligent men make a big deal about thinking. They purse their mouths, close their eyes, and say hmmmm, or they massage chins, or rotate their pens between their fingers – while you breath-lessly await the jewels of cerebration that will fall from their lips. He, on the other hand, had a natural fluency of thought to speech. When he needed to stop and think, he merely stopped. No big deal, no hmmmms. 'Even all those rich guys,' he continued, 'the master-criminals-egomaniacs who steal millions: Whenever they move on, they usually leave a lot of pissed-off people behind. Ultimately, those people talk and the guys get caught.'

'So you're thinking the other woman is dead, too?'

'Just sitting here like this, talking? Yes. But if I was a Jersey cop without too big a caseload, I'd keep looking.'

'For a Courtney connection?'

'Sure. But mostly I'd want to look at her whole life.'

264

'So you don't think it's a wild-goose chase?'

'I'd say it's something we should look into.'

'"We" meaning . . .'

'Not you and me, Judith.'

My salad and his clam chowder arrived, which was fortunate because I couldn't think of a withering rejoinder. I speared a small leaf of romaine and suggested that in all the information he'd heard about the Courtney Logan investigation, there might be a byte or two he could pass along that wasn't Eyes Only or whatever big cop secrets are called. 'Like your Homicide guys are apparently all excited because Greg Logan withdrew forty thousand dollars from their joint account and put it in his own name. That was only in response to Courtney having taken twenty-five thousand out of their joint accounts to throw away on StarBaby or cashmere bathrobes or whatever.'

'Don't you think his lawyer mentioned that?' Nelson asked.

'So?'

'So, maybe someone did follow up.' Except for an occasional flare of temper, he'd always been a low-key, don't-show-your-cards kind of guy. To another person, the 'someone' following up would be interpreted as a reference to a detective in the Homicide unit of the Nassau County Police Department. But despite his low key, I knew the way Nelson played the game enough to realize he was the 'someone' he was referring to.

'What did you find out?'

He gave me a small smile of acknowledgment and said: 'The twenty-five thou she took: A buddy of mine in Homicide looked into it. There was no trace of it in any business or personal account. They couldn't find any photography equipment that would come to anything near that. Twenty-five thousand bucks just disappeared.'

I left my fork in the salad, put my arms on the table, and leaned toward him. 'Nelson, doesn't that tell you something?'

'What?'

'I don't know,' I admitted.

'Listen –' I think he was on the verge of calling me 'my sweetheart,' which he'd often called me during our affair. But instead he said, 'Judith, sometimes what looks like a clue is just a plain, old fact.' I was about to argue that twenty-five thousand bucks would be a big, fat fact, but he held up his hand. 'And sometimes cases don't get solved. Sometimes killers go free.'

'I know, but I don't think Greg –'

'Why not?'

'He's too smart to have done it so stupidly.'

'Let me tell you something.' He clunked down his spoon alongside his soup bowl. 'A lot of killers are stupid. Those cases almost always get solved in less than seventy-two hours. And sometimes a pretty smart person kills and thinks he's covered it up in a genius way, like the bad guy in Sherlock Holmes –'

'Professor Moriarty.'

'– except they get arrested within seventy-two hours, too. Now take your friend Greg Logan.'

'I'm not even going to bother saying he's not my friend.'

'Good. He seems to have gotten everything he might have wanted: No wife, no nagging. Control over all his property, custody of his kids, bank and stock brokerage accounts. Okay, that's minus twenty-five thou, but either it's his cost of doing business or he found it and stashed it someplace. In any case, we would have solved this case in seventy-two hours, too, if the idiot who was in charge had done his job.'

'Looked in the pool, you mean?'

'That? Sure. You know what almost seven months in a three-quarters-filled swimming pool does to a body?'

I pushed my salad plate away and asked: 'Are you going to give me a graphic description that will make me realize this sort of thing is too ugly for me and I should stick to history?'

'I'm going to try.'

'Don't they put chlorine in the water?'

'Fifteen gallons of liquid chlorine and algacide.'

'You read the reports!'

'Reports, autopsy findings, a fast look at the video and crime-scene pictures. I did it for you, my sweetheart.' He said it in a mocking way, but couldn't carry it off. Two red stripes of embarrassment appeared on the tops of his cheeks. 'So do you know what all that time does to a body, even with the chemicals?' he challenged. 'See, it decomposes from inside out, so the gases made it float to the top. It's *really* disgusting after months in cold water. What's left of the outside of the body gets a waxy look. You wouldn't have wanted to see Courtney Logan after they pulled her out.' He paused, waiting for me to tell him to stop. When I didn't, he took a couple of ostentatious spoonfuls of clam chowder. 'Of course her face wasn't identifiable, and part of her head had been blown away by the two bullets. But we had her dental records. Hey, do you know how the skin on your hands and feet get when you're in the water a long time?' I nodded. 'Well, imagine how it would look after seven months.'

I pulled back my salad plate, stabbed a crouton, and ate it. Nelson looked annoyed that I didn't seem at least mildly nauseated. 'How can you tell whether a homicide victim has been murdered someplace else and then moved if it's been in water for months? I mean, if she were shot right by the pool, would it be different than if she were shot someplace else and brought back?'

'There could be trace evidence at the scene. You know, signs the body had been dragged from a short distance. Or an out-of-place bit of material that indicates some distant location. Like a really unusual soil sample that could tell us she wasn't killed on Long Island. But after seven months, it's unlikely, and in Courtney's case, it didn't happen.'

'Was there enough left of her to take fingerprints?' I asked.

'They got two or three, I think. Matched prints on her stuff in the house.'

I picked up a bread stick. 'You read everything?'

'I read a lot of it,' he answered cautiously.

'Did anything in all the evidence you read about strike you as odd, or worth exploring further?' Slowly, he rocked his head from side to side: maybe yes, maybe no. 'What?'

'I'm not going to tell you.'

'But you're good at this and the guy in charge of the case isn't!' He shrugged. 'Wouldn't you want to see it solved? An innocent man may be –'

'I knew you would say that,' he remarked.

'So what's your response?'

'If I see anything that can point to someone as the killer or exonerate your boyfriend's son, I'll be sure to mention it to one of the nonassholes on the case. Okay?'

'Nelson.'

'What?'

'Are you ticked off with yourself for calling me your sweetheart or with me for staying on the case even though you warned me off?'

'You know what women always say?' he finally said.

I smiled. 'What do we always say?'

'I feel like I'm being used.'

'That? You know I'm not using you.'

'Yes you are.'

'Nelson, I'm talking to you as a . . . coworker.'

'No. You're jerking me around to get information you shouldn't have.'

The pigtailed waiter approached, tray in hand, and eyed us in the way a disapproving parent might look at children who didn't clean their plates. 'Do you want me to hold your entrées?' he inquired, so overly polite as to be rude. Nelson was still giving me the evil eye, so I indicated to the waiter that he could take my plate. While he was at it, he grabbed Nelson's bowl, then promptly replaced it with his dinner, fried scallops and french fries. Finally, huffing as if he were used to serving a more sophisticated clientele, the waiter set down my fish and left us to our own devices.

'How about this?' I said. 'I'll tell you some of my thoughts and you do with them what you want.'

'Like . . . ?'

'Like first seeing if the New Jersey woman and Courtney

had any connection. Didn't you say in the week or so before Halloween, Courtney put seven hundred plus miles on her car? She could have gone to Cherry Hill and back a few times.'

'Maybe she drove to Colonial Williamsburg.'

'Maybe Miss New Jersey had financial dealings with Courtney. All her money had been cleaned out of the bank. And Courtney was down twenty-five thousand.'

'Even if they had some dealings, then we'd likely be looking for a third person.'

'But the woman might have killed Courtney,' I objected.

'Or Greg Logan could have done the job on both of them, stashed the bucks someplace, and is biding his time.'

'If Phil Lowenstein had even an inkling his son might have killed Courtney, do you think he would want me looking into this?'

'Aren't you hungry?' Nelson inquired.

'I love lukewarm fish. Listen to me. Courtney Logan embezzled from her high-school candy-bar sales.'

He started to laugh. 'That's fifteen to life.'

'Shush. Something was wrong with her. She told the young woman who did the videotaping for her that she had another person working for her. But there's absolutely no evidence of him. Courtney was lying.'

'Maybe she was trying to puff herself up.'

'And when she went out and the au pair didn't know where, she was supposed to tell Greg that Courtney was out shopping.'

'What did you tell your husband three afternoons a week when we –'

'Not shopping, but how tactful of you to ask.' When he didn't apologize I said: 'Courtney told the au pair that Greg had too much on his plate. Except no one else, including the au pair, ever saw him as pressured or stressed. And as far as an affair goes, only one person thinks she could have been having one: her best friend.'

'Well,' Nelson said, 'you're the historian. How often in the history of the world does a woman *not* tell her best friend?'

'That's my point. Courtney didn't. The best friend is very pretty and sweet but probably not the sharpest knife in the drawer. She said Courtney never told her anything about a guy. She just suspected it because Courtney seemed so distracted. Except I don't see them as best friends. Like everything Courtney did, there was this quality of superficiality to it.

'Nelson, over and over, people keep saying something was missing in her. At work she was this bundle of ambition but never gave it a hundred percent. StarBaby wasn't thriving and she lost interest. She tried to get Greg to open Soup Salad Sandwiches on the West Coast, but that was too big for him and my guess is she thought of him as small potatoes. She did all the suburban lady things, but dropped out of organizations she'd been really active in. I'll bet anything if she hadn't been killed, 1999 would have been the year of her last pumpkin cake. Baking, interior decorating, shoe buying, Mommy and Me classes. She wanted bigger things than just that. And I'll bet quiet, nebbishy, smart Miss New Jersey offered her a chance to satisfy some ambition that needed satisfying.'

'You're telling me a story. "Once upon a time there

was a little girl named Courtney who looked at her candy-bar-sale balance sheet –"'

'I'm telling you a theory. I'm telling you what I know deep down is true, and don't say anything like "Oh, the DA will really be impressed."'

'What's New Jersey's name?' Nelson asked.

I found myself in the middle of another staring contest. I lost. 'Emily Chavarria.' And I spelled it for him.

When I got home, I set my alarm for six A.M. I wanted to get to New Jersey early, before all the Sunday-morning beach traffic.

Chapter Thirteen

All the way down the Turnpike, I kept pushing thoughts of Nelson out of my head. I was nervous that in the midst of some erotic reverie, I'd swerve into another lane and hit one of those interminable silver tank trucks, the ones with huge 'Flammable' warnings. Instead, I sang along to a Dinah Washington CD and pondered how come New Jersey, an otherwise normal state, would elect to honor its notables by naming after them the service areas at which travelers urinate and eat suspect frankfurters.

I exited onto Route 73 and finally, despite my Internet driving directions, found The Meadows, Emily Chavarria's town-house complex, just outside Cherry Hill. I hadn't foreseen a gated community. How the hell was I going to get past the guard? Lowering the Jeep's window, I felt a droplet of sweat trickling from behind my ear down my neck. My mouth went so dry I was surprised I could part my lips. In a white shirt with a gold shield that proclaimed EVERALERT, the private security guard scowled at me with bulging eyes, then looked away. His Adam's apple bounced. 'Yah?' Apparently he'd decided I was not an imminent threat to The Meadows.

'Hi!' I smiled. He didn't. I cleared my throat. 'Uh, did

Sergeant Wilson get here yet? To the place where Emily Chavarria lived?'

'*Again?*' The guard sighed with the weariness of an old hand who's seen it all far too often. 'I thought they got done with that months ago.'

'I guess not.'

'No,' he said at last, 'nobody's got here yet.'

'Oh,' I said, trying to appear deflated, a performance that was lost as he was eyeing some sort of screen in his booth. 'I'm supposed to give him . . .' I patted a brown paper bag on the seat beside me that contained an apple core and an empty water bottle. It made a crisp, official sound. 'From the lab.'

'Name?' he mumbled, picking up a clipboard.

'Dr Singer.' One of the boons of being a woman of a certain age is that we are often viewed as terminally lackluster and, thus, incapable of any interesting vice, including guile.

'You from the lab?'

'Yes.'

I was already looking ahead. The complex was a series of wood and fieldstone structures that looked more than substantial enough for an upwardly mobile assistant bank manager. He wrote down my name, directed 'First left, first right,' raised the barrier, and even managed a one-finger salute.

Emily herself, or the new owner of 807 Squirrel Court, had set a huge stone squirrel beside the front door of the town-house to greet visitors. Despite its toothy smile, I moved on and rang the bell of the attached house next door. A woman about thirty, with purplish-red hair – the result of that rinse that makes everyone who uses it look as if their ancestors hailed from a part of the British Isles with extremely peculiar climatic conditions – answered the door.

'Good morning!' I said, in a jaunty, dropping-in-at-nine-thirty-on-a-Sunday voice. The woman tightened the belt on her pink, waffle-weave bathrobe. 'I'm Judith Singer. I've been hired by the family to look into Emily Chavarria's disappearance.' I didn't say whose family, a sign of my growing skill at subterfuge. I suppose it was to my credit that I felt a pang or two of guilt.

Maybe the woman picked up my discomfort because she opened her door wide and stepped back so I could come in. 'Hey,' she greeted me. 'Beth Cope.' A man about the same age strolled into the hall. 'Judith Singer,' she introduced us, 'my husband, Roberto Anello. Hon, Judith is a detective. She's looking into Emily's disappearance.'

Roberto, in a corresponding bathrobe in blue, flared his nostrils, but he was only suppressing a yawn. Lacking the hair for a purplish-red rinse (or for anything else for that matter), he scratched his scalp. Then, having come to some sort of decision, he asked with considerable courtesy: 'Do you have any ID?'

Oy, I thought. 'Sure,' I said. I opened the latch on my handbag, took out my car keys, cell phone, and Palm Pilot and poked around in the utterly ID-free abyss.

I was saved by Beth's 'Hey, no problem' and Roberto's silently seconding the motion, because, within seconds, I was in their kitchen. I sat across from them at a table between a red leatherette booth, the sort found in diners. As the walls were festooned with an Eskimo Pie clock and archaic signs like PEPSI COLA'S THE DRINK FOR YOU! and OBERMAIER'S YUMMY PIES, I concluded they were 1950s aficionados. Ergo, I fit right in.

'You were living here last October, when Emily supposedly left for her trip?' They nodded simultaneously. 'Did she talk to you about it at all?'

'Not much,' Roberto said. 'It's like we – Beth and I – met that night after work like we always do and went grocery shopping. Friday shopping.' Beth beamed as her husband spoke. 'We came in around sevenish.' She nodded vigorously in agreement. They seemed such a pleasant couple, and obviously pleasant to each other. I found myself wishing that Kate would have a relationship like that instead of with MTV Adam and his zoot suits.

'I guess we remember because we told the police all about this sometime in . . . I guess back in November,' Beth added. 'It was incredibly spooky. I mean, Cherry Hill is not the kind of place people vanish from.'

'So Emily's putting a suitcase into the trunk of her car –' Roberto went on.

'Which was . . . ?' I asked.

'A Toyota something,' he replied. 'I think an Avalon.' I noticed, he wasn't actually bald. A layer of pale fluff covered his scalp, the sort of near hair you often see on a newborn. 'And I said, "Hey, Emily, need any help?" because the suitcase was half the size of her and she looked like she was struggling. She said no thanks. Then we asked her where she was going. She said Australia and New Zealand. For three weeks. I thought, Hey, what a great trip!'

'And you know what I thought?' Beth chimed in. 'Three

weeks on one suitcase? She's a better woman than I am. She only had that one suitcase in the trunk and then she closed it.'

'She was driving herself to the airport?'

'I guess,' Roberto said. 'Personally, I'm not a great believer in long-term parking.'

'Did she seem excited about the trip?' I asked.

'Not that I could see,' he responded. 'She had a flattish personality. Besides being quiet. I mean, she wasn't quiet and weird or quiet and nervous. Just . . . quiet. She wasn't, what do you call it? A big talker.'

'It's like this,' Beth added. 'We were just "Hey, how's it going?" neighbors.'

'Okay,' I said. 'Even if she didn't say anything, do you have any sense how it did seem to be going for her around the time she left and didn't come back?'

'I couldn't tell,' Roberto answered, 'but Beth has a theory.'

I looked to her. 'Well,' she exhaled meaningfully. 'I feel bad saying this but she was as close to being totally dull as a person can get.' I nodded. 'And she looked dull. No makeup except this kind of awful frosted coral lipstick that must have been a freebie, one of those cosmetic company mistakes that become gift-with-purchase. You know what I mean. Anyway, Emily wasn't homely or anything, but she didn't have lots to work with. Small eyes. Hair about here' – she indicated the middle of her neck – 'which is neither here nor there. Except in the last couple of months she started to look better. Much better. Not noticeable makeup, but whatever it was worked because she suddenly looked like she had some life in her face. And she let her hair grow and it was definitely, definitely highlighted. I mean, September, October, and it kept getting blonder and blonder instead of darker.'

'She still wasn't what anyone would call a babe,' Roberto interjected.

'But I told Roberto: "I bet she's someone's babe!"'

Beth and Roberto turned out to be the best The Meadows had to offer. One woman screeched from behind her closed door: 'What? What? Who? What?' I shrieked 'Emily Chavarria' until my throat hurt and I began to worry that someone six town houses away would call the cops. Across Squirrel Court, another couple knew her, but not as a neighbor – only as a photo in a newspaper captioned MISSING. Everyone else was out praying or golfing.

Unable to figure out what to do next, I longed for guidance, *Detection for Dummies*. I drove around Cherry Hill aimlessly. Eventually, I wound up in the parking lot of a giant mall, the kind of place that has too many stores selling the sort of candles whose scent is so belligerent no packaging can contain it. I opened the car window, turned off the engine, leaned back in the seat, and closing my eyes, thought about what it takes to go to Australia besides a fondness for marsupials.

Arrangements. Had Emily bought a ticket and then simply not shown up? Were Australia and New Zealand a cover for other plans, like establishing a new identity in some far-off place? Maybe she'd bought a ticket to Lima, Peru, or Lima, Ohio, and was, at this very minute, snickering over her *rebanada* or Froot Loops as she contemplated her successful murder of Courtney Logan. Or was I being too hasty? Was Emily also a victim? Was there some evil genius preying on FIFE members or on smart women or some other category I couldn't figure out? Were any other members of FIFE mysteriously missing or murdered? Was some rogue FIFEer running amok? Was there some connection between Greg Logan and Emily Chavarria I'd missed?

Before I finished each question, another would pop up. I opened my eyes for an instant just to make sure there were no Hannibal Lecters sautéing fava beans outside the open window of my Jeep. Safe. I tried to imagine Emily's life. Coming to an Ivy League school from a small town in Oklahoma. Whether shy or nerdy, quiet. Living a quiet life, seemingly brightened only by coral lipstick.

Yet according to Beth and Roberto, she'd begun coming out of her shell. As the days grew shorter, her hair grew blonder. Her face brightened. To me, this Emily didn't sound like someone singing the blues. In fact, Beth had suggested the possibility of a man. I could relate. Was it a coincidence that with the mere notion of Nelson back in the general vicinity of my life, I'd gone to the hairdresser the previous week to become a bit more intensely brunette? If I'd had blond tendencies, the way Emily apparently did, no doubt I, too, would have spent fall getting sun-streaked.

So who was the new guy? Definitely no one I could come up with on a late Sunday morning. In fact, the only man I could think of mentioned in connection with Emily was the bank client Joshua Kincaid had called Pharmaceutical Container Man. What the hell was his name? In noir whodunits, the detective calls his secretary and says, 'Listen, doll-face, what was so-and-so's name?'

And with two cat-claw nails, doll-face takes the chewing gum out of her mouth and says . . .

Right! Richard Gray or Gray Richards. And he owned fifty-one percent of his family's company. Could Emily have been yearning for one of those plain-girl-takes-off-her-glasses-and-rich-guy-who'd-overlooked-her-goes-hubba-hubba moments? She sounded too serious a careerist to mix business and romance, but Josh Kincaid had mentioned something about her hitting the glass ceiling, so I wasn't going to rule it out – especially since I had nothing else.

I checked my voice mail. Four messages! To many, no big deal. To me, a wildly eventful morning: Fancy Phil reported that Greg had never heard of anyone named Emily Chavarria. My son Joey announced he'd been hired by the *New York Times*'s Arts and Leisure section to do an article on the Coen brothers. Nancy, her Georgia tones sugary as pecan pie, demanded, 'Where the fuck are you?' And then Nelson, in his bland cop voice: 'I'll see you at noon today, Sunday –' I glanced at my watch. Nearly eleven. Even flying, there was no way I could make it back to Long Island. '– at Carlo's Big Cheese Pizza, Forty-seven Donovan Street, Cherry Hill.' Cherry Hill?

If stomachs can have seizures, mine did, contracting over and over before finally solidifying into a pain-producing object north of my navel. How the hell had he known? I tried some relaxation breathing I recalled from a yoga video I'd watched two or three times: in through the nose, hold, hold, hold, out slowly through pursed lips. All right, he'd called at ten forty-two, so clearly he was in or near Cherry Hill. Either there had been a magic moment when he'd spotted me tooling around in a red Jeep with New York plates and a St Elizabeth's College faculty parking sticker or he, too, had gone to check out Emily's house and discovered from Everalert or Beth and Roberto that a lady from the lab/investigator for the family had left just a short time before. From the tone of his voice, it didn't sound as if he were planning on a fun lunch.

Being one of those drivers who needs very specific directions – 'Immediately after an off-white stucco house with a cutesy mailbox decorated with little girls holding a daisy chain, bear right onto North Peanut Street . . .' – I spent a good part of the next hour locating Carlo's Big Cheese, then trying to outwit a traffic circle in order to reach it. So when I walked into the place in a state well beyond frazzled, I felt grateful that Nelson had always been one of those people for whom noon meant precisely that. I'd have time to select a table not in direct sunlight, check to see if the ladies' room was go-able in, and lighter of bladder and spirit, sit down and breathe some more.

Except there he was. No casual short-sleeved, extensor-muscle-baring shirt like the night before. Gray suit, white shirt, blue tie. While it didn't shout 'Cop,' it said something loud enough for Carlo, or whoever the guy in the tinted glasses behind the counter was, to have seated him at a discreet corner table.

'Sit down, Judith.'

Although it occurred to me to inquire 'Is that a command or an invitation?' I merely sat. What I finally did say was: 'You didn't mention last night that you were going to Cherry Hill.' When that did not produce a response, I got up, left my purse on the chair, and went to the ladies' room. When my return received no reaction, I stood beside my chair and said: 'Listen, I've lived through a not-great marriage and both my children's adolescences. So if you're planning on continuing the silent treatment, know that I'll find it incredibly boring and I'll be forced to lunch elsewhere.'

'I wasn't giving you the silent treatment,' he finally replied.

I sat down. 'What was it, then?'

'I was at a loss for words.' I wasn't ready to smile yet, which was fortunate, because he was in ice-cold mode. 'I was amazed at how stupid you were,' he continued, 'going to the guard and saying you're from the police lab.'

'It got me in,' I retorted.

'It got you in, but if you're going to pull that kind of crap, you shouldn't leave your real name.'

'Next time I'll have an alias ready.' Nelson stood. I thought he was walking out, but he only strode across the restaurant and said something to the man behind the counter. When he came back I said, 'Can I assume you didn't tell him to call the Cherry Hill cops and have them come and arrest me for false something?'

'I told him a plain pizza.' I nodded. 'Are you still drinking Diet Coke?'

'Still. So, did you just hear about me from the security guard or did you get a chance to meet Beth and Roberto?'

'I met them.'

'Good. Nice couple. So you know that Emily left with a suitcase.'

'I know,' he said, hooking his finger over his tie,

loosening the knot, then opening the top button of his shirt. 'Now tell me what you make of all this.'

'Then will you tell me?'

'Come on, Judith. I gave up a day off to look into this business. I don't have time to fool around.' God knows what kind of a smirk crossed my face, because he added: 'Cut it out.'

'Fine.'

'Talk.'

'I wish I had a lot to tell you,' I began, 'but all I've done so far is speak to the neighbors. So you probably heard what I heard: Emily was acting as if things were looking up. I don't know what was going on with her at the Red Oak Bank. Come to think of it, I don't know what was going on with her *not* at the Red Oak Bank. But at the very least it seems to me when a woman changes her appearance for the better, she has a different sense of herself, or some new expectations. Maybe she'd gone for therapy and had new feelings of self-worth, which for her meant lightening her hair and contouring her cheekbones.'

'What?'

'Never mind. Some makeup thing. Or it could be she found a man.'

The pizza guy came from behind the counter, set a Diet Coke before me and a beer in front of Nelson, both in giant red, green, and white paper cups with the slogan EAT A PIZZA spiraling from bottom to top. 'Did you happen to find out if there was a man?' Nelson asked.

'No. Does that make us even or are you ahead of me?'

'Even.'

'Let's talk about Emily's travel plans,' I proposed.

'Go ahead,' Nelson said.

'Well, I was sort of hoping that after last night when we'd discussed how Emily seemed to have made plans and how Courtney seemed to have made none – beyond buying apples for her kids – you might have come up with some information on where Emily did go. From credit cards or something.'

'You're really an ace at this detective stuff, Judith.' For the first time since I'd walked in, he smiled, openly, generously, as if he'd forgotten he was angry. '". . . credit cards or *something*"?'

'Go ahead,' I said. 'Talk about whatever you want to talk about.'

For a little longer than was comfortable, he looked into the foam on his beer. 'You know, I have a problem about talking to you.' I started to be amused, but then he added: 'I'm serious.'

He was. 'What's the problem?'

'I have to think about anything I say to you, Judith. I could be more, whatever, open with you. Except there's a direct line between you and your friend Phil Lowenstein.'

Maybe I shouldn't have been stung by this remark, or stunned either, but I was. 'Do you think I would betray you, Nelson?'

'No; no, I don't. But like I tried and tried to tell you, Phil isn't a nice man. He's a dangerous and sometimes violent man. Look, under normal circumstances, even though all these years have gone by with us not seeing each other, I know . . .' For a second he put his hand over his heart. 'I know you would never do anything to hurt me. Even under abnormal circumstances. But what if this guy put a gun to your head? It wouldn't be out of character, you know. What if you reported certain information to him and he wanted to know where it came from? So you'd say, "Sorry, Phil, it's a privileged communication." Do you think Phil is just going to say, "Okay, I respect your right to protect your sources"? Or do you think he'll grab you by the throat and start squeezing until you manage to cough up my name?' He took a paper napkin from the napkin holder and folded it in half, then in half again. 'Listen, my job is on the line. Other than my kids, it's pretty much my life. If it somehow got out that information I gave you found its way to Fancy Phil Lowenstein, I lose my living, my reputation. Forget being shamed. I'd be risking jail.'

'I want to live to see grandchildren,' I said quietly. 'So if there were a gun to my head, well, I don't know what I would do. So I guess it's best if you don't tell me anything.'

We sat in the sort of silence that is only possible between two old friends or two lovers so assured of the other's admiration that there is no need to charm or even to speak. I don't know how long we didn't talk, but finally the guy in the tinted glasses appeared beside our table and set down the pizza. I was getting busy fighting the mozzarella when Nelson said: 'Just on the basis of a preliminary check, Emily didn't use the Amex or Visa that were in her name after Thursday, October twenty-first, the day before her final day of work at the bank.'

'You don't have to tell me this.'

'And forget her not getting on a plane. There's no record of her even buying a ticket to Australia or anyplace else since before Christmas 1998, when she went from

Philadelphia to Oklahoma City to visit her family. So if things were looking up for Emily, or she had big expectations, I'd like to know what they were.'

We sat in Carlo's until the leftover slices of pizza congealed. We left the Courtney Logan case and chatted about safer subjects. The public's Gore–Bush blahs versus the electricity we'd known as kids watching JFK run against Nixon. Police-department politics compared to the politics of academia. Who was worse, Kate's boyfriend or his son's fiancée (whom Nelson referred to as the Syosset Slut), who wore microscopic leather miniskirts and too-tight tube tops. Neither of us got near the topic of Nelson's having a wife.

When we got outside it was not only hotter, but more humid. I didn't want to leave, but I didn't want to stand there and feel my hair growing into a deranged frizz. At that instant he touched my arm and said: 'I'll drive.'

The words 'I think I'd better be getting home' seemed to be on their way from brain to mouth. Nevertheless, I found myself opening my handbag and dropping in my car keys. I don't remember much about the short ride except staring at the blank screen of one of those global positioning systems and thinking, What if he can't? What if I don't? What if it's awful? What if the motel room or wherever he was taking me smells of insecticide? What if one of us (no doubt him) really doesn't want to see the other again afterward? Would there have to be one more tryst for courtesy's sake? What if he'd been imagining me as I was twenty years ago? What's going to happen when we leave and I have to go home alone and he goes back to the guidance counselor? In matters of the heart, I've always had a tendency to look on the bright side.

He pulled into a Holiday Inn. Since in our earlier days we'd met in one of his friends' apartments, I immediately started agonizing over motel protocol. Check in together? I linger while he goes to the front desk? He pays? Dual, egalitarian credit cards? Untraceable cash? 'I have the key,' Nelson remarked as we pulled into a parking space.

'I guess that makes you an optimist.'

'About you, yes.' As we walked through the halls and took the elevator upstairs, he held my hand. His skin felt so hot I knew, besides his excitement, that my fingers were freezing. 'Judith,' he said as he slipped the magnetic key card into the slot, 'this isn't going to be painful. You're not going to need anesthesia. Relax.'

I stood beside the low, king-size bed that overwhelmed the small room. A sliver of sunlight slipped inside where the curtains didn't quite meet and made a diagonal across the bedspread. I was saying, 'God, don't you wish we could get past the next couple of minutes and –' when he kissed me, a gentle, leisurely kiss to show me No, I don't want to get past anything.

Amazing, I suddenly realized, how completely I remembered his lips, the prickles of his beard, the same aftershave that smelled like lemons and witch hazel. He was only a couple of inches taller, so it was the easiest thing in the world to kiss him. I thought, I want to do this for hours, but I found myself pulling off his jacket, his tie, unbuttoning his shirt. After he eased off my cotton sweater, I was the one who threw back the spread, hauled off his undershirt, drew him onto the bed before I'd even bothered to slip off my shoes. 'Please,' I whispered.

'Listen,' Nelson told me, 'I don't know about you, but I don't have to be anyplace until tomorrow.' He slid his hand behind my back and, in a move I hadn't forgotten, unhooked my bra and tossed it aside in a single fluid motion.

All through the afternoon we kept murmuring the helpful hints lovers offer each other: 'Easy,' 'Slower,' 'Faster,' 'Harder,' 'More.'

At the end of the day, he said, 'You know how women are always needing reassurance and how men aren't supposed to be good at giving it?'

'I've heard words to that effect.'

He propped himself up on his elbow. 'So, here goes. I loved you way back when. I love you now. And I loved you all those years in between.'

'Same here, big boy,' I told him.

'No. You have to actually say it.' So I did.

I left him an hour later. I can't say the possibility of intimacy hadn't occurred to me, because even before having dinner with Nelson the previous evening, I'd shaved my legs so closely I'd taken off the first two layers of the epidermis. However, I didn't want to stay the night with him. Toothbrushes, deodorant, and makeup were all buyable in New Jersey, but I didn't want to have to bear the chilly loneliness of day-break after a night of his warmth. He drove me back to the parking lot of Carlo's Big Cheese and we parted with soft-spoken I-love-yous.

I got back to Shorehaven with time to spare until sunset and drove over to Nancy's without even calling first.

Maybe subconsciously I wanted her to wag her finger at me and howl 'Adulteress!' but instead, after agreeing to stay for Larry's barbecued swordfish kabobs, an admittedly high price to pay, I dragged her upstairs to her computer and asked her to access a couple of *Newsday*'s databases, like Lexis and Nexis.

'Have you taken leave of your senses? No, don't even bother answering. Do you have any idea how much the charges are? How can I justify –'

'You don't have to justify anything. Just say you used it for some personal research and pay them back.'

'Why can't you go to the library?'

'Because it's seven-fifteen on a Sunday night, that's why.'

'Wait till tomorrow.'

'Now.'

'Oh Lord! I can't –'

'Nancy, I don't have time for your Butterfly McQueen act. You know how a person should be willing to lay her life on the line for her best friend? Just access Nexis and we'll call it even.'

Muttering 'shit-ass-rat-fuck,' she got on-line and typed in all the permutations of Gray or Grey and Richard or Richards, the Pharmaceutical Container Man. It took only seconds and some scrolling backward to discover that in April 1998, Richard Grey and his sister Marlena Grey Eugenides offered shares of their family's company, Saf-T-Close, in a public offering.

'Let me think,' I said. 'That's one of those IPOs. Initial public –'

'I know what it means, turkey. But what does it *mean*?' Nancy asked.

'I think . . . I'm not one hundred percent positive, or even seventy-five percent positive, but I think it means that Emily Chavarria knew that the bank's big client, Saf-T-Close, was going to sell stock to the public. Maybe she got in on the ground floor and made a bundle.'

'What's wrong with that?'

The truth was, I had no idea. 'Keep looking,' I ordered her, a little imperiously, but I was standing beside her aching to get on-line and she refused to relinquish control of either her chair or the mouse. 'Boring, boring, boring,' I muttered as she clicked on various thrilling items, such as Saf-T-Close hiring Charles W. Swarski Jr as its new director of marketing and its earnings per share increased by eight percent in the quarter ended December 31, 1998. Then I said, 'Look!' On October 11, 1999, Chapman-Bohrer, a major drug manufacturer, announced its acquisition of Saf-T-Close at fifty dollars per share. '"At close of business the previous Friday,"' I read off the screen, '"Saf-T-Close's final price on the NASDAQ was thirty dollars per share."'

'All right!' Nancy cheered. Almost immediately, she deflated. 'What does this have to do with Courtney Logan?'

'Insider trading!'

'What about insider trading?' she persisted.

When I tried to explain and the words didn't come, we agreed to reconnoiter and meet again in five minutes. Nancy made a beeline to her bedroom phone to call her broker at home and I stayed by the computer and called Kate on another line. Fortunately she answered, making it unnecessary to expend enormous stores of energy being civil to Adam.

It used to be, Kate explained, that insider trading applied to sales or purchases of stock by a company's employees, people who have confidential information about the company's plans. These days, she said, it also applied to people who are tipped off by an insider even if they don't work for the company or owe it any legal duty. A banker like Emily could be one of these people. If Richard Grey tipped her off about the sale, she couldn't buy Saf-T-Close at a lower price and then flip it the next day or week and nearly double her money.

I said good-bye to my daughter and sat down at the computer and went back to the April 1998 announcement. The price of the IPO was eleven dollars per share. If Emily had a piece of the IPO, which was probably legal, she could have made a nice profit on Saf-T-Close. But what if she wanted more? What if, besides her profit on the IPO, she wanted to put even more money on a sure thing, the acquisition? How would she work it?

Nancy returned and took off her imaginary hat to me. 'The broker says the deal with insider trading is that you get someone else to buy the stock and not set off the SEC's computer alarm or whatever.'

'So Emily could have gotten Courtney to buy the stock,' I mused. 'But how much good would that do? Courtney only had twenty-five thousand.'

'For someone smart you're so fucking muddle-headed,' she said with her usual delicacy.

'What are you saying?'

'I'm saying, peabrain, that if indeed any of this is true and not a figment of your overheated imagination, then Emily might have given Courtney some bucks, big bucks,

291

with which to buy said shares of Saf-T-Close and maybe agreed to give her a nice percent of the profit for her trouble. And maybe, you nit, Courtney wanted to keep the money all for herself. I mean, what less can one expect from a person who has the panache to embezzle from a Crunch-Munch sale? And maybe Emily got pissed, made some careful plans' – she took a deep breath and kept going – 'came to Shorehaven for a tête-à-tête with Courtney, and two shots later –'

'Courtney is dead and Emily is free to start a new life where there aren't any glass ceilings!'

Chapter Fourteen

The woman from FIFE sounded unduly nasal, as if she were holding her nose in a juvenile attempt to disguise her voice. 'You're the second call about this today,' she said. For a second I was flummoxed, not a reassuring state of mind on a Monday morning. Who? What? Why? Who else could possibly . . . ?

'Oh,' I replied, 'you mean Captain Sharpe of the Nassau County Police Department.' I did my best imitation of a warm chuckle. 'I guess he's one step ahead of me this morning.'

'I'm sure if he wants to share the details, you can get them from him,' Ms Lovely said, clearly not finding my warm chuckle either credible or endearing.

'Probably not. It would take me a week to convince him to give me the correct spelling of Emily Chavarria's name.' The day before, Nelson had been willing to share information with me (to say nothing about what else he'd shared). But not only didn't I want to rely on his generosity again, I didn't like the idea of being a damsel in distress who needs saving by a hero. 'Look,' I went on, 'I'm doing this on behalf of the family. Obviously they're frantic. All I need to know is if Ms Chavarria and Ms Logan were at the same meeting at any time, if they could have met. Please. For the family.'

'All right, all right. I told the captain . . . They were at the same meeting in '94, in Baltimore. It was in April. FIFE East. But as I explained to the captain, there were over forty delegates. I, personally, have no way of knowing if they ever said two words to each other. I wasn't even here in 1994.' Both times she said 'the captain,' she got a little breathy. I figured Nelson had been troweling on the gruff charm.

'Is Ms Chavarria still active in the organization?'

'The captain asked that, too.'

'I suppose there's a certain investigatory mind-set.' I figured 'mind-set' was one of those corporate words coined to evade the need for actual thinking and would warm the cockles of Ms Lovely's heart. 'Was she still active?'

'Yes, in the South Jersey chapter and in FIFE East. Not in National.'

'And what about Courtney Logan?'

A hurricane of a sigh came over the phone. 'Paid her dues. Was she active in the Wall Street chapter? I'm afraid you'd have to call them.'

'Okay, whom should I call?'

'I can't give out such information.'

In movies, private investigators are always slipping people twenties to get information. I couldn't imagine saying, Hey, Ms Lovely, if you cooperate, I'll stick a couple of sawbucks in the next mail. So I merely said: 'Look, I know you must be horrendously busy –'

'I am and I really have to –'

'– and I wouldn't be bothering you if not for the family.

If you could tell me the name of the head of the Wall Street chapter –' Before she could slip a word in edgewise I added: 'And also, if you could email or fax me the list of people who were at the Baltimore meeting, I know they'd be grateful.' With another whooshed exhalation, she gave me the name and agreed to fax the list. I was on the verge of asking what, if any, other questions Captain Sharpe had asked. But at that moment she got another call and got rid of me fast.

The president of FIFE Wall Street was a hotshot at Merrill Lynch, so I wasn't expecting anything. But she took my call and told me no, Courtney Logan hadn't been to any meetings or events that she could remember. She herself had of course heard the name and about the murder, though couldn't recall ever meeting her. However, she really should write a note of condolence to the husband, poor guy. I was nearly in shock over her acute niceness, but nevertheless was able to give her Greg Logan's name and address.

Shortly after that, a faxed list of the Baltimore attendees arrived. Now that I had it, I didn't know what to do with it short of entering every name on a search engine and seeing if any articles on serial killers or missing women came up. But I decided I had other fish to fry first, so I shoved it into the desk drawer I used for papers and clippings I really wanted nothing to do with yet couldn't bear to throw out.

Then I paced around the room for the seven whole seconds such a circumnavigation took. When I'd returned to graduate school after Bob and I decided not to have another baby, I'd taken over the fourth bedroom as an office. It was so small that whenever I felt guilty about only having two kids, about not adding another Jew to the world to help replace the lost ones, I'd think that the third child would have untold resentments at having gotten stuck with what, essentially, was a cell with sheer white curtains.

I sat back down and returned to the *Courier-Post* Web site, where I downloaded the piece about Emily's mysterious disappearance. Then I spent a half hour muttering 'Shit!' until I finally figured how to extract the photograph from the body of the article. Ten minutes later, after reaching Steffi Deissenburger, I emailed the photo to her. I thought it was a pretty nifty idea until the increasingly familiar dread returned – that I actually was on Fancy Phil's wild-goose chase, and in the end, Emily would have been a side trip to nowhere. The killer would turn out to be Steffi, or Steffi + Greg. Having thus screwed up, I would incur Fancy Phil's fury and Nelson Sharpe's contempt. Or vice versa.

On that happy note, the phone rang. 'This is Steffi Deissenburger.' I probably thanked her twice. 'It is not a bother,' she said. 'I cannot tell one hundred percent if this woman was a visitor. But' – I held my breath – 'I think she could be, or might be, someone who was visiting Courtney. I did not see her for long. Only for a minute.'

A tingle of excitement, followed by the warm flush of hope that feels too good to be a hot flash. My heart began to pound. But wanting to sound composed, I said, with over-the-top sincerity, à la Judd Hirsch as the shrink in *Ordinary People*: 'Tell me about it.'

'Sometimes when Courtney had a friend visit,' Steffi said, 'she would ask me to take the children from the house. So she and the friend could enjoy a quiet conversation. Did I tell you that already? This is what I did on that day. I took Morgan and Travis to the library, then to lunch, then I think to the big playground in Christopher Morley Park.'

'When was this?'

'I believe it was in . . . I cannot say exactly. It could have been the end of summer.'

'Please,' I urged her, 'go ahead.'

'I brought the children back earlier than Courtney had asked. Travis was – he was crying. From being cranky, you see. He had not had a nap and he was a child who needed one. Sometimes he even took a nap in the morning.'

'What time was it when you got back to the Logans'?'

'Before four. Courtney asked me to keep the children out until four o'clock so she and her friend –'

'Did she mention the friend's name?'

'I don't think so. Or I don't remember. I am not sure.'

'Sorry to have interrupted you. Please go on.'

'I drove home, and as I am parking the car, a woman comes out from the front door. Courtney is there and they kiss good-bye.'

'A hugging kiss?' I asked.

'No. A fast kiss like Americans do who do not know each other so well.' Steffi made the staccato smack of a social kiss. 'The woman sees the children, so Courtney waves to me to come over. She says, "This is Morgan and this is Travis."'

'She doesn't introduce you?'

'No. I believe she is a little angry that I came home

297

before four o'clock, although she may just be tired. And the woman says something like "They're so cute," even though Travis is crying. He was very, very cranky and it was a long day for him. Then the woman gets in her car and drives away.'

'Did Courtney say anything to you about your coming back early?'

'No. I started to apologize, but she said to forget about it, that it was all right and she had a nice visit with her friend.' I got a clear mental picture of Steffi at that instant: her contrite expression, her heavily made-up face, her placid posture, her nervous hands.

'Courtney didn't call the woman Jane or Mary or anything? Just "my friend"?'

'I think just that. I don't remember.'

'Okay, you said the woman got into a car. Do you remember what kind it was, or the color?'

'No. I don't think it was a German or a Swedish car. I have been to both countries and their cars are familiar to me. And the color . . . ? I don't remember. It may have been dark.'

'Did you notice the license plate?' I ventured. 'Was it from New York or some other state?'

'I don't think I saw. Travis was crying and I felt, you know, bad about coming home early. Courtney had asked me to please to keep them out and if they got to be a problem to go to Baskin-Robbins and buy them ice cream.'

'That doesn't sound like her,' I remarked. 'Ice cream?'

'Well, you see, she understood how young children were. She wanted to make it easier for me to handle them. She was very thoughtful in this way.'

'Right. Now, would you say the woman was younger or older or the same age as Courtney?'

'I would say a little younger, but not too much. Thirty or thirty-one.'

'And what did she look like?'

'Like the woman in the photograph you emailed to me. Very plain. Dark blond or light brown hair. She wore it back, like a chignon, but not so elaborate, if you understand. Not very tall, but she wore shoes with those high but very heavy heels. I don't know what you call them. And a plain gray business suit with a white blouse under it. Not well cut, the way Courtney's suits were. Like a little gray mouse the woman looks, was what I was thinking. She – what is the word? – oh, carried. She carried herself as though she did not wish to be seen.'

'Would you say shy?'

'Maybe shy, someone who is not easy at being friendly – except with a few who know her well.'

'Was she easy with Courtney?'

'I did not see her enough to know.' She paused, and I held myself back from throwing another question at her. 'It is like this,' Steffi continued. 'I watched her when she was looking at the children and I thought, She is fond of them not because she likes children but because she thinks so well of Courtney and they are Courtney's. So she has admiration for Courtney. Maybe I was wrong and she is still shy, even with children. But she did not seem to know how it was with them, or even to like them. She kept looking at Travis as though he would see her and understand he had to stop crying.'

'What was your general feeling about her?'

'Perhaps lonely,' Steffi said cautiously. 'She did not act like a woman with a husband or nice boyfriend. You know? As if there is someone in the world who wants you. Still, I did not see her longer than one minute. I cannot even tell you more than maybe, *possibly*, this woman was the woman in your email.'

After speaking with Steffi I found myself at loose ends, only in part because I couldn't figure out what to do next. Her offhand remark about the confidence of a woman with a husband or boyfriend who knows there is 'someone in the world who wants you' kept replaying in my head.

At ten-twenty (according to the perpetually erroneous clock on the lower right of my computer screen), I was at the height of aggravation at myself. I hadn't been able to dismiss the why-doesn't-he-call anxiety about Nelson as well as the so-why-don't-you-call-him-and-stop-the-playing-hard-to-get-game response (to which I added a schmuckette-that's-what-you-get-for-sleeping-with-a-married-man kick in the ass). I was starting to get unusually inventive, constructing a scenario in which Nelson drove home from the motel the previous afternoon, slept with his wife out of guilt or desire, had a heart attack, and at that very moment was being laid out with a boutonniere in his lapel in some Methodist funeral home. The phone rang as I was subtracting the carnation and adding an American flag because he'd been in the air force and was a cop.

It was Nelson. Alive. His greeting was the one he'd always used two decades earlier, saying I love you, to which I responded with my customary 'Who is this, please?' He told me he'd like to come over, I said good. Thirty-five minutes later he came through the door. He

300

kissed me thoroughly before saying 'I'm here on business.'

'I could tell,' I answered, trying to ignore the hideous hounds-tooth jacket he was wearing again. I led him through the living room into the sunporch, a small room common in Tudor-style houses built in the 1920s and '30s, the old-time equivalent of a den. It was there I watched my old movies, listened to music, stretched out on the couch to read mysteries and the occasional literary novel, biographies, magazines – anything not having to do with being a historian. I gestured to a seat on the couch for Nelson.

I sat cater-cornered to him in Bob's old leather recliner, a chair that had begun making embarrassing squealing sounds not long after he died, no matter how much silicone and oil I offered it. In my weirder moods, I thought of the chair as haunted, though not malevolently so.

Anyway, I told Nelson what Steffi had said about the emailed photo, that she had seen someone resembling Emily saying good-bye to Courtney and driving off. Then I offered him what I'd found out about the Red Oak Bank's client Richard Grey and about Saf-T-Close's going public in '98 and its acquisition by Chapman-Bohrer on October 11, 1999.

'That's fantastic!' he said. 'How did you find that out?'

'Luck. And the Web.'

'I'm impressed, Judith.'

'Wow. Now I am, too,' I told him. 'Nelson, can you look to see if Emily or, more likely, Courtney bought any of this stock? If Emily did it, it would be a clear case of insider trading. So she couldn't do it legally. But if

Courtney knew about Saf-T-Close's being acquired early enough, through Emily, she might have made a killing.'

'On that twenty-five thousand she pulled out of those joint accounts?' Nelson asked.

'Well, I don't know about that. I mean, if the stock went from thirty to fifty, I figured that's about a sixty-six percent profit. But what I'm thinking is that – assuming there is an Emily–Courtney connection – that Emily gave Courtney her money to invest.'

'And then?'

'And then maybe Courtney held on to it. And Emily, who had planned to disappear from the bank, made a side trip to Shorehaven. I don't know if she got back her money, but maybe she got back at Courtney.' Nelson did not make a big production out of thinking. Still, I knew. 'What are you thinking?' I demanded.

'I'm thinking that if this story you're telling me turns out to be true, which I'm not saying it will, then it will be a stinkeroo to figure out. These two weren't teachers, or cops. They were financial sophisticates.'

'And we're not.'

'Unless you sneaked in an MBA along with your Ph.D.'

'Nope.'

'Okay now, my turn. I may be onto something also.' Late morning light streamed through the louvered windows and lit up his hair. With his snub nose and large, choir-boy eyes, he looked vaguely angelic. He reached into the inside breast pocket of his jacket and extracted a folded sheet of paper. 'Listen to this.'

'Can I see it so I know what you're talking about?'

'No. Listen, Judith . . . The last thing I want to do is hurt your feelings, but I'm going to say it straight out. You're not my partner in this.'

'So how come you're here?'

He flashed one of his annoyed looks. 'To talk.'

'To talk about stuff you really shouldn't be talking about?'

'Probably.' He seemed remarkably casual about such a lapse, although I supposed that anyone doing the sort of work he'd done for all the years he'd been doing it could not be easily flustered. 'Do you want to listen?'

'Of course.'

'This is just between us.'

'You don't have to tell me that, Nelson.'

Instead of countering with anything smug or scathing, as almost anyone else would do, he simply opened the paper and ran his finger down what appeared to be a column. Naturally, such a showing of cool impressed me exponentially. 'I was checking out incoming calls to Emily's house and office. Okay, five of them came from the same number in the 917 area code. You know what that is?'

'The code for a lot of pagers and cell phones.'

'Right. It's used around the tristate area. So, a couple of things. The cell phone was bought on September seventeenth, 1999, a Friday, at an AT&T place on West Thirty-ninth in Manhattan. That was over a month before Emily Chavarria and Courtney Logan disappeared.'

I leaned forward. 'Was it in either of their names?'

'No. It was bought and paid for by someone named Vanessa Russell.'

'Cash or credit card?'

'A Discover card,' he replied. 'First of all, whoever

303

Vanessa is or isn't, she – or someone who used her cell phone – made those five calls to an 856 area code, which is –'

'Cherry Hill,' I said. 'Home of the lovely Holiday Inn overlooking – Okay, who did Vanessa call in Cherry Hill?'

'Only Emily Chavarria's voice mail at the bank. Now let's see how good at this you are,' Nelson said. 'The calls varied in length from a little over a minute to almost four minutes. What does that tell you?'

I did some hmmming. 'Does your watch have a second hand?' I inquired. He nodded. 'Okay, time me: "Hi, Nelson. This is Judith Singer of Sixty-three Oaktree in Shorehaven. I'm calling you about the whole business with Emily Chavarria and Courtney Logan. I'd appreciate getting whatever information you have. You can call me at 516–537–1409."'

'Twenty-one seconds.'

'Which means either she was leaving a hell of a long message –'

'You got it. Checking Emily's messages.'

'Which would most likely have to be done by Emily, because she'd have to know the password or code or whatever to retrieve them.'

'Most likely,' he agreed, 'but not definitely.'

'Were any of those calls made after Emily disappeared?'

'Three of them.'

'If the phone is in the name of Vanessa Russell . . . How did you find it so fast?'

'Doesn't take long if your contact from the phone company feels like being a nice guy. Everything's computerized. Almost all of the other calls to access Emily's voice mail were made from Emily's house. One was made from a pay phone at a restaurant in Manhattan. The rest were from that cell phone.'

'So Emily was around even after she didn't go to Australia but disappeared.'

'I'd give it a seventy-five percent shot,' Nelson said.

'I'd give it a ninety,' I retorted.

'In a homicide investigation you shouldn't give anything those odds. If you were a guy, I'd say you haven't been doing this long enough to know a pile of shit from a hot rock.'

'But I'm not a guy.'

'Right. So maybe you're being a little overoptimistic about your deductive talents. But I still haven't gotten to the good part.'

'What's that?'

'That someone using Vanessa Russell's cell phone called Courtney Logan's house on Sunday, October twenty-fourth, and then again on Thursday, October twenty-eighth, three days before Courtney disappeared.'

'Oh my God! That definitely ties Emily to Courtney.'

'No, that ties a user or users of a certain cell phone to both Emily and Courtney. Maybe it was Emily herself calling. Maybe not.'

I bounded out of the chair, muttered 'Excuse me,' and hurried to the kitchen. Returning with a bag of organic celery hearts, I plopped down on the couch beside Nelson and offered him one. Looking at me as if I'd proffered a bag of rocks, he shook his head. I pulled off a stalk and began to munch. 'Eating calms my nerves,' I explained.

'You think I don't know that?'

'Oh, shut up! Now, Vanessa Russell of cell phone and Discovercard fame: Is there really such a person?'

'I don't know yet. There was no answer at the home number that she gave on the application for cell phone service, a 718 Brooklyn number. I called her where she supposedly works, with a 212 area code, but there's no such number. I'm having someone check out her home address and number and also with Discover to look at her credit history, if any. But I can't take too much time on this. Courtney is a homicide and Emily is a missing person in New Jersey. Not my jobs.'

I set down my celery and put my hand into his; I'd always loved the way his hand made mine look dainty. 'You wish it were your job, don't you?' He nodded. 'Can you try to make it yours? Like on the theory it involves an organized crime figure you're already investigating for . . . whatever. I mean, Fancy Phil was Courtney's father-in-law.'

'I already tried that the day after they fished her out of that pool. The powers that be knew exactly what I wanted to do, which was to horn in on a homicide case. They said leave it alone.'

'Was it an actual order?'

'No, it was one of those friendly suggestions that if you don't take to heart, your ass is grass and you wind up getting an unfriendly suggestion that it's time to start filling out the pension papers.' He gave a what-the-hell shrug that was utterly unconvincing.

'So what are you going to do?' I asked.

'What I'm doing. A little looking here and there. A little listening. Mainly to you. And to a couple of my old friends still in Homicide – though not on this case.'

'They're part of the old regime and don't get the juicy cases? That's department politics?'

'Smells like it.'

'Nelson, do you honestly think Phil Lowenstein had anything to do with Courtney's murder or Emily's disappearance?'

'Damned if I know.'

'You know,' I told him.

He rose from the couch and I did, too. 'Twenty percent chance,' he said.

'Two percent, and I'm not going to split the difference. Even if he wanted to find out what I was doing ringing Greg's front doorbell and offering my services –'

'You did that? Are you nuts, Judith?'

'Marginally. But if Fancy Phil was interested in hearing what I had to say, he could have done exactly what he did do, hang out in a corner of my garage until I pulled my car in and closed the door. "Hi! Wanna see my new pinkie ring?"'

'He surprised you in your garage?'

'He's such a playful fellow. Look, if he'd wanted to get me wiped out, I'd have already been run over by a cement truck. No, he *hired* me. I'm working on his behalf, even though I refused to take any money from him.'

I suddenly realized I was following him to the front door, without a detour to the upstairs. He gave me a fast kiss on the forehead. 'Gotta go. Can I see you tonight?'

'I can't.' He looked on the verge of asking me to change my plans, so I added: 'It's a long-standing date with friends from high school. There's no way I can weasel out of it.'

I said nothing about not wanting to weasel out. After he

left I went back onto the sunporch and sat where Nelson had been sitting. The cushion was still warm from him. Did I really *not* want to see him? Of course not. Doing anything with Nelson was better than listening to my friend Marcy's unfailing lament over what managed care was doing to her practice of medicine and hearing Helena's ode to the golfing life in Boca Raton. (I suspected my descriptions of St Elizabeth's History Department Frolics were equally electrifying for them.) But I was afraid of an overnight with Nelson, not only that all the nights after that would be unbearably lonely, but that somehow I would wind up being the lever to pry him out of his supposedly lousy marriage. If anything was going to happen between me and Nelson, it would have to be on a separate agenda from whatever was going on between Nelson and the guidance counselor.

Naturally I had an almost irresistible impulse to bring the entire matter before Nancy, except I wanted to avoid her inevitable harangue even more than I wanted to hear her advice. Instead, I made notes on the case for the rest of the day, went into the garden to cut some roses, and left for dinner in Manhattan with my pals. As expected, nothing was new with them, beyond a new grandchild for Marcy and new moisturizing regimen for Helena. I heard about both at great length.

Driving home from Manhattan, I was so exhausted I blasted a rap station and turned the air conditioner to its iciest to keep from nodding off. I'd never been one of those frisky types about whom it is said: If you want to get a job done, give it to the busiest person. A full day for me was teaching a class, making egg salad, and watching a Bette Davis movie. While I did crave the sense of being alive that I got from murder, all the exhilaration and agitation of the past month had worn me out more than I wanted to admit.

I was heading down Oaktree Street. Even before I got to the driveway, I saw my way to the garage blocked by a colossus of an automobile. I got alert fast. And turning in, I spotted a heavy, hairy braceleted right arm as the front passenger door of the giant car swung open. Fancy Phil. It was like a massive intravenous shot of caffeine.

'What's up, Doc?' He at least had the decency not to guffaw at this allegedly humorous reference.

Glancing at his Cro-Magnon driver, I turned to Fancy Phil: 'How come I have the pleasure of your company at this time of night?'

'Let's go inside and we'll talk.'

His multichinned face, illuminated by the outdoor lights, was one large, friendly smile. Around his neck he wore a star of David so unavoidably huge on his black knit shirt, so goldly garish that I could only assume it was not only meant to be noticed, but also to reassure: My people = thy people. 'Not inside,' I said, smiling back. 'It's such a beautiful night.' I gestured upward to what was either Venus or a satellite and took a deep breath of rambling roses and car exhaust. 'Let's stay out here.' I walked up the path to the three steps that led to the front door, sat, and patted the flagstone beside me.

Fancy Phil followed me slowly and somewhat stiffly, as if he were Frankenstein walking after just a few moments of life. He did not sit. 'What's the matter? You scared of me again? I thought you got over that.'

It's always hard to choose when your gut says one thing and your brain says another. 'Phil, do you have your driver's number?' In case he thought I was referring to the man's ID from Ossining State Penitentiary, I added: 'His phone number.'

'Yeah. Why?'

'Then please tell him to take a ride for a half hour or so. You'll call when you need him.'

He glanced down and saw my house keys in my hand. If he was even half as brainy as I believed he was, he'd realize the electronic gizmo on my key chain was a panic button for the house's alarm system. He flashed me a look that said, Hey, if you want be ungracious, fine by me. Then he wiggled his index finger and his driver/goon opened the window. 'About half an hour,' Fancy Phil said. 'I'll call you.' Quietly and elegantly, the great, dark car backed out and drove off. Fancy Phil turned back to me. 'So, you gonna invite me in now?'

'I'd rather take the night air.' For some reason, I was not afraid. Uneasy, sure. Maybe even apprehensive. But no chill of fear, no shiver of panic.

'What kinda crap is this, Doc? If I was up to something, I wouldn't be hanging out in my car in your driveway, so all your neighbors could memorize the license plate. You think you can't trust me?'

'I think you've got something on your mind and I'd prefer to hear it under the stars.'

The residue of his smile vanished, but he lowered himself down and, with a barely perceptible grunt, sat beside me on the step. His white linen slacks were stretched so tight around his thighs they looked about to explode from fabric fatigue. 'So?' he inquired.

'So what do you want?' I asked.

'I want to know everything you got.'

'I'm not planning on keeping it a secret, Phil. I'll tell you as soon as I feel I can present a coherent narrative.' I saw the look he flashed me, but I also realized he understood exactly what I'd meant.

'Listen, Doc. I like you a lot.'

'Good. I like you, too.'

'If I didn't have a wife and, you know, a good friend already, I'd actually ask you out on a date. So liking you so much, admiring your smartness, I don't want to make you upset. Or angry with me. Or even, God forbid, afraid of me.'

'Where do you come from, Phil?'

'What? Way back? Brooklyn.'

'Me, too. And we had an old saying there: You're pickin' on the wrong chicken.'

'I never heard that.'

'But you understand what it means,' I said.

'Yeah.'

'For several reasons, none of which I want to elaborate on, it would be best for you if we could resume our old, friendly relationship and cut the business of "God forbid, afraid of me," which translates into "You should be scared shitless." Now, do you want a report on what I've been doing?'

'Yeah.' He pretended to scan the sky for glorious celestial objects. 'Can I come inside now? I swear I'm not gonna hurt you or make a pass. I'm just upset, is all.'

It is rarely wise to ignore your head and your gut and proceed on faith, but I sensed this was one of those times. 'Let's go.' I took him into the living room, turned on all the lamps, and left the curtains open. The place smelled of the roses I'd cut before I left for the city, and any trepidation I may have had disappeared when I saw him gazing from vase to vase to vase, from red to apricot to yellow. 'Beauty-ful,' he commented.

'Thanks.'

Fancy Phil lowered himself onto a club chair and pointed to a hassock. 'Can I put my feet up there if I take off my shoes?'

'Sure, even if you don't take them off.' I was about to sit a few feet away in a matching chair, but I asked, 'Do you want something to eat? Drink?'

'No.' He patted his belly, not without fondness. 'I gotta take off a few. You got any sour balls or anything?' I peered into the depths of my handbag and picked out the two mints wrapped in cellophane I'd taken from the restaurant where I'd just had dinner as well as an almost full pack of sugarless gum. 'Thanks, Doc.' When he finished ripping the cellophane with his teeth and gulping the mints whole instead of chewing them, he said: 'Look, I didn't want to scare you. I just wanted to catch you when you got home. It's that the clock is ticking. They called Gregory and wanted him to go back to their headquarters and go over his information.'

'Again?'

'Yeah.'

'The cops from Homicide?'

'Yeah. His lawyer told them, you should pardon me, to

go take a flying fuck. But you know and I know, they don't got anyone else waiting in line to take the hit for this thing. Their not making any arrest is an embarrassment for them. I'm . . . I'm scared any minute they'll trump up some phony crap just to make the public think they solved the case. What Morgan and Travis have already gone through . . . How could they take their father getting dragged off?'

'It would be a nightmare,' I agreed. I didn't want to think about Greg behind bars for Courtney's murder, his children seeing him in an orange jumpsuit on their increasingly rare visits.

'Okay,' I said. 'We've got to give them something that will divert their attention from Greg. So let me give you a rough sketch of what I've found out.'

Chapter Fifteen

The moon was almost full. Outside the window, across the street, the mist over my neighbor's front lawn glowed in the light; it looked as if a Spanish colonial had risen from a swamp on some extraterrestrial landscape. 'I don't see the end to this yet,' I told Fancy Phil.

He slipped off his white suede loafers and put his bare feet up on the hassock. 'See?' he said, wriggling his toes for emphasis. 'Feet don't come cleaner than this.'

My duties as hostess apparently included smiling my approval of his personal hygiene, so I did. Then I went on: 'It's not only details of what happened with Courtney that we're missing. It's the big picture, too. There are so many blanks to fill in. I want to be able to give you a chronology or some kind of logical progression.'

An enormous pink jewel set in a ropy gold ring on Fancy Phil's right hand gleamed in a cone of light cast by the lamp. 'Do I look like a guy who's gotta have a progression?' he inquired.

'Maybe not, but that's the way I work.'

He placed his right arm in front of his sizable waist and, with surprising grace, considering he was sitting, offered me a magnanimous bow. 'You're the doctor, Doc. Go ahead.'

'Okay. Let's start with the assumption that Courtney had an aspect of her life she didn't want Greg to know about. That's not to say there was some deep, dark secret, like an affair or a complicated financial deception. It could have been that she was going to a friend's house and smoking marijuana and watching dirty movies. Or going to Bloomingdale's and trying on clothes all day.'

'I got news for you, cookie,' Phil said, twisting around his ring to better admire it. 'Nobody's got a life that's an open book.' He saw me eyeing his ring and held up his meaty hand for me, fingers splayed, so it could catch every photon of light and better show off the gem. 'Is this a ring or what?' he demanded.

'I've never seen anything like it.'

'Quinzite opal,' he declared. His nails looked far better manicured than mine, topped with a clear polish with a hint of pink to echo the color of the opal. 'Those stories about opals being bad luck? Craziness. But I guess it keeps down the price. Not that I care. I pay top dollar for quality.'

I gave him a look I hoped would say: Sadly, we must leave the subject of your jewelry. 'About Courtney's life,' I said. 'She told Steffi, the au pair, that if Greg ever called and she wasn't around, to tell him she was out shopping. No big deal. Not the kind of lie that if Greg found out would shake the marriage to its foundation. Still, something was going on. In the week or two before Halloween, Courtney was away three or four times for a whole day, from after breakfast until seven or seven-thirty at night.'

'That don't sound like marijuana,' Fancy Phil reflected. 'And not Bloomingdale's either. Because you know what happens, you try on clothes for ten hours? Seriously, you could end up in traction.' He unwrapped a few pieces of the gum I'd given him earlier and popped them into his mouth.

'You're probably right,' I said. 'Anyhow, according to Steffi, on those days, Courtney dressed up, nicely, elegantly. Not in anything sexy, not the kind of thing she might wear if she were having a sizzling affair.' (Twenty years earlier I'd worn jeans or corduroys to mine, though I concede I did go flambé in the underwear department.) 'It sounds as though she was dressed for business.'

'Maybe she had some guy who wanted class, not tits and ass.' Delighted by his rhyme, Fancy Phil smiled, albeit a reserved gangster smile that displayed only the hint of teeth.

'Do you really think so?' I inquired politely. He shook his head hard: no way. 'Then I'll go on. According to one of StarBaby's clients, when Courtney came to talk about the company, she wore a simple pair of slacks and a silk blouse. Not a suit with a skirt and high-heeled shoes, not with her hair up. The au pair confirmed that.'

Fancy Phil smoothed down the chest hair in the V made by his open-neck shirt. His gold chain and star clanked. 'Courtney was platinum card all the way. I told you, Doc, for someone who liked simple, that girl spent a fortune – like on clothes. Gregory and me was talking about it last weekend. He came over for supper with Morgan and Travis. My wife made her own pizza. Can you believe that? Plain for Morgan, with all kinds of fancy mushrooms for us. Not canned mushrooms. Fresh. Macaroni for Travis. Anyway, Gregory was never cheap, like about Courtney's clothes. A guy wants his wife to look like a million bucks.'

'But not necessarily cost it.'

'You got it, sweetheart. Listen, if you're in the money, sure, why not? Buy your wife a fur down to the floor, a diamond bracelet that says "diamond bracelet" loud and clear – not one of those crappy tennis things. But Gregory don't have those kind of bucks yet. Maybe he won't ever, what with everything having to be legit. Not bucks for the big-time stuff Courtney was dying for. Not to rent a house in Italy for a month with not just a maid, but a cook. A *cook*? Tell me, what does it take to make spaghetti? And the money Miss Simple pissed away – she should rest in peace. Eight hundred dollars for a pair of pants. That's what Gregory told me, and that was just for starters.'

'She'd been an investment banker,' I remarked. 'I'd have thought she would have a more realistic understanding of what their finances were.'

Fancy Phil shook his head sadly. 'It was like this. It wasn't about Gregory. Courtney was positive I had all the money in the world. So whenever she had to have something, she'd hint in front of me. And to tell you the truth, sometimes Poppy Phil would reach into his pocket. Like one time she hinted about a new car to drive the kids around with, with more safety things. Could I say no? Of course not. I got her that Rover. And okay, the TV screen that comes out of the ceiling and gets projected on. For that dumb StarBaby. When she saw I wasn't going to go for it, she said she really meant it for the kids to watch *Sesame Street* on. Okay – so call me a schnook – I got it for her. But if she wants a sable? She has a mink already. But she was hinting big time: One of her girlfriends' husbands bought her' – his voice rose to a falsetto squeal – '"the most beautiful sable coat for her thirty-fifth.' That was how Courtney hinted. Never said *I* want. I'm thinking to myself, a squirt like her puts on sable, she'll look like a sable holding a pocket-book. And I'm also thinking: *No way*. Not a sable, not a fox, not even – pardon me – a fucking bunny rabbit. I don't wanna cut off my son's balls and buy my daughter-in-law a fur. Also I got a wife. Third wife, and she's the kind of girl who thinks number three means she gets to have three furs.' Having gotten that off his chest, Fancy Phil said: 'What am I talking? Go ahead. Any more on Courtney's secret life?'

'On October fourteenth, she had her Land Rover serviced. The thirty-first was the last day she could have possibly driven it, right?'

'Yeah? So?'

'Between those two dates, she put seven hundred sixty-two miles on her car.'

After two seconds of calculation, Fancy Phil asked: 'Where the hell did she go?'

'Remember when I was talking to some of Courtney's former colleagues in the financial community, how one of them happened to mention what he called a weird coincidence: that a banker in New Jersey, someone he dealt with once, had also been reported missing. Emily Chavarria.'

'Yeah. The one you asked me to ask Gregory about. He never heard of her.'

'Right. Thirty-one years old, had gone to a good school. She was supposed to be smart, though not extroverted like Courtney. Quiet. Or maybe just shy. From what the guy who'd worked with Courtney at Patton Giddings told me, Emily must have been more than competent because she was hand-holding one of the bank's biggest clients. Yet she seems to have hit a glass ceiling that was set pretty low.' Fancy Phil's head cocked to the side with an unspoken 'Wha'?' So I explained: 'A glass ceiling is about discrimination. It's an obstacle nobody inside a corporation will admit to that keeps women and minorities from rising to positions of power. But even though she was young, Emily didn't find another job and take a hike. So maybe she was resentful. Maybe she felt entitled to more than she was getting or going to get from the bank.'

Fancy Phil put his feet down in the space between hassock and chair and leaned forward. 'You're just guessing at that.'

'Absolutely.'

'Keep going. I'll stop you when you start sounding stupid.'

'So far so good?' I asked.

'So far.'

'From Shorehaven, it's about a two-hundred-twenty-five mile round-trip to where Emily lives and works. Or worked. Now, one of her bank's biggest clients was a man who'd inherited the majority interest in a family company. And there came a time when he took his company public, sold shares –'

'You don't gotta explain the market to me, Doc. The SEC once tried to get me for stock manipulation, those dumb-fucks.'

'Anyway, later on, the company was acquired by a large corporation. Of course, if you're a banker for a company and you know this sort of thing is going to happen –'

'Insider trading,' Fancy Phil cut in. 'Yeah, yeah. The goddamn SEC makes such a big stink about it.'

'I think they call it a felony,' I replied.

'They're so stupid. Anyhow, what's the name of the guy's company?' he asked.

'I'm not prepared to tell it to you right now, Phil.'

'C'mon.'

'I'd rather not.'

'Why not, goddamn it?' he suddenly bellowed. No suburban niceties for Fancy Phil; no 'Quiet so the neighbors won't hear.'

I never had anyone angry at me who had a criminal record, one element of which was smashing somebody in the face with a brick. At the sight of the fire in Fancy Phil's beady eyes, my guts began to turn liquid. His face was a dangerous red, getting redder. I had to steel myself not to turn away from his glare. 'Why won't I tell you?' I demanded, surprised at finding my own voice rising. 'An insurance policy.'

'Cut it out!'

'No, Phil. Not after I get home late from the city and Surprise! There's Phil Lowenstein and some muscle-bound moron waiting for me.'

'He's not that dumb.'

'Look, it would make me incredibly happy to help Greg, so you and I can be friendly after all this is over.'

'I'm friendly now!' he bellowed. Placing his left hand over the star of David, he raised his right high: I swear to God! 'Hey, aren't I sitting here with you? Listening polite.'

'You're very polite. And very intelligent. Greg's lucky

320

to have you in his corner. And I like you, Phil. I don't want to get you angry or hurt your feelings. But when I saw your car and got a look at your driver . . . So this is just a way to make myself feel more comfortable.'

'I'm not gonna argue with you, even though you're wrong.' He sniffled once, noisily, to show the hurt I'd inflicted. 'Keep talking.'

'It looks like this Emily had a tie to Courtney, besides that FIFE meeting – that's the organization they both belonged to. After Emily disappeared, someone called her voice mail at work from a cell phone a few times. Now unless she'd given her password to somebody else, she was alive and curious enough to check her messages.'

'Whose name was the cell phone in?'

'A name that appears to be a phony, although it's being checked.'

'I hate it when the flavor of gum goes south so goddamn fast,' Fancy Phil muttered as he added another piece to the wad already in his mouth. 'Who's checking the name of whoever bought the cell phone?'

'Someone with easier access to that sort of information than I have.'

'Which means that's another thing you're not telling me.' No rage this time. He merely grumbled.

'Right. But listen. Here's the Courtney–Emily link. Whoever had that cell phone also called your son's house two times, and the last time was a few days before Courtney disappeared.'

'No shit!' he exhaled.

'No shit. Maybe they were just trading rice pudding recipes. But it's my gut feeling that there was some business deal between Emily and Courtney. There's the matter of the company being acquired by a larger one, and also the matter of Courtney making twenty-five thousand dollars disappear. Who knows what else? If I had to guess, it's that Courtney fronted for Emily in buying that stock of the company before it was acquired. They knew, because of insider information, that the price would go way up. I'm not saying that's exactly what happened. For all I know it could be some other shady or unshady deal. The question is, how do I find out? Could there possibly have been a brokerage account Courtney had that Greg hasn't mentioned to you?'

Fancy Phil gave me a who-knows shrug, but was silent. I waited while he buffed the stone of his ring on his white slacks. Then he said: 'If those two girls was in cahoots and this Emily was smart enough to buy a cell phone in some alias –'

'The credit card she used is probably a phony.'

'Sure,' he said offhandedly, as if such methods were kindergarten tactics to him. 'So if she's got the brains to buy a cell phone in a phony name, she and Courtney sure in hell aren't going to trade in their own names.'

'Right. Do you have any idea how they might have done it? Trading the stocks?' I figured Fancy Phil wouldn't get insulted if I assumed he had knowledge of the illegal.

He didn't. 'Maybe do that Internet trading, someplace where they don't ask too many questions. Except that's usually Amateur Hour.'

'Not with these two,' I suggested.

'Yeah, you could be right. If it was me? Offshore corporation.'

'I've read about it, but I don't think I really understand.'

'You could trade in your name: Dr Judith Singer. But if you do that, what's the point? The point is hiding yourself. The way I *heard* it's done' – I couldn't swear, but I think he winked – 'is that you set up a corporation in the Bahamas or Cayman Islands or British Virgins. Okay? You with me? Their laws basically say they can't give out the name of the person or the people behind the corporation. Trust me, it's done all the time. That way, it means the pig people at the IRS can't trace you and those bastards at the SEC can't go for your throat. See, it's the corporation that buys and sells stocks or whatever. No names.'

'But Courtney was murdered. Wouldn't the police or FBI be able to get those islands' governments to give up information on who's behind the corporation?'

'Do I look like a lawyer, sweetheart? But the answer is, even if they get the name or names, what good is it gonna do them if this Emily was smart enough to start the corporation in an alias?'

'Don't you need to show ID to start up a corporation?'

'Yeah, you do. But, Doc, if a lady banker from a good school has got the smarts to figure out how to get a fake credit card, and then has the balls to use it, don't you think she's already got a phony ID? You come up with a halfway decent-looking birth certificate, you got your new identity, and a passport is a piece of cake. It costs, sure, but it can be done.'

'So if we don't know the alias Emily chose to set up the corporation, we'd have a hard time tracing her.'

Fancy Phil's mouth turned down at the edges. He looked as glum as I felt. 'Hard time? Impossible time.'

'You mean even the bank or lawyer or wherever she has the phony corporation won't know who she truly is?' I asked. 'There really would be no way of tracking her down then.'

'Right,' he conceded.

'If Emily set up this corporation to buy the stock, and if she gave Courtney the money to do it for her – beyond whatever money of her own Courtney may also have invested – would both of them have had access to that corporation?'

'Could be,' Fancy Phil said.

'Why wouldn't Emily just use the corporation and bypass Courtney entirely?' I asked. 'I mean, if she created a corporation using a false name and fake ID.'

'Maybe she wasn't convinced that she couldn't be traced. If she was a shy girl, maybe she was scared to go someplace like the Caymans, deal with a local lawyer. Maybe Courtney had more brains about this stuff than this Emily: She'd been at a big place that did international deals. The other girl was stuck in some dipshit town in New Jersey. Or maybe Emily talked over her plan with Courtney and then Courtney put on pressure not to be left out of the deal.'

'Blackmail-type pressure?'

'Could be. She wouldn't have had to say it out loud. No "Include me out and I'll rat to the feds." This Emily would be smart enough to understand without words. Know what I mean? Or maybe they were happy partners in this thing, but each of them set up their own corporation.'

'Why?'

'Because after this deal, Emily planned to disappear. Why else all that business with Australia? Or because even happy

324

partners can learn to hate each other. Or because this Emily was smart enough not to trust Courtney.'

'But then why would she kill Courtney?'

'Because Courtney *knew*.'

'Knew what?'

Fancy Phil took a gum wrapper from his pocket and spit out the wad of gum. 'Courtney knew the money from insider trading existed, right? Courtney knew Emily existed. And Courtney might not have been satisfied with what she got. You told me she lost her interest in that dumb StarBaby after the summer, that she seemed to have her mind on something else. She could have tried to get the hook into Emily for more: "Fork it all over or else."' He wrapped the gum carefully and stuck it in his pants pocket. 'Of course, that's if your story's right: "Once upon a time there was a bad girl named Emily who led a good girl named Courtney down the garden path." You make it sound real possible, even though it's hopeless to find this bitch.'

'Maybe hopeless is too strong a word,' I suggested.

'I said "hopeless" and I mean "hopeless,"' Fancy Phil retorted. 'Shit, I can't believe that little blond pipsqueak Courtney could get messed up with something like this.'

'At least we have a link between these two women, Phil. You can have Greg's lawyer bring it to the cops. For my part, I'm still going to try to dig up more.'

'How?'

'Should I tell you I have secret methods? Or should I tell you I have no idea, but maybe I'll think of something?'

Putting his hands above his knees, Fancy Phil managed to launch himself out of the chair. 'I hope you can think of something. Because remember that wild-goose chase I was worrying about? For my Gregory's sake, let's pray you don't got us both on it.'

After he left, I walked around in a haze, fluffing up the cushions on the club chairs, rearranging perfectly satisfactory arrangements of roses, turning off lamps. Hopeless, he'd said. I couldn't believe this was the end of the line. I trudged into the kitchen to set up the coffee machine so all that would be required of me in the morning would be the push of a button.

When a few lucid thoughts returned, they were random ones: Regret that I'd chosen to investigate murder rather than teach a quickie summer course on the social and intellectual history of the United States, a subject I was completely unqualified to teach (not that that would deter Smarmy Sam). Fear that Nelson would not be proud I'd gotten as far as I had, but rather, disappointed that I'd turned out to be irrevocably second rate at the one thing at which I had hoped to excel.

Then I made myself sick over how awful it was that Emily Chavarria had not only outfoxed me, but the police as well. Greg Logan could still wind up paying for her crime with the rest of his life. When I went to bed (as always on my half, as if lying on Bob's side would be an act of flagrant discourtesy), I fell almost immediately into the deepest sleep.

Arising with the sun, I had an intuitive awareness that something lousy could be happening in my life, much like the way I'd woken up mornings as a teenager when my period was overdue. I could almost hear Fancy Phil's 'hopeless' echoing through the house. I dragged myself into the bathroom, and sparing myself a confrontation with my own image, I turned my back toward the mirror as I brushed my teeth. Who knows what happened next? Maybe the whirr of the electric toothbrush diddled a nerve fiber on some brain cell, or maybe I was just thinking 'teeth.' But teeth led to chew, and chew led to gum, and suddenly my mind's eye was watching Fancy as he spit the gum he'd chewed into a wrapper and then managed to poke it down into the pocket of his too-snug slacks.

Used gum led me to more used gum. I recalled the night I'd called on Greg Logan and how, in taking out my curriculum vitae from my handbag to show him, I'd also pulled out an ancient wad of Trident wrapped in a random piece of paper. The one minuscule globule of moisture left in the gum had glommed on to my CV and I'd almost handed it over to Greg.

What was it about gum? By this time the toothbrush had nearly abraded the enamel of a molar, so I turned off the brush and rinsed my mouth. Gum? I turned on the shower, waited till it went from ice-cold to scalding to its usual lukewarm, and stepped in. Oddly, the thick fog of my melancholy began to lift. No mopey standing under the water hoping to be washed clean of whatever was plaguing me, no sniffling 'I Gotta Right to Sing the Blues' as I soaped up.

It wasn't until I was drying off my nether reaches that I stood up straight and said, 'Oh my God!' Dropping my towel, I pulled my ratty bathrobe off the hook and raced downstairs and into the sunroom. There, in one of those idiotically oversized wicker baskets that look so deceptively felicitous in decorating magazines, was my 'Check it out!'

book bag from the library. I'd stored the evidence from Courtney's closet in it, the stuff I seized the day Fancy Phil took me to the Logans'.

There it was: grape bubble gum. A child-sized piece, not a great wad like Fancy Phil had been chomping on. Still, from what I knew of Courtney, this was not a treat she would allow her daughter. In fact, had she picked up Morgan at her Nuclear Physics Readiness Playgroup and espied her chewing something purple and sweet smelling, she would have said: Spit it out.

Since at that hour the sunroom was not living up to its name, I hurried into the kitchen and examined my find under the brightest light. My memory hadn't failed. The gum was wrapped in the customer's copy of a charge receipt. American Express. Whatever had been bought cost $3,078.62. However, the nature of the purchase and the name of the buyer was stuck to the gum and therefore unreadable. No reason to give up, I thought. The gum could have been so dried out after months in Courtney's cordovan shoulder bag that it would no longer have a gummy nature. I tugged gently on the paper. Nothing.

After turning on the coffee machine, I walked across the room and studied an article I'd clipped years earlier, one of Nancy's first freelance efforts. I'd taped it onto the inside of the door of the broom closet. 'Go, Go Goo,' it was called, with advice for removing common stains, candle wax, and, yes, gum. Naturally, from Kate and Joey, I remembered the ice-cube-on-hair trick, but she'd also recommended putting a gum-ridden object in a plastic bag in the freezer, then chipping the gum away. Or dry-cleaning it. Or using peanut butter as a solvent.

But should I, could I have a go at the evidence? I went to call my lawyer. Kate answered first, then an instant later Adam picked up an extension. From the woolly sound of their voices, I realized they were only moments into the getting-up process. I posed my question anyway. First they both made a huge to-do that *they had nothing at all to do with criminal law* and *I should not rely on them for a legal opinion.* Then their best guess – *and it was only a guess* – was that as long as I was brought into the Logan house by a member of the family who possessed keys and the alarm code, and since I had not done this snooping on behalf of the authorities, it was okay to have the receipt in my possession. I saw no point in mentioning the grape gum. When Adam hung up to get ready for work, Kate said: 'Mom.' Her voice was gentle, maternal.

'What?'

'Consider not doing it.'

'Doing what?'

'Let's put it this way,' she remarked. 'When I was in high school or college, say I called you about having something like this receipt in my possession. If I'd asked vague questions about its legality, and you knew that receipt was either remotely or closely connected with a murder investigation, what would you have said?'

All I could truthfully say to her was: 'I would have said, "Are you nuts, Kate? Leave it alone!"'

'I rest my case,' my daughter said softly.

The minute I hung up, however, I went right back to the degumming dilemma. Peanut butter was a substance, along with bittersweet chocolate, that I dared not allow in the house. Not that I would employ something so blatantly gooey as peanut butter to separate paper from gum. However, I did stick the receipt into a plastic bag, pop it in the freezer, and got busy quartering an orange. I'd only halved it when I retrieved the bag.

What should I do with this evidence? Turn it over to Nelson so he could give it to a police laboratory – if he thought it a lead worth pursuing? That made sense, except the police lab might turn it over to Homicide, and they, in their proven idiocy, might conclude that the Jane Doe who'd bought a $3,078.62 sable boa or whatever had absolutely zero to do with Courtney Logan's murder. Thus the cops would continue on their merry way, looking for a smoking gun to help them nab Greg.

A laboratory, I was thinking as I returned to the orange. A laboratory I could trust. I considered calling Fancy Phil and asking if he knew any drug kingpins and whether they might have a rogue chemist on their payrolls. But what if the kingpin had an unstated beef with my client? Or what if there was a DEA bust and the receipt was seized along with forty-three tons of cocaine? Besides, I concluded, a rogue chemist might not agree to chat with the cops if he/she discovered anything worth pursuing.

It wasn't until a few hours later, when I was in the middle of the householder's chore I most detested, bill paying, that it dawned on me that although I didn't know a lab, I did know a chemist. Jenny McFarland and I had been on a committee to try to improve the lot of adjunct professors. I'd always felt that she and I could have been great friends if not for vast differences in age, politics, religion, marital status, and cultural interests. We disagreed on everything except that we were awfully fond of each other. So I called her at her house in Forest Hills Gardens, in Queens. While I baby-sat for her five children (who were so well behaved I wondered if Jenny had been sprinkling some tranquilizing chemical over their Cocoa Puffs), she drove over to St Elizabeth's to try to separate American Express receipt from grape gum. She didn't even ask why. I'd told her it was important and a personal favor and that was enough for her.

Three hours, six diapers, and untold readings of *Where's My Teddy?* later, Jenny returned with a huge grin and a piece of purple gum in a small, transparent container – as well as a slightly holey, somewhat oily receipt from Louis Vuitton on East Fifty-seventh Street in Manhattan for three-thousand-bucks-plus worth of luggage. For all I knew, that could wind up being one small duffel bag. The lucky owner was not Courtney Logan, not Emily Chavarria, and not Vanessa Russell. Standing beside Jenny, gazing at the receipt, I experienced what the heretofore meaningless cliché – jumping out of one's skin – meant.

'Another name! Samantha R. Corby!' I crowed into my cell phone as I sat in my Jeep in front of Jenny's house. When I explained who Samantha R. was and how I'd learned about her by going into the Logan house, and finding and ungumming the receipt, Nelson threw a fit that included using every curse word he'd learned since fifth grade. I promised him I would go straight home and call no one, especially Fancy Phil, until he came over after work. He ordered me to put the receipt on top of a piece of plain paper, not paper towel, not newspapers, and *leave it alone.*

Well, I needed to get back to what that ass Warren G. Harding called a 'return to normalcy.' When I got home,

I returned to my month's stack of bills and praised myself for being, unlike Samantha R., so restrained a consumer. I spent the rest of the day pruning whatever tree or bush happened to get in my way. Then I sat on the patio listening to Louis Armstrong and Ella Fitzgerald sing together. When they got to 'I Won't Dance,' I thought how easy it was to say that in song, how hard in life. I was dancing. Having started again with this man I felt I'd been born to dance with, what was going to happen to me? An endless adulterous whirl? A gentlemanly thank-you to me as the song ended, then a return to the lady he'd brought to the ball? It wasn't that I was trying to avoid thinking about the receipt. The truth was after so many years of lifelessness, I was so overstimulated I couldn't think straight.

The last thing on my mind was sex — except around five-thirty I admit I did take a second shower, then spritzed a little Femme in strategic areas. But having exhausted myself thinking about my future or the lack of it, I somehow found the energy to obsess about the case again, trying to figure out a way to discover if 'Vanessa Russell' or 'Samantha R. Corby' had left any trace at all. I couldn't imagine calling some banker in the Bahamas and saying: Listen, I know you're not supposed to give out information on your depositors, but could you make an exception in this case because I'm a nice person? I don't need much, just the address where you send the statements.

A little after six, I opened the door for Nelson. His slow step over the threshold and his pulling me toward him in the most leisurely way was a clue I didn't have to be a detective to decipher. I was about to suggest Work first, play later, but the warm path his hand made as it snaked under my blouse and made its way up my back changed my mind.

The only awkward half-moment was when we reached the top of the stairs. I realized I couldn't bring him into my bedroom. God knows why. Rationally, I knew Bob's ghost would not suddenly materialize in his customary stance – arms crossed over chest, lips compressed in vexation. Still, I stood unmoving, until Nelson suggested quietly: 'How about one of your kids' rooms, or a guest room or something?' I led him into my office, where I took *Mr Truman's War: The Final Victories of World War II and the Birth of the Postwar World* off the couch. We made such splendid love that when it was finally over, I virtually floated down the stairs, back to the American Express receipt on a piece of white printer paper on the kitchen counter.

I didn't mention I'd already made two copies of it and put one of them in the mailbox to Fancy Phil. As *Cosmopolitan* used to instruct us girls in the sixties, there's no need to tell your man everything. The two of us gazed down at the receipt. I said: 'Now don't tell me getting out the grape gum is a felony with a minimum ten-year sentence at a maximum-security institution because I won't believe it.'

But Nelson wasn't listening. He was mechanically buttoning his shirt and staring at the receipt. 'This is the place for the expensive pocketbooks, right?' he asked.

'Right.'

'And you found this in one of Courtney Logan's pocketbooks.'

'Yes. In a shoulder bag. Not a Vuitton. Nice leather, though, if I remember correctly.'

'Let's get back to this.' Nelson pointed to the receipt.

'Either the card she used was a fake or stolen or a legitimate card she got using a false name. Unless it turns out it was Emily's card, and Courtney just happened to pick up that receipt. Or maybe there really is a Samantha R. Corby around, and when the kid or whoever spit out the gum, Courtney just picked up that piece of paper.'

'They're all possibilities,' I agreed. 'But listen, Nelson. Under normal circumstances, you get a receipt, you put it in your bag. It's yours. If you're insanely organized you keep it. Or you throw it out when you get home. But most of the time a receipt just lives there for a while, until spring-cleaning or whatever. Now, if you're preoccupied with more important things – the way Courtney was after the summer – and you catch your kid chewing gum, you reflexively wrap it up in whatever you've got – a tissue or in any piece of paper you've thrown into your handbag.'

'So you're saying that in your opinion, most likely Samantha R. and Courtney are one and the same.'

'Well, this isn't a normal situation, what with suburban women being missing or getting murdered and fake credit cards and questionable stock trades and all that, but still, yes, in my opinion they're one and the same.'

'So how come' – he broke down and borrowed my reading glasses – 'how come it says "Luggage" here?'

'Because they sell luggage, too,' I explained.

'Courtney was murdered on the thirty-first?'

'That's right.'

'Doesn't it strike you as funny,' Nelson said, 'that six days before she was killed, at a time of year hardly anyone takes a vacation, and a little too early for Christmas shopping, she was buying luggage? Where was she planning to go?'

Chapter Sixteen

I beamed at Nelson. 'You can find out where Courtney was planning to go!' Standing motionless about two feet apart in front of the cabinet where I stored my mixing bowls and baking gear, we were gazing down again at the American Express receipt. I'm not sure why we couldn't seem to move from it – whether we were still awed at finding that rectangle of paper that could prove a memento of Courtney Logan's secret life or if each believed the other would make a grab for the receipt and run like hell: him to police headquarters, me to Fancy Phil.

'What do you mean, I can find out?'

'I mean, don't you have a number to call and get a printout of whatever charges were on that card?'

His eyebrows strained toward each other. He couldn't figure out how come I was asking a question that had such an obvious answer. 'Of course I do.' If he'd been his children's age, he would have said Duh.

'I don't get you,' I told him. 'I know it's not your unit, and maybe if this case gets solved you won't get enough credit, or any credit. But don't you have an overwhelming need to know? *Now?*'

'My sweetheart,' Nelson said sweetly. He'd always been

a lot of good things – thoughtful, friendly, intuitive, tender, fair. Loving, too. But sweet he wasn't.

'What's the bad news?'

He put his arm on my shoulder and pulled me close so my head bent to his shoulder, the kind of playful embrace football players give each other. 'Judith,' he said so warmheartedly that I immediately understood why a criminal would confess to him. 'I've already done much more than I ought to. Going to New Jersey, checking Emily's phone records, the cell phone purchase. And then talking to you about them. You may not think so, but I've gone out on a limb.'

I pulled away not so much in anger, though I was less than delighted, but because I couldn't converse with my neck stretched out and my head resting on a shoulder that felt surprisingly bony for a guy with actual muscles. 'I know you have. I appreciate it. I'm grateful for the faith you have in me.'

Thankfully, he dropped the sweetie-pie and good-buddy acts. 'I haven't told my guys in Homicide how come I'm so interested in the Logan case. They think it's because of the Phil Lowenstein connection, or because I miss the unit so much. I definitely haven't told Carl Gevinski. He's the asshole in charge of the investigation. It's been just you and you alone.'

I leaned against the cabinet, but far enough from the receipt that he'd be assured I couldn't execute a deft spin and snatch, though I suspect he knew that for me, deft was not an applicable adjective. 'I don't know what to say, Nelson. The last thing I want is for you to get into trouble on my account. And I understand that it probably wouldn't look good for you to be consorting with a person who has ties to Fancy Phil, a guy involved in a case you're investigating – although obviously that could be explained.'

'Explained is one thing. Believed is another.'

'I don't want you to compromise your integrity or your livelihood.'

'I know that.'

'The only solution I can think of is to let you call the shots if you can promise me an honest and thorough reinvestigation of Courtney's murder. If you can't, I have a responsibility to Phil and his son –' He didn't like the last remark. He slammed his hands down into his pockets and began one of his staring contests. 'If you can't share any of this information with me, then I'll write up whatever I already have and let Phil turn everything over to Greg's lawyer.' Naturally, he was still looking directly into my eyes. Supposedly with men the staring business is about who gets to be the alpha male, but since I was willing to yield to Nelson the right to the biggest chunk of woolly mammoth, I didn't have to feel like a bug-eyed fool. So I signaled my beta status by glancing back at the receipt. Nevertheless, I wasn't about to forgo my argument. 'Greg and his attorney have an absolute right to know what I've found,' I informed him. 'Look, she won't like it; no criminal lawyer is going to be thrilled that Fancy Phil has had a secret, parallel investigation going on, except her detective hasn't produced any miracles. But chances are, the guy being a pro, he has a contact at American Express who's either sympathetic or bribable. He can find out what Samantha R. was buying before Halloween.'

While Nelson stayed in the kitchen to make some calls, I went upstairs to slip into something more comfortable, which in my case was a pair of baggy navy shorts (my legs being fairly sensational until three inches above my knees), a big white shirt, sleeves rolled up, and thongs. Still, I didn't know if Nelson was staying or going until I came back down and saw him standing before the open refrigerator with a bunch of tired parsley in his hand. 'Believe it or not,' he told me, 'you have a better refrigerator than most single women.'

'That's because I eat more than most single women. Are you cooking?'

'Sure.' Right after high school, Nelson had gone into the air force and been assigned to a stove instead of a jet fighter. He bragged his most brilliant dish was barbecued chicken for three hundred, though he'd always claimed he could pull together a decent meal for a smaller group, like two.

'What are you making?' I asked.

'Pasta with a sauce made out of whatever you got.' He pulled out an onion, a stray clove of garlic, and a red pepper so old it had imploded upon itself, then opened the freezer and discovered half a French bread I had no memory of buying, eating, or serving.

'How do you know so much about single women's refrigerators?' I asked.

'From when I was between marriages. And you know, on the job.'

With that cheerful thought, I got busy setting the table. 'Do you know what I'm thinking?' I asked.

'You're going to tell me, aren't you? Where do you hide your canned tomatoes?'

I pointed to the pantry and said: 'About Emily. That Josh Kincaid I told you about, the one who'd worked with Courtney at Patton Giddings, who met Emily at a real estate closing? The way he described her –'

'"Her" meaning Emily?'

'Yes. He made her sound so bland and quiet that she must have been close to invisible. I guess she had a good relationship with the bank's big client, that Saf-T guy. But I don't know about other relationships. When I spoke to her mother, she didn't know anything about Emily's friends. Maybe there weren't many, or any. By the way, the mother was not from the big conversationalists, to put it mildly. And Emily's neighbors, that nice young couple you spoke to also – Beth and Roberto – their description was of someone really quiet or extremely shy.'

As Nelson was opening the cans of peeled tomatoes, I got to thinking that this sort of intimacy was probably more threatening to my peace of mind than the sex part of the relationship. Such welcome coziness, and from the very man I'd yearned to be cozy with for much of my adult life. I recalled that in the first years after we parted, I'd often excuse myself when the family was watching TV together in the evening and go upstairs to a bathroom, lock the door, and sob. 'So what about her being quiet or shy or unassertive or whatever?' he asked. 'How many hundreds of times have you seen neighbors of a guy who's just gunned down ten people being interviewed? They all say, "But he was such a nice, quiet person." Quiet people kill. Shy people kill.'

'I know. But it's so weird to me to have to think of someone that retiring as a criminal mastermind. Look, she accepted the glass ceiling at work. Her whole career she'd been at only one job, and it didn't sound like a particularly thrilling one.'

'Not everybody is ambitious.'

'I know that. She could have done better, but she stayed and stayed in a boring, safe job. Sure, maybe that was how she was, someone who didn't like challenges. But that's what's so amazing, that she plotted this whole criminal scam, using insider information. She had Courtney, or Courtney and some offshore corporation, buying the stock low and selling it high.'

I had to give him credit; he could listen and chop the onion with the boldness of a television chef at the same time. 'First of all, my sweetheart, this is just your theory. It could be that Emily Chavarria and Courtney Logan met each other at that women's thing in Baltimore and became friendly. The reason Emily called Courtney a few days before Halloween was that she was going to a party and couldn't decide whether to go as Snow White or the Seventh Dwarf.'

'I know it's just a theory,' I conceded. 'Anyone could have killed Courtney. Greg, the au pair, the high-school classmate who wound up taking the blame for the candy-bar-money theft, Mr or Mrs Fancy Phil, the guy who built and serviced the Logans' pool. Just give me another theory that fits as many facts as mine does. I'll be glad to consider it.' He turned away to think and chop.

All I wanted to do was stand there and watch him, so I made myself go upstairs to my office. I got on-line and did one of those People Searches. A few Vanessa Russells, though I sensed none of them was Emily since killers probably prefer unlisted numbers. Still, I printed out the page.

I pushed back from the desk to avoid one of my flake-out attacks: I'd begin at a music site ordering a Sinatra CD, wind up reading personal accounts by Japanese-Americans of life in internment sites during World War II, then shut down the computer having no memory of why I'd turned it on in the first place. Focus, I ordered myself: Even a big baby like Josh Kincaid had landed himself a job at Patton Giddings. True, after a year he'd been asked to leave, but if he hadn't had the family mortgage company to fall back on, he probably could have chosen from a couple of non-dead-end, semi-interesting jobs in finance. I had no idea how much discrimination against women there was in the field, but even assuming a great deal, Emily might have gotten out of the Red Oak Bank and gone elsewhere. Well, I thought, maybe she had a mad crush on an unattainable man there and couldn't bear to leave. Or maybe, despite having the Mr Saf-T seal of approval and thus kept on by Red Oak, she was a noticeably dim bulb or a bad egg nobody else would hire.

The aroma of sautéing onions wafted into the room and I felt myself getting teary – not from the onions but from the perfection of having Nelson in my house and the knowledge that sooner or later he'd be leaving for his own. For his wife. From wife, it was just my usual happy hop to contemplating the possibility that she'd decide on a late-in-life baby – Surprise, honey! – thus guaranteeing their marriage for the next twenty or so years.

I pulled my chair back to the computer and typed in 'Samantha R. Corby.' Eight S. Corbys, with addresses and phone numbers. I printed out that page, too, then switched to a general search engine and gave 'Samantha R. Corby' a shot. Nothing, which didn't cause me to reel with shock. However, knowing the mindless literalness of computers, I typed in 'Samantha Corby.' One item came up.

I double-clicked and there I was, at the Web site of the Wiggins, Idaho, *Star*, a newspaper that made the *Shorehaven Beacon* read like the *Christian Science Monitor*. Right there, in the November 19, 1999, issue, in a small box titled 'Welcome New Neighbor!' between 'Arlene and Arnold Chester' and 'Dr and Mrs Alwyn Rossi' was 'Samantha Corby.' I had no idea of what to do next, but since no mellifluous calls of 'Dinner!' were rising up the stairs, I pulled up a map of Idaho and made Wiggins the center of that universe. Just a few millimeters above it, a direction some might call north, past towns called Bellevue, Hailey, and Ketchum was Sun Valley. Resort, I thought. Famous resort. Hadn't some Olympics been held there?

I got on the phone. The woman at the *Star*, who sounded as if she might be the paper's entire staff – or the only one there so late in the day – said the names for 'Welcome New Neighbor!' came from local real estate brokers. She gave me a few numbers. I kept making calls until Nelson bellowed: 'Ready when you are!'

I came down bubbling about my Samantha Corby discovery. 'Could be,' Nelson said, actually pulling out a kitchen chair for me.

Whatever parsley he hadn't used he'd stuck in a glass and set it on the table as the centerpiece. 'When Steffi talked about the woman she saw leaving the Logans', the woman who might be Emily,' I said a few minutes later as

I pierced a couple of pieces of fusilli, 'she described her as a little gray mouse.' Busy admiring either my shirt or my cleavage, Nelson nodded in a polite, uninterested way that was almost husbandly. I thought I deserved a little more heed, having already lauded his tomato sauce at length, with absolute sincerity. He was a natural cook, at home in any kitchen. He'd even discovered my vegetable patch and picked some lettuce and radishes for the salad. 'Nelson.'

'What?'

'I want you to pay a lot of attention to me right now.' He smiled, nodded okay, took a bite of the garlic bread he'd made, then refilled our glasses from the bottle of red wine I always kept on hand for Nancy so she wouldn't get d.t.'s or bitchy or whatever. 'Okay,' I said, 'remember "little gray mouse," but put it on the shelf for a minute.'

'It's on the shelf. I'm listening, Judith. I'm fascinated by everything you say.'

'Good.' I made a big deal of clearing my throat, probably because I wasn't completely clear about what I was going to say and I guess I wanted Nelson to approve of every syllable. You think you get to a point in life when other people's opinions don't matter. You are who you are; you won't be destroyed if someone doesn't like you or mocks your ideas. I knew Nelson liked me – loved me – and he wasn't going to laugh his head off if he thought I was wrong. He'd say straight out that he disagreed with me. At best he'd be kind. At worst, polite. Sure, if I'd say something blatantly idiotic he'd respond with 'Give me a break,' but I knew he was well aware I wasn't a blatant idiot.

'Come on,' he said encouragingly.

'To me, it seems that when you're searching for the

whodunit in a murder case, you have to have the pertinent facts. But if the facts aren't enough to help you to solve it, you also have to search out the emotional or psychological truth. I keep thinking about the sort of person Courtney was and I keep coming up with the feeling there was something fundamentally wrong with her.'

'Homicide victims are dead because someone perpetrated a crime against them,' Nelson retorted. 'They're no better or worse than anybody else. Saints get murdered. So do monsters. If you're right about Courtney, she was involved in a serious mess. She was greedy, arrogant, and a lousy judge of character.'

'Right, but let me go on from this. At first I thought of her as a perfectionist, but I think it's equally about control. She wanted to be in charge. She was the one who set the rules. No sugar for the kids. Only an hour of TV. The au pair had to wait until after the kids were asleep before she could watch television in her own room. The young woman who did the videography for StarBaby told me that until Courtney lost interest, Courtney practically breathed for her. She didn't hire an interior decorator the way a lot of women in her economic class do. She did it herself. Perfectionism or control, but nothing was left undone. The chandelier in the front hall: it had teeny lampshades over each bulb, and each shade had a scalloped trim. She lined the bathroom wastebasket with a doily.'

'I can't believe someone thought she deserved to die for that,' Nelson said.

'No. That's not why Mack Dooley got a big surprise when he took off the pool cover. But before I get to that, let's talk about how other people saw Courtney. Greg? He's not going to say he hated her. There's no way of knowing what he felt. The same with the au pair. She seems to have genuinely idolized Courtney, but if she had a mad pash for Greg, requited or unrequited, she's not going to tell me that Courtney was a domineering pain in the ass.'

'Do you have a mad pash for me?' he asked.

'No, I'm just toying with you until I can find something better.'

'That's what I figured you'd say.'

'Courtney was pretty, or at least cute, kind of a Princeton amalgam of Sandra Dee and June Allyson.' Nelson laughed, but then he'd always reacted that way to my movie analogies, so I flicked my hand to brush him off. 'But so many people seemed to think there was something not right about her.

'First and foremost, that woman she went to high school with, Ingrid Farrell. Ingrid took the hit when Courtney stole that candy-bar money. It's really not a juvenile prank, because everyone believed Ingrid was guilty. Even Ingrid's parents believed she'd done it, and so they made restitution. The cloud of that incident has been hanging over her ever since. It was a terrible thing for Courtney to do. Okay, next: Jill Badinowski, one of StarBaby's clients: She described Courtney as being an ice-cold businesswoman, that she could be selling videos of babies or poison gas, it made no difference. Fancy Phil told me that if you looked for personality in Courtney, it wasn't there. He described her as *lukshen*, Yiddish for noodles.'

'Noddles are a no-no?'

'No, they're a yes-yes, but plain, without seasoning or sauce, they're really blah. So Fancy Phil saw Courtney as bland. On the other hand, he recognized how manipulative she was, trying to get him to buy whatever she and her husband couldn't afford: a Land Rover, a super-duper TV. She even tried getting Fancy to buy her a sable coat.'

'So what are you saying?' Nelson wasn't challenging me, just trying to find out where I was going.

'I'm not one hundred percent sure yet. What does it sound like to you?'

'I don't know. So far, what strikes me is that candy-bar thing. I know I kidded you about it, but it's not cute or pretty. It stinks. The sable coat is pushy, but it's not the end of the world.'

'One of the women in her group of about seven or eight mothers of little kids didn't really know Courtney very well. But she was very smart, very insightful, plus she used a movie analogy in describing Courtney.'

'Always a sign of high intelligence,' Nelson observed.

'Of genius. She compared Courtney to a pod person in *The Invasion of the Body Snatchers*, just a shell of a person, drained of all humanity.' I waited for a laugh or a good-natured shake of his head, but he merely sipped his wine and waited. 'Zee Friedman, the videographer, said that when little Travis came into the room while they were talking, Courtney got this blissed-out look on her face, like a Madonna. And when Greg came home from playing golf, Courtney acted as if he were the hottest guy in the world.'

'What's wrong with that?'

'I love my kids with all my heart and soul,' I said, 'but when they were little and came running into the room and interrupted what I was doing, believe me, it wasn't Mary and Jesus time. And after you're married for six or seven years or whatever, and you're with a business associate, you don't get all steamed up when your husband comes home. The au pair picked up on it, too; she said when Greg was around, Courtney acted like a bride on her wedding day. And her best friend Kellye Ryan noticed the "Ooh, isn't he hot?" bit. She didn't buy it for a minute. In fact, she thought Courtney was having an affair – although she's a minority of one. Most everyone else didn't see her as sexual at all.' I rested my head against the back of the chair. 'Is she coming through clearly to you yet?'

'No.'

'Cecile Rabiea, who came to Patton Giddings the same time Courtney did, said her work was good, but she wasn't able to go the full route, to court the client, help the client. It wasn't that she was lazy, it's that somehow she couldn't get the human element right.'

'Fine, but she's still not clear.'

'Courtney didn't comprehend other people's needs, not really. She could have been immature or insensitive. On the other hand, she could have been seriously deficient or defective. And another thing: She wasn't showing people her true colors. Maybe she didn't have any colors. Too many people described her in terms of being slightly off. You know, like a pretty good actress playing roles like wife, mother, neighbor, investment banker. When you're talking about a person's essence, a pretty good imitation isn't good enough. That's why people were struck that there was something off about her.'

'Where you taking this, Judith?'

'Where do you think I'm taking this?'

With his fork he made tracks through the tomato sauce on his plate, around, rather than through, the pasta. 'That Courtney was some kind of . . . Whatever they're calling it these days. Psychopath? Sociopath?'

'I think so. I know I shouldn't take that one incident with the Crunch-Munch sale in high school as emblematic, but it showed a coldness that's scary.'

'But that's not fair to Courtney. She isn't around any-more to defend herself.'

'I know. But if she were a sociopath, she'd probably be articulate and have a smooth defense – the way she convinced her high-school principal that Ingrid Farrell stole the Crunch-Munch money. Courtney didn't have a conscience.'

'How do you know?' he insisted. 'If she did steal the money, maybe it was bothering her all these years. What could she have done? Gone back to wherever she came from – Washington – and confessed? That's not realistic. She had a husband, kids, a position in the community.'

'I know. Stable family life. And she wasn't violent or argumentative the way a lot of wackos are.'

'Right,' Nelson said.

'But if she's turned out to be such a good person, full of remorse but unable to apologize without jeopardizing everything, then how come she got involved with Emily?'

Nelson reached out and put his hand over mine. 'But that's just a theory, Judith. All you have on that is that when Emily was supposedly on vacation, the cell phone that was used to call her office was also used to call Courtney's house. And also that about six years ago the two of them went to the same conference in Baltimore.'

I set down my fork so I could cover his hand. 'A hand sandwich,' I noted. He smiled. 'I know you're being kind, Nelson. Thank you.'

We took our hands back. 'It's okay.' His tone was gentle. 'Listen, don't be hard on yourself. Nobody, including me, would want to give Phil Lowenstein bad news.'

'I want to give you another theory.'

'Sure.'

'It's about little women,' I began. 'Not the book –'

'The movie?'

'Be quiet. You know, I saw pictures of Courtney in the papers and on TV. She wasn't a beauty, but she was really good to look at.' Nelson nodded cautiously. 'Then I went to try and convince Greg to hire me, and don't shake your head and mumble "I can't believe you did that." I did it. Period. End of discussion.'

'Not quite. You were a jerk to do that, Judith, knocking on the door of someone who's pretty obviously a murder suspect. Now it's end of discussion.'

'Fine. Anyway, I was sitting in his living room and on the table next to me was a framed photograph of Greg and Courtney in tennis clothes. They looked adorable together. Both were clean-cut, athletic looking, but there were nice contrasts, too. He's dark, she's fair. He's tall, she's short. I remember, her head was resting against his chest. Actually, he's not all that tall. She was just short. My guess is about five-feet-one or so.'

Nelson swirled the wine in his glass. 'Uh-huh.'

'So I was thinking again about that picture. And also, when I went through her closet, which I don't want to dwell on because just the thought of it probably makes your cop hackles rise, whatever hackles are. Anyhow, her shoes were a size six.'

'Well, that solves the case, doesn't it?'

'You know who else was short? Emily. When Beth and Roberto were talking about her, they said she only had one suitcase for her trip. He offered to put it in her trunk because she was, you know, a little woman, but she said she could manage. And remember the "little gray mouse" Steffi talked about?'

'Where are you going?' he demanded. 'Do you think she was carrying body parts or gold bars in the suitcase and didn't want anyone to feel how much it weighed? Or she had little bitty Courtney inside? Maybe Courtney went to buy apples but then drove down to New Jersey and Emily, who hadn't gone to Australia, killed her, then brought her back to Long Island and slipped the body into the pool.' His manner wasn't sarcastic, but tough-minded, the devil's advocate.

'No, I'm not saying that.'

'Good.'

'I'll get there, Nelson. Just hear me out. Emily had brown hair. But after the summer, she started letting it grow. And voilà! It started getting blonder. Beth told me she suddenly looked like she had some life in her face.'

'A boyfriend?'

'Could be. Or maybe she was all charged up about the new life she was going to have, financed by whatever scheme she and Courtney had cooked up, and yes, Nelson, I know it's just a theory. Here's another theory: Maybe Courtney was giving her a makeover.'

'Okay.'

'Little Courtney was making over Little Emily to look like Little Courtney.'

He was gazing right at me, but this time it was no staring contest. He was looking for an answer. I think he was close to realizing what I was trying to say, except he was slowed down by simultaneously reasoning it out and thinking of reasons why I couldn't be right. 'What are you trying to say? What do you think was going on?'

'I think Courtney was creating a substitute Courtney. I think the body in the pool –'

'Impossible!'

'– is Emily Chavarria.'

Chapter Seventeen

'Don't just say "impossible." Think about it,' I pleaded with Nelson. 'Emily coming to Shorehaven and shooting Courtney doesn't make sense.'

'It makes a hell of a lot more sense than –'

'I'm talking about character. Personality. Whatever you want to call it. When I found out there was an Emily and decided there could be a link, I thought, Hot damn! She did the dastardly deed. But the more I learned about her, the less likely she seemed to be capable of carrying off this kind of a murder and cover-up.'

'What about the money side of this, if there was one?' Nelson asked. 'Was Emily capable of that?'

'Intellectually, without a doubt. But I bet even there, Courtney took over and was calling the shots. But what Emily did or didn't have is find-outable. Even if all her money disappeared from her bank and brokerage accounts, you can find out how much was in them and when she took it out.'

'You think her timing for withdrawing everything would have to be before that bigger company took over Saf-T-Close?' He seemed not so much attentive as tolerant, letting me express myself.

So I did. 'Sure, she wanted to get all she could to buy that stock she knew was going to go way up. But forget her for a second. Look at Courtney. She was assertive, she was ambitious. She was athletic, for God's sake. Do you think Emily the mouse would have been strong enough to kill a Courtney wherever and then get the body into the pool?' He was shaking his head: pure speculation. 'Give me a break, Nelson, come on.'

'I'm giving you a break, believe me. But what do you want me to do? Throw out any rational thought that comes into my head because it doesn't fit your theory?'

'No. Not at all. Just give me a little more time.' It struck me that the request for more time might sound obsequious or pathetic, as in 'Don't go home to your wife yet.' To make up for that, I heard myself breaking into my I-am-Woman-hear-me-roar voice that was so thunderous I unnerved myself. 'Listen to me! Emily was obviously struggling with that suitcase.' I quieted down a bit. 'That's why Roberto offered to help her. She wasn't that strong. But I bet if you check out Courtney some more, you'll find out she could lift . . . whatever Emily weighed.'

Nelson pushed his chair away from the kitchen table, sat back, and crossed his legs in that triangle shape men make, so their privates remain on display in case anyone has doubts. He gave his mouth a curl to the side that I knew meant: I hate to say this, but . . . 'Fingerprints, Judith. Remember fingerprints? The ones in Courtney's house and car they got after she was missing match the prints they were able to get from the body.' I started clearing the table, not to run away from the conversation but to organize my thoughts. 'And another thing,' he said.

'What?' He drew back his lips and tapped on his teeth. They appeared to be in good shape. 'Teeth?' I said. 'Oh, you mean the dental records.'

'They seem to go with the teeth from the body in Courtney's pool.'

I made a big deal of putting the leftover pasta in a plastic container so he'd know I'd cherish it for days to come. I was beginning to see why prudence suggests not mixing romance and business; it's hard to think straight when desire and pique mix. 'Don't worry,' I said, too brightly for my taste, 'I can fit all of this into my grand synthesis of unprovable hypotheses.'

He lifted his glass in a toast. 'I'm a good listener.'

'Think about the little gray mouse again. She was in Courtney's house.' Seeing he was about to interrupt, I added: 'Okay, she *may* have been in Courtney's house. I bet if you gave Steffi some more pictures of Emily she could identify her even more positively.'

'So Courtney did what?' Nelson inquired tactfully. 'Wiped every surface in the house so only Emily's prints would be there?'

'Probably, although I'll bet if Nassau County's finest had really been conscientious, they would have found other little prints from some other little adult. Don't forget, when they picked up those prints, they were looking for a missing person, not a murder victim. And they probably did it days or even weeks after Courtney disappeared.'

'We'll never know, will we?'

'Maybe not.'

'What about the car?' Less tactful now, and on the road to bluntness.

'The car . . .' I said slowly.

'Because you yourself told me the au pair said that gray mouse who might be Emily . . . Her car was in the driveway.'

'That doesn't mean she didn't drive Courtney's car some other time. Look, I'm Courtney, okay? I don't want my own prints on my car. So I wipe the steering wheel, the window buttons, the gearshift, the seat belts, the car seat for the kid really, really well. What else? Oh, the door handles, inside and out, the back gate on an SUV. Now every time I use it, I either wear gloves or something over all my fingertips. Pieces of Band-Aid or something.' He mumbled either 'genius' or 'ingenious' in a sardonic tone which I naturally ignored. 'I also have my husband drive it,' I continued. 'But at some point I ask Emily to drive. Maybe instead of going for apples I met her in a central location and said, "Hey, I've been driving car pools all day. Give me a break," or some such thing. So to the Missing Persons cops, the Land Rover will look like a normal family car because the parents' prints will be up front and the kids' and their friends' prints will be all over the back. No prints from a kidnapper or carjacker or killer or whoever supposedly snatched Courtney.'

'I like that,' he said. 'Very creative.'

'Oh, go stuff it!'

'You're making Courtney out to be a master criminal.'

'No, not a master criminal, but a damn good one. Why not, Nelson? If I can imagine all this, she certainly should be capable. She's a *magna cum laude* graduate of Princeton. That means she was more than smart in college. She was organized. Meticulous. You could see it in her house. Everything was *done*. Every lampshade was the platonic ideal of that particular kind of lampshade. She had botanical prints matted and framed and hung on a ribbon. There wasn't one empty table; every single knickknack was planned, not too many, not too few, size and color-coordinated. It was a flawless, soulless house.'

He rose from the table and kissed me just as I was coming up from fighting with a bowl that didn't want to go in the bottom dishwasher rack. 'Is that it,' he asked, 'or is there more?'

The night before, when I'd momentarily wakened for a bathroom intermission, I'd promised myself that whatever happened in this relationship, I was going to behave like a grown woman – not a middle-aged girl. No innuendos. No cutesy hints. I would not refer obliquely to his marriage in the hopes he'd respond with a declaration that included the words 'getting a divorce' and 'redecorate your big bedroom upstairs.' If I wanted to discuss his status, I'd promised myself, then I had to say it straight.

Thus, I stifled the emerging Are-you-sure-you-have-time-and-don't-have-to-get-home? and told him: 'I've got a lot more.' We sat back at the table, clear now except for the glass of parsley. 'The gift Courtney had for analysis, for looking at all the angles of a problem, was sharpened at Patton Giddings. Numbers crunching, evaluating businesses. Remember, her work was good. It was her people skills that didn't make the grade.'

'Okay, but what about the dental records?' He caught the look in my eyes. 'Oh no. Don't tell me you're going to say she switched them, Judith Eve Bernstein Singer.'

'She did switch them, Nelson Lawrence Sharpe. The X

rays that they slip into those cards? Emily's has got to be in Courtney's and vice versa. I bet if you locate Courtney's dentist, you'll find a new female patient . . . probably in September or early October. A new patient who was about Courtney's height, with blond streaks, a little younger than Courtney. Is that creative, too?'

He had that annoying tender look people give to klutzy, big-footed puppies. 'Yes.'

'Good,' I responded. 'Well, we can solve this difference of opinion very easily.'

'Excellent. How?'

'Get Courtney's dental records from Olympia, Washington. I bet they won't match the teeth on the body. Or Emily's records from Leesford, Oklahoma. They will match.'

'Jesus H. Christ,' he said softly, and shifted in his seat. Now he was looking away from me, viewing the wall with my arrangement of framed California fruit-crate labels, although I don't think he saw them. After what seemed a long time but was probably only a minute, he turned back to me. 'I don't know what to say. This is a theory. A long shot.'

'What's the downside? You annoy a couple of dentists?'

'I'd need a subpoena to get those records. And this is an interstate matter.'

'Can't you wangle a subpoena? Or just make a call and be charming?'

'I'm not charming.'

'You are, too.'

'I've got to think about it,' he stated with finality. Then he stood.

'By the way, Nelson, there may be another way to solve our difference of opinion.'

Maybe he thought I was being too overbearing, or attempting to keep him from leaving. Still, he behaved kindly, even indulgently. 'I'm still listening.' He even smiled.

'All that fingerprint evidence and the teeth business are considered conclusive, right?' I asked.

'In a lot of cases.'

'So did anyone on the Logan case bother to compare DNA from the body with DNA from Morgan or Travis?'

Nelson sat back down. 'Oh shit!' he replied.

By the time he left, he was still wavering. Though taken with what I had to say, he was not completely convinced that he hadn't fallen for a story, my diverting fusion of random facts. Nevertheless, he was intrigued by the Courtney–Emily link: the Baltimore meeting; the cell phone that had made calls to Emily's office and Courtney's house; the possible identification of Emily by Steffi Deissenburger. He was aching to bust open the case. But I'd studied the FDR years long enough to have a pretty good feel for politics. I understood that the last thing Nelson would do was go out on a limb and risk making a fool of himself in front of the department's top brass and the new chief of Homicide.

The next couple of days were rough. I was never much good at waiting around for things to happen, but I didn't dare try anything rash. So I kept a lid on it. Just to show Fancy Phil I was still on the case, I had another breakfast with him. Raisin Bran for me. For him, two stacks of pancakes, a plate of French toast. His morning jewelry was a ring with a giant seal that looked as if it had been snitched from the Vatican, and a double length of huge gold chain links that might have been a combo of jewelry/equipment for a sex game I did not want to envision. I kept my Emily-in-pool theory to myself, but reported to Fancy that I was pursuing leads on the two women in both Shorehaven and Cherry Hill.

Nelson called mid-afternoon. I could hear him trying to keep the excitement out of his voice. He'd been able to get a copy of Samantha Corby's charges from an ex-cop he knew who was now working in the compliance department of American Express. Heavy-duty purchases in the best of the best stores in Manhattan during October, a car rental there, and meals at some pretty tony restaurants. For a few minutes I puzzled over why she hadn't shopped locally, then realized, given her spending habits, she couldn't pass herself off as Samantha Corby on the north shore of Long Island, being well known already as Lady Bountiful, aka Courtney Logan. Among the other charges were some first-class tickets to Miami and a hefty Miami hotel bill. I couldn't believe she had the gall or carelessness not to worry about running into someone from her New York life there. Then to – *Bingo!* – Nevis in the British Virgin Islands for two days. Offshore whatever! I gloated. Visiting her money! Nelson countered with: How about scuba diving? After that interlude, Samantha Corby had gone back to the Miami area, to Key Biscayne, for two weeks, then on to Boise, Idaho – about one hundred fifty miles away from Sun Valley – where she spent over four thousand dollars on ski gear.

'The charges stop the end of December,' Nelson said.

'What?' Since he wouldn't fax me the list of charges, I'd been cradling the phone between ear and shoulder and scribbling notes as fast as I could. 'What do you think happened?'

'I don't know.'

'But you have a theory.'

'Come on, Judith,' he said. 'I can't stay on with you. I've got a lot to do.'

'What's your theory, and don't give me your I'm-being-tolerant sigh. Why no charges after December?'

'If there's actually a Samantha R. Corby – and so far there isn't any – I'd say she overdid it on her Christmas spending and needed time to recoup.'

'But if it's Courtney?'

'Then she could be as smart as you think. All the American Express bills were paid in full.'

'Why is that smart?' I asked, musing if I was a sociopath and had no qualms about murder, I could probably live with stiffing Neiman Marcus.

'Because if you're going to get lost, you pay your bills. The last thing you want are bill collectors or skip tracers hunting you down. They stay at it longer than cops can and they have more money to search with.'

'Then what happened after December?' I asked.

'You know as much as I do.'

'No, Nelson, you know more. You're a detective.'

'I thought that's what you are.'

'Don't banter with me now. I'm not in a bantering mood. Just tell me what you think.'

'If it's Courtney? She's either dead or, more likely,

using another name. And if she dropped Samantha, which would be super-cautious but also super-smart, she probably dropped Sun Valley, too.'

All that kept me from going into a complete funk was the belief that even if Courtney had gotten away, there remained the possibility of clearing Greg Logan of the murder charge that had been hounding him since his wife's disappearance. A DNA test would do it. Actually, the other thing that kept me out of funkdom was Nelson's calling at seven-thirty that evening asking if he could come over for a while.

This time we made love in Joey's ex-bedroom, under a *Metropolis* poster. He waited until he was dressed again to give me the news that Courtney Logan had been cremated. Before I could howl in despair, he added that the medical examiner's office always kept tissue samples for later testing. In this case, with the body so decomposed after all those months in the pool, they'd kept teeth and bone instead of tissue. The pulp cavity of a tooth and the marrow of a bone would retain blood elements that could be tested. Not conventional postcoital sweet nothings, I admit, but I was exhilarated – until he said he was going to wait to get dental records from Washington or Oklahoma before he put his ass on the line and pushed for the DNA test. Also, he was swamped with his own cases, so please, no pressure.

The next morning I tried Fancy Phil. No luck with him. Maybe he really had turned over that new leaf and was at that moment studying Talmud. Or if he was still the same old Fancy, he could have been occupied with some new white-collar crime or with his old, reliable: assault with intent to kill. He finally responded to his beeper after noon. Just to keep him from getting too inquisitive, I asked him to get the names of Courtney's gynecologist, dentist, and accountant, figuring that with Fancy Phil, teeth (and their implications) would be overlooked when bracketed by vagina and money.

Having not much to occupy me after Fancy, I called the Red Oak Bank, said I was working for Dewey and Bricker, and asked for the person who had done secretarial work for Emily Chavarria.

'Helloooo,' I heard at last. Gina Berke trilled so high her voice probably fell more into the hearing range of rodents than humans. 'How may I help you?' I gave her a story about Emily being missing for so long now, and how the family had scrimped and saved and had come to Dewey and Bricker Investigations in Oklahoma City. Would she know offhand who Emily used as a doctor and dentist in New Jersey? Before she put me on hold, I considered saying Thanks, ma'am to sound more western, but decided not to push my luck. When Gina picked up the phone again, she gave me Dr Alan Jerrold, D.D.S. – 'Can you believe he's still on my computer?' – and Jack Goldberg, M.D. While I had her at her screen, I asked if she'd ever made any hairdresser appointments for Emily.

'God, it's funny you're asking that. Not till the last couple of months. You should have seen her before. Very plain Jane. You wouldn't have ever thought of her as a blonde, but she started looking so good.'

'A new boyfriend or something?'

'I don't know. Emily didn't talk all that much. Very, very, very shy socially.'

'Could she talk for banking business?'

'Oh yeah. Sure. She was . . . I forget the word, but really, really good at what she does. Did. Sorry.'

'I heard she was close with Richard Grey,' I said.

'I don't know if she was close. He's engaged.'

'I meant in a business sense.'

'Oh, sure, Mr Grey would have trusted her with his life. When she didn't come back . . . He was beyond the valley of upset, if you know what I mean.'

'Right. And her hairdresser?'

'Mane – M-A-N-E – Magic.' And she gave me the number.

'By the way, just out of curiosity. Was Emily sickly or kind of weak? Or strong?'

'She never, ever missed a day of work.'

'So I've heard.'

'But she looked like if you'd blow her over, like, she'd get blown over.'

When Fancy Phil called back with the names of Courtney's accountant, gynecologist, and dentist, he wanted to know why I needed them. Greg was curious, too.

'Does Greg know about me yet?' I asked.

'Look, Doc honey, I'm asking him a lot of questions, you know? So he must know I got someone looking into something, but he don't know it's you. How come you're asking about her gyno and her dentist and CPA?'

'No reason. I guess I'm grasping at straws, Phil.'

'You know, that's one of those stupid sayings, "grasping at straws." Not that I'm blaming you. But who the hell invented something that goddamn stupid?'

'Beats me.' I took down the names and said I'd get back to him.

Courtney's dentist in Shorehaven was Winslow Gaines, D.D.S. I had a hazy recollection of hearing the name from Nancy. Assuming Gaines hadn't been Ginsberg a generation earlier and speculating that between the Millers' church and Larry's country and yacht clubs, she, of all my friends, would have the best chance of knowing a Winslow Gaines anyway, I called her at *Newsday*. After both of us vented our spleens about the disgusting attacks on women and girls by forty men in Central Park and made a date for dinner that night, we got to Winslow. Not only did Nancy know Win, a member of North Bay Yacht Club, she'd *known* him, chuckle-chuckle, about ten years earlier. Didn't she ever mention him? The knowing had lasted less than a month because of his fondness for dental humor. Without too much of a fuss she said, All right, I'll call him. I know he'd adore hearing from me again. As always with Nancy, I simply could not imagine an American girlhood that could have engendered that much ostensible self-esteem. If I'd had a hat I would have taken it off to her. Anyhow, she commanded me to meet her at his office around six o'clock. I asked if she didn't want to check with him first. She said, Oh, please!

For a man in his early sixties, Winslow Gaines was quite a hunk. Tall, broad-shouldered in his white dental tunic, with white at the temples of his light brown hair and a cleft in his chin. He had the ho-hum handsomeness of a soap-opera star. He certainly was friendly enough, though it was hard to get his attention, as it kept wandering to Nancy, who, I could tell, had changed from the usual slacks and shirt she wore to work into a sleeveless beige linen dress cut to bare a little shoulder and a lot of leg.

'The last time Courtney came in?' he said as he sat down at the receptionist's computer. His staff was gone. The waiting room, with its pictures of sailboats and copies of *Yachting World* and *Classic Boat*, along with *What's New in Tooth Whitening?*, was empty. The dentist was not a natural cyberguy, hitting the keys slowly with his index fingers. Nancy, standing behind him, hands familiarly on his shoulders, rolled her eyes at his bumbling. When he turned back to glance at her, she flashed him a provocative smile. 'Let's see,' he muttered. After poking a few more keys, he swung his office chair around to me. 'How did the dentist break his mirror?' he demanded.

'I don't know,' I told him.

'Acci-DENTAL-ly!'

I chortled along with him while Nancy said, 'Come on now, Win. You're looking for Courtney Logan.'

Finally, he pointed to the screen. 'Here she is! Last came in on October twenty-sixth, in 'ninety-nine. Complained of tooth pain, but it was periodontal. I remember telling her that her home care was pretty far from exemplary, and she was on her way to serious gum disease if she didn't mend her ways.' He shook his head sadly. 'You know, after she disappeared, and then all that stuff later, finding her . . . You remember things like that. Nice, nice woman.'

'How were her teeth?' I asked.

'Not bad at all. But like most people with good teeth, you think everything will be fine forever. Oral hygiene is way, way down on your list of priorities. You can't live like that.'

'Around that time,' I told him, 'someone else might have come in, probably a new patient. A woman. Also on the small side, like Courtney. Streaky, blondish hair, on the quiet side.'

'Do you know her name?' he asked. I suggested Emily Chavarria, Vanessa Russell – the name of the cell phone's owner – and Samantha R. Corby. He typed in the names, but none came up on the screen.

'Do it by date,' Nancy directed him. When he turned around looking befuddled, she shooed him off the chair, sat herself down, and began to type.

'Why did the guru refuse Novocain at the dentist's?' he asked me. He was lounging against the wall, arms crossed over his chest, looking incongruously bon vivant.

'I give up.'

'Quiet!' Nancy demanded. 'What does NP mean? New patient?' Win nodded. 'Seven new patients in October. Look at these names,' she commanded him.

He whispered 'He wanted to transcend dental medication' to me, gave me a wink, then leaned over toward Nancy until the side of his face was touching hers. He pointed to a box that said AGE and immediately eliminated four from the group as being children. Of the others, two were women, one of whom was fifty-seven years old.

The other was twenty-eight. 'Polly Hastings,' Nancy announced. 'An alias if I ever heard one. Win, do you remember Polly?'

'I don't think so.'

'Twenty-eight, angel. You must have some memory.'

'Doesn't ring a bell,' he answered.

366

'Look! She came in on October the twenty-sixth!' Nancy said.

'What time?' I asked.

'Two o'clock.'

'And Courtney?'

'Two-fifteen.'

'Oh my God!' I said. 'She could have snatched Emily's file for a minute. All she had to do was go into the room Emily was in to say hi.'

'Or while the X rays were drying,' Nancy chimed in.

'What's going on?' Win asked. 'Who's Emily?'

'Or she found a way to get into the records room,' Nancy said.

'Patients don't walk into the file room,' Win said. He looked as much confused as disturbed, although in either case, handsomely so. 'This new woman was just in for a checkup. Oh, Wendy gave her a cleaning and took X rays.' I took out the photograph of Emily Chavarria I'd gotten off the Web and emailed to Steffi. He studied it and shook his handsome head. 'I mean, she's not really, uh, that memorable, is she? Well, maybe it's not a great picture.'

'Imagine her all dolled up,' I suggested. 'Longer, blonder hair. Makeup. Does she look at all familiar?' I asked.

'I'm sorry, I have no recollection.'

'Well, give us a copy of her X rays, then,' Nancy directed him. I think he was about to explain about doctor-patient confidentiality when she took his hand and led him farther back into the office. I assumed she was taking him to the file room, or (if the good Dr Gaines was still having compunctions) for a few magical moments on a chair in one of his examining rooms. To while away the time, I sat down at the computer and managed to retrieve Courtney's record. Good health, it appeared. No allergies. In the four years she had been a patient, she'd only had X rays, cleanings every six months like clockwork, and what I guessed was some sort of custom-fitted gizmo made for teeth brightening.

'I hate to ask what took you so long,' I said to Nancy later.

'Then don't ask.'

'Fine.' We were sitting at the town dock watching the day wind down before going out to dinner, although the gulls were busy with theirs. They flew, then rode the wind, then zoomed down to the water for their entrée.

'Besides having to work my wiles to get the X rays, do you know what else I got from Win?' she asked.

'I hope nothing that will require medication.'

'Dubious. I got "What ride in amusement parks do dentists like most?" Don't bother to guess. "A molar coaster." The man cannot control himself. And his wife: I see her at the club and she always looks vague. She probably punctured her eardrums. Well, in any case . . .' She waved a manila envelope. 'We have Polly Hastings's X rays. What are you going to do with them?'

'If he swears to give them back or have a copy made for me, I'll give them to Nelson. To see if they match Courtney's childhood and teenage records from Olympia, Washington. I bet they do, because Courtney went and switched the X rays, hers for Emily's. If Nelson can't get the information, I'll give it to Fancy Phil, and maybe Greg or Greg's lawyer can work out some deal with the Washington dentist.'

368

'Let me be clear. These really aren't Polly's teeth,' Nancy drawled. 'Well, Emily's teeth. These are what you were talking about, from the old switcheroo, so they're actually Courtney Logan's. Right?'

'Right. If they aren't, I'm making a major fool of myself.' Her silence spoke loudly. 'I'm not making a fool of myself with him, Nan.'

'Still the same old fire?'

'Still the same. It's not just fire. I love him.' Way out on the bay, we watched as a sunfish bounced happily through the wake of a grand sailboat.

'This is the strangest relationship.'

'Nancy, loving a man is not strange. Some might say sleeping with so many men that you stopped counting because you couldn't remember if it was seventy-one or seventy-two is a bit peculiar.'

'It's not peculiar,' she said somewhat huffily. 'It's promiscuous. What did our man in blue say about his wife?'

'I didn't want to talk about her.'

'Why not? Afraid he'll say he's staying?'

Clearly, although I didn't say so.

The next morning, to get away from Nelson and Captain Sharpe, both of whom seemed to be exerting an undue influence over my life, I got on a flight leaving La Guardia Airport for Salt Lake City. By mid-afternoon Idaho time, I found myself on an exceedingly small plane being piloted by an excessively young woman over the Sawtooth Mountains. It landed in Hailey. That's about ten miles from Sun Valley. And six miles from Wiggins, where I found Samantha R. Corby's rented condo.

Chapter Eighteen

At the fourth real-estate office, I got the news: Yes, they had rented to Samantha Corby. But she was long gone. 'God, she left . . . Why do I think before Christmas? If I'm thinking of the right person. You understand this is not the field if you're looking for long-term relationships. The rental market, I mean.' Doreen Brinkerhoff, the agent in charge of renting the furnished condos in Knob Ridge Villas in Wiggins, stood beside a file cabinet. She stuck a ruby-nailed finger through her tangle of shoulder-length black corkscrew curls and scratched her scalp. 'Even if they buy. Usually it's an investment property, so they're hardly here.' Probably in her early forties, Doreen was firm to a fare-thee-well. Her skin was so tanned that it had the color and texture of the tobacco leaf outside a cigar. 'Let me look one place more.' She shoved the drawer shut and, despite a minimal denim skirt and platform sandals, squatted down for a look in the bottom drawer. She struck me as the sort of woman to whom life has offered many reasons to be cynical, yet her hard-featured face was benevolent.

I took out the photos of Courtney I'd gotten from the Web and from Fancy Phil and bent down to let her see them, not daring a squat on general principles, and additionally not after all those cramped hours on airplanes. I gave Doreen a choice: tennis Courtney, bridal Courtney, mommy Courtney holding baby Morgan, baker Courtney holding lattice-top pie. 'Does this look anything like the woman you think could be Samantha?' I asked.

Her turquoise eyes – the color, I suspected, not of her irises but of her contact lenses – swept over the pictures. 'I . . . think . . . it . . . could . . . be. I only met her one time.' She went back to the file drawer, though it was so choked with folders I didn't know what she could possibly find.

'What makes you hesitate?' I asked.

'Honestly? I don't remember. Maybe . . . Shorter hair? Younger?'

'Samantha Corby looked younger than this woman?'

'I think so. God, if you got to rely on me, I hate to say it . . . You're in deep you-know-what. Oh! Look! Do me a favor. You see where it says '2BR 99'? That's the two-bedroom units in 1999. Pull it out for me. I just did my nails this morning.' After a fair amount of tugging I was finally able to jerk out a thick file. 'Depending on how the season is going,' Doreen said, 'we sometimes have to rent by the week. That makes for a real fat file.' Swiftly, she was standing and flying through the pages. 'Here! Hallelujah! Look, Judy. Samantha rented through December thirty-first, but she left on the twenty-first.' I had long since given up correcting Judy to Judith when dealing with people who were not likely to be soul mates.

'Does it happen to say why she was leaving early?' I asked. Doreen shook her head. 'Okay, big question: Did she leave a forwarding address?'

371

'Uh . . . No. It says . . .' She took a page from the file folder and handed it over. In schoolmarm penmanship someone had written 'Will call re security deposit.' Since Doreen didn't stop me, I turned over the page. The paper trembled. That was because my hand was shaking. On the back was a photocopy of a check from Samantha R. Corby to Wiggins Way Realty drawn on the Key Biscayne Bank & Trust – as well as a Florida driver's license with her photograph.

In the mountains, it was a cool, windows-open day, but I started to sweat. After I wiped my face with the tissue Doreen handed me, I took out my glasses and stared at the full face picture. I couldn't tell if it was Courtney. A resemblance, sure, but the formerly blond hair now appeared dirty blond or light brown in the black-and-white photocopy. It was shorter, too, curling under mid-neck. The once clear brow was covered with a fringe of uneven bangs. It could have been Courtney. Or Courtney's younger, less attractive sister, had she had one. Or someone completely unrelated. I copied down Samantha's home address on Key Biscayne, her height, five-two, and her date of birth, 08–04–71. On the bottom of the card it indicated that Samantha, a caring soul, was an organ donor.

'Do you want to fax it somewhere?' Doreen inquired. 'You can use my fax.'

I faxed copies of both sides to myself and also to Nancy at home, in case I needed it sent anywhere before I got back. 'This is really awfully nice of you,' I told her.

'Please. It's been real slow and it's exciting having a detective –'

'Researcher.'

'Oh, come on, Judy!'

I accepted her knowing smile. 'Well, if it is so slow, Doreen, would you mind seeing if the condo she was in is rented now?'

'Sure. But look, after she left, maybe there were five, ten, fifteen other people between then and now.' She seemed to think I had some private-eye purpose in mind, like lifting fingerprints or searching for money under floorboards, and as I could see she was relishing the notion, I didn't set her straight. Strolling over to her computer, she typed in an address. 'Sorry. Summer people in it now. How about this? How about I show you where it is. It's a short walk. And if you don't say I sent you, maybe you could knock on a few doors.'

I should have known from Doreen's calf muscles that a nice walk for her would be at least two miles. After fifteen minutes bouncing along at an altitude over five thousand feet, I was convinced I was going to faint, or at least swoon. It wasn't only being higher than zero feet above sea level. I felt so detached from everything and everyone I cared about. I could have been renting somebody else's life, somebody whose job was to chase down a woman who might have called herself Samantha R. Corby.

But the country was glorious. The cloudless sky was a shade of brilliant blue new to me. And there really were purple mountains majesty rising behind downtown Wiggins. Notwithstanding, I held back from humming a few bars because from the little I'd seen I sensed this might not only be the whitest town in America, but also one content with the distinction.

When we got to the other side of Wiggins, Doreen said: 'Listen, Judy, off-the-record? Girl Scout's honor? With someone clean-cut like Samantha Corby whose bank says okay, the check won't bounce, we sometimes don't bother with references — not if we're under the gun like we are in November when she rented.'

'Now that you mention it,' I said, 'you're right. I didn't see any references on the sheet you showed me.'

'That's because whoever first showed her the place probably didn't ask for any. I mean, it's not like this is New York, nothing personal.' Before we said good-bye, I wrote down my number for Doreen, although we both agreed that if Samantha hadn't called for her deposit since December, she was unlikely to now.

The Knob Ridge Villas were a series of flat, off-white two-story buildings with gray roofs, unremarkable in any way except, I supposed, in their ability to disappear against a backdrop of snow. In June, they simply looked wan. I could not picture the Vuitton Queen, the Land Rover Lady, the Armani Madonna living in a Knob Ridge Villa. On the other hand, if months earlier Courtney Logan had wanted to disappear without having to hide out in a trailer park in Rapid City, South Dakota, if she wanted to ski or have a first-rate martini or be just a few miles from *al dente* pasta and urbane men, well, this could be the place.

It was getting late in the afternoon, and chilly. Already I was yawning. But since I hadn't rented a car and wanted to walk back to the Wiggins Inn having made some progress, I started lifting the brass door-knockers on the villas of Knob Ridge. Most of the condos had the comatose air of a resort off-season, after the end of snowtime and just before the summer rush. Only four people answered their doors, although I surmised a few more were at home. Two of the four had only been renting since the end of April, when the ski season ended.

H. Jurgen opened her door about three inches, keeping her hiking booted foot planted right behind it, in case I tried to smash my way inside. No, she had no idea where Samantha had gone. They'd shared a chairlift a couple of times. She hardly knew the woman. She looked at two of the Courtney photos, then back to me, shook her head, and without another word, closed the door. I heard the fall of a deadbolt.

H.'s neighbor, Victor Plummer, was a scrawny man in his seventies with a few tufts of white hair. He lived two condos up from where Courtney had been. While not a gent of the old school, he appeared to be marginally more courteous. He didn't know where Samantha had gone either, but she'd been a nice girl. He'd heard Vivaldi coming from her place once, and not *The Four Seasons*. He looked at all my photos. 'Could this woman be Samantha Corby?' I asked.

'Can't tell,' he said. His gaunt face was shadowed by its old handsomeness, like the photographs of FDR at Yalta, although you'd have to picture FDR with a very deep tan and a Denver Nuggets T-shirt. 'Who's she?' he asked, pointing an arthritic finger at the photographs.

I was on the verge of finding him endearing, albeit brusque. 'She's a woman named Courtney Logan. She's been missing since –'

'What is this?' he demanded angrily. 'I don't have time for this kind of crap.'

'Look, Mr Plummer, the family is very concerned about her.' I pulled out my notepad and hurriedly wrote my name and phone number on it. 'Please, if you remember anything about Samantha, or if you hear anything, I'd be grateful – and so would the family – if you'd call me collect.' He, too, closed the door in my face, but at least he grabbed the piece of paper first.

By the time I made it back to the Wiggins Inn, I was shivering. Exhausted, too. A long day and a useless one. The inn didn't believe in room service, so I had a bowl of pretty good mushroom soup and a roll, and called it a night.

The mattress in my room had been shaped into a V by previous guests. I know I slept because I opened my eyes and was startled to discover it was morning, but I felt I had witnessed every second of the night. I kept thinking how stupid I'd been to spend my own money coming across country to discover that Courtney Logan was no longer in Wiggins, something I'd known before I left my house for La Guardia. Could she have moved to some other part of the Sun Valley area and was living under another name? If she'd left, where would she go from here? Back to Washington? To some other country? How much money did she have to invest in her own disappearance? And naturally, what if this whole thing came down to nothing and I'd been on Fancy Phil's wild-goose chase?

On the first half of the plane trip home, I finished the book on Truman I'd been reading, then slept from some-place above Sioux City, Iowa, back to New York. When I got back to the house, there were three messages. One was from Nancy: 'I'm assuming you are either schussing down mountains with a dude named Chet or you are back and holed up getting your brains banged out by that cop who will inevitably break your heart, you besotted, romantic fool. In either case, I would appreciate a call just to know how things went.' That meant she was worried, especially after receiving the fax with Samantha's name and picture on a driver's license. I called and told her that while I might be besotted, I was not a fool, romantic or otherwise.

'Oh please!' She heaved a vast southern sigh. 'You might as well walk around in a jester's costume. In any case, I have had a thought.'

'"So rare as a day in June." Can you remember what it was?'

'I was thinking about how Courtney or that little mouse person died. Just because they found her in the pool, you get the image of a watery death.'

'But in fact it was a gun,' I remarked.

'Yes, two bullets. The more I thought about it, I remembered an offhand remark either you or I made at the time, that the second shot was for insurance. And I thought — I being a woman of constant cogitation — damn, isn't that just like everything you've told me about Courtney Logan.'

'Which is?'

'Thorough. All the lampshade gewgaws, the bric-a-brac, everything just so. One shot in the head would do it. All right, if you were Fancy Phil or one of his associates, you might think something like: Remember in 1977, how Vinnie the Vulture got shot in the head but was still able to identify his assailant by dribbling his name in spittle. But if I were going to kill someone by shooting them in the head . . . Judith, once is enough, especially if you're going to stick them face-down in water and tie back the pool cover nice and tight.'

'It does go with her personality,' I agreed.

'So following up on that thought, on *Newsday*'s time and money, I called Summit High School in Olympia and thoroughly beguiled the assistant principal. He toddled over to the yearbook office for me and found *The Apex* – isn't that clever? – for the year Courtney graduated.'

'And?' I demanded.

'Many, many, many activities and honors for our girl, as you can well imagine. Including a rating of Distinguished Expert in the NRA – as in National Rifle Association – Marksmanship Qualification Program. Not that it takes a Distinguished Expert to shoot someone in the head point blank.'

'Not at all.'

'But it does show a certain degree of comfort when it comes to pulling a trigger.'

'Wow. Thank you. I'm really grateful that you –'

'Judith, don't go effusive on me. There's more. I could get no satisfaction from the old battle-ax at Emily's school in Oklahoma. But I called the mother – who was no America's sweetheart. She did manage to string enough words together to tell me that Emily – and I quote – "never messed with guns."'

I recalled Zee Friedman remarking how she'd overheard a one-sided conversation Courtney had a week before she disappeared, in which she'd said, 'You promised.' Zee had thought she sounded desperate. Had the caller been Emily and had Emily pushed Courtney too far?

Nancy's message was followed by two from Nelson. 'Just calling to say hi. By the way, I found out something interesting about your home-town girl. Call me at work. If I'm not there, leave a message.' In his second call, his voice gave away his concern by trying to come across as cool: 'Hey, hope you're having a good day. I'm working late, so you can beep me whenever you get in.'

After I beeped him, I took the portable phone, placed it on the edge of the tub, then soaked in a hot bath, usually a fine place for bright ideas to bubble up. But nothing much bubbled. Oh, I'd check the Key Biscayne address to see if it was authentic and if anyone named Samantha R. Corby had lived there and left a forwarding address. And of course I'd give Nelson a copy of the fax so he could, if he wanted to, call or subpoena the Key Biscayne Bank & Trust and see if they had information on Samantha – any other checks she'd written, her balance, and so forth.

I knew that if Courtney had executed the perfect crime, I would never have thought that the body in the pool was anyone but hers. Still, it was a damned good crime, as crimes go. Good enough, because of her thoroughness, to ensure her freedom. Deciding to delete the possibility of a wild-goose chase from my consciousness, I pumiced my feet and wondered how long she'd been planning her escape from marriage. Why couldn't she have just said 'enough' to Greg? Or simply taken a powder?

My guess was maybe that was what she was originally planning. Being the quintessential suburban wife, the perfect mother, after all, had not worked out. Maybe after her final throw pillow there was simply nothing left to buy. Perhaps Greg, with his refusal to try to open Soup

379

Salad Sandwiches on the West Coast, had proven unworthy of her awesome efforts. Possibly she found child-rearing not only draining, but incredibly boring – a conclusion that would inevitably be drawn by someone who could not love.

But Courtney being Courtney, she couldn't endure failure. Greater New York hadn't been so great for her. First the knowledge that she'd failed at Patton Giddings, then the realization that being a housewife would bring no applause, no money. The only reward was satisfaction. How could she break free? She could resign from Patton Giddings, or wait to be asked to leave; in either case, she'd be done with them forever.

But even if you quit as a wife, you're still stuck with an ex-husband, a nuisance almost by definition. And the children! Be rid of them, give over custody to Greg, and you'd still be obliged to return to the scene of your failure to visit them, or worse, have them intrude upon your new life. Not only that: You would have a legal obligation to contribute to their support.

And people would gasp, How *could* she? If she went to Sun Valley or Milwaukee or Beijing as Courtney Bryce Logan, someone from her old life, hearing about her, spotting her, might say to someone in her new life: Do you *know* what that woman did? So she had no choice but to disappear, to be missing. Emily Chavarria could have been part of Courtney's original scheme or an afterthought, but at some time it became clear that Emily, knowing about the insider trading and who knows what else, could not be allowed to live.

I climbed out of the bath, enveloped in a cloud of freesia,

and grabbed a towel. How well could Courtney hide? A magazine article I'd read recently said it was impossible to become a new person through plastic surgery; to some degree you would always be recognizable. Still, I'd passed by several longtime acquaintances around town within the last year or two not recognizing them after what one of them referred to as 'a little work.' They'd had to tap me on the shoulder and say, 'Judith, it's *me*.' Karen or Linda or Jean. So who knew?

Nelson's call caught me in my closet as I was making the cataclysmic decision between white or beige underwear. 'Where were you, for Christ's sake?'

Since I couldn't come up with a clever response to show him I was very much an independent woman, I told him: 'In Sun Valley.'

I chose beige and held the phone about a foot away from my ear as he yelled 'What the hell is wrong with you?' while he banged on something several times, hopefully his desk. While Bob almost never shouted, he could hold a grudge longer than the Hatfields and McCoys. If Nelson still had the temper he had years before, it would soon blow over. 'What if Courtney had been there?'

'See? You already know she wasn't,' I pointed out. 'Not just because I'm alive. Because we both knew there was at least a ninety-nine percent chance she wouldn't be. Otherwise, trust me, I wouldn't have gone.' I told him about the photocopy of Samantha Corby's check and license I'd gotten from Doreen in Wiggins and about the cold shoulder I'd gotten from both H. and Victor, Samantha's former neighbors. 'Now you,' I said. 'You said you found out something interesting.'

'I'll come over in a while. To pick up that photocopy.' I went back into the drawer, came out with black underwear. Obvious, perhaps, but also effective. 'Is that okay?' he asked as I ditched the beige.

'Sure.'

'I'll tell you what I came up with when I see you.'

It was getting near the summer solstice, so it was still light out when Nelson arrived. I'd already set a couple of citronella torches on the grass around the patio and made sangria with the wine we'd left over a few nights before – once I'd sniffed and determined it wasn't vinegar. I had just dried my hands after slicing up a peach when he came around the back. 'Hi,' he said, and from behind his back brought out a great bouquet of daisies, although I'd seen several of them peeking around his sides. They were beautiful, and we went into the kitchen and spent a few minutes kissing and finding the right vase. By the time we got outside, the daylight had turned softer and more gold, the lovely silkiness that comes to the light before dusk. We wound up sharing a chaise and a glass of sangria. 'I've been thinking about how to handle this Courtney business,' he said.

'You mean politically, for you.'

'And for you. If anything comes of it, you should get credit from your boyfriend.'

'Fancy, you mean?'

'Fancy. So first let me tell you what I've done while you weren't answering your phone and I didn't know what . . . You should have told me you were going, Judith.'

'I don't know about that,' I said carefully. 'But that's a subject we can talk about some other time.' I squelched:

If you want there to be another time and you're not here to say good-bye.

'I told you I wasn't ready to go to the brass on the DNA. But unless I had something concrete, I couldn't go to them at all.'

'What if I told you I got X rays from Courtney's dentist here in town?'

'You didn't.'

'I did.'

'How?'

'My friend Nancy got them. The dentist is a former lover of hers, but then, who isn't?'

'Not me.' We spent a minute or so sipping sangria and making out, then went back to the case.

'So what are you going to do?' I asked.

'You mean, what *did* I do. I thought about calling Courtney's parents out in Washington, making some excuse about needing her dental records for the investigation and not wanting to waste time having to get a subpoena for them.'

'How long does a subpoena take?'

'An investigative subpoena from the DA's office? A few minutes. But then I thought, no, they already must have a relationship with somebody from Homicide. They might call to check on me. And who knows what kind of a kid Courtney was? Maybe her parents knew bad stuff about her that other people didn't know. They'd have the presence of mind and the experience to call a lawyer before doing anything.'

'So, what *did* you do?'

'I called Emily Chavarria's house. Got the father –'

'I hope he's better than the mother.'

'Sounded like a decent guy who's been through hell. Anyway, I commiserated with him and told him the last thing I wanted to do was scare him, but if he could get Emily's Oklahoma dentist to overnight me her records and X rays, it would help rule her out.'

'And?'

'And they got here this morning.'

'*And?*'

'I brought them over to this great guy at the medical examiner's office, somebody I've known for years, and asked him for an unofficial opinion.' I waited. 'Judith, they match the teeth from the body in the Logans' pool.'

It was only a combination of relief, too many sangria-soaked peach and apple slices, and jet lag, but I gave the glass over to Nelson and closed my eyes, too wiped out to say anything more than 'Congratulations.' I heard the clink of the glass as he set it on the patio and rested against him while he stroked my hair, something he'd figured out years earlier to bring me back when I was ready to go over the top. 'Now what?' I finally asked.

'Now I'm going to go to the brass, tell them what I've found out. I'll also let them know that I've heard whispers about Greg Logan's lawyer having some questions about the ID of the body. And in case it hasn't dawned on them, I'm going to tell them very delicately that someone had his head up his ass on this case because no DNA test was ever done.'

'That will make them do it!' I enthused.

'No. Not right away. What that will do is make them wait a day or two – till they figure out how to cover themselves. Or it may make them hem and haw and want to get rid of me. So I'd appreciate it if you'd ... Shit, I hate to do this. But let Fancy Phil know you have some doubts that the body was Courtney's, that it could be someone else's who had zero to do with Greg Logan. Trust me, by seven A.M. Monday morning, all over Nassau County, you'll hear the sound of Greg's lawyer screaming for a DNA test.'

A little later, after I realized that if I made and/or ate dinner I might die of fatigue, I told Nelson to go, that I had to go upstairs. Though I was sure I'd go straight to sleep, this time he walked me upstairs, came into the master bedroom with me, and stayed for an hour. No shade of Bob came to haunt our lovemaking, no shadow of Nelson's marriage held us back.

'When do you want to talk about us?' he asked before he said good-bye.

'Tomorrow,' I mumbled. 'Whenever we both want to.'

'Want to what?' he inquired, in a sensual murmur which usually means: I want to do it again.

Once again I told him good night, sent him home, and slept until the phone rang the next morning. 'Is this Judith Singer?' a woman's voice asked.

I cleared my throat to get the languid sleep hoarseness from my voice. 'Yes it is.'

'Hi, my name is Ellen Berman. I live in Garden City. One of my friends in town went to Princeton with Courtney Logan. She heard something about your looking into the case. Anyway, she gave me your number. I really feel funny about doing this. But I worked at Patton

Giddings until the end of last year. I knew Courtney. I don't want to get involved, but I feel — I don't know, an obligation . . .'

I sat up and quickly told her, 'Oh please. There's no reason to worry about getting involved.'

'Well, this may be a big nothing. I hate to waste your time. But I was talking to my friend about some of the conversations I had with Courtney and a couple of bells rang. Maybe I could meet you for a cup of coffee sometime?'

'Sure. How about later today?'

'Today? Well, I'll actually be near Shorehaven. I have to go to that big picture-framing place. Just tell me where to meet you.'

'Would you like to come over here?' I asked. 'I can guarantee you a semi-decent cup of coffee.'

'Are you sure it wouldn't be —'

'No trouble at all!' I gave her directions to my house from Main Street.

'Around eleven or so? Is that okay?' Ellen asked. 'God, I hope I'm not wasting your time and your coffee. But there are a couple of things about Courtney' — she hesitated for a minute — 'that somebody ought to know.'

Chapter Nineteen

Ellen Berman rang my doorbell at ten-thirty, a half hour early. Since I would have wasted the next thirty minutes alternately fantasizing she'd give me a major lead like, Oh, Courtney's dream was to live at 43 degrees latitude and 98.6 degrees longitude, or dreading she'd have an insipid tale like, Courtney shoplifted a teaspoon in her Old Master pattern, I was glad to see her.

'Am I too early?' She was pretty, a little like Audrey Hepburn in *War and Peace* – the thick browed Audrey. She had those great, dark doe eyes.

'No, this is fine,' I assured her, opening the door wide. 'Glad you're here. I didn't put on any eyeliner, but if you can survive that horror, I'll put up a fresh pot of coffee.'

'Thanks!' No sweet tremulousness like Hepburn: Ellen had the easy manner of the naturally outgoing. Her clothes were outgoing, too, in that astutely mismatched designer way. Cropped orange pants, a shocking-pink cotton sweater, snazzy cork-bottomed clogs in pink, red, and orange. Her jewelry was a simple gold watch and thin hoop ear-rings. Instead of heading for the living room and into the sunroom, I led her toward the just-straightened-up kitchen. Just then she asked: 'Would it be okay to use your bathroom?'

'Sure. It's straight through –' When I turned back to point her in the right direction, I saw she had another accessory. A gun.

No matter how many scenes you've seen in movies where the camera looks straight into the barrel of the gun, it doesn't prepare you for the ugliness of looking into that long metal nose with its single nostril. It's a creature out of Hell. My body told my mind that I didn't have long to live; whatever force holds cells together began to weaken. I'd heard that people lose control of their bladders or defecate in this kind of horrific moment. Others simply black out. My body considered all three options, but instead crashed against the wall right where we were, just outside the kitchen. Even though the answer was obvious, I asked with disbelief: 'Courtney?'

No answer. Her eyes darted back and forth over that five-foot-long passageway between center hall and kitchen. I glanced around and saw what she was looking for. Yes, this was the perfect spot. No windows, not even a small, ornamental pane of leaded glass. No windows, no witnesses.

'Is that –' I began.

'No questions,' she snapped, though still in that chipper, extrovert voice. No more peppy little blonde: She had the deep gold tan of a wealthy brunette. She'd lost weight, too, and now was model-thin if not model-tall.

'Is that the gun you used on the . . . other person?'

'Of course not,' she said dismissively.

Her thumb moved, or maybe it was only my head

388

shaking in denial of what was happening. But though I had no knowledge of guns beyond seeing Nelson's in its holster and watching *Shane*, I had the sense she was flicking the gizmo that would take off the safety lock. 'Not the other person. Emily!' My words exploded, and the force made her head jerk back. 'Is that the gun you used on Emily?' No answer. In that second of silence that followed, I thought how terribly sad it was that I would never know how it would have turned out with Nelson. But since that was a future I wouldn't have, and I had almost no more present, I sent up a silent blessing for Kate and Joey. Then I got out the first four words of the *Shema*, the prayer Jews are supposed to say twice a day and right before their deaths. But I stopped myself because I was still alive, and where there is life I was obliged to fight for it. Thinking 'I'm dead' would doom me.

'What do you know about Emily?' she inquired, as if asking about a mutual acquaintance.

Slowly, not so much because I did not want to startle her but because I didn't have much strength, I pushed myself from the wall into an upright position, regretting the year I'd picked Learn to Crochet over Tae Kwon Do. 'Do you mean the Emily Chavarria who was found on May fifteenth in your family's swimming pool?' I asked her. Just then, a thought flashed into my head: How the hell did she find me? I didn't go around thumbtacking index cards on bulletin boards or sending out 'Wanted' posters with RSVP JUDITH SINGER in the lower left corner. 'Oh,' I said. 'Did you find out about me from that man in Wiggins I gave my name to? Your neighbor Victor?'

'You got it!' she replied brightly. I was still having

trouble thinking of her as Courtney Logan. I didn't dare look directly at her any more than I'd make eye contact with a slobbering Doberman. But after a couple of glances, I saw her hair had been dyed, very skillfully, the darkest brown, with a touch of auburn. My color. Her eyes, too, were like mine, somewhere between dark brown and black. Of course, I looked like one of those late-nineteenth-century photographs you see at Ellis Island, Pensive Semite in Babushka, and she like Audrey Hepburn. What I couldn't figure out was what kind of loyalty a man like Victor would feel toward Samantha/Courtney. 'When I moved in,' she explained, as if she'd heard me ask, 'I told a couple of my neighbors I was on the run, that my husband had been abusive.' Maybe she wanted me to tell her how clever a strategy that was. I didn't, so she explained: 'I said he was very rich. He'd been stalking me. He'd hired detectives. I told them about beatings. I told them he'd threatened to kill me. I begged them to let me know if anyone came looking for me.'

'How were they able to reach you? You moved, didn't you?'

'Question time is over.' The horror of her was her niceness. She had a gun and was about to kill me. Her Audrey Hepburn eyes were still shining. Her voice was cheery: Life is really neat! What made me even more terrified was my knowing the buoyant gunslinger standing less than two feet away had once earned an NRA Distinguished Marksman qualification.

But the next second brought a respite: Though question time was over, answer time was still going on. 'I gave them a number in St Louis where they could call me or leave a message,' Courtney was saying. 'Of course, I'm not in St Louis. But I call that number twice a day, religiously.' Well, I had called her thorough. 'And I'm going to keep on doing it until the second anniversary of my escape, just to be extra sure.'

'Escape out of where?'

'Out of *here*! Trust me, the only thing that could drag me back to Shorehaven was to deal with you.'

Because my credo is that it's always better to know the truth, I decided to give Courtney a dose of it – not for her own good, but for mine. 'Your problem is bigger than me, Courtney. Your father-in-law knows all about you. The Nassau County cops just got onto you. *Newsday* could break the story any minute.'

She gave a heh-heh chuckle I supposed qualified as the 'mirthless laugh' villains are forever emitting in noir mysteries set in Los Angeles. 'You're trying to buy time,' she observed. 'Sorry, I'm not selling any.'

I lost my fight to keep my eyes away from the gun. She could see my fear was exhausting me. It was hard to get enough air to push out my words. 'They know about how you switched dental X rays at Dr Gaines's office, how you –'

'Listen to me,' Courtney commanded. 'Don't even attempt to match wits with me. I know all about you, how you got involved in that dentist case here in town, whenever, a hundred years ago. Well good for you. You get an A for this one, too – for all you found out all by yourself.' I wish I could say that in looking at her I could see the wickedness or the madness. Truth was, she looked pretty and well put together, though more *Elle* than Long

Island. Only her eyes looked somewhat lifeless despite their luster, a hint that something about her was not a hundred percent. However, I guessed it was less an emanation of evil or sign of pathology than the brown contact lenses.

I prayed Fancy Phil was right in his where-to-hide-money theory and that she hadn't gone to the Caribbean to scuba dive. 'How would I be able to find out about the offshore corporation in Nevis? The federal authorities traced that.' I can't say Courtney looked scared, but for the first time she looked disquieted. With the index finger of her free hand, she stretched out the collar of her pink sweater – even though it was loose fitting enough that it couldn't be annoying her. 'And what about your dental X rays? The Nassau County cops are checking the ones from Emily and the ones supposedly yours from Dr Gaines against yours from Olympia, Washington.'

'What else do they know?' I couldn't believe she still had that read-any-good-books-lately? breeziness.

'Why should I tell you?'

'Because I have a gun,' Courtney said reasonably. She did one of those perky, apologetic shrugs – Sor-ry. Her gold hoops sparkled in the light from an overhead fixture in the passageway. 'And you don't.' Just as I had begun to feel safer, seeing an extra minute or two of life, she suddenly seemed to be growing taller in her cork-bottomed clogs, more resolute. 'What else do the cops know?'

'Listen, Courtney, New York's got the death penalty again. Do you want to add another murder so if you're caught it's guaranteed?'

'Stop it,' she said with an indulgent smile. 'I'll live a long and happy life. Unfortunately –'

'I don't want to hear about your life!' I told her. 'I don't want to hear any big bullshit about how clever you were, because you weren't.'

'Listen to me!' she ordered. 'I —'

'No. You listen to me, Courtney. I don't want to hear what a brilliant plan you conceived. And I don't want to hear that the whole thing really wasn't your fault. I've seen too many movies where the killer explains why it's never his fault. Her fault. It *was* your fault. But unfortunately this is life, not a movie. You have the gun. I don't have the agility to knee you in the balls even if you had balls. I don't have the strength to twist your arm so you wind up killing yourself. But know this: You're not that smart. You're a screwup, plain and simple. If you weren't, we wouldn't have found out about it. Meanwhile your husband has been living under a cloud —'

'It so happens,' she hissed at me, 'that even before the whole thing with Emily, I was planning on leaving after I took Morgan trick or treating. I didn't want to disappoint her by not going. And I also did it on the thirty-first because I knew, I *knew* Greg would be at a dinner meeting in the city with Jim Cooley from Upper Crust. I *wanted* him to have an alibi.'

Maybe she was waiting for me to tell her how thoughtful she was, but I decided to disappoint her. My only chance at getting out was to be able to make some clever move, although with her standing a couple of feet away and the gun pointing somewhere in the general direction of my heart and lungs, clever wasn't coming. The only way I could buy time was to keep her talking, since I doubted she'd be the type to appreciate the Bergmanesque qualities of a meaningful silence. 'Not that I'm being critical,' I went on, 'but didn't it occur to you that the trick-or-treat experience for Morgan might be tainted by the trauma of having a mother disappear and never return?'

'See? This is why it's useless to talk to you.' I tried to swallow so I could speak, but I found myself choking on my own gulp. 'It so happens I gave it my all. You and everyone else will never know how hard I tried to be the best mother there is. Maybe I wasn't the best wife in the world, but I tried there, too. Part of it was I didn't have the best material to work with.' There was no need to ask Courtney what she meant, because she was on a roll.

'He was the biggest disappointment. Good-looking in that exotic way, very intelligent, a real natural athlete. You look at those blobby parents of his and you wonder how in the world did they produce someone with such amazing hand-eye coordination. And his speed! He's all the way back and suddenly he's at the net. And money. He had money and an MBA, which can be an unbeatable combination. Except what did he do about it? Next to nothing. He had no daring. He took a really good idea and worked and slaved and turned it into a mediocre business.' I decided it best not to bring up StarBaby. 'And do you know the most pathetic thing about it? Greg was perfectly content to be second rate.' Courtney rubbed her lips together the way you do before you blot lipstick. 'He knew damn well he was settling for safety and security over the chance to be a player. And he knew that sooner or later someone was going to come in and copy his formula and make it the next Starbucks. Do you know what he said?'

'What?' Her right arm, the one with the gun, must

have been getting weary because she was propping up her forearm with her left hand. All I could think of was what in the world I could do to disarm her. For once, I was overjoyed to be sixteen pounds over the legal limit, except I couldn't come up with a way to throw my weight around that would result in both my getting the gun and staying alive.

'He said he could live with that. I told him in kidding-around way that I didn't know if I could. And he said, "Well, Courtney, you're just going to have to *learn* to live with it." And then his whole fixation on being legitimate. Believe me, when I told him I was proud that he wasn't interested in the family business or the family values, if you know what I mean, I meant it. But it permeated every aspect of his life. He was panicked about anyone thinking he was coarse. Panicked. Half the time we'd go out with other couples, really terrific, successful couples, and he'd hardly say anything because he was so panicked. Except his excuse was that he was reserved. Reserved? And taxwise there were probably hundreds of deductions he could have made legitimately, but he wouldn't let the accountant take them. You can be understanding for a while, but for how long? And the really sick thing? He was on the phone with his father at least once a day, even on weekends. Talking about baseball and the market, like his father was a normal person. Greg never heard of the term "arm's length."'

I was tempted to ask her about her children but was afraid of setting her off. Sooner or later, unless she decided to fire in the meantime, I'd have to do something. But my legs were performing a pathetic shimmy and it was all I could do just to keep standing. The unsettling thing about

Courtney, as if I needed more unsettlement, was that for an egocentric crazy sociopath, or whatever the diagnostic term is, she was as intuitive as she was.

Just as I was thinking, Huh? What about your kids?, she said: 'As far as the children go, they're better off without me. I know that may sound like a rationalization, but it's the truth. They always loved Steffi, our au pair, better than they loved me. I felt badly I couldn't leave Steffi a letter with some instructions or guidelines, though that was obviously out of the question.'

'What about Emily?' I inquired. Courtney did her lip-rubbing business again, then kept them pressed together, as in 'mum's the word.' 'I know you two met at a regional FIFE meeting in Baltimore. But I couldn't piece together how the relationship developed.'

Her lips parted. 'I wouldn't call it a *relationship*.' Each time she began talking again I'd get an instantaneous flush of hope, followed by a growing desperation and paralysis. The reverse psychology which had worked earlier, telling her I didn't think she was smart and that I didn't want to hear her version of events, might not work again. 'There was much too much of a hero-worshiping aspect to it,' she was saying. 'I mean, the woman was a *tabula rasa* looking for someone to write on her. Self-confidence in negative numbers. Which was sad, because she had a mind. But if I hopped on one foot, she'd hop. I bought a Lana Marks bag and guess who else did? One time I told her, 'Emily, you can wear a really great pants suit and the bank won't fire you, I guarantee it.' So of course she had to buy a couple of pants suits, but I got sixty thousand emails asking where she should buy it and what designer and all that.'

'Her name wasn't on your database,' I said.

She laughed, throwing back her head, although not so far that she still couldn't keep her eye on me. And the gun didn't move a millimeter. 'That's because the month before I left I got a new hard drive. My nightmare was that Greg would spare no expense trying to find me and hire one of those computer people who can read stuff you think you erased.' She shook her head in weary recollection. 'You wouldn't believe how long it took to import a lot of that stuff and reenter the rest. Not just database stuff. My other files, too, minus what I didn't want to show up. Days and days and days I was my own secretary.'

'You weren't involved with on-line trading?'

'You mean day-trading? No. That's so dilettantish. For total losers and a couple of geniuses. I admit I'm not that kind of a genius.' For a moment she looked pensive. 'Emily traded on-line, but she didn't sit around all day staring at a computer screen like a day-trader. I wouldn't call her a genius, but she was terrific at it. She made herself some good money.'

'What was her nest egg? From the first public offering of Saf-T whatever?'

'Very impressive,' Courtney remarked. 'How did you track that down?'

'Someone else did.'

'Who? All right, play games. I don't care. You'll see where it will get you. Well' – she grinned – 'technically you won't see.' With her first real smile of the morning, I noticed the old Courtney dimples. 'What were we talking about? Oh, Emily. Emily got in on the ground floor with the IPO, invested her life savings, thirty-five thousand.

She doubled her money the first week. Then she sold all her Saf-T-Close stock and began making serious money. I mean, from something like her initial seventy thousand investment, she ran it up to almost *seven hundred thousand* in on-line trading by the next summer. She'd get home from the bank and that's all she'd do, not that she had a lot of other opportunities. Anyhow, every time she made a killing she had to call me up and boast. Well, finally this boring person in New Jersey was worth almost three-quarters of a mil! That's when I said, "Let's have lunch. We haven't seen each other in ages."'

'When was this?'

'I don't know,' she said irritably. 'So we kept having lunch. And then she told me about the Chapman-Bohrer buyout. Anybody would think, Oh, Courtney's the evil genius behind all this, but Emily was the one who suggested it.'

'Suggested what?'

'You know. That I should buy stock for her in my name and she'd give me fifteen percent of whatever she netted. The naïveté, the gullibility. That she could trust anyone, even me. Then she said if I wanted to buy for myself, whatever money I wanted to put into it – *She* said, "Why don't you have your parents buy your shares for you? They have another name." Like a couple who makes fifty grand or so a year would be buying twenty-five thousand dollars' worth of Saf-T-Close. For someone smart she was not smart.'

'That was the money you took out from your joint accounts?'

'Right again. Very, very good. But buying under another

name gave me the idea of the offshore corporation. So I set that up and gave Emily the papers to sign as coprincipal, except three guesses what I did with those papers.'

'Why did you have to kill her?'

'I take full responsibility for that,' Courtney said. 'I just didn't think something through that I should have.'

'What was that?'

'That once she comprehended – and that took forever – that we weren't best friends and that I hadn't bought tickets to Australia for us and that there was no chance in hell she was going to get her hands on the money, she wasn't going to take it lying down. She threatened to blackmail me.'

'How?'

She did not directly answer. 'Well, I didn't want her to go back to her bank and say, "I didn't go to Australia and New Zealand because my friend Courtney fucked me over." I wanted her to make a clean break so they'd think she was missing. So I got her a hotel room in the city and told her there was some problem with the offshore corporation because our lawyer had left the island. I said, "Just sit tight. We'll take our vacation as soon as I clear this up. I'm working night and day on it." I got her a cell phone so she wouldn't make calls to my house from the hotel. I said, "We can't afford to have any phone records if the SEC ever decides to take a look."

'But then she finally figured out something was wrong. And then the blackmail threats began: She was going to tell Greg. Then she'd go to the SEC, which I personally doubt she would have done. But of course that would have totally fucked up my plans about getting away. And then she came out to Shorehaven. Unfortunately, she'd been to the house a few times, so she knew where it was. She could practically get there on automatic pilot.'

'And?'

'And, I said, "We can't stay here, Emmy. You're making too much noise, carrying on like this. Let's go for a walk." And of course she said okay. She even waited while I ran back upstairs to get out the gun. I told her I had to change my shoes and she believed me. I even got her to drive my car one last time.'

'Where did you shoot her?'

'Where? In the head.' She spoke with exaggerated patience, the way an unkind person might do with someone who is slow.

'I mean, where were you?'

Courtney exhaled, as though exhausted by the memory. 'In Piney Woods Park, behind the old Fiske mansion, on one of the trails.'

'You shot her twice.'

'One for good measure. Just to be sure. That's how I am. This was just a couple of days before Halloween, the day I was planning my escape. But I had to put everything else aside. Anyhow, I shot her and I put a pile of leaves and branches over her and said a little prayer that I wouldn't screw this up. Then I had to go home, pick up Emily's car, and drive it to one of those dumpy car cemeteries with all the old wrecks. Isn't it amazing, how the mind works? I must have passed the place a year or two before, going somewhere. All of a sudden, on my way home from the park right after I'd shot her, it came back to me. Then I had to get rid of the plates. I threw them into a Dumpster at a construction project.'

'And her body?'

'I was so nervous. You should have seen me! But I knew I couldn't let it stay where it was. But then on Saturday after it got dark, Greg was still at the office and I told Steffi, the au pair, to take the kids to Roosevelt Field and go to F.A.O. Schwarz and the food court for dinner. She was so good about working on weekends if I needed her. So I wrapped her – Emily – in one of those green plastic things you put on the floor when you paint. What do you call it? A drop cloth. I put my watch and rings on her. I got her into clothes similar to what I was planning on wearing on Halloween, wrapped her in the drop cloth, and put her in the back of my car –'

'But her fingerprints were on your car. And in your house. You obviously wiped your prints off in order to make the police think that Emily's fingerprints were your fingerprints – the same fingerprints that would match the body. She visited you at least a couple of times, right? When you had Steffi take the children away for the day, and again when you went to the dentist.'

She shook her head, smiling at a recollection. 'If you're dying, no pun intended, to know how I did it, I had her drive me to the dentist's office. I'd made an appointment for her under a made-up name, and when we got there I said, "Ooh, your teeth need to be cleaned." Cute? She didn't even know she had an appointment. I just said, "Go in, Emmy. They'll take you. Oh, listen: I made the appointment under another name. I don't want anyone being able to connect the two of us." Steffi was with the children.'

'I guess there were other times she came to your house, too.'

'So?'

'So what I'm thinking is that maybe you planned out this . . . Emily's death a little more than you're describing.'

'Did you ever hear of "FO and D"?' Courtney asked too sweetly. I shook my head. 'No? We used to say it in school.' For the first time she looked angry. 'Fuck off and die!'

I spoke right away, trying to keep my voice soothing. 'Did you ever consider that the pool wasn't a good place? That they might have found her before she' – I wasn't able to come up with a euphemism, so I said – 'decomposed?'

'Of course I thought about it. But this wasn't how I'd planned to do it. She came to the house and I had to improvise. All you can do in any situation is your best. I had to shoot her in the goddamn middle of nowhere. What if there'd been a hiker around? Then the next night I had to go back and get her, which was incredibly spooky. I bet you're dying to know how I got her into the pool.' I nodded. 'I drove my car. It's a Land Rover. Greg said a Range Rover would send the wrong message, which just about sums him up. I drove across my neighbor's property after dark with the car's lights off. I got to ten feet away from the pool, then I carried her. In the dark. Talk about deadweight. But she was out of the car, into the drink, pool cover tied back down in five minutes.'

'You weren't worried that once you were gone the police would look in the pool?'

'Of course. I agonized. But my escape plan was in place. Worse comes to worse, they'd pull back the cover and say, "Gee, that's not Courtney. It's someone who's her size and who has blond hair, or almost blond, but – gee, where could Courtney be?" It was a calculated risk. But I'd be in another city. I'd be in another life! Let them look for Courtney. They wouldn't find her.'

The blond business. Was Emily simply mimicking the woman she venerated? Or had Courtney talked Emily into going blond? If so, she'd formulated the pool burial not at the spur of the moment, but in early September, when Emily started changing her hair color. 'How had you originally planned it, before you had to use the pool option?'

'FO and D.' She was getting bored with me.

'Where did you get the gun?'

'Oh, that was about two, three years ago when we were skiing in Utah.' Her manner turned reflective, as if reminiscing about a pleasant vacation. 'I was a nervous wreck, sending it home in my luggage, but it was the only thing I could think to do. Like the airline really noticed. But I just thought that with someone like Phil Lowenstein in the family, we should be armed.'

'Did he or anyone else ever threaten you?'

'No. But why not be protected?'

'Greg didn't know you had the gun?'

'Of course not. He probably would have thought it was coarse or something. And he was definitely too much of a wuss to have a gun in the house.' She combed her hair off her face with her left hand. 'I know you've been playing for time, trying to think of some way out. Not that I blame you. You're smart, but as I said, not as smart as I am. I hate to say it, but –'

With my left arm I slammed her gun hand against the

wall. With my right, I jerked her gold hoop earring down. She screamed as it tore through her earlobe – I think as much with horror as with pain – and covered her ear with both hands. Now the gun was pointing toward the ceiling. Blood began oozing out between her fingers and down her neck. Reaction time was a factor, I knew. With mine being sluggish and hers fast, it would only be a second or two until she'd get back enough control to wrest her right hand from her ear, aim, and shoot.

I grabbed for the gun, but she tightened her grip. I couldn't get it loose and found myself swaying as she writhed and screamed, 'My ear! My ear! You ripped my ear!' With one hand I grabbed onto her wrist and tried to keep the gun pointed up, although her wrist was slick with blood. Then I remembered something I'd heard at a self-defense forum at a Take Back the Night rally on campus: If you're trying to release someone's grip, don't go for his thumb. So I grabbed Courtney's pinkie and bent it back, and farther back, until her next scream told me I'd broken it.

Although I already knew that because now I had the gun.

Except we were at a standoff. I had the gun, but I needed the phone, which was in the kitchen. Courtney alternated between holding her ear and howling 'I'm going to bleed to death!' and 'My finger!' and making swipes toward me to try to get the gun back. The shoulder and sleeve of her bright pink sweater were blood-soaked, and for an instant it brought to mind Jacqueline Kennedy's suit after JFK was shot. My teeth started to chatter and I clamped my jaw shut.

But then I had to open it. 'Courtney,' I shouted over her cater-wauling, 'you better hear me. This isn't a democracy. I rule. Either you come into the kitchen or I'm going to shoot you, and with any luck, I'll kill you.'

I pulled out a chair into the middle of the kitchen. I must have had a reason for that, though I don't recall. She sat. After throwing her a dishtowel for her ear, I grabbed the phone. God knows what I shrieked to the 911 operator. Then began the endless wait for the cops to arrive.

The vibrations from my chattering teeth spread downward until I was shivering all over. I have no doubt she saw it, because I wasn't more than five feet from her. Nevertheless, she did not try to take advantage. Instead, hunched over in the chair, both hands pressing the towel over her ear, she seemed to have withdrawn for a consultation with herself. No more bawling, no more attempts to get back the gun.

When the two cops came, one gingerly took the bloody gun from me. It was evidence and I suppose I wasn't radiating an Annie Oakley aura of expertise in the firearms department.

With that, Courtney began to weep. Loud sobs, buckets of actual tears. 'Thank God you're here!' she cried to them. 'Thank God!'

'Listen,' I warned them, 'she's the one who killed that woman they found in the pool last month!'

'Don't listen to her,' Courtney exhorted them. 'My name is Amy Carpenter and . . .' She stopped to weep some more but only for a moment. 'She thinks I'm having an affair with her husband and I swear to God I'm not. Look what she did to me! Please, let me get to a doctor. Oh please.' She looked up at them. Her doe eyes, only slightly red, brimming with tears, were so moving they almost tugged on my heartstrings. The two men glanced at each other, then back to Courtney. She showed them her ripped earlobe and then held up her broken, swollen pinkie.

It occurred to me that what I might be seeing in their eyes was sympathy. 'She's not Amy Carpenter,' I told them. 'She's used lots of aliases. She's Courtney Logan, for God's sake!' A mistake.

Tall cop spat out: 'Courtney Logan is dead.'

'No, no,' I told him. 'She's not! The woman who's dead is –'

'Oh God! Please don't make me sit here like this. Please, get me to a doctor,' Courtney wept. 'I'm so scared I'll bleed to death.' Shorter cop, gazing at her, looked as if his pity was turning to love, mixed with a dash of horror that someone would drop dead on his watch and he'd have to fill out the reports. Sensing this, she looked up at him, a lovely crystal tear resting on her lower lashes, on which, somehow, she'd had the luck or foresight to apply waterproof mascara.

Two more cops arrived. Second tall cop was grimacing at the blood-soaked towel and therefore didn't bond with Courtney. His partner, Female Cop, looked over at the first two and inquired, 'Hey, guys. You call an ambulance?' A perfectly reasonable question, I thought.

'This lady,' Tall Cop said, pointing to me, 'is saying the other one –' His somewhat icy tone thawed as his finger moved toward Courtney. 'She's saying this one is Courtney Logan. The one that got shot in the head and put in her own swimming pool.'

'If you'll just listen for a minute,' I began.

'Shut up, lady,' the short cop barked.

'Hey, guys. Yes or no? You call an ambulance?'

'I'm going to throw up,' Courtney announced with a note of genuine nausea in her voice. 'Please, could someone get me to the bathroom fast?' All four cops took a step toward her.

'Not before one of you calls Captain Sharpe at headquarters!' I shouted. Four heads turned to me. I saw four faces with foreheads creased, as if they'd only taken one semester of the language I was speaking. As I was repeating myself, Courtney made a run for it.

Cleverly. Instead of standing, turning, and rushing for the kitchen door, like a person escaping, she rose from the chair in a crouched position. It barely seemed as if she had moved. Then she raced toward the door. The cops took a long instant to comprehend she was not making a run for the bathroom. Too long. Courtney was out the door and crossing the patio. 'I have to get to a doctor,' she cried. 'I have to!' God, she was fast!

She had almost reached the grass when two of them got to her. But instead of kicking or biting, fighting to get free, as I'd expected, Courtney collapsed, falling to the flagstone, arms limp, torn earlobe lying on the stone. Tall and Short knelt beside her and called out 'Ma'am?' over and over. After a minute, when she didn't stir, each took a side and tried to help her up. However, despite her being not much heavier than a paperweight, they could only haul her up so that she was on her knees.

I was calling out to Female Cop, 'Could you please call Captain Sharpe and tell him you're at Judith Singer's house with Judith and Courtney Logan?' when Courtney made her mistake. Grabbing onto Short as if attempting to draw herself up, she tried to open his holster to take his gun. I had to give him credit. Before I could see it coming, he either swatted or smashed her so she was down on the patio again. Then he flipped her over onto her stomach and handcuffed her.

At that point Female stepped back into the house and said something about calling for an ambulance and backup and what was that captain's name at headquarters? I can't recall what else she said, because when I next opened my eyes I was on my living-room couch and the emergency medical technician who was taking my blood pressure was saying, 'Everything's fine, dear.'

Chapter Twenty

'I hate to say it, but you're going to have to regrout your tile.' Nancy stared down at the black and white tiles in the passageway. 'All that blood.' She glanced over to me. 'Are you sure you're all right?'

'Just a little shaky.'

'Seriously, how about a double Absolut? It won't turn you into me.'

'I already had a double Xanax,' I told her.

We strolled back outside and sat on an old beach towel I'd spread on the grass on the side of the house. A cool day for a picnic, but the sky was radiant and the vision of the gun looking down its nose on me seemed fainter in the brightness. Cops were still in the kitchen and out on the patio, although all the crime-scene work seemed over. They chattered the way coworkers do on mornings after the Oscars or a World Series game: Can you *believe* what happened?

'Did Courtney look anything like the shot of her we originally ran?' Nancy asked. 'Or did she look like that nauseating, nostrils-on-parade picture that was in the *Beacon*?'

'Neither. She dyed her hair dark brown, got really dark

brown contact lenses, and lost weight.' Nancy's eyebrows lifted. 'She didn't mention which diet. You know those corky clogs that add a couple of inches? She had them on, so I got the impression of someone five-three or five-four.'

'What was she wearing?'

'You always go right to the heart of the matter,' I said. 'A pink and orange getup. It could have been Ralph Lauren, but you'll probably tell me it wasn't.'

'Describe it.' I did. Wearily, she shook her head. 'No, no, no, you poor, benighted fool. It sounds like Escada. By the way, where is your Little Boy Blue? Or Big Boy Blue? Does he know what happened yet?'

'Of course. He was here for a while.'

'Holding your hand, no doubt.'

'No doubt. But he went back to headquarters to have some jurisdictional dispute over the case. He worked on it, he wants it – for its own sake and as a way back into Homicide – but the *schmendrick* from Homicide who screwed up the case wants to keep it. He said he'll be back.'

Though Nancy didn't change her expression, I somehow found it necessary to add, 'He *will*. And not just for that.' When she did not reply, I changed the subject. 'I can't believe I actually fainted.'

'So Victorian of you.'

'I know. And one of my least favorite eras.'

'You forget Dickens, but you're in shock. God, you were so incredibly brave. To say nothing of effective. Can you talk about it some more or are you just going to stare up at that tree?'

'The noble oak,' I murmured.

'Noble sycamore, you ass. If you want to sit here in

410

comfortable silence, that's all right with me, even though I came here so you could ventilate.'

In the capacity of official best friend, Nancy had arrived in time to hear me giving most of my statement to a young, gum-cracking detective. I'd spoken about the Ellen Berman pretense, the gun in Courtney's hand and all she'd told me, my tearing off the earring, breaking her finger, and then the gun in my hand. For good measure I'd thrown in Courtney's break for freedom, the scuffle, the handcuffs. 'No,' I said. 'I'd like to talk about it.'

'Do you think Emily just surprised Courtney by coming over before Halloween and that's why she got killed?' Nancy asked. 'Or was the whole thing planned?'

'Planned is my guess,' I said, 'although I'm still not sure how detailed the plan was, especially about Emily. Certainly the killing wasn't a whim. Listen, whatever Courtney says is suspect. Maybe Emily did surprise her. Maybe she invited Emily over to get a few more fingerprints on things, have a nice drive with more fingerprints, then murder her in the woods. But it seems to me she'd used her charm to get Emily to go blonder and blonder for a reason, to be a better Courtney substitute. So she must have been thinking of the pool, hoping she'd be left there till the cover came off and the body would be in lousy shape. Or maybe she'd planned on burying Emily in Piney Woods Park, but digging a deep enough grave was too much of an effort. She did seem to spend the fall making plans – getting credit cards and fake ID, probably driving back and forth to Cherry Hill and maybe scouting out places to ditch Emily's car, getting Emily a cell phone in Vanessa Russell's name. And one of the days she sent the au pair Steffi out of the house with the kids: She told Steffi to take them to Baskin-Robbins if they started to kvetch. That was totally out of character. But she wanted to be sure no one could possibly connect her with Emily.'

'Do you want my two cents?' Nancy asked.

'Sure.'

'I think that the minute she had the opportunity to make some serious bucks with Emily's on-line skills and the insider trading, Courtney started planning her own takeover – of the money – and Emily's murder. She strung Emily along, but once she got her mitts on all that money, there was no way she was going to share. Dead Emily was a given the minute Courtney got the money in a nice, warm off-shore account.'

'It was only a matter of timing, then?' I asked.

'Timing and opportunity. Courtney probably wanted out for ages.' Delicately, Nancy picked a few blades of grass off her brown-and-white spectator flats. 'Anybody else would think she had the perfect life, or at least a decent one.'

'I know. But to her, it was a failure. She hadn't made a mark in investment banking. She got turned down for a loan for StarBaby. And StarBaby itself: It wasn't going to tank, but it does sound as though it was going no place fast. Her best friend, Kellye Ryan –'

'Our Lady of Prada?'

'Yes. Kellye and the young woman who was videotaping for her, Zee Friedman, the one I'd love to fix up with Joey: They seemed to think that by the summer Courtney was depressed. And then by the fall, her mind was somewhere else. A new lease on life – that didn't include StarBaby.'

'Don't forget the husband,' Nancy interjected. 'I bet she didn't see him as a man who started a new business and was making a go of it.'

'Of course not. She saw him as a loser, a guy who didn't have the guts to be big.'

'Big was an issue for Courtney,' Nancy observed. A uniformed cop walking by nodded politely. Suddenly, dazed by the power of Nancy's innate man-attractant, he tried to smile suavely. By that time, of course, Nancy had lost track of his very existence.

'That's part of why I think Courtney was planning something before StarBaby's lack of success got her down,' I went on. 'Look, she took twenty-five thousand dollars out of their joint bank and brokerage accounts last spring and summer. I'm sure the police will subpoena her bank records, but she didn't put that money into her StarBaby account.'

'Maybe she spent it on something worthwhile, like clothes,' Nancy suggested. 'Or – listen to this – she took the on-line plunge and lost the whole damn bundle trading stocks on the Internet!'

'That was one of my guesses.' The tranquilizers were starting to take effect. I stretched out on the towel and watched leaves swishing in the breeze. 'Or she could have used some of it to buy fake ID and open bank accounts. I bet that would be hard to find out, though. She used so damn many different names. Nelson said it looked to him as if Courtney had a great source of phony ID. From that ID, she was able to get credit cards and driver's licenses in different names. Usually, good ID like that costs a bundle. So either she was willing to spend a

413

healthy amount of money on it or she got some sort of quantity discount.'

'Where would you buy ID like that?' Nancy asked.

'Why? Whom do you want to be?'

'I don't know. Someone thirty-five. Remember when I was thirty-five? I was thinking, Holy shit, I'm old. Next stop, Death. Now? I would start over somewhere, pass myself off as a thirty-five-year-old – Okay, a thirty-five-year-old who's lived hard. Not in Snore Valley. I suppose it's a cliché, but I'd pick Paris. What I can't comprehend is where did a mommy from Shorehaven come up with first-rate fake ID? She wasn't a criminal.'

'Of course she was! And smarter than most. As far as the ID, there's supposed to be some on the Internet,' I reported. 'Except Courtney strikes me as being too smart to order something like that, a birth certificate or a driver's license – and then go present it to get a passport. She'd be risking arrest. She'd be risking a police or FBI sting. And she'd be risking blackmail by the scumbucket who sold it to her.'

'So where else?'

'She probably could finagle a birth certificate with a raised seal from some county in a sparsely populated state . . . I don't know. Like Montana maybe. Some functionary in New York or Florida wouldn't be able to say "Hey, that's not what a Montana birth certificate looks like." Maybe she just made it her business to find someone who sold high-quality stuff. It shouldn't be different from drugs or any other contraband. Unless you really trust your source, it's terribly risky.'

'So the source could have been some sewer sludge guy

414

– or Courtney herself getting a phony birth certificate?' Nancy asked.

'Right. If it was Courtney, she'd need mail drops. I'm not sure if municipalities would mail a birth certificate to a box number. For all I know, it's the same with end-of-the-month statements from on-line brokers. But considering what else she was willing to do, I suppose a mail drop would be easy enough.'

'She certainly had a sense of entitlement,' Nancy observed. 'Princeton.'

'Please, you don't need three credits in sociopathy to graduate from Princeton. She was – she is – a bad person.'

'Can you imagine, stealing from your joint account with your husband while you're still sleeping in the same room? Tacky. What's fascinating to me is that when her best wasn't good enough, what did she do? Turned around and became another person.'

'Unmitigated chutzpah,' I murmured.

Nancy twisted her hair into a topknot, then let it fall back onto her shoulders. 'Too bad she became disagreeable.'

'The murder business, you mean.'

'Yes, that poor mouse woman. And you, almost!'

'But Courtney was always willing to do whatever it took for her own ends. Remember how she took the Crunch-Munch money and put the blame on Ingrid Farrell?'

'You've got to wonder,' Nancy reflected, 'what kind of a guy Greg Logan is. Not only putting up with her sticking her hand in the till. She must have shown her true colors at some point. Couldn't he know or intuit she was a bad seed?'

'Some people thought she was fine. Kellye Ryan seems to have been genuinely devoted to her.'

'Possibly Kellye is not the person for whom the phrase "Still waters run deep" was coined.'

'That's true,' I agreed. 'Courtney's pool man thought well of her.'

'Always the authoritative judge of virtue.'

'So did her au pair. And Emily, of course. Although the pool guy didn't know her very well. And Emily, may she rest in peace, is dead. And the au pair is so good-hearted she'd probably think . . .'

'What?' Nancy asked. 'You were going to say something about her thinking Hitler was a nice guy, but then you remembered she was Austrian. Am I right?'

'You're in the right neighborhood,' I muttered. 'Okay, yes. But getting back to how people viewed Courtney. A lot of them thought there was something not quite right, not the real McCoy about her. But it's still possible Greg was conned the way Emily was. Listen, it's significant she betrayed the two people who were emotionally dependent on her. One she killed, one she left with a shattered life. Not just that, even though she claimed she was being kind by giving him an alibi, she made him top suspect by putting the body in the pool. And I'm not even mentioning her two kids.'

'Was it the emotional dependency itself that drove her bonkers?' Nancy inquired.

'Could be. She is really, really sick. Nelson said he's met more than his share of those. Psychos or sociopaths or whatever. Most people think of them as madmen like Charles Manson, or obsessed losers like Timothy McVeigh. But he says a fair number of them are smart, attractive, charming. Like con men, who don't just need the money;

416

they need to pull the scam, to destroy lives. And I think with Courtney, her craziness –'

'Or overwhelming greed.'

'Or need. Whatever it was, it gave her the power, the energy to be convincing.' I got up from the towel and straightened out my shirt. 'Guess what?' I said.

'You're going for a nap.'

'How did you know? Seriously?'

'Give me a break. And after the nap? Him?'

'No. My client, Fancy Phil Lowenstein. And Gregory Logan.'

It took me nearly two hours to tell Greg and Fancy Phil all that had happened from the beginning of the case. We sat in the Logan living room the way I had the last time. Not a speck of dust, the nap of the rug vacuumed to attention, but it didn't look as though it had been used since my last visit. The room was still a shrine to Courtney's grimly impeccable sense of design. But as I wound down my story, I noticed the tortoiseshell-framed photograph of husband and wife, Courtney and Greg aglow and agleam in their tennis whites, was no longer on the table beside the antique leather-bound books and the fat-bottomed onyx vase.

'I don't know what to say,' Greg told me at last.

'Say you're sorry,' Fancy Phil boomed from his side of the striped couch.

'Dad, you and I made a deal.'

'So don't say you're sorry.' Fancy Phil was dressed conservatively: only a flat, half-inch-wide gold chain and its matching bracelet. His shirt was Hawaiian style with a repeating pattern of Gauguin's *Tahitian Women on the Beach*.

Greg, in khaki slacks, white cotton cable-knit sweater, and sailing moccasins, sat in the wing chair where he'd been the last time I was there. He looked even more worn than the month before. His tan had faded to parchment, perhaps because he could no longer find golf partners, perhaps because he was now spending all his free time with his children. 'I am sorry about how I treated you,' he said.

'Listen, I was out of order, coming here the way I did,' I told him. 'It was just that I felt I had a chance of finding out at least something in this case. It didn't dawn on me that I'd be viewed as another in a long series of nuts intruding on your privacy. I should have been more sensitive.'

'I'm not only sorry, I'm grateful. I owe . . . well, if not my life, then everything else to you.'

'I'm the one who went over to her house and talked her into doing it,' Fancy Phil announced.

'I'm glad you did, Phil,' I told him. 'You're a great father.'

Greg nodded his agreement. 'How do you think she was able to get away Halloween night?' he asked. 'That's what I still can't understand. The car was in the garage.'

'My guess?' I said. 'She probably left the garage door open, backed out, and waved good-bye. She came back a little while later without her headlights on. It was dark by then. Sunset was before five that day.'

'So what the hell did she do? Walk to Sun Valley?' Fancy Phil demanded.

'No,' I said. 'She'd rented a car in Manhattan a week or two before. On the Samantha R. Corby credit card. Maybe she had that car parked close by. A couple of blocks' stroll and she was off. Not to Sun Valley right away. She spent some time in Miami –'

418

'Bitch!' Fancy Phil said. Before his son could say a word, he said: 'Sorry, Gregory. I'll leave it alone.' He turned to me. 'Before you got here we was talking. About a lot of things. About what he should say to the kids now.' Then to Greg he said: 'Whatever you tell them, kid, it'll be as good as anybody can say it.'

'I'd have to check with Steffi Deissenburger,' I went on. 'But I wouldn't be surprised if the bye-bye Mommy game started in September.'

'Why?' Greg asked.

'So she could have an adult witness to her driving off. Then she went to Florida. My guess is she already had at least a bank account set up there and some kind of address or mail drop. She might have even made a trip down there earlier, setting up whatever needed setting up. We know she charged tickets to Miami. She could do that in one day, fly there and back, and be home by seven-thirty.'

'Do you think she had someone there?' Greg asked quietly. 'A man?'

'I have no idea. I assume she went down there just to rest and establish a tan. Her story was she lived on Key Biscayne.'

'What about . . . with Emily Chavarria? I mean, their relationship.'

'Most likely a case of hero worship by a lonely young woman that Courtney exploited. But instead of being a good role model, she turned out to be a Svengali.'

Greg nodded. Fancy Phil said: 'A *what?*'

'How long do you think . . . How long a sentence will she get?' Greg asked.

'I haven't a clue,' I told him. 'Unfortunately, she can

probably afford a good lawyer. Let's hope she can't charm a jury.'

'Do you think there's a chance she could get off?' Greg went from looking pallid to looking ill.

'Gregory.' Fancy Phil leaned forward toward his son. 'Don't worry about a jury. Guilty, not guilty, she's never gonna get off.'

On Long Island, roses are at their sumptuous best in the middle of June. At the end of the day I was out by the bushes clipping away when Nelson came by. I showed him a pale pink one with silvery outer petals. 'I never remember the names of them,' I said, 'but this is an antique rose – brought over from France in the early nineteenth century. You know, around the time the pirate Jean Lafitte stopped plundering ships. He took time off to fight for the United States. He helped defend New Orleans during the War of 1812.'

'Is that a history lesson or are you asking me to see the good side of Fancy Phil?'

'Both, I guess.'

'If it's any comfort to you,' Nelson said, 'that week when we were tailing him . . . That particular time, we were actually after the guy he was supposed to meet.'

'But Fancy never met him, did he?' I tried not to sound overly triumphant.

'I don't know. He was able to shake the tail. He's made tail-shaking into an art form.'

I clipped another rose. Nelson took it from my hand and put it into the bucket of water with the others. 'Are you ready to talk about us?'

'Today was a little on the stressful side, what with having to rip someone's flesh and grab a bloody gun and then a finger.'

'I want to *un*stress you. Let's go sit down and talk.'

I glanced toward the patio. 'I want to stay outside, but I'm not in the mood for looking at Courtney Logan's blood droplets.'

'Here's okay, then,' Nelson said. 'Look, I know you had more than your share today. I'll make it quick. I'm going to get a divorce.'

'Listen, before you –'

'With you or without you, Judith, it was going to happen. It's not only that we're not happy. We're not – how the hell can I put it? We're not even good companions to each other. I married her because she was a decent person and pretty and I couldn't take dating anymore. At the time I thought that was love.' He glanced away, then looked back. 'I was kind of screwed up for a while.'

'So was I. Probably from the day we said good-bye.'

'Me, too,' he said quietly.

'Maybe even before.'

'Maybe me, too.'

'But listen, Nelson. We've only known each other in one way.'

'Which is . . . ?'

'As adulterers.'

'God almighty! Do you think I'm a compulsive . . . fucker-arounder?'

'Not at all. Do you think I am?'

'No,' he said. 'Of course not.'

'All that I'm saying is, if at some point you do get free –'

421

'It's a done deal.'

'– and that's entirely between you and your wife, then you and I can see what it's like truly being together. Leading real lives together. Legit.'

'Living together?' he asked.

'I don't know. Is that what you want?'

'Yes.'

'Well, it's probably what I want. Or to be more truthful, I love you more than you'll ever know. I want you body and soul. But let's see how it works in the real world. I may hate your taste in music. You might hate my friends or your friends might hate me. We might love or detest each other's children.'

'So we'll start out how?' He slipped his hands into his pockets, a casual pose, a way of looking cool at the start of a negotiation.

'We'll go on a date. We'll spend a weekend together. We'll be single. Free. Legit. We'll each go to work, we'll call each other. If I remember correctly, we'll talk more about the Mets than about politics because political discussions weren't our finest hour as a couple. What I'm saying is, we'll be –'

'Natural?'

'That's good. Natural.'

'Judith, I want to marry you.'

'I want to marry you, too. But before we buy the rings and send out the invitations, we should go for a walk, go to the movies.'

'And then more,' he said softly.

'Maybe.'

Magic Hour

To my best friend,
Susan Zises

Acknowledgments

I sought advice and information from the people listed below. All of them gave it freely and cheerfully. I want to thank Arlene Abramowitz, Janice Asher, Peter Corwith, Lawrence Goldman, Maddy Kahn, Susan Lawton, Neil Leinwohl, Tony Lepsis, Fr Thomas McCarthy, Bob Mitchell, Catherine and Robert Morvillo, Saundra and Herschel Saperstein, Cynthia Scott, Abby Singer, Dustin Beall Smith, N. T. Thayer, Sr, William Wexler, and Frank and Lisa Cronin Wohl.

A hug and a kiss to my great pal, Frank Perry, who taught me about making movies.

A salute to the police officers who answered my technical questions. Unlike Detective Stephen Brady, they were all straight shooters and gentlemen. I apologize if I twisted the facts to fit my fiction. Thanks to Detective-Lieutenant Eugene Dolan of the Nassau County Police, Captain William Kilfoyle and Officer Alan Paxton of the Port Washington (New York) Police, Lieutenant William P. Kiley and Captain John McElhone of the Suffolk County Police, and Sergeant William Crowley of the Southampton Town Police.

The staffs of The Hampton Library in Bridgehampton and the Port Washington (New York) Public Library were unfailingly courteous and helpful.

A special thank you to Paul Brennan, who was generous enough to share his memories of growing up in Bridgehampton with me.

My assistant, AnneMarie Palmer, deserves cheers,

bouquets, standing ovations, and whatever else she might want for her hard work and grace under pressure.

Owen Laster, my agent, manages to be both hard-headed and kindhearted. He is truly a class act.

Larry Ashmead is a great editor. All writers should be as lucky as I am.

My children, Andrew and Betsy Abramowitz, are no longer children. I thank them for their wise and perceptive editorial comments and, of course, for their love.

Finally, in case anyone is curious about who the best person in the world is, it is still my husband, Elkan Abramowitz.

CHAPTER 1

❧⊙❧

Seymour Ira Spencer of Manhattan and Southampton was a class act. Hey, the last thing you'd think was 'movie producer'. No herringbone gold chain rested on a bed of chest hair; there was no fat mouth, definitely no cigar. If you could have seen him, in his plain white terry-cloth bathrobe (which he was too well-bred to have monogrammed), standing on the tile deck of the pool of his beachfront estate, Sandy Court, sipping a glass of iced black-currant tea, talking softly into his portable phone, you'd have thought: *This* is what they mean when they say good taste.

I'll tell you how tasteful Sy Spencer was. He actually might have hung up, strolled inside and picked out a Marcel Proust book to reread. Except just then he got blasted by two bullets, one in his medulla, one in his left ventricle. He was dead before he hit the deck.

Too bad. It was a gorgeous August day. I remember. The sky was a blue so pure and powerful you almost couldn't look at it. Who could take that much beauty? Down at the beach, where Sy was, silver-white gulls soared, then dive-bombed into the ocean. The sand gleamed pale gold. Farther north, out beyond my backyard, potato fields gave off a rich, dark-green light.

It was the kind of perfect Long Island day that makes the summer people say: 'Darrr-ling [or *Ma chère* or Kiddo], this is *such* a glorious time out here. And do you know what's so pathetic? All the little social climbers are so busy being upwardly mobile that they never get to appreciate' – taking a deep, sensitive sniff of fresh air through their dilated nostrils – 'such breathtaking loveliness.'

Jesus, were they full of shit! But they were right. That day, the sun bathed the entire South Fork of Long Island in glorious light. It was like a divine payoff. For the last five years, one of the secretaries in Homicide had been bestowing the same benediction on me: 'Have a nice day, Detective Brady!' Well, God had finally come through. This was it.

For Sy Spencer, of course, this was not it. And to be perfectly honest, the day, wonderful as it was, wasn't so nice for me either. Nothing as dramatic as Sy's day. Definitely not so fatal. But the events of that sunny summer afternoon changed the ending of my story almost as much as they did Sy's.

I was home in the northwest corner of Bridgehampton, six miles east and five miles north of Sandy Court, in considerably less impressive circumstances. My house was a former migrant worker's shack. It had been renovated by a hysterically ambitious, pathetically untalented ponytailed Brooklyn Heights architect, who comprehended, too late, that the place would never be considered a Find. He had been forced to sell it cheap to one of the locals (me) because even the most gullible smoothie from New York would not buy a low-ceilinged, Thermopaned whitewashed hovel with a six-burner restaurant stove and aggressively cute fruits and flowers stenciled along the walls and floors, situated on a rutted, geographically undesirable road between a potato field and a stagnant pond.

Anyway, somewhere around the time the bullet blasted through the base of Sy's skull, my life also blew up. Our two lives – ka-boom! – were joined. Of course, I didn't

10

know it. Unlike movies, life has no sound track; there was no ominous roll of drums. For me, it was still a nice day. A fantastic day. There I was, with my fiancée, Lynne Conway, lying on a blanket on the grass in my backyard, having moved outside from the bedroom for a little postcoital sun, conversation and iced tea. (I'd even thrown a couple of lemon circles into our glasses, to show that, okay, Lynne might have gone to Manhattanville College and known about fish forks, but I could still be a gracious host.)

Of course, if I had been truly gracious, we would have been stretched out on lounge chairs, but in the last few years I hadn't had time for amenities like towels without holes, much less outdoor furniture. So what? I knew all that would change in three months, when we got married. We'd have lounge chairs on a brick patio. A barbecue with a domed cover. Tuberous begonias. I would stop referring to the bacon-cheddar cheeseburgers I ate in the greasiest diners in Suffolk County as dinner; I would come home to poached salmon with parsleyed potatoes, fresh asparagus. I would, at age forty, be a newlywed.

I turned over onto my side. Lynne was so pretty. Dark-red hair, that Irish setter color. Peachy young skin. A perfect nose, slightly upturned, with two tiny indentations on the tip, as though God had made a fast realignment in the final seconds before her birth. She wore khaki shorts that revealed her fabulous long legs. It wasn't just her looks, though. Lynne was a lady.

She came from a good family . . . well, compared to mine. Her father was a retired navy cipher expert. His retirement seemed to consist of sitting in a club chair, his white-socked feet on an ottoman, reading right-wing magazines and getting enraged at Democrats.

11

Lynne's mother, Saint Babs of Annapolis, went to Mass every morning, where she probably prayed that the Lamb of God would strike me dead before I could marry her daughter. Babs Conway needlepointed all afternoon while she watched *The Young and the Restless* and *Geraldo;* she was eight years into her masterwork, a gigantic 'The Marys at the Sepulchre' throw pillow.

So there was Lynne: a nice Catholic girl. And a good woman. A beauty. Believe me. I knew precisely how lucky I was to have her. My life had not been what you'd call a charmed existence. Happiness was a blessing I'd doubted I deserved and never believed I would receive.

'For the honeymoon,' she said softly, adjusting the shoulder seam of my T-shirt, 'what would you think – this is just another option – if instead of Saint John we spent a week in London?'

'You want to snorkel in the Thames in late November?'

Lynne smiled, and the smile made her look even lovelier. She offered no wisecracks. No: Do you think I want to spend my honeymoon with some schmuck in flippers? What she said, without a trace of sarcasm, was: 'I think I get the point. Saint John.' I gazed into Lynne's fine brown eyes.

And then I stopped having a nice day.

Because there I was with a wonderful, kindhearted, titian-haired, honey-skinned woman, and all I was having was a nice day. I wasn't having fun.

This is nuts, I said to myself. I had to understand that Lynne was young. She didn't quite get me yet. To her, I was a man of the world. It was kind of sweet. Okay, I wished she'd loosen up just a little. I admitted it. I even admitted I was a little tense. I should have wanted a drink. But listen, I told myself, I *don't* want a drink. I'm doing fine.

12

Still, that was why, when Headquarters called fifteen minutes later and said, There's been a homicide reported in your neck of the woods, ha-ha, on Dune Road in Southampton — that's *the* high-rent district, right? — a movie producer, Somebody Spencer, was shot . . .

Jesus H. Christ, I said. Sy Spencer.

You know him?

I know about him. My brother's doing some work for him on the movie he's making out here.

Hey, is it true he won an Oscar a couple of years ago?

Yeah.

I bet I saw him! On TV, you know, one of those guys saying: I wanna thank my agent and my parents and my late cat, Fluff. Listen, it's your day off, but you're the only one who lives way the hell out in the Hamptons, and we just got called in on a mess in Sachem where some computer nerd got into a fight with his old man and strangled him and tried to hide him under the compost heap, so could you get over and establish a presence? Keep the village police eager beavers from playing cops, sticking everything not nailed down into Baggies. You know how they can fuck up a crime scene. Thanks, pal.

. . . Well, I felt a certain gratitude toward Sy Spencer.

I walked Lynne out to her car and kissed her goodbye. 'Sorry, but this one sounds like it's going to totally screw up our weekend.'

She squeezed my hand and said, 'Come on. I'm an old pro by now. I just feel awful about your brother's boss. What a shock!' Then she added, 'I love you, Steve.'

I thought: This woman is going to be a wonderful wife. A terrific mother. So I said, 'I love you too.'

A homicide would be a snap compared to this. Which shows you how much I knew.

*

13

The night was as beautiful as the day had been. But neither the moon that rose four hours later nor the floodlights from the Emergency Services truck shining on the crime scene could make cheerful what was, in fact, gruesome: a corpse.

Although a corpse in a spectacular setting. Sy Spencer's lifeless body sprawled facedown on his tile deck. These were no ordinary exorbitantly priced tiles; about one out of every five of the deep-blue squares was hand-painted with a different fish, all of them too fashionably thin and richly colored to truly exist in Long Island coastal waters. But as some New York exterior decorator probably explained to Sy, they combined an oceanic motif with tongue-in-cheek chic.

The pool itself was long, luminous aqua. In the cool night air, a mist, like a rectangular cloud, hovered over the water. Sy's graceful, sprawling gray-shingled house, built in the early twenties, in that lost era of huge families and happy servants, rose up three stories high behind the pool. If you turned the other way, you saw soft sand and the Atlantic.

'How's your beautiful bride-to-be?' Sergeant Ray Carbone asked me. We were standing right near Sy's head. Carbone wore a blue serge suit and Clark Kent glasses. With his small frame, potbelly and hunched-over back, he looked more like an overtaxed accountant than a disguised Superman.

'Still beautiful,' I said.

'She's a lot more than beautiful. Rita and I were talking about you two the other day. Lynne gives you just what you need. Stability. Stability's the name of the game.'

'For me, it has to be.'

'Don't think I was talking about the drinking.'

'It's okay. You can talk about it.'

14

'As far as I'm concerned, that's history. Look, I know there's no such thing as a re*cov*ered alcoholic. You're always recover*ing* – for the rest of your life. But, Steve, you were classic emotionally labile.' Carbone, who had a master's in forensic science, was going for a second one, in psychology. 'You'd be Mr Nice Guy, and then you'd become so withdrawn – like no one was home inside – and then you'd start with the belligerence. But the past few years: what a difference! You're as solid as they come. Trust me. You don't have to worry.'

'No. I always have to worry.'

'Wrong. But you know what? Your not being complacent is a sign of wellness.' That's what happens to a guy after twenty-four credits at the State University at Stony Brook. 'Actually,' he went on, 'what I meant by stability was a fire in the hearth. Good company. A nice bowl of soup. We need something normal, healthy to come home to after what we have to look at.' Twenty-four credits couldn't entirely knock out Carbone's basic common sense.

A technician from ID elbowed his way past us, knelt down beside Sy, and slipped bags over the lifeless hands. (Paper bags. In movies, they use plastic. Scary when the camera moves in close, those lifeless hands wrapped like last week's Oscar Mayer pimento loaf. Very visual. But very phony: we never use them. Plastic traps moisture and screws up any chance of doing an FDR test, to see if the victim fired a weapon.)

'What did you find inside?' I asked Ray.

'Nothing. No signs of robbery, no violence. Sy had packed a carry-on bag to go to LA for some meetings. There was an unmade bed in the guest room. He could have taken a nap.' The button on Carbone's too-snug suit jacket popped open. Not counting his midsection, he was thin. But his clothes were always a size too small for his basketball of a belly. 'The cook was downstairs the whole time,' he continued. 'Nice lady. She gave me a bowl of clam chowder, the red kind. She's making something now for all the guys. All she heard was the shots. Nothing before that.'

'Nothing after?'

'No. She looked out the window, saw Sy, ran out to him, saw he was dead. The way his head was turned, she could see that one eye, open.' We both glanced down. The hood of Sy's bathrobe was pulled back far enough that you could see his quarter profile and a bit of his hair: short, tight gray curls, cut middle-aged-gladiator style. The one eye that was visible was wide open. Because of the position of his head, the eye stared downward, as though it had found a hideous flaw in one of the fancy fish tiles. 'She called the village police.'

'From the portable phone?'

'No. She said she knows not to touch anything near a murder victim. She went into the kitchen.'

Okay, I thought, what kind of homicide do we have here? Not a heat-of-the-moment crime of passion, a murder arising out of jealousy or a family quarrel. And so far there was nothing to indicate a felony murder, a killing that occurs during the commission of another crime, like a burglary.

I knew I should hang on for forensic results – the autopsy report with photographs and videos, the toxicology and serology reports – but there I was, itching to figure out what kind of a guy/gal (I'm an equal-opportunity detective) the perpetrator was.

Well, it was easy to figure out that this killer wasn't some impulsive jerk who, in a moment of madness, grabbed a stake from the flower garden and turned Sy into a human shish kebab. No, this killer was extremely well organized, bright enough to plan the murder, bring his own weapon and take it away with him. His getaway had been slick too: completely uneventful. Judging from the lack of any physical evidence so far, he hadn't gotten rattled.

Another thing that struck me – from the first minute I saw Sy – was that although the killer had a brain, he had no heart. I always notice how the perpetrator treats the victim; it tells so much. This one didn't seem like a psychopath. I knew I'd have to wait for the autopsy, but it didn't seem like there would be mutilation – no sicko ritualistic marks, no deranged slashing. So he was heartless but no sadist; there was no need to terrify, no gun shoved in the victim's mouth or gut or genitals. Sy had been shot from a distance, from behind, impersonally.

But just as there were no indications of cruelty, there were no signs of decency either: no concern, no remorse. The killer had not covered Sy's face, or closed that awful, staring eye, or picked a flower and tossed it toward the body.

Of course, it could be a stranger murder, a nut case unknown to Sy. 'You hear about anybody else getting taken out this way?' I asked Carbone. I did my homework if I was in the mood; he always did his. If there was a serial killer operating within fifty thousand miles of Suffolk County, he'd have read about it. 'Rich people? Movie people? People shot from a distance?'

'I'll check with the FBI, but I don't think so. Unless this is number one.'

'We've got a cool cookie here,' I observed. 'An organized fucker.' We'd wait for the post-offense behavior, to see if it was a Son of Sam-type wacko

17

who'd want to declare his genius to the police. 'Good shot too. Got to give him credit.'

'So what do you think the weapon was?'

'Low-gauge rifle?' I asked the ballistics guy, who was standing a couple of yards away, opening his case.

He nodded. 'Looks like a .22.'

Carbone muttered: 'Damn. That's not going to make our life easy.'

He was right. Here on the South Fork, .22s were a dime a dozen. Everybody had one; locals used them for target practice, small-varmint shooting. Or anything. If a farmer wanted to kill a pig, he'd get out his .22; my father had owned one.

'What background were you able to get on this Sy guy?' Carbone asked me.

'Fifty-three years old. Dartmouth College graduate. From a rich family – kosher provisions business. The ones with that commercial where they all sit around the kitchen table in crowns: "Bologna for the Royal Family!" But it sounds like he wasn't all that turned on by lunch meats. He wanted culture. He started a big poetry magazine, *Shower of Light,* about twelve years ago. Put a pile of money into it. But then he seemed to have decided that poetry wouldn't get him what he wanted.'

'What was that?'

'Who the hell knows? What do most guys want? Excitement. Fame. Fortune. Superior ass. I mean, who would you rather hit on, a receptionist in a pastrami factory or a poet? Or a movie star?' Carbone the Thoughtful looked like he was actually beginning to contemplate the alternatives. 'Ray, the answer is: Movie star with giant boobs.'

'I don't like those big, big ones,' he said, thoughtfully.

18

'What do you like? A girl who looks like she's got two Hershey's Kisses glued on her chest?'

'No, but you see a young girl with giant ones, you figure that when she's thirty-five . . .' He shook his head in sadness.

'When she's thirty-five,' the ballistics guy interrupted, 'you trade her in for two seventeen-and-a-half-year-olds.' He chuckled at his own wit, then added: 'Move back a little, out of my way.'

'Anyway,' I continued, as we moved back, 'all along, Sy Spencer was pretty much a man-about-town, one of those people who pop up now and then in the gossip columns. No dirt: just some guy with major bucks who gave money to the right causes, went to all those jet-setty charity benefits. That seems to be where he met the movie types who have houses out here. And he got it into his head that he wanted to be a movie producer. Apparently, so do half the people in his world. But he got what he wanted.'

'You know, I've heard his name. Good movies, right?'

'No doubt about it. The guy had class.'

'So, Steve. Gut reaction.'

'It's going to be a media circus. Plus a major pain because we're dealing with hotshots who expect heavy-duty ass-kissing: "No, thanks, sir, I don't drink while I'm on duty," when they offer us the cheap-shit Seagram's they've been keeping from before they became famous. And – unless we get lucky in the next seventy-two hours and find someone in Sy's life stroking a warm .22 – it's going to be an absolute bitch to crack. Sy was the ultimate fast-track guy; he probably had fourteen Rolodexes, and those were just for personal friends.'

'Where would you start?'

'The movie he was producing, I guess. It's called *Starry*

19

Night. They're shooting it over in East Hampton now.'

'No kidding! *Now?*'

Having spent my whole life being local color in what people called the Fashionable Hamptons, I was used to rubbing shoulders with celebrities. Well, not exactly rubbing. But from the time I was a kid, besides the regular rich and semi-rich summer people, there'd be famous models squeezing tomatoes at a farm stand, or TV anchormen picking out a toilet plunger in the hardware store in town – right next to you. We knew to pretend they were just plain people, but we also knew it was okay to ogle as they paid the cashier. Neither they nor we wanted them so plain as to be overlooked.

But Carbone came from the *plain* plain world, suburban Suffolk County, a world peopled by ex-third-generation Brooklynites – shoe salesmen and IRS auditors and junior high school social studies teachers – a world that, if plopped down outside downtown Indianapolis or Des Moines, would not seem an unnatural part of the landscape. 'East Hampton's only – what? – ten, twelve miles away,' he was saying. His eyes were lit by a starry sparkle. 'We may have to go over there to question some people on the movie set.' Carbone was normally so levelheaded, so thoughtful, you'd think he'd have been glitz-proof, but at the thought of Lights! Camera! Action! he was loosening his tie, unbuttoning the top button of his shirt. If there'd been a straw hat and cane, he'd have grabbed them and high-stepped over to East Hampton, belting out 'Hooray for Hollywood'.

'Who's starring?' he asked, much too casually.

'Lindsay Keefe and Nicholas Monteleone.'

'No kidding!' Then, fast, he switched back to his I'm-a-regular-guy mode. 'I always liked him,' he said. 'Reminds me of a young Gary Cooper. Good without being a

20

goody-goody. And she's a good actress.' Carbone shook his head in sadness. 'But too left-wing for my taste.'

'With her body, do you care what her position on disarmament is?'

Suddenly it hit Carbone. 'Is Lindsay Keefe *here*?' he asked, his voice a little hushed with awe. 'In the house?'

'Upstairs, with her agent. You didn't hear her? He's trying to calm her down.'

'Can you believe it? I was *in* there, interviewing the cook. I didn't even know she was here, in the same house.'

'The agent brought her back from the set. Heavy-duty hysterics.' Carbone's eyebrows began drawing together in sympathy, so I added: 'Let's not forget she's an actress. Anyway, according to the agent, for the last six months Lindsay's been living with Sy. Here, and he has a duplex on Fifth Avenue. They're madly in love. Perfect relationship. Never a harsh word between them. Blah, blah, blah. The usual. Oh, and they were going to get married the minute the movie was finished.'

'You believe the agent?'

'He's not a slimeball. He's an older guy named Eddie Pomerantz. Late sixties, early seventies. You can't miss him. A color-coordinated hippo: pink polo shirt and forty-eight-waist pink madras slacks. He was the one Sy was on the phone with when he was killed. Claims they were discussing some minor problem about photo approval. A movie star gets to approve any picture before it's handed out to the press, and Pomerantz said someone on this movie slipped a shot of Lindsay drinking coffee with her hair up in curlers to *USA Today* and she started crying when it got published because it's detrimental to her career to be seen in hair curlers.' I shook my head. 'For this the guy gets ten percent.

21

Anyway, Pomerantz said he heard two shots over the phone.'

'You buy his story?' Carbone asked.

'I buy that he heard two shots. He sounded pretty definite on that. But he kept eating nuts like a fucking maniac. There was a giant bowl of nuts on the table in the library or den or whatever it's called, and he must have glommed two pounds of pistachios in five minutes. I was going to tell him not to eat potential evidence, but he was such a nervous wreck I didn't have the heart. He was upset about Sy, and *very* worried about his client.'

'Could it be normal professional concern?'

'Could be.'

'Listen, in this situation, concern would be an appropriate response. You know and I know and this Pomerantz must know that murder may mean publicity, but in the long run, being the mistress of a homicide victim isn't going to help anyone's career.' I nodded in agreement. 'What's the matter? Do you think he's afraid of something specific?'

'Couldn't tell. But we've got to consider if this business is in any way related to Lindsay Keefe. A jealous ex-boyfriend. Or some jealous ex-girlfriend of Sy's who got pissed off that Lindsay came into the picture.'

'And we have to find out if things were really that hunky-dory between Sy and Lindsay,' Carbone said.

'Yeah. Maybe Sy did something so terrible she felt she *had* to kill him.'

'Like what?'

'How should I know, Ray? Maybe he left dental floss with last night's corn on the cob on the sink. Who the hell knows what sets people off, makes them kill? Do you?'

'No.'

22

'Me neither. Maybe it was just something boring, like Sy was getting it on with the script girl.'

'You can't wait to start with the hypotheses, can you, Brady?'

'No. Now listen: someone on this movie besides Lindsay might have had a grudge. Or from some other movie. Or it could have been a cold-blooded hit. We've got to find out what kind of life Sy had – beyond his movie life. Did he gamble? Was he cooking the books? Into weird sex? Doing drugs?'

A video tech stepped in front of us and, walking around Sy's body, aimed his camera on the white robe. Then he zoomed in on the two small splotches: the one on the hood, where a bullet entered just above Sy's brain stem, and another by his left shoulder blade.

'You'd never think of a man like Sy as a victim of anything,' Carbone mused. 'He seems like the ultimate winner.'

'I know. Look at all this,' I said, glancing around the pool area.

White wood tubs overflowed with trailing ivy and deep-purple flowers that gave off a light, spicy scent: nothing too perfumy, nothing too obvious. The chaises lay back, deep, welcoming. Small stone tables were carved like diving fish. You'd put your drink on the tail. White umbrellas on bamboo poles stood tall, like giant parasols. Almost-invisible quadraphonic speakers peeked up from the velvet grass.

'Ray, I bet your wildest fantasy isn't as good as what Sy actually had. What was missing that any reasonable man could want?'

Carbone started mulling it over, probably thinking something like a cohesive family unit or Self-knowledge.

What I was thinking was: If Sy had stuck with kosher salamis and not had all his dreams come true, would he

23

now be alive, dressing for dinner, buttoning a three-hundred-dollar sports shirt, or sticking his pinkie into the salad dressing to check whether his cook was using enough basil or chives or whatever this month's most fabulous herb was? Why, on this spendid summer night, was Seymour Ira Spencer, the Man Who Had Everything, playing host to a bunch of cops who were swabbing between his toes, tweezing fluff off his bathrobe and cracking Lindsay Keefe tit jokes over his dead body?

Look at a map. Long Island resembles a smiley but slightly demented whale. Its head – Brooklyn – butts against Manhattan, as if trying to get into some hot party from which it was deliberately excluded.

But unlike bubble-brained Brooklyn, the whale's body wants no part of the high life. Queens, Nassau and suburban Suffolk County just swim, eternally, in the bracing waters between the Atlantic and Long Island Sound, yearning to reach mainland America. See how the whale's hump arches up in longing? All it wants is to be part of the US of A, where life resembles a Coke commercial.

Okay, now check out the rest of Suffolk County, the whale's forked tail. The tail isn't swishing a salute to either Manhattan or Middle America. No, it's raised high to greet Connecticut and Rhode Island. The East End of Long Island is, really, the seventh New England state.

See? On the North Fork of the tail, there are Yankee-style farms, fishing fleets and a few intensely quaint colonial villages that lack only a hand-carved 'I am unspoiled' sign. And now look at the South Fork, my home. Our accents closer to Boston than the Bronx. Solid Anglo stock, augmented (most would say improved) by Indians, blacks, Germans, Irish, Poles and Others. More farms again. More cute towns. But unspoiled like the North Fork?

No, spoiled beyond comprehension.

For over a hundred years, artists and clods, geniuses and jerks, have been coming out here with their ways – and their money. To the Hamptons. 'We summer in the Homp-tons,' they say. Do they ever: in oh-so-social Southampton, don't-say-rich-say-comfortable Water Mill, bookish Bridgehampton, belligerently down-to-earth Sag Harbor, show-bizzy East Hampton, home-of-the-boring Amagansett (I think the last truly interesting person to live in Amagansett died in 1683) and I-am-one-with-the-sea Montauk.

This summer paradise isn't my South Fork, though; it belongs to men like Sy and to the legions of lesser New Yorkers who yearn to walk in his footprints in the sand. It is the Eden of the urbane: beach clubs, tennis clubs, yacht clubs, golf clubs; power breakfasts in the designated-chic local coffee shop, power softball games, power clam-bakes, power naps.

But along this narrow strip of trendy whale's tail, there are also hamlets called Tuckahoe and North Sea and Noyack and Deerfield. And there are people who neither know nor care that the copper beech is the Tree of Choice and the Japanese maple is Almost Out, or that duck is a passé poultry. There are people who are here not to vacation but to live lives: farmers, supermarket cashiers, dentists, welfare recipients, librarians, truckdrivers, short-order cooks, lawyers, housewives, carpenters, lobstermen, hospital orderlies. Oh, yes – and cops.

My name is Stephen Edward Brady. I was born in Southampton Hospital. A few days later, I went home with my mother to Brady Farm in Bridgehampton. It's still there. Not the farm, of course. My father sold everything but the farmhouse and two acres in 1955, a little more than a decade before the big land boom that would have made them rich, the only thing my mother had ever wanted to be.

I was born on May 17, 1949, to Kevin Francis Brady, farmer and (in the great South Fork tradition) drunk, and to Charlotte Easton (of the Sag Harbor Eastons) Brady, housewife and social climber. In 1951, my brother Easton was born.

I went to Sagaponack Elementary School, a one-room school-house. (The summer people say: 'I love it! It's so *real*.' So okay, A for ambience. C− for education. B for freezing dampness that makes your fingers throb in the winter. And A+ for smells from decomposing rodents under the foundation in late spring.) Then I went to Bridgehampton High. And then the State University of New York at Albany.

It wasn't that I'd been such a saint in high school, but at least I'd known who I was and that I'd belonged. Sure, I was a bad boy in Bridgehampton − a little driving while intoxicated, a little breaking and entering. In my heart I knew it was a phase, that someday I would become a solid citizen, buy back my father's farm, sit on the school board.

But I picked the wrong generation, and the wrong genes. Up at Albany, I became just another whacked-out asshole with sideburns. I embraced my generation's holy trinity: sex, drugs, and rock and roll. I was a true believer. I screwed and drank and drugged along with Jim Morrison and Jimi Hendrix and Janis Joplin. I didn't die, though. I flunked out.

So I enlisted in the United States Army. Why? To this day, I have no idea. I can't re-create the boy I was, the boy who could do something that dumb and self-destructive.

On my first day of basic, they clipped my hair with a machine that left it less than a quarter inch long. I remember standing at attention and having a five-foot-three Filipino drill sergeant reach up and grab those hairs between his thumb and index finger, pull at them, and scream up into my face, 'Fucking hippie!' All I wanted to do was go home. I knew I wasn't man enough to take it. Except I had to take it. In those eight weeks, the army's goal is to break you down, then build you up again into a machine that obeys all commands without thought or argument. Well, they broke me down. I cried myself to sleep every night. There I was, a big guy, a soldier, boo-hooing into my pillow so that no one, especially all the other crybabies, could hear me.

But I went off to war an infantryman, a master of the M79 grenade launcher. I fought for God and America and the honor of the Brady bunch. No. Actually, I just fought to stay alive. I fought even harder not to feel alive. Feeling dead was a major asset in Vietnam. I moved on from hash and pot to smoking opium joints. And after about a month, skag.

Skag is heroin. Five or ten percent pure on the streets in the States. Ninety-six percent pure in Vietnam. No needles: cigarettes. You just had to inhale, so you weren't a junkie. We were all very clear on that. We were just a bunch of grunts sitting around smoking at night after a hard day's work in the jungle: a little patrolling, a little shooting, and then stacking up stinking dink corpses so we could get our body count and move on for more.

Skag was cheap: three bucks a hit. Skag was good for us grown-up GI Joes, better than pot, because pot makes time go very, very slow. Heroin lifts you out of your body, takes you out of time. It got me through those three hundred and sixty-five days in hell. No, I wasn't caught. If you had brains and a little foresight, you could get a buddy to pee for you and were home free. (Ha.) I was discharged, honorably.

I hadn't been doing skag every day. Just almost every day. I said to myself: You're not addicted. But when I landed back in the States after the eighteen-hour flight, I was sick — leg pains when we refueled in Guam, stomach cramps, the sweats in Hawaii. Terrible diarrhea the whole time, banging on the door of the airplane bathroom, doubled over, screaming at the top of my lungs: Please, oh God, let me in!

In San Francisco I had to buy heroin on the street. Three days, five hundred bucks. I couldn't handle a needle. The dealer had me wait in the basement of a burned-out grocery store; after the high started to wear off, I'd stand there shivering in the dark, my head twitching. I could smell the wet, charred wood and the decay, hear the deranged scurrying of rats. When there was a lull in his action, the dealer would clomp downstairs, hold a flashlight in his mouth and shoot me up. He had hunched shoulders and a thrust-forward turtle head, like Nixon. His damp, hot fingertips probed for a vein; there were crescents of green-black dirt under his nails. He told me: Don't expect me to keep doing this. This is a special introductory service.

It was that night I lucked out. I came up for air about two a.m. and ran right into a San Francisco PD street sweep. A big, mean-looking black cop grabbed me. He was about to pat me down when he took a second look and said, Army? I said, Yeah, and he said, You dumb piece of white shit, but instead of taking me in, he dropped me at one of those free clinics in Haight-Ashbury.

28

The clinic was run by a woman doctor. It took almost a week to get detoxed. Then I spent another two weeks in bed – with the woman doctor. Her name was Sharon. 'Positive reinforcement', she called it. Sharon panted a lot; I kept feeling her hot, moist spearmint Certs breath. She always gazed deep into my eyes the second it was over. Aren't I *marvelous*? her eyes demanded.

Marvelous? Somehow I was getting it up and, apparently, getting it off. But my dick could have been Novocained; I swear to God I felt nothing.

By the end of the second week, Sharon was after me to go back to College – in San Francisco. Hey! I could move in with her! What a fabulous idea! Together we could bang our brains out! Detox the toxed! Refinish her floors!

I did not leave my heart – or any other part of me – in San Francisco. I was back home for Christmas.

Two days of my mother and brother, and I moved out. I needed a job. One of my buddies from high school had joined the Southampton Town PD. No degree necessary. Decent pay. I applied, but there was a waiting list, so instead I joined the Suffolk County PD. I became Guardian of the Suburbs, Keeper of the Peace for the lawn-tenders and split-level dwellers.

I soon began showing my true Brady (as opposed to Easton) colors, popping a few beers a day. Then a six-pack. I was an alcoholic – not that I knew it – and an armed officer of the law. But hey, I was a terrific, ambitious cop. My job meant everything to me. In the beginning, I was even snowed by the dumb stuff: the uniform, the shield, the gun, the siren. Finally, I was part of something good. Law and order. With a little effort, I felt that my life, like Suffolk County, could be brought under control.

Mainly I worked. I spent my days off in Bridgehampton, picking up women and getting laid or watching the Yankees. (In an ideal world, it would have been both.) In eighteen years, I don't think I had a relationship that lasted longer than a month. I worked my way up to drinking two six-packs and half a fifth of booze a day. Scotch in winter, vodka in summer.

Like every other drunk, I was absolutely positive I wasn't a drunk. My mind was so sharp; I could give you every single stat from Thurman Munson's entire career. And at work, when I was on a hard case, I could lay off booze completely. Hey, I had no problem.

By 1984 I was a detective sergeant in Homicide. I was working eighteen, twenty hours a day. I'd go on the wagon and stay on for a couple of months; then I'd slide off. But I was good at hiding my drinking.

Finally, not good enough. Fourteen years after I'd been an alcoholic, someone in the department noticed that what even my friends had been calling my short fuse might be a bad drinking problem when I got into a fight with some guy from Missing Persons in the parking lot at headquarters in Yaphank. I pulled my gun, aimed and shot out his side mirror. I have absolutely no memory of it. They told me I started up because this guy had parked over the line, too close to my car, an indigo '63 Jaguar, E-type. It could go from zero to fifty in 4.8 seconds. I loved my car.

My commanding officer, Captain Shea, suggested a vacation at South Oaks, the department's favored drying-out spot. Vacation: They took away my suitcase and searched it; they strip-searched me; they took away my razor.

I was so scared. No one else there was. This was the place to see and be seen. Anybody who's anybody is drying out, all the hip guys and gals in sweatpants and slippers seemed to be saying. They all loved group; they loved to talk about their sodden daddies, their stinko moms. They couldn't wait to tell about waking up caked in their own vomit. They cried. They laughed. They hugged each other. They all seemed to think they were auditioning for the lead in their own TV bio-movie: *Debbie [or Marvin]: Portrait of a Long Island Alcoholic*.

I remember always being cold at South Oaks, and talking as little as I could get away with. But I thought all the time. I thought: My life is shit. All I have is work – death – my dick and TV. Listen, when you're sitting in a therapy session at a funny farm with seven substance abusers and a psychiatric social worker and you look back and realize that the highlight of the last decade of your life was getting cable so you could watch Sports Channel, you begin to realize you might be a little deficient in the humanity department.

I dried out at South Oaks. After I left, I stayed with AA. The department told me they wouldn't can me, but I would have to go back into uniform.

That was terrible. No, humiliating was what it was. Forget that I'd once been thrilled to be the boy in blue. Now I was a man. So what was I doing all dressed up like Mr Policeman for Halloween? Was I doomed to endless, mind-numbing cruising in a patrol car for the rest of my life?

I fought like hell for half a year to get back into Homicide. Besides the Yankees, my work – putting together the puzzle – was the only thing I really cared about in the world, the only thing that made me feel alive. I finally made it back in, mainly because Shea and Ray Carbone knew they needed me and went to bat for me. But I lost my rank of sergeant. I was clearly not a leader of men. Shea said, 'Bottom line, Brady. I don't give a rat's twat that alcoholism's a disease. That's your problem. If I hear you even walk within a mile of a bottle of anything, I'll bust your ass for good. Hear me?' Yeah, I said. Fair enough.

In January 1989, on my way home from an AA meeting, I met Lynne, age twenty-three, originally of Annapolis, Maryland, a teacher of learning-disabled kids at Holy Spirit Academy in Southampton, when I stopped to help her with a flat tire. Lynne was intelligent. Serious. Classy. Pretty. And competent: she really didn't need me to help her change the flat. And yes indeed, she was stable. On July 4, we got engaged.

There it is. *My Life,* by Stephen Edward Brady. Not precisely a sterling character. In fact, something of a not-so-good guy. Maybe even a bad guy. But a man who, like all men, holds within him the possibility of redemption. Right?

Anyway, my autobiography until that not-nice day when Sy Spencer was murdered and when I realized that – till death do us part – I would find peace and quiet and even happiness with Lynne.

But I might never have fun.

CHAPTER 2

'Come *on*,' I urged the kid, hoping for an argument. 'Sy and Lindsay were the perfect couple.' Jesus, I wanted *life*. Believe me, I'd worked on enough homicides to know that the first interviews set the tone for the whole investigation. You had to charge up your sources; any passion – rage at the killer, outrage, grief, hostility to the police – was better than slack jaws and lead asses. I paced back and forth. 'Sy Spencer and Lindsay Keefe. A brilliant show-business couple: successful, in love, making a great movie.'

'No,' Gregory J. Canfield whispered. He had actually uttered a word. That meant he was metabolizing. But it was hard to tell; he was about as animated as the average homicide victim. Gregory was Sy's personal production assistant, hired through some work-study deal with NYU film school. Poor guy: not only was his personality bordering on inert, but he was a born creep. He was the world's skinniest human being, and his tight maroon T-shirt, which clung to his rib cage, and his wide-legged shorts with pleats didn't help. Also, he had those spooky blue-white, almost colorless eyes, eyes that belonged to some slime-bellied animal that crawled along the sticky, grape-soda-splattered floors of dark movie theatres. 'Uh, Mr Spencer and Ms Keefe – they weren't any Irving Thalberg and Norma Shearer.' I could hardly hear him.

In comparison, my voice sounded overly strong – like

an announcer on a toilet-bowl-cleaner commercial. 'What are you saying? They weren't happy?'

'Maybe Lindsay Keefe told you something else, sir,' Gregory J. Canfield mumbled. That seemed as close to authoritative as he could get. 'But I think, you know, maybe they were headed for disaster.'

'What do you mean? Personal disaster?'

'Well, um, more with the film. Maybe the personal stuff would follow.' He bent down and ran his finger under a too-tight strap on his leg. He was wearing sandals, handmade things with leather thongs that crisscrossed up his stick legs.

'What was wrong with the movie?' I asked. But I'd lost him; his attention was riveted on Sy and the crime-scene crew. His eyes panned the activity and then bugged out for a close-up of a couple of ID apprentices who were unreeling a tape measure from the corner of the pool deck to the back of Sy's skull. Gregory's skin got a little green; he swayed: a potential fainter. 'Let's move,' I said, grabbing his shoulder and steering him away from the action, down toward the stillness of the dune heath. 'Talk to me. That's it. Concentrate. Now, what makes you think *Starry Night* was in trouble?'

'Uh, the dailies. What they used to call the rushes. They weren't . . . good.'

'Not good, or lousy?'

'Um, more than lousy. Actually, more than horrendous.'

His head had swiveled back to watch an ME tech swabbing Sy's nose with a giant Q-tip. I turned him around so he was facing the ocean and held my hands up on the sides of his face for a second, like blinders. 'Stop looking at all the cop crap, Gregory. You're a movie guy, not a Homicide guy. You'll just make yourself sick. Now tell me about *Starry Night*.'

'Lindsay was killing the film. You should have seen Sy's face after dailies: it went from disappointed to . . . traumatized.'

'What did he say?' I asked.

'Uh, well, you see, nothing. He was very – how can I put it? – reticent.'

'What do you mean? Reserved? Cold? Nasty?'

Gregory swallowed to clear his throat; his Adam's apple bobbled. 'No. He just didn't . . . didn't respond. It wasn't one of those comfortable Gregory Peck silences, you know? More brooding De Niro – if De Niro was playing an Ivy League type. Something was going on underneath, but you weren't sure what. Anyway, Sy's secretary was staying in his New York office, so my job was to always be there for him: place phone calls, keep lists of whatever he wanted people to do, run errands back and forth to the set that his personal assistant – the assistant producer – was too important to do. I was in the house a lot, sometimes in the same room. But he never said anything to me unless it was some specific request. Like get a glass of Evian; he liked it plain, no lemon. Or find out what kind of flowers the costume designer likes, because Lindsay had gotten pretty nasty over a red lace teddy; Sy wanted to smooth things over.'

'He never talked to you personally?'

'No. Just hello in the morning and goodbye when I left – if he wasn't on the phone.'

'Did you ever see him angry?' Gregory shook his head. 'Did you ever see him show any emotion at all?'

'Well, he'd laugh at someone's joke on the phone, that sort of thing. One time, when he was talking to someone who I guess was very important, he was doing William Powell. You know, roguish charm. But *nothing* else. Not while I was around, sir.'

'Sounds like he must have been rough to work for.'

'He was kind of like a combo William Hurt–Jack Nicholson. Classy-scary-cold. I think if you had some value to him he could be very nice. But I had absolutely no idea if he liked me or hated me.'

'But still, even though he didn't show emotion, you say you sensed he wasn't thrilled with the dailies?'

'Yes. The last couple of nights, he was white as a sheet after the lights came back on. He *had* to have known that Lindsay was running the film into the ground.'

'But do you know that for a fact?'

'No. I could just . . . intuit it.'

'Had Lindsay and Sy been fighting?'

'No direct confrontation. Not that I ever saw. But most of this week, the air was charged. I'm sure, with you being in Homicide, sir, you know better than most people that anger isn't always expressed verbally.'

'Yeah, I know that. But if you're trying to sell me a charged-air theory, you've got to give me some substantiation. Come on now. How angry was Sy? How angry was Lindsay? Angry enough to have pumped two bullets into him?'

Down near the beach, there was just enough light from Emergency Services for me to see Gregory's white skeleton arms start popping goose bumps. 'Please, Detective Brady, Ms Keefe may have been wrong for this particular role, but I have the greatest respect for her not only as a performer but as a human being. I'm sure someone of her intellectual stature and – '

'Can it, Gregory! This isn't some NYU film school fucking seminar. Now, you'd been shooting the movie for three weeks. Isn't that early to know a picture's in trouble?'

'No. Everyone sensed it. You know how there's a

feeling of intense community? Did you ever see *Day for Night?*'

'No. And don't tell me about movies or actors. Tell me about life.'

'On the set, the cast and crew were just going through the motions, talking about all the other movies they'd worked on. Not about this one.'

'But what about Lindsay Keefe? How could she stink? She's supposed to be one of the best actresses around, right?'

'She *is* a good actress. But her role calls for vulnerability under a brittle exterior. The *only* thing that came through in dailies was brittleness. And not sophisticated, Sigourney Weaver brittleness. Just hardness, shallowness. Very TV miniseries.'

'You personally saw these dailies?'

'Yes.'

'Well? Was she bad?'

'Yes, sir.'

'Did Sy ever express displeasure over her, either to her or to you or to anyone else?'

'Not . . . really. But he was so circumspect, you never had any idea what he was thinking unless he specifically told you.' Gregory hesitated. I couldn't tell if he was trying to come up with something – anything – to please me or whether he was honestly trying to remember something. But just then, Robby Kurz came sauntering down the lawn.

Detective Robert Kurz. Rain, shine, sleet, hail. Gunshot, strangling, knifing, poison. Man, woman, child. No matter what the conditions of a homicide were, Detective Robby lit up every crime scene with his big Howdy Doody smile, his endearing, snub-nosed face and the bright white light of his enthusiasm.

'Yo, Steve!'

'Hi.' To get away from his relentless exuberance, I walked toward the beach, pretending I wanted to think. Naturally, Robby hurried after me.

Lucky for me, Robby was thirty. That provided some distance. I'd had almost ten years more on the force than he did. While he was still sitting in his patrol car, waiting for some commuter in Dix Hills to run a stop sign, I'd been the rising star of Homicide. In rank, having been busted, I was his equal. In fact, being lead detective, I was his superior.

He tried not to acknowledge it. Robby – despite the shiny bald spot he tried to hide by combing his hair sideways and spraying it into paralysis, despite his desperately-eager-to-cheat wife (Mrs Howdy Doody, with a silver heart dangling in her freckled cleavage) and, more important, despite his arrest record, which was, embarrassingly and unfortunately, almost triple his conviction record – had determined that he was the perfect cop. This notion filled him with pleasure; it was impossible to pass him in the john, on the stairs, at the coffee machine without getting a rapturous grin. Every morning he handed out bagels and crullers and Danish to the squad like the Pope bestowing blessings.

Robby stood beside me near the dune, one foot higher than the other, his body on an awkward slant. He was definitely not an outdoor guy; the security of Suffolk County-issue linoleum was vastly preferable to sand.

'What've you got?' I asked. I ran my hand over the spikes of some tall beach grass.

'Footprints on the grass near the house!' he enthused. 'From rubber thongs. The regular, cheap kind. Mitch from the lab says they're a man's size ten or eleven, although obviously' — Robby paused, probably so I could prepare myself for a blast of deductive brilliance — 'those kind of shoes can be worn by *anyone*. But if we can track them down —'

'Where exactly were the footprints?'

He pointed past the pool and the lawn, to the corner of the big porch that ran the entire length of the back of the house. I stretched my neck and squinted. A guy from the lab was straddling an area of grass right up against the house. He was just finishing photographing the footprints, getting ready to apply the dental stone we use for making molds of them.

At that particular corner, the crawl space, neatly covered in lattice, rose about five or six feet high, with the porch above it. From up on the dunes, not far from where we were standing, a hundred feet away, it would have been easy to spot a man with a rifle. But not from the house. Unless you were deliberately leaning over the porch rail, looking right down at the spot where lawn met lattice, someone with a .22 could probably crouch in the shadowy safety of the grand old house and you'd never see him.

'This could be *major* important!' Robby announced, nodding his head in agreement with himself. His sprayed hair didn't move.

But despite his excitement, I wasn't ready to have an orgasm over the footprints; good investigators shouldn't come too fast. I wanted to rule out all other possible explanations for the footprints before I wasted two days on a *major* thong hunt.

'See if you can get someone to check out the gardeners,' I said to Robby. 'Find out if any of them wore thongs. Also, take a look in Sy's closet. I didn't notice any in there when I did my walk-through, and I don't think he'd do anything like wear them, but this could have been the summer that guys like him decided K Mart was *très* amusing or some shit, and he'd have bought fifty pairs.' I thought for a second. 'Except maybe not a size ten or eleven. He was a little guy: little hands, little feet, probably little –'

I stopped before I even started. It was no fun being immature and dirty around Robby. His idea of humor was Polack knock-knock jokes. His concept of sex talk was to confide that he and Freckled Cleavage had gone on a marriage encounter weekend. 'Anything else?' I asked him.

Robby grinned (boyishly) and fiddled with a cuff of his sports jacket, a shiny blue thing that had a half-belt stitched around the waist in back. He dressed as though he made an annual haberdashery pilgrimage to suburban Peoria. 'There were hairs. In one of the guest bedrooms, although there weren't any guests.'

'Were they all from Sy?'

'There was one pubic hair, probably his. Four head, someone leaning back against one of those wicker headboards. The hairs got caught.'

'Any with roots?' With the new DNA typing, you can get a genetic make on someone from any cell with a nucleus. But to test hair, you need the follicle cells that cling to the root, and although you can sometimes make do with one, it helps if you have a clump of ten or twelve hairs.

'Complete roots on two of the head hairs from the headboard. They were *not* Sy Spencer's hairs, because they were black or very dark brown, and longish. He had short gray –'

'Yeah, I saw.'

I'd also gotten a fast look at Lindsay Keefe when her

agent had half escorted, half hauled her out of the car, and she'd been what I'd remembered from movies. Blonde. In fact, the blondest.

'That's all you found?' I asked him.

'Come on,' he said. He was so goddamn chipper. 'You know how long it takes to get anything resembling an opinion from ID.'

'So while you were inside with Carbone you didn't happen to ask if there were any live-in people who might have had a quickie in the bedroom? Maids, valets – that kind of thing?'

'Relax. Where are you going? To a fire? I was just about to ask about servants, but I thought I'd fill you in first.' Robby paused. It had been three minutes since he'd displayed any disarming boyishness, so I got a lopsided smile. 'Look, we both know this is a major case, Steve. I want the brownie points on this one – and so should you. If we can close this neat and fast, it could mean *big things*.'

When you work with a bunch of cops, or any group of people, there are always some who are going to irritate you. Either with lousy character traits, like laziness, dishonesty, sloppiness, or just with irritating personal habits like teeth sucking, cuticle nibbling or superfluous grinning. But Robby wasn't awful. He wasn't hateful. Sometimes, like when he was talking sports, especially hockey, he could actually be interesting; nobody knew as much about the Islanders' offensive strategy as he did. And so what if behind all the smiles he was a self-righteous dick? I just steered clear of him.

But what I couldn't steer clear of was the fact that I thought he was a bad cop. And he thought he was Suffolk County's anointed Good Guy. Days, even weeks, before the assistant DAs felt they had a case, Robby would be pushing to arrest, because he *knew* who the bad guy was. And he was going to get him.

The smiles and the crullers he handed out to cops disappeared for suspects; most of his interrogations turned into finger-jabbing accusations. Sure, he could intimidate some kid into spilling his guts. But he'd alienate suspects other detectives had softened up, and instead of agreeing to a videotaped confession, they'd be screaming for a lawyer.

One time, my best friend on the squad, Marty McCormack, and I had a young guy whose new wife had disappeared. I knew – Christ, everybody knew – that he'd killed her and dumped the body. But how could we find out where? We played it as if this guy was the anguished husband; Marty kept him looking for his wife, thinking of possibilities where she could be. I kept him talking. One night, we stepped out for a bowl of chili and asked Robby just to come into the interrogation room and baby-sit. In the half hour we were gone, he came on tough. Hostile. Aggressive. He knew this was a bad guy. Who didn't? But he almost ruined it.

And I'd lost it when I found out, banging walls, calling him a stupid piece of shit in the squad room. 'You almost fucking blew it!' I yelled. He'd said, 'Just cut it out, Steve,' and even managed a boyish shake of the head that said: Jeez, that Brady and his darn ole temper.

It wasn't that I hated him. We were just oil/water, fish/ fowl, day/night. And so without making a big deal over it, we'd pretty much arranged our lives – and our desks – so we stayed apart.

Until Sy.

'Steve Brady!' Marian Robertson, Sy's cook, exclaimed.

Then she made a twirling motion with her index finger. Spin around, boy, it said. And, obediently, I turned around so she could get the three-hundred-sixty-degree picture. 'I can't say you don't look a day older than you did in high school,' she went on, 'though you are that same boy – but with a man's face. I said to myself the minute you walked in: "That's the boy who was shortstop on Mark's team," although I went blank on your name. I do see your brother. Easton Brady's your brother, right?' I nodded. 'Such a handsome boy. Could be a movie star himself.'

Mrs Robertson babbled away with the absolute self-confidence that came with the conviction that she was the South Fork's Most Unforgettable Character. In fact, I'd totally forgotten her until I walked into Sy's kitchen.

And what a kitchen – especially if you were a big eighteenth-century fan. Strings of garlic, wreaths of herbs, copper pots and straw baskets hung from the walls and the beams. An iron kettle hung in a six-foot-high brick fireplace; it was so gargantuan Sy could have played hide-and-seek in it.

Mrs Robertson turned away from me to finish cutting the crusts off the sandwiches she was making for the crime-scene crew and began arranging them in a perfect, intricate pile: some creamy-colored cheese on the bottom, pale-pink pâté next, and then dark smoked ham, so the platter looked like a spiffy architectural model of a ten-million-dollar beach house. 'Isn't this something?' she inquired. 'One of my specialties. Anyway, Steve, the minute you showed me your badge, of course I remembered hearing you had become a policeman, although as you may imagine, between you and I and a lamppost, you were pretty near the last boy at Bridge-hampton High I'd expect to see in uniform, so to speak.'

She gave me a nose crinkle that (I think) meant: You may have a gun and a badge, but to me you're still a teeno with Clearasil dots. 'I see being a detective you can wear regular clothes. Rank does have its privileges, and that's nice, because you are looking fit.'

Marian Robertson looked the same as when she sat in the first row of the stands at every high school baseball game: dark-brown skin, short, with rounded features and a cute, pudgy body, as if, through interracial marriage, she was half sister to the Pillsbury Doughboy. The only change I could see was her hair; it looked like she'd slapped a gray wig on her head as a seventh-inning joke to give the Bridgies a laugh. Back in high school, she'd acted Unforgettable too, bringing cookies for 'you young fellows', handing each of us a chocolate-chip or a pecan sandy as we trotted off the field, calling out, There's more where that came from!

'Mrs Robertson, I know you gave your statement to Sergeant Carbone, but I have a couple more questions. What does the maid look like?'

'The maid? She's very plain.' Mrs Robertson opened one of the glass doors of the giant restaurant-style refrigerator, eyed the melons and took out an enormous beige ball that was probably a twenty-five-dollar, genetically engineered cantaloupe.

I glanced at my pad. 'There's only the maid, Rosa?'

'That's right.'

'Is she black, white, Hispan –'

'Portuguese.' Marian Robertson cut me off. 'Short, but taller than me. Maybe five foot two. You know, there used to be a song.' She cleared her throat: '"Five foot two/Eyes of blue/But oh what those five two can do . . ." Oh, Lord! Steve, that I'm singing! I apologize. How it must look! But I've been working for Mr

44

Spencer for fourteen summers, and it's so . . . Murdered!'

'Listen, you're upset. You have every right to be.' I paused. 'Were you very fond of him?'

'Well . . . fond enough. I mean, he was so polite. That's what everyone said: "Sy is *so* divinely polite. *So* courtly." You know how those Yorkers talk.' I nodded; all of us who were born here shared the knowledge that we were more decent and more down-to-earth than the slickers from New York City. When you really came down to it, we knew we were better human beings. 'Let me tell you, you can double the phoniness in spades for movie types. But Mr Sy Spencer himself seemed to be genuine silk stocking – not at all flashy or fresh.'

'But did you like him?'

'Well . . . now that I think about it, I'm not sure. He was one cool cucumber.'

'Was he cold? Withdrawn?'

'No. Very toned down, but decent enough. Smiled a lot. Didn't laugh. Never treated me any different the first summer or the fourteenth. But it was like he had a script of how to act with a cook, and that was that. Teasing, like about how he was going to have to mortgage the house to pay for my chickens; I make a *very* rich chicken stock. But the same joke for fourteen years.

'And let's see. He was indeed polite: a compliment after every dinner party, and if he didn't like something, which was hardly ever, he wasn't rude. He'd just say, "I am not entranced by chocolate-dipped fruit."' She opened a plastic container and handed me a cookie. 'Viennese almond wafer.'

'Thank you. Getting back to the maid, Mrs Robertson. What does she look like?'

'Short, like I told you. Yellowish skin, but with pockmarks, poor baby.'

The cookie was good. I smiled. 'What color is her hair?'

'My, are you handsome when you smile! You should smile more often. It lights up your face like a Christmas tree.'

'Rosa's hair, Mrs Robertson?'

'Originally, only the good Lord and her mother know, although my guess is your basic brown. For all the time she's worked here' – she shook her head sadly – 'fire-engine red.'

'And you and Rosa were the only people who work here? I expected valets or chauffeurs or butlers.'

'No. He hired waiters and bartenders for dinners and parties. He had a driver in the city, but he took a helicopter out here and drove himself around in that Italian sports car of his.'

I held out my hand for another cookie. As she gave it to me, I asked: 'Who was in the guest bedroom today with Sy Spencer?'

'What?' She looked startled.

'Someone used the guest bedroom.'

'Besides Mr Spencer?'

'Yes.'

'Really? I have no idea, Steve. You know, he and Lindsay Keefe were living together. But they're in the master suite. What makes you think someone was in the guest bedroom?'

I took another bite of the cookie. 'Just some indications,' I answered. 'Did you hear anyone upstairs?'

'Only Mr Spencer. He was here all afternoon, packing to go to Los Angeles, on the phone. He had been supposed to leave this morning, but then he had to go over to the movie set, so I guess he was changing a few plans.'

46

'No one with him?'

'No.' She thought for an instant and then added: 'I mean, I won't cross my heart and hope to die, because to tell you the truth, you can count the times on one hand that I've been on the second floor of this house. But as far as I know, he was alone.'

'Where was Rosa?'

'She cleans and does a laundry every morning, then goes home for the afternoon . . . she has a little girl. Takes whatever ironing. She comes back about six, to tidy up from my cooking – scours pots, damp mops the floor, takes out trash, that sort of thing. Then she stays through dinner and does the dishes and sets the table for breakfast.'

'Mrs Robertson, I don't want to embarrass you, but in a police investigation we have to ask some pretty direct questions.'

'Go ahead.'

'Was there any indication that Mr Spencer had sexual relations in any other room beside the master bedroom?'

'I go home after dinner. So for all I know, he could be making hay in the sauna or in the screening room or in the wine cellar. All I can vouch for is not in my kitchen, because I would know in two seconds flat. *Nobody,* not the boss, not God himself, is allowed to mess with my kitchen. Got that, Steve?'

'Got it.'

'Good.'

Local cops – in this case the Southampton Village PD – secure the perimeter of a crime scene. One of them, a gangly kid my grandmother would have called a long drink of water, came into the tent on the far side of the pool where we were inhaling Marian Robertson's sandwiches. He called out: 'Is there a Steve Brady on duty tonight?' I put down my mug of coffee. 'A guy's out front. *Real* shook up about the murder. Says he's your brother.'

So I went over to Ray Carbone to tell him about Easton's connection to Sy, even though I had to interrupt Carbone while he was lifting up a triangle of sandwich and eyeing it suspiciously, clearly having deduced that it was, in fact, pâté. 'Can we talk outside for a minute?' I asked. He slid the sandwich back on the platter.

The green-and-white-striped tent we'd been in was a three-sided thing. I guess it was either for changing, if you were an exhibitionist, or for just lying out of the sun and wind. It was about ten feet away from the shallow end of the pool, a perfect distance for a police snack – far enough from the crime scene so that you wouldn't have to pretend Sy's body was a scatter rug while you were woofing down his food.

'Listen, Ray, my brother – his name is Easton – he's out front. He wants to see me.'

'Let him come back, take a look,' said Carbone. In the shadow of Sy Spencer's house, he'd suddenly become Long Island's most gracious host. He even did a be-my-guest sweep with his arm. Then he added: 'Easton?'

'Yeah.'

'What kind of a name is Easton?'

'My mother's from this Yank family up in Sag Harbor. It was her maiden name. They do things like that.'

'I thought you were Irish.'

'My father was Irish. About my brother –'

'What does he do?'

'A little bit of everything. Classy stuff.'

'Like what?'

'He sold Jaguars. I bought mine from him. Then he

sold expensive real estate. Worked in a bunch of hot-shit boutiques around here.'

'Sounds as if he never settled into a defined role. How come?'

'I'm a borderline personality myself. How the hell should I know what's wrong with anybody else?' Over in the tent, the men were still swarming around the table laden with Sy's food. 'Ray, put a lid on the psycho-analysis for now. I want to get this over with. It has to do with the case.'

'The case? Your brother?'

'Yeah. I mentioned the connection when Headquarters called, but I forgot to tell you. Easton was working for Sy. Listen, about three, four months ago he was out of a job: not exactly news. Anyway, he heard about how Sy was going to be making a big part of *Starry Night* in East Hampton, so he wangled an invitation to some jazzy charity party. To make a long story short, he got introduced to Sy and made a big pitch about how he'd been born and raised here and knew everybody and could be helpful. Sy liked him and hired him to be a kind of liaison with the locals – I guess to spread a little money around and keep things happy and get things ready for filming. He did so well that Sy kept him on for the movie.'

'Any problems?'

'No. It was really working out. That's the shitty thing; my brother finally seemed to have found something he was enthusiastic about, plus something he was actually good at. Sy had even made him one of the assistant producers, with his name right up there. Not at the beginning, but at the end when you see all those names. Anyway, sooner or later someone will be taking his statement. I'm just letting you know about him because the department's so big on all that ethics crap.'

'Well, maybe let Robby take it.' I guess he saw my face. 'Steve, Robby's not a bad kid. Okay, too bright-eyed and bushy-tailed for your taste.'

'He has no balance.'

'He has enough, and if not, you'll make up for it. Robby is with you on this one. You'll see, it'll work out. He's really gung-ho. Anyway, it looks better if someone who isn't your closest friend takes care of your brother. But listen, I have no objection if you want to sit in the background. Quietly.' He paused. 'Is your brother, you know, a stable guy?'

'No. He's a demented twit who took a .22 and blew Sy Spencer away because Sy had become his mentor—father figure and Easton has such a low sense of worth that anyone who respected him and helped him self-actualize was ipso facto worthless and had to die.'

I'm not bad. Easton is handsome. Although we resemble each other, I look like an Irish cop and he looks like an Episcopalian lawyer. In other words, my brother is a WASPier, more refined version of me: his eyes a truer blue, his jaw more squared-off, his hair shinier, plus he actually is six feet. I'm just a shade under, which has always annoyed me because girls — women — always ask 'How tall are you?' and if I say six feet I feel like a fraud, but if I were to say five eleven and five eighths, I'd feel like a buffoon.

Easton was standing in the gravel driveway, not far from the stairs that led to the front door. He wasn't in one of his typical getups: a bright-colored blazer, or a pale-pastel sweater, looking more the leisured Southampton aristocrat than the real ones ever did. He was wearing a dark-gray suit with an impeccable paisley tie. His cordovan shoes, illuminated by the unobtrusive low

50

beams that lit the circular driveway and entrance, were brighter than his face. Upset? Even in the dim light I could see he was very upset. Skin waxy. Eyes red not so much from crying but, as I saw as I came up to him, from rubbing them, as if in disbelief.

'Hey, East,' I said. He jumped. 'You okay?'

'Sorry. Do you know what's so odd? Here I am, actually waiting for you, hoping you were here, but my mind was going in ten different directions at once, and just now, when I heard your voice, my first thought was: What the hell is Steve doing at Sy's house?'

'When did you hear about what happened?'

'When I got back from New York. I drove there today, to do some odds and ends for Sy, and when I got home, there was a call on my machine. From this perfectly awful film-school type who's his PA Production assistant. Something like: "Um, uh, you might wish to know that Mr Spencer was, like, murdered at his home."' All of a sudden Easton stopped talking. He got the shakes. 'Damn. It's nippy,' he managed to say. Like my mother, Easton used words like 'nippy' instead of 'cold' or 'cool' or 'chilly', words to distinguish him from the proles. 'Oh, good God.' He rubbed his arms, but it didn't help. Then his teeth started to chatter, fast, like those stupid wind-up teeth in novelty stores.

'Did you speak to Sy today, East?'

'Last night.'

'Any indication of trouble?'

'No.'

'Had any threats been made against him that you know of?' He shook his head in answer – and in disbelief. 'Do you have any reason to think he was afraid of anything, or anyone?'

'No.'

51

'Any change at all in his behavior?'

He couldn't stop shaking. 'He was fine, I'm telling you.' For my brother, trembling was the absolutely perfect, tasteful way to fall apart: so proper. It didn't make any noise, and unlike sweating or barfing, you could have your breakdown and then go right on to a cocktail party without messing up your clothes and having to change.

'They can get your statement tomorrow. Why don't you go home? You look pretty shitty.'

'I don't even know why I'm here.' He glanced up at the house. 'Actually, I suppose I thought I should show up. In the back of my mind I was thinking: With all the chaos – police, God knows what else – maybe I can give Sy a hand. It's an insane reaction, but Steve, I have to tell you, this is such a shock. I mean, to get that message.'

'It must have been a real kick in the nuts.'

'It knocked the wind out of my sails. I can't believe it. Who in God's name would murder Sy?'

'Who do you think?'

'No one would want to kill him,' Easton announced. He was positive. He stuck his hands in the pockets of his New York City fancy pants.

'The facts seem to indicate otherwise, don't they?'

'Probably a burglar.'

'No.'

'How do you know for sure?'

'What are you talking about? It's my job to know.'

'And you're never wrong, are you?'

As usual, after more than sixty seconds in each other's company, we were into our regular sibling routine – being irritated by each other. I decided this was one time I should be unirritated. More than that. He was my brother. He was genuinely upset; I should be gentle.

52

'There doesn't seem to be any evidence of a burglary attempt,' I said, as softly as I could.

'How was he killed?'

'Shot. From some distance. Most likely with something like a .22. It doesn't look like an impulsive act.' We had a long moment of silence. 'Listen, one of the other guys will interview you, probably tomorrow. Go on home.'

He shivered again. 'He was really good to me.'

'Yeah. Listen, I'm sorry. Oh, East, one more thing. Forget fights, threats. Did Sy give any indication that he was having problems with anybody?'

To give him credit, my brother really seemed to think about it. 'I've only been working with him for three and a half months. I can't set myself up as an expert. But from what I've seen, when you're producing a movie, you have problems with *everybody*. You're dealing with a cast and crew of a hundred prima donnas – and their agents, and their unions. And then you have the money-men, who always make life a living hell. A producer has to be tough-minded – and tough. And Sy was. He never backed off from a confrontation. He just kept going.' A small, affectionate smile passed over Easton's face for a second. 'Sy was like a steamroller. He wouldn't stop. You either moved or got crushed. At some point, just about everyone involved probably told him, or wanted to tell him: Drop dead.'

'Son of a bitch!' Carbone blew up in front of me and Robby Kurz. He was yelling about Eddie Pomerantz, Lindsay's agent, now safely on his way home, who, two minutes earlier, had informed him that Lindsay had taken a couple of Valium and was out like a light, but who then admitted, when Carbone started screaming at him, that she'd had four or five. Possibly six, although he wanted it clearly understood that his client was seriously not into drugs. Carbone explained to us: 'I had that doctor from the ME's office – the one with the Dumbo ears – go up to her room. He says she could be genuinely knocked out for more than eight hours. Passive-aggressive bitch.'

We sat in Sy's office, a room on the second floor that had probably been a kid's bedroom. You knew it was an office because there was a phone with so many buttons that it looked like it could launch a satellite, and a small computer. But that was it for modern stuff. The rest of the room looked like some fish-crazy English gentleman's study: there was a stuffed marlin on the wall, some washed-out paintings of salmon leaping out of the rapids, a bunch of gleaming, never-used rods, perfectly, casually arranged in a corner.

Carbone scanned his notepad. 'Now listen, no matter when we get out of here tonight or tomorrow morning, I want both of you back at ten to interview Lindsay Keefe. I'll probably be stuck in a meeting with Shea on how to handle this thing. This thing's bigger than *Newsday*. It's national. International. Now, Robby,' Carbone went on, 'before ten, get what you can from Steve's brother, Easton. Then meet Steve here, for Lindsay. After you're through with her, you work on Sy's business associates. First from this movie. Then start working back.

'Steve, you concentrate on all the nonbusiness-type movie people. Oh, and his women. Look into if he was currently involved with anyone besides Lindsay. And check his ex-wives. He had two of them. One lives in Bridgehampton, so maybe you can get to her before ten.' He glanced down to his pad. 'Bonnie Spencer.'

I shook my head. It sounded vaguely familiar, but I was sure it wasn't anyone I'd actually met.

54

'A movie writer.' He handed me a piece of paper with an address. 'You know where it is?'

'About two minutes from where I grew up.'

'The other ex lives somewhere in the city. She was the first, and we'll have a name and address on her by tomorrow. All right? We'll use Southampton Village's squad room as a command post for the next day or two. I'll meet up with the two of you as soon as I can get out here tomorrow.' He stopped, looked right at me, and sighed. 'I think this is going to be it. The case where I find out that I'm too old for this kind of work.'

I stood in Sy's gym, talking to Lynne from his wall phone. All the not-fun stuff I'd been bugging myself about since the afternoon now seemed stupid. Engaged-guy nerves, a last-ditch defense of bachelorhood. Because, objectively, Lynne was so terrific.

One of the things that had always knocked me out about her was that she acted as though I had a normal, not-terribly-exciting job. I could be a manager of an Aamco transmission franchise. She deliberately did not focus on what I actually did. I understood why; homicide is the ultimate breakdown of law and order, and Lynne's whole life, as a teacher and as a person, was dedicated to being constructive. She was there to give someone a chance, not take it away. Murder wasn't exciting. It was sinful, and it was also outrageously unfair. In the deepest sense, killing wasn't nice.

Another thing: despite her career and her really astonishing competence, she was enough of a traditional female not to want to hear the details of a fatal beating, or how the scalp is peeled back from the skull during an autopsy. So she concentrated not on the subject of my work – the dead and how they got that way – but on the living.

So we were not chitchatting about the murder, other than the briefest summary of what had happened and where I was. Instead, we were talking people. We'd done thirty seconds on how Carbone managed to be an intrusive pain in the butt and a terrific guy at the same time, a minute and a half on why I couldn't stand Robby, and now we were on to my brother.

'Did you say anything like: "Gee, Easton, I'm sorry about Mr Spencer. I know how much you liked him and how important he was in your life"?'

'Don't bust my chops, Lynne.'

Except for the floor, the entire gym was mirrored. I was the only thing in the room that didn't gleam. Besides a stationary bike, a treadmill and one of those stair-climbing things – all with glowing red or green digital displays – there was a bunch of Nautilus equipment. I stood up straighter; either Sy had a lot of vanity to work out in front of all those mirrors, or he needed tremendous incentive.

'Steve,' she said patiently, 'did you say anything at all to comfort your brother?'

'Yeah. I said I was sorry.'

'That's all?'

Just when I thought I looked okay in one mirror, I'd see my reflection in another. I pulled my shoulders back. I knew I didn't have a gut, but in the ceiling mirror I seemed to, so I sucked it in. 'Don't get on me about Easton now. I just called to say good night and I love you.'

'Well, good night and I love you too. It's just that I know how much you want a decent relationship with him. Wouldn't this be the perfect time to reach out?'

I told her I guessed it was, and then we did the good night and I love you business again because I'd been on with her for almost five minutes and wanted to get back.

After we hung up, I lay down on the gray-carpeted floor and closed my eyes for about ten seconds, probably my total rest for the next forty-eight hours. I know it was sentimental — and probably inaccurate — to say Lynne had saved me, but I really felt she had. Sure, I'd been staying sober with AA. And since getting back into Homicide I was working better than I ever had before.

But by the time I met her, I was feeling scared. I was standing all alone, no crutches. No booze. No drugs at all. Two months after I got out of South Oaks, I got the flu. I sweated out a hundred-and-four-degree fever rather than risk becoming a Tylenol junkie. Hardly any women either: I had lost almost all desire. In the old days, almost anything that produced estrogen could get me going if I was in the mood to get going, but most of the time now I couldn't seem to find anybody who made me want to unbuckle my belt. And yeah, there was football — the Giants, who I liked a lot. But no Yankees: it was January. I was running at least five miles a day to stay in shape and get that chemical going in the brain; I forget the name of it, but at South Oaks they told us it was the body's natural narcotic and was okay. Running ten, twelve, sometimes fifteen miles on my days off, to get that high — and to exhaust myself because I was nervous about what I'd do with too much time and energy.

See, at the funny farm the shrink talked to me about what deep down I always knew — or, if I didn't know, sensed. That the drinking and the drugs and the womanizing were all pretty much the same thing, part of what he called my self-destructive pattern. Sure, I had been going for the high, but (a big but) the high hadn't

57

been my real goal. What I'd really been searching for all that time was to feel nothing. Oblivion.

So there I was, finally, trying to turn my back on oblivion, to face the world, to take one day at a time.

But all that summer and fall, after those first heady years of sobriety, I started having nightmares: I was drinking again. I'd wake up from a dream about taking a bottle of icy, syrupy vodka out of the freezer, pouring it – almost against my will – and taking a deep, desperate sip. I'd feel panicked, sick to my stomach with despair. Because I knew how fragile my stability was. And I also knew I wasn't a resilient kid anymore. If I lost my grip again, I could fall into a bottomless pit, and I wouldn't have the strength or the courage to try and climb back out. I would be lost for good. I would die. Talk about oblivion.

And suddenly there was Lynne, standing by the trunk of her car, assembling the jack. She was cautious as I pulled over, but she looked me right in the eye and said, 'Thanks. I can handle it.' I showed her my shield and told her that was fine with me; I'd hang around and watch. I liked watching women change tires.

She handed me the jack, and when I finished I took her out for a hamburger. All of a sudden, I found I was having a genuine, normal conversation. Not just talking to a woman to prove I wasn't only out to screw her. Real discussion. About the emotional problems kids with dyslexia can get. About whether a person's body language can make them more or less likely to be the victim of a crime. About public schools versus Catholic schools. And about how I was an alcoholic.

And two weeks later, we went to bed. I lay there afterwards and thought: Oh my God! I'm having a *relationship*.

CHAPTER 3

◦═◦◦═◦

Bonnie Spencer's dog barked with joy: Hiya, hiya, wonderful to see ya! Its tail made giant circles of jubilation: Whoopee! We got company! It was a huge, happy thing, like a fat, black English sheepdog.

'Steve Brady,' I called out, and flipped open my ID.

Her dog interrupted its woofing only long enough to lick my hand and my shield: Hiya! Love ya! But Bonnie Spencer stood silent and motionless in her front doorway – and gaped. It was seven forty-five, the morning after her ex-husband had been murdered. She obviously hadn't been expecting condolence calls; she was wearing turquoise second-skin biking shorts, a huge, shapeless faded pink cotton T-shirt and sweat socks. A pair of sneakers dangled from her hand, as if she'd been about to put them on for a run.

'I'm a detective with Suffolk County Homicide,' I added. Her lips rounded as if she was going to say Oh!, but she didn't. She didn't do anything, not even glance at my ID. She simply gawked. 'Bonnie Spencer?' The dog poked her leg with its snout, as if to say: Come *on*, talk to the guy. But she didn't.

I put my ID away, stuck my hands into my pockets. Even though it was a warm, end-of-summer morning, the moist, leafy smell of fall was in the air. Bonnie Spencer didn't seem to want to look at me; instead, she seemed mesmerized by my car in her driveway. Listen, the '63 XKE is a truly great car, but when there's a detective from Homicide on your doorstep first thing in the morning, that should be the attention-grabber. 'Are you Bonnie Spencer?' I repeated.

She blinked, shaking off her daze. Her eyes brightened. 'Am I Bonnie Spencer?' She laughed. But then she did an awkward box step of embarrassment, probably sensing her manner wouldn't win any awards for Most Seemly Display of Wistful Sadness in a Situation in Which an Ex-Spouse Has Been Offed. She switched to subdued. 'Of course I'm Bonnie.' Then she added: 'Gee.'

Gee. Bonnie Spencer.

Okay, picture the ex-wife of a celebrated movie producer. What comes to mind? A cold, elegant bitch with tobacco-colored arms who wears jewelry to the beach. A stunner with pointy, polished nails that tap all the time, sending out the coded message: Fuck you; I'm dissatisfied.

But Bonnie Spencer didn't seem dissatisfied. And she definitely didn't come across as elegant, especially with that goof of a dog slobbering with happiness at her side. Looks? No glamour girl, not by a long shot. More like one of those girl-buddy types, tall – five eight or nine – broad-shouldered and clean, probably from some clean town where all the girls said 'Gee.' Nothing to write home about. Not much to look at. But the weird thing was, I couldn't keep my eyes off her.

Her best feature was her hair, glossy and dark, pulled back into a ponytail. Other than that . . . well, okay features. Deep laugh lines around her eyes. She had the high, healthy color men have more often than women: that rosy brownness that comes to the naturally fair-skinned who spend a lot of time out of doors. In other words, Bonnie Spencer, sneakers in hand, looked like someone you never really got to know in high school: the big, strapping girl jock who gets over mourning the end of field hockey season by spending the winter stroking her lacrosse stick.

Except she was no girl – not anymore. The strong body and the shiny hair were deceptive. At first glance I had put her in her early thirties. But her neck was a little too lined, her lips a little too pale. She was in her late thirties, maybe even forty.

In relation to Sy she made absolutely no sense. To have seen the compact, richly robed, perfectly groomed Mr Spencer and his exquisite world of hand-painted pool tiles, and then to look at big, all-American Bonnie standing on the planked wood floor of a pretty but definitely not show-stopping old saltbox house . . . The question was not why Sy had dumped her, but how such a man had come to marry such a woman in the first place.

She was staring at me again. Her eyes were dark gray-blue, a deep, mysterious color for such a straightforward girl, the color of the ocean. I looked into them; that how-come-*you're*-here expression had returned.

'Ms Spencer?'

'Please,' she said, almost shyly. 'Bonnie.'

And then, once more, ka-boom, her mood changed. Suddenly she became friendly, easy. She gave me a smile. A great, generous smile. Perfect white teeth, except for a slightly crooked one in front, as though her parents had run out of money a month before the orthodontist had finished. Listen, it can make you so happy to get a warm, uncomplicated smile like that. But why the hell was she smiling? Why the hell was her face lit up like that? What did she think I was going to do? Ask her to the senior prom?

'You've heard about your former husband, Seymour Spencer?'

'Oh, God,' she breathed. The smile vanished. Her eyebrows, the kind that slant up, like a bird's wings, drew together; they were eyebrows meant for a more delicate woman. 'It was on the ten o'clock news last night. One of those god-awful stories about famous people you don't know. Except it was about Sy.' For a minute, her expression reflected the normal disorientation of the average citizen confronted with murder: a flash of horror, then a fast flare-up of incomprehension. 'You probably hear this all the time, but I can't believe it.' Her voice was filled with fervent emotion. 'I'm *so* sorry.'

Too much emotion. Too goddamn fervent. Look, I'd been in Homicide a long time. Every working day of my life was spent with the distraught, the agitated, the grieving, the indifferent. And so I knew that something wasn't right about Bonnie Spencer. First of all, her 'I'm so sorry' was overly personal; it's hard to explain, but even the world's most extroverted person doesn't respond to a cop with that kind of familiarity.

And another thing: just standing there in the doorway, she kept changing her mood. Not in the usual way, like a dazed person trying to come to grips with a too-terrible reality, but as though she were searching for the perfect, appropriate emotion to show off to me.

How did I know all this? Any decent detective knows when to turn off his mind and tune in his gut. And my gut was saying: Something's going on with this woman.

So all of a sudden, instead of a routine interview with a dead hotshot's ex-wife to see if I could come up with any leads, I was on the alert.

'Would you like to come in?' she was asking.

'Thanks.'

It was a good-size, solid house, built for a farm family. I followed her — and the dog — into a roomy kitchen and, naturally, said 'Yeah, great' when she offered to make me coffee. (Saying yes to coffee during an investigation makes people feel you've accepted them; it makes them relax, open up. Unfortunately, half the time you wind up drinking stuff that tastes like lukewarm liquid shit, but in the long run it's probably worth it.)

She cleared the morning's papers – the *Times, Newsday,* the *Daily News* – all with their stories about Sy's murder, off the table. She must have gone out for them when the coffee shop opened, at six; they'd all been read. I tipped the chair back and sat quietly, the way I usually do. I wanted to see what Bonnie Spencer would reveal. But she turned away to put the water up to boil and measure out coffee, so for a few seconds the only thing she revealed was nice thighs – a little over-developed, but muscular, tight. Meanwhile, the dog put its head on my lap and gazed up into my eyes – the soulful look a dumb girl who wants to be taken seriously would give in a bar.

Bonnie turned around. 'Moose,' she ordered, 'go to place!' She pointed toward one of those small, oval braided rugs. The dog ignored her. Bonnie shrugged, half to herself, half in apology: 'The dog has the IQ of a cockroach.' Then she opened a cabinet and took out a little white pitcher shaped like a cow. She was waiting for me to begin questioning her. I didn't. She asked: 'Did Sy . . .' She stopped and started over. 'The TV said he was shot.' I nodded. She held open the refrigerator with her hip while she poured milk into the pitcher. I glanced inside: no chilling white wine or goat cheese in there. God knows over the years I'd made it with enough summer women to recognize that, at least in the food department, Bonnie was not a typical New York woman. She was either on a budget, on a diet, or had given up all hope of

63

visitors; she had a pint container of milk, whole wheat bread and a big, Saran-wrapped glass bowl that looked like she'd gotten overenthusiastic about broccoli. 'Was his death instantaneous?' Her voice was high, hopeful.

'We'll know more after the autopsy.' Just then, Moose gave a deep, lovelorn sigh and lay down at my feet. On my feet, actually.

'Everything I can think of to say is a cliché – but I hope he didn't suffer.'

'I hope not.'

'Well,' she said, 'I guess you weren't just cruising the neighbourhood and felt like a cup of coffee.'

'I guess not.' All of a sudden I realized I had seen her before. Probably at the post office, getting her mail.

'I guess you have some questions,' she said.

'Yes.'

But I didn't ask any. I got busy pretending to formulate a question while studying her cow pitcher. What I was actually doing was checking out if Bonnie had a body worth writing home about under that big T-shirt. Naturally, when I caught myself doing it, I got pissed because I'd always made it a point never to think about sex during work hours (which is generally a snap, homicide not being generally conducive to hard-ons), and also because wanting to know what was under her T-shirt made me feel ridiculous. If she were in a movie, she'd be the heroine's good-natured girlfriend, a tomboy with a heart of gold. But for someone who wasn't attractive, she was so attractive. Here I was, half hoping she'd need something on a high shelf. She'd have to stretch up her arms; her shirt would rise and I would get to see her ass. It made me feel like a louse. Since AA and especially since Lynne, I'd stopped my bad-boy crap, my automatic concentration on anything female, my reflexive coming on to almost every woman I met.

'Tell me about you and Sy Spencer,' I said quickly. 'How long were you married to him?'

'Three years – 1979 to 1982.' She poured the boiling water through the coffee filter. 'You don't take notes?'

'I think I can manage to remember 1979 to '82.' I'd forgotten to take out my pad. Suddenly it felt like a block of lead in my jacket pocket. 'Amicable divorce?'

'Even if it hadn't been, do you think I'd shoot him seven years later?'

'I'm open to all possibilities.'

'Well, I didn't shoot him.' Her manner was solemn, sincere, proper; if Bonnie Spencer's mouth was from the city, the rest of her had grown up in that nice non-New York hometown, wherever it was.

'Good. Now, do you want to answer my question? How was the divorce?'

'Amicable.'

'Fair settlement?'

'I got this house.'

'Just the house?'

'Yup.'

'Was there any litigation?'

'No. Both of us were just overflowing with amicability. "Bonnie, *please* take the alimony." "No, Sy, but thanks *so* much for thinking of me."'

'Why no alimony? He was rich.'

'I know. But back then, I didn't care about money. Oh, and I was in my wronged-woman phase: "Do you honestly think a monthly check will make up for the loss of a husband, Sy?"' She shook her head. 'God, was I morally superior. You can imagine Sy – and his matrimonial lawyer. They must have been shouting

"Hallelujah!" and jumping up and down and hugging each other.'

I didn't like this. At the same time I was being vigilant, trying to figure out just what was wrong with Bonnie Spencer — because I *knew* there was something wrong — I was finding there was something about her I really liked. Maybe I was just intoxicated by the homey atmosphere — being at that bright-polished wood table in the fresh-smelling country kitchen, watching a woman open a cupboard and think for a second before choosing from a bunch of mugs. Maybe it was that big hairy black mop, Moose, warming my feet. I could just feel myself letting go, my brain turning to mush. Bonnie put the cow pitcher and a sugar bowl down on the table and handed me a mug of coffee. The mug said 'I love' — the 'love' was one of those hearts — 'Seattle!' and had a cartoon of a smiley animal with funny-looking flippers.

'I know it's tacky,' she said. 'It was a choice between tacky and chipped.'

'You didn't get any alimony at all?' I tipped the pitcher. The milk came out of the cow's mouth. It was so dumb.

'I never dreamed I'd need it. See, when I met Sy, I was a hot screenwriter. My movie — *Cowgirl* — had just opened. It got great reviews, did decent business. And during the time we were married, I wrote five more screenplays. Three of them were in development.' She sat down across from me at the table. 'When you're a big success right off the bat, you assume it's going to go on forever.'

'It didn't?'

She shook her head. 'No. *Cowgirl* was my first and only movie. Nothing ever happened with any of the others. Anyhow, Sy offered to pay me alimony at least three times. But I wanted to show him I could be

66

independent. And you know what? In the long run, it really was better this way.'

'Why did the marriage break up?' She was clearly not a New Yorker, because instead of giving me a socio-psycho-feminist analysis of the relationship, she clammed up. 'Come on,' I urged. 'I know this may seem like an invasion of your privacy, but someone's been murdered. I need a picture of this man's life – a complete picture.'

It took her a while, but finally she opened up. 'When we met, in LA, Sy was trying to produce his first movie. I guess I was the important one – the toast of both coasts. Okay, the semi-toast. He loved coming along for the ride. He met a lot of people. You know, contacts.

'I don't want to make it sound as if he was using me. I think he truly thought I was . . . well, wonderful. And he was so smart and worldly that when he proposed I thought: Gee, if this man is in love with me, maybe I *am* wonderful. Anyway, pretty soon he made his first movie, and then his second. And let me tell you, Sy earned his success. He wasn't just another rich guy who wanted to get into the movie business to date actresses or impress his friends in Cleveland. He was a born producer.'

'What makes a born producer?'

Bonnie didn't have to think for much more than a second; she'd done her legwork on Sy a long time ago. 'He has to have a good story sense; Sy had a great one. And the ability to get people excited over his vision. And be a trendsetter. If everyone else was making heartwarming movies about farm families with lovable old grandpaws and alfalfa blights, Sy would make something stylized and science-fictiony because he loved the script and believed it would make a great movie.'

'So he became a big producer. What happened to you?'

'Nothing much. I stopped needing an unlisted number.'

'You're not saying he dropped you when you stopped being a hot screenwriter?'

'Yup.'

Yup? 'Where are you from?' I asked.

'Ogden, Utah. Is Moose bothering you?'

'He's okay.'

'She. Can't you tell? She loves men. She drops me in two seconds flat for anything in pants. She's the town slut.' Real fast, Bonnie's doting dog-lover smile faded. She glanced away, up at the wall clock, but she wasn't interested in the time. I made a mental note to check on her reputation.

'How did Sy drop you?'

'How? Not too hard, considering how much he wanted out. He told me – very gently – he had been having an affair with someone. Some society lady, like his first wife, except this one didn't look like she ate oats and neighed. Anyway, he told me he was in love with her and it was causing him enormous pain to be hurting me, but that he would appreciate a divorce so he could marry her.'

'But he didn't marry her.'

'No, of course not. He just wanted out. He was having the affair anyway, so he used it. I guess he thought it would be easier for me if there was another woman; he knew I could accept love a lot better than him saying, "Hey, Bonnie, I hate taking you places because you're taller than me and a has-been."'

'And you weren't angry at this kind of treatment.'

'Of course I was angry! If you go back seven years, I

68

bet you'd find twenty witnesses who heard me yelling: 'I hope you die, you louse.' But time passes. And the fact of the matter is, we wound up being friends.'

'When was the last time you saw him?'

'I'm not sure.' But she was! Damn it, I could feel it. She lifted her chin, examined a pot holder on a hook and pretended to think. 'A few days ago, I think. I dropped in on the set.'

'And before that?'

'Let's see . . . Oh, about a week before. He asked me to come over, to see his house.'

'Did you stay long?'

'No. He just gave me the fifty-cent tour.'

'How good friends were you?'

'Pretty good friends.'

'Did you spend a lot of time with him?'

'Not all that much.'

'Did he visit you here?'

'He dropped by once or twice. But we were mainly phone friends. He was my colleague, my collaborator. See, I hadn't written any screenplays for a few years, but last winter, when I gave it another shot, I sent it right off to Sy. I mean, I hadn't seen him since the divorce, but I knew he'd give me a fair reading. And he really liked it!' She massaged her forehead. 'Oh, God almighty, I can't believe he's dead.'

'What about the script?'

'What? Oh, we were developing it together. It was a kind of female-buddy spy movie.'

'What exactly does "developing" mean?'

'It means working on a project – the script, the financing, trying to get a good director or a star involved. But Sy never moved on a project until he was satisfied with the script. And mine – it's called *A Sea*

Change – wasn't quite in shape to be sent out. But he had a lot of great suggestions. I was rewriting based on his suggestions.'

'And then he'd produce it?'

'Yup.'

'Was he paying you a lot?'

'Well . . . he wasn't actually paying me yet. But if I'd asked, he would have given me option money.'

'Why didn't you ask?'

'I guess the same reason I didn't want alimony. I didn't want to seem greedy. I know, that sounds stupid. No, it *is* stupid. But Sy always worried that people – women – were out for what they could get from him. I didn't want him to think that of me, either time. Anyway, I knew he'd be fair once we got rolling.'

'How do you support yourself? Family money?'

She laughed and looked around the kitchen. 'Does this look like family money?'

'You live in Bridgehampton all year round?' I was really surprised.

'Sure. Oh, I see; you thought this was my sincere little summer cottage where I go to get away from my forty-room Sutton Place triplex. No, this is it. I support myself by writing. I do the "Happy News" column for the *South Fork Sun*. I'm sure it's the high point of your week: weddings, babies, anniversaries. "Penny and Randy Rollins of Amagansett's famed Wee Tippee Inne celebrated their nineteenth anniversary with a gala extravaganza – featuring Penny's world-famous fish chowder!" And I write copy for mail-order catalogs. Stuff like "White swirls of rayon chiffon set aglow by luminescent faux-pearl buttons."'

'You didn't resent Sy, that you had to give up

screenwriting, give up all that high living for something
. . . less exciting?'

'Resent? A woman tends to resent a man who says, "I
don't desire you anymore."' She looked away, embarrassed. Then she went on: 'But that's on a personal level.
Professionally, how could I resent him just because
other people weren't hiring me as a screenwriter? That
wasn't Sy's fault. Eight studios and fifty thousand
independent producers rejected my scripts. They said
they were sweet. Sweet is movie speak for insignificant.
But in all those years I never doubted that Sy wished me
well.'

'Did you ever talk about anything beyond this new
project?'

'Sure. Look, I know his friends, his family.'

'Any brothers or sisters?'

'No. Just Sy. Both his parents died since the divorce.
But he had aunts, uncles, lots of cousins. I knew them
all; we went way back. When I met him, he was still
publishing his poetry magazine and trying to get his first
movie produced, and his office was still in the Spiegel
Crown Kosher Provisions building.'

'Spiegel?'

'Spiegel was his name originally: Seymour Spiegel.'
She shook her head. 'He changed it the summer before
he went to Dartmouth. I never understood why. I mean,
what did he think he would say at graduation? "These
are my parents, Helen and Morton Spiegel. Their name
used to be Spencer, but they Judaicized it." Or if he was
going to change his name, why not go the whole route
and call himself Bucky? I mean, Sy is not a quantum leap
from Seymour.'

Just then, Bonnie got stopped by some memory of Sy.
Her eyes opened too wide, the expression people use

when they're trying not to cry. She stood up and got busy sponging off what looked like a clean stove.

And then it happened again: the imposition of self-control, followed by the conscious shifting of the gears of her personality. When she turned around, she was composed – but with just the appropriate degree of concern. 'Do you have any ideas about who killed him?' she asked. Sincere. Saddened. Full of sympathy. Full of crap.

'Do you?'

'No,' she said. For a woman her age, she looked like she had a great body. I tried to figure out where I'd seen her before. Maybe running. She had the slim, muscular legs of a runner.

'Think back over the last few weeks. Was Sy angry at anybody?'

She leaned against the kitchen counter and smiled. 'Everybody. When he was making a movie, anyone who gave him a hard time was an enemy. It was funny, because for all his charm he was aloof, and always in control. When we were married, we'd have fights where I'd yell, kick the refrigerator, and Sy would watch, like he was watching an actress doing an improvisation: Wife Losing Her Temper.

'But when he was producing – God, that was another story! Goodbye charm. And forget aloof. His money and his reputation were on the line. He never yelled – that wasn't his way – but he'd lace into people in this icy voice. It could really get scary – all that fury expressed in this absolutely cold manner. Let me tell you: he got his way.'

'Was he angry at anyone the last time you talked?'

'Lindsay, I guess.'

'But they were living together. They were supposed to be in love.'

'Well, I've got to tell you: the love part is debatable. But even if they had been, this is the movie business. An executive producer doesn't love an actress who's jeopardizing a twenty-million-dollar project. Sy told me the dailies were awful, which really surprised me because her success isn't just based on blatant beauty; she's a talented actress.'

'But you think Sy got disillusioned with her?'

'Sy had a gift for falling in and out of love pretty easily.'

'Let's put love aside. Was he annoyed with her? Angry?'

'Furious. He said she was just coasting – not putting any thought or energy into the role because it wasn't an "important film". That *really* ticked Sy off, because it was an article of faith with him that any movie that's true, that moves audiences – even a screwball comedy – is an important film. He believed in *Starry Night*. And Lindsay didn't. What made the problem even worse was that she has such a monumental ego she couldn't see how flawed her performance was. And naturally, she wouldn't try to fix what she'd decided wasn't broken. Let me tell you, if he hadn't gotten killed, he would have made her life a living hell.'

'So he was ready to steamroll Lindsay?'

'Yup. And the director too.'

'What's his name?'

'Victor Santana.'

'Why was he mad at him?'

'Because Santana had gone gaga over Lindsay and couldn't or wouldn't get her to change.'

'Anyone else?'

'Oh, his usual hate list. The director of photography they'd hired – a French boy genius – was shooting too

pastelly. The line producer was bellying up to NABET –
the film technicians' union – too much. Sy was angry at
everyone.'

'Okay, then who of the movie people was seriously
angry at Sy?'

'I don't know. I'm not part of the *Starry Night*
company.'

'How about Lindsay Keefe?'

'My guess is if you tell a critically acclaimed actress –
a movie star – that her performance is putrid and then,
no matter how many little adjustments she makes, that
the dailies are still awful . . . well, you figure it out. But
even *I* wouldn't believe she'd shoot him because he
criticized her work.'

'Who else?'

'I don't know.'

I looked her straight in the eye. 'He was your ex-
husband. He could talk to you.'

'We didn't talk all that much.'

'You talked enough. What else was on his
mind?'

'He never really said anything specific.'

'Tell me anyway.'

'Well, I just want you to know this is my interpretation of what he *didn't* say.'

'Go ahead.'

'This is a very expensive movie for an independent
producer. I think maybe he was a little concerned that
his backers were upset. The people who invested might
have heard about trouble on the set, and they might
have gotten anxious.'

'Who were they?'

'Specifically? Beats me. I think a couple of them may
have been from his days in the kosher meat business.'

She paused. 'You know there are some rough people in that industry.'

'Yeah, there's mob money in it.'

'From the little Sy said, though, these guys didn't sound like out-and-out goons. More like businessmen in suits and ties, except with five-pound gold ID bracelets.'

'Was that all? No one else with a grudge?'

'I'm pretty sure.' I waited while she thought. 'Nope,' she said at last. 'No one else. Definitely.'

I stood and faced her. She lowered her head so I was looking down at her dark, shiny hair. Her breathing became quick, shallow. I knew I was getting to her. Not just the cop: the man.

'Bonnie, you're smart, observant. Sweet too, and I mean that as a compliment.' She tried to look me in the eye – casual. But her face had flushed bright pink. 'You're not being straight. I get the feeling you're holding back, and that concerns me.'

'I'm not holding back anything.' Just for an instant her voice caught in her throat.

I moved in closer. 'You could help me solve a murder, Bonnie.'

'I can't. Honestly. I've told you everything I know.'

'Listen, if things were going lousy with Sy Spencer's movie, with Lindsay, who would he confide in? Who knows the business? Who knows him? You.'

'Please. I've told you everything he told me.'

'I've got to tell you: something about you doesn't feel right. What are you hiding?' She turned her head away from me. 'Come on, do you want me to start thinking maybe you were involved?'

'Why would you think that?' She wasn't exactly scared, but she wasn't at ease either.

'Open up, Bonnie.' I stepped toward her. She inched

backward, until she was pressed against the sink. I moved in until we were almost touching. 'Tell me what you're *not* talking about. Be smart. Because if I start to think you were involved, I'll go after you – and I won't stop.'

I had a few minutes after Bonnie, so I drove down to the beach. I hadn't liked the way the interview had ended. A little official charm is one thing. That final minute, that simultaneous coming on to her and threatening her, was another. And I hadn't come on to her just for leverage; I'd really wanted to be close to her. I needed to clear my head.

Down at the beach, a stiff wind was whipping up the sand, blowing sharp, scratchy grains against my face and neck. Summer people were scuttling around, on the verge of hysteria. Nature was behaving badly. They closed their inside-out umbrellas, folded their chairs, picked up their coolers and rushed past me, back to their cars. There could be no grain of sand under gold spandex bikinis, or in eyes that had to be wide open for the next hostile takeover.

I took off my shoes, squatted down by the dunes near a patch of jointweed, pretty much out of the worst of the wind, and watched until all the New York bodies had run away.

Back in the late fifties, when I was a kid, people still slept on the beach, right where I was, on hot summer nights. Grownups would pitch tents, but the rest of us would lug out the blanket rolls we'd learned to make in Boy Scouts. Sometimes we'd tell scary stories about the Cropsey Maniac or whisper dirty jokes, but by eleven, we'd fall silent and just lie on our backs, staring up at the night sky. The stars were so beautiful they shut us up.

I must have been about ten when I started sneaking out of the house one or two nights a week to sleep on the beach after the summer was over. I did it all year round, except for the winter months. Once the house was dark, I'd tiptoe down the steep back staircase and out the door, grab the blanket roll I kept in the toolshed behind the house, take my bike and race like hell for three quarters of a mile over the pitch-black road.

I don't know why I had to get out. Okay, even back then, my brother and I didn't exactly revel in each other's company; but our relationship was more mutual annoyance than animosity. At his worst, Easton was just a pain-in-the-ass prig who ironed his T-shirts.

My mother? A lady. She didn't hit me or scream at me. She just didn't like me, and probably didn't love me. I was the mirror image of the drunk farmer who'd fucked her over and then taken off. Just being myself – dangling my legs over the arm of the couch while I read, whistling a tuneless few notes when I was doing something mindless like washing windows – pissed her off. She'd pass by, and there'd be just a sharp expulsion of air through her nose, an irate snort. When I was younger I'd ask, 'Hey, Ma, what's wrong?' Her answer would be 'nothing' in the form of a high-society chuckle – a throaty heh-heh of denial. Then she'd say, 'Steve, sweetheart, *please. Anything* but "Ma." Did I raise a hillbilly?' My mother always made me feel like total shit.

I know. She didn't have it easy. The farm was gone, and so was my old man. There was no way near enough money to feed me and Easton, and keep us in jeans and sneakers, much less for her to lead the gracious-lady life she aspired to. So she got a job – at Saks Fifth Avenue in Southampton, selling expensive dresses to expensive women. And when she wasn't involving herself in rich lives by zipping up their dresses or stroking their embossed names on their charge cards, she was busting her chops doing scutz work for their charity groups. My mother would do *anything* – set up three hundred bridge chairs in the midday sun, lick one thousand envelope flaps until past midnight – to be allowed into their swan-necked, high-cheekboned society.

I don't know where my mother got her obsession with the upper crust. Sure, her family was an old one in Sag Harbor, and to hear her you could practically see portraits of bearded Eastons in the brass-buttoned uniforms of whaling boat captains. But there were no portraits; I'd biked up to the Sag Harbor Library in eighth grade and learned there was absolutely no basis for ancestor worship. Early Eastons might have gone to sea, but they'd obviously been ordinary sailors: guys with bowlegs and black stumps for teeth. Her old man, who died before I was born, had sold tickets for a ferry company that had the Sag Harbor and New London, Connecticut, route.

Still, my mother was convinced, despite all hard evidence to the contrary, that she was a gentlewoman. She didn't give a damn about the local South Fork female elite, the wives of lawyers, doctors, successful farmers, or even the moneyed Yanks – maybe because they all knew who she was, or wasn't. No, she lived for Memorial Day, when her 'friends' opened up their summer houses out here. Even when we were kids, she'd sit at the supper table and talk about her New York 'friends.' Quality People.

Her friends, of course, were not her friends but her customers, summer women who came to the grand old houses, 'cottages' in Southampton – like the one Sy bought – for the summer. She'd go on and on about Mrs Oliver Sackett's hand-embroidered-in-England slips ('Divine, teeny stitches!'), or the thirty-one ('Norell! Mainbocher! Chanel!') dresses Mrs Quentin Dahlmaier had ordered from the main branch in New York, one for every night of the month of July.

Bottom line? My mother felt fucked every single day of her life because she didn't have a driver (*'Never* say "chauffeur"!' she warned Easton; 'it's *nouveau riche'*) and a maid and a sable coat. She didn't even have a roof that didn't leak.

And I think that's why I got out from under her roof as often as I could. Sitting over a plate of her *spécialité de la maison,* macaroni and undiluted Campbell's Cheddar Cheese Soup (which, of course, she knew was not Quality, but which she announced was Great Fun), listening to her go on to Easton in her throaty voice – she was a heavy smoker and wound up sounding like Queen Elizabeth with laryngitis – Jesus. She'd talk about how Mrs Gabriel Walker ('one of the Bundy sisters, from Philadelphia') was mad for nubby linen, absolutely mad . . . Her conversation was directed to Easton, never to me. But then she knew and I knew that would be a waste of time.

I did not belong in that house. Like my old man, I was not Quality.

'Had Mr Spencer to the best of your knowledge received any threatening messages or phone calls?' Robby Kurz was asking Lindsay Keefe.

You could tell Robby had gotten up extra early to get spiffy. He'd arranged a yellow handkerchief in the breast pocket of his brown plaid jacket into points. The smell of his double dose of hairspray overpowered the scent arising from a huge bowl of white roses on the table in front of the couch he and I were sitting on.

'Of course there were no threats.' Lindsay exhaled, a sharp, pissed-off breath between pursed lips. She was trying very hard to be patient. 'What do you expect? That his killer went up to him and announced: "You're a dead man"? And there were no heavy-breather phone calls either.' For a woman in shock, Lindsay sounded clearheaded. In fact, completely self-possessed, not a hint of hysteria. The bat-shit, Valiumed, sensitive *artiste* her agent had described could have been some other person.

Even though I'd caught a glimpse of her the night before, in the back of my mind I must have been expecting a fifteen-foot-tall Goddess of Film, a gargantuan babe with enormous, glistening lips and colossal legs that could crush any man caught between them. But Lindsay, standing by the window, fingering the sheer white curtain, was of ordinary height, although so small-boned and petite (except for her world-famous tits) that she looked as if she'd been created solely to make men feel big, important. In her daintiness, she must have been a perfect match for Sy. Two exquisite pocket-size people: a separate species.

But Sy had been an ordinary-looking man. Lindsay Keefe's looks were extraordinary. No wonder she'd gone from doing Greek tragedies in little theaters in little midwestern cities to making avant-garde films in Europe to being an American movie star. Her features were beautiful. Okay, they didn't add up to perfection, but they came damn close. (Movie stars usually have one annoying flaw – a wen, a strawberry mark that you can't ignore, one defect that makes you wonder why they couldn't pop a few thou for a plastic surgeon.

Lindsay had a black mole on her neck, at the spot where a guy's Adam's apple is. It was a thing you'd never think about on a regular person, but I couldn't keep my eyes off it.)

Her skin was the palest possible, the kind where you can almost picture the whole blood vessel network underneath. Her hair was some miraculous white-blonde, but with half silver, half gold overtones. And the eyes: pure black.

She'd gotten herself up all in white. A long, filmy skirt and a plain, schoolgirl blouse. The living room was all white also, like a stage set designed solely to flatter blondes. There were a lot of what I'm sure were antiques, but solid stuff: fat couches and chairs covered in different materials – but all whites too, various shades of it, so it became a kind of color.

'If you want to know the truth,' Lindsay went on, '*nothing* could scare Sy. He was a man in control, at the peak of his powers. Intellectually, emotionally, financially . . .' She stopped for a second. When she continued, it was with disgust, as though she'd caught us sniggering over the notion of Sy's 'powers'. She seemed exasperated with what she'd decided were our infantile, dirty cop minds. 'All right, I'll fill in the blank for you: at the peak of his powers sexually.'

Forget that her words were unfair, to say nothing of blunt, brusque and bordering on the stunningly snotty; it hardly mattered. Robby and I sat motionless as she spoke. Her voice had a deep, sensual undercurrent, a hypnotic hum. You wanted to hear whatever she had to say. She could be talking about Sy's death, or reciting erotic poetry, or reading the ingredients off a Kaopectate label. You couldn't resist being Lindsay Keefe's audience.

You wanted to applaud everything. Because besides the Face and the Voice, there was the Body. She had positioned herself perfectly in front of the window. With the curtains open, the late-morning light behind her was so strong you could practically see what she had for breakfast. Everything was lit up: her legs, the line of her bikini underpants stretched over her flat stomach, her hand-span waist – and most of all, the fact that she wasn't wearing a bra. Incredible: her boobs were flawless, the awesome ones that defy gravity and point north. And naturally, she stood slightly sideways, making sure the sunshine lit her up so you couldn't avoid seeing the pokes her nipples made as they pushed against the gauzy fabric of the tightly tucked-in blouse.

'Sy was a great success artistically *and* financially. You must know that this is not an industry where people wish each other well. But would someone murder him because his last film won the Gold Palm at Cannes and grossed ninety-two million? *Please.*'

Robby was nodding at everything Lindsay said, but it was nodding run amok. His head kept bobbing up and down, nonstop, like one of those jerky dolls with springs for necks you used to see in the backs of cars.

I wasn't nodding at all. Because, number one, although I might have been spellbound by the Voice, I still had enough brains to realize all we were getting from Lindsay were words. She was giving a brief (but wonderfully well lit) personal appearance that would satisfy two uncouth cops – without revealing anything.

And, number two, my nodding reflexes weren't working so well because I was genuinely stunned at Lindsay Keefe's absolute indifference to us. Hey, we hadn't dropped in to discuss delinquent parking tickets. You'd think, being an actress, she'd offer a few chest-heaving sobs, or at least sniffle. All she was doing, though, was going through the motions of an interview so she wouldn't get marked down as uncooperative – and keeping us titillated while she was at it, only because it would have been against her nature to be in the same room with a human dick and not titillate. But she totally didn't give a shit about what we thought about her. I'd never come across that before.

Homicide is not a common circumstance in most lives and, therefore, neither are homicide detectives. I'd always gotten *some* reaction: respect, hostility, obsequiousness, guardedness, guile, cooperation. Forget personal qualities: to anyone remotely connected to a murder, Robby and I were figures of authority, symbols of the Law. But not to Lindsay. To her, we were clowns in cheap sports jackets.

She lifted her hair out from under her collar, letting it fall over her shoulders. 'Is there anything else you want from me?' Lindsay demanded.

Robby tried to be cool. He didn't get anywhere. He started giving off a sour wet-wool smell; he was in a sweat of nerves and desire. 'Did Mr Spencer ever mention anyone from his past who might not wish him well?' he asked. Lindsay took a slow, deep breath, presumably to show us how she was trying to retain her composure so she could continue the ordeal of questioning. 'Miss Keefe?' To be fair, Robby's voice didn't quite squeak, but it wouldn't have won any prizes for resonance.

She left her position near the window and came and sat on a chair opposite us, her legs curled under her, her hands clasped in ladylike fashion in her lap. 'Look, I've given you all the help I can,' Lindsay said. 'I don't know anything more.'

That voice! It was one of those voices you read about in old detective stories, which girls with names like Velma have: rich, luscious, like warm cream. Except the funny thing was, for all her cream and translucent skin and superior tits and blonde hair and black mystery eyes, Lindsay Keefe wasn't knocking my socks off. Sure, if your taste ran to devastating blondes she wasn't bad. But on or off the job, I was never the kind of guy who gets off on contempt. Okay (to be fair), maybe this was Lindsay's tough act, to hide some vulnerability – or some real or imagined indiscretion she was afraid was incriminating. Or (not to be fair) maybe Lindsay was just an insolent, contemptuous, cold, emotionally defective twat.

'Well?' she asked. 'Any more questions?'

Robby wasn't completely star-struck, but he seemed to have forgotten momentarily, that he was the killer interrogator of the Suffolk County PD Homicide Squad and the beloved husband of Freckled Cleavage. He gulped. 'I think that about covers it for now,' he said.

'Fine,' she said, and stood. Robby stood too, although not without banging his shin on the white marble coffee table.

I stayed on the couch. 'Did Mr Spencer ever mention seeing any of his colleagues from his days in the kosher meat business?' Lindsay eyed me a little curiously. I hadn't said anything beyond a 'Hello' and an 'I'm sorry'; until now, I'd been letting Robby do the questioning. 'Why don't you sit down just for one more minute, Ms Keefe.' She sat, and then Robby did too. 'The meat business,' I prompted.

'No,' she answered. 'I'm almost positive he didn't see any of them. For him, that was another life.

84

But let me say this, Detective . . . I forgot your name.'

'Steve Brady. Did any people he knew from the meat business invest in this movie, Ms Keefe?'

'Yes. One or two.'

'Do you know their names?'

'Just one. Mikey. Michael, I suppose.'

'Any last name?'

'I don't know it.'

'Did you ever hear of Mr Spencer meeting with this Mikey?' She shook her head. 'Having a phone conversation with him?'

'Sy made most of his calls from his study.'

'Right, but did you ever happen to be passing by and hear any call to this Mikey?'

'Actually, once. And I *was* passing by – not eavesdropping. Don't condescend to me.'

'Okay. What did you happen to hear, passing by?'

'Sy was reassuring this man that everything was going well.'

'Was Mikey worried that it wasn't going well?'

'No, of course not. It was one of those soothing, stroking, you're-so-important phone calls. Sy was a master of those.'

'No problems with *Starry Night*?' I asked. She shook her head, allowing a curl of her long platinum hair to fall in front of her shoulder. She started twirling it around her index finger; I assume my eyes were supposed to follow the little circles until I was mesmerized. But I couldn't stop watching the mole on her neck; it was so black it looked like an undeveloped third eye. 'Mr Spencer was pleased with how it was going?' I asked.

'Yes.'

'No problems with the director? Any of the actors?'

'Nothing that wasn't routine.'

'He was happy with your performance?'

'Of course.' Emphatic. Clipped. 'Why do you ask?'

'Just trying to get the lay of the land,' I said.

'Let's be straight with each other, Detective Brady. I don't know what you've heard, but there's always on-set gossip about the star of a film. Sometimes it's more than petty nastiness. I'm sure there are people saying terrible things, like that I'm a tough bitch. That's because I'm serious – *passionately* serious – about my work. Or that my performance is somehow lacking. Or that my relationship with Sy was . . . well, one of mutual convenience. The truth is, yes, I am tough. But I also happen to be a vulnerable human being.'

'I'm sure you are.'

'And I loved Sy very, very much.'

'I understand.'

'I hope you also understand that Sy loved my work.' She bowed her head for an instant, a second of silence. Then she looked me right in the eye. 'And he loved me.'

'I don't doubt that for a minute,' I said, and thought about the long, dark hairs that had gotten caught on the headboard in the guest room.

'We were going to be married.'

I asked: 'What do you know about his ex-wives?'

'I haven't met either of them.'

'Did he ever talk about them?'

'Not very much. The first was named Felice. He married her right after college. She was getting her PhD at Columbia. Supposedly very brilliant. Came from a distinguished family. A great deal of money.'

'What happened?'

'Truthfully?'

'Please.'

86

'Bor-ing.'

'Did he have any contact with her recently?'

'No. I'm almost positive. They were divorced in the late sixties. She's remarried.'

'What about his second wife?' I asked.

'Bonnie. From out West someplace.'

'Do you know anything about that marriage?' Robby asked.

'A mismatch.' Lindsay placed the fingers of one hand in the palm of the other; they needed a rest, or else she was examining her nails. 'She's a writer. Well, she had one movie produced, and that's when Sy met her. I think he was enamored of what he thought was a lively, unpretentious intelligence. All zip, and hero-worshipping quotes from Joseph Mankiewicz's screenplays. That appealed to him – for five minutes.'

'And then?' I asked.

'The truth? She had one movie in her. She was yesterday's news by the time they were married.'

'Do you know if he saw her at all?' Robby asked.

'No. Of course not. But she lives around here. When they split, she got their old summer place. Actually, though, Sy did hear from her a few months ago. She sent him some new script she'd written.'

I asked: 'Was he going to produce it?'

'God, no.'

I found myself swallowing hard. 'He told her no?'

'Of course. He told me he had to. Kindly, probably generously. But I'm sure very, very firmly. Oh, but wait a second. That's right. I'd forgotten. She came onto the set in East Hampton, *pursuing* him. I didn't see her, but she went and knocked on the door of his trailer. It was awful. But he said he told her in no uncertain terms: 'Goodbye. Stay off the set of my film. And keep your screenplays to yourself.' That may sound harsh, but he had no choice. This business is a magnet for all sorts of unstable people.'

'He knew her, though,' I said. 'She was his ex-wife. Did he think she was unstable?'

'No. As far as I know, he just thought she was a loser. But if Sy had given her the least bit of encouragement, she'd have been all over him: Love my screenplay. Love me. Do for me. Make me rich, famous. Make me a star. People like her are *desperate*. Sy had to get rid of her.'

CHAPTER 4

The Homicide team meeting turned out to be six cops sitting around a blackboard shrugging shoulders. Robby hadn't been able to interview Easton because he'd been tracking down the kosher-meat guy, Mikey, who turned out to be Fat Mikey LoTriglio – a real sweetheart. Like the Spiegel-Spencers, Mikey's family had owned a major meat-processing plant, but he also had ties to another family – the Gambinos. He had a dandy record of arrests for extortion and aggravated assault – our kind of guy – but he'd never been convicted of anything.

Ray Carbone announced that all he'd been able to do, because he'd been busy calming down the higher-ups and helping write a press release, was find out that Sy's first wife's name was Felice Vanderventer and she lived on Park Avenue.

Our man at the autopsy, Hugo Schultz, the Sour Kraut, reported that not counting his death, Sy had been in great shape. No diseases. No traces of alcohol or drugs. His last meal seemed to have been bread and salad. There was evidence of recent ejaculation, probably post-salad. Oh, he'd been killed by the first bullet, which had gone through his head; the one that had gone through his heart was unnecessary: Target practice, Hugo said.

The other two guys listened and drank coffee. I briefed everyone on Bonnie's story on her screenplay versus the opposing Lindsay version – and how there was something not right about Bonnie, something that bothered me. Oh, and that Lindsay's claim of giving a stellar performance was countered by both Bonnie and Gregory J. and how I thought *Starry Night,* the twenty million dollars it was costing and, possibly, Lindsay's reputation might be headed for the crapper.

In other words, what I got from the meeting was not much. It was then that I thought about my movie man. Jeremy. Germy.

Jeremy Cottman, the most famous movie critic on TV, was my one rich and famous friend. Okay, so it wasn't exactly a big-ass buddy friendship. In fact, it had been over twenty years since I'd laid eyes on him.

Jeremy had been a Bridgehampton summer kid, the son of rich but not famous parents. His father had been a stockbroker whose only customer seems to have been himself. Mr Cottman played perpetual golf; his skin had the texture of a grilled cheese sandwich. Mrs Cottman, who called everyone 'cutie-pie,' had spent whole summers in a sunbonnet that tied under her chin, clutching a pair of clippers, pruning anything that didn't run away. Their house, a rambling white wood Victorian, overlooked Mecox Bay.

Rich kids like Jeremy played all summer: swimming in each other's pools, going to parties at each other's beach clubs, taking riding lessons in those puff-thigh pants. Kids like me worked. I started out scraping duck shit and sorting potatoes for the farmer who had bought our land. When I was twelve, I graduated to cleaning swimming pools, and later to caddying at one of the local golf clubs.

But in spite of work, summer had always been an enchanted time. It didn't get dark until late, so we'd grab a bite of supper and rush down to the ball field. We were in the four thousandth inning of a baseball game that had been going on since the summer after third grade: shirts and skins, our shirts getting progressively scruffier as the fifties gave way to the sixties, our skins darkening from the white, stick-out-ribbed chests of nine-year-olds to the broad, tanned, hairy torsos of high school seniors.

It was a strictly Bridgehampton game. Every once in a while, a summer kid would ride past – on an English racing bike. After a few nights of bypasses, he'd brake, knock down his kickstand and get really busy inspecting a tire. Usually we'd ignore him, as in: This is one club you can't join, fuckface. But if he looked like a terrific jock, we'd be a little less exclusive. Sure, the kid would have to have the balls to grunt the opening 'hi.' But then, if he wasn't too well-dressed, we might ask him if he wanted to hit a few.

Jeremy (I was the one who started calling him Germy) made our team. He was an incredible power hitter, a so-so outfielder, and a cruel and funny mimic. He'd pick some movie star or a baseball player and have them say terrible things about one of the kids, so it was like being dumped on by Marilyn Monroe or Carl Yastrzemski (the greatest human being Bridgehampton had ever produced, even though he'd played for Boston).

I'd never met anyone like Germy Cottman. To be able to hit those line drives. To have discovered a way to say *whatever* was on his mind. God, how good that must feel! We became great summer friends, eventually trusting each other enough to share our most intimate sports fantasies. We were the best of buddies from about the time we were twelve until we went off to college.

Germy went to Brown. I went to Albany State. I

looked for him that summer after freshman year, but his mother, clipping roses that were doing something to annoy her, said, Sorry, cutie-pie, Jeremy is in Bologna, learning Italian. I saw him around once or twice after that, but we didn't have much to say; by then, he was an intellectual, I was a druggie, and neither of us was playing ball anymore.

But every now and then Germy's name came up around town. I heard he was in graduate school in Chicago for something; he was working on a newspaper in Atlanta; he was working on a newspaper in Los Angeles; he was writing long movie reviews – film criticism, I suppose – for some high-minded magazine.

And then one night on TV: the Germ! I remember lying on my couch, pretty drunk but not totally gone, slugging down a beer, thumbing the remote control. There he was, swiveling back and forth in a big leather chair, legs crossed, telling us folks at home – in his familiar, clothespin-on-the-nose prep school nasality – why *Out of Africa* was such an overrated movie; then he did a brief, mean, but exceedingly accurate, imitation of Meryl Streep.

Germy was on the map. A celeb. And over the next couple of years, his show actually got better. He wasn't only negative. Sure, there were still his killer reviews and his snide imitations, but he stopped showing off his intellectual superiority and started displaying his real intelligence. He'd run a film clip in slow motion and explain exactly about how a certain shot was done, or describe precisely why So-and-so was a good editor, or a bad production designer. He knew the players too; he'd report how some internal fight at a studio affected a particular movie.

All America watched Germy: seven-thirty, Friday

nights. And read about him too, in *People, Time, Newsweek*. I read he'd married the daughter of a famous 1940s director; that he had a house on a cliff overlooking the Pacific; that he'd moved back to New York; that he'd divorced his wife after fifteen years and married some very famous Broadway lighting designer – not that I'd ever heard of her. Around town there was talk that his father had had a heart attack on the eighteenth hole and had died before they could get him back to the clubhouse and that his mother had died too, and Germy had inherited the house. But although I kept up with what he was doing, I hadn't spent any time with him since I'd played shortstop and he'd played outfield.

I felt a little nervous about calling him, but then I thought: I've got to give it a shot. It being a glorious, sunny Saturday afternoon, Germy could actually be a couple of miles away. He might be spending the day practicing a cruel Clint Eastwood imitation or banging the lighting designer or (I smiled to myself as I pulled into his driveway) sitting cross-legged on his bed the way he used to, working neat's-foot oil into his mitt.

A minute later, there he was at his front door, his hands braced against the frame, as if he were defending his house from some intruder who might push him aside and ransack his living room, or demand to know what Chevy Chase was really like. 'Yes?' Chilly, about to cross the border into absolute iciness.

'You don't recognize me, Germy?'

Then he did the Oh-my-God! I-don't-believe-it! bit, followed by our mutual finger-squishing handshake. It was for real. We were both pretty touched at seeing each other, although not comfortable enough to follow our natural inclination, which was to give each other one of those acceptable, non-homo, World Series hugs. 'Steve! Come in!'

I followed him through the front hall, toward the living room. It was like stepping back into 1959: the blue-and-white umbrella stand filled with tennis rackets, the dark, scratched-up old mirror in a carved wood frame. 'I can't believe it,' I said. 'It looks exactly the same. Any minute your little sister's going to come running in and spit at me.'

'That's right!' Germy said in his slow honk. 'I'd forgotten. She spent a whole summer spitting at you. She was madly in love.'

The Cottman house still had the we've-been-rich-forever shabbiness it had when we were kids: faded flower print cushions, threadbare rugs with flowers that skidded across wood floors, old wicker chairs. Out on the back terrace, there were flowers blooming in his mother's mossy clay pots, and the old, white-painted wrought-iron chairs, chipped in the same places.

Like the house, Germy hadn't changed much. He was tall, about my height, but he hadn't outgrown his round-chinned baby face, with its button nose and wide-open eyes. Sure, his forehead was a little lined, his brown hair had a little gray, but in his horn-rimmed glasses and white tennis sweater, he looked more like a tall kid in a daddy costume than a full-fledged adult. He made a take-a-seat gesture. 'Can I get you anything? A cup of coffee?' Then he remembered. 'A beer?' I shook my head. 'Steve! God! Tell me about yourself. Where are you living? What do you do?'

Germy had much too much class to ask: What do you want? although it must have been in the back of his mind that maybe I was there for a handout, or with some obnoxious request: Can you get me an auto-graphed picture of Goldie Hawn?

'I'm here, in Bridgehampton, north of Scuttle Hole – '

'Married, single, div – ' He interrupted both me and himself with his own enthusiasm. 'I got married again last year!' He paused as if to give me time to prepare myself for something wonderful. 'To Faith Armstead!'

I nodded respectfully, as in: Oh, of course, I'm always dazzled by Faith Armstead's lighting. 'Congratulations.'

'She's stuck in a theater all day today. Can you believe it?' His second marriage was working; I could hear the pleasure as Germy pronounced his wife's name. And he seemed proud, almost awed by her dedication; she could have been the first wife since the dawn of history to work on a Saturday. 'Now, what about you?' he demanded.

'I never got married. I was pretty screwed up when I got back from Vietnam.'

'Vietnam,' Germy echoed.

'And then I got used to being single, being free. But I finally met a great girl. We're getting married Thanks-giving weekend.'

'You were in Vietnam,' he said softly. The new quietly moved reaction. After all those years of being Asian-baby butchers, we had somehow turned into national treasures. 'Did you see action?'

'No, you jerk-off. They needed a shortstop on the Saigon intramural team, so I spent the whole war on the ball field. Listen, I really want to catch up, but I'm actually here on business . . .' I saw his face fall a little, his round kid-cheeks flatten. 'Eat it, Je-re-my. You think I'm going to give you a life insurance pitch?'

'Well . . . ' His embarrassment evaporated. 'No.' He

became his real self, his caustic TV self. 'You look more like redwood decks, actually.'

'I'm a detective with Suffolk County Homicide.'

'*You?*'

'Yeah. Never thought I'd wind up on this side of the law, did you?'

'Homicide!' he said. 'Steve, that's exciting. Glamorous!'

'Yeah, well, the violence is fantastic, and I've always been crazy about decomposition.'

'Seriously, do you like what you do?'

'It stimulates my intellectual processes.'

'I said seriously.'

'Yeah, I like it. A lot. Now, do you know why I'm here?'

It took him less than a tenth of a second. 'Sy Spencer.'

'I need background, foreground, whatever you've got. Did you know him?'

He turned his chair so he was facing me; his back was to the bay. 'Slightly.'

'You didn't hang out with him?'

'No. He ran on that middle-aged fast track: a little old money, a *lot* of new money, and writers, restaurant owners, fashion designers. All those emaciated, face-lifted women and their beefy men.'

'Sy wasn't beefy. Five six, a hundred thirty-two pounds.'

'He was an exception.' Germy hesitated: 'Oh. You know how much he weighed from . . . ?'

'Yeah. The autopsy. Listen, the guy was in fantastic shape. I should have his liver. If he hadn't backed up into those bullets, he'd have lived till a hundred. The thing is, Germy, I know more than I want to about all his organs. But I want to know about *him*. So I need

96

you. Even if you weren't his best friend, you must know about him, about what he was doing.'

'Of course.'

'Okay, what do you know about *Starry Night*?'

'Gossip or substance?'

'Both. Substance first; get it over with.'

Germy took off his glasses and gave the earpiece a thoughtful chew. 'All right. I actually read an early draft of the script. It's an action-adventure-love story about a charming heel who marries a very rich woman for her money. Superficially she's the frosty, sophisticated sort – a "Hamptons" type, if you'll forgive me. She's overwhelmed by the heel's magnetism and sexuality. Well, to make a convoluted story short, his past – dealing a little cocaine – catches up with him, and some Colombian types kidnap his wife for reasons the script does not adequately make clear. The heel doesn't care at first. Then slowly he realizes he has fallen madly in love with the wife, and she . . . she's tied up in a basement in . . . I'm a little foggy here, but I think in Bogatá. Maybe Brooklyn. In any case, it dawns on her that he's more than a charming stud; he's the first true love of her life. He goes after her, she escapes, there's a gratuitous car chase, the bad guys seem about to win. But in the end they live happily ever after.'

I sat still for a minute, staring out at the shimmering golden reflection of the sun in the bay. 'Would a guy like me shell out six bucks to see it?'

'Hard to say, Steve. It's a film about breaking through your shell, discovering your humanity. The script has some of the best dialogue I've read in years. Genuinely witty. And some fine straight moments, before the kidnapping, when each starts to reveal himself to the other and then pulls back, as if they realize they're

97

violating some unwritten Law of Superficiality of jet-set marriages. But it certainly doesn't cover any new ground. And as far as I can recall, the plot is pedestrian. But the characters are unusually well drawn for a postliterate script.' He slid his glasses back on. 'In case you don't know it, we are living in what is, essentially, a postliterate era.'

'Oh, I do know it. It's a tragedy I've got to live with every day of my life.'

'I knew you'd feel that way.'

We sat in comfortable silence for a minute. When you know someone since you've been kids, you have a kind of ESP. I could sense Germy, like me, relaxing, lifting up his face to feel the sun, and wanting – really, desperately wanting – to talk about all the amazing things that had happened to the Yankees since Steinbrenner.

But I had a your-guess-is-as-good-as-mine homicide hanging over my head, so I made myself stick to the subject. 'It sounds like maybe you have a qualm about the *Starry Night* script.'

'Well, it could make an exciting, stylish film. But it's all in the execution. Will the actors be credible? Will you believe in the possibility of a great love between Lindsay Keefe and Nicholas Monteleone? His appeal has always been more emotional than sexual. He's essentially a man's man; all his best movies have been about relationships between men – rodeo riders, Amazon explorers . . .' He grinned. 'Homicide cops. But the question about whether the movie will work goes beyond the two principals: Will the Colombians be offensively stereotypical Latino greasers or genuinely terrifying? How good a job will the director do on the action sequences? Will the big chase scene come off? Also, the real problem – the reason Sy didn't get studio financing – is that it was felt there is a limited audience for this type of vehicle: Cary Grant *cum* balls. It probably won't play to the under-twenty-fives. It's not moving enough to be another *The Way We Were*. And it's not a sizzler; even if Lindsay does bare her breasts once again, or decides it's time for a change and moons the camera, it won't help. First of all, audiences have seen her body too many times; there's a strong inclination to say: "Please, madam, keep your shirt on." In the script, the compelling sex is verbal, lighthearted man-woman word play, not sex play.' He leaned back and clasped his hands behind his head. 'Is that substantive enough?'

'Yeah. Now what about money? I've heard twenty big ones. Where does that kind of dough come from?'

'Private investors. Or banks who had faith in Sy's track record.'

'If you were a bank, what kind of faith would you have?'

Germy unclasped his hands, then crossed his arms over his chest. 'I'd invest – although not twenty million. That seems awfully high for a film that will be shot primarily out here and in Manhattan, even with all the lavish set decoration and costumes and an anxious director who's known for a lot of retakes. But forgetting dollars and cents, Sy's films were really good. Bankable. He believed in starting with a polished script. He'd go for the gifted actor over the big name. I always admired his movies.'

'Just admired? You ever love any of them?'

He took a minute to consider the question. 'No. I can't really explain it, but there was something a little smug about every picture he produced. Each one seemed to be saying: 'Aren't I sensitive? Provocative? Don't I have superb production values?' There was always intelligence and care, but never any real spirit. I suppose his films were like Sy himself.'

'From the little you knew him, what did he seem like?'

'Intelligent. Polished but not slick. And for the movie business, where hugging and kissing and screaming "Dahlink, you're a very great genius" is an institutional requirement, he was notable because he was so restrained. A gentleman.' Germy stopped short.

'What are you thinking about? Even if it seems totally irrelevant.'

'Well, Sy wasn't definable. He struck me as something of a chameleon. Man-about-town with men-about-town. Lover boy with women. Tough negotiator with the unions – a real dirty street fighter. And full of Jewish show-biz warmth with a couple of the old-time reporters, dropping Yiddish all over the place. The few times he and I talked, he was very professorial – as if the only thing he lived for were discussions of Fritz Lang's deterministic universe. It made me laugh because I knew he had to have gotten me confused with another critic: I never gave a flying fuck about Fritz Lang.'

'Which one of his personalities came closest to being the real Sy Spencer?'

'I haven't the foggiest.'

'What do you think drove him, Germy? Money? Sex? Power?'

'Well, he certainly seemed to have enjoyed all of those. But he didn't *seem* driven, even though he must have been. He could be pleasant – even charming. But some integral part of his circuitry – the part that reaches out and makes human connections – seemed . . . disconnected.'

'What do you know about his ex-wife Bonnie

Spencer?' Germy shook his head: never heard of her. 'She wrote the screenplay for a movie called *Cowgirl*.'

'I remember that one. It was a nice movie.'

'What was it about?'

'A widow of a small-time rancher literally puts on her husband's boots. It deals with her relationships with the ranch hands, the neighbouring wives. Some moving dialogue about her passion for the land. Beautifully photographed.'

'A major motion picture?'

'No. But a really decent minor one.' He took off his glasses again and did some more gnawing. 'Her name wasn't Spencer when she wrote it. Something else.'

'Sy married her after it came out. But then none of her other screenplays ever got made.' I had this vivid image of Bonnie in her bicycle shorts and too-big T-shirt leaning against the sink in her kitchen. It was not an image of a person who could in any way be in the movie business. 'Ever hear anything about her?'

'No,' he said.

'It sounds like he cut her loose when he realized she wasn't the hot property he thought she was.'

'That sounds fairly typical. Of the industry and of Sy.'

'What about Lindsay Keefe? I've been hearing her acting wasn't very good this time around.'

'Well, now we move on to gossip. I've heard the same thing, and I don't doubt it. She's a very cerebral actress. Her characters tend to be focused women, intelligent, passionately devoted to whatever they're doing, sometimes capable of deep emotion: abused women who write poetry, missionaries who join obscure revolutionary movements. That sort of thing. The character in *Starry Night*, though . . . she's different. Soft, endearing, the poor little rich girl. My guess is, Lindsay may be enough of an actress to project endearingness. But she's mostly head, no heart. The role would be one hell of a stretch.'

'Will they stop making the movie now that Sy's dead?'

'Are you joking? Making movies is a *business*. For an actor, a director, they'd have to stop for a few days until they could get a replacement. For an executive producer . . . they won't even stop for a cup of coffee.'

'Did you hear anything else about what was happening on the set?'

'The usual malicious innuendos.'

'Good. What are they?'

'That Sy was dissatisfied, and he and Lindsay may have actually fought over her performance. Or, even if there was no confrontation, she sensed she was in trouble with him. In either case, she took a deep breath . . . and pointed her major artillery at the director, Victor Santana. Made him an ally.'

'How did she get him on her side?'

'Her side? Her side was the least of it.'

'No shit! Lindsay was making it with Santana?'

'Steve, when the executive producer leaves the set for the day and the director and the leading lady then proceed to hold a script conference in the director's trailer for forty-five minutes with the blinds drawn *and* they don't ask a production assistant for coffee *and* the trailer is observed rocking back and forth, what do you think?'

'Fuck City.'

The real question was, what did Sy think? What did he know? And what had he been planning to do about Lindsay Keefe?

We sat in his kitchen eating ice cream out of pint

containers, the way we used to. Halfway through, we switched; I got Germy's cookies 'n' cream and he got my coffee Heath bar crunch. Neither of those flavors had been invented when we were kids.

He told me how his mother's cancer had metastasized and how excruciating her pain had been and how she'd finally ended it by OD'ing on the Seconal she'd accumulated over a month. I told him I always thought she'd go on forever with that funny old bonnet and the pruning shears and how truly sorry I was she wasn't around anymore to call me cutie-pie.

He put down his spoon. 'Steve, when we were kids, I never had the courage to ask you . . . Your father just walked? Your mother supported the family?'

'Yeah. After he sold the farm, he had a few different jobs, but he'd always get canned for coming to work drunk. I'm not talking a little slurring; I'm talking pissed out of his mind. When you're working over at Agway, it isn't a plus to puke all over the biggest farmer in Bridgehampton. Anyway, he took a hike when I was eight.'

'You never heard from him again?'

'No. For all I know, he could still be alive somewhere, although I wouldn't make book on it.'

My father was a lazy, disgusting, dirty drunk. He was also, in rare, semi-sober moments, a sweet man, talking sports to me, buying a buck's worth of bubble gum so I could have the baseball cards. And he'd sit beside Easton as he built his model ships and say 'Good work,' although he couldn't help, because his hands shook with perpetual DT's. And once in a while he'd come up to my mother and say, '"Ah, love, let us be true to one another,"' or '"Shall I compare thee to a summer's day?"' – and for that second, you

103

could see there had once been something between them.

'You never let me come into your house,' Germy said quietly, as we walked back onto the terrace. 'You always had an excuse. The painters. Your mother was expecting company.'

'We didn't have any money. I couldn't have even offered you a soda. And the place was falling apart. You lived here, in all this richness, and this was just your summer house.'

We fell silent for a minute because, although we had often discussed Roger Maris's troubles, we had never spoken about our own; we had no idea where to take the conversation next. I got up, walked to the edge of the terrace and, for a minute, watched the brilliant red-and-white sail of a Windsurfer skim across Mecox Bay. I turned back to Germy. 'Remember your Sunfish? You got it for your sixteenth birthday.' He nodded. 'You let me sail it, and I took it out so far I was sure I was going to die or get in deep shit with the coast guard. I remember I was more afraid of the coast guard than of death.'

'That was when you were starting to get pretty wild. I remember the next summer, before college. You were drinking too much, even for a rebellious kid. I started . . . not to feel comfortable with you.'

'I know.'

'You were bragging about breaking into houses over the winter, trashing them – for fun.' He looked straight at me. 'Were you just bullshitting?'

'No. And it wasn't just a little vandalism. I'd gone bad, Germ. I was stealing. Color TVs, stereos. Sold most of the stuff to a fence over in Central Islip. I pissed the money away. Booze. Records. A leather jacket. Except one time I went to Yankee Stadium. Got a terrific seat, right near first. This was going to be my perfect day. But we lost. A shitty game.'

'When was that?'

'July of '66.'

'A shitty year,' Germy recalled. 'We finished last.'

'I remember. The first of many shitty years. For me. The Yankees got better. I didn't. Not for a long time.' I separated my thumb and index finger by maybe an eighth of an inch. 'This much,' I explained. 'I missed being dead or in the slammer by this much.'

'That must be scary.'

'Yeah, it was.' I thought for a second. 'Still is.'

CHAPTER 5

By the time I finished with Germy, it was after three o'clock. And it was a Saturday afternoon and the set of *Starry Night* was closed down. So I had the movie people come to me in our temporary headquarters in the Southampton Village PD. I'd gotten use of the Xerox/coffee machine room for interviews – with the understanding that I could be interrupted in the event of a catastrophic copying crisis.

The room was no more or less ugly than any other small, windowless, fluorescent-lighted, metal-and-green-leatherette-chaired government-bureaucracy utility room. Its stale air was perfumed with the aroma of prehistoric coffee grounds and the fumes of copier fluid, its floor decorated with the pink and white and blue confetti of torn-off ends of Sweet 'n' Lows, Equals and sugar packets, as well as with a dusting of white powder that was not a controlled substance but non-dairy coffee lightener. It was no different from any other room where cops work: a place that was habitable yet degrading to the human spirit at the same time.

Victor Santana, the short-haired, thickly mustached, spiffy dude of a director who sat across from me, was willing himself to rise above his surroundings. He was doing a damn good job. He did not seem to belong in the room. In fact, he did not seem to belong anywhere except in a three-star restaurant, a four-star movie or a five-star hotel. The guy was one suave package: a white shirt with a dark red tie, pale gray slacks and a charcoal sports jacket made of some priceless fabric so exclusive a guy like me would never have heard of it.

Santana's name was Hispanic, and he was a pretty intense beige, but his accent wasn't Spanish. He sounded as if he was trying to have been educated at Oxford. It didn't quite work; his diction, like his sideburns, was a little too clipped. My guess was he wouldn't deny his heritage, but neither would he cry '*Caramba!*' to an offer to be grand marshal of the Puerto Rican Day parade.

He came off as urbane, the sort of guy James Bond would banter with at a chemin de fer table, whatever the hell chemin de fer is. But despite his civil smiles and even his I'm-so-accommodating dark-eyed glints, I knew I was getting nowhere fast. He seemed to be spouting the same essential script as Lindsay: *Starry Night* was great; Lindsay was a great actress; Sy Spencer had been a great producer. 'Making a film,' he was explaining, veddy Britishly, each consonant a pearl, 'is a collaborative process. I cannot tell you what a joy it was – artistically *and* personally – to work with Sy and Lindsay.'

So I said: 'Mr Santana, please cut the shit. We know for a fact that you and Lindsay Keefe were having an affair.'

His torso twitched, as if I had, for an instant, electrified his chair. 'That is absolutely untrue!' he declared. He pronounced the word 'ab-so-lyutely.'

'We have witnesses.' Of course, all we had was a secondhand report of a rocking trailer. But it was worth a shot. 'Witnesses who can testify to you and Ms Keefe – in your trailer.' Suddenly he appeared to be studying the veins in his hand. After a second, though, I realized he wasn't into veins; he was communing with his wedding ring. Santana was in his mid-thirties and had had a couple of successes. Maybe he was calculating how much each lurch of the trailer would cost him if his marriage blew up. Had Lindsay been worth a hundred thou per hump? Or maybe he just felt guilty. 'Why not tell me about it?'

'All right,' he sighed. Total mush: here was this cosmopolitan guy who didn't have the presence of mind to ask who the witnesses were and what they had witnessed. It was going to be a cinch, because Santana was dying to Tell All. He settled his perfectly tailored ass back in the chair but leaned the rest of himself forward. 'We were having an affair,' he confided, real whispery, as if to say: Swear to God you won't tell. 'Please understand, this is no superficial run-of-the-play liaison. It is . . . well, it is a love affair. I wouldn't want you to think . . .'

'No problem, Mr Santana. Listen, normally, what you do is your own business. Two people working together can fall for each other. Happens all the time. It's just that in this case, the lady's boyfriend, fiancé, whatever, was shot through the head and heart. So I have to ask a few questions.'

'Maybe . . . Do you think I should speak to an attorney?'

'You can speak to whoever you want. Hire a whole law firm. You're a sophisticated man. You know what your rights are. But why? You're not guilty of anything, are you?'

'Of course not.'

'So just answer a couple of questions. Now, to make my life easier. Or later, if you want, with your lawyer.' I really wasn't trying to trip him up. I just didn't feel like hanging around until the middle of the following week when some dork in a dark-blue three-piece pinstripe could manage to get here from Manhattan, hook his thumbs onto his vest pockets and give me a harangue on prosecutorial discretion. 'Did Sy know about you and Lindsay?'

'No. Of course not.'

'How do you know?'

'I asked. I was a bit nervous, but she said she was certain.'

'Everything seemed lovey-dovey between them?'

'I'm quite certain he thought so.'

'Which means what?'

'Which means he didn't know how Lindsay felt about me – and I about her.' You know those hearts-and-flowers stories you read where the hero's eyes shine? Well, Victor Santana's eyes started to shine. He glowed with the glory of love. You wouldn't think a grown-up guy with such an expensive sports jacket could be such a sap, but he was.

'Was Sy happy with her acting?' This clearly was not Santana's favorite question. His glow dimmed. He sat up straight, tense. He tried to calm himself by stroking his tie; it had lots of little shield designs that I guess were supposed to be club insignias, or family crests. 'Hey, Mr Santana, I've been talking to a lot of people. I have an idea of what's going on, so do us both a favor. Don't get creative. Was Sy happy with what Lindsay was doing?'

'He was not thrilled.'

'Objectively, how was she?'

'She was *won*derful. I mean that sincerely.' He stopped whacking off his tie; he started rotating his wedding ring.

'So Sy Spencer was wrong?'

'Yes. Completely.'

'Why would a smart producer like him think an actress – someone who he's also supposed to be in love with – is crapping up his movie? Especially if she's not?'

'Sy wanted total control over every aspect of Lindsay's life. When she started showing the smallest signs of independence, he began to undermine her – so she would be more dependent on him.' Santana's script was a little different from Lindsay's, but it was pretty clear from his mechanical delivery who had written his lines. 'Sy was terrified of losing her. So he played on her vulnerability. Superficially, Lindsay seems strong. But she's a very vulnerable woman.'

'What did Sy say to you about her acting?'

'He indicated that he felt Lindsay was cold.' Santana shook his head as if unable to comprehend such insensitivity – except the gesture was way overdone, like an actor in a silent film.

'What did he want you to do?'

'He told me to warm her up.'

'Did you try to warm her up in the acting area?'

'No. Truly, it wasn't necessary. She was giving a smashing performance.' Come on, I wanted to say. Get real, Santana. Your old man was probably a building superintendent, and here you are saying 'troooly' and 'smahshing'. 'The warmth was there,' he was explaining. 'Not in words. But in a million tiny gestures. The camera really doesn't lie, you know.'

'You saw this warmth in the dailies they show?'

'Definitely.'

'Who else saw it? Besides you and Lindsay?' In his silence, I could feel Santana's embarrassment. So I changed the subject before he could start resenting me. 'What about your work? Was Sy happy with it?'

Santana let go of his wedding ring and glanced up. 'Other than our disagreement over Lindsay, I think he was pleased. This was only our third week of shooting.'

'Did he ever have it out with you over how you were directing Lindsay?' More silence. 'Come on. Why should I hear a lot of fancy stories from third parties when I should hear the plain truth from you?'

'He said . . .' He shook his head as if refusing to give words to the unspeakable.

'What?'

'He said if Lindsay didn't start showing some real warmth . . .'

'He'd do what?'

'He'd replace me with someone who would be able to . . .'

'Say it.'

'He was . . . crude. What do they say about men like Sy? You can take the boy out of Brooklyn, but you can't take the Brooklyn out of the boy. He said, and I quote: "Give her a kick in the clit and get her to act like a real woman."'

'End quote,' I said.

'Oh, yes indeed,' he agreed. 'End quote.'

I wasn't really sure why Nicholas Monteleone was such a famous actor. It's not that he was bad-looking. Dark-brown hair, matching eyes. Big lips that critics probably called sensuous. And for a slim guy, lots of muscles, even in unnecessary places, like his forearms, as though he moonlighted as a blacksmith. If he'd worked in Homicide, he'd be second or third best-looking. But that someone was paying him a million bucks a movie because he was such a hunk? I'd seen a couple of his pictures, and he'd never looked like a leading man to me. He had no intriguing dark corners; despite his sleepy, heavy-lidded eyes, he was all sunshine and light.

But he did look like his part in *Starry Night*: a playboy. His thick, almost shoulder-length hair was moussed back on the sides. He'd rolled up the cuffs of his pale-pink shirt just once, and miraculously, they stayed that way. But sitting in the Xerox/coffee room, Nick wasn't playing it smooth. More: Forget I'm a world-famous star. I'm a regular guy. Come on, let's be friends!

Temporary friendship was fine with me. He seemed genuinely good-natured, and what the hell, it's nice to have a movie star trying to grin his way into your heart. But for all his pleasantness, Nick Monteleone didn't seem to know anything worth knowing. Had he seen Sy angry? Hmmm. No, didn't think so. Had anyone been angry at Sy? Ummm, not that I know of. That type of thing for twenty minutes.

'Uhhh,' he finally said, 'I know this is a serious business, and I'm probably acting like a self-centered asshole, but I've gotta ask. By any chance did you happen to catch me in *Firing Range*? I played one of you guys.'

'Yeah,' I told him. It wasn't anything I'd go to the movies for; I'd caught it on cable, although I wasn't about to tell him that. 'You were very good.' In fact, he had gotten a lot of it right: the camaraderie of a homicide squad, the compulsive twenty-four workdays and, especially, the fatigue. But he'd worn a shoulder holster – which hardly anyone I know wears – and he'd been physically slow, almost clumsy. By the time he'd have drawn his gun, he would have been dead about

112

forty seconds; he hadn't moved right. And now, watching him, I realized he couldn't even sit right. He was doing the relaxed, manly, lean-back-on-the-two-rear-legs-of-the-chair, when suddenly he lost his balance and almost crashed over backward. He saved himself, barely, but couldn't admit defeat by bringing the chair down on all four legs, so for a minute his feet did a hysterical cha-cha until he regained his balance. Forget his expensive muscles; I saw that Nick had the co-ordination of a Frankenstein windup toy. When he was a kid, the guys probably muttered, 'Not Monteleone!' when they were picking teams.

'Did you get what my character was about?' he asked. 'I mean, did *you* buy him?'

'Sure.'

Actually, thinking about it, I remembered shaking my head, wondering how come this white Chicago homicide lieutenant (in movies, homicide-cop heroes are always lieutenants) had a combo black-New York-Rambo accent: Yo, mothafucka, put that .38 (which came out like 'dirty-eight') on the table and get those hands up high. *Now,* putz.

'I mean, you probably think I'm just another narcissistic actor – and you're probably right – but I am just honestly curious: Could I have been someone you work with?'

What he wanted, I realized all of a sudden, was unconditional acceptance. Not just as my friend. As my colleague. I had to love him totally – and prove my love – or he wouldn't open up to me. So I gushed. 'You know, it was the goddamnedest thing! You really were one of us,' I told him. 'No shit, you could have had the desk next to mine at Headquarters.'

Nicholas's entire body eased. He let up on his macho

113

chair routine. He stretched out his legs, crossed his feet at his ankles. He was wearing some kind of step-in shoes made from lots of thin strips of leather; they probably had some foreign name my brother would know.

'Tell me about dailies,' I asked him, now that we were practically best friends, to say nothing of partners. 'What are they exactly? The whole day's worth of film?'

'The film has to be processed, so what you're seeing is the footage shot the day before. All the takes. The director and the editor sit in the back and talk – whisper, actually – about which take is good, which isn't, what coverage they'll use, what kind of light and color corrections they'll want to order.'

'Who else goes to see them?'

'Actors. Sometimes. Personally, I'm *super*analytical about my own work, and I like to see what everybody else is doing too. You know. Like how is my lighting? My costume? My makeup?'

'Did Lindsay go to dailies?'

Nicholas compressed his big lips. 'No. She always rushed back to Sy's house to work out. Swam laps in his pool. Had to keep those pecs toned.'

'How come she didn't want to see her acting? She's supposed to be smart. Isn't she analytical about her work the way you are?'

'The real truth? Lindsay is an egomaniac.' This said by a guy who went every night to watch his makeup. 'She's totally convinced she can gauge her performance as she gives it, so why bother to see herself? Besides' – Nicholas shook his head wearily – 'if she wants a reaction, all she has to do is look into Spanish Eyes after each take. You get what I'm saying? She can see her brilliance reflected.'

'She really got to Santana?'

'Got to him? She had him in a chain collar, on a leash. "Roll over, Victor. Good boy! Stay!" A *tragedy* for the rest of the company. The first week, Victor was very strong, full of ideas, energy, really exciting to work with. And actually giving Lindsay a rough time because from day one – well, day three or four – he was under the gun. Sy was not happy with Miss Keefe's work. Naturally, Lindsay being Lindsay, she *immediately* picked up that the balance of power had shifted – away from her. She needed a new ally. So she sniffed out Victor's weakness. *That's* her greatest gift, finding a guy's most sensitive area.'

'What was Santana's?'

'Oh . . . being allowed to live in Movieland. I mean, Victor Santana was a damn good cinematographer and then moved to directing. He's directed two really well-received films, right? But beneath his "I'm *so* sophisticated" façade he's still wide-eyed about being in the business. Deep down, he can't even believe he made it out of East Harlem. And here's Lindsay, with her classical-theater background and her Commie Chic reputation and her half-naked *Vanity Fair*. Supremo nympho. The only guys who get into her are *major* lefties – or very heavy hitters with a net worth of at least fifty mil. So Victor thinks: If the same woman who screws the world's most interesting men – that Latvian novelist, Fidel Castro's minister of defense, Sy Spencer – well, if she wants to screw me, I must be in their league.'

'How did she get Sy? What was his weakness?'

'Oh, easy. Sy was the ultissimo intellectual snob. And even though she manages to take off most of her clothes in every movie she makes, Lindsay is still considered a very serious actor; she's convinced everybody she's getting naked as an *hommage* to the First Amendment.

She gets brilliant reviews in all the right little magazines – the ones with French names and cheapo paper – and the big ones too. And she was politically correct on Nicaragua before anyone else knew you were even supposed to think about a Nicaragua. Also, she's a genuine beauty. No plastic surgery. And that for-real blonde hair.'

'No shit. The hair's real?'

'I've been told by highly placed sources that the bottom – it's a match.'

'Wow.' Then I said: 'Okay, we'd bettter get back to the dailies business. Did Sy see them all the time?'

'He had to. First of all, he genuinely cared. And also, they were the only way to monitor his investment.'

'Did he ever say anything about being dissatisfied?'

'No. I mean, it depends on the director, but usually it's not just the inner circle at dailies. There's the director of photography, the writer, cameramen, sound men, assistant directors, production assistants, hair and makeup, set designer. The whole cast and crew, if they feel like it. Usually about fifteen people show up, sit around, stuff their faces with trail mix and watch. So Sy – who prided himself on his classiness – wouldn't sit and bitch about Lindsay in front of an audience.' The skin around Nicholas's eyes glistened, almost raccoonlike, in the fluorescence. At first I'd thought it was some weird trick of the light. Then I realized it was face cream.

'So how did you know he wasn't happy with her?'

'Well, one day about a week ago, we'd been shooting *very* late. Hardly anyone came to dailies. Most people, Santana included, were wiped; they got the hell out the second after the lights came on. I was kind of hanging around, wanting to get a minute with Sy to talk about something – '

'What?'

'I forget. I'm sure it was nothing important. In any case, Sy starts letting loose to a few of his people. Not loud, and not even angry, which shows you how under control he was, because when you looked at Lindsay up on that screen it was like looking at Big-Tit Barbie. I mean, not one single spark of life. Anyway, Sy was supercool, just kidding about the scene and what a fortune it was going to cost to have an effects man add lightning, and did we really need lightning. Everybody started talking about lightning. All of a sudden, Sy laughs and says how the best thing that could happen to this movie would be if lightning struck *Lindsay*. Then he said, "Just kidding." But naturally, everybody knew what he meant.'

'What did he mean?'

'If anything really happened to her? It's what the moneymen always say when one performer is crapping up a movie; if lightning struck, the completion guarantors – the insurers – would have to pay so they could begin production again with another actress. Sy was being lighthearted, but the subtext was: Forget the two-hearts-that-beat-as-one shit; he wished to hell he could be rid of her.' Nicholas paused. He was working up to something big. Inhale. Exhale. Inhale. Finally, he got it out: 'Can I call you Steve?'

I wasn't any actor, but I flashed my most engaging cop-friend smile. 'Yeah, sure.'

He smiled back. 'And you call me Nick. Now, Steve, just between us. About Sy's wanting to get rid of Lindsay. This last week, I think Sy *might* have been taking meetings off the set.' Nick had heavy eyebrows. He lifted them significantly. 'Do you get my drift.'

'He had someone else?'

'I'm not sure. But you could see Lindsay trying too hard to please him, and him not interested in getting pleased. I mean, she'd put an arm around him, and he'd put his arm around her. The movements were right, but hell, I'm an actor. Why do I get the big bucks? Because I'm intuitive. I *know* body language, and his was saying, "I have a headache tonight, dear."'

'Maybe he was just upset about her performance.'

'Maybe. But the first two weeks, he'd always be sniffing around her, hanging around the set most of the day. He knew then that she wasn't doing her best work, but he was so goddamn hot for her he couldn't be angry. I mean, you should have seen him: canned heat. But suddenly he's looking at his watch. He's leaving by eleven.'

'Did you hear any talk – vague rumors, even – about this from anyone?'

'No. It's just my theory.' Nicholas the Graceful stood up, stretching his arms, and – whammo – slammed his hand against the wall. He sat down again and pretended his knuckles weren't throbbing. 'Listen, can I *really* trust you, Steve?'

'You bet.' I leaned forward and gave him a light, male-bonding arm punch. 'You know you can.'

'You know Katherine Pourelle?'

'The actress? Yeah, sure.'

'This is not for public consumption, but I used to have a thing with her, when we were both starting out. She was living with this guy from ICM. Her agent, in fact. Well, she was more than living with him. She was married to him. Anyhow, we had this big love, big breakup, big hate. But last winter we met in Vail. New husband – real estate developer. New agent. But you know what goes down. We stopped being silly and

118

became . . . I guess you'd call it friends.' I assumed what he was trying to tell me was that he fucked Katherine Pourelle in Vail while her husband was out schussing. I gave him what I hoped was a knowing smile. 'Well, I got a call from her Tuesday night. From LA. She wanted to know what was with the production. At first I thought she'd heard about how lousy Lindsay was doing and just wanted to dish. Kat *hates* Lindsay and *loves* to dish. She did a play with her, years ago. Everybody who ever worked with Lindsay *loathes* her. Fine, I figured, so we talked about Lindsay and Santana, how he was her first non-Commie Hispanic. Oh, and about how Lindsay always closes her eyes when the director is talking, like she's concentrating on the voice of God, and how you wish you could smack her. Anyway, we had this long, really great talk, but there was something left unsaid. I could *sense* it. I mean, Steve, I earn my living by being open to feelings.'

'Right,' I said encouragingly.

'So I said to her: "Come on, Kat. Tell me what you heard." So she makes me swear not to tell a soul. She'd gotten a call from Sy that morning!'

'And?'

'He asked if she would give *Starry Night* an overnight read. *Super*secret. Do you get what I'm saying?'

'He wanted her to look at the part Lindsay was playing?'

'You got it!' Nick said. 'I think Sy knew that this was a potential twenty-million-dollar catastrophe. *And* I think he'd also found himself someone with blonder hair, or *plus grande* boobies. Lindsay had lost her hold on him. You know what, Steve? I think Sy was getting ready to pull the plug on Lindsay.'

*

When Lynne took me on, she knew we had a lot going for us. I wanted what she wanted: love, companionship, a family, plus – since she seemed to average one marriage proposal every two weeks – a chance to stick it to her stick-up-the-ass family. But in taking me on, she knowingly, willingly and of her own free will bought the whole package: recovering alcoholic (to say nothing of a guy with a former fondness for pot, hash, barbiturates and heroin), recovered fuck-arounder, about-to-be-old fart, compulsive runner, workaholic. Her acceptance of me was absolute, unquestioning.

Was she perfect? No. She was a pain in the ass about order, the type who in sixth grade would have won Neatest Three-Ring Binder. I was neat; she was nuts. She had to restrain herself from making the bed the minute I got up to go to the bathroom. She actually inspected her pencils every night to make sure they were all sharpened for the next day. Lynne's idea of wild spontaneity was going out for a nude moonlight swim – after she finished her lesson plan but before the eleven o'clock news. Still, as much as I bitched about it, deep down, her order comforted me. I needed a structured life filled with perfect pencil points and lights out immediately after Johnny Carson's monologue. Her imperfections turned out to be virtues.

So why was I less than wild with happiness? Why couldn't I accept Lynne without reservation, the way she'd accepted me? How come I couldn't say: Sure, she's a little serious, but who gives a shit with that hair, those legs? Why was I wasting time worrying that I wasn't one hundred percent ecstatic? Wasn't ninety-nine percent enough? What was wrong with me? She had five million sterling qualities. Why was I zeroing in on the one she lacked? Why the hell was I waiting for Fun?

120

It wasn't that Lynne didn't have a sense of humor. She did. But it was a sense of other people's humor. She'd smile whenever I'd say something even mildly clever. She'd laugh at Eddie Murphy and Woody Allen movies, at my friend Marty McCormack's stupid minister-rabbi-priest jokes (where the priest, naturally, always got the punch line) and at any attempt at comedy by any member of grades K through 6 at Holy Spirit Academy, especially her kids, the ones with learning disabilities.

What Lynne lacked was liveliness. I knew it wasn't fair to hold it against her. It was like saying to a woman, I want you to be five foot two and built like a brick shithouse, when she is, in fact, tall and willowy.

Still, I couldn't shake the low feeling that had come over me on the blanket in my backyard the day before. More than disappointment, less than dread. I didn't know what the hell it was. But there I was, taking a phone break, my feet up on the Xerox machine, making it worse – giving her an opening I knew she didn't have the capacity to fill. 'Okay, who do you think is sexier? Me or Nicholas Monteleone?'

And as Lynne, predictably, was responding, 'You,' I found myself ashamed of myself for wanting: 'Are you *kidding*? Nicholas Monteleone!'

She asked: 'Is he a nice person?'

'Yeah. Friendly; a good talker for someone who speaks other people's lines for a living. When I finished questioning him, I felt: Too damn bad he has to leave; he's great company. But he's *so* terrific that you start wondering whether it's him or it's an act. Like, if he thought that running around the room and imitating an aardvark would put him in a better light with Homicide, would he forget the congeniality bit and start licking up ants?'

121

'What do you think?'

'Ants,' I said. I looked at my watch. It was after five. 'Listen, honey, were you counting on lobster?'

'No, but that's what you told me you were counting on.'

'Did you melt the butter?'

'No, of course not. And you didn't buy the lobsters. I know you. I know you so well that right now I know I'm going to have a Lean Cuisine and then about ten you'll pop in – just to say hello.'

'I'm a very friendly guy.'

'Guess what? You won't be able to be too friendly. My roommates are home tonight.'

'Shit. All right, if I get finished by ten, ten-thirty, can I pick you up and take you over to my place?'

Just as Lynne was saying, 'Okay, but not too late a night, because I have a huge pile of test results for next year's kids I have to go through,' a Southampton Village cop appeared at the door with a surprise guest: Gregory J. Canfield.

Gregory gaped at the room, slack-jawed, trying to register everything, as if the decor – including the brown-stained hot plate of the Mr Coffee machine and me with my feet up – was going to be the subject of his final in Advance Set Design at NYU film school. Now that there was no corpse to upset his delicate balance, he was Mr Movie Man.

I said, 'People. Speak to you later,' to Lynne and 'Thanks' to the cop who'd shown Gregory in. Then I hung up, swung my feet off the Xerox machine and told Gregory to sit. But he barely got through the door when he stopped short. You could see his mind moving in for a close-up; he stood before the bulletin board, staring at a yellowing FBI Most Wanted list, at hand-printed signs

122

offering Doberman-mix puppies, an '81 Datsun 280 ZX and a model 12 Winchester pump-action shotgun, probably wishing someone else from NYU was there to share this Moment of Authenticity.

'Okay, now you know what lower middle class looks like, Gregory. Time to sit down.' He did. 'You're here to help me. Right?'

He nodded. He looked slightly less repulsive than the day before, mainly because instead of baggy shorts, he was wearing baggy slacks. His skeletal white legs, with their bulbous kneecaps, were covered. 'I remembered what I couldn't remember last night.'

'Great,' I replied. I waited. He was staring at my holster, which was clipped onto my belt. 'You remembered something?'

'You asked me if there were any threats made to Sy Spencer.'

'And?'

'I don't know if you'd classify this as a threat. I mean, a genuine threat.' Gregory hesitated. Now he was gazing at me with the same passionate intensity he'd directed at the bulletin board. He'd obviously decided I was the star of this movie. He flushed. He fidgeted. He beamed at me. I was his True Detective.

'Listen, Gregory, anything you think is even remotely threatening — a dirty look — is something I want to hear about.'

'Did you know Sy had an ex-wife who lives in Bridgehampton?'

My heart gave a thump. I sat up, alert. Damn it, I'd been right. There was something about her. 'Bonnie Spencer,' I said. His face fell. 'Hey, if by this time I didn't know Sy had an ex in the neighborhood, what the hell kind of detective would I be?' Gregory still looked like he was debating whether or not to be clinically depressed. 'Now come on. You're my key man in this investigation. Okay, I gave you a name: Bonnie Spencer. But now it's your job to fill me in.'

'Well, Sy married her right at the beginning of his career as producer. She'd written the scenario . . . That's another term for screenplay. It's more common in Britain. In any case, she'd written a movie called *Cowgirl* in the late seventies. Unpretentious film. Her credit was Bonnie Bernstein.'

That big Utah jockette didn't strike me as a Bernstein. 'Had she ever been married before Sy?' I asked.

'I don't know.'

'Okay, go on.'

It's funny; as he was talking, I realized that Bonnie had been on my mind since I'd left her that morning. I couldn't shake the images I had of her. One was the real Bonnie as I'd seen her. The other one was even more vivid, and unconnected with reality; she was in some sort of sleeveless thing, a dress or a tank top, that bared part of her broad shoulders. I could see her arms and shoulders: strong, smooth, with the sheen of a deep tan. Incredibly silky skin. It was really, well, an exciting image – and a strange one, because the bare-shouldered Bonnie in my mind's eye was so incredibly desirable, and really had nothing to do with the big girl in the big T-shirt I'd interviewed.

'The marriage broke up,' Gregory reported, 'and she went into total eclipse as a writer.'

'How come?'

'I don't know.'

Maybe, I thought, Bonnie Spencer reminded me of someone else, some large, bewitching girl out of my past. That made sense. But my house was no more than four miles from hers; I could have passed her one summer evening on one of my runs and focused in on her best few square inches. Or maybe I'd given her a half second of consideration in my bar-hopping days, before moving on to someone better. Who the hell knew? In all those years of drinking – especially toward the end – there were black holes in my memory. We could have met at a cocktail lounge and discussed Truth and Beauty all night, and it would be a total blank.

'From what I've heard,' Gregory went on, 'Bonnie is pretty much of a zero. Her only real significance is that she used to be married to Sy. But even then, I probably wouldn't have heard about her if she hadn't come to the set.'

Right. Bonnie had mentioned she'd dropped in to see Sy. 'What happened?'

Gregory rubbed his palms together as though he was heating them up for a passionate prayer. 'One of the other PAs came running over to me, saying Sy's ex-wife was there and what should he do. But he couldn't do *anything*, because she was right there behind him. She'd *followed* him. To see her, she's this very plain Jane type, but you could understand how she must have learned a thing or two from Sy, because before I could say a word or go get one of the assistant directors, she walked right past me and knocked on the trailer door. I said, "Excuse me, miss, but that trailer is *private*. I'll have to ask you to please wait over by the craft services table." Well, that *second* Sy opened the trailer door. He took one look at her and . . . you would not believe his face!'

'Tell me.'

'Beet red, and I mean b-e-e-t. She said something like "Hiya, Sy!" as if she expected him to give her this major warm welcome, which, of course, he didn't.' Gregory drew in his sunken cheeks. He seemed to be waiting for applause.

I didn't clap. 'Gregory, you came in to tell me about a threat.'

'Oh. Right. Yes, well, Sy gave her this *withering* look and said, "This is not a Bonnie Bernstein production. You know you do not come onto a set unless you are invited." And believe me, the way he said it was not exactly *sotto voce*. I mean, Sy could be *heard*.'

Shit. Even though I knew there was something wrong about Bonnie, I felt lousy for her. 'How did she react?' I asked.

'Jolted. Absolutely jolted. I mean, for whatever reason, she had been expecting a red carpet. She must have thought he'd welcome her with open arms and – '

I cut him off. 'The threat, Gregory.'

'Right. Well, she stood there for a minute, paralyzed. I mean, you can *imagine* the humiliation. For a second, I thought she might cry. But she didn't. No. Quietly, and I mean *quietly*, like probably I was the only one close enough to hear, do you know what she said to him? She said, "Sy, you've just been a rotten bastard for the *last time*!" That's what she said. *Days* before he was murdered. And then she just turned her back on him – and walked away!'

CHAPTER 6

❦⦿❦

Jesus, what a day! Trying to dope out what was under Lindsay's sheet of ice, behind Nicholas Monteleone's cloud of congeniality. Feeling upset that my brother was so upset, wondering if he'd be able to find another job. Seeing Germy again, seeing my past. Lynne.

And Bonnie Spencer. The hardest part of the whole day. Ever since the morning, I'd been fighting her off – the desirable, bare-armed fantasy Bonnie and the real Bonnie, big, plain. Okay, so with fantastic, gold-medal thighs. But I wanted her out of my mind, and she wasn't cooperating.

After Gregory had gone – although not before he'd announced, in front of about ten guys in the squad room, that I was a 'fascinating combination' of Scott Glenn and Keith Carradine – I lifted the phone to call Marty McCormack, at home. I wanted to fill him in, ask him if he thought I should bring Bonnie in for questioning, scare her a little. Actually, I just wanted to talk to a friend.

But all of a sudden, I'd started feeling . . . It's hard to describe, but every drunk knows the sensation: a slight tightening in the throat, a fluttering of the heart, and then weariness, edginess. It all happens in that micro-second before your brain says, Hey, I *really* would love a drink. I hung up the phone and drove over to Westhampton Beach.

And at five o'clock, I was sitting on a brown metal

127

folding chair in the basement of the Methodist church in the usual repulsive fog of cigarette smoke at an AA meeting. But I seemed to be doing everything I could to avoid making the old searching and fearless inventory of myself. Instead, I found myself easing into a real hot reverie – reliving my morning meeting with Bonnie, then improving on it. I was in her kitchen again, moving in on her. Her back was pressed against the sink, but now I was rubbing up against her. I kissed her, and she let out a cry of relief and desire and put her arms around me. Her arms felt so incredibly wonderful.

I became aware that I was breathing a little too deeply, crossing, uncrossing my legs. I forced my attention straight ahead.

The smoky basement haze softened the too-lipsticked dark-red mouth of the speaker. Her name was Jennifer. She had wide maroon makeup stripes on her cheeks and dark-brown eye shadow that went up to her eyebrows. But although she looked hard, she didn't sound it; she had that high, silly, sweet voice of a girl who asks you to make a muscle and then squeals 'Oooh!' She couldn't have been much older than Lynne.

'See, I used to empty out the saline solution for my contact lenses and put vodka in the bottles!' Jennifer explained. We all laughed, applauded; that was one we hadn't heard. 'Anyhow, I kept three bottles in a drawer at work. Two or three times a day I'd start blinking like crazy and rubbing my eye.'

Usually I hated meetings in the summer. Somehow, when I wasn't looking (or was too drunk to notice), AA had become a nonalcoholic version of a singles bar. Dingy church basements were packed with yuppies exchanging degradation stories and slipping each other business cards. Despite all warnings, pickups were

128

common. 'Hi, babe. Need a sponsor?' AA had turned into the new Hamptons scene, and locals like me felt like . . . well, locals. Jennifer giggled. 'I'd grab a bottle of saline solution, toddle down to the bathroom and chug the vodka! And after work, I'd sneak the bottles into my purse, take them home and refill them for the next day!' This meeting wasn't all that bad; along with most of the others, I nodded with recognition at Jennifer's desperation and – despite her lack of anything resembling intelligence – her enormous ingenuity. I thought: We're all so cunning when we're desperate to fuck ourselves over.

I stretched out my legs and leaned back in the chair, forcing myself to relax, to listen, understand, learn. But just as I was thinking an enlightening thought – about how so many drunks have this almost religious belief in the superiority of vodka, its odorless innocence, its purity – Bonnie pushed her way into my head again.

Beneath that straight-shooter veneer, behind the savvy, self-effacing humor, what the hell was she? A *Fatal Attraction* psychopath pursuing Sy, hounding him to produce some hunk of junk she thought was a screenplay – or to get him to love her again? Or was she simply a no-talent loser who had barreled onto the set after pumping up her courage with cocaine or booze or some dopey assertiveness training book?

And what about the threat Gregory had overheard? Look, telling someone it's the last time he's going to be a rotten bastard is, to a homicide cop, somewhat less significant than a vague 'I'm gonna get you' or a specific 'I'm going to hack your balls off and make them into cuff links.' Still, when I'd interviewed her, Bonnie had tossed off her visit to the set in a couple of words, giving the impression that dear old Sy had asked her to drop by just to be friendly: a little cheek-to-cheek air kiss, a little 'Oh, Bon, you must meet Johnny, our key grip,' a little chat about some dangling participle in her screenplay.

And what about her story about being invited to Sy's house, getting the fifty-cent tour? Why would a smart operator like Sy Spencer risk the Wrath of Lindsay by bringing home his tall-in-the-saddle ex-wife to have a look around the master bedroom suite with its king-size closets, its emperor-size bed? Why would he offer Bonnie a tour of a house that had to have pointed out to her: Sweetheart, did you get fucked over on alimony! Was he that insensitive? That much of a prick? Or had Bonnie pushed her way in there too? And why had she told me about it? Good old honesty? Or had anyone seen her, maybe making an unseemly fuss? rifling through drawers? taking something that didn't belong to her? Had she been smart enough to know we'd be dusting everything – from the doorknobs to the blade of Marian Robertson's Cuisinart – for prints and knew hers were there?

Goddamn Bonnie. It ticked me off that all day long I hadn't been able to get her out of my mind. When I thought about it, she was the one who'd ruined Lindsay Keefe for me. Here I'd been expecting at least a cheap thrill, and what happened? I'd actually gotten turned off because Lindsay, posturing in front of the window, had seemed so false after Bonnie's 'naturalness'.

Big deal. She was in great shape and she'd . . . I don't know. She'd amused me. But I knew, as I sat there, tuning out the AA meeting, that I was acting nuts, fixating on Bonnie. By any rational standard, I'd never had it so good. Lynne was great-looking, sweet, young. But there I was, eyes closed, imagining running my hands over the flawless satin of Bonnie's arms – even

130

though, for all I knew, she could have clammy, fish-belly flesh or rough lizard skin, or her entire body could be dotted with dime-size brown freckles.

I wasn't sure what was going on. Had Bonnie Spencer gotten to me? Or had I gotten to me? Gregory, after all, had been right on target about her: a plain Jane. Barely nice eyes – okay, an interesting color. An ordinary nose. A forgettable mouth, most likely with chalky, premenopausal lips; I really hadn't noticed. So what the hell was I doing wanting to . . . I can't even say wanting to see her again. Just wanting her.

Forget reality. I wanted my fantasy too much to open my eyes: I had dropped my jacket onto her kitchen floor. My tie was unknotted, my shirt was open, and I was tearing off Bonnie's bra so I could hold her against me, skin to skin. Applause startled me. I looked up. Jennifer, smiling with lipsticked teeth, was stepping down.

Engaged-guy nerves. That was my problem. Definitely. After more than half a lifetime of drinking – and womanizing – of being a master self-deceiver ('Only three beers tonight') and a consummate liar ('Oh, sweetheart, oh, you're so beautiful, oh, I love you'), it was so hard to keep it simple.

Willie, the leader, a big local guy in a plaid shirt who was a motorcycle mechanic, stepped to the front. Years before, he'd gotten his teeth knocked out in a fight; his dentures looked as if they'd been molded for a giant; they made him lisp. 'Thith hath been a great meeting!' he boomed. 'Time to clothe now. Would all thothe who feel like it join me in the Therenity Prayer?'

Was it only that I was having the normal alcoholic's trouble of keeping it simple? Or was I in deeper shit, really looking to self-destruct? To throw over Lynne, which equaled throwing over happiness, stability, a

131

chance to be a human being? Was I still drawn to oblivion?

Forty-five of us stood and held hands. I squeezed tight. I felt warm I'm-with-you squeezes back, even from the yuppie jerk in tennis whites on my right. I thought: *This* is what I'm here for. Support. I can't do it myself. I need these people. I need God. I need . . .

I couldn't fight Bonnie. Something is wrong about her, I thought. Plus, objectively, there is absolutely nothing about her to turn me on. And yet now I was imagining kissing her soft, warm skin.

'God grant me the serenity . . .' My voice was embarrassingly loud.

Maybe I could keep it simple: Just admit she was one of those women who, despite the most commonplace looks, had always been an erotic genius, even now, even as she was getting too old for anyone to want. A not-homely, not-pretty woman you'd overlook on the street but who, in close quarters, knows exactly how to get to you. Or maybe she wasn't devious. Maybe she did it unconsciously: she gave off primitive, subliminal signals or secreted some subtle female animal smell. Whatever it was, I wasn't going to let it affect me.

'. . . To accept the things I cannot change,' I prayed. 'Courage to change the things I can; / And wisdom to know the difference.'

Amen.

On the basis of its architecture, my mother's house, an old place with weathered cedar siding and a deep front porch, should have been charming or quaint or inviting. But it wasn't. There were too many trees too close: overpowering oaks, dark, drippy maples, grim spruces; their humid shadows spooked the house. And inside . . .

well, it was always dank, especially in the living room, with its never-quite-dry upholstery; sit there long enough and your pubic areas felt about to mildew. No wonder I'd gone off to Vietnam, come home for three days and then never gone back. But my brother had never moved out.

Oh, right, you could say, hearing that: He still lives with Mommy. But it really wasn't like that. Easton was no mama's boy. Sure, with his navy-blue blazers and golden color, he might look like some harebrained heir to a Southampton fortune. But in truth, he was very unindulged. My father had given him almost nothing, except an occasional unbankable belch, and in any case had cleared out soon after Easton's sixth birthday. My mother, although she clearly preferred him to me, spent every cent she had on upping her own Quality Quotient, not his; she would never pass up buying a hundred-dollar ticket to a benefit for hyperkinetic Maori Anglicans held on some rich socialite's lawn (with shrimp in sculpted-ice swan boats) in order to do something nice for her son. Still, Easton had inherited my mother's grand dreams, although unlike her, he had never lost touch with the truth. He was not the typical Bridgehampton local who falls in with the summer crowd; he did not get dizzy drinking rich people's champagne. No matter how much time he spent in their perfect houses, he knew he wasn't one of them, that he was, essentially, poor and, in addition, not blessed with that mysterious personal magnetism that attracts money.

So forget Easton buying his own place, or even renting an apartment. Both assumed a steady income, and my brother understood that long-term job retention – unlike cutting lemon peels into translucent twists –

was not one of his fortes. I'm sure he never actually sat down with my mother and said: Listen, I can play golf, tennis and croquet, sail a boat. I know the correct dress shoes to wear from Memorial Day to Labor Day. But for some reason I keep getting canned after six or eight months. So if you don't mind, I'm going to stay put here. Why go through the embarrassment of setting up housekeeping somewhere and then getting evicted? Right, Mom?

Actually, Easton's living at home suited them both. No rent for him, just whatever he could contribute, whenever. And living in the big house set far back from the road, he could pass himself off as a Bridgehampton blueblood. Who among his city slicker acquaintances would get out of their Porsches to inspect the house — and discover we did not own the adjoining farmland? Who, over the course of a lazy summer, would bother to check his credentials, to find out that his father had been not a gentleman farmer but a drunk given to pissing on the floor of the local tavern?

(I call Easton's friends acquaintances. Just like my mother, he lived for the summer people. From the time he got his driver's license, he ignored the kids at high school and hung out with a semi-social Southampton crew: the Daddy-is-on-Wall-Street-and-by-gosh-so-am-I fraternity. It didn't seem to matter who they were individually; they all had boats to invite him on, golf clubs to take him to, wives' college roommates to fix him up with. They were interchangeable: extremely tan, mildly wealthy and slightly stupid.)

Anyway, the domestic arrangement suited Easton. And I guess my mother liked having him around because he could do all the man jobs: mow the lawn, put up the storm windows, check the mousetraps in the cellar.

134

She'd never been much of a farm wife, even when she'd had a farmer.

Living with Easton gave my mother an audience for her compulsive monologue no one else would be willing to listen to. She'd sit at the table, push her food around her plate, light up a cigarette and – puff, puff – talk about the French five-thousand-dollar dress Mrs Preston Cortwright had tried to return the Monday after her big party; the rumor that Mr Edward Dudley, husband of size-three Mrs Edward – puff, puff – had taken up with their Experiment in International Living seventeen-year-old fatso fräulein from Munich. Or – my mother would tap off the ash – how she herself had made all the right diplomatic moves and had *finally* been named deputy associate chairlady of the Southampton–Peconic Museum of Art's annual cocktail party.

My mother's pretentiousness, her coldness – her absolute nothingness – never got to my brother. Unlike me, he could listen to her expound on Quality without wishing she'd choke to death on one of her goddamn Protestant watercress sandwiches.

Not that they spent a lot of time together. My mother used the big back bedroom on the first floor, and Easton took over the second floor. I don't think either of them longed for more companionship. Okay, compared to me, Easton was my mother's pride and joy, but compared to what she had expected of him – the presidency of a major brokerage firm, senior partner of a Wall Street law firm – he was a loser.

But a well-dressed one.

Robby Kurz did a major double take after we rang the doorbell. 'Easton Brady,' my brother said to Robby, and shook his hand.

135

Robby stared at Easton. Then he blinked a couple of times, as if expecting his vision to clear. He had probably been imagining me minus two years, and that was sort of true. But he was also face-to-face with a gent in gray flannel slacks, a pale-blue Oxford shirt and a sapphire-blue V-neck sweater, a rich-looking Waspy guy who was combing back his hair off his forehead with his fingers – hair that was just slightly too long. Not hippy or scruffy hair, but hair that seemed to be saying: Forgive the length, but I just got back from sailing home from Bermuda.

Half an hour later, Robby was still sneaking fast, disbelieving glances from Easton to me. He sat at a folding card table across from Easton in my brother's sitting room; it had once been my bedroom. As a kid, Easton had used the table to build his model ships; now it was covered with a huge, square fringed gold cloth, like one of those scarves you see on pianos in old movies. It almost hid the table's skinny metal legs. I sat directly behind my brother, on a nice old cracked leather couch he must have picked up at some yard sale; the shrink at South Oaks had had one like it, the same dark brown.

My deal with Ray Carbone was that I could be at Easton's interview without being there. But every now and then my brother would turn his head and glance at me for reassurance as Robby questioned him about the cast and crew. What the hell: I'd nod, letting him know he was doing fine. Well, he was.

'What exactly were you doing in New York yesterday?' Robby was asking.

'I was meeting with our casting director. Going over deal memos and negotiating a price on some extra work we wanted done. Sy and Santana felt we had to cast the

136

Colombian drug kingpin as threatening, but quietly threatening.'

'You mean all the parts weren't filled yet, even after they'd started making the movie?' Robby asked.

'That's right.' Easton sounded casual, like someone who'd been in the business for twenty years instead of a few months. 'It happens fairly often. We knew we could always sign an actor we'd already read, but we were hoping for someone special. The problem was where to look.' I rested my head on the back of the couch's cool leather, crossed my arms over my chest and checked out my brother. I was impressed: no more of his sweaty, eager, fast-talking bullshit, like when he was selling houses or Jaguars or hand-knitted boat-neck sweaters. Easton had become a genuine movie guy. 'We'd seen just about every over-fifty swarthy actor in New York and California. No luck, but we weren't ready to give up. Well, not yet.' He really seemed to know what he was talking about. I was proud all of a sudden.

He kept plucking at the neck of his sweater, probably to realign the V in front. 'The casting director wanted to start looking at actors in Chicago, to farm the work out to her associate there. But the price she quoted us seemed out of line. Sy thought it would be better to negotiate with her in person than over the phone, but he couldn't do it. He was busy on the set and getting ready to go to LA, so he asked me to.'

'How long did that meeting last?'

'From before two until – I'm guessing now – three-thirty, four. I'm not sure. You could check with her.'

'Did you speak to Sy on the phone at all during that time?'

'No. I was going to drive over to his house after

dinner, around nine, and tie up whatever loose ends there were.'

'Was he expecting any company for dinner?' I interjected.

'No,' Easton said. 'Just Lindsay.'

'Did you come straight back here after your meeting?' Robby asked.

'No. I went to Sy's shirtmaker to give him a swatch of Egyptian cotton Sy wanted to use and to pick up some other shirts that were ready.' I couldn't see my brother's face from the couch, but Easton must have smiled at Robby because, suddenly, Robby had on his super-toothy grin. 'Assistant producer,' Easton continued, 'and swatch-carrier. My whole job was to smooth things out for Sy. I went to meetings, made phone calls, wheeled and dealed in a minor way. And even played errand boy.' He fell silent for a minute, then added solemnly: 'It was the best job I ever had.'

Outside my old bedroom window, the leaves on the oak tree were almost black against the blue-gray twilight. It's usually a down time for ex-drunks, but there I was, all of a sudden, feeling pretty up – about Easton.

My brother, obviously, had always had some inner aberration that had screwed up his chances at a career. But outwardly he'd been Mr Moderate. Balanced, temperate, neat, controlled. No fires burning in his soul. You couldn't believe he wasn't able to get a grip on his life, because he *seemed* so balanced. He did nothing to excess; when he drank, it was a watered-down Scotch or a couple of glasses of wine. When he drugged, it was one puff of a joint. Even the women he went out with were understated – to the point of invisibility: well-bred, well-dressed, with boobs barely bigger than their tiny noses.

But strangely, the movie business, famous for its bullshit, had managed to make Easton more real. He was much less pompous. Okay, still not the kind of guy you'd ask over for *Monday Night Football*, but friendlier, looser. A decent man instead of Charlotte Easton Brady's finely featured, immaculately groomed, elegantly dressed prig of a son. Maybe, I started thinking, after all these years, we could really be brothers. Lynne would say, Let's have Easton to dinner, and I'd say, Great.

'Why was Mr Spencer going to Los Angeles?' Robby asked.

'He had four or five different projects he was interested in. He had a lot of meetings lined up.'

I broke in. 'Isn't it a little unusual for a producer to leave town while his movie is being made?' -

Easton turned around, giving me the profile that demonstrated who'd gotten the best of the genes. 'Not necessarily. Sy was executive producer. He had what's called a line producer to supervise the whole production, take care of the day-to-day problems. And he had me to put out smaller fires. So he could afford to get away for a couple of days.'

'Except things were pretty lousy here.'

'What do you mean?'

'The business with Lindsay.'

'Lindsay.' Easton seemed a little ill at ease, as if by confirming trouble he'd be letting Sy down. 'I see you've heard the rumors.'

'We heard about the lousy dailies,' I told him. 'Were they that bad?'

He shrugged. 'I can't be a hundred percent sure, Steve.

I haven't been in the business long enough to really know. I mean, when Sy asked, I pretended to have an opinion and crossed my fingers and hoped I didn't sound like a complete fool. But whatever reactions I have, they're still pretty much the same as the man who buys a ticket and sits in a multiplex with a box of popcorn: either bored or enjoying himself. As far as I could see, Lindsay was doing all right. And she looked – there's no other word – breathtaking.' Robby started his compulsive Lindsay nodding. 'But I *think* I understood what Sy was talking about. Whenever Lindsay was on the screen, I wasn't riveted – except by her beauty. I looked, but I didn't really listen. My attention wandered. And to be honest, it probably would have wandered more if I hadn't been involved in the movie.'

'But she wasn't a disaster?' I inquired.

'Not her acting *per se*. But I think from Sy's point of view the movie itself was a disaster-in-progress, because the audience *had* to love this woman. And even I could see you did not love Lindsay in those dailies. Actually, you didn't even like her all that much. You just didn't care.'

Robby took over. 'Was Sy going to Los Angeles to speak to Katherine Pourelle about taking over Lindsay's part?'

Just before Easton whipped his head around to face Robby, I saw his reaction: absolutely stunned at how far we'd come so fast. 'Jesus, who told you that?' Neither of us responded. Finally, Easton spoke. 'Well, congratulations! Whoever your source was knew what he was talking about.' He turned back to me, really curious. 'Who told you?'

'I can't, East.'

'Oh, right,' he said. 'Sorry. I didn't mean to be

pushy . . .' He smiled. 'Well, not too pushy. In any case, Sy *was* going to see Katherine Pourelle. But as far as I was concerned, it was just a typical Sy maneuver. You see, he would let word leak out that he was speaking to Pourelle and her agent. That would put the fear of God into Lindsay, make her wake up and start – well, start acting. But I swear to you, Sy *never* would have fired her.'

'He told you that?' Robby asked, then cleared his throat. He was getting hoarse. It had been a long day, and he looked like one exhausted Howdy Doody. Even the perky points of the yellow handkerchief in his breast pocket had gone limp.

'No. But you see, I'd gotten to know Sy. He could be objective, tough, even callous about Lindsay the actress. But he was completely vulnerable to Lindsay the woman. She had an enormous hold over him.'

'Sex?' I asked.

'Yes,' Easton responded.

'Was it just a sex thing, or did love enter into it too?' Robby inquired.

'It must have been both.' Easton lowered his head. His shoulders rose and fell with each of his sighs. And all of a sudden it hit me. Easton, like Sy, was being objective about Lindsay's performance – but not about Lindsay herself. He couldn't hide it. He'd actually fallen for her.

'It's not just that she's beautiful, or talented or intelligent,' he was explaining, trying to sound detached, 'although she's all those things. She has a way of getting to a man.' Robby was bobbing his head again: Yes! Yes! Yes! 'Sy . . . Sy needed Lindsay too much to fire her.' I heard Easton swallow. He seemed to have needed her too. He had one hell of a lump in his throat.

'He needed her even if it cost him twenty million dollars?' Robby asked.

'Yes.'

But what about Nick Monteleone's theory that Sy had chilled on the fair Lindsay and was, in fact, getting his toes curled elsewhere after he left the set every morning at eleven? I thought about those long, unblond hairs caught on the headboard in the guest room.

'Were you there for that conversation about if lightning struck Lindsay?' I asked.

Easton's posture went ramrod straight. Once again, he seemed amazed that we actually had been doing what we were supposed to be doing: being detectives. Finally, he said: 'God, you two are thorough! And . . . well, yes. I heard Sy say that. But that wishing Lindsay were out of the picture − literally − was just Sy's way of blowing off steam.'

'What do you mean?'

'She was a big disappointment, but he wouldn't have fired her. Trust me, Steve. There was no way he would have been able to cut her loose.' Easton's tongue came out to moisten his lips. 'He was helpless when it came to Lindsay.'

Normally, I would have gone after him, half kidding, half zinging it to him, saying: *Him* helpless? What about you, sucker? I'd have given him a lot of shit about falling for a movie star. But I wasn't going to embarrass my brother in front of Robby. Also, I realized that even if this was a hopeless crush, it was important; this was the first time in Easton's life where he was showing some passion. It was not something to laugh about.

'What about the other investors?' Robby asked. 'It wasn't just Sy's money, was it? What about Mikey LoTriglio?'

142

'Mikey!' Easton said. 'Yes, of course. He'd slipped my mind. God, you should see him. What a tough act. Makes Marlon Brando in *The Godfather* look like a pussycat.' He stopped and considered what he'd been saying. 'But maybe that's not fair. He has a thick New York accent. And he looks like such a . . . hood. Maybe that makes him seem tougher than he is.'

'Was Sy afraid of him in any way?'

Silence. Easton must have been chewing his lip over that. I peered around. There was a script on the coffee table in front of the couch. I picked it up. My brother turned at the sound of paper. He saw what I was holding. His body sagged; his poise deserted him. He seemed to have forgotten about Robby. 'See that script, Steve?' He sounded like a kid a few seconds from tears. 'Sy gave it to me Thursday, the day before . . . He handed it to me and said, "Our next movie, Easton. It just might make history."'

'I'm really sorry,' I said. 'Things were going great with him, weren't they?'

'I finally – ' He cut himself off, realizing Robby was there. 'My life was tied to his,' he said quietly. He took a deep breath, and when he spoke again he was the old Easton, aggressively cheerful. 'Well, I guess I'll have to beat the bushes, find something else.' He shook his head. 'I'd hate like hell to have to move to California, but I may have to. Be closer to the action, to people in the business.'

Oh, shit, I thought. Easton had lucked out with Sy. He'd found a patron who liked his Southampton style and who had the rare and good instinct to trust Easton, to allow him to rise to all sorts of occasions, to prove himself. But Sy couldn't give a reference. And what the hell kind of résumé could my brother hand out in

Hollywood? Failed car salesman? For years Easton hadn't even been able to sell madras Bermudas to congenital preppies. He lacked something – conviction, balls. What would he do in Los Angeles? How would he maneuver in a city of sharks?

'Uh, where were we?' Robby wondered. He was massaging the bridge of his nose as if it were some newly discovered acupuncture point that would induce bright eyes and a clear mind. Except it didn't work. Christ, he was wiped. I thought: Thirty years old is too young to get that tired that fast. Maybe that was why he was always trying to jump the gun, pushing for an arrest. The guy had no stamina. He couldn't keep it up for a long investigation.

'We were on Mikey,' I reminded him.

'Right. Mikey.'

'Sy did get . . . on edge when Mikey called,' Easton admitted to Robby. 'But "on edge" for you or me might mean losing our temper, biting our nails. For Sy, it was just a slight tightness in his voice. You'd have to know him quite well to pick it up.'

'Did he seem afraid?' Robby asked.

'I don't know. There was just that hint of tension. Although that in itself was a bit unusual. I mean, Sy never *got* anxiety. He gave it – to everybody. But every time Mikey would call, Sy would shake his head and mouth: "I'm out."'

While my brother talked, I opened the script. It said: 'Night of the Matador' and 'An original screenplay by Milton J. Mishkin.' I turned the page and read a little:

LOW-ANGLE SHOT of MATADOR, huge, commanding, menacing against black BG.

I am Roderigo Diaz de Bivar – El Cid. And I am Francisco Romero, seven hundred years later, piercing the bull with my sword.

SFX: Thunderous animal breathing. Is it the matador? Or the bull?

And I am Manolete, gored to death. And the young El Cordobes.

CAMERA RISES. BG brightens and WE SEE Matador in the center of the bullring, surrounded by PICADORS on horseback and BANDERILLEROS. He brandishes his red muleta.

I am Spain.

CAMERA MOVES IN to Matador's muleta for ECU and as WE HEAR flamenco music:

I am man.

BEGIN OPENING CREDITS against red.

I thought: They couldn't pay me to read this shit, much less see it – which probably means it's a true work of art.

'Did Mikey LoTriglio call Sy a lot?' Robby was asking.

'The last week or so, yes. About two or three times a day.'

Robby began playing with the fringe on the scarf that covered the table, running his fingers through it. 'What were Mikey's calls about?'

'I gather he'd been hearing rumors that the movie was having problems. Sy kept denying it, of course.'

'Do you think this Mikey made any threats?'

'I never heard his part of the conversation,' Easton said. 'But whatever his message was, Sy found it . . . disturbing.' He paused. 'Sy's upper lip would get those little beads of sweat. You can't imagine what that was like. Sy was *not* a man to sweat.'

Inducing perspiration is not, in the State of New York, grounds for arrest, but you couldn't tell that from Robby's face. Suddenly he was awake, alert. Mikey was his guy. You could see the gleam of handcuffs shining in Robby's eyes.

'Hey, easy, Robby,' I said.

'Steve, this is a good lead,' Robby responded, ignoring Easton, as if he were another cop – or a member of the family. 'Mikey's bad.'

'Sure, but he's no moron. Would he shoot Sy over a bad investment?'

'Come on. He's Mafia.'

'Yeah,' I acknowledged, 'but this doesn't look like their kind of hit. They tend to be more personal, more close-up than a couple of long-distance bullets from a .22.'

But Sy might have had other enemies, I thought: a pissed-off poet from his old magazine; an old show-biz connection with a grudge; some South Fork local he'd insulted – a gas station attendant, an electrician, a swimming pool contractor – some guy with a snootful of sauce and a pocketful of ammo. And what about Lindsay? Calculating, egotistical, arrogant, maybe ruthless, maybe about to be bounced in her dual role as star and concubine. Could she fire a rifle?

And, damn it: Bonnie. How much research had she done for *Cowgirl*?

'What about the ex-wife?' I asked Easton. 'There's some talk that Sy was developing her screenplay.'

Easton shook his head. 'No. Sy gave me her script fairly soon after I started working for him, before we were in production. Asked me to find some nice things to say about it. My guess is that when he told her no, he wanted to be able to say: "Oh, but the dialogue was so fresh, so honest."'

'How was the dialogue?'

'I don't know. Not horrible. But Sy said she was born forty-some-odd years too late, that she wrote 1942 women's B movies.'

'Did she ever call him?' Robby asked.

'Yes. A couple of times a week, as a matter of fact. And she dropped in on him on the set, which did *not* amuse him. I know; I was in the trailer with him. You know how cool Sy always was? Well, I thought he was going to have a fit.' Easton stopped. He turned around in his chair to face me.

'What are you thinking?' I asked my brother. 'Woman Scorned?'

'I don't know,' Easton said thoughtfully. 'I'm not a cop. I don't know how to weigh these things. But, Steve, I have to tell you: I didn't like the look on Sy's face when he saw her. I had a feeling something wrong was going on.'

CHAPTER 7

If I wanted to be on time, I had two minutes to make the ten-minute drive to Lynne's. So what did I do? I drove right to Bonnie Spencer's, parked around the corner and then stood diagonally across the road.

Her house was plain in that no-nonsense, almost severe colonial style – not much more than a large two-story box with a roof and chimney. But a big, soft willow stood in front, and, in the moonlight, the old gray shingles shone silver against the dark sky.

The curtains were drawn, although not so tightly that I couldn't see the blue flicker of a black-and-white TV. Jesus, what had I promised Lynne when I'd called from the Southampton PD? That I'd be at her house by ten, ten-thirty? It was ten twenty-eight. I walked across the road and up the stone path toward Bonnie's house.

That Moose was some watchdog! There wasn't even a mild grrr until I rang the bell; then, through the long, skinny windows that framed the front door, I could see her tail going so fast it made her rear end shimmy.

The outside light went on. I stuck my hands in my pockets. I took them out. Finally, Bonnie walked into the front hallway. For a second I thought maybe I'd interrupted something that she and a guy had been doing with the TV on. But as she got nearer to the door I could see there was no guy. She had on baggy cotton sweats and a red sweater. No makeup, but then maybe she never wore makeup. Her hair was loose, down to her shoulders, but it stood up on the back of her head, as though she'd been lying on a couch for a couple of hours.

I tried to read her expression when she saw it was me. Relief that I wasn't some night-crawling creep, maybe mixed with some apprehension about what was I doing there again, and maybe – although it's a lot to read through a skinny window – anticipation. It could be that moving in on her that morning had worked.

Except, I thought, as the door opened, who needed it? I felt like such a jerk. I couldn't believe I had wasted a whole day fantasizing about this woman. 'I know it's late,' I said, before she could say anything, 'but this is a homicide investigation.'

'Uh, would you like to come in?' The corners of her mouth wiggled for a second, deciding whether or not to smile; she opted for not. Then she turned and led me toward the right, into the living room. She switched on a couple of lamps, turned off some old movie she'd been watching on her VCR.

I could see the indentation her head had made on a pillow on the couch. I sat down next to it; the cushion was warm. Moose stood by my legs, stretching her thick, hairy black neck, clearly contemplating the possibility of leaping up beside me. Finally, realistically, she lowered her big butt onto the floor, threw me the doggy equivalent of a come-hither look and, once again, lay down over my shoes. The girl may have turned out to be mediocre, I mused, but the dog was as fantastic as I'd remembered. I swiveled my foot back and forth, rubbing her belly.

Bonnie sat across the room from me, on a rocking chair. The room was nice – yellow and peachy pink and white – but not what I would have expected from her.

Sure, it was comfortable, but it was a Manhattan interior decorator farmhouse. A room like this should be plain, nice at best, not charming. But it was all there: braided rag rugs on the pegged oak floor, old quilts, pillows made from more old quilts, samplers in frames and a lineup of old white water pitchers on the mantel. Plus, off to the left of the fireplace, a painted bellows big enough to inflate the fucking Goodyear blimp. She saw me eyeing it.

'When we bought the house, Sy got interested in American folk art.' To illustrate, she pointed out some shelves: books interspersed with wood decoys. 'If it looked like it could quack, he bought it. He even put in a bid on an 1813 hand-carved loom. What did he think he was going to do? Spend his weekends weaving? Anyway, then we had our first party out here. This famous book editor walked into the room, looked around and said, "*Very* cute!" The man was so mean! Why did he have to say that? But from that minute on, Sy hated the house.' I didn't respond; she filled in the silence, fast: 'So here I am – with a lot of ducks. Um, can I get you something? Coffee? A drink?'

'Why did you go to see Sy on the movie set?'

She took an instant too long to answer. 'Just being friendly. And I guess I felt some nostalgia for the good old days.'

'Between you and him?'

'No. Between me and the movies. Sometimes . . .' Her voice got a little scratchy. '. . . I miss it so much. The writing – writing something better than "A yummy cloud of almost-silk." And I miss the people and –'

I cut her off before she could get into an 'I'm So Alone Blues' number. I didn't want to hear it. 'You went onto the *Starry Night* set. What happened? Was Sy happy to see you?'

'I guess you must already have the answer to that.' The lamplight made a patch of brightness on her dark hair, just where it grazed her shoulder.

'I want your answer.' I pulled my feet out from under Moose; the dog peered up at me, surprised at the sudden withdrawal of intimacy. 'What's the problem? Was he happy to see you or not? This shouldn't be something you have to think about.'

'He seemed upset that I came uninvited,' she said at last. 'Not furious, like he'd want to beat me to a bloody pulp and stomp on my head and – ' Suddenly her eyes grew wide with embarrassment. 'Oh, God, for a minute I forgot what you did for a living. I'm really sorry. I didn't mean to make fun of . . .'

'It's okay. You were saying he wasn't about to do you permanent damage.'

'Right. But he wasn't about to be polite and say: "Tsk-tsk, you might have called first, Bonnie, dear."'

'What was his attitude?'

'Something between – let's see – nonchalance and rage.'

'Do you want to be a little more specific?'

'He didn't yell.' I did a speed-of-light survey; her red sweater was just tight enough to show she had standard, conventional tits. If you took the entire female adult population of the world, Bonnie Spencer's tits would mark the median. 'But maybe that's because he was trying so hard not to spit.'

'If you were such great friends, why would he act that way?'

'I don't know. Maybe he was in the middle of a tantrum about something else and I just showed up at the wrong time.'

'Maybe.' I wanted to give myself a swift kick in the

ass: to think that over the day I'd built up this Marlboro Man's sister to be an embodiment of sensuality.

And then Bonnie reached up and smoothed back her hair. For just a second, she held it up in a ponytail. The undersides of her forearms were pearly, flawless. I pictured her stretched out on the couch beside me, her head on the pillow, her arms lifted, showing off that soft skin. I'd bend over and kiss it. Run my tongue over it.

I coughed to clear my throat. 'Did you drop in on him to ask about your screenplay?'

'No.' She let her hair drop. The action was beautiful, graceful, like a slow-mo replay of a perfect catch. 'We'd gone over all his notes. I was working on the revisions.'

'And you say he liked it?'

'Yes.'

'Did you ever think he might be saying nice things about your work to lead you on?'

'Why would he do that?'

'The truth?'

'Go ahead.'

'Maybe he found you more interesting than your screenplay. Maybe deep down you sensed that and – '

Her face turned a hot pink. 'Let me clue you in to something. I am not one of those typical New York neurotic dames, just dying to believe the worst about herself. And Sy wasn't some sleazo who'd say, "Ooh, baby, love your montage." My work was good, and Sy liked it. I knew he did.'

'Hey, I'm not trying to hurt your feelings. It's just my job to probe. Okay?'

She calmed down. 'The fact is, Sy and I were friends. Look, I wasn't his type, not even when he married me, and ten more years didn't do much for me in the lusciousness department. I know what he went for. A

152

Lindsay, someone breathtaking. Or someone wispy and intellectual and twenty-two from Yale. Or a jet-setty type with a French accent who could quote Racine — with hair under her arms and a château. I was his ex-wife; he had no reason to hand me a line. He knew better than anyone what I had to offer — and he'd already said no thank you.'

'What about for old times' sake?' She shook her head hard. Her hair swung softly. 'Bonnie, were you sleeping with Sy? Is that why you felt so free to drop by? Maybe just a nice, spontaneous gesture?'

'No!'

'Or maybe to let the world know you were back on the map?'

'No!'

'Because if you were, that wouldn't bring you under any suspicion.' Bullshit, of course. 'Here you were, two adults who knew each other very well, who liked each other . . .'

'Nothing personal, but that's a lot of bull.'

'Okay, no more questions,' I said, getting up and walking over to her. Moose, the town slut, stayed by my side. 'For now.' Then I laid it on thick. Smile. Wink. Charm, charm. 'I'm sorry if I offended you.'

'It's all right,' she said, her voice softening. Charm, charm was working. She looked up at me; her eyes actually became a little misty, almost as if she expected to be kissed.

'Good,' I said. 'Glad you understand.' I reached over and ruffled her hair. Too bad: the button on the sleeve of my sports jacket got caught in her hair. 'Sorry,' I said, really sincerely, and tried to get the button free. Her hair smelled of some spring flower I couldn't identify: lilac, maybe, or hyacinth. I grasped the button and got it

153

away, but unfortunately it yanked on her hair. 'Listen, this doesn't count as police brutality.'

She smiled. A great, wide-open, western smile. 'I know.'

'See you around, Bonnie.'

When I got back to my car, I slipped four strands of Bonnie Spencer's hair into a small plastic envelope. Three had roots. Enough for a DNA comparison analysis.

I always hated making it with women who couldn't shut up. Listen, no guy minds an encouraging word here and there, a helpful suggestion, a sincere scream of enthusiasm. But for the longest time before Lynne came into my life, nearly every woman I picked up was a Gray Line tour guide of sex.

They'd all memorized the same script. About how the trip was going: Oh, it feels so wonderful. Oh, don't stop . . . Directions to the driver: A little harder. No, easy, slow. No, up higher, higher . . . And what tourist treat was just around the corner: I'm going to take you/it in my mouth (an offer I never sneezed at, since it embraced the twin joys of gratification and silence) . . . And of course, they'd always let you know when the tour was over: Oh, it's happening. Oh, yes. Wait, just a second. Oh, this is too much. Please, no, God, Jesus.

Lynne, though, was quiet. What a relief. Of course, she had the self-confidence of the young and the lovely: she knew she didn't have to keep up a monologue to hold a guy's attention. And she was quiet, also, because somewhere – maybe at Manhattanville College – she'd learned that nice young ladies do not shriek 'Fuck me harder!' when in the arms of gentlemen.

But that night, her quiet had some measure of the

154

silent treatment. She was angry at me for ringing her doorbell at eleven-fifteen, saying, 'Oh, shit, I'm sorry,' when I saw she'd given up hope of seeing me that night and had gotten undressed. Plus she was pissed at herself for letting me go to her closet, grab her raincoat, put it over her nightgown and lead her out her door with a tired line like 'Please, I just want to be with you tonight.' She hadn't said a word in the car.

But she wasn't only getting back at me by being uncommunicative. As I unbelted her raincoat and eased it off, she reached over and turned out the bedroom light. She was denying me the pleasure of seeing her.

'You're really mad,' I said. I took my gun off my belt and laid it down on my chest of drawers gently, so she wouldn't be further put off by its offensive clunk. 'Why don't you say it?'

'All right. I'm angry.'

'Tell me why.'

'Because you just assume I'm always available to you, any hour, day or night. I understand that you work crazy hours. But you don't seem to understand that I have to make a life – a structure – for myself. No. You want sex, you want to talk, so you expect me to drop whatever I'm doing. That's not fair.'

'I'm sorry.' I came up beside her and slid my hands under the feathery cotton of her nightgown, easing it up and off. I pulled her to me. She was softening, but she wasn't yet at the point of offering assistance. I held her with one hand and took off my clothes with the other. 'I love you.' I waited. There was no 'I love you too' response.

Okay, a romantic, sweep-her-off-her-feet gesture was called for. I was so goddamn tired. But I lifted her up, carried her to the bed and laid her down. A little risky in

155

the dark, what with guys my age slipping disks, developing hernias. But Lynne was light, I was desperate and, hey, it worked. She didn't say 'All is forgiven.' She didn't say anything. But she reached up from the bed, felt for me and pulled me down beside her.

So in the blackness we started making love. Lynne's silent treatment wasn't so bad, I thought. Better, in a way, than her usual quiet, where she might say a couple of words; it enhanced the pleasure. I could concentrate on everything – the sound of her body against the sheet as she started to squirm, her breathing as it grew deeper.

This had potential; it might be more than a routine roll. But just as I was about to call out, 'Lynne,' I lost all sense of her.

I was no longer making love with my fiancée. I was screwing the way I used to: It didn't matter at all who it was beside me, on top of me, beneath me, just so long as it had all the stock parts. I just wanted to get it in and over with. And then . . .

Big surprise. Well, it was to me.

The faceless female disappeared. Bonnie Spencer was in bed with me. She was wild. The soft, stroking hands may have been Lynne's, but the Bonnie in my mind had her legs wrapped tight around me and was clawing at my back. Then she groaned with pleasure, letting out the same animal sounds I was making. Louder. Her dark hair was spread out all over the pillow; the flower scent was intoxicating. As I entered Bonnie, she let out a sob. Oh, God, I thought, this is the best. I called out, 'I love you. Oh, God, how I love you!' and I heard Bonnie cry out, 'Help me!' as she started to come, and then, 'I love you so much.'

It was perfect.

It was over.

Lynne finally spoke. 'That was nice.'

'Yeah, it was.'

'Wake me at six. Okay? I want to get home early. I have a ton of reading I have to do.'

'Okay,' I said. Then I closed my eyes against the darkness.

I spent Sunday going over the lab and autopsy reports and doing my paperwork. Then, first thing Monday morning, I pushed open the heavy glass-and-brass door at five after nine and strolled right over to Rochelle Schnell, first vice-president of South Fork Bank and Trust, Bridgehampton branch.

'I respect your mind,' I told her, and sat on the edge of her desk.

'You gave me that line about twenty-five years ago.'

'Did it work?'

'No. Of course not. But I liked it that you tried.'

Rochelle was forty years old. I knew that because we'd started Sagaponack Elementary School together, in kindergarten, and since we'd been born two days apart, we'd had to share our class birthday party. (Her mother, Mrs Maziejka, was supposed to bring the cupcakes and mine the Kool-Aid, but since my mother worked, Mrs Maziejka had always brought both. She'd never bitched about it; in fact, she even wrote 'Rochelle!' in pink icing on half the cupcakes and 'Steve!' on the other half in blue.)

Rochelle sat behind her immense wood desk in a dark-gray dress-for-success suit. But then – as she strode over to kiss me and say 'I haven't seen you around in months. You look fantastic!' – I noticed her skirt was one of those stretchy, midthigh things that look like an overgrown support bandage.

'Yeah? Well, so do you, Ro-chelle, except you've got a real problem. No one is going to hand out their life savings to a banker whose skirt's so tight you can practically see her pudenda.'

'Don't bet on it. Now, what can I do for you? Or did you just drop in to check out my skirt?'

I put my hand on her back and guided her to her chair, then sat down across the desk from her. 'Off the record. I want to know if you have a depositor named Bonnie Spencer – '

Rochelle cut me off. 'Big no-no. You know I'm an honest woman. I can't even give you a name. I'll verify it with our lawyers, but I'm sure you have to give me a subpoena. Then, if she does have an account, I'll have to call – '

'All I want to know is if she has an account here. No details. Please. A personal favor, Rochelle. It's not like I'm some jerk you don't know.'

'No, you're a jerk I do know.' She exhaled slowly. Then she swiveled around in her chair, faced the computer terminal on her desk and put her hands on the keyboard. Her giant diamond ring, courtesy of Mr Schnell, who'd bought the bank to get her attention, sparkled; her long red nails clicked as she typed. 'Yes, she's a depositor.'

'Thank you.'

'You're welcome.'

'Tell me how much is in her account.'

'No. You're a cop. Comply with the law. And don't think you're going to charm it out of me. I've already told you more than I should. Not one more thing. Just go to the DA and get a subpoena.'

'But, Rochelle, with all that Bank Privacy Act shit, that means you're going to have to notify her that there's been an inquiry by a law enforcement agency.'

'Is that *so* terrible?'

'Yeah. Just hear me out. It's terrible because Bonnie Spencer is a genuinely nice lady and I don't want her to get hurt in this investigation. Her ex-husband – '

'Oh, *that* Spencer!'

'Yeah, well, the powers that be are getting a little antsy, and it would help if I could just find out – fast, without waiting for a subpoena and notification – that she really is as okay as she seems to be, that no big money was going in or out of her account. I'd like to see her name out of this. You know what I mean? This woman's a real sweetheart. She had nothing to do with a homicide. She had nothing to do with *him*. All I need are some numbers to back me up, so we can cross off her name. Time's a factor here. I don't want to risk some gung-ho first-year detective calling her employer and saying, 'I'm from Suffolk County Homicide and I'm checking up on Bonnie Spencer.' Please, Rochelle. Help me help her.'

Rochelle's nails went click-click again. 'She has a hundred and five in her checking account. There's regular activity, so I guess we're her banker.' Click. 'Six hundred thirty-four in a savings account, that last month had a balance of a little over seven hundred.' Click-click. 'And her Visa card . . . she hardly ever uses it.'

I pointed to the computer screen. 'What does all that tell you?'

'That her ex-husband was *very* behind on his alimony payments.'

'She wasn't getting alimony.'

'In that case, she's just plain poor.'

*

The only thing appealing about Bonnie's next-door neighbor, Wendy Morrell, was her name; it conjured up a dewy virgin gamboling in a field of clover. In fact, in the morning light, Wendy looked less like Snow White and more like the witchy stepmother – in an olive-green jumpsuit. She had a face full of those air bubble things that grow under the skin. There was one large one on her left cheek, and I found my finger reaching up toward my own cheek, maybe trying to perform a symbolic bubblectomy; I put my hand down at my side.

'I mean, naturally I've been reading everything there is to read about the murder,' she said, 'but in a million years it would never have occurred to me that *Bonnie* Spencer had any connection with *Sy* Spencer.'

Wendy Morrell was probably in her early thirties. Manhattan thin, a body that if seen in the Third World would evoke pity but that probably commanded admiration in the city. Under the wide gold bracelet on her forearm, you could see the outline of her radius and ulna. Wendy's hair was cut in that chopped-off style that only guys just out of basic training (or very, very beautiful women) should wear.

We stood by the front door of her modern house. She had not invited me in. Maybe she was an elitist bitch. Maybe she was embarrassed; houses like hers, million-dollar exercises in solid geometry, had, overnight, become Out on the South Fork. They'd been replaced by postmodern whiz-bangs, country houses so enormous that they seemed to have been built for a race of giants instead of the periodontists and pocketbook designers who lived in them. Wendy had planted herself smack in the middle of her doorway, as though afraid I'd elbow her aside in an attempt to see how rich people lived – or, if I was hip, to get a look at her

160

hopelessly outdated high-tech kitchen and snicker at it.

'That those two Spencers lived on the same planet was a miracle,' she went on. 'I mean, I don't mean to denigrate her, but it's such a contradiction of style: elegance versus gaucheness. You know? Look, she goes running. I'm the last person in the world to be a spokesperson for jogging suits. Am I going to make a case for pastel sweatpants and matching zip-ups? I know this may not mean a lot to you, but if she's got a house in the Hamptons, not Kalamazoo or wherever she comes from, she should manage to have a little pride in her appearance, not wear clothes that look like she raided the boys' locker room at the end of the school year. I mean, *some* sense of appropriateness must have rubbed off from Sy.'

'You knew him?'

'Well, we were never formally introduced. But you know what they say: there are basically three hundred people in the world.' She suddenly realized she was talking to a member of the four billion minus three hundred, because she explained: 'That's a New York–Hamptons concept: You know there are certain places in SoHo or East Hampton and you'll walk in and there'll be Calvin Klein or Kurt Vonnegut or Sy Spencer. Sy happened to be the friend of a very dear friend. Teddy Unger. Commercial real estate. You know who he is? Well, he owns half of New York. The better half. So even though we never got to meet formally, Sy and my ex-husband and I were all of the same world.'

Even if you stretched the definition of the Beautiful People beyond any rational limits, Wendy Morrell would not have fit in.

'So what's with the ex-wife?' she demanded. 'Is she under suspicion?'

'No. This is strictly a background check. I'm just trying to get a sense of the sort of person Bonnie Spencer is.'

'I can't help you. I am not a neighbor type.' Wendy glanced over at Bonnie's, then at her own driveway, where I'd pulled my Jag all the way up, almost to her garage, so Bonnie couldn't see it from her house. She gave my car a suspicious look, as if it represented something nasty, sexual and, above all, unforgivably pushy, since it was not a car a cop should be driving.

'But maybe you might have picked up something, just out of the corner of your eye,' I suggested. 'Did she entertain guests with any frequency?'

'I wish I could give you a full report, but my days are *very* full. Believe me, I don't spend my time watching Bonnie Spencer.' She touched the gold pin that, thank God, held her jumpsuit closed. It was at the point of her body that, on a woman who hadn't starved herself, would have been called a cleavage. 'I have a business to run.' She said 'a business' as if she meant General Motors.

'What do you do?'

'Wendy's Soups. I'm president and CEO.' As in: Everyone knows Wendy's Soups. Well, everyone who's anyone, as I clearly wasn't. 'There have been major articles about me. *New York Times, Vogue,* et cetera. *Elle* . . . You know *Elle*? The piece was called "Superb Soups!"'

'Do you cook them here?'

She smiled. Big mistake. God had given Wendy Morrell the gift of gums. 'No. The plant is in a cute little ethnic neighborhood in Queens. I employ forty-six people.'

'So you don't live here all year round?'

'No. East End and Eighty-first. Just long weekends here. It used to be all August too, but then there was that cover story in *New York Woman*.' With, I assumed, a photo of a bowl of split pea superimposed over her ugly puss. 'We went through the roof. You can imagine!'

'Look, Ms Morrell, obviously you're a very busy person, but busy people tend to be the most efficient.' She obviously agreed. 'You're not the nosy neighbor type, but . . .'

'I don't know anything about her. We nod hello. That is all. When I'm out here I'm still plagued. The phone, the fax. My office cannot leave me alone. The pressure *never* stops. I have to *force* myself to relax. I do not do coffee klatches.'

'Does Bonnie Spencer have coffee klatches?'

'Not that I've ever seen.'

'What I'm getting at is, are there any frequent visitors?' She glanced at my Jag again. 'Men in sports cars?'

'Men in sports cars. Men in sedans. Men in all *kinds* of vehicles. Is that news to you?' She paused. 'Once . . . I saw a pickup truck. I happened to notice it because it was late at night. Well, let's be generous. Maybe she needed some emergency construction done by a kid who couldn't have been more than twenty-two, in tight jeans and work boots.'

'I'm going to be direct, Ms Morrell, but I feel I can be direct with someone who's a CEO.' She acknowledged the tribute with a brief flash of gums. 'Is it your impression that Ms Spencer is promiscuous?'

'Maybe she's just interviewing half the men in Bridge-hampton for that happy-news column she writes. She came over once, asked if she could interview me! I was very pleasant. I told her I was horrendously tied up, but

I'd love to. Some other time.' She stopped. 'Are you sure you're with the police?'

I handed her my shield. She brought it up close to her nose, breathing what was probably disgusting, humid, lentil-dill breath on the plastic, and studied it. Then she handed it back.

'Have you seen any one car at Bonnie Spencer's recently? A black sports car?'

'Detective Whatever' – she smiled – 'I *know* what a Maserati is. My ex-husband drove a Ferrari 250 GT, '62. Believe me, I had sports cars burned into my brain during *that* marriage.' She looked over at mine. 'I know an E-type Jaguar roadster when I see one. The English don't say "convertible", you know.' I hated it that this witch had any sort of intimacy with great cars. 'And the answer to your question is yes.'

'Yes, what, Ms Morrell?'

'There was a Maserati in her driveway. Last week. Every morning that I was here. A quarter to twelve. Like clockwork. And a *fabulously* dressed man got out of it. I realize now that it must have been Sy Spencer. But I'm sure there's an innocent explanation. Maybe she just served an early lunch.'

'Maybe. When did he leave?'

'Two, three, four.'

'Any sounds of fighting?'

She shook her head. 'I cannot believe it! He was so fine – and *re*fined. I mean, this man could have any woman he wanted. Why would someone like him waste his time on a nothing like her?'

'Maybe she's nice.'

Wendy Morrell cocked her head, drew her eyebrows together, as if she were hearing about a sensational new trend for the first time. '*Nice?*'

CHAPTER 8

Nice Bonnie Spencer.

Well, fuck her and the horse she rode in on. All along I'd known something was wrong. All along I'd known she was lying to me about Sy. Still, somewhere I'd kept a candle burning, a flicker of hope that she was a good person, that whatever ties she had to her ex-husband had to do strictly with making movies. Because if I ever was going to be friends with a woman, Bonnie would have been exactly the kind of woman I would have picked. She seemed so straight that in spite of all my doubts, when Wendy Morrell opened her gummy mouth, I truly believed she was going to say: A black sports car? No! The only car *I* ever saw in her driveway was the Lilco meter reader's — and he was never there for more than ninety seconds.

To hell with Bonnie. I shifted into third.

The trip from Bridgehampton to Headquarters in Yaphank was thirty-nine miles, most of it along straight-arrow, four-lane Route 27. Once it had been my own personal test track. Since sobriety, though, I'd become an old fart and never pushed much beyond seventy-five mph.

But now, going west against beach traffic, I decided I needed speed. I couldn't believe how badly I'd mis-judged her. Moose wasn't the town slut; the animal wasn't the animal. The stupid bitch, Bonnie, couldn't keep her legs together. I shifted into fourth, heard the deep, throaty hum of the exhaust, watched the tachometer go into redline. I eased up when I got to a hundred and five. Fuck Bonnie Spencer! This was fantastic! In most sports cars, when you're in last gear, you feel like you're skyrocketing, leaving the pull of earth's gravity. But the XKE kind of squats, fuses with the road. It's the ultimate down-to-earth experience.

There just isn't anything like speed to take you away, especially sober. (Driving drunk, you know in your gut that Death, carrying a scythe, in that hooded bathrobe – sort of like Sy's, although not as good-quality terry cloth – is standing over the next rise.)

So fuck Bonnie. And fuck this case. The minute it was over, I'd say to Lynne: Come on. No waiting till Thanksgiving weekend. Let's find some priest whose dance card isn't all filled up the way your guy's is. We'll get married right away. And forget Saint John. We'll go to London. I'll go to museums with you. To Shakespeare. I'll visit English schools and stand by your side and learn all about the newest methods for combating dyscalculia. I swear to God, I'll even go to the opera.

Sergeant Alvin Miller of the Ogden, Utah, Police Department talked re-e-e-eal slo-o-o-ow, as if each word had to mosey down a long dirt road before it could come out. 'Well, now, Detective Brady. One of the boys passed on your message last night. 'Bout ten. I'm not with the department anymore. Re-tired, you know. Have been for eleven years.' I transferred the phone to my other ear. 'But seeing as you said it wasn't urgent, I wasn't going to call you up there in Noooo Yorrrk, where it was midnight.' He said 'New York' in the resentful way guys in my company in Vietnam did, as if ordinary people and ordinary places – suburbs, farms, beaches and forests – were just camouflage for a state whose sole business was mocking the rest of America. 'Hope my not calling back right away didn't hold you up.'

'No problem.' Across the room, Charlie Sanchez sat at his desk holding aloft a cheese Danish from the daily love-me bag of bakery goodies Robby had brought in. Charlie was sticking out his tongue, licking the yellow cheese in the center. The crime-scene photographs on my desk, showing Sy with his two small, neat little wounds, were less revolting than watching Charlie tongue a pastry. 'I appreciate your calling back,' I said to Sergeant Miller.

'You bet. Now, you wanted to know something about the Bernstein girl. Don't tell me she's in trouble?'

'No, she's okay. Her ex-husband – '

'She got a divorce?'

'Yeah. A few years ago.'

'No kiddin'. What was her first name, now?'

'Bonnie.'

'That's it, all right. Bonnie Bernstein. She living in New York?'

'No. In Bridgehampton. It's a little town on the East End of Long Island.'

'Oh. I heard she went to Hollywood. She made a picture, you know. I forget what they called it, but I saw it. Not bad.'

'The detective I spoke to said you might know the family.'

'Yup. Knew them. Pretty well, at one time.' I wanted to grab this fucker by his string tie and shake him, make the words come out faster.

'Can you tell me about them?'

'Sure.' I licked my fingertip and erased a coffee ring while I hung around and waited for his next word. 'If memory serves me, the Bernsteins – that would be Bonnie's grandparents – opened the store.'

'Uh-huh,' I muttered encouragingly.

'Called it Bernstein's.'

'Did her parents keep it up?'

'Kept it up real nice.'

Out in the anteroom, Ray Carbone was handing one of Homicide's two secretaries a piece of paper. From the pained look in his eyes, it was probably a draft of the next press release, which would say, essentially, that we knew nothing. The secretary glanced around for her glasses, didn't find them, and so stretched out her arm and pulled back her head to read. Hanging above her head was the giant banner that no one could miss when they walked into Suffolk County Homicide: THOU SHALT NOT KILL.

'What kind of a store was Bernstein's?'

'A sporting goods store.'

'Bats, balls?'

'Nope. More like guns, fishing gear.'

'Handguns?'

'Sure, handguns. This is Utah.'

'Rifles?'

'Yup.'

'Is the store still around?'

'No. Mrs Bernstein – that would be Bonnie's mother – died. Dan – that's her father – sold the place and retired. I believe to Arizona, but I won't swear to it. Maybe New Mexico. And the boys – three or four of them – didn't stay in Ogden. One of them is a college professor at UU, and I don't know what the others did.'

'Bonnie was the only girl.'

'So far as I can remember, and I remember her because she was friends with the boys and girls in my Eddie's Mutual. I guess you don't know what that is.'

'No.'

'It's a group for Mormon junior high and high school kids.'

'Were the Bernsteins Mormons?'

'Of course not. You're from New York. You should know that.'

'Right. Okay now, let me be straight with you, Sergeant Miller.'

'Best way to be.'

'The incident I'm investigating – '

'I know what kind of an incident. They told me you were on the Homicide Squad. You need a whole department out there on Long Island just for homicide, huh?'

'Yeah. The victim was Bonnie's ex-husband. He was shot with a .22. The perpetrator was a good shot. I'd like to rule out Bonnie.'

'What are you asking me?'

'I'm asking you whether you have any idea if she could shoot a .22.'

'I don't know.'

'Your best guess.'

'My best guess is, a girl like Bonnie – a tomboy kind of girl – whose family owned a sporting goods store and whose dad was probably the damn finest shot in Ogden . . . I used to go up to Wyoming with him and a couple of other fellas, hunting elk. Well, she was the apple of her father's eye. Possible he or one of her brothers taught her to shoot a .22.'

'Thank you.'

169

'Well now, you expect me to say she couldn't have done it, don't you?'

'I wouldn't be surprised if you did.'

'Well, I won't say it. She left Ogden. Went to Hollywood, then New York. Can't issue any guarantees under those conditions, right?'

'Right.'

'But just between you and me, Detective Brady? You may be from Noooo Yorrrk and think you're pretty wily, saying you're trying to rule out Bonnie Bernstein. Sounds to me like you've got it in your head that she shot her former husband. With malice aforethought. Maybe.' He took a long and very slow breath. 'But if the girl you suspect is anything like the nice, smiley girl in my boy Eddie's Mutual, you know what I think? I think you got yourself one lousy theory. You get me? I think you're pissing into the wind.'

Robby Kurz placed his bet: 'Fat Mikey LoTriglio. Okay, never convicted of anything, but his name has been linked with two mob hits. All he has to do is raise his fat finger, and someone dies.'

'No way,' I said. 'Bonnie Spencer. Motive. Opportunity.'

Ray Carbone added his twenty to ours. 'Who's left? Lindsay Keefe? All right. She may have felt cornered, her job, her reputation on the line. And she probably has a lacuna of the superego. It would be too much like a movie if she did it, but I'll go with her anyway.'

Charlie Sanchez was about to retire and didn't care enough anymore to join the pool. He wrote down our bets, folded the money and slipped it into the pocket of his beloved suede vest.

The interrogation room we were in at Headquarters

was better than a naked light bulb and a chair, but it wouldn't win any awards for design excellence. Headquarters itself had originally been a county social services agency, and in the heart of the soft green and brown fields of Yaphank, the building rose up, uncompromisingly ugly. Inside, it was full of gray asphalt tile and orange plastic furniture – just to remind the meek that while they might be in line to inherit the earth, their actual lives were shit and likely to remain that way.

Four of us sat around the fake-wood table. Charlie, who'd been with the department for twenty years and was within weeks of becoming head of security for a shopping center in Bay Shore, stroked the vest his girlfriend had given him for his forty-second birthday. He wore it inside and outside, even in ninety-five-degree heat. He loved the vest almost as much as he loved his girlfriend. (His wife had given him a snow-blower for his birthday, probably in response to the electric pencil sharpener he'd given her for hers.)

'We got a missing-one-thousand-bucks situation,' Charlie began. He'd been doing background on Sy. 'Here's what I found out. At fourteen minutes past eight on Friday morning, Sy was at the cash machine at the Marine Midland Bank over in Southampton.'

'His secretary in New York said he told her he'd be getting cash for his trip to LA,' Ray added.

Charlie went on: 'Sy had one of those preferred-customer cards, so he could withdraw up to a thou. Well, that's what he withdrew. Did any of you guys come across a thousand bucks?'

Robby shook his head. 'No. There was' – Robby checked his notebook – 'a hundred and forty-seven bucks in his wallet.'

I closed my eyes, concentrated. Then I said: 'Hey! Hold on! Listen to this timetable. Sy went to the bank at eight-fourteen. He got to the set in East Hampton eight thirty-five, eight-forty, which is about what it takes from Southampton to East Hampton if you don't make any stops. When he got there, he stayed pretty much in his trailer, talking to people. Right? That Gregory kid was around a lot, and we talked to everyone else who talked to Sy. Did anyone say anything about any cash changing hands? No. The people he was seeing were mainly technical – a special effects guy who was doing a fire and some gunshots, Nick Monteleone and his makeup lady. Spent a few minutes with Lindsay, but she was being fitted for a dress, so a seamstress and the costume design lady were there the whole time. He wasn't talking to union guys or local cops or politicians – people he might pay off. You with me?' Robby and Ray nodded. Charlie caressed his vest some more. 'Okay, assuming he didn't slip anyone a wad of cash, he leaves the set about eleven-fifteen with a thousand bucks in his pocket. Doesn't stop at Bonnie's this time. Instead, he seems to have gone straight home; he was there at ten of twelve. We have the cook's word on that, because he asked for a green salad and bread for lunch, ASAP.'

'That's lunch?' Charlie shook his head. 'Can you believe it? A guy has a cook all to himself and he says, "Give me a salad." New York faggots, I swear to Christ. Makes me sick.'

'What does all this add up to, Steve?' Ray demanded.

'It adds up to that after he got home, Sy saw only one person besides the cook: the person he as a practicing nonfaggot seems to have humped in the guest room. Now, there was Bonnie Spencer-type hair on the pillow in the guest room – okay, we have to wait till Lifecodes finishes the DNA analysis, but I'll bet you anything it's hers.'

'Why are you fixating on her?' Ray asked.

'Because this is an intelligent murder, and she's very intelligent. Because he used her – twice – and I don't think this is a broad who allows three strikes. I think she's got a tough streak in her. And because she's been hiding something from me from the minute she opened the door Saturday morning. And because she was *there* Friday, at his house. Motive and opportunity, Ray.'

'You know what I can't figure out? He was cheating on Lindsay Keefe with his ex-wife,' Charlie said. 'What was he? Nuts?'

'Keep your eye on the missing thousand bucks,' I reminded them. 'Ask yourselves: Where was the wallet we found that *did* have some money in it?'

'In the inside pocket of his blazer,' Ray said.

'Where?'

'In his and Lindsay's bedroom, on a hanger outside the closet door. Stuff for his trip was all set out – a packed carry-on, a leather envelope with a couple of scripts.'

'Right,' I said. 'But the pockets of the pants he was wearing that day were empty except for some change and his car keys, and those pants were in the guest room. My guess is, he packs, then has an hour or so, decides he wants to get laid and calls Bonnie to get over. He sneaks her past the cook, upstairs, into the guest room. He throws his pants over a chair, fucks her, then . . .'

'Then what?' Ray asked. 'This is the first serious speculation I'm hearing about this person – other than the fact that she was his ex who lived nearby. What do you think went on?'

173

'My best guess? They had words. He tells her to get dressed and get out. Or he doesn't have to say it; she figures it out for herself. Whatever. But he grabs a robe and leaves her there while he goes for a fast swim before the plane ride. In any case, she feels she's been had. She goes through his pants, takes the thou.'

'And then she goes outside, finds a .22 and shoots him?' Charlie asked. 'A lady writer is able to score two bull's-eyes from fifty feet?'

'Could you do it, Charlie, if you had the rifle?'

'From fifty feet? Why not?'

'Yeah, well, why not her too?' I said. I told him what I'd learned about Bernstein's inventory from Ogden's finest.

'Well, *I* can't buy Bonnie as a serious suspect,' Robby said. He shifted, and his rayon pants rubbed against the plastic of the chair and gave off a squeaky fart sound. 'Even if she has long dark hair, even if she was sleeping with him, even if she can shoot that well, which I seriously doubt, why would she kill him?'

'Lots of reasons.' I was starting to like this, the explaining, the persuading, the idea that things were coming together. But most of all, I was liking the realization that I had no trouble making a case against Bonnie, that finally, where she was concerned, my head was harder than my dick. 'First of all, she's living hand-to-mouth,' I explained. 'She got shafted in the divorce. She's gotten a look at Sy's way of life, sees how he's given up the humble Farmer Spencer bit he was doing when he was married to her, the denim overalls and butter-churn crap. Now he's living like an out-and-out multimillionaire, which he is. She sees the richness of his life, compares it to the poorness of hers. Probably has already told him how rough things are, asked him for

174

help. And expects it too, what with her probably giving him a blow job and soup and sandwiches every goddamn day that last week. Except he says no.'

'Why didn't she just keep at it?' Ray asked. 'Play on his sympathy? Or make him feel guilty?'

'Maybe she's already given it everything she has – which isn't that much. She fucks and she's nice. What else does someone like her have to offer? And anyway, it wasn't just money. She could have been in love with him and really believed she could get him back. But no matter what she wanted from him, Sy said, No way.'

'He just turned off on her, so she kills him?' Robby asked. He didn't sound convinced, but then again, he had his twenty on Mikey LoTriglio.

I pushed harder. 'All she's been doing is covering up, lying to us. Why? So we don't think she's a fast girl who lets a man put his thing into her you-know-what? No. Because she has something important to hide. A murder.'

Robby turned that over for a minute. Then he asked: 'But *why* would she shoot him? Revenge?'

'Revenge. Plus desperation, plus greed.'

'Where would she get the .22?' Charlie asked.

'She lives alone. Probably had it for years, a present from Daddy Bernstein. Could be she sensed this was the final fuck and brought it along in her car. Or maybe she left, went home, got it and came back. Come on, guys. Sy was wearing his pants at the movie set, so no one took the thousand off of him there. Then he gets home, sticks it to the as-yet-unknown brunette we *know* has to be Bonnie, goes for a swim and bang. He's gonzo – and so is the money.'

'Even if she was there, it could have been someone else who shot him,' Carbone said.

'It could have been. But who? Why? We already know about Bonnie.'

'So she killed him for a thousand bucks?' Robby asked. 'I've got to tell you, Steve, that still doesn't compute. Not with the way you described her. She doesn't sound like a really bad person. Except for the screwing around, and what the hell, she's lonely.'

'But *why* is she lonely?' Naturally, I didn't look at Ray Carbone, even though I was playing to him, trying to get the psychology vote. 'Ask yourselves, what kind of a normal single woman stays in a town she has no roots in, a town that's deserted three quarters of the year except for locals like me and some antique-dealer types who talk about stuff like the bleak beauty of the winter seascape and shit like that. How come she didn't sell the house, which could bring her big bucks even with real estate being what it is, and move to Manhattan, get a decent job?' Charlie rubbed his chin, Robby looked mildly intrigued and Ray leaned forward. 'I'll tell you why not. She's a loser, and she knows it. She had one minute of success that might have been a fluke, and in that minute she lands Sy. You know what that marriage said to her? It said: "Bonnie, babe, you're terrific." But then he gets bored and takes a walk. She stays in that isolated house because she knows if she moved to the city, she'd have no excuse for being a loser. This way, she lives hand-to-mouth – but she can keep up her illusions. That Sy will come back. That one of her shitty screenplays will get made into a movie. That she's worth something. And then what happens?'

Despite the fact that Mikey LoTriglio was due any second with his lawyer, Robby was getting hooked. 'What happens?' he said, as if waiting for the end of a bedtime story.

I gave it everything I had; I knew it would be a major asset to have Robby on my side, not off after the Mafia. 'Sy starts sleeping with Bonnie again, gives her hope. Suddenly she's thinking: I *am* terrific. I can have a life. I'll have my husband back and live in New York, on Fifth Avenue, and in a seven-million-dollar mansion on the beach. And she must have started sharing her dream with Sy, because all of a sudden he blows her off. Maybe nicely. Or maybe he just tells her the truth: "Bonnie, baby, I was PO'd at Lindsay and felt like a grudge fuck, and you were available. It didn't mean anything."'

Ray was breaking his empty Styrofoam coffee cup into white chips. 'All right. His rejection might hurt her. Destroy her. But would it push her over the edge?'

'Yeah, because this time he didn't leave her with any illusions. He didn't want her. He didn't want her screenplay. Don't forget: He humiliated her, treated her like a two-bit whore when she came to visit him on the set. And he didn't value old times' sake enough to help her out of a crappy financial situation. Look, two strikes: he'd used her once, to get a foot in the door of the movie business, and he'd used her again, to get his rocks off when he got mad at Lindsay. And now it was kiss-kiss, sweetie, I'm off to LA. I'm telling you, he walked out of that guest room leaving her with *nothing*.'

'It's just a theory,' Robby murmured. But he sounded on the verge of being convinced.

So did Ray. 'Okay, Steve and Robby,' he said, 'keep your other options open, but follow up on this Bonnie. It sounds like she needs a little extra attention.'

Fat Mikey LoTriglio looked like a Sicilian version of Humpty-Dumpty. He had no visible neck; his silk tie, a dark blue dangerously close to purple, seemed suspended from one of the chins that rested on his chest. 'I grew up wit' Sy,' he was explaining to me and Robby. 'He was like a brother to me. Let me tell you, you find the guy who took him out, you call me. You tell me, "Hey, Mikey, we found the guy who blasted Sy," and I swear to God, I'll – '

'At the time Mr Spencer was murdered,' Fat Mikey's lawyer interrupted, 'Mr LoTriglio was having cocktails with several business associates, who, naturally, can vouch for his whereabouts.' The lawyer, a guy around my age, wore round little glasses with wire frames, as though hoping someone would assure him that he didn't look like the sleazy mob lawyer he'd become, that he still looked like John Lennon.

'Hey.' Mikey turned to the lawyer. 'I don't have cocktails, okay? I have drinks.' He looked back at us and explained: 'This is a new lawyer. My old one, Terry Connelly. Ever deal with him? Massive stroke. They got him in some hospital in Rhode Island, poor vegetable. Sad, sad. And now this fuckin' murder . . .' He shook his head in disbelief. 'It's a knife in my heart, Sy gone.'

'What's going to happen to your investment in *Starry Night*?' I asked.

'Mr LoTriglio's participation in that venture has not been established,' the lawyer said.

'We know Mikey invested four hundred thousand in the movie and got his brother-in-law and an uncle to put up another six hundred thousand,' Robby said, but reasonably, not with his usual I'm-gonna-see-you-fry vengefulness. At some moment between the time Ray and Charlie left the interrogation room and the time Mikey and his lawyer walked in, Robby had switched to Bonnie Spencer. I smiled to myself. I was really happy.

178

I'd won Robby over. I could stand back; she was his girl now, and he would do anything to get her.

'How was your investment going, Mikey?' I asked.

Mikey fluttered his eyes, a single flutter: his naive expression. 'What do I know about producin' movies?'

'You must know something if you put up a million bucks.'

'Hey, my friend Sy asks me to put up some money, I do it.'

'Mr LoTriglio's accountants were impressed by Mr Spencer's track record,' the lawyer said softly. 'They felt *Starry Night* was an excellent investment – albeit any investment in filmmaking entails a certain degree of risk, of which they were fully cognizant.'

'Did Sy let you know how the movie was coming along?' I asked. Fat Mikey shook his head; his chins jiggled. 'A million bucks, Mikey. Weren't you curious?'

'Nah. What do I care? Sy says this is gonna be an Oscar winner. He says, "Mikey, get your tuxedo cleaned for a year from March." That's all I needed to know.'

'You didn't hear anything about any problems with the movie?'

Mikey smiled. Well, the corners of his lips moved upward. He crossed his arms and rested them on his belly. 'What problems?'

'Problems like the movie was looking like a piece of shit.'

'Fuck you. I didn't hear *nothin'* like that.'

'Problems like the only way to save it was to get rid of Lindsay Keefe, which would have put the producers – that's you – a few million deeper into the hole before they even began again.'

'Bullshit,' Mikey said.

'You were on the phone a lot with Sy Spencer

last week. What were you talking about?' Robby inquired.

Mikey looked at his lawyer, who seemed to be lost in wonder, beholding his shoelace. 'You from Harvard!' he bellowed. 'Look alive. My memory isn't so good. I need a reminder. Maybe I happened to mention it to you. What was I talkin' to Sy about last week? I think Sy and I *might* have been on the phone a couple of times, but for the life of me I can't remember what we said.'

'I think you did mention that you had the most general conversation with Mr Spencer. Hello, how are you, how are things going – and he assured you all was well.'

'That's right,' Mikey said. He rotated his head and looked Robby right in the eye. 'All was well. And then – a fuckin' bullet. *Two* fuckin' bullets. I gotta tell you, a piece of me died when Sy went. We were like flesh and blood. When we were kids we'd follow his old man and my old man around through one of the processing plants, and while they talked about all the cheap shit they could stuff into one salami, Sy and me talked about . . . Life.'

'*Life?*' I repeated.

'Yeah. Life. Like philosophy. *Now* I remember. We were talkin' about philosophy last week, on the phone.' His lawyer put a restraining hand on Mikey's huge, sausagelike thigh, but Mikey either didn't feel it or was ignoring it. 'There we were, two businessmen, but we're such good friends we don't talk business. We talk . . . Plato!'

'Where were you last Friday night, Mikey?' Robby asked.

'You mean what's my alibi?'

'Mr LoTriglio was at Rosie's, a bar in the meat

180

district,' the lawyer said. 'He is widely known there. A good many people saw him, and several engaged him in conversation.'

'Talking Plato?' I asked.

'No, you stupid asshole,' Mikey answered. 'Talkin' fuckin' liverwurst.'

One of the guys I sometimes ran with, TJ, a marathoner, owned a couple of video stores on the South Fork. He was in love with my Jag, so I made a deal with him. Whenever I wanted to be inconspicuous, I could take one of his married-man cars – his Honda Accord or Plymouth Voyager – and leave my car in his garage. At a little after four in the afternoon, I parked the Voyager across from Bonnie's house and waited.

Surveillance had always been a snap for me. I'd bring along a bottle of club soda, a Thermos of coffee, and a jar to pee in, sit back and enter into some kind of twilight state. It was like being asleep with my eyes open; I could keep watch, but my mind was someplace else, and I'd be totally unaware of the passage of time. I'd know that I'd sat through a whole night when the sky turned red at sunrise.

But now I was itchy, looking at my watch every couple of minutes, as if to encourage it, wishing that I'd stopped at the luncheonette on the way over for a sundae because I felt like I needed a hit of chocolate. I was annoyed with myself that I hadn't sent one of the younger guys to do this job. Finally, though, it wasn't that long a wait.

She came out at five o'clock, dressed for a run. The weird thing was, she was dressed exactly the way I would dress for running. Shorts and a T-shirt, wool crew socks, with a light sweatshirt tied around her waist, in case it got cool down by the ocean. She was carrying a red ball; Moose was barking with joy at her side. I slid down in the seat. She braced herself against her mailbox, stretched her calf muscles and then her quads. What a pair of legs! They looked like she'd been captain of the girls' soccer team since nursery school. She and Moose started out at a nice clip, picking up more speed as they rounded the corner and headed down toward the beach.

Jesus, I thought, as they disappeared, I really am in love with that dog. Maybe because it was black, it reminded me of a Labrador we'd had at the farm when I was little, Inky, a dumb, sweet-natured bitch who treated me and Easton as if we were her puppies, watching us play, barking if we wandered off too far, growling at anybody who drove up to the house and approached us.

I pulled on a pair of the thin rubber gloves we used for crime-scene work, turned off my beeper and checked out the area. Clear. I crossed the street, studying the house. I could probably sneak in through a basement window; even if I had to break a pane, she might not notice for days. Or I might be able to jimmy open the back door. But, as I suspected, neither was necessary. Bonnie had left the front door unlocked.

Even if she ran like hell and just threw the ball once down at the beach, I had a clear twenty minutes. But I worked the upstairs first, in case I heard her and had to get out the back door.

Bingo! She used one of the bedrooms as an office, and there, under a big framed poster from the movie *Cowgirl*, beside a computer half-covered with stickum notes, in a messy, overstuffed folder marked 'Pending,' was a Xeroxed real estate listing for her house. It was dated August 4, so she'd decided to put it on the market while there were still summer people around to come, look and oooh: 'Oh, Ian, the exposed beams!' Had she taken up with Sy yet? Was she selling it because she was already having dreams of a grand house by the ocean, a screening room, charge accounts, a wedding ring? Or was the real estate listing pre-Sy? Had she been at the end of her rope? I jotted down the broker's number.

I had to work fast – and neat. Neat wasn't too much of a problem since Bonnie's papers were just this side of chaotic. Still, this was not exactly what you could call a legal search, so I couldn't risk leaving any trace.

I went through her bedroom too, finding, mainly, that she kept the local library in business, that although her tangle of bras were what you'd expect from a female jock, utilitarian and uninspiring, her panties weren't: little string bikinis, black, red. I was starting to imagine her, but I cut myself off. Time. Also, there was something about being in her bedroom, its peacefulness, with its tied-back white lace curtains, plain four-poster bed and old-fashioned dresser with a white doilylike thing on top of it, that made me uneasy. I wanted out of there. I was half out the door, on my way downstairs, when I turned back to check out her closet.

Bingo again! Inside the toe of a pair of boots – one of those places women inevitably hide their valuable stuff – I found it: a wad of cash rolled up in a rubber band. Eight hundred and eighty dollars. More than she had in her savings account. Big bucks for a poor girl like Bonnie.

Change from a thousand.

CHAPTER 9

What was so terrible? Sex, even with someone as fabulous as Lynne, can become routine. So big deal: you superimpose another woman over your dearly beloved and suddenly a predictable quickie becomes the Fuck That Shook the World. It can happen, especially if a guy's pattern has always been to step out a lot. Is that so bad? There is no betrayal. Nobody gets hurt.

But it wasn't just that one brief late-night fantasy. My whole life – not just the case – was starting to focus on Bonnie. Like when I'd gone to the bank to speak to Rochelle, I stopped at the cashier's for a couple of rolls of quarters. More than a couple: enough to hit every pay phone on the South Fork. And so once or twice – all right, three or four times – a day I'd drop in a quarter just to hear Bonnie say 'Hello.' Once, when I heard the tightness in her throat (she must have known it would be another hang-up, because who the hell else would call her?), I stood by the phone outside the East Hampton post office and got this terrible lump in my own throat; I wanted to cry for her.

Maybe I was so overcome with pity because an hour earlier I'd been looking over all the records we'd pulled on her, and discovered on the printout from Motor Vehicles that besides being five foot nine inches, which was not exactly a feminine asset, she was forty-five years old. Forty fucking five! I did the math three times. I couldn't believe it. But what kind of sense did it make for me to be getting all choked up with pity for a put-upon, middle-aged loser if I was the schmuck standing out in the rain, praying she'd give me another 'hello' before she slammed down the phone?

Listen, I told myself, this is definitely one of those sexual obsession things. But instead of ignoring it, or figuring it out, I kept borrowing TJ's cars, so Bonnie wouldn't spot my Jag. I drove by her house on the way to work and on the way home. Sometimes in between. All I had to do was spot a shadow passing by an upstairs window, or catch the flutter of a white curtain, and I would feel God's grace upon me. One time, Moose was lying on the front lawn, giving her front paw a manicure with her big pink tongue, and I had this dizzying, blood-to-the-head flush of joy.

And when I'd searched her house, I'd looked in her garage right before I left and saw an old Jeep Wrangler. It made me so incredibly, stupidly happy that Bonnie drove a four-wheel-drive recreational vehicle.

But I felt the same degree of happiness when I found the wad of cash in her boot. I thought: Fantastic! I've really nailed the bitch.

So when Carbone and the lieutenant, a guy named Jack Byrne, who was so shy or weird that he whispered instead of talked, called me in and said, Listen, here are a couple of people to see in the city. The first wife and Sy's divorce lawyer. You'll have to go, not Robby. We need someone with a little finesse . . . Well, I should have been relieved. Here it was: a chance to get the hell off the South Fork, shake off the fixation, stop the Bonnie mania, cut the shit.

Except as I drove west on the Long Island Express-way, all I could think about was her dark, shiny, sweet-smelling hair. I wanted to stroke it back off her forehead, play with it, wrap it around my finger after we finished making love. But also, I wanted to see it inside a small plastic envelope: Government Exhibit D.

Goddamn, I wanted to take TJ's minivan, park it down the street and watch her house all day, catch a glimpse of her. I didn't want to work. And I definitely didn't want to go to Manhattan.

Imagine a cartoon of a snooty, stick-up-the-ass rich WASP. That's what Felice Tompkins Spencer Vanderventer looked like, except in 3-D. Yes, she'd heard her first husband had been murdered. Sorry.

Not really sorry or terribly sorry; she didn't gush. Everything about Felice was austere, from her face (which was very long and rectangular, like a gift box for a bottle of booze, except instead of a ribbon on top she had a thin figure eight of gray-brown hair tacked down by a couple of bobby pins) to her dress, which looked as if it were made out of a humongous brown Kleenex held together by a narrow brown belt.

She was Sy's age, fifty-three. Maybe when they were twenty-one they'd looked like a couple, but now, had he been alive and had they stayed married, she would have had to handle embarrassing references to her son; they had separated not only into different worlds but into different generations.

Like Felice, her Park Avenue living room was out-moded. But it wasn't austere. First of all, it was so big you could play basketball in there, except you'd break your neck because it was so chockfull of stuff. The place looked as though someone had bought out the entire inventory of a store specializing in dark, ugly antiques. There was no faded, restful old-money homeyness like at Germy's, just a lot of very high, overstuffed, heavy furniture with claw feet. It would have taken five moving men just to lift one of her hideous black carved-wood chairs. The pictures were heavy too, fancy gold-framed oil paintings of fruit and pitchers and dead rabbits.

'When was the last time you spoke with Mr Spencer?' My left shoe squeaked every time I shifted my weight. She hadn't asked me to sit.

'About ten years ago.' Even in the early-afternoon glare, the room was so shadowy it was hard to make out her features — except for her teeth. They were double normal human size; it looked as if she'd had a transplant from a thoroughbred mare. Felice was so aggressively unattractive that, considering her surroundings, you knew it was her, and not Mr Spencer or Mr Vanderventer, who owned the sixteen-foot-high ceilings and everything under them.

'Did you ever meet or speak with his second wife, Bonnie Spencer?'

'I saw them together briefly, once, in front of Carnegie Hall. Sy introduced us.' Outside Felice's window, the only bright spot in the room, Park Avenue stretched out like a parade ground for the rich. The island in the middle of the street had huge tubs of bright-gold flowers; they gleamed like piles of money. Past the traffic, over at the curb, elderly doormen opened limousine doors and helped out the rich and able-bodied.

'During the time you knew him, did Sy ever mention a man named Mikey LoTriglio?'

'I believe so.'

'What did he say about him?'

'I don't know. Something about their fathers having

been in the meat business.' She said 'meat business' with distaste, as if Sy had been in wholesale carrion. 'I never paid attention to that aspect of his life.'

I gave it another five minutes, but all I could get was that Felice had married Sy because he could quote all of Wordsworth's 'Intimations of Immortality from Recollections of Early Childhood.' She'd divorced him because she finally found out he was more interested in 'social advancement' than in poetry. And all right, yes, since I'd asked (her upper lip curled, covering about half of her giant teeth), because she caught him cheating. Who with? With her first cousin Claudia Giddings, a trustee of the New York Philharmonic. He told her he'd fallen in love with Claudia, that he wanted to marry her, but of course he never did.

The trip to Manhattan looked like a waste. What had I gotten? Corroboration that Sy couldn't keep his pants on, especially when there was someone screwable who could boost either his status or his career. And that Germy had been right on the money: Sy was a chameleon. A refined poetry-spouter to Felice. An 'I care' Down-to-Earth Human Being to Bonnie. A cool, masterful mogul to Lindsay. And not just to women: somehow, he became whatever anyone wanted him to be. A remote God of Cinema to Gregory J. Canfield. A congenial producer-pal to Nicholas Monteleone. A blood brother to Mikey. A savior to Easton.

I walked down Park Avenue to stretch my legs and let my shoe desqueak, twenty-five blocks from Felice's brown fortress of an apartment house to a silvery glass-and-granite office building. Nature had given up on this part of Manhattan and was hiding out in Central Park. On Park Avenue, there were only too-flawless horticulturists' gold flowers, and a thin, bleached-out strip of sky. Jesus, I hated New York.

Well, maybe not hated. When I was a kid I'd gone on a class trip to the top of the Empire State Building and to see the Christmas tree in Rockefeller Center, and I'd let out an 'Oooh!' of honest delight. But after that, I could never figure out what to do with myself in the city, except that I always felt I should do *something* – like take advantage of Culture. Once I'd been down at NYPD Headquarters on a case and then had taken a couple of subways uptown and wound up at the Metropolitan Museum of Art. But it was so big. And I'd had to check my gun with security. The guy there had treated me with a combination of suspicion and contempt, like I was some Bible Belt anti-smut loony who was going to shoot the dicks off the Greek statues. Finally, I'd found myself in a room full of Egyptian mummies, and when I'd asked where the pictures were, a guard, who I'd actually smiled at because he looked like an older Dave Winfield, had said, '"Pictures"? Do you mean "paintings"?' That had been it for Culture.

And just walking through the streets, either I'd see nothing but the homeless, and sick whores, and drug deals going down, or – today, as I pushed open the heavy door of the office building – swanky, Sy-like people saying, throatily, 'Hiiii' to each other. I always felt like a rube. All dressed up with no place to go. And no matter what jacket I put on in Bridgehampton, when I got to Manhattan my shirt cuffs were too short.

Jonathan Tullius Esq's cuffs were, of course, just the right length. He'd been Sy's divorce lawyer, both times. It looked like business was good. His office, filled with soft-looking leather furniture, smelled like the inside of an expensive loafer. 'Sit down, Detective Brady.' He had a deep, melodic voice and the barrel chest of an opera singer. He said: 'I called your offices immediately after I heard about the murder, and spoke with a Sergeant Carbone. And I see now I was right to do so. You people must have some interest in Bonnie Spencer, since you are, in fact, responding to my call.' He was crazy about the sound of his own voice. 'To get to the point, Detective Brady: Sergeant Carbone agreed this conversation would be strictly off the record and disclosed *only* on a need-to-know basis.'

'Right.'

'You see, on one hand the attorney–client privilege survives death.'

'Yeah.'

'Therefore, I should not be talking to you.' He swiveled around in his throne of a leather chair and then rested his elbows on his desk. 'On the other hand, Sy was a dear friend as well as a client. He called me last Thursday. The day before he was killed. He was quite, quite concerned.' Tullius had one of those soft, pampered, self-satisfied faces you see at Republican National Conventions.

'What was he concerned about, Mr Tullius?'

'Money.' I waited. 'And his former wife. Bonnie Spencer.'

I thought: Oh, fuck it! 'Was she holding him up for money?'

'No. But Sy was concerned that she might. You see, he'd run into her out in the Hamptons. She lives there full-time. Got their old summer house. He had nothing to do with her after the divorce, but then she'd dropped him a note about some screenplay she'd written . . .' He paused. 'You do know that she had been a screenwriter at one time.'

'Yeah,' I told him. 'I'm the squad's Bonnie Spencer expert.'

'They had one or two telephone conversations about it. He was trying to be nice, encourage her. And then he was out there almost the entire summer, filming *Starry Night*. Well, just on a whim, he dropped by her house. One thing led to another.' The lawyer cleared his throat.

'Sexual congress,' I suggested.

'Yes. He called me about it. Apparently, she's in a bad way financially, and Sy – *post hoc ergo propter hoc* – was worried that she might attempt to make some sort of a case for alimony because they had resumed sexual intimacy. I assured him she could not. The marriage was over, as was his responsibility toward her.'

'He said they only slept together once?'

'Oh, yes. Absolutely. You see, he was living with Lindsay Keefe. Why, under that circumstance, he chose a dalliance with Bonnie is one of those conundrums only the Higher Powers can unravel, but there you have it.'

'Did Bonnie make any threats?'

'No, but Sy seemed unduly concerned over her. Disquieted, guilty. And over a single lapse. It didn't "play", as they say in the film world. That's why I decided to phone your office. There was *something* about Bonnie. I met her during the divorce proceedings and, quite frankly, did not care for her. That rampant good nature; there was something so false. I simply did not trust her. My guess is, Sy finally smelled something fishy too. He might have been worrying about the possibility of extortion: Pay me or I'll tell Lindsay. Or he might have been thinking she would seek revenge against him, against his property. You see, he was quite taken aback by Bonnie's poverty. He said he'd seen holes in one of her pillowcases. Just a symbol, naturally, but he *did* say about his little tryst with her, his little one-afternoon stand: "I wonder what this is going to cost me?" What's been bothering me ever since his murder is . . . did he have any intimation that the cost would be his life?'

What a toad-load, I thought, as I walked up Park Avenue again, back to my car. I couldn't believe Carbone and Byrne had insisted I piss away a day on these two fuckheads. The entire bureaucracy of the County of Suffolk was losing its grip, peeing in its collective pants over the media exposure the case was getting. CBS, NBC, CNN and ABC were showing helicopter shots of Sandy Court, and some photographer in a boat had taken long-distance shots of Lindsay walking on the beach. Plus there seemed to be thousands of close-ups of Captain Shea in front of a bouquet of microphones, saying, 'We are at the present time investigating a variety of possibilities.' Neither Peter Jennings nor Bryant Gumbel sounded hopeful of an immediate solution. The *New York Times* came right out and said that the Suffolk County PD 'appeared stymied'. And *Newsweek* agreed: 'The police seem not to have a clue . . .' The department only wanted to look good and to protect itself, and that meant following up every single lead, even the most idiotic. So a whole day shot to shit. A hundred miles to New York and a hundred miles back, to find out that Sy Spencer liked to fuck rich and/or famous women and that some supercilious lawyer was sure Sy had foreseen his doom in a threadbare pillowcase.

I turned up a side street, went into a drugstore, got out a couple of bucks' worth of quarters. I stared at the colossal condom display, wondered what kind of a moron would buy blue, ribbed rubbers and dialed 1-516, the area code for Long Island. But instead of dialing Headquarters, I dialed Bonnie's house. She answered. 'Hello.' Her tone was cautious, weary, as though she expected another hang-up. I didn't say anything. *'Hello?'* she repeated. I hung up and called Robby. No DNA report yet. No nothing. To kill time, so I wouldn't have to drive back during rush hour, I had Robby give me the names, addresses and phone numbers for Mikey LoTriglio's known associates that he'd gotten from the FBI and the NYPD.

Three of Robby's names were the guys who had sworn and deposed that Fat Mikey had sat with them in a booth at Rosie's Bar in the meat district on Friday, August 18, from approximately three in the afternoon to – at least – six or seven. A couple of the other known associates were unavailable, currently residing in Allenwood federal correctional facility in Pennsylvania. Mrs Fat, Loretta LoTriglio, had checked into Mount Sinai Hospital two days before the murder and was still there, recovering from a new silicon breast implant because the old one had slipped and her tit had wound up in her armpit or something.

So for lack of anything better to do, I decided to check out Mikey's girlfriend, Terri Noonan, a part-time receptionist for an optician, who lived ten minutes from the Triborough Bridge in Jackson Heights, Queens.

I had an image of a gun moll with blonde, teased hair and a wad of chewing gum. Terri Noonan had plain curly brown hair and no makeup. She wore a starched white blouse with a little round collar and a pale-blue cardigan sweater buttoned at the top. No jewelry. She looked like she belonged to an order of nuns that had given up the habit but not the vows. Except when you looked twice – and you had to because she didn't show it off – you could see she had an absolutely spectacular, long-legged, big-boobed showgirl body. My guess was that Mikey had gotten it mixed up: he'd married the bimbo and kept the sweetie pie on the side.

Terri tried a whispery 'Mikey Who?' but gave up after I said 'Come on, Terri.' She asked me in and made me a cup of tea. The apartment, like the woman, was comfortable, simple, although as I'd passed the bedroom, I'd spotted a round bed with a quilted violet cover. But the living room had a green-and-white-striped plaid couch, green tweedy club chairs, a couple of trees in giant pots and green wall-to-wall carpet. Nice, comfortable. The kind of stuff a cop's wife who had good taste would buy. She poured the tea from a pot with flowers, then went back to the kitchen and returned with a plate of bakery cookies; she probably bought them fresh every day in case Mikey dropped by. I couldn't help staring; instead of the nun cardigan and the plain navy skirt, she should be wearing tassels and a G-string. She said, 'God, Mikey was so upset about Sy. No kidding.' She pointed to a Linzer torte. 'Raspberry jelly inside that one.'

'You mean Mikey was upset because they were fighting about the way the movie was going?' I didn't think Terri was trying to look dumb; Mikey probably hadn't told her a thing. 'You know,' I said. 'The movie Sy was making, *Starry Night*. The movie Mikey invested in.'

'I swear to God, Officer, he never said anything about any movie or any investment.'

'And he never said he and Sy had words?'

She crossed her heart, held her hand up and said, 'Cross my heart, my mother's life to die. Not a word. I

194

mean, I knew about Sy because he was kind of famous, and one time when Loretta – Mikey's wife – was out at La Costa we went to a premiere and a big party after for one of Sy's movies. But they was friends from the old days, and Mikey didn't talk about him all that much, except, like, to reminisce. But when he died, Mikey came right over.' Terri blinked. 'He was in tears, and Mikey's not one of these phony guys who cries all the time. I never, ever saw him like that before.'

'When was that, Terri?'

'Uh, let me think. Saturday morning. That's when I make him my cheese omelet.'

'You know Sy was killed late Friday afternoon. About four-twenty.'

'I didn't know the exact time,' she said, and broke off a tiny end of a chocolate chip cookie and put it in her mouth.

I put down the teacup and looked straight at her. 'Terri, this is important. Where was Mikey at the time of the murder?'

'Friday?'

'Friday.'

'Why is it important?'

'Do I have to draw you a picture?'

Terri readjusted the stiff little collar of her blouse so it lay flat over the cardigan. 'Mikey was here. In this apartment.'

'With you?'

'Yes.'

'What was he doing?'

She glanced down at her flat-heeled shoes. 'It was personal.'

'You and Mikey were having relations at or about four p.m. last Friday?'

She raised her right hand. 'From three till six,' she swore.

'Mikey must be quite a guy.'

'He's a little on the large side, but he's in very good health.'

'Will you sign a statement to the effect that he was here with you?'

'In blood,' she said. Instead, I handed her my Bic and watched as she began writing 'I, Theresa Kathleen Noonan, do swear . . .' 'See,' she said, after she signed her name, 'Mikey couldn't have been out in the Hamptons when Sy was killed, because he was here with me!'

But now Mikey had two alibis – which was as good as none at all.

So I should have felt better about Bonnie, right? It ought to be comforting to know that your sicko obsession may, in fact, be a nice, nonhomicidal girl.

Driving home on the Northern State, somewhere around the middle of Nassau County, I started having this fantasy about knocking at Bonnie's door and saying, Thank me. She asks why, and I say, Because I blew Mikey LoTriglio's alibi out of the water. And then, We put a tap on his phone and guess what? He got a call from some two-bit, piece-of-shit wise guy who, it turns out, pulled the trigger of the .22 – on Mikey's orders. You're home free, Bonnie.

Then I had an alternate fantasy where she's back from a hard run, her face rosy, her breath coming in gulps, and I pull up, get out of the car and tell her, Listen, everything's okay. We did a routine check, and it turns out that Victor Santana, the director, was renting a house that had a gun rack – and the owner confirmed a

.22 was missing! Oh, no – not Santana. Lindsay! She knew Sy was going to California to replace her, and she just snapped. Can you believe, she went to a sporting goods store five minutes from the *Starry Night* set and bought ammo. She was wearing dark sunglasses – like the guy at the store had never seen a movie and wouldn't recognize her! Listen, I tell Bonnie, I know it's been hell for you. I'm sorry. And Bonnie says, Thank God, and she's so grateful she puts her arms around me and I say, It's okay, but then I rub my face against the softness of her skin and one thing leads to another and we're inside, in her bedroom, having incredible, sweaty sex that lasts the whole night.

The daydream lasted all the way to Southampton, to the point where I was crying out Bonnie, baby! and about to come for the fourth time, when, out of the corner of my eye, I spotted the turnoff to Lynne's. That's when I cooled down enough for my brain to start functioning again.

And it told me that no matter how many phony alibis he had, it wasn't Mikey or Lindsay who killed Sy Spencer. In my heart I knew it was Bonnie.

It was confirmed. It was confirmed by Bonnie's real estate agent that Bonnie had been expecting big things from Sy. I finally reached the agent at home. She answered her phone with a hearty 'Hi! Regina!' She sounded like one of those fervently friendly divorcées, women abandoned by rich men, stuck on the South Fork, who con other women with rich husbands into houses so expensive that the husbands will feel fucked over and so, after an exorbitant season or two, leave, thus creating still more real estate agents.

She was saying: 'I told Bonnie, "Hon, this is *not* a

seller's market. Hold on to your house. Wait." ' It was after nine at night, but the agent's voice was still horribly hearty, although a little mushy around the edges, probably from two or three gimlets. 'But she said she really needed the money and to try.'

'Did she say what she was going to do if she sold it?' I asked.

'Let me think.' I waited. 'Something about going back to wherever it was she came from, even though I told her, "Bonnie, you can't go home again." Right?'

'Any interest in the house?'

'One or two offers, but very low-ball, and she was holding out for the asking price, which was very unrealistic, and believe me, I told her so.'

'And then?'

'I called to ask if I could come over and show the house to people, and all of a sudden she was saying, Sorry, I have guests. This happened two or three times. Well, finally I said, Bonnie, they're not beating down the door to buy an upper-midrange listing, because you literally have hundreds of them from Quogue to Montauk, so the next time I call maybe you can take your guests to the beach or into town for a half hour. And then she laughed – she's got a sense of humor – and said it wasn't guests, it was a man. And the next day she called me to put the deal on hold, because things were really looking up. I asked her if that was French for man, and she said yes. Like, he was a very high-powered type, but he was still managing to see her *every single day* for the last few days, and so she wasn't about to have people looking at the house with that kind of interest. So I said, Marriage-type interest? And she said she'd settle for someone's hand to hold on New Year's Eve. Sweet. Right? But the thing of it was, she was staying put. To me, that meant she was thinking about more than a New Year's Eve date; it had a certain ring of seriousness. You know? I remember, I kidded her and asked if her man had a friend, and we had a good laugh about two old dames like us – not really *old*, we're in our forties – having a double wedding.'

So Bonnie had expected something from Sy. Well, why not? She was putting out plenty. That, too, confirmed: the DNA report was on Carbone's desk first thing the next morning. The hair I had gotten off Bonnie's head was a genetic match to the hair on the headboard in Sy's guest room. She had been in the house with Sy the afternoon of his murder.

Motive? Yeah. And now, definitively, opportunity.

CHAPTER 10

I'd gotten Bonnie out of the tub. She was wearing a blue-and-white-striped bathrobe, and the bottom of her ponytail was wet. Her wrists glowed from too-hot water. I guess she'd been trying to soak out the tension. Maybe she'd succeeded, although her eyes were puffy, probably from sleeplessness, possibly from crying. She had to know she was on our Hit Parade. Maybe she even knew she was Number One.

But she wasn't doing any wounded-petunia number. She crossed her arms and stood up straight, an I'm-not-taking-any-shit stance. 'I'd be grateful if you could come by during normal business hours,' she said. Her crossed arms pushed her breasts up. She saw me staring and, slowly, trying to look casual, lowered her arms and slipped her hands into her pockets. I pictured myself standing behind her, kissing her sweet-smelling hair, the nape of her neck, then slipping my hands into her pockets and feeling her.

It was one of those she-knows-that-I-know-that-she-knows moments. We both knew she wasn't wearing anything under the robe. We both knew I was aware of it. And we both knew if I tugged at the sash, the robe would open. We'd do it standing up in that front hallway of her house because we were so wild for each other we couldn't wait.

I said: 'I understand you don't like being disturbed this late. But these are my normal business hours.'

She said: 'All right. Excuse me for a minute. I'll put something on.' She walked upstairs. I closed my eyes, leaned against the wall and began to imagine I had pulled the sash. The robe opens and I pull her up against me – she's still hot from the bath – but before I can ease the robe off, she goes for my pants, unzips them, takes it out, holds it in her hands and . . .

I heard her on the landing and opened my eyes fast, in time to watch her walk downstairs. She'd put on jeans and a white T-shirt, a man's V-neck undershirt of washed-out cotton, only hers was tucked in tight, so you could see every stitch of the white lace of her bra. I hadn't seen this one on my illegal search; it was one of those tiny bras women wear not for support but for men. I thought: Over-the-hill bitch. Except she looked fantastic. I caught myself rubbing the pads of my fingers together, in anticipation.

'Uh,' I said. Oh, was I one cool cop.

'Beg your pardon?'

'Where's your dog?' That was the only thing I could think of to say.

'My *dog*?' She started to relax. Even to get playful. 'Why? Do you want to question her?'

'Yeah. I want to know about her relationship with the deceased.'

'I got her at Bide-A-Wee about two years ago, so I don't think she ever really got to know Sy. I mean, beyond the usual social superficialities. "Hi, angel. *Fabulous* haircut."'

I started to smile. 'I just asked where your dog was.'

Bonnie's tone stayed teasing, light. 'I shot her.'

'Stop it.'

'Ha!' she exclaimed, like a TV lawyer who's just

elicited a damaging admission in front of a jury that will help his client. 'See? Deep down, you don't think I'm capable of murder.'

'No. I don't think you're capable of murdering your dog.' Bonnie laughed a little too hard. She took a step back; this was too real, and suddenly she was comprehending how terrified she was. But she made herself take a deep, deliberate breath. Easy, she was telling herself. Relax. She stuck her thumbs into the belt loops on her jeans, cowgirl style, as in, Get off my ranch, mister. 'Where is she?' I hated to keep asking the same stupid question, but having made a fool of myself asking about the dog, I now had to treat it like it was a key to the investigation.

'She likes to go out at night.' A cool, matter-of-fact response. No, cold. 'Sometimes around ten I open the back door and yell for her. She's back inside in two minutes.' Bonnie turned away from me, probably to hide her fear. Despite her laid-back, home-on-the-range posture, it was stealing over her face – jaw a little rigid, eyes too wide. She strode into the kitchen, opened the door and yelled: 'Moose! Milk-Bone!' While we waited, she went to the refrigerator and took out an Amstel Light. She did not offer me one, so I wasn't able to say 'No, thanks.' By the time she popped off the cap, Moose came barreling up to the screen door. I opened it. She let out a blissful bark and started licking my hand.

But Bonnie was hardly blissed out. She was busy being tough. She pulled the dog away from me, patted its head, then took a doggy bone out of a cookie jar and put it in Moose's mouth. For that instant, Bonnie forgot herself and was tender, a mother offering her child a lollipop. Moose, meanwhile, glanced up. She may have been nuts about me, but I wasn't part of her nightly ritual; she decided I might want to grab her treasure, so she hightailed it out of the kitchen, bone in mouth. I grinned. Bonnie didn't.

'What do you want to know?' she demanded. She tilted back her head and took a swig of beer. I stared at the arch of her throat, the rise of her breasts. I wanted her so much. 'Well?'

All right. She wanted it, I'd give it to her. 'Can you shoot a .22 rifle?'

In a movie, Bonnie would have shown her shock by spritzing out the beer. Real life lacks grand gestures, or even spectacularly messy ones. She just swallowed a little harder than normal. 'That's not funny.'

'I'm not being funny. You're the funny one. I'm the cop. And I'm very, very serious. I want to know whether you can shoot a .22.'

'I don't have to answer that.'

'You already have. You didn't say no.'

'I didn't say yes, either.' Suddenly her fear turned to anger. She slammed the beer bottle down on the counter. 'Just let me tell you something. I've been watching detective movies since I've been eight or nine years old. I know hard-boiled and soft-boiled. I know you're supposed to frighten me so much that I spill whatever beans there are to be spilled. Or you're supposed to charm me, so I'll get giddy and babble all my girlish secrets. Well, guess what, buster? You're no Humphrey Bogart. And guess what again? I didn't do anything wrong. I have nothing to confess. You're wasting your time.'

'Yeah?' I shouldered an invisible rifle. I sighted. I pulled the trigger. 'Bonnie Bernstein-Spencer. Her family owned Bernstein's Sporting Goods in Ogden, Utah, a store which did not sell junior lacrosse sticks. No: rifles, handguns. Ms Bernstein-Spencer grew up with several older brothers and was reputed to be a tomboy. Her father was known as a fine shot; he even used to go up to Wyoming to shoot elk. Tell me, Bonnie, is Ogden a nice place to visit? Because if you don't answer my question now, I'll be on the next plane out, spend half a day in town, and I guarantee you, I'll come home with whatever's left of the rabbit you shot between the eyes in 1965, plus affidavits from ten witnesses who saw you shoot it.'

She started to cry, those round, silent tears that drift down cheeks and leave trails. 'Please,' she whispered, 'don't do this to me.'

'I just have to get to the truth.' I realized I was whispering too. 'Bonnie, can you shoot?'

'Yes.' I could barely hear her. 'But I swear to God, I didn't kill Sy.'

Jesus, I thought, I almost have her. Almost. 'You have to understand,' I told her gently, 'people swear to God all the time. "I swear to God, I'm innocent."'

'But I am.'

'Prove it to me.'

'How?'

All I had to do was pull her in very slowly, lovingly, as though seducing the most reluctant of women. 'We can rule you out with a simple little test. Come with me. I'll drive you down to Headquarters, stay with you the whole time. You just give a small sample of saliva and blood – a pinprick, nothing more. And then you're in the clear.'

For a long moment there was silence. I heard the deep hum of the refrigerator and then the click of Moose's paws as she toddled back into the kitchen, across the tile, to look up at us. She didn't understand why we weren't having fun.

'Come on, Bonnie.'

I imagined her beside me in the Jag on the way to Headquarters, our arms and shoulders touching when I took a curve; I thought about the heat that instant of friction would give off. Shit, I don't want this fantasy.

But then, at Headquarters, my bewitchment would finally be over. In that hard fluorescent light, I'd see Bonnie Spencer for what she was: a killer. Of course, she hadn't meant to do it. Of course, if she could live the moment all over again, Sy would still be alive. And of course, she was, without a doubt, honestly and profoundly sorry. But still, a killer. And seeing her in that merciless light, I would no longer be able to desire the thing I most hated. Murderer.

I would no longer spend every goddamn obsessed minute creating different scenarios of kissing her, caressing her, fucking her: in beds, in chairs, on tables, in showers, on floors, in cars, on the beach, in the ocean, in the woods. I would be relieved of my madness. I would save thousands staying away from pay phones. I would go to my wedding with a peaceful mind and a loving heart.

All of a sudden, I felt sick, awful – the opposite of dizzy: heavy-headed. Despair settled on me. In that terrible moment, I wondered, How the hell am I going to live out the rest of my life without this woman? For a minute I truly could not speak. Then, I don't know how, I got it together: 'Let's go, Bonnie.'

'No.'

'Come on. You've got everything to gain, nothing to lose. Let it be over.'

'I want you out of here.'

'Bonnie – '

'Don't come back. I won't speak to you again.'

'Honey, I'm sorry, but you'll have to.'

'No. And I'm not your honey. Not by a long shot, you son of a bitch. If you have any more questions, you can speak to my lawyer. Now *out*.'

Robby Kurz came swishing over to my desk, licked his pinkie and ran it over his eyebrow. I told him: 'Hey, you're not telling me anything about yourself I don't already know.'

'Gideon is outside,' Robby simpered, in an exaggeratedly faggy way. Well, what do you expect from a cop? A gay rights button? 'He's simply *dying* to see you.'

'Gideon who?'

'Are you ready for this?' He waved a business card. 'Gideon Isaiah Friedman, Esquire. Of East Hampton, sweetie. Attorney for Bonnie Spencer.'

Gideon Friedman walked toward me. He didn't take little mincing steps. And he didn't lisp or wave a limp wrist. Still, you knew what he was. Maybe it was that his getup was impeccable country lawyer, English style: awesomely casual, perfectly cut brown tweed suit with a tattersall shirt, green knit tie and shoes that looked like wing tips, except that they were brown suede. Or maybe it was the flawless haircut, where every single strand of brown hair lay smooth against his head, as if his skull were magnetized. Or maybe it was that he was too boyishly handsome for a guy in his late thirties, with that innocent, round-eyed, ultra upper-class queer look male models have, the ones who always have very long scarves tossed around their necks in interesting ways. Forget his name; he had the look of one of those guys

206

with a wood racquet who leap over the net at the Meadow Club.

Or maybe it was just the way he checked me out when I stood up to shake his hand. 'Hi,' he said.

'Hi,' I responded.

'I'm here representing Bonnie Spencer.' He had a breathy voice, like a waiter in one of those trendy, expensive seafood restaurants, Fish Hampton or whatever, that open and close every summer because nobody, not even the most pretentious schmuck from New York, would voluntarily eat rare scallops more than once. I looked at him and thought: Oh, Christ, Bonnie's going to sit in Bedford for twenty-five to life.

'Why don't you sit down?' I suggested. He sat in the plastic chair next to my desk and glanced around the squad room. I figured he'd murmur, Oooh, how butch! or at least cross his legs at the knees. 'Well, Mr Friedman, what can I do for you?'

'Well . . .' And suddenly he stopped being a homo. He became a lawyer. 'Why not start by telling me what this bullshit is about Bonnie coming in and taking blood and saliva tests to "rule her out" as a suspect.'

'I meant that. Sincerely.'

'Give me a break. You were referring to that DNA testing, right?' I shrugged. 'What's the story here? Sy Spencer was shot from a distance. Are we talking about some perspiration that dripped onto the murder weapon? A little saliva? Did the perpetrator drool?' It was weird, the hard-edge-lawyer sarcasm presented in that whispery waiter's voice. 'Or was there some kind of a fight, and you have blood – or skin cells from under Sy's nails?' For a lawyer with no leverage, who had no idea what we had or where we were going, he was pretty good.

'I'm not prepared to discuss the evidence at this time.'

'Why not?'

'You should know why not. There's no percentage in it.'

'Okay,' he said. 'Then I suppose there's no percentage in anyone taking any blood tests.' He stood, regretfully, as if he hadn't been able to save me from making the most grievous misjudgment of my career. 'I'm going to have to advise my client to stand on her Fifth Amendment privilege against self-incrimination and not take the test.'

It was only then that it hit me that Gideon probably represented dress designers. 'You're not a criminal lawyer, are you?' I asked.

I waited for him to get pissed or, minimally, petulant, but to his credit he stayed composed; serene, even. He sat back down and examined the nap of the suede on his English shoe. 'Why do you ask?'

'Because a criminal lawyer would know that a suspect in a murder case can't refuse a blood test.'

'Why not?'

'Because blood tests and other medical tests are fact, not testimony. They aren't covered by the Fifth Amendment.'

'Says who?'

'Says the US Supreme Court.'

'Really? Recently?'

'Within the last five or ten years.'

'It must have happened after law school. I'll check it out.'

All right, so maybe he represented a hairdressers' lobbying group. But he wasn't that bad a guy. Not full of shit. And not full of himself. Except what the hell would he do when he got to court? Go fancy dress, show up in a black robe and white wig? And what would he do when the chief of the Homicide Bureau of the DA's office cross-examined Bonnie? Take smelling salts?

'What kind of lawyer are you?' I asked.

He smiled. Perfect, even white teeth, like Chiclets. 'I specialize in real estate.'

'Real estate,' I repeated. 'Must be busy, over in East Hampton.'

'Let me tell you what you're thinking,' Gideon said. 'Okay?' I shrugged. 'You're thinking: Oh, goody! I can send Bonnie Spencer up the river for life and that land-use faggot lawyer who represents her won't be able to do a thing except wave bye-bye as she goes.' I sat back in my seat, trying to look astounded at such a ridiculous — no, prejudiced — notion. It was not all that easy since, basically, that was what had been going through my mind. 'Well, that's not the way it's going to be, Brady. Let me tell you how it's going to be. If you're just toying with her, I would hope you'd be smart enough to stop right now. Before I make a scene in front of your superiors.'

'You think I give a shit? Go ahead. Make a scene. The captain's in that office off the reception area.'

'You should give a shit, don't you think?'

'No.'

He paused for a second. 'All right. If you sincerely think you have any kind of a case, I'd appreciate it if you'd let me know. Because then I'd have to step out — and bring in Bill Paterno.' I picked up a pen and twirled it between my palms; Paterno was the best criminal lawyer in Suffolk County.

'Do you think Bonnie Spencer can afford Bill

Paterno?' I asked, trying to sound casual, as though I didn't know how broke she was.

'No. But I can.' Gideon put on a little-old-man Jewish accent. 'I make a very nice living, tanks God, and have some vonderful inwestments.' Then he added: 'Bonnie is one of my dearest friends.'

Well, it figured. I could see them. Giddie and Bonnie. He'd have her over to his place in East Hampton for Mexican beer and guacamole or whatever nouvelle hors d'oeuvre had replaced it, and they'd giggle and gossip and talk about James Stewart and Henry Fonda – or Share Deep Feelings.

'You can hire Paterno, Mr Friedman. You can resurrect Clarence fucking Darrow. Bonnie's still going to have to take the tests. And then we've got her.'

'Why? Because she told you she could shoot? *Please*. Girls in Utah do that sort of thing.'

'They hand out a .22 with every box of Kotex?'

'Where's the rifle?' he inquired. I said nothing. 'Bonnie doesn't own a rifle. She doesn't have access to one.' Gideon waited. 'You don't have the murder weapon, do you?' I kept silent. 'Why Bonnie? Why not Lindsay?'

'Lindsay?'

'Lindsay can shoot. You don't believe me? Go rent *Transvaal*. Bombastic dreck, but you'll see her with a rifle.'

'She's an actress. Holding a rifle doesn't mean she can shoot it.'

'Why not find out?'

'Mr Friedman, we know where Lindsay Keefe was at the time of the murder.'

'And?' he asked, lifting a nonexistent speck of lint off

his tweedy sleeve. 'Are you implying my client was anywhere *near* Sy Spencer's house?'

'Possibly.'

'I don't believe you.' I shrugged again. 'Stop that shrugging!' he said. 'It's very irritating. Now let's get serious. You don't want to torment this woman, do you? You just want to get her a little agitated. Well, you've done it. She is agitated to the extreme. Now why don't you let me know *why* you want the tests. Be big about it. Maybe I can recommend taking them – if it's not unreasonable, or damaging to her interests.'

I thought about it. The only reason to let a suspect know what evidence you have is when you decide to short-circuit an investigation and go for a confession. I wasn't in that much of a rush; I could wait another twenty-four hours. I sensed there were still more leads to follow. And I had to cover my ass on the illegal search of Bonnie's house by getting a warrant and then 'finding' the real estate listing and the money in her boot. Those two items would give the DA's office more rope to hang her.

'You know,' I said to Gideon, 'the perpetrator was a very intelligent person. But not that intelligent. He or she' – Gideon made a sour face – 'left so many loose ends we're still tripping all over them. The evidence box on this one is going to be so heavy the court clerk will need a goddamned moving van to bring it in. So what's the point of telling you what we have, when by this afternoon we'd have to give you a major update.'

'You're playing poker,' Gideon commented.

'Do me a favor, Mr Friedman. Give your client a message for me. Tell her that if she did it, she should

211

come in now. Maybe we can bring the matter to a conclusion that's mutually advantageous.'

'Why won't you be decent? She's a truly good person. Why won't you give her the benefit of the doubt?'

'Let me continue. If she lets this thing play out, if she doesn't come forward with a confession, it's going to be harder for her.'

'Tell me something,' Gideon said. 'Do you honestly think you can be objective about my client?' I didn't like the way he was eyeing me; I got a quick, bad, pukey feeling. Had he picked up something from me? Had Bonnie told him anything? But what could she tell him? That once I stood a little too close to her? That a couple of times she'd sensed a bulge under my clothes that wasn't my gun?

'Yeah, I can be objective. She's a lovely lady. Good sense of humor. Friendly. Personally, I think she's a sweetheart.' Gideon listened, alert. 'But she's a sweetheart with a mean streak.'

'You're wrong.'

'Hate to say it, but I'm right. You see, I think Bonnie got — what's the word? — piqued at Sy. She was lonely, divorced, poor, unsuccessful. And along came her ex. He winked, then fucked her a few times . . . Hey, we know about that, even though she swears she didn't. She lies all the time. Anyhow, he fucked her. And then he told her goodbye. No companionship, no marriage, no money. Oh, and no movie. No nothing. So she blew him away.'

'You don't really believe that.'

'I do.'

'You have no evidence.'

'We've got plenty of evidence.' I put my feet up on the desk. 'I've got to tell you, I find homicidal behavior

212

not worthy of a sweetheart. But what I think isn't important. The lady's going away. So be prepared. Maybe make her a nice bon voyage party.'

Marian Robertson, Sy's cook, was being paid by the movie production company to remain on her job until Lindsay finished *Starry Night*. 'Cook?' she sneered. 'Lindsay Keefe needs a cook? Do you know what she eats? Fruit. All right, an occasional nut. No wonder she looks like a glass of milk. I sit here all day so that maybe, when she gets home, I can make her seven Crenshaw melon balls. What kind of person can live on melon balls?'

For a second I couldn't answer because my mouth was full. She'd insisted on making me bacon and eggs, to say nothing of a tower of English muffins and coffee. 'You don't like her,' I managed to say.

'There are worse.'

'Who?'

'Oh, the pushy ones. The braggarts. And the ones who come in two minutes before a dinner party for twenty and tell me they're on Pritikin. The ones who have to explain to a colored woman what *mille feuilles* is.'

The marmalade was in a tiny white crock, like a soufflé dish for midgets. I spooned some onto another muffin. 'What about someone like Bonnie Spencer?' I asked. Marian Robertson started to gnaw on the inside of her cheek. 'Remember Bonnie? Sy's ex-wife.'

'Oh, of course! Nice girl.'

'Mrs Robertson, this is very difficult for me. I've known you since I was a kid. I look up to you.

I would hate to see you in trouble.'

'Me?'

'Yes. We have physical evidence that Bonnie Spencer was in the house the afternoon of Sy's murder. Now, you can tell me you didn't know she was here, but sooner or later we're going to confront Bonnie with our evidence. And she may say something like: ". . . and that nice Mrs Robertson, who knew me so well when I was married to Sy. She always made me my favorite . . . whatever. Kumquat pudding. Well, Mrs Robertson and I had a nice chat that afternoon." And then you'd have a legal problem, because in your statement you said no one was here.'

'More coffee?'

'Mrs Robertson, withholding evidence, lying to the police – it's a crime.'

Finally, she said: 'You're barking up the wrong tree, Steve. Bonnie's as good as they come.'

'If she's that good, why did you lie to protect her? Don't you think it would be better to let her goodness shine through?'

'If she wanted to tell you she was here, it was her business, not mine.' She cleared the cream and the marmalade off the table. I was no longer a welcome guest.

'Was she here last Friday afternoon?' She took away the sugar bowl.

'Yes.' Clipped. No, Steve, you're looking fine. No, you were the best shortstop the Bridgies ever had.

'Did you speak with her?'

'Just hello, how are you, and just a couple of minutes of catching up.'

'Was it friendly? Did she kiss you hello? Did

you make a fuss? "Good to see you, Mrs Spencer!"'

'I call her Bonnie. And I was glad to see her and she was glad to see me. I gave her a big hug. What are you going to do about that? Put me in the electric chair?'

'Mrs Robertson, I'm just trying to get the feeling of the afternoon.'

'The feeling was, Mr Spencer must have gotten tired of Madame Melon Balls, because he actually brought Bonnie into the house. And he was smiling, happy to be with her – like the old days. And they didn't stay in the kitchen to chat. My guess is they had other fish to fry upstairs. But that was all right, because I got the feeling Bonnie would be back. Then we could catch up. I know her; Mr Spencer would get busy on the phone, and she'd wander down to the kitchen and we'd have ourselves a good gabfest.'

'I'd like the truth now. Were there any sounds of fighting coming from upstairs?'

'No.'

'Any sounds of anything?'

'No. Listen to me. He wouldn't have gone out to the pool to relax and make his last-minute phone calls if Bonnie was still upstairs. Say what you will about him, his manners were perfect. It wasn't in his nature not to drive a lady home, or if she'd come on her own, escort her to her car. Believe me, after Bonnie and before Lindsay, there was quite a parade of women going upstairs to see his ocean view or whatever. He *always* said a proper goodbye.'

'Then how come you didn't hear him escort her out?'

'I don't know. Maybe I was beating egg whites. Maybe I was powdering my nose.'

'Did you hear Mr Spencer come down and go out to the pool?' She did a cheek chew before she nodded. 'And what about Bonnie? Did you hear her leave after he went outside?' She didn't answer. 'Okay, between the time Bonnie went upstairs with Sy and the time you heard the shot, what precisely did you hear? Her voice? Her footsteps? The sound of her car?'

'She didn't kill him.'

'What did you hear, Mrs Robertson?'

'I didn't hear anything.' She took away the muffins and my plate. 'Does that make you happy, Steve?'

I knew the old saying was true: You don't remember pain. Physical pain, like in Vietnam, when some new kid from North Carolina heard enemy fire, aimed his M-60, and blasted me through the shoulder. The medic shot me up with a ton of shit, but they had to stuff a gag into my mouth so I wouldn't scream and give away our position when they cut open my shirt. Me, who'd always looked at wounded, screaming guys and thought: Sure, it must hurt like hell, but can't he just bite the bullet, control himself? I kept moaning so loud that they kept the gag in, and they took it out only when I puked and almost choked to death on my own vomit.

I can recall thinking, when they joggled my shoulder as they put me on the stretcher to get me to the helicopter: I will not live through this flight because the pain will kill me. I truly cannot take it. I kept howling, 'I want a priest!' Me, whose last confession pretty much coincided with my first communion. But I don't remember the pain itself.

And you don't remember emotional pain either.

Like being a seven-year-old kid playing ball and my

216

father drives onto the field in some farmer's tractor he's doing day work for, and he cuts the engine, stopping between the pitcher's mound and first base, practically breaks his neck getting down and then grabs a bat out of the hands of one of my friends and insists on hitting a few.

More pain? Being a thirty-five-year-old and seeing my pal, my confidant, the only person I ever really spoke to outside work, the one person I thought to buy a Christmas card for – the guy who owned the liquor store – flash his wife a look of revulsion when I walked through the door.

You know all that pain and more occurred. Recalling it, you might feel sad or even cringe. But you do not remember the pain itself.

So when I rang Bonnie's bell and got no answer, and then ran to her garage to see if her car was missing, and then, finally, spotted her in her chicken-wired garden, picking vegetables, I almost laughed at the panic I'd felt, the horror, the stab in the gut – the pain – when I thought she'd gone. So what if she had? You do get over these things.

And when Moose barked a welcome and Bonnie looked up and saw me and shuddered – a violent, uncontrollable shiver of fear – I wanted to disappear, or die, it hurt so much. But I said to myself: I'll get over it.

She was squatting over a basket of eggplants. 'What are you going to do with all those things?' I asked.

'Get out of here.' Her voice was a hoarse whisper. She braced her hands on her knees and slowly, as if it were too much of an effort, pushed herself up. All her energy, all her fire, all her humor was gone.

'Look, I just want you to understand . . .' What

217

was I going to say? Nothing personal. 'You lied, Bonnie.'

She walked out of the garden, leaving the eggplants, a plastic bucket full of tomatoes, Moose – everything – behind. She headed toward the house, awkwardly, without any of her great jock grace, as if she'd lost her center of gravity. I followed her. 'We have a neighbor who can not only identify Sy's car as being here every day the week he died, but who can identify Sy himself. I mean, we can place you with him enough times . . . Why did you lie about a thing like that?'

She didn't answer me, didn't acknowledge that I'd grabbed onto her arm, trying to steady her or just hold on to her. 'And why did you lie about your screenplay? Didn't you bother to think that he'd tell the people he worked with that it was a piece of shit?'

She tripped over a tree root. I lost my grip on her, and she fell on her hands and knees. 'Are you okay?' I asked. She couldn't get up. She sat back on the ground, breathless, and looked down at the pebbles and grass embedded in her hands, at the little rivulet of blood that ran toward her wrist, but she didn't wince or weep. 'Bonnie,' I said. Her spirit was gone.

Moose wandered over, wagged her tail and licked Bonnie's hand, but Bonnie didn't acknowledge her. 'Please,' I said. I pulled her up. She didn't stop me. When she was on her feet again, she continued her unsteady journey toward the house. 'Listen, your lawyer friend . . . He's going to pay for the best criminal lawyer around.'

I felt sick. Empty. But I'd lived through too much. I knew. Part of me understood that in two weeks, I'd be hoisting an alcohol-free beer, eating potato chips, and Lynne would be saying: 'Forget that you're going to get the fattest gut in Bridgehampton. Do you *know* what those chips look like on your insides?'

You forget pain. You really do.

Bonnie opened the screen door to her kitchen. 'Congratulations,' she said softly.

'I don't want congratulations. Believe me, I'm sorry.'

'No. You did what you set out to do. You got me. That's it. My life is over. What you did isn't homicide, but the effect is pretty much the same: a dead person.'

There was so much grief in her voice, as if she was mourning someone she had loved very much.

'It has to be,' I said.

'Why?'

'Because you killed someone.' She walked inside and closed the screen door. I looked at her, blurred, distant, through the mesh. 'Don't try and leave. There'll be a twenty-four-hour watch – '

'Where could I go that you wouldn't find me?'

'That's right.'

'It's so sad.'

'It is,' I agreed.

'No. It's sad because I didn't do it. You know I didn't.' It was about sixty-five degrees. I began to shake. I knew: This would be pain I would never forget. 'Don't worry,' Bonnie said, just before she closed the kitchen door. 'You'll get over it.'

CHAPTER 11

We got to Bonnie's house before eight the next morning. Less than thirty seconds later, she looked up from the fine print on the search warrant, swallowed and said: 'I'll have to call my lawyer.'

'Feel free,' Robby said magnanimously, a second before he and the other detective, a short bodybuilder type in his late twenties, tried to push past her, into the house. The kid's thighs were so overdeveloped that he couldn't get his legs together. He walked like a chimpanzee.

'You can't do this!' Bonnie shouted, trying to block us. I was the one who finally shoved her aside.

'Reasonable force,' I said. 'Call your Civil Liberties Union.'

At first I'd expected hysteria. Then – especially when I noticed she was wearing those tight turquoise bicycle shorts and a T-shirt – I did a fast fantasy number. She'd faint. I'd grab her, lead her over to her couch and mumble something calming, like 'Easy, Bonnie,' as, slowly, I let her out of my arms. Easy, Bonnie: I liked the idea of saying her name out loud.

But she'd just stood near the staircase, completely still. She was there, but she wasn't there. The world she was living in was so awful that she withdrew and entered some other, kinder universe. At last, she drifted past me, into the kitchen to call Gideon. I could have been a ghost, just air and vapor. Moose picked up

Bonnie's mood, staying right beside her, concerned, not giving me so much as a wag of the tail.

I followed them into the kitchen and started going through her cabinets as if assuming I'd find a cupful of .22 bullets behind the Down Home Gourmet barbecue sauce. For someone who was close to broke, Bonnie was spending too much money on mustard: honey mustard, tarragon mustard, green peppercorn mustard. I looked over at her. Maybe I'd try a little mustard humor, clear the air. But her back was toward me, and she was speaking quietly into the phone.

I shook a jar of popcorn hard and loud, like some maracas-playing fool in a Latin American band. I wanted attention. Maybe if she acknowledged I was alive I would be able to feel alive. I was so goddamn down.

Fuck this sadness shit, I told myself. Your obsession's dead. Be glad. But I couldn't let it rest in peace. And I couldn't stop trying to get a rise out of Bonnie.

I made a big production out of going through her pocketbook. Obnoxious. Intrusive. A deliberate invasion of privacy. I examined each key, flattened out a couple of linty tissues, studied a supermarket cash register tape. In slow motion, I took apart her wallet, laying out her seventeen bucks in bills, her forty-four cents in change, her driver's license, her Visa card, her library card, her video store membership card. And the pictures: father in a plaid shirt holding up a prizewinner of a trout. Father and mother – tall and broad-shouldered like Bonnie – all dressed up, like for a wedding, smiling, but starched, stiff. You just knew they'd rather be in their plaid shirts. Brothers and sisters-in-law on skis. Nieces with horses. Nephews with dogs. All the Bernstein pictures had mountains in the background.

I waited for her to show some spirit: run, try and punch me, scream out something like 'I hate you!' Nothing. So I made a big deal of opening a purple plastic case that held a couple of Tampax. I held each one – Super – up to the light, as if anticipating a fuse instead of a string. Zero response. Should I taunt her? Say, No shit. You still have a period? and then deny it if her lawyer bitched about my being insulting? But I kept quiet. Thighs, the kid detective, was around; I didn't want him to think I was anything other than neutral.

Bonnie hung up the phone. I went back to the pocketbook. There was some powder on the bottom of her purse, red, obviously the blushing stuff women put on with those big fluff brushes. But I did a major number, sifting it into a plastic envelope, like it was a new, killer form of cocaine that made crack look like aspirin. She made no snide remarks. Clutching the warrant in her hand, she simply walked out on me. I stood there, a complete jerk, helpless, yearning, watching her turquoise ass until it disappeared into the hall.

I was like a husband whose wife has just walked out on him. I sank into the same chair where I'd sat that first day, having coffee. I was still holding her pocketbook.

About ten minutes later, when I finished the kitchen and found absolute squat, I went looking for her. She was sitting on the brick ledge in front of her fireplace, the search warrant beside her. She was hugging herself, as if waiting for logs to blaze up and thaw her out. Of course, there was no fire. Outside, it was already over seventy. The sky was too bright, an almost painful blue, the brilliant morning light of the end of August. The sun poured through Bonnie's living room window, making shining squares on a dozing Moose and on the dark wood floor beneath her.

Bonnie's head was down, so she didn't notice Thighs rush over and hand me a heavy shopping bag. Since all he'd turned up so far was one of Moose's half-chewed rawhide bones under the couch, he was clearly longing for some significant sign of Bonnie's guilt.

I emptied the shopping bag onto the coffee table. Bonnie glanced over. There were two unopened boxes: a coffee grinder and one of those expensive espresso-cappuccino machines. In the bottom of the bag was an American Express receipt: Sy Spencer, card member since 1960, had paid for them.

I walked over to her, sat down on the other side of the search warrant and fluttered the receipt in front of her. 'Sy like a cup of espresso afterwards?' I inquired. 'Or before? Some guys need a little stimulant.' She didn't answer, but then I hadn't expected her to. I didn't exist. Plus Gideon had obviously warned her not to say anything, and she was taking him literally. 'Is your lawyer coming over?' I asked. She picked up the warrant. She looked for a pocket for it, but since she was wearing the shorts and T-shirt, she didn't have any. She just held on to it. I shifted so I could at least look at her. Her T-shirt was from some film festival, probably a feminist thing. Across her breasts it said WOMEN MAKE MOVIES in red and green and yellow and blue.

I rested the receipt on top of the warrant she was holding and pointed to Sy's name. 'Three hundred and fifty-five bucks for a cup of coffee,' I said. Across

223

the room, Thighs sniggered; he probably thought the sound was a manly detective laugh. Bonnie brushed away the receipt with the back of her hand. It floated onto the floor.

It was so quiet. The only sound was the dog's snoring and then the clunk, clunk of Robby walking around upstairs. I'd wanted him to be the one to find the money in her boot, the real estate listing. I told him: I'll stay downstairs, keep an eye on her.

But she wasn't going anywhere, and I couldn't move anymore. I just sat there beside her. We could have been a heartbroken couple waiting for some sad appointment together, cancer specialist, marriage counselor. I kept sneaking glances at her; instead of wearing her hair loose, tucked behind her ears, or in a ponytail, she'd put it into a braid. I had the urge to reach over and, with the tip of my index finger, stroke each one of the shiny intertwinings. I'd say, It'll be all right.

What I actually said was: 'Where'd you hide the rifle?' She didn't move. 'Bonnie, your window of opportunity is closing. You make it tough on us, we'll make it tough on you.'

Just then, Gideon Friedman came striding in. Ninja Lawyer: baggy, rolled-at-the-cuff black cotton slacks, a black sweater, hair combed back with slickum. I stood up. 'Hey, Counselor Friedman,' I said. 'Good to see you.'

He walked past me and hunkered down in front of Bonnie. 'Did you say anything to him?' he asked her. 'Anything at all?' She shook her head. 'Good girl.' He picked up the search warrant, stood, and read it over. He saw it was okay. He wanted it out of sight, but since he didn't have any pockets either, he held on to it and, with his other hand, pulled Bonnie up and steered her into the kitchen.

They must have been talking softly in there. I couldn't hear anything, not even the hum of muted conversation. I walked over to her bookshelves. Most of them were paperbacks: hundreds of mysteries and novels. There were books about movies – biographies of actors and directors, *Cinematographer's Handbook, Farce in Film* – and about nature stuff. *Flowering Plants of Beach and Dune. Hiking Long Island.* There were no sex books tucked behind *Birds of North America,* no *Memoirs of a Victorian Serving Wench,* and no *Stop Being a Compliant Cunt and Get Him to Marry You,* one of those books single women always seem to have.

Just then Robby clomped down the stairs. His beige loafers had thick black heels with what sounded like metal taps. He was grinning, brandishing a plastic evidence bag with the wad of bills that had been in Bonnie's boot. I walked over to him. 'Eight hundred eighty!' he announced.

'In tens or twenties?' I tried to look amazed, thrilled. 'Like from a cash machine?'

'You got it.'

'Anything else?'

'Not really.' Robby seemed a little disappointed. He'd probably been hoping for a smoking rifle.

'No vibrator in the night table?' Robby shook his head. 'No interesting papers?'

'Nothing.' Shit, I'd have to go up to have a casual look-through and then find the real estate listing. Unless she'd thrown it out. 'Just a lot of movie script stuff in her office,' he said. 'Rejection letters in a file. But listen, we have enough! This money is the stake in her heart. And once we get her blood samples, it's all over.'

'Any rejection letters from Sy?'

'No, but we don't need any. Where is she?'

'In the kitchen with her lawyer.'

'Think we should stick it to her now?' He was like a leashed, drooling Doberman; he couldn't wait.

'Yeah,' I said. 'Might as well get it over with.'

My throat felt swollen. My chest rose, but I couldn't get enough air.

We walked into the kitchen. Robby waved the bag of money in front of Bonnie's face. 'Eight hundred eighty dollars in twenties,' he said to her.

'If you have any comments, please address them to me,' Gideon responded.

'Oh, *sorry*,' Robby said, giving him a big, shit-eating grin. 'We found this hidden in your client's boot. All I want to know is where this money came from. Maybe she could tell us.'

'Oh,' Bonnie began, 'it's – '

'Quiet,' Gideon snapped at her.

'But, Gideon, it doesn't have anything to do with Sy.'

Gideon did not look thrilled with her. 'Would you please leave us alone for a minute?' he asked. We walked into the hall outside the kitchen, heard whispers. I took deep breaths, but I just made myself dizzy. Then Gideon called, 'All right. You can come back in.' When we did, he nodded at Bonnie.

She spoke to Robby, as if there was only one cop in the room. 'The money you found is what's left of twenty-five hundred dollars I got last December. I do a lot of work for a catalog company, and the owner pays me once a year. In cash.' Then she added, 'Off the books.'

'So there's no record of your having received the

payment,' I said. Bonnie made herself look at me, except her eyes did not meet mine.

'That's the point of being paid off the books,' she explained, too patiently, as if talking to someone with an IQ in the minus column. 'There isn't supposed to be any record.'

'So we just have your word that that's where the money came from?'

'Where else would I get eight hundred and eighty dollars?'

'On the morning of his death, Sy Spencer withdrew a thousand bucks from a cash machine. It was gone when we found him.'

Gideon broke in. 'Do you call this police work? You don't investigate. You just drop whatever you can't explain at Bonnie Spencer's front door. Obviously Sy gave it to someone. Or he bought something.'

'No,' Robby said.

'Don't say no. I knew the man. He had a great eye, and he loved to indulge himself. If he saw a hundred-dollar tie he liked, he'd buy one in every color.'

'Believe me, we checked,' Robby continued. 'There was no time for him to buy anything. And he didn't give anything to anyone. Whoever was with Sy Spencer last took the money. And we know that person was Mrs Spencer here.'

'You *know* that? How do you *know*?' Gideon asked, as if he couldn't believe our stupidity. But I could tell; he knew too.

'Because they were in bed together in the guest room of his house that afternoon.'

'Really?' There's nothing like watching a desperate lawyer trying to do an amused act.

'Yeah, really,' I broke in. 'There was some hair in the bed that wasn't Sy's. We're betting that when we get a sample of Ms Spencer's blood, it'll be a perfect DNA match.'

Bonnie's hand flew up to touch the top of her head. She remembered. She understood. She looked at me with a terrible mixture of fury and grief.

'Now, you want to know what happened the afternoon Sy was killed?' I could only talk to Gideon. I didn't have the courage to look at Bonnie anymore. 'Your client had relations with Sy Spencer. They had a disagreement. He left the bedroom. She took the thousand bucks from his pants pocket. When he went for a swim, she put on a pair of rubber thongs – '

'I don't have rubber thongs,' she said to Gideon.

' – and went downstairs. At some point, she walked to a spot right by the back porch, where she – '

I could feel Bonnie staring straight at me. Her eyes were huge. 'No. I did not do it. That money . . . I got it – '

'Okay,' I cut her off. 'Give me the number of the guy at the catalog company.'

Bonnie looked over at Gideon but didn't wait for a signal. Just as he started to shake his head no, she said, 'The man's name is Vincent Kelleher. He lives in Flagstaff, Arizona. I do three catalogs for him. *Country Cookin'*, *Juno* – that's for heavy women – and . . . God, I'm going blank on the other one right now. Oh, *Handy Dandy*. Hardware, gadgets.'

Before I could say anything, she hurried out of the kitchen, upstairs, to her office. I followed. Her hands were shaking as she leafed through her address book. 'Here.'

I dialed the number. The place wasn't open yet. Gideon came upstairs, into the office, followed by Robby. Finally, I got Kelleher's home phone from Information and woke him up. Yes, he was Vincent Kelleher. Thighs must have sensed something going on, because he came upstairs too, but the small office was too crowded for him to fit in; he stood outside the door, staring at Bonnie's *Cowgirl* poster. Yes, Vincent Kelleher affirmed, he owned several mail-order catalog companies. Yes, Detective Brady, a Bonnie Spencer had done some work for him. Off the books? I demanded. In cash? No! Did you pay Ms Spencer two thousand five hundred dollars in cash last December? No! At any other time? No! She'd done some work for him a couple of years ago, and he'd paid her . . . by check. Was she in some sort of trouble, Detective Brady?

I hung up the phone. I turned to Robby. 'He never made a cash payment to her.'

'That's what I figured,' he said.

Bonnie grabbed onto the lapel of my jacket. 'I swear to you – ' It was the first time she'd touched me. I pushed her hand away.

'Out of curiosity,' I continued, 'Mr Kelleher wants to know if the lady's in some sort of trouble.'

'I'll say she is,' Robby said. 'Big trouble.' He looked at Gideon and smiled. 'In fact, by tomorrow, I think the lady could find herself under arrest.'

'I think you and I should talk,' Gideon said to me.

'I think it's too late,' I said.

'The man's right,' Robby told Gideon. 'It's too late. Deal time is over.'

'There are not going to be any deals,' Gideon said.

'You're right,' Robby told him. 'No deals. You know why? Because your client is dead meat – and all of us know it.'

Oh, right. Vietnam vet with Purple Heart and Bronze Star. Big, brave cop with brass balls so big they clang. Except when the cars lined up in front of Bonnie's house like a cortège – Bonnie and Gideon in Gideon's BMW 735i, Robby and Thighs in Robby's silver Olds Cutlass, which was actually gray, and me – to take Bonnie to Headquarters for a blood test. I couldn't force myself to go along for the ride; I didn't have the guts to watch Bonnie being driven to her own funeral. As soon as we passed the two-block-long run of stores that was downtown Bridgehampton, I cut north off the main street and tore along the back roads until I got to the highway. Then I floored it. A hundred and ten.

Big stud in a Jaguar. When I got to Headquarters, way ahead of them, I couldn't even make myself go into Homicide. I went into a stall in the men's room and sat down on the can.

I was afraid to face Bonnie.

No, I was afraid to face what I had done. I sat there, heart hammering, realizing I was the butt of some Almighty joke: This woman who somehow had come to mean a lot – no, everything – to me, this woman who I couldn't imagine living without, was, due to my sharp investigatory skills, my crafty persuasiveness, my flawless logic, going to go to jail and would come out an old lady. I would never see this woman, this enchantress, again.

Whatever the hell her magic was, this woman was able to do what no one else had ever done before: bring me to life. But before I could solve the mystery of what her power was, I solved the mystery of Sy Spencer's murder. Oh, I was one shrewd dude. I'd broken her spell.

So now I was totally, wholly and entirely without her, without any hope of touching her or talking to her, for the rest of what will be, at best, thirty or forty years of my lifeless life. I would move through marriage, kids, more homicides, grandchildren, retirement, as though moving through a thick and dirty fog.

There I was, a real man. A homicide detective, sitting on a toilet because I was afraid to face some killer with a shining braid who makes good coffee and has a wonderful dog.

But I got myself under control, except for one or two trembling breaths. Still, I couldn't leave for another five minutes because some guy from Sex Crimes or Robbery could come in to take a leak and when I passed him, I might suddenly get the shakes, or even burst into tears. He would realize then that, somehow, I was not the tough guy he and I and everybody else were so convinced I was.

So I just hid out in the toilet until I could become a man again.

Bonnie and Gideon, while not true locals, had probably lived on the South Fork long enough to know how to get to the Long Island Expressway without having to wait in the summer traffic caused by Yorkers, who, while normally the world's pushiest people, were totally feeble when it came to driving: sitting passively in their overheating cars, moving at the speed of a slug, on their way to buy a bottle of balsamic vinegar for thirty dollars. Their city brains could not comprehend the concept of turning off main roads. Naturally, all this would change the second *New York* magazine published an 'Insiders Tell Their Secret Hamptons Shortcuts' article.

But Bonnie and Gideon wouldn't take a shortcut. What was waiting for them that would make them want to rush over to Headquarters? And Robby and Thighs weren't going to push them; they knew just enough about the South Fork of Suffolk to know that a road on a map did not necessarily mean a road in reality. Why risk a wrong turn, wind up in the middle of a field of cauliflower and have Gideon reconsider and decide to spend a few days fighting the blood test, litigating the unlitigable? So they'd creep along with all the other cars. They could be another thirty, forty minutes. An hour even.

I left the men's room and dragged myself into Homicide. Since we work on shifts, two or three guys share a desk. Hugo the Sour Kraut was at mine. I waved at him to stay put and sat down at Robby's. Two minutes later, Ray Carbone stuck his head into the room. He was wearing his congenial expression, like he wanted to talk about the exit wound in Sy's skull, or the Jungian theory of personality, so I picked up the phone, dialed the number for time and made a show of holding on, expectant, like I was waiting to speak to some Ultimate Witness. 'Eastern Daylight Time, ten-fourteen . . . and twenty seconds,' the computer voice said. Carbone saluted goodbye and left. I was too exhausted to even hang up the phone, so I just sat there, listening to time passing. 'Eastern Daylight Time, ten-sixteen . . . and thirty seconds.'

I opened Robby's drawer, searching for a pen so I could look like I was taking notes. No pens, but there were a couple of near-empty bottles of breath freshener drops, a business card from Mikey LoTriglio's lawyer and, toward the back, Robby's file on Mikey. I took it out: Michael Francis LoTriglio, aka Mikey LoTriglio, aka Fat Mikey, aka Mickey Lopkowitz, aka Mr Piggy, aka Michael Trillingham. Faxed forms and computer printouts from NYPD and the FBI showing his arrest record: extortion, loan-sharking, conspiracy to sell stolen securities, tax evasion. And homicide, twice. Richie Garmendia of the Retail Butchers Union had been found floating under a West Side pier with his skull battered in. And Al Jacobson, an accountant for a carting company, was missing and presumed dead, death reportedly caused by being dropped in a cement mixer and thereby becoming part of Battery Park City in Lower Manhattan.

With all his arrests, Mikey had been brought to trial only once, on tax evasion. Well, twice. Two hung juries, and the government had severed him from their case.

'Eastern Daylight Time, ten-eighteen . . . and ten seconds.' I closed my eyes and pictured Bonnie as I'd last seen her; she had changed clothes to come to Headquarters. I'd watched her walk downstairs in a black cotton sweater tucked into a straight white skirt, and black-and-white high heels. She must have put on some makeup, because her eyelids had turned bronze and her lips looked like she'd been eating raspberries. It wasn't Bonnie; it was a tall and very tasteful tragic figure. She wore long gold earrings and looked heart-sick.

I opened my eyes but couldn't shake the vision of her, so I made myself look down at the file again. Robby had made lots of notes in his rounded fourth-grade penmanship: about Mikey's mob associations, including known hit men, about his use of his family's business as a front for Family business, about his friendship with Sy and his investment in *Starry Night*. Detailed notes, pages and pages. I could see how he'd prepared for Monday's Homicide meeting, for making his case that Mikey was our guy.

But at the meeting I'd convinced him our guy was Bonnie. And starting after the meeting, the pages had become paragraphs, the paragraphs, phrases. '8/22. 4:10.' That was about a half hour after Mikey and his lawyer had been in, not that Robby or I had cared all that much. We both knew by then who'd killed Sy. 'Spoke to Nancy Hales, bookkeeper for Starry Night Productions, Inc.,' he'd written. 'Finally admitted Mikey tried bribe for info re movie $$.'

I turned to the next page, but it wasn't there. I hung up on 'Daylight . . .' Something wasn't sitting right. No more notes? Even if Robby had a videotape of Bonnie pulling the trigger, he should have asked some more questions. Like what did 'Finally admitted' mean? Like how much was the bribe? Like how had it been offered to the bookkeeper? On the phone? In person? Like had this bookkeeper known what a bad guy Mikey was? How had she said no? Or hadn't she? I put the file back in the drawer, leaned back and closed my eyes. Relax. Not my problem.

But then I opened my eyes, leaned forward and called Nancy Hales in the *Starry Night* production office at a film studio in Astoria, Queens. I gave her a song and dance about Robby being assigned to another case; I was just checking up on his notes.

'How many times did you speak with Detective Kurz?' I asked casually.

'That once in person.'

'In your office?'

'Yes. And two times on the phone.' Her voice was husky and overly slow. She was dull-witted or southern, or maybe she was into phone sex.

'Tell me about Mikey LoTriglio.'

'I told – '

'I know, but I want to hear it in your own words, not rely on his notes.' Then I added: 'Believe me, it'll be better for you.'

'He said . . .' She was nervous. 'The detective said I wouldn't be in any trouble if I cooperated.'

'You won't be. Now tell me what happened.'

'Mr LoTriglio came up to the office one day looking for Mr Spencer, but I think he knew Mr Spencer wouldn't be there. Do you know what I mean?'

'Yeah.'

'He asked for the bookkeeper, and someone brought him over to my desk. He pulled over a chair and asked if anything funny was going on. I said, "Funny?"'

'What did he say?'

'He said, "Don't shit me." So I told him I couldn't discuss business with him and he told me he was a major investor and I said I knew that but he'd still have to get Mr Spencer's okay.' She paused. 'He was . . . I kind of knew he was a gangster. Not like *Scarface*, but still, I was scared. That's why I did it.'

'Took his money?' I asked.

'Uh-huh.'

'How did he give it to you?'

'He sort of slipped it under my telephone.'

'I mean, in what denominations?'

'Fifties.'

'How many fifties?'

'Didn't the other detective tell you how much it was?'

'I thought you were cooperating,' I said.

'Ten fifties.'

'And what did he get for his five hundred dollars?'

'The Lindsay Keefe business.'

'Do me a favor, Nancy. I'm making my own notes. Let's start fresh. Spell out the Lindsay business for me.'

'That the extra location scout and the two extra trailers and Teamster drivers and Nicholas Monteleone's bonus on signing and four interior sets we built . . . well, all that didn't exist. Sy just had me put in some invoices and . . . kind of move some money around.'

'Move some money to Lindsay?'

'Yes.'

'How much did it come to?'

She whispered: 'Half.'

'Half a million?'

'Uh-huh.'

'Why did Lindsay Keefe get an extra half million?'

Her whisper became even softer. 'I don't know. I guess she was threatening to quit.'

I didn't get it. Sy had wanted to get rid of her. 'When was this?'

'Three days before the start of principal photography.'

I took a deep breath. 'Nancy, why would he give her a half million more? She had a contract, didn't she?'

'Yes.'

'So?'

'So he was crazy about her. I mean *crazy*. Like he would have done *anything* to keep her happy.'

Or, at that point, to keep her in his bed. No big deal.

He was Sy Spencer. He could get creative with the budget, and when *Starry Night* made ninety mil, who'd miss a few hundred thousand? And so, for a million plus another half million, Sy had bought himself a truly superior lay – and a lemon of an actress who was killing his movie. That must have been some kick in his arrogant ass. 'Did you get the sense that Mikey LoTriglio had heard any of the negative talk about Lindsay's acting that was going around?'

'I think . . . There *were* a lot of rumors. I'm pretty sure he heard about them.'

'How?'

'Probably by paying off someone in the crew.'

'Like who?'

'I don't know.'

'And then he found out from you that Sy had diddled the books to give Lindsay a five-hundred-thousand-dollar bonus.'

'Yes.'

'And how did Mikey react?' Silence. 'Didn't Detective Kurz talk to you about this?'

'No. I would have told him, but he didn't ask.'

'And you didn't volunteer.'

'No. I was scared.'

'Tell me what Mr LoTriglio said.'

'He said . . . when he heard the exact figure on what Lindsay had gotten, he said, "My friend Sy is goin' to get his nuts chopped for this." And then he walked out.'

CHAPTER 12
❧≈◦⋐❦

What the hell was wrong with Robby? Jesus, if I'd been the one assigned to Mikey LoTriglio, I'd have been kicking chairs, screaming at the cop who kept insisting the perpetrator was the ex-wife. So what if Bonnie slept with Sy, I'd yell. There's a law against that? She humped him, kissed him goodbye, told him to call when he got back from LA, and then went home. Period. Oh, your she-can-shoot theory? Is that your problem, jerk? Well, what about Mikey – or one of his boys? And what about Lindsay? Turn on your VCR and watch her toting a rifle, in loving color.

And even if the ex-wife had, in fact, slept with a .22 between her legs all the years when she was a kid in Utah, could she still bag Sy? Could such a nice, warm lady plan such a mean, cold killing? This is life we're talking about here, not goddamn Agatha Christie, where Lord Smedley-Bedley's black-sheep cousin gets murdered after crumpets with the vicar on a rainy afternoon.

And listen, jerk, I'd bellow, and maybe jab my pen toward him, like it was a dart, *listen*! What about the criminal personality? Who is more likely to shoot when betrayed? A kissed-off screenwriter who's slept with every other guy on the South Fork, who's so used to hearing guys tell her goodbye that she could write their rejection speeches for them? Or a Known Bad Guy who's just discovered his alleged good friend is screwing him out of half a million bucks?

If I were Robby I'd have fought. I'd have built up a terrific case against Fat Mikey. Against Lindsay, come to think of it. She was a movie star, a professional egomaniac, and Sy was about to blow her out of the water.

So what the hell was wrong? When I'd sat at the meeting, stacking up the cards against Bonnie, why hadn't Robby knocked down a few of them? It would have been so easy.

I had a fast thought: Oh, Jesus, could I have destroyed an innocent life?

But then I told myself: Asshole, look what she's done to you! Miss All-Natural is a brilliant con artist. First she looks up from the warrant, gives you that look of pain, then that disbelieving how-can-you-hurt-me? stare. And then the cold shoulder. She's got great ESP, that Bonnie. You thought you were so cool, but she's known all along you've had a major thing for her. So she sits and shivers by the fireplace on a hot day. Lets her mouth quiver. Swears she didn't do it. Why shouldn't she swear? She knows how the conned want so desperately to keep being conned. But then she sees she can't get to you . . . Well then, okay, too bad; she gave it her best shot. So she goes upstairs and puts on a sexy skirt and gold earrings.

But what if she's telling the truth?

Then why did she lie so much?

Well, what if she lied through her teeth . . . but still didn't kill him?

Didn't kill him? Take Bonnie Spencer, Mikey LoTriglio and Lindsay Keefe. Which one of the three is most likely —

Robby came in just then and hurried over. He didn't like my feet up on his desk, near his pen set, but he was too excited to waste time in a protest. 'Bonnie's in the lab!' Only his nervousness that the side of my shoe would smear the 'Detective Robert Leo Kurz' brass plate kept him from positively gurgling with delight. 'She's down there now. With the lawyer.' I didn't budge. 'What's wrong? Don't you want to go?'

'What about Mikey's payoff?' I asked him. He gave me a village idiot look that was so completely moronic I knew it was fake. 'His payoff to the bookkeeper at the *Starry Night* office.'

'Who cares?'

'I care. We know Mikey's alibi sucks shit. So he had opportunity. And now, from what the bookkeeper says, motive. Why the hell didn't you pursue that line of questioning and – '

Robby held up his hand, swift, full-palm. Stop! Aggressive, angry, like one of the neo-Nazi cretins in the police academy who demonstrate how to direct traffic. 'Wait just one second here, Steve.' Huffy. Definitely huffy. 'We *have* our perpetrator, who we all agree is our perpetrator, over in the lab, as we speak.' He did an about-face, marched out of Homicide, down toward the lab.

I kept up with him. What a born dork Robby was, with his white Tums crust at the edges of his mouth. He radiated hairspray scent. His suit matched his pale-beige loafers. A fucking dork suit: the fabric was supposed to look luxurious, like nubby linen, but instead it looked as if it was cut from a bolt of cloth that was having an allergic reaction to its own ugliness. You could see its unhealthy sheen; it was covered with minuscule bumps.

'Hey, I want to talk to you for a second,' I called out. He didn't stop.

We got to the door of the lab just as Bonnie and Gideon were leaving. She was pressing a gauze pad against the bend in her arm where they'd drawn blood, so she didn't see me until I said 'How'd it go?' She glanced up, startled, terrified, the nice girl in a horror movie who had just seen the monster.

I might as well have been one. She tried to get away so fast that she wound up stepping on her own high-heel shoe and would have fallen if Gideon hadn't grabbed her arm. She slumped against him for just a second, until she regained her balance.

For that one second, though, Bonnie's eyes were on my face. Finally, there it was: absolute fear. Eyes floating in the whites, unfocused, in terror of the monster who was stalking her. And then she was rushing away, down the hall. Her long, fast strides were restrained only by the knee-hobbling hem of her skirt, so Gideon was able to keep up.

After they disappeared around a corner, Robby said: 'I'll go over to court, get the arrest warrant.' He started to go.

I grabbed the sleeve of his repulsive suit. 'Not yet.'

'What do you mean, not yet?'

'I mean, we'd be making a mistake to push it.'

'No, we wouldn't.'

'Yes, we would.'

'No!'

'Robby, how many man-hours have you put in looking for that .22? Not enough. We've got to give it a better shot.'

His upper lip drew up, so he was almost snarling. His bared teeth were the same color as his beige suit and

241

shoes. 'What the hell's the matter with you?' he demanded. 'You going soft? You going to risk letting her run?'

'Where is she going to run to?'

'Anyplace. Listen, I was in her closet. She has hiking boots! A backpack!'

'For crissakes, she's a Jewish broad. What the hell is she going to do? Go to ground in the wetlands?' I didn't tell him that was precisely it: the waking nightmare that had stolen five hours off my sleep the night before. Bonnie *could* get away. I'd almost choked myself with my sweaty, twisted rope of a sheet as I tossed around. She could disappear, live off the land, gradually make her way north, steal a boat, get off Long Island. 'Or you think the fag lawyer's going to hide her in his wine cellar?'

'She could go back to Utah!'

'And do what? We've got the addresses of all her brothers, and her old man in Arizona. There's no place for her to hide.'

'If we bring her in now, before the weekend, we're heroes. Damn it, don't you care about your career?'

'Blow it out your ass, Robby.'

Robby banged the wall with his fist. It made a dull, undramatic thud. But his voice made up for it, blaring, amplified by the narrow corridor so the whole floor could hear him. 'You're gonna fuck up this case!'

'No! I'm going to do my job, follow up *all* the leads. I'm not going to be some ass-kisser who cuts corners because he can't wait to pucker up.' I made a wet, kissy sound in the air. ' "Yoo-hoo, Captain Shea. Here is the solution to the heinous murder that has so captured the attention of the national media. Please, *you* take all the credit. I only want the satisfaction of a job well

242

done – "' Robby brought up his fists and bounced on the balls of his feet. His keys jingled in his pants pocket. 'Holy shit! Don't hit me, Robby!'

'Shut your fucking mouth, Brady.'

'Don't hurt me! I'm forty years old.'

'Listen, you loser, son-of-a-bitch drunk, I'm going to court to get a warrant. Now.'

'Good. Get the hell out of here. And while you're on your way, I'm going in to Shea and telling him what a lazy bastard you've been, and how you're jumping the gun and handing him a case that could fall apart five seconds after it gets to the grand jury.'

It was more like a movie than life, almost a freeze-frame. I didn't move. Robby kept his fists up, but finally, slowly, opened them. His fingers spread out; it looked as though he'd decided to throttle me. Finally, I said: 'Calm down.'

'Fuck you, you dipso.'

'Listen to me. Don't rush this. You're gonna push Shea, and then the DA will find fifty loose ends – like Mikey LoTriglio. Like Lindsay.'

'Lindsay,' he sneered.

'Don't you get it? Some rag newspaper in the supermarket is going to print a picture of her from *Transvaal* holding a rifle. "Is Lindsay Keefe Trained to Kill?" Don't you get that the *Daily News* is going to do a big piece on Sy's mob connections? And don't you get that unless we can respond to every single question that could come up with one single answer – Bonnie Spencer – the department could be made to look like it's trying to pin it on some poverty-stricken sweetie-pie of an ex-wife, and you and I are the ones who'll get creamed for it?'

Robby didn't answer. And he didn't choke me. He

just lowered his hands, turned and, in his clunk-heeled beige loafers, stomped back to Homicide.

'Don't ask me about the case, Germy,' I said into the phone.

'I am not asking you about the case,' he honked in his hundred-thousand-dollars'-worth-of-New-England-schools voice. 'I am a film critic, not a gossip columnist. And I didn't ask what was wrong with your case. I asked what was wrong with you. You sound − it's hard to describe − flat. Tired.'

'I'm too old for this shit.' Having bounced the Sour Kraut from our mutual desk, I had my files fanned out in front of me, all unopened. 'Tell me about Lindsay Keefe.'

'I love it. Classic film noir. The uncouth cop falls for the ice-blonde sophisticate.'

He did it; he made me smile for a second. 'I just want to know about *Transvaal*.'

'Why?'

I hesitated, but then I said: 'I know you long enough to know you'll keep your mouth shut, Jeremy.'

'That's right, Steve.'

I saw I'd been doodling on the cover of Bonnie's file. Shaded 3-D boxes. Her initials: I realized they were mine, backwards. 'Okay, I heard Lindsay was shown shooting a rifle in the movie.' Germy made that upper-class exhaling sound that comes out between Ah! and Oh! 'What I'm asking is if − without raising bi-coastal eyebrows − you can get me the name of someone who knows what went on while they were making that movie.'

'Someone who knows whether Lindsay could actually shoot or if she just pulled the trigger and the sound editor went "Bang!"'

'Yeah.'

'Call me back in an hour.' He paused. 'And listen, from an old friend . . . You sound something less than yourself. Take it easy. All right?'

'Sure,' I said. 'I'll be fine.'

I called Lynne, hoping I'd get her machine. But she picked up. 'Hello!' Cheery, welcoming. I had nothing to say to her. I hung up the phone and dialed my brother.

'Easton, come on. *Listen*. Remember you told me Sy would never have fired Lindsay?' I asked.

'Um, he would have let her think it, but he never would have.' Easton sounded thick-tongued, slightly dopey.

I'd obviously woken him from one of his ritual marathon sleeps: striped pajamas on, phone on a pillow on the floor to muffle the ring, curtains safety-pinned to ensure unending darkness. His sleeps were escapes that would last for weeks, except for shuffling excursions in flapping leather slippers down to the kitchen, where he'd spoon soft food – ice cream, canned fruit cocktail – into his mouth listlessly, as though feeding a baby who wasn't hungry. Occasionally, he'd offer a thin excuse: The doctor says it's probably mono, and then give a feeble cough. Easton's sleeps came whenever he realized he wasn't going to be superstar insurance agent, or hero of men's wear. He'd start going in to work late, coming home early – sometimes after lunch. A boss would call, first to lecture, finally to fire him, and Easton would simply mumble, If that's how you want it, and hang up the phone and go back to sleep.

Well, what did he have to stay awake for now that Sy was dead? 'East, come on. Focus for a second.'

Irritable. 'I *am* focused.'

245

'Do you think there was any chance Lindsay knew that Katherine Pourelle had been sent the *Starry Night* script, or that Sy was going to see her out in LA?'

Easton tried to rise to the occasion. You could almost see him shaking his head, clearing out the fog. 'Did she know?' he repeated. Suddenly he sounded alert, interested, protective. 'Why do you want to know about Lindsay?'

'Look, I know you're – you know – kind of attracted to her, but try to be objective, East. This is a homicide.'

'And you think if Lindsay had found out somehow . . . Steve, that's idiotic.'

'Probably. But I can't leave any loose ends untied.'

'Give me a second,' he said. 'I must have dozed off for a couple of minutes. I'm still a little groggy.' I reached into my drawer and retrieved a combo key ring–nail clipper I'd gotten at a grand opening of a car wash and gave myself something resembling a manicure. It seemed I'd have time to take off my shoes and socks and do my toes, but finally Easton spoke, although hesitantly. 'Lindsay had . . . a certain curiosity about Sy's business.'

'What does that mean in real life? She was nosy?'

'If you want to look at it superficially.'

'Give me a for-instance.' He didn't reply. 'Stop the chivalry shit. I'm not looking to arrest her. I'm just looking to finish the paperwork on this case.'

'Is Lindsay a real suspect?'

'No.'

'Who is?'

'Not for public consumption, okay?'

'Of course not.'

'The ex-wife, Bonnie. But Lindsay shot a rifle in a movie called *Transvaal*, so I've got to check her out some more. Now, how was she nosy?'

'The word I used was "curious". You see, Sy usually swam his laps after she did hers. So when she came back into the house, supposedly to take a shower, she'd actually go into his study.'

'And?'

'And pretend to be looking for a stamp or a paper clip, but actually go through whatever papers were lying on the desk. Oh, I just remembered. Sy had one of those pocket computer calendars. One time, I saw her pressing some buttons on it. My guess was she was reading off all his entries. I know this makes her sound like a sneak. She really wasn't. Sy was more than her lover; he was her employer. She knew as well as anyone how brutal he could be with anyone he wasn't pleased with, and he definitely wasn't pleased with her. So she was protecting her own interests, so to speak.'

'Bottom line, Easton. Do you think she knew why he was going to LA?'

'Bottom line?' He gave it real thought. I waited. 'She *was* getting curiouser and curiouser. Extra visits to his study. Checking out the fax machine early in the morning, before Sy was up, before she went to the set.'

'How do you know what went on so early?'

'I liked to get in early. This is . . . embarrassing.'

'Listen, do you think you're the first guy in human history to get stupid over a girl? I'm your brother. You can tell me. You went in early because you wanted to see her?'

'Yes. But she never really tried to hide her curiosity from me. Either she thought I was so much a part of the household that I was like wallpaper – there, no threat – or she sensed how I felt about her, and felt safe.' Easton sighed. 'I think that must have been it. But in any case, what you want to know is if I think Lindsay knew Sy was

247

going to take some action. And the answer is yes. I do.'

Germy called back a half hour later. He'd spoken to the producer of *Transvaal*. They had hired some South African game warden as a technical adviser, and he'd given Lindsay a couple of hours of lessons with a rifle. The producer had no idea what kind of a shot she was, but he'd added she'd had a quickie affair with the game warden but then switched over to a black actor who was playing an anti-apartheid activist.

Gideon called around noon. He was back in his office. He'd hired Bill Paterno for Bonnie, but wanted one last talk with me. In person. Man to man. He said that without self-consciousness. Could he come back to my office? I glanced over at Robby. He was hunched over his desk, going over all the DNA and lab reports, index finger inching down the pages, lips moving, calling on the God of Science to bless his crusade against Bonnie Spencer. He looked pasty and intense and a little nuts, so I gave Gideon quick directions to the nearest diner, told him to meet me there at one-thirty, that he could have as long as it took me to finish a chicken salad and bacon sandwich and a vanilla malted – which, when I was minding my manners, took approximately four minutes.

The Blue Sky had once been a regular greasy spoon, but the Greek guy who'd bought it had done it over, so now the spoon was hardly greasy at all. The walls were paneled in fake oak, the ceilings dripped with fat-globed chandeliers and hanging plastic plants. The menu, a listing of every food product capable of being microwaved, was almost as thick as the Bible. The owner hovered over us, pad open, ready to transcribe whatever we happened to say.

I looked at Gideon. 'The cook usually washes his hands

248

after he takes a dump, so you can have the chicken salad or tuna fish and not die. The hamburgers taste like snow tires. They nuke everything else.'

'Don' listen to him,' said the owner. 'He's a stupid cop. All my food's good. Today the special is nice flounder on a bed of spinach wit' feta cheese.'

Gideon said no thank you, he'd already eaten. Just an iced coffee. I ordered, and the owner strolled off, toward the kitchen.

'Go ahead,' I said. 'Make your pitch.'

Gideon adjusted his knife, fork and spoon and took a minute to make sure the edge of his napkin was absolutely parallel with the edge of the table. Once that was accomplished, he immediately opened the napkin and put it on his lap. I noticed that for all his clean-cut, square-jawed handsomeness, the bridge of his nose appeared to have gotten squished in the birth canal or in a fight and never popped back into place. 'I was hoping this conversation wouldn't be necessary,' he said quietly.

'It's not. You could have saved yourself the trip – and acid indigestion from the iced coffee. All we're doing now is neatening up a few loose ends. Probably by tomorrow we'll be arresting your client.'

'Her name is Bonnie.'

'I know that.' My cheeks began to ache; I could feel the pressure of tears someplace way behind my eyes. I wasn't going to lose it, but if I was, it wouldn't be in front of this guy. 'Let's get on with it.'

'Why are you out to get her?'

'Mr Friedman, with all due respect, you're her friend. And this is not your field. You're personalizing a criminal investigation. And you're wasting my time and not doing your client any good. Do everybody a favor: wait till tomorrow. Let Paterno handle it. He's used to dealing with us and the DA.'

The owner came back with the iced coffee and a little bowl of teaspoon-size containers of half-and-half. Gideon waited until he was gone. 'You're the one who's been personalizing it,' he said.

'What are you getting at?'

'I'm getting at that it is morally and ethically wrong to investigate someone you've – '

Put up the umbrella, I thought, because here it comes: a shower of shit. 'I've *what*?'

'Slept with.'

Heat rises. Blood rushed up to my forehead, my ears. I was so fucking furious. Disappointed too: I couldn't believe she'd resort to something that cheesy – which shows the state I was in. I'd had no trouble believing that, with evil intent, she could plan and execute a homicide. But tell a tacky lie? Not my Bonnie! 'That's total and complete crap,' I said.

'No, it's not crap.' He was calm, at peace. Whatever shit he was dropping on me, it was shit the bitch Bonnie had made him believe.

'Your friend has a little problem in the truth department, counselor. I never laid a hand on her. I never made a suggestive remark. Nothing.'

'Now, *that's* crap.'

'Look, you don't really want that iced coffee. Go back to East Hampton, practice some real estate law, forget this conversation.' He stayed put. 'Okay, the head of Homicide's a guy named Shea. Go ahead. Talk to him. Or file a formal complaint with the department.'

'What happened between the two of you that makes you want to get her so badly?'

I looked up and saw the guy coming back with my sandwich and the malted. The food looked pale, puffed-up, dead – like something pulled out of the water, something that, before you can stop yourself, makes you gag. 'Look,' I said to Gideon, 'obviously she has you believing something went on. I'm not going to try and talk you out of it.' A piece of bacon hung out of the roll, dark, curled, wormy. 'But I'm not going to ruin my lunch and sit here listening to you tell me I copped a feel when I was questioning her, or showed her my shield and said, "Fuck me or go to jail." Okay? So take a walk, Mr Friedman.'

I could hardly hear him. 'I'm not talking about the investigation. I'm talking about what went on five years ago.'

'What?'

'Five years ago. You . . . I wouldn't call it an affair. But it wasn't just a typical one-night stand.'

'Wrong guy,' I snapped.

'She called me about it the next day. I remember. She sounded elated. She said, "Gideon, I met this wonderful man!"'

'She's lying. Or maybe she's just . . . Maybe this whole experience has made her a little crazy, if she wasn't that way to begin with.'

'Bonnie's as uncrazy as they come.'

'So maybe it's an honest mistake, and she just thought she saw me under her covers. Look, I'm sure you know it isn't any secret that a lot of guys have rolled around in that bed.'

Gideon had put a lightweight olive-green blazer over his ninja outfit. Silk probably. He rolled down a sleeve, then recuffed it. 'Bonnie told me, "He grew up here in Bridgehampton. On a farm. About two minutes from here."' I didn't say anything. I shook my head. 'I remember this conversation, Mr Brady. I'd never heard her so high. She said, "He's a cop, of all things. A detective. Very bright. And a wonderful sense of humor. I had *fun*."'

'Not with me she didn't.' He started working on his other sleeve. 'I'm sorry. I know you believe what you're saying, but it wasn't me.'

Gideon peeled the top off a little container and dumped cream into his glass. 'She said –'

'Please. There's really no point to this.'

'Let me finish. She said, "His name is Stephen Brady."' I sat across from him in the booth, still shaking my head no. 'I remember your name, because we had this long . . . well, amusing discussion about whether Brady is a WASP or an Irish name and about the . . . sexual proclivities of each group. Bonnie said she'd ask you what you were the next time she saw you.' Gideon took a packet of Equal and sprinkled a dusting of the powder into his coffee. 'She had no doubt that she'd see you again. That was the funny part: her absolute certainty that the night had been special. She'd been around a long time, knew the ropes. She was never given to self-deception. She knew what happens when you ask someone you meet in a bar –'

'What bar?'

'The Gin Mill. Over on –'

'I know where it is. Go on.'

'What else is there to say? Bonnie knew that when you invite a man you meet in a bar to come back to your house, you don't expect him to send flowers the next day.'

'She said I sent flowers?'

'No. A metaphor for romance. But she felt something had happened between the two of you. Something out of

252

the ordinary.' I rested my forehead in the palm of my hand and rubbed, back and forth. 'You can't have forgotten. Or even if she had been just another pickup to you, seeing her, seeing the house –'

'I'm telling you, I have no memory.'

Gideon's young, handsome, squished-nosed face looked more uncomprehending than angry. 'Why the vendetta if you have no memory?'

'There's no vendetta. She's guilty.'

His spoon clanged against the glass as he stirred, but his voice was very gentle. 'Why didn't you ask one of your colleagues to take over the Bonnie aspect of the investigation?'

'There was no reason to have someone else step in. I never met her before.'

'But you did. It happened.'

It took a very long time, but at last I said: 'Look, I'm an alcoholic. I've been sober for almost four years. But there are blanks in my life. Days, maybe weeks I'll never be able to recall. Maybe . . . There were a lot of women. For all I know, she might have been one of them. I had this feeling almost from the beginning that she looked familiar. I figured I'd seen her around town.'

'You don't deny it, then.'

'No. But I don't admit it either. Maybe I spent the night with her. Maybe I told her she was a terrific person. It was one of the things I always said: "It's not just the sex, babe. It's *you*. You're a terrific person." But if I did spend some time with her, I'll never know what I did or what I said.'

'For the record, you told her you loved her.'

'But I never saw her again, did I?'

Gideon sat back in the booth and crossed his arms over his chest. Relaxed, conversational. 'She said you were heavier then.' I'd dropped twenty pounds after I'd stopped drinking and started running. 'And you had a mustache. Thick, droopy.' Yes. 'That's why it took her a minute to realize it was you at her door. And do you know what went through her mind then? She thought: Who cares why he never called? He's back!'

'Mr Friedman, don't you get it? Either she did a little research on me in town and made this whole thing up – or it actually happened. But it doesn't matter. They can take me off the case, put someone else in my place, and the outcome will still be the same. Bonnie Spencer will be brought to trial on – yeah, sure – circumstantial evidence. But *strong* circumstantial evidence. Most likely she will be found guilty. And she will go to jail. And whether I slept with her or gave her a line about loving her or never met her before I rang her front doorbell won't matter one goddamn bit.'

'Bonnie was right. You are very, very bright.'

'Thanks.'

'Hear me out. You've constructed an intelligent, imaginative theory about how Sy was killed. All I ask now is that you look back at your data, put that same creativity to work again.'

I shook my head.

'Try it. Build another case. A real one this time, not a myth.'

'I can't.'

'You have to.'

CHAPTER 13

❦

I left the diner, my lunch untouched. The afternoon had
turned from plain August hot to sweltering. I thought
about finding an AA meeting but instead drove north,
aimlessly, farther from Headquarters. I pulled into the
parking lot of a shopping center. Suburban heaven, with
its open-twenty-four-hours Grand Union, its nail salon, its
frozen-yogurt store and its card shop featuring Charlie
Brown paper tablecloths, plates, cups and guest towels.

I put the top up, locked away my gun and changed into
the shorts and sneakers I kept behind the two front seats,
on the parcel shelf of the car – my gym locker on wheels. I
hooked my pager onto the elastic waistband of the shorts. I
had used my running shirt with the Clorox-eaten sleeve to
clean the dipstick, so I had to run shirtless.

The humidity was suffocating. I would gladly have
taken one of those blue bandannas I'd been laughing at all
summer, the kind New York runners were twirling and
wrapping around their foreheads, trying to look like
construction workers instead of rich idiots. And I'd even
take one of their ass packs too, with its plastic bottle of
mineral water.

For the first couple of miles through central Suffolk –
past tract houses sided with cheap, already-pitted
aluminum, where nobody, apparently, had enough
home-owning pride to stick a mailbox with a painted 'The
McCarthy's' up on a post, or plant a crab apple or a
rosebush or anything beyond the token scraggly juniper

the builder had stuck in the front lawn, past about ten acres of open grassland with a For Sale sign – I didn't think about Bonnie at all. I didn't think about anything.

I ran past a small farm, just like any on the South Fork, although here there was no sweet ocean tang in the air to obscure the harsh perfume of fertilizer and pesticides. Pretty, though: a brown field of russet potatoes, almost ready for harvest. It was edged by a border of dark-pink clover and white trumpet vines. The potatoes look good, I was thinking. A lot of Long Island farmers don't like russets because they can get all knobby, but there'd been just enough rain –

Bonnie! Not a fantasy this time. A true recollection.

Labor Day, about four in the afternoon. Inside the bar – yeah, Gideon, the Gin Mill – it was murky, and packed, like the Friday night of Memorial Day weekend. But the season was over, and the too-old-to-be-yuppies were no longer cruising loose, happy, expectant. The same hot-shit Yorkers now jammed against the bar, pushing each other. They were overtanned and overdesperate, with stiff, extended, sun-dried arms, hands grasping for their margaritas ('No salt!'), drinking too hard to hide their despair that another summer had passed without their falling in love, or at least finding someone who wouldn't humiliate them by guffawing – Har! Har! Har! – in a movie on the Upper East Side, or by being fat in TriBeCa, or by wearing brown suede Hush Puppies on Central Park South.

It was the perfect time for a local like me, bored with a June, July and August of receptionists and nurses, who wanted (for one night) a grown-up, dressed-for-success lay. Easy pickings: By that first Monday in September, I knew the thirty-five-year-old lady corporate vice-presidents would have stopped playing the Geography

Game, with an automatic You're Out for Hamptons hicks. I also knew all those frosted-haired, lip-glossed, scrawny-necked financiers would no longer be muttering 'Really?' and then two seconds later going to the ladies' room when they heard I was a cop. These women at the Gin Mill hadn't caught themselves a banker or a doctor or even an accountant without his CPA. So now it would be: 'I envy you, living here year round' and 'A *homicide* detective! Tell me, how can you stand looking at . . . what's the best way to express it? Looking at the dark side of the human condition day after day?'

Except instead of hitting on one of those, I spotted Bonnie. If I had to say why I chose her, it could have been because it was the Summer of the Perm, and she was the only woman without cascades of frizzles. Or because she wasn't wearing an outfit, one of those things with plaids and stripes and flowers, where nothing matches on purpose.

Bonnie leaned against the bar, foot up on the rail, standing tall among the other women. She was working her way through tissues and keys in the side pocket of a short red-and-yellow-plaid skirt, on her way to money to pay for a beer. She wore a red tank top. As I maneuvered toward her, I could see the sheen of her broad, tanned shoulders. Silky skin, I thought, not leathery. I put my hand on her shoulder. It was silky. I said: 'I'll buy,' and gave the bartender three bucks for her beer. She smiled. 'Thanks.'

But that was all that would come: an image. I kept on running, sweat dripping down onto the blacktop, for another two miles, all around the farm, then back past the grassland, into that pathetic stretch of aluminum-sided Long Island. I'd been hoping to clear my head. But all I could recollect in that killing heat was Bonnie

Spencer in the crisp, conditioned air of the Gin Mill, holding her beer in front of her with two hands, the way a bride would hold her bouquet. Her hair was short then, a little choppy; maybe she'd tried to give herself a sophisticated haircut, but she'd wound up looking like a wood nymph's older sister instead. The recessed lights over the bar made her arms and shoulders gleam.

I walked around the parking lot a few times to cool down, except the air was so thick and humid all I was able to do was stop wheezing. I hung around for another five minutes, hoping for a breeze, but none came, so I got into the car and used the oil-streaked T-shirt as a towel. The pager had rubbed against my skin, and there was a dark-red bruised spot on my right side.

I got into the Jag, sprayed a little Right Guard under my arms and then contorted myself to get back into my shirt, tie and suit fast, before some housewife could peer down and catch me humping the steering wheel as I pulled up my zipper. I kept replaying the scene in my mind.

'I'll buy.' Putting down my drink — vodka with a wedge of lime — and handing three folded singles to the bartender.

Bonnie's smile, so radiant that for a second I felt light-headed. 'Thanks.'

I went into the supermarket and bought a big bottle of club soda. My face must have been close to purple, because the expressline cashier said, 'Y'oughta watch it, hon. This heat and all.'

'I'll buy,' I said to Bonnie.

'Thanks.'

I sat in the car again, glugging down the soda, trying to recreate what happened next. Logically I would have said 'Steve Brady' and she would have said 'Bonnie Spencer,' and a couple of minutes later maybe we would have chuckled about two Bridgehampton rubes having to meet in East Hampton, in a phony 'genuine' gin joint with a bullshit ceiling fan and bartenders who deliberately didn't shave because scruffy was a Great Look, surrounded by city slickers in two-hundred-dollar sandals.

Except I couldn't remember anything more. Maybe nothing more had happened. Maybe, for some reason, she had just recalled what turned out to be an aborted pickup attempt. Being a screenwriter, she'd whipped up a little love story around it and, casting herself in the leading role, said to her lawyer: Here, maybe you can use this. Except Gideon had remembered her euphoria, remembered hearing my name. Whatever else he was, he was a smart man, and a savvy, probably even an ethical, lawyer. I didn't think he would lie to a cop during a homicide investigation, not even to help a friend.

Well, whatever had happened with Bonnie, it was lost to me. Too bad. I would have liked to know what it had been like, screwing her. I drove back toward the farm, put the top down again, took a leak by the side of the road and got back into the car to drive to Headquarters. I put my hand on the stick.

God almighty, it began to come back.

We took a sip of our drinks and then exchanged names and discovered we both lived in Bridgehampton, although on different sides of the tracks. 'You weren't born here,' I said.

'Which means you must have been.'

'Right. Where are you from?'

She must have said the West, or Utah, because somehow – and this came back so vividly – we got to talking about trout fishing. It turned out that she could tie her own flies. I said, I'm not much of a fisherman. I've only gone for fluke and blues a couple of times, but maybe we could go together one day. And she said, Night's better for trout, and smiled and added, Tell you what. Give me a call when you can tie at least three leader knots as easy as you tie your shoelaces, and I'll take you to the perfect mountain stream. I said, Can't I give you a call before that? and she flashed me a beautiful smile.

Just as I was thinking to myself, This is one incredible woman, somebody pushed to get closer to the bar, knocking me into Bonnie. Oh my God!

Electricity. Magnetism. Whatever the hell it was, I couldn't believe it was happening. We stood there, body against body, unable to pull apart, like victims of an uncontrollable mob, crushed together. Except we could have parted, without too much trouble. We were just being jostled by a crowd of ordinary, pushy New Yorkers. But I was so aroused, and the pressure felt so good.

And clean-cut Bonnie — courteous ('Nice of you to pay for my beer'), amiable, humorous, lover of mountains and fisher for golden trout — was as hot and irrational as I was. Her hand slid between my legs. Jesus! In the dim, smoky light of the bar, in the press of bodies, in the dehumidified, perfume- and aftershave- and mouthwash-scented air, in the noise of raised voices and clanking glasses, she was tuning out everything — and going for it. Not just to provoke me, but for her own pleasure, which, of course, became my pleasure. She let out a small, low sound. She was going to be a noisy one, a wild one.

'Let's get out of here,' we both said at the exact same time. Normally, when that happens, you laugh, but we had crossed some boundary and gone where there was no kidding around.

What happened next? We took my car to her house. I

must have been in a white heat, because I couldn't remember any conversation or anything about her street, or the downstairs of her house – only following her ass up to the bedroom and pulling off her clothes the minute we passed through the doorway.

We were just starting, but both of us were so inflamed we tore at each other, groaning, the way people do in that moment before the end. We parted for a second; Bonnie's hands were trembling, and she couldn't manage my buttons, so I undressed myself. She watched me, spellbound, and I became so excited by her intensity I couldn't finish the slow strip I'd begun. I threw off my khakis, my undershorts, my shoes.

Bonnie moved close to me and touched me for a second, to verify that what I had wasn't going to go away. Then she moved in even closer. She raised her hips, straddled me. No teasing, no foreplay; we were way past that. I pushed in right away and we stood, her back against the bedpost, screwing our brains out.

She came first. I lowered her onto the bed. I wanted to finish on top. Her arms and legs wrapped around me, and we became the two halves of a greater person.

I'd never had sex like that before. It wasn't that I was voluntarily letting go; it was that I had no control. Just when I thought that I'd ridden out the last wave, that I could catch my breath, slow things down, speed them up, subdue her, another, bigger wave knocked me senseless.

At last, her whimpers and moans turned to shrieks of pleasure. I joined her. I heard myself screaming so loud it scared me.

We lay there on top of the white popcorn bedspread, not knowing what to say to one another. It was that moment where my foot or my hand would inevitably begin to drift along the floor, searching for a sock or my shorts. Except I couldn't move. And I didn't want to go. Finally, Bonnie said: 'Think of a way we can get over the awkward silence.'

'Tell me more about fly-fishing.'

'You need an eight-foot glass rod,' she murmured. 'Don't let them talk you into bamboo.'

I held her lightly, running my hand up and down her back. Her skin was like velvet. A breeze that had a hint of autumn in it fluttered the white lace curtains.

'This is wonderful,' I said.

'I know.'

'I meant the breeze.'

Suddenly she noticed the window was open. She sat up. 'Oh, God.'

'What?'

'We were kind of loud. Just watch. One of my neighbors will think I was being murdered and call the police – after she serves the carpaccio.' I started to laugh. I hadn't told her what I did for a living. 'You won't think it's so funny when you hear the sirens.'

'Want to bet?' I pulled her back down, so she was lying facing me. 'I'm a cop. A detective on the Homicide Squad.'

'No. That would be too interesting. You're not.'

'Of course I am.' She shook her head. 'Okay, what am I?'

'I don't know. You sort of have a macho style, but you probably do something adorable. Sell children's shoes. Teeny size-two Mary Janes, with a free balloon.' She bit her lip. 'God, I'm going to die if that's what you really do.'

I forced myself out of bed and retrieved my pants from where I'd tossed them, between a little stool and one of those old-fashioned makeup tables with a skirt. Bonnie looked bewildered, then hurt; she combed her short hair with her fingers, as if preparing for a dignified goodbye. But I tossed her my shield. She caught it, too, and it had been a lousy throw. Her left hand shot out.

'Good reflexes,' I said.

'I need them. You're not exactly Sandy Koufax.'

We stared at each other across the room, she amazed that I was a cop; me, that she knew baseball. For some crazy reason, after all that had transpired, this was too intimate. Real fast, we began to talk over each other, she saying something pointless about loving whodunits, me asking if she had anything to drink. She offered iced tea or Diet Coke, but then I said '*drink* drink.' All she had was light beer and a bottle of one-step-up-from-rotgut red wine she'd bought to use for sangria, for a picnic, but it had rained. I settled for the wine. She threw on a bathrobe and went downstairs.

The minute she was gone, I got claustrophobic; I wanted out. It wasn't the room. I knew that much. It was sizable, appealing, all white except for the old wood beams and the painted blue-green chair rail. It definitely wasn't over-stuffed; there was a four-poster bed with plain wood nightstands on either side, the little stool and vanity table with its ladylike yellow-and-white-striped skirt, and a clumsy, cozy-looking club chair, covered in a shiny cotton – big yellow flowers with blue-green leaves – a stand-up lamp beside it.

But even though there was that cool breath of air coming through the open windows, I wanted to get outside. Go home, have a couple of drinks, maybe drive up to the bay afterwards, watch the sunset. I put on my shorts.

I heard her coming upstairs, so I picked up the phone. I'd say 'Damn. Yeah. Right away' when she walked in, and then tell her a fast-but-grisly homicide story: maybe a stabbing followed by arson. Something nice and graphic, full of gaping tracheas, mutilated genitals. Run while she was still gagging.

Except she came in carrying a can of Diet Coke, a wineglass, the bottle, and holding a corkscrew between her teeth. She looked so goofy. I hung up the phone and took the corkscrew. 'Calling your office?' she asked, and handed me the wine.

'Yeah. No emergencies that can't wait.' I opened the bottle, poured, drank. The pressure to escape eased a little. I'm sure we must have talked for a while, because if I had taken her in my arms again, I would have been lost. I remember stretching out on my side, letting my fingers graze over her fabulous skin, but not getting too close. It was perfection, lying there like that, feeling the warmth of her, the coolness of the breeze. The sky had lost its daytime glare and had become softer, finer: blue tinged with pink and gold.

I whispered, not to disturb the beauty: 'I love this time of day.'

Bonnie glanced at the window. 'Magic hour.' She kissed me on the mouth, but sweetly, almost daintily. 'It's a term in cinematography. The time after dawn or before dusk. Enough light for shooting, but there's a fineness, a tranquillity to it – magical light. You have to work fast, because before you know it, the enchantment is over, but while it's there . . . you can get something beautiful.'

I drank some more wine. I must have fallen asleep for a couple of minutes. When I woke up I caught Bonnie studying my face. She averted her eyes and said too fast: 'I was just wondering how you'd look without the mustache.'

'No. You were thinking: This is one hell of a man.'

'Yes.'

I let my fingers glide down, over her throat and breasts. I caressed her stomach and felt her muscles contract. Two or three good, deep kisses. And then we were at it again,

264

this time with a lust that made the last go-round seem a lighthearted tease. We were biting and clawing at each other. I heard myself growl.

Bonnie pulled back. The wildness disturbed her. She wanted to be civilized again, a sexy woman, not an animal. She got cool and urbane on me, did a couple of cute maneuvers with the tip of her tongue. Then she got to her knees to climb on top. I knew what would happen: She'd arch her back, toss her head, let her breasts bounce. Then she'd bend over and do some more tongue tricks. She wanted what I wanted: mastery.

But I didn't want well-bred sex games. I pushed her down, onto her back. We were animals, and I was the male. I wanted her to know that. I pinned down her arms, pried open her legs with my knee and started giving it to her. She was strong, and she struggled to get free, but at the same time, she was sobbing one word over and over: More.

After it was over she turned away from me. She wasn't making any noise, but I could feel her back shaking as she cried. I was kind of shaky too. I hadn't been in control at all. What if she hadn't cried for more? What if she'd wanted me to stop? Would I have?

I rested my cheek against the nape of her neck. 'Bonnie, it's okay.' She didn't say anything. 'Too rough?'

'No.'

'Too what?'

'Too much.'

'Too much what?'

'I don't know.'

I rolled her over onto her back and kissed her. Her cheeks were wet. 'Next time I'll be real suave. Okay? You'll think: Jesus, what technique!' Bonnie's face softened as she smiled; I knew she wasn't pretty, but for that second, she was so beautiful. 'I'll come up with some position where I'm all twisted up, with my head coming out of my ass and my dick pointing east. You'll have to slide on sideways.'

She wiped away the last tear with the tip of her index finger, a lovely ethereal gesture from such a big, hearty girl. 'When you were holding me down . . .'

'Tell me.'

'What if you'd been a bad person?'

'But I'm not. I'm a great person. Now let's talk about something else. Are your eyes blue-gray or gray-blue?'

'Please. I'm serious.'

I turned the pillow over to the cool side. 'Well, if you are serious, maybe you should think twice before inviting guys you've just met to come into your house.' Until I said it, I hadn't realized how much it bothered me. Angered me. Goddamn it, she had been so easy. I hadn't wanted her to reach out and touch me, a stranger. Play with me. In a public place, for crissakes. Here she was, tall and clean and fine, and she tied her own flies: a wonderful woman. But instead of a light kiss, a smile to turn down the thermostat after we'd been pushed together, she'd cupped my balls, stroked my dick; her hand was still cold from holding the beer. 'You knew absolutely zilch about me, and you said, "Let's get out of here."'

Bonnie didn't get that guilty, You-think-I'm-a-whore look I'd expected, maybe wanted. 'I thought you were better than this.'

'Hey, I'm not talking about morals. I'm talking as a cop who's seen some nice girls get hurt when things got out of hand.'

'I can take care of myself.'

'You're strong. Mountain woman, right? If someone you meet at a bar gets out of hand, you'll just use some self-defense shit you read in *Ms.* magazine. Let me tell you something, sister. Before you can stick your finger into his eyeball or crash down on his instep or knee him in the nuts, you could be raped – or dead.'

'I'm a good judge of character.'

'You think all those nice, dead girls said to themselves: "This guy's a psychopath, but he's got cute dimples"? No, they said: "I'm a good judge of character."'

For a minute she didn't say anything. Then she propped herself up on her elbow and said: 'Aren't you *starved*?'

'Yeah, come to think of it.'

'Scrambled eggs? An omelet and toast?'

I took a fast shower while she went downstairs to make supper. I put my clothes back on but went downstairs barefoot. Sitting in the kitchen and watching her in her bathrobe, flipping an omelet, I felt snug; I thought: This is what husbands must feel like. But it was strange: the homebody with the spatula didn't seem to have any connection with the wild woman I'd been fucking upstairs. Then she turned around, and I saw her mouth was swollen from all the kissing.

Bonnie handed me a blue-and-white plate with the omelet and the toast, buttered and cut in triangles. I went to the refrigerator and took out a couple of her crappy light beers. I remember we sat there in the kitchen talking for an hour or more, but I don't remember what we said.

Later, I remember thinking, as I followed her back upstairs, that Bonnie had grace. Physical grace that born athletes have. The surefooted walk, the upright, easy posture. And commonsense grace. When to kid around and when to be serious, when to talk, when to shut up.

And sexual grace. She loved having sex – and having it with me – and every kiss, every touch, every thrust was something she wanted. She didn't posture: didn't stick her ass out for admiration, even though it was admirable, didn't offer her tits up like they were twin trophies in some erotic contest. It was all natural. Graceful. No strings attached.

We must have been too exhausted to fuck, so we made love. Afterwards, I lay on my back, stared at the beams in the ceiling and thought: I did more than satisfy her. I'm important to her.

'Can I go to sleep now?' she asked.

'Sure.'

'I hope you'll stay till morning.'

'Of course I will.' I got mad, though. Did she think I was some goddamn one-night stand who was going to tiptoe out at three a.m.?

'Don't be angry,' she said. 'It's not you. It's me. I needed a little reassurance.'

'Be reassured,' I whispered.

At about three a.m. I woke up for a minute. She was sound asleep. 'Bonnie.'

Her head was resting on my arm. I could feel the flutter of her lashes as she opened her eyes. 'Hi.'

'Hi. Listen,' I said. 'I want to tell you something.'

'What?'

'I love you.'

'I love you too.' Then she asked me: 'Aren't we too old for this?'

'No. Go back to sleep.'

I got up about six-thirty. She made me coffee. I said it again: I love you. I promised I'd call her from work or, if things got crazy, the second I got off.

I got into the Jag. It had been out all night, and the leather seats were wet with dew. I drove home, wet, limp, but filled with what I suppose was joy.

I got home. Yawned. Wished I was back in bed, wrapped in Bonnie's arms. Really tired. Needed a pick-me-up. Made a double screwdriver. Drank it, then another. Called work and coughed. Said I had some lousy virus. A hundred and three. Ray Carbone said, You sound terrible. Yeah, I said. I feel like hell.

I went on a five-day bender. By the end of it, Bonnie was just a vague, irritating memory.

By the end of the following year, when I was forced to check into South Oaks for treatment for alcohol abuse – plus pancreatic insufficiency and malnutrition caused by my drinking – I had managed to wipe out her memory completely.

Bonnie Spencer never existed.

CHAPTER 14

I got back to Headquarters a little before four o'clock. Even before I saw Ray Carbone, flushed an ominous crimson, I saw Julie, the receptionist, pick up a pen and draw it across her throat. So I knew I was about to be declared dead. But since noncompliance with official department guidelines was standard operating procedure with me, I had no idea what I was going to get killed for this time. Then Carbone jerked his thumb toward the captain's office; I knew it had to do with the Spencer case – and I knew it was not going to be a routine reprimand.

And seeing Frank Shea, Captain Shea, tie knotted tight, jacket buttoned, jabbing his index finger toward a chair was not exactly reassuring. Despite the American and Suffolk County flags in back of him, Shea usually looked more like a lounge singer than a cop: a lock of Brylcreemed hair trailing over his forehead, his tie hanging unknotted, his shirt half unbuttoned, displaying a huge gold Saint Michael's medal, a crucifix, a long, curvy tooth from what must have been some large, pissed-off animal, plus three chest hairs. He put on his jacket only to see the commissioner and for funerals.

Carbone took a chair and put it beside Shea's desk, so they were both arrayed against me. 'What's up?' I asked.

'I warned you, Brady,' Shea responded.

'About what?'

'You know! Look at you!' Okay, I'd been running,

then sitting in the car with the top down, thinking about Bonnie. So maybe I was on the verge of sunstroke; I'd glanced in the rearview mirror just a couple of minutes before, in the parking lot outside Headquarters, and noticed that under the sunburn, my skin was gray. And I had a headache and couldn't stop sweating. But I didn't look *that* bad. 'Look at you!' Shea bellowed.

'What? The department has some new good-grooming directive?'

'Fuck you and die, Brady!'

I peered over at Carbone. 'Do you want to tell me what's going on?'

'Steve.' Now that Shea was playing bad cop, Carbone could get compassionate. He sounded like a cross between shrink and priest. 'Robby told us.'

'Told you what?'

Shea picked up a paperweight and slammed it down on his desk. 'That you wouldn't get a warrant!'

'Yeah? Well, goddamn right. I'm not ready to arrest yet.'

'Who the hell do you think you are?' Shea demanded. 'We've got enough evidence to send her away for life. She knows it! She's gonna flee!'

'Where?'

'Shut up! She's gonna flee while you're babbling theories about Lindsay Keefe!'

'Listen, we've been . . . a little hasty. My fault, probably more than anybody else's. But we've got to think about Lindsay. And Fat Mikey too. Shea, just cool it a second and –'

'You bastard, I listened to you once.'

'What are you talking about?'

'Remember? You told me how you were going to stay sober.'

271

'Well, fuck you. I am sober.'

'Robby Kurz says you're not.'

'I'm drinking? Bullshit.'

'Robby was genuinely upset. It killed him to tell me.' Shea paused for a second. 'He *swore* it was true! Robby saw how I kept shaking my head, not wanting to believe it, and he swore. Vodka. Drunks think there's no odor, but believe me, there's an odor. I've smelled it on people, and he said the smell was rising off your skin.'

'Robby can take a goddamn fifth of Smirnoff's and shove it up his lying ass. Listen, we had a few words. Maybe I flew off the handle. But to say I was drinking is such slander – '

'He *smelled* it. You were weaving when you walked, and – '

'No!'

'He realized it two days ago. His only mistake was holding out, trying to protect you.'

I really thought I was going to be sick. I felt the acid burn of vomit in my throat. I got very quiet. 'You think I'm drunk now?'

Carbone looked sad for me. Shea said, 'Stinko.'

'I want one of you to walk over to the lab with me. I want a Breathalyzer test.' They shot a glance at each other; they knew you could only get accurate readings for about two hours after drinking. So I added: 'Blood, urine too. Right now. I want you both to understand: I've been sober for almost four years.'

'You're all red!' Shea accused. 'You're sweating like a pig.'

'Why the hell didn't you ask me how come? Don't you think you owe me that? You want to know why I look like I'm going to get sick?' I thought fast. 'I've been out at Old Town Pond in Southampton – less than a quarter of a mile from Sy's house – walking over every goddamn inch of marshland. You know and I know that we need the weapon, and that rat-ass Robby Kurz – who's been in charge of finding it – has been sitting on his behind, shoving Danish into his mouth, writing his acceptance speech for his commendation, instead of looking for the goddamn .22. Excuse me: writing his speech and making up lies.'

'You're accusing *him* of lying?' Shea asked, with a nasty, unamused chuckle.

'Yeah.'

'Why would he lie, Brady?'

'Because he's a fanatical, ambitious, self-righteous turd. You *know* what he's like when he goes after somebody. He wears blinders; he refuses to see reality. And he's lying because he knows if he can put the lid on this fast, he can make sergeant by next month – and be first on line for your chair when you retire. Plus he's a sneaky ass-kisser who doesn't like the way I operate and wants me out of the way. He wants me out of the way so I won't stop him from arresting her. Because I've got to tell you, Frank, I might stop him. I have real doubts, and if we false-arrest her, she can make trouble. She has a big mouth.' Shea and Carbone glanced at each other. I went on: 'And Robby wants me out of the way because Bonnie was my idea to begin with – as Ray can attest – and he doesn't want me to get any credit.' All Shea did was sneer. Carbone hung his head. He really liked me. He wanted to believe me. But he'd had too much Psychology 205; he knew alcoholics are infantile, egocentric, that they lie as naturally as most people tell the truth. 'Come on, Ray. Walk me down to the lab.'

273

'Brady,' Shea said, 'you know what this bravado shit — "Take me to the lab!" — is gonna get you?'

'Yeah. Exonerated.'

'No. Because I am going to call your bluff, you son of a bitch. I want you in the lab *now*. You hear me? You built a great case, and all of a sudden, when the commissioner, the county exec, the goddamn national media is at my throat, you're sabotaging it. What are we gonna look like when the press finds out we had her and we let her slip through our fingers?'

'Frank, ask yourself: Why would I let a thing like that happen?'

'Because you've been on a binge and you've lost all sense of judgment, of decency . . .' His voice got louder, more theatrical. He grabbed the paperweight, held it in his fist and shook it at me. '. . . of obligation to the department. And to me! I stuck my neck out for you.'

I stood and turned to Ray. 'You're the psychology genius. Why would I . . . Even if I'd fallen off the wagon and went on the biggest bender of my life, what motive would I have for screwing up a case? If I thought Bonnie Spencer killed Sy, why wouldn't I drink four or five toasts to justice and arrest the bitch?'

Shea didn't give Carbone time to answer. 'Because Robby saw you with her in her house when you went in with the search warrant. He saw how you got rid of him, sent him upstairs. And he saw you nosing around after her, following her from room to room. And then, when you asked her about where she got the money in the boot, you put on kid gloves. *So* gentlemanly. Wimping out: You called that catalog guy like it was killing you. Like the *truth* was killing you.'

'Shea, this is nuts.'

'And then all of a sudden, you're onto Lindsay theories, Mikey theories. Onto *anything* that will keep Robby off Bonnie Spencer. So to answer your question: Why wouldn't you arrest the bitch? Because for some stupid, drunken reason, you've fallen for her.'

I passed the Breathalyzer test, of course. Then I walked a painted line, from heel to toe, picked up a nickel, a dime and a quarter without fumbling, recited the alphabet. It took a couple of minutes more to pee into a cup and get blood drawn. Ray stood by while the tech stuck the needle in. He said, 'Shea will be glad to hear about the breath test, and if the others come out all right – '

'You believe that feeling in love shit?'

'I don't know.'

'You know Lynne, Ray. I'm asking you, do you think when I have someone like her I'd go for an old broad that every guy in town has had a piece of?'

'I saw her when she came in for the test. She's not bad.'

'She's no Lynne.'

'Look, all I know is you have a beautiful, well-constructed case against her – I heard you present it – and suddenly you're throwing it away. *Why?*'

'Because I don't think she did it.'

Carbone shook his head. 'I can't buy that, Steve.'

'Where's Robby?'

'Why?'

'Because I want to know why he didn't have the balls to face me.'

'He would have.'

'Except?'

'Except he's down at Southampton Town Court

getting a warrant. And then he's going to arrest Bonnie Spencer.'

Bonnie opened the back door a crack. 'Do you have a warrant?'

'No. Listen, Bonnie – '

She shut the door hard, just short of a slam. I rang the bell. Nothing, except Moose right by the door, barking, trying to sound like a watchdog but giving away the game by the ecstatic wagging of her tail. I squinted, trying to see past the lace kitchen curtains. Bonnie had disappeared into the house.

I love the way cops in movies whip out a credit card, diddle a cylinder and the door springs open. I wasted about five minutes with a card, my Swiss Army knife and every key I had on my key ring. It was a bitch, because I had to do it quietly, so she wouldn't call Headquarters and claim I was harassing her. Finally, the lock clicked open and I was in.

I didn't have to do a room-to-room; Moose led me to an open door, then downstairs, to the basement. Bonnie stood by the dryer, folding a dish towel. When she looked up to greet Moose, she saw me. Jesus, did she scream!

'Bonnie, please, listen to me. I'm not here to hurt you.' Her head swiveled in a frantic search for something to protect herself with, but you can't fight off an armed and dangerous psychopathic cop with a plastic bottle of Downy. I took a step toward her, I suppose wanting to touch her, reassure her I was there to help, but she drew back, as if trying to disappear into the narrow gap between the washer and the dryer. So I kept my distance. 'I know you think I'm insane or something, but just listen, because there's not much time.' Shit. 'Not much time' was the wrong thing to say. Bonnie's eyes clouded, as if she comprehended she had only a few minutes more to live. 'Bonnie, pay attention. The guy I'm working with on this case, Kurz, the asshole with the hairspray. He left Headquarters before I did. He's going to court to get a warrant for your arrest. So time is a factor here. If he knocks on your door in the next couple of minutes, I can't . . . I can't help you. Understand?' She didn't say anything, but she was listening. She looked straight into my eyes. It was such a probing gaze I felt she could absorb all my thoughts, understand precisely what I was there for. But she just waited for me to go on. 'I have doubts. I mean, I don't think you should be arrested yet. There are still too many questions about Sy's death for us to be saying, The case is closed. I want those questions answered. I want the case to stay open. But it's your call. You can stay here, go with Kurz when he comes here for you.'

'Or?'

'Get the hell out of here. With me. Now.'

Smart girl. She thought to toss all the folded laundry back into the dryer, so it wouldn't look as if she'd run on a moment's notice. We raced out her back door, and I led her through her yard, across an open field to a small wooded area where I'd hidden the Jag, in case Robby showed. Moose sprinted after us, if something with that big a butt can be said to sprint. Bonnie got into the car, and while the door was still open, the dog leapt in, over her lap and into the driver's seat.

'Get her *out*,' I said, at the same moment as I opened the driver's door and grabbed her collar.

'When will I get back?'

277

'How the hell should I know. Two minutes, if you don't convince me.'

'What if I do?'

'I don't know.'

Suddenly she brightened. 'If you put the top down, I could hold her in my lap and there'd be room for the three of us.'

'If I put the top down, you idiot, there'd be a hundred witnesses who could say, "Oh, I saw Bonnie and her dog. They were tooling over to Steve Brady's, in his car." A hundred witnesses to my hindering prosecution. A Class D felony.'

'You mean this isn't legal?' But before she'd finished the question, she knew the answer. 'I can't let you do this.'

She put her hand on the door handle. 'Don't move,' I ordered.

She shook her head. 'No. I'm getting out of here.'

I drew my gun. 'You move, Bonnie, and I'll shoot you between the fucking eyes.'

'Oh, stop it.'

Jesus Christ. My head was pounding, I was nauseous from dehydration, I was standing there holding a gun on a murder suspect I was helping escape, and there was a hundred-pound black, hairy mongrel with its tongue hanging out sitting upright, its claws gripped nice and tight into the leather, gazing out the front window, as if waiting for a traffic light to change. 'I'm not going to talk about this now! Your goddamn life is on the line, so get that mutt out of here and let's move.'

Bonnie's voice was so low I could hardly hear her. 'The back door is closed. She can't get to her water, and if I'm not there . . .'

I stuck my gun back in my holster, hauled Moose out of the car and climbed into the driver's seat. Which of course was the cue for Bonnie to open her door and get out. 'Get back in!' I shouted. She shook her head. I started the engine. 'Goodbye.' Bonnie whistled, two high, quick notes. Moose raced around to her side and Bonnie pushed her in.

And that's how we came to drive to my house with Bonnie in the passenger seat, me in the driver's seat, and fatso Moose stretched over both our laps, barking with pleasure at this wonderful game.

Migrant workers' shacks not being known for expansive rooms or cathedral ceilings, the architect-entrepreneur-loser I'd bought my house from hadn't had much space to work with, so he'd made most of the place into a 'family area,' one main room that served as kitchen, den, dining and living room. Then he hacked off a little at each end, so that when he was taking potential buyers around, he could make one of those *Voilà!* gestures with his hand and say, 'To sleep . . . ,' then wait for the Yorkers to say, '. . . perchance to dream,' and they could all be good friends and bask in the radiance of each other's culture, plus make a nice, civilized deal. Except I'd rather have gotten strung up by the nuts than say '. . . perchance to dream', and the architect had gotten real nervous because he knew I was a cop and therefore I might think the 'To sleep . . .' meant he was making a pass, because he wore a ponytail, and this could queer the deal in every sense. So he'd just added, 'The bedroom,' real fast and left it at that.

The master bedroom, like the rest of the house, had come furnished – since this was to be the model for the hundreds of migrant-worker shacks he had dreamed of renovating. But the bed he'd put in was just large enough for midgets to do it in the missionary position, so I'd gotten rid of it and put in a king-size bed. Once I did that, there was just enough space to get to the closets and the bathroom.

On the opposite side of the house, he'd taken the same amount of square footage and stuck in two guest rooms, connected by a bathroom. I led Bonnie into the first, which wasn't much different from the second, except instead of scallops and conch shells stenciled on the floors and around the top of the walls, it had pineapples. Since I hardly ever went near this part of the house, I'd forgotten about them, and about the hideous lamp with a green shade and a base of some fat sticks tied together with rawhide the architect had told me was a rustic touch I might conceivably wish to change. The poor guy was such a basket case because he couldn't sell his house; I wound up putting in a bid that same day.

I pulled down the shades. 'Don't get the wrong idea,' I said, my back to Bonnie. 'This is to make sure you're not seen.'

'I won't get the wrong idea.' Her voice had a tremor. That was the only sign she was as terrified as I sensed she was.

'Not that I get a lot of company, but just in case.' When I turned back to her, she was sitting, primly, on a small ladder-back chair. I sat on the edge of the bed, but because the room was so small, our knees were about four inches apart. 'Now, I want to hear what actually happened, right from the beginning. Every detail, from the minute you first spoke to Sy or laid eyes on him again. Unless you'd been in touch with him all the years since the divorce.'

'No.'

'Okay, but first, I want to clear up something.'

'You mean about — '

'No.'

But she couldn't let it be. 'Gideon called. He told me you have no recollection that you and I . . . that you and I had met.'

'Look, I don't have time for that now.' I was detached. Professional. 'What I want to clear up is your last lie.'

'You make it sound like it's the last of a hundred thousand.'

'It is, give or take a few.'

'If I'm such a liar, why would I tell the truth now, when the police are closing in on me?'

'Because you're desperate.'

'Well,' she said, in that trembling voice, 'I guess I am.' She dropped her head and stared down at her hands, folded on her lap. She had beautiful, long-fingered hands, with nice, no-polish oval nails, hands you would see in commercials for hand lotion.

'Okay, why did you make up the story about the eight hundred eighty bucks we found in your boot?'

'That *was* the truth.'

'Bonnie, understand one thing. You shit me, you're out of here.'

'Please, call him again.' I shook my head. 'Try to understand,' she pleaded. 'Vincent Kelleher is a very nervous, not-too-successful businessman who sells pot holders that look like armadillos, and size fifty-four sweatsuits in pink, aqua or lilac with appliqués. All of a sudden, this nebbish gets a long-distance phone call from a detective asking him about money he slipped me off the books. An illegal payment. He was always nervous about doing it, and when you called, he must have been convinced Eliot Ness and the tax squad would swoop down and arrest him.'

'You're good, Bonnie. Really good.'

'No. If I were that good, you would have believed the lies I did tell. I wouldn't be in this mess now. Please, call Vincent Kelleher.'

But just then my pager squeaked: 'Brady call Carbone ASAP.' I told her not to move, and I hurried across the house, into my bedroom, and closed the door.

Carbone asked where I was, and I told him I'd gone home after sixty hours of being on, because I was wiped, and sick of the shit he and Shea had handed me, but did he want me in for another Breathalyzer test, to make sure I wasn't sitting around with a bottle of Canadian Club and a straw? He said, Look, maybe we were too hasty, and Robby, not being a drinking man, might have misread some of the signs and . . . And *what*? I demanded. There's no sign of Bonnie Spencer, he said. Is Robby hysterical? I asked. Yes, and so is Shea, and if you think the commissioner isn't shitting a brick, then you're not thinking. Hey, Ray, everybody should calm down. It's six-thirty. The cool of the evening is upon us. Maybe she's down at the beach. Maybe she's having dinner with a friend. Tell everybody to relax. Have a drink – on me. Look, you want me to check around? He said, Maybe that would be a good idea. Okay, I said, I'll surveil her place until you can get someone else over there, then I'll check around, make a few calls. Just do me a favor. Page Robby. Get him the hell away from her house, because if I see him, I swear to God I'll kill him. Carbone said all right. He was about to hang up when I inquired: They finish my pee and blood workup yet? You're okay, Steve. Thanks. Be reasonable, he said.

We've got an anxiety-provoking situation here. A lot of pressure. Sometimes people make errors in judgment. I asked him if Shea realized he had made an error in judgment, or would I have to piss into a Dixie cup every day? Carbone, being patient, said, Shea knows the results of the tests, and he's not a stupid man. But let's face it: the two of you don't have a natural affinity. He let you back on the squad because he needed you, not because he liked you or trusted you, which I guess isn't news. Not by a long shot, I said. Carbone said, So do yourself a favor, Detective Brady. Earn a gold star. Bring in Bonnie Spencer.

The engine on Robby's car was running as I drove up to Bonnie's, and when I pulled over beside him, he flung the arrest warrant into my car and peeled out — as fast as an Olds Cutlass can peel — before he had to look me in the eye or hear what I had to say. He knew what it was, though: I was going to get him. And I knew what his response would be: Not if I get you first.

A few minutes later, two Southampton Town PD squad cars pulled up. They were supposed to hang around until someone from Suffolk County Homicide came to relieve them, so I handed them the warrant to pass along and told them I was just going to check out the house one more time. I slipped on a pair of rubber gloves carefully, ostentatiously, as if getting ready to perform neurosurgery, and went in. Five minutes later I came out with some of Bonnie's underwear and a T-shirt folded flat in one pocket, along with her toothbrush, and a Ziploc with Purina Dog Chow in the other. I swung two evidence bags with a pair of sneakers and a hairbrush as I walked down the front path, then gave a mock salute to the Southampton cops before I drove off.

Some blithe spirit. My hands were clammy, my stomach churning. Not for any rational reason, like I knew I was destroying my entire professional and personal life, to say nothing of risking two years in the can for hindering prosecution by rendering criminal assistance to a person who has committed a Class A felony — like second-degree murder. I was actually very clear about the consequences of the devastation I was bringing on myself. I remember I contemplated what a felony conviction could do to my pension rights, wondered whether they had AA meetings at the Green Haven Correctional Facility and decided that because I had a couple of good friends in the Suffolk County DA's, maybe they'd only go for a misdemeanor. But the drippy palms, the twisting gut, had nothing to do with these objective considerations.

No, I drove back to my house with an unswallowable lump in my throat because I was afraid Bonnie would be gone. She'd think fast, as she had the week before, at Sy's, when she'd killed him, and do what she thought she had to do: run. *No.* She hadn't killed him. I did believe her. But she'd have visions of the jury nodding, convinced, as the People summed up its circumstantial case against Spencer, and she'd run. Or just be frightened, and want someone to hold her, comfort her, kiss the top of her head, like her friend Gideon, and she'd run. Or knowing Bonnie, be a good, chin-up American, face the music, trust in God and the Constitution, and she'd run, find a phone, call Homicide and ask, Is Detective Kurz in?

Oh, Jesus. What would I do if she wasn't there?

It was Thursday night, but weekenders were already pouring in. Traffic had gotten even heavier than when I'd left for Bonnie's a half hour earlier; it was like one endless, metallic reptile snaking its way east. And every person in those thousands of cars was an important person, with important things to do. They *had* to hear what last-minute truly fun invitations were on their answering machines so they could break the dates they'd already made. They *had* to change into the three-hundred-dollar black gauze shirt. They *had* to refresh their potpourri before their houseguests arrived. There was fresh mozzarella oozing in the shopping bag on the back seat, wetting their baguettes, an intolerable situation that *had* to be stopped.

Not a single car would defer and let me cross Montauk Highway. I honked and flicked my brights at a new 560SL, made eye contact with the driver and then didn't look back at the road; I kept staring at him – and driving. It unnerved him enough that at the last possible second, he slammed on his brakes. Hatred disfigured his jowly face, but he knew I looked demented enough to actually hit a Mercedes.

Then I floored it back to my house. Except I had to stop when the guardrail went down at the train tracks. It was the longest fucking train in the history of the Long Island Rail Road.

I rushed into the house and tripped over Moose, who was running to greet me. I said, 'Get out of my way, you goddamn bag of shit.' She wagged her tail. I patted her head. Okay, I thought, Bonnie left the dog. Clever: she knew I'd take care of it. The house was absolutely silent. I trudged toward the pineapple room and called out 'Hi' against the emptiness. Still a little hope. 'Hello?' Not a sound. 'Bonnie!' I yelled.

'Hi,' Bonnie called back. Did I jump! 'It's you! I heard you say "Hi", and I thought it was your voice, but I couldn't be sure. I thought: What if it's one of his friends, or a burglar?'

My whole body was flooded with relief, and it left me so empty, that sudden decrease in tension, that I had to lean against the wall for a minute to get my equilibrium back. Then I went into the pineapple room.

She was curled up on the bed reading *This Date in New York Yankees History*, the only book that had been in there. She put it down on the floor, then sat up on the bed, Indian style. 'Who is the all-time leader for career grand slams?' she asked.

'Gehrig,' I mumbled.

'It said Henry Gehrig. Is that the same as Lou?'

I nodded and said, 'Here.' I handed her the sneakers and hairbrush and took the underwear and toothbrush out of my pocket. I was still too emotional. I couldn't make conversation.

'Thanks.'

I jiggled the bag with the dog chow. She smiled and waited for me to say something, so I told her I'd give it to Moose, take a quick shower and be back. I was amazed; I sounded so matter-of-fact. Like a normal person. Did she want something? I had a bunch of TV dinners. She said, No, thanks, she wasn't hungry.

I shoved two Hungry Man dinners in the oven, figuring when push came to shove she wouldn't be able to resist an aluminum-foil tray of greasy, breaded chicken, or worst case, I'd eat it. I got into the shower. Water, a lot of soap, the nice pine smell of shampoo. This was better. A cool, clean man instead of a sweaty, feverish, overwrought wreck. I reached out for the towel, a little disappointed Bonnie hadn't sneaked in to hand it to me; in the back of my mind, I'd been imagining getting out of the shower and having her there. I'd say, Get the hell out of here, and she'd say, Let me do your back. But then, resting her body against me, she'd reach around to the front, stroke me, murmur, Oh, Stephen.

I got dressed, took out my notebook and called Vincent Kelleher, the catalog king. 'Detective Brady again.'

'Yes, sir?'

'Mr Kelleher, I don't know you, but somehow I get the feeling that you weren't being straight with me, and that makes me very upset.' Silence. 'Now listen, I'm not interested in your tax situation. You want to pay off the books, on the books, I don't give a damn. But I do give a damn if you lie in response to a simple question.'

'Why do you think I lied?' he whispered in Flagstaff, Arizona.

'Because I'm a cop. I *know*. You want to tell me about your financial arrangements with Bonnie Spencer?' Silence. 'If you're straightforward with me, we'll both hang up and that will be the end of it. If you dick me around, I'll pass on my suspicions to a buddy of mine in the IRS in Washington.'

'I paid her . . .' His voice faded. This guy had an Irish name; I couldn't believe he could be such a wimp. Fucking assimilation.

'How did you pay her?'

'In cash.'

'How much?'

'Twenty-five hundred dollars. She was the one who asked to be paid in cash. I swear to you, I never offered it.'

'How did you get it to her?'

'Her father lives outside of Scottsdale. She visits him once a year, then drives over, sees the mock-ups for new

287

catalogs. We talk and . . .' If this guy went through a red light, he'd probably handcuff himself, turn himself in and beg the judge for the max.

'You talk and what? You hand her the money?'

'Yes, in an envelope. But I promise you, it won't happen again.' All right! I thought, as I hung up. Score one for the good guys.

I searched around and finally found a couple of paperbacks, Stephen King and Clancy, and brought them into her room. I didn't want her to hate it, being stuck in there, and I didn't want her to think I was a semiliterate jerk who, when he read at all, read statistics – although that was more true than not. She was a writer; she had full bookshelves. What was I going to say? Hey, Bonnie, I may not read books much, but I read three papers a day and watch all the historical documentaries on cable. You want to know about the Battle of Midway? Metternich's life story? Just ask me.

'These are for later,' I said. 'Now it's time to talk.' I pulled back the shade and looked outside. The last of the soft, magic daylight was fading.

'Okay, but . . . I'm not telling you how to do your job . . . maybe you could give Vincent Kelleher a call.'

'Why?'

'Because he wasn't telling you the truth. And *I'm* going to tell you the truth. I know how badly I've messed things up for myself, and now you're giving me another chance. Well, I want to be worthy of your confidence. And I want you to believe me about everything.'

This time, the cop beat out the man. She shouldn't

think she had me on her side; she should convince me. I said: 'Maybe I'll call him later. For now, tell me how you hooked up with Sy again.'

CHAPTER 15

❖❖❖❖❖

'When you and Sy split, was there a lot of bad feeling?'

'No.' Bonnie leaned back against the headboard, one of those cheapo woven wood jobs that squeak every time you inhale. She was wearing what she'd worn when I found her folding laundry: red nylon running shorts and a black tank top. The white socks she'd had on had gotten filthy on the run through the field, so she'd taken them off. She hadn't been wearing shoes.

She drew her knees up together, folded her arms over them, then rested her head on the arms. Jesus, was she flexible; it was the kind of position that normally only an eight-year-old can be comfortable in. 'The day I signed the separation agreement, he took me out to lunch. Le Cirque. Soft lights, soft linen napkins. Soft food, so you wouldn't crunch when you chew. We were sitting on the same side of the banquette. He held my hand under the table and said, "It's my fault that I wasn't able to love you enough. But I'll always be there for you, Bonnie."'

So, obviously, would Moose. The dog rested her face on the blanket until Bonnie patted her. Then she lay down on my feet.

'Did you throw up when he said that?'

'No, it was before the appetizer. But see, in his own way, Sy was sincere. He truly believed what he was saying, even though twenty seconds after he dropped me off at Penn Station so I could get the train back to

Bridgehampton, I ceased to exist. But since I hadn't given him a hard time about splitting up . . . I mean, I cried a lot and asked him to go to a marriage counselor, but that was all. I didn't want alimony. So he felt kindly toward me. If someone had asked, "Sy, what was your second wife like?" he'd have said, "Hmmm, second wife. Oh, yes. Bonnie. So *sweet*. Down-to-earth." It was funny: If you crossed him, he'd never forget you, but niceness made no impression on him.'

'Why didn't you fight harder to stay together?'

'Because . . .' She put her hands together, prayer fashion, and touched her forefingers to her lips. Finally, she said: 'Because I knew he didn't love me anymore – if he ever had. Sy could fall in love, but it was like an actor immersing himself in a character. The week I met him, in LA, he must have just come back from a John Ford retrospective – so I became his cowgirl. He walked around wearing a denim jacket, squinting, smoking; this was before his decaffeinated days. He broke off the filters and lit his cigarettes with those matches you'd strike on the bottom of your boot; he actually took to wearing an old pair of shit-kickers, which wasn't so terrible because he was three inches shorter than me. God knows where he got them – probably in some Madison Avenue antique-boot boutique. We'd go riding a lot. Western saddle. He said, "The English saddle is so effete." But after three weeks back in New York – six weeks into our marriage – he got tired of being Hopalong Cassidy. And he got tired of loving me. I knew it.' She turned away from me for a minute and got busy folding over the pillow, so it made a better support for the small of her back. 'There was no percentage in fighting him on the divorce. He'd tried to be a decent husband, and it got to be too much of a burden.'

'How was he a decent husband? I thought you said he cheated on you – with some socialite.'

'Decent for Sy. He held doors open. He remembered birthdays, anniversaries. He had great style; one Valentine's Day he bought me a new tackle box, and when I opened it, there was a beautiful long strand of fourteen-millimeter pearls.'

'What are fourteen-millimeter pearls?'

'*Big* pearls.' Her hands described a sphere that was about the size of the average classroom globe. It annoyed me that she liked such an expensive gift. I wanted her to say, I told Sy to take back the pearls; I only wanted the tackle box. But she didn't. 'You have to understand Sy,' she went on. 'He couldn't be faithful. He couldn't be straight. He *had* to be . . . I don't know if "crooked" is the word. He had to manipulate every situation. Some of it was money. He was always afraid someone was cheating him, so he played one stockbroker, one lawyer, one accountant, against another. But *he* cheated people all the time. He hid personal expenses in movie budgets. I'm not just talking about a sweatsuit and a set of barbells; his second movie paid for a gym and a hot tub in our apartment in the city. And you couldn't use words like "illegal" or "immoral" with him, because in a weird way, he took them as compliments. He saw his finagling as an adventure and himself as a kind of swanky Robin Hood. But all he was doing was robbing from the rich to give to the rich.'

'You didn't see any of this when you agreed to marry him?'

'No. I just saw this charming, cultured man with

crinkles around his eyes who was crazy about *Cowgirl* and who knew all about westerns. Not just a superficial knowledge: I remember him describing one of Tom Mix's silent movies – *Cactus Jim's Shop Girl*. Actually, he seemed to know about everything: Cambodian architecture, the Big Bang theory, the linguistic connection between Finnish and Hungarian. But I think what got me most about Sy was that he *appreciated* me. My work. My eyes. My hair. My . . . All the usual stuff. This man was such a connoisseur, I thought: Lord, am I something!'

She concentrated on massaging her knee, a slow back-and-forth motion, the way you do to ease an old injury. Suddenly she glanced up at me, then, quickly, back down to her knee. I knew what she was thinking: despite our very different résumés, I was like Sy. Oh, how I appreciated her that night: I swear to God, I've never met anyone like you, Bonnie. Bonnie, your skin is like warm velvet. You know what, Bonnie? Your eyes are the color of the ocean. Not a summer ocean. Like on a bright winter day – so beautiful. I could talk to you for hours, Bonnie. Bonnie, I love you.

'But Sy's enthusiasms never lasted. He had a closet with equipment from sports he'd tried a few times and given up: golf, racquetball, scuba diving, polo, cross-country skiing. And if he could have put women in a closet, he would have; he was on to other enthusiasms by our two-month anniversary.'

'I'm sorry.'

'Don't be. Actually, it got to be amusing.' She lifted her chin and gave a little closed-lipped smile, a superior city-slicker expression that overflowed with *savoir-faire*. It was fake as hell. 'I could tell who he was having an affair with by the way he dressed. One day he put away his nipped-in-waist Italian suit and took out a torn T-shirt and bleached jeans, and I knew he'd stopped with the production designer with the surrealist jewelry and taken up with the third-string *Village Voice* movie critic, this girl with a lot of hair who was about ten minutes past her Sweet Sixteen. You couldn't help but laugh.'

'Don't bullshit me.'

The blanket on the bed, which the architect had probably decided was a grand bucolic design statement, was a pukey green plaid. Bonnie traced a thin, dark-green line with her finger. 'All right,' she said quietly, 'what he did to me stank. More than that. It broke my heart. I'm not the kind of woman men fall for. Then, finally, one did. I was so happy. But before I could even finish the love poem I was writing to him, a sonnet — fourteen lousy lines — he stopped loving me.'

'So the marriage was over before it was officially over.'

She nodded. 'We still had sex, but there was no love, and not much companionship. On the nights he was home, he'd hole up in his study and read scripts or make phone calls. After the separation, I went on with my life. It wasn't hard to do; we hadn't really been a couple.'

'But your economic situation, your social status, changed. What was your life like?'

'What do you mean?' She got very engrossed in following another, thicker line in the plaid.

'Happy, sad, wonderful, terrible?'

'It was okay.' She didn't look up at me.

'Come on, Bonnie.'

'Why is this necessary?'

'Because I want to know the circumstances surrounding your taking up with Sy again.'

'The circumstances were that I was — am — an independent woman. No ties. My mom died when I was seventeen: a brain tumor. My dad remarried — to a woman from Salt Lake who gets pedicures. He sold his store and they moved to Arizona, to a retirement community; they play bridge. My brothers are all married, with families of their own.'

She got quiet, thoughtful. She stopped with the blanket and reached back and played with the end of her braid. Absentmindedly, she unwound the rubber band. She unplaited her hair, and, as she began to talk again, stroked it, as if comforting herself. In the light of the green-shaded lamp, it gave off soft copper glints.

'My life: I live in a lovely town by the ocean in a part of the country I don't belong in. I have Gideon and his lover, two women friends, and a lot of pleasant acquaintances. Summers are a little better; I kept a couple of friends from my Sy days — a film editor, a *Wall Street Journal* entertainment industry reporter — and they have houses around here. We have some good times. I do volunteer work with illiterate adults and for every environmental cause that comes down the pike. That's how I met Gideon. He was representing a land rapist, and we started out screaming at each other because roseate terns have become an endangered species, but we wound up great friends. You want more? I make eighteen thousand dollars a year writing pap for catalogs and the local paper and industrial publications like *Auto Glass News*. What else do you want to know? Sex? Until AIDS, I slept with any man who appealed to me. Now I read and watch two movies a night and run five miles a day. I had an abortion when I was married to Sy because he said he wasn't ready to have children. I wanted to have a baby more than anything. From the time I was thirty-eight, when it dawned on me that I'd never get married again because no one would ever ask, I stopped using birth control. I was never able to conceive; I found out my fallopian tubes were scarred closed from a dose of gonorrhea I'd gotten from my husband about six months after the abortion. Well, that's it.' Bonnie clasped her hands on her knees. 'I guess you expected something a little more upbeat.'

'A little.' I had to be professional. What was the alternative? Taking her in my arms, hugging her, whispering tender words of condolence? I asked: 'We found two condom wrappers in a wastebasket in Sy's guest room. If you couldn't get pregnant —'

'AIDS, chlamydia, gonorrhea again. If I could have found a way of slipping a Trojan over his head before I kissed him, I would have, but it would have lacked a certain subtlety.'

'Tell me more about your life.'

'What's there to tell? I had such a happy childhood. And then my screenplay became a movie and got wonderful reviews, and then Sy came along and married me. Sure, I knew there'd be bumps. Tragedy even, like losing my mom. But it didn't occur to me that life wouldn't basically be wonderful. Well, it's not. It isn't terrible, but I never thought I would be so lonely.'

'But now you have to deal with something a little more serious than personal happiness,' I reminded her.

'I know.'

'Like the possibility of a murder conviction.' My voice was grim, deep and low, like a 45 record playing at 33. The small bedroom suddenly felt tight, airless, like a cell.

Bonnie seemed determined not to succumb to the gloom. She flashed one of her great grins. 'So worse comes to worse, I get convicted for murder. After twenty, thirty years in jail, think of the script I could write. None of those *Blondes in Chains* clichés for me. You know: the dyke matron, the ripped uniforms so breasts peekaboo out. No, I'll write a socially significant screenplay and maybe get on *Entertainment Tonight*.'

'Tell me about the screenplay you were working on with Sy.'

'Oh, right. *A Sea Change.* It's based on a real incident during World War Two. A German submarine surfaced off the coast of Long Island, and a couple of saboteurs slipped in. In my story, two women spot them down by the beach: a middle-class housewife and a bargirl who turns tricks on weekends. Anyway, it's about their helping catch the Nazis, but also about the friendship that develops.'

'You sent it to Sy when you got finished with it?'

'I called him.'

'What happened?'

'Well, first I spoke to his secretary, asked that he call me back, which he did a couple of days later. Kind of wary, to tell you the truth: I guess he was nervous I might be asking for money. But when I told him what it was, he was nice: You sound fan*tas*tic. Send it Fed Ex. Can't *wait* to read it.'

It wasn't only that she didn't wear makeup, or that she did have incredible calf muscles; Bonnie was simply

297

like no other woman I'd ever met. She seemed to be incapable of womanly wiles in any form. I looked her straight in the eye and she made no defensive feminine gestures. Her hand didn't fly up to touch her nose to check if it was oily, or up to her head to smooth down or fluff up her hair. She didn't make cow eyes or wounded-doe eyes, spread her legs an intriguing inch, thrust out her pelvis. No, she just looked straight back at me. I thought: Maybe it came from growing up with all those older brothers and that elk-shooting father and that rangy, broad-shouldered mother. Maybe she'd even tried batting her eyelashes or giggling, and nobody noticed. Maybe she'd acted wide-eyed and inept around all those Brownings and Remingtons and Winchesters in the store, or gazed upon the engine of the family Buick and said, 'Oooh, what's all that?' and got a swift kick in the butt, real or symbolic. She wasn't feminine. She was female.

'You say Sy liked your screenplay?'

'Yup.'

I thought about what Easton had said about it. 'Then why would he have told one of his people to find something nice to say about it, so he could get you off his back? And why would he have told Lindsay . . .' I tried to think of a way to say Sy thought the script was a piece of crap without actually having to say it.

'I can't say for sure. With Lindsay, I think it was natural he'd try and cover up any relationship with me.' Bonnie rotated her ankles, making circles with her feet. 'I mean, Lindsay has perpetually twitching, super-sensitive antennae that can pick up any other woman within a fifty-mile radius. Sy was so careful; he did everything except wear sunglasses and a false nose when he came over.' She stopped twirling her feet and started

298

to do toe touches, flexing her calves as she bent over. She could have been stretching for a marathon; she was ready to run. She was not someone who could tolerate being confined.

'Why would he ask his assistant to find something nice to say?'

'Busywork, maybe.'

'No.'

'When did he ask his assistant to read it?'

'A couple of months ago.'

'I'd just handed in my second draft then. Sy *said* he liked it a lot but that he wouldn't have time to really go over it until *Starry Night* wrapped.'

'This was the rewriting you did based on his suggestions?'

'Yes.'

'Knowing Sy, was it possible he didn't like it, even though he told you he did?'

She considered the question. 'Knowing Sy, yes. Maybe he – I don't know – wanted me back in his life for a while.' She looked disheartened, as if she'd just gotten a brusque rejection letter in the mail. 'But he did write me this nice note. Something like: "Skimmed it. Adore it. Can't wait to *really* read it."'

This could be another one for the good guys; if Sy had liked the screenplay, and if she had written proof, she'd have every motive for wanting him alive; a dead executive producer can't make a movie. 'He wrote you a note?' I demanded.

'Yes. He has little three-by-five note cards with his name. He used one of them.'

'Typed or in his own handwriting?'

'I think he wrote it.'

'Did you save it?'

'It should be in my *Sea Change* file. In my office.' She stopped cold. 'Oh, wait a second. You want proof that he liked it originally too. Right? Fine. Look in that same file. There's his original memo, the one he wrote after he read the first draft. Typical Sy. Eight pages, single-spaced, multisyllabic. Talking about everything from character arc to how I misused the subjunctive mood. But filled with "brilliant" and "trenchant" and "poignant".'

'What does "trenchant" mean?'

She chewed her lip for a second. 'I don't know, to tell you the truth. It's one of those words that nobody in human history has ever said out loud, and you don't see it written that often. He also wrote it was "au courant". *That* must have been a shock to him. Sy had always told me I was born too late, that I belonged under contract to RKO – if there still was an RKO – because my writing talent was for great 1941 movies. He couldn't get over that I'd finally written a screenplay that would appeal to someone besides my Aunt Shirley, and a perverse USC film professor. An eastern, not a western.' She got off the bed and began to pace, which isn't easy when you can only pace three steps forward and three steps back. 'You know, you had a search warrant. How come you didn't read that file?'

'Robby Kurz probably looked at it and decided it wasn't important.' I took out my notebook and jotted down: 'Bon's Sea file.'

'Not important? You're hearing from people that Sy hated my work, that he rejected me – which would give me a motive to kill him if I was a homicidal maniac, which I'm not. And you say it's not important?'

'It's not our job to dig up exculpatory evidence.'

'No. It's your job to railroad people.'

'Sit down.'

'I don't want to sit down,' she snapped. 'God, I feel so cooped up in here.'

I was pissed. I wanted her to like being with me. 'Want to try a jail cell?'

'Do you? Maybe you can have the one next door. You know, when you go up the river for your Class D felony.' Bonnie's pacing got faster, more desperate. Suddenly she stopped short. Smiled. That phony, movie-biz smile, falsely warm, fraudulently agreeable. 'Listen, I have a great idea. We can share a cell! Have a hot affair after lights-out. Not just your conventional hot affair. I mean, a *love* affair. We'll actually talk! Tell each other our life stories. The true ones, even when they hurt. Not the slick ones we make up to entertain people. And sex! We'll do it standing up, sitting down, frontways, sideways – '

'Bonnie, stop it!'

'Why? I'm telling you, it could be magic. Like we were creating something the world had never known before. And then the next day – '

'I asked you to stop it.'

' – the next day you'd be free. You could forget it happened. You could forget it meant something.' She hoisted an imaginary glass. 'Hey, I'll drink to that!'

'I'm sorry if I hurt you,' I began. 'That time of my life, I was a mess.'

I got up and walked into the bathroom. Moose followed. No tissues, so I brought her a wad of toilet paper, knowing she was going to cry. I came back and put my arm around her shoulders, ready to absorb her sobs. But she pulled away and turned from me; she

301

wasn't crying, and she didn't want me comforting her.

'Bonnie,' I said to her back, 'in AA, one of the things we do is to make a list of all the people we've harmed. Then we've got to be willing to make amends. I know I harmed you. I'm not going to make excuses – '

'Gideon said you didn't remember what happened.'

'I didn't. But later, after he left . . . I remembered some of it. I know I'll never be able to know what really went on between us – what we talked about. But let me just say how sorry – '

She turned back and gazed at me so straight I looked away. 'No amends, okay? I don't want any magnanimous Twelve Step gestures that will make you Feel Good About Yourself. Yes, you hurt me. But I let myself get hurt. I was playing a raunchy sex scene, and I tried to score it with violins. Well, I was the dope.'

'You know it wasn't any scene.'

'I know it's history.' She sat down on the bed again, feet on the floor this time, hands in her lap. Mormon schoolmarm posture, not Bonnie posture. There was a long silence. It was broken by the screech of a gull flying toward the water. Bonnie finally said: 'I apologize for the outburst.'

'No problem.'

'I don't want to be a bitter person. I lost control for a second. I'm exhausted. I haven't been sleeping, not since Sy was killed. Not since you rang my bell. I'm scared. I wake up and the sun is shining and I yawn and stretch – and suddenly I'm overwhelmed with terror. I'm trapped inside a nightmare, and the sunshine doesn't give me any light. And you: I can't resolve my memory of you and my fear of you. It's very hard being here in your house.'

'I understand, and I just want to say how sorry – '

'Let's drop it now.'

'Can't I – '

'Please, don't.'

It was getting dark. I knew I had to call Lynne. I walked into the kitchen, but instead of picking up the phone, I put Moose's dog chow in a bowl and got her some water. Then I took the dinners out of the oven and brought them back into Bonnie's room on plates, with forks and napkins. I thought she'd say, No, thanks, I'm much too upset to eat, but by the time I got back again with Cokes, she'd woofed down a drumstick and half the mashed potatoes and corn.

I sat there holding a wing, like I couldn't figure out what to do about it, thinking that there were approximately a million subjects I wanted to talk to this woman about: what teams she liked, although I had a dread suspicion she would be a Mets fan; what Mormons were all about; whether she read about stuff like Eastern Europe and the national debt in the paper or just articles about movies and saving marsh grasses; what was her favorite running route; how had she hurt her knee; did she only like the John Wayne and Katharine Hepburn stuff or did she ever watch a good horror movie; did she believe in God and did she feel guilty or only regretful about her abortion; had it simply been the sex – amazing, all-star sex – or had she fallen in love with me in the course of that night.

What I asked her was: 'When did you begin sleeping with Sy again?'

'That last week.'

'Why?'

'"Why?"'

'What was it, a casting couch kind of thing? You

thought if you slept with him, he'd make your movie?'

'You know,' she said, and reached for another napkin, 'there's an old show-business joke: A gorgeous, talented actress walks into a producer's office and says, "I want that part. I'll do anything, and I mean *anything*, for that part." She gets down on her knees and says, "I'm going to give you the world's most incredible blow job." And the producer looks down at her and says, "Yeah, but what's in it for me?"' Bonnie wiped the bread crumbs from the chicken off her hands. 'So what was in it for Sy? Nothing. There was nothing I could do for him that would entice him into doing anything he didn't want to do.'

'But how could you sleep with such a bastard? Okay, he let you have the house, but other than that, he left you broke. He made you get an abortion – '

She cut me off. 'No one held a gun to my head.'

'Maybe he didn't, but he gave you the clap, didn't he? Forget that it's proof positive of adultery. It took away the chance for you to have the one thing you wanted more than anything in the world.'

I'd just hit her most painful spot. She didn't wince; she just stood, holding out her plate. 'Why don't I bring this into the kitchen?' Her voice was artificially high, as if she were being stretched too tight.

'No. I don't have curtains or anything on the windows. I can't risk having you seen. I'll take it in later.' I took the plate from her and put it down on the floor. 'You're going stir-crazy, aren't you?'

'And this isn't even stir,' she said softly.

'Put on your sneakers.' When she did, I turned off the lamp, took her arm and steered her out of the bedroom, through the dark main room and out the back door. It was nearly night; the sky, already dotted with stars, was a uniform blue. Dark, indigo, like my Jag. I sat her down on the back step and murmured, 'Keep your voice down.'

'You're worried about nocturnal farmers, plowing out there, right past those bushes, listening in?'

'I always worry about nocturnal farmers. Or a friend could drop over. So what do you want? To sit out here or go back inside?' In response, she leaned against the doorframe and took a deep breath. Whatever she'd had in mountains, this had to be better. The bracing salt of the sea, the fragrance of pine, the deep, musky smell of the earth. 'More questions, Bonnie.'

'Okay.'

'Why did you sleep with Sy after what he did to you?' She didn't answer; I think she was still with that lost baby. 'Come on,' I pushed her. 'You don't strike me as one of those masochistic broads who lets herself be used. You seem to play more by men's rules than women's rules. You have a good time, you say thank you and that's it. You don't wake up the next morning feeling like a piece of shit; you wake up and say to yourself, "Hey, I got laid. It was good. Cleared my sinuses." And that's that.'

'That is never that.'

'But it's not that far from the truth, is it? You're not saying, "Sweet Jesus, help me. I hate myself."'

'People of my persuasion generally don't say "Sweet Jesus."'

'You know what I mean.'

'Am I one of those women who sleeps around to degrade herself? No. I sleep around – or slept around – for sex. Sometimes to be held.'

'So answer my question.'

'I slept with Sy because he was there, a real, live

person who *knew* me. He came to the house to go over his memo on my screenplay, and we wound up talking about my brother Jim's wife, who Sy had always had a little crush on, and about his Uncle Charlie's bypass surgery, and about all the movies he wanted to make after *Starry Night*.'

Talk about stars. The night was so clear that the stars were not cold, distant lights but twinkling points of warmth: Hi! Welcome! Nice universe we've got here!

Bonnie went on: 'When Sy saw the pitchers on the mantel, he reminisced about the trip we'd taken to Maine, where we bought a couple of them. It was so nice – a shared memory. What else? He said my script looked like hell and he couldn't believe I was still using a typewriter, and he picked up the phone and called his assistant and had him order a computer and printer for me.' I made a mental note to ask Easton about that. 'Let's see. He brought me flowers. So I guess you're wondering, was I had for an IBM-compatible and a bunch of day lilies? Partly. Sy swoops into your life, takes over everything. Let me tell you, it's very seductive, having someone come and care for you: buy you electronic toys, brush your hair, ask you how your day was. So that was part of it. And the other part was, I slept with him because I was so unloved. I couldn't stand it anymore.' Before I could say anything, she added: 'And don't ask if I really think he loved me, because we both know what the answer to that one is.'

'Why you? Look, I'm not putting you down, but he was living with Lindsay Keefe.'

'I'm sexier than Lindsay Keefe.' She wasn't being falsely immodest. She was being matter-of-fact. She meant it. Then she stretched out her legs and got busy doing toe touches again. She couldn't sit still; she had too much energy. I wondered how she sat for two hours to see a movie. It was such a dark, sedentary passion for someone who seemed all daylight and outdoors. 'It wasn't just sex for Sy,' she was explaining. 'He was screwing me literally to screw Lindsay figuratively. He was always so much happier when he was cheating. Somehow, his women always suspected, and he liked their scrambling to hold on to him. He liked their anguish too. And he *loved* the logistics of sneaking around. But with Lindsay, it was more than his usual infidelity. He was *furious* at her.'

'Why? Because she wasn't good in the movie?'

'Because she wasn't good – and she wasn't trying. See, Sy had his own money, the bank's money and some of his friends' money invested. It was a real risk. He knew this kind of sophisticated adventure-romance doesn't do fabulous business unless there's something very special about it. But he felt he had that in the *Starry Night* script. For all Sy's baloney, he truly believed in what he did.'

I remembered that Germy had liked the screenplay. 'Did you read it?'

'Yes. It was terrific. But Sy needed box office clout *and* ecstatic reviews: "An American classic! See it!" And Lindsay Keefe was his ticket. She's a star. Men, especially, love her. But more important, she's made quality movies. The critics take her seriously. Also, Sy knew that with the wrong stars, actors with a limited emotional range, *Starry Night* would be just another one of those 1950s Eastman Color-style rich-adventurers-on-the-Riviera movies, except set in the Hamptons and New York. But with actors who could show innocence, sweetness, under elegance, who could really deliver lines – because the dialogue is *so* good – he'd have a major commercial and critical hit. He was on his way; from what he said, Nick Monteleone was born to play this role. He was debonair without being too Cary Grant; he was manly, exciting. But Lindsay just ruined it. She walked through the part as though it was beneath her, and that was showing contempt for Sy's judgment, and for Sy. You didn't do that to him, not if you had any brains. It was a major no-no.'

'Why didn't he kick her out of his house? Fire her?'

'Well, he wasn't going to fire her until he had a replacement, which was going to be terribly expensive. Lindsay had a pay-or-play contract: she got paid in full whether she made the movie or not. But he was looking for someone else. That's why he was going to LA. As far as kicking her out of his house, he was first and foremost a smart operator. If for any reason he couldn't make a deal with another actress, he'd be stuck with Lindsay, and while she was living with him and having sex with him and getting little ten-thousand-dollar trinkets from him, she'd at least be semi-manageable. If he gave her the heave-ho, she'd be blatantly hostile.'

'Do you think Lindsay knew Sy was seeing you?'

'Me specifically? No. Seeing someone? Definitely. Not that Sy told me, but he'd call her trailer from my house; they have those portable phones. She'd come to the phone and obviously ask where he was, and he'd take a long beat and then say, "Oh, I'm, uh, having lunch with an old friend from college, uh, Bob, just ran into him. We're at this little hole-in-the-wall." And she asked him where, and he took another beat and said, "Uh, uh, Water Mill." He was lying but letting her know he was lying.'

'Did you get any sense from Sy that Lindsay might have someone on the side?' Bonnie smiled and shook her head, as if the possibility was too ridiculous to even consider. 'Why not? Was he that terrific in the sack that she wouldn't want anyone else?' I confess: this was not strictly a police question. I wanted to know.

Maybe she knew I wanted to know. But she didn't want to tell me. 'That's really not relevant.'

'Yes, it is. I've got to know everything about him. I've got to know how he behaved toward people, toward women. It's important that I know what kind of number he was doing with Lindsay Keefe. Why are you so sure she wasn't stepping out?'

'Because Sy could satisfy anyone.' She sat up, eyes right on me, trying to act detached, trying for a clinical look, like a woman in a white coat on TV selling April Showers douche. If she'd worn glasses she would have taken them off and looked sincere. 'Sy was extremely adaptable with women. He could be whatever they wanted. Well, he couldn't be six three, with a thing that went from here to Philadelphia. But he could talk dirty or romantically. He could be an animal, or he could be Fred Astaire to your Ginger Rogers. Forget real passion, or real warmth – he wasn't capable of either. But he could be a sensational animal, a fantastic Fred Astaire. Or whatever it was you wanted.'

Moose came to the door and started barking. She wanted to join the conversation. I couldn't risk letting her run out and setting off my neighbors' dogs in the dark. So we went back inside, back to the pineapple room. I switched on the lamp, and we took up our previously staked-out positions. But since we were getting along better, I decided it was safe to put my feet up on the bed. 'What if I told you Lindsay was having a go at Victor Santana?' I inquired.

'No!'

'Well?'

'I'd say . . .' Bonnie gave it about five seconds' thought. The fresh air had brightened her eyes, cleared her head. 'She probably could have gotten away with it. You know why? Sy would never believe it.' She pulled up her legs, hugged her knees. 'But if he did, that would have been it for her. He was *so* vindictive. If anyone – an agent, a studio executive – crossed him, he'd go on Sy's list. Seriously, he had this mental list, including a top ten, that kept changing. Whenever he could zing it to someone on his list, no matter what number, he would. And once you were on, you never dropped off.'

I kept thinking Sy's vengefulness had to mean something. Maybe he'd confronted Lindsay, worked her over about her crummy acting. Or he'd found out about Santana. Maybe she sensed he was about to do damage to her: not just fire her but try and destroy her career, let everyone know she'd lost it as an actress. Would she have gone after him then? It added up, I thought. No. But almost.

Bonnie said: 'I honestly don't think Sy knew. He wasn't in one of his I'll-rip-out-her-heart-with-my-teeth moods. He was very optimistic about his trip to LA. Very relaxed too. He'd planned on taking the ten-fifteen morning flight, but instead he decided to go over to the set, to make nice to everybody because he knew morale wasn't all that high. Then he called me to meet him at his place. I'd never seen it before. He gave me the grand tour. Wanted to hear me say "Gosh! Gee! My God!"'

'Did you?'

'Sure. If you're going to make a fuss over a house, this was the one to do it with.'

'He was relatively relaxed?'

'He wasn't tense. He said he'd done everything but wave pom-poms and cheer on the set, and when he'd left, he could feel the change in atmosphere. Much more positive. And as far as the LA trip, he'd gotten copies of the screenplay to three different actresses, and he was going to take the seven o'clock evening flight, get a decent night's sleep, and the next day he was going to have breakfast, lunch and dinner with them. He was going to make one of them an offer that same night. He told me, "I'm a little in the hole right now with *Starry*, but watch. I'm going to pull it out. It's going to be my biggest. My best."'

I put my feet down and pulled the chair closer to the bed: straight talk time. I didn't like being so charmed by her. 'Tell me why you threatened Sy.'

'What are you talking about?'

'Bonnie, come on. You went to see him at the *Starry Night* set. We have witnesses. You said: "Sy, you've just been a rotten bastard for the last time."'

'You call this an interrogation?' Too cute. Like a snotty Upper East Side bitch.

'Fuck off, Bonnie.'

'No, you eff off. Don't you know *anything* about people? Here's Sy Spencer, my former husband who's been coming to my house every day, having sex with me, telling me how he's missed me, how wonderfully *human* I am, how there's been an emptiness in his life since I've been gone despite all the other women and he's beginning to think he made a ghastly mistake. "Ghastly" was his word. Sure, I knew it was almost all bull, but he said, I

311

want you to come down to the set one day soon; I want you to see what I'm doing firsthand. So I went. Okay, it might have been better to wait for an engraved invitation: big deal. But when I got there, he told me to leave — so everyone could hear. I wasn't hurt. I was furious. And that *was* going to be the last time he was a rotten bastard. He came over to my house later and I wouldn't let him in. Over. Goodbye.'

'Except it wasn't over.'

'He called about two seconds later from his car phone. He said he felt *terrible*. He explained that if he had invited me on the set, it would look like we had something going, because he never took anyone to the set except big banker types. And he couldn't afford to have Lindsay focus on me; it would give the game away, and he wasn't ready for that yet. So he had to disavow me publicly. Naturally, he apologized all over himself and swore he was getting rid of her. As soon as she was gone, I'd have *carte blanche* to visit anytime I wanted. He said he was proud of me. I'd created *Cowgirl*. He wanted to parade me around, show me off to the crew.' I didn't say anything. I didn't have to. She acknowledged: 'Even if you were dying to believe him, you couldn't. For a sophisticated man, he could be such an ass.'

The day's heat was finally rising off the land. The first night breeze blew through the window. The shade flapped, and Bonnie shivered. 'Let me get you a sweatshirt or something.'

'No, thanks. I'm fine.'

Okay, I would have liked to see her in my old SUNY Albany sweatshirt. I would have liked to take her hands between my hands and rub them. The fact was, I liked having Bonnie in my house. Despite the insane circumstances, despite the occasional angry sparks that flared up between us, it was so comfortable. So much about her pleased me, from her not making cholesterol remarks when I handed her the TV dinner to her courage to her wonderful, glossy hair. But the great thing was, I realized, that in spite of the pleasure of her company, I had recovered from my obsession with her.

Maybe by allowing myself to remember what had gone on between us, I had broken her hold over me. Here I was, able to sit in a box of a room, inches away from her, question her, behave like a real cop. Her power was gone. I could relax, not fantasize about kissing her. Or about licking her lips, putting my tongue in her mouth. I was past that hump of desire. Hey, I thought, about time.

In that instant of self-congratulation, I glanced away from her mouth. If the shade hadn't been pulled down, I might have looked out the window, leaned back and watched the moon on the rise. But since there was no night sky to admire, no stars, I looked elsewhere and noticed the tautness of the nylon shorts stretched between her legs.

If we'd been characters in some porno cartoon, the God of Passion would, at that moment, have hurled down a bolt of lightning; it would have slashed across the sky, forked into two jagged spears and, at the exact same moment, zapped each of us, right in the pubes.

Just as my breathing deepened, Bonnie reached behind her, took the pillow and placed it in her lap. It was one of those unconscious gestures of self-defense. But without realizing it, she began fondling the edge of the pillow, rubbing the protruding corner with her thumb. Oh, God, I thought, she could be doing that to me. I got more and more excited. I could almost feel the soft pressure of her thumb.

I tried to picture Lynne, use her as a magic charm against what was happening: auburn hair, I said to myself, and big brown eyes, peaches-and-cream complexion. The waist, the gorgeous long legs. But I couldn't get the parts to add up to anything. I couldn't break Bonnie's spell.

But she could. Either she suddenly realized what she was doing or she simply sensed the change of climate in the room, because she tucked the pillow behind her again. 'What else would you like to know?' she asked, all perky, cheerleadery, like she was going for the Miss Teenage Ogden title.

'Why did you lie to me?'

'You mean, when you first came to my house?'

'I came in, asked a simple question: When was the last time you saw Sy? You said you weren't sure, but you thought a few days before, at the set. I asked when you'd seen him before that, and you were kind of vague, but you thought it was about a week before, when he gave you the fifty-cent tour of his house. You said you hadn't spent much time with him.'

'For someone who can't remember, you have a great memory.'

If I looked at her, I'd see her crotch, or her breasts, or the hollow of her collarbone where the neck of her stretched-out T-shirt drooped. So I looked right past her and concentrated on the weave of the crappy wood headboard. 'I asked if Sy had visited you at your house. Again, vague, but then you said maybe he had dropped by. Real casual. Just two old pals working on a movie script together. So what I want to know is, did you construct an alibi before I showed up? Or were you winging it?'

'Aren't you going to give me one of your warnings? You know: "If you don't tell me the truth, I'll bust your head open."'

'No. It's "I'll bust your fucking head open." Now, can we get on with it?'

'What's wrong?'

Just because I was making major eye contact with a headboard, she thought something was wrong? 'Nothing's wrong. I asked you a question. I'm waiting for an answer.'

'I had an alibi, but I was winging it too.' She took a deep breath. 'After Sy called, I drove over. He showed me the house, and – big surprise – we ended up in bed.'

'Yeah, big surprise.' I could picture him, his arm around her, leading her from room to beautiful room, the 'This could be yours again' unspoken. I could see his hand on her ass, guiding her into the guest room, closing the door. 'When did you start screwing and when did you finish?'

She snapped: 'Why don't you just come right out and ask me exactly what we did and how it was?'

'Why don't you shut your mouth? Understand something: you're here to work. I didn't bring you over for the pleasure of your company or to get off on hearing about your sex life.' Thwarted desire is great for the disposition. 'Now, from when to when?'

'From about one until two-thirty. Do you want to know if it was good for me?'

'I'm sure it's always good for you, sweetheart. Otherwise you wouldn't do it so often.'

Well, I'd said it to hurt her. And it worked. Nothing

like a deep, wounding insult to snap a woman out of enticing you, put her on the verge of tears. Works like magic. 'It wasn't necessary to say that.' Her voice quavered; it was costing her to fight back.

'Did anyone see you while you were at Sy's?'

'Mrs Robertson. She's the cook.' She spoke to the green blanket.

'Did you have any conversation with her?'

'Yes. Sy went to call California for a minute, to make sure all his meetings were in place. She and I talked.'

'What about?'

'About our families, Sy's family. She'd begun working for us the second summer we were married. I hadn't seen her since the divorce.'

'Was that before or after you got laid?'

'Don't talk to me like that.'

'Before or after? Hurry up, Bonnie. There's a time bomb ticking. Robby Kurz is out there looking for you.'

'Before.'

'So you talked with Mrs Robertson, went upstairs, had sexual intercourse . . . Is that better?' She didn't answer. Just then I got another picture of Sy, with his tight cap of short gray hair, climbing all over her, petting, fondling, squeezing, feeling her skin. 'And then what? Come *on*. Any conversation?'

'Only about the three actresses he was seeing. Who I thought would be best for the part, and why. He said he'd call me from LA and give me a report.'

'That's it?'

'Pretty near.'

'What else?'

'He said he loved me.'

'Did you believe him?'

'I believed he believed it for that second.'

'Did you believe him?'

'No.'

'Any signs he was under pressure?'

'Not really.'

'So you kissed goodbye, and what?'

'He went to shower and pack, I guess. I went down to say goodbye to Mrs Robertson, but she wasn't in the kitchen. So I went home.'

'Did you speak to Sy again?'

'No. Never again. The next thing I know, I was out in the backyard, cutting some dahlias. The phone rang and it was Mrs Robertson, telling me what had happened, that the police were there. I was just . . . I don't know what I was. What she was saying wasn't making any impact: it was like dialogue that doesn't ring true. Then Mrs Robertson said, "They asked me if he had anyone with him, and I told them no. What they don't know won't hurt them, so keep your lip zipped." And I thanked her.'

'That was some favor.'

'She meant it to be. Please, don't hold it against her.'

Like I'd really arrest Mark Robertson's mom, impound her rolling pin, throw her into a cage with a bunch of hookers and crack dealers. But I just said to Bonnie: 'Go on.'

'I was too upset to cry. I put on the news. And then I began to think: What if the cops question me? I read police procedurals. I'm a natural: the ex-wife. I didn't sit down and plan anything, but during the night – I couldn't sleep – I realized my fingerprints would be in his house and his in mine, so I shouldn't lie about that.

And also to say I'd been to the set – although I didn't realize anyone had heard me mouth off to him.'

'So you decided to tell the truth and just fudge a little on the details.'

'Yes. That's right. I thought I'd be smart, not mention that I'd been sleeping with him, avoid a lot of embarrassing questions. But I wasn't sure about saying I hadn't been in his house that afternoon. There was no reason *not* to admit it: I certainly had no motive to kill him; I wouldn't be a suspect. But Marian Robertson had already said I wasn't there, so I thought: Well, if worst comes to worst, I'll tell the truth, but if not, I'll keep quiet – for her sake and mine.'

'But worst came to worst, and you didn't tell the truth.'

Bonnie stood, pulled the shade back about an inch so she could see out into the night. 'I opened the door the next morning and . . .' She turned, leaned against the wall, faced me. 'Please don't interrupt now. It's going to be hard for me to say what I have to say.' I nodded. 'I only spent that one night with you, but it was significant. Well, significant is an understatement. I fell in love with you. When you didn't call, I tried to call you. Your home phone is unlisted. And at your office, I left my name four times. I assumed the Homicide Squad is geared up so that its detectives get phone messages and either they answer them or . . . they don't.

'I was in pain beyond anything I want to talk about. And so ashamed. It took me a long time to get over it. But I did.

'And then there you were, five years later, on my doorstep. I didn't recognize you for a second, or maybe I just couldn't believe it, and then . . . I was so happy! I

318

mean, Sy had been murdered the night before, a shocking, horrible thing. I'd lost a good friend, or at least an ex-husband, a lover, a producer. But all I could think was: Stephen is back! But instead of showing any . . . affection, you showed me your badge. It suddenly hit me why you were there. And you were so correct. So I got myself together. I figured this must be as awkward for you as it was for me. But the odd thing was, you didn't *seem* awkward. You were businesslike but nice. Every once in a while I saw a flash of the man I'd known that night. You have a wonderful smile, which you use to great effect. And I . . .'

Again she turned to the window. I kept quiet, because she'd asked me to and because I didn't know what to say. 'I wanted you to want me again. I wanted your good opinion; I didn't want to be a tramp.'

'You're not.' I wished she would turn back again, but she just stood there, facing the drawn shade.

'It's my turn. You agreed. Fact: You picked me up in a bar. I came on to you; to put it mildly, I wasn't subtle. Fact: I brought you back to my house and, to use your terminology, got laid before I knew what you did for a living. Fact: I didn't even know what your last name was. I didn't know that until later, when you showed me your police ID. But all that didn't matter. I *knew* you were right. This was a miracle – and it was happening to me. So I just let go. I gave everything I had. Why hold back? It never occurred to me that you wouldn't understand completely, approve of me, rejoice in what we were doing, because we had this magic. You understood that.

'But five years after the fact, I was just some woman who felt you up in a bar, who couldn't wait to get you home. Then you asked me when was the last time I saw

Sy. I wasn't going to say, Oh, yesterday afternoon, in his bed. Because I didn't want you to know I was still easy, that I'd dropped my drawers less than twenty-four hours before, for a man who was living with another woman: Lindsay Keefe, a world-famous beauty. You'd think that all I could possibly be was a quickie; I knew you'd assume that I had about as much value to Sy as I had to you, to any man: zero.

'I guess I wanted retroactive chastity. I wanted your respect. I wanted you to appreciate that my openness with you was exceptional, that you brought it out, that I wasn't a bimbo who'd do it for anybody. I never was like that. Well, maybe I'm not being totally honest. I don't know how many men I've been with: thirty, forty, maybe more.' I remember telling the shrink at South Oaks that the women I'd had were into triple digits, but I didn't know whether it was two hundred or five hundred. Summers in the seventies and most of the eighties, I'd fucked my way from Hampton Bay to Montauk. Bonnie said: 'You knew I was easy, promiscuous, whatever. You knew I had a past. But I thought: I have another chance now. Maybe he can come to understand that what happened between us was unique.'

At last, she turned back. She was so tired; her face was puffy with fatigue. I thought: She's old and now she looks it. Lynne is so young.

'You know,' Bonnie went on, 'you never asked me what I did. The morning you came to question me and it came out that I was working with Sy, I was so glad. Because I wanted you to be impressed. I wanted you to think, Gee, she's a screenwriter. She's not a slut; she's an interesting woman. A good woman. She has worth.' Bonnie stood tall and straight. 'I wanted to be a woman you would be able to love. And that's why I lied to you.'

A sharp breeze billowed the shade. It banged it against the windowsill. Bonnie jumped as if it had been the crack of a gun. I stood up and told her: 'I know I've contributed to your unhappiness. I'm sorry.'

She moved away from the window, until she was standing near the wood cube of a nightstand with its lamp, just inches from me. 'How about this?' she proposed. 'Instead of apologizing, why don't you just act with a little more decency? Stop talking about my fucking and screwing and getting laid as if I'm the Whore of Bridgehampton and you're a dumb, pig redneck in line for a gang bang. I'm a human being, and I'm in terrible trouble. If you're going to help me, why not be generous? Do it with a little kindness.'

'All right,' I said. The breeze was changing to a chilly late-August wind. I felt cold. 'Sorry.'

'Thank you.'

Bonnie had goose bumps on her arms and legs. I went into my bedroom to get a sweater and some stuff for her. Moose trotted beside me. I tried to put a pair of socks in her mouth so she could bring them in to Bonnie, like a retriever. It would be funny. But Moose didn't get it; she let the socks drop out of her mouth and threw me an injured look, like I'd been leading her on to think she was getting a Big Mac.

When I turned out the light to leave, I noticed the red light flashing on the answering machine. Two messages. Loud ones: I lowered the volume. One was Germy, saying he had a good source for Yankee tickets. They were on the road, playing Detroit, but did I want to go when they got back? And Lynne: 'Hi. I love you and I'm thinking about you. Honey, I *know* how busy you are, but could you call for just a second? I have to tell my mother if we want breast of chicken stuffed with wild rice or roast beef for the reception. You'll say it's up to me, but please, I want you to feel a part of this.'

I called Headquarters and got Carbone. No trace of Bonnie yet, he reported. I haven't found her either, I said. But I'd checked her house and it didn't look as though she'd left in a hurry or taken stuff with her. My guess was she'd gone out for the evening and would be back later. Meanwhile, I had my list of her friends and acquaintances and was going house to house, checking them all out. So far, no luck. I asked if Robby had gone home, and Carbone said no, he was still in the office, reading over the files.

I went back inside and gave Bonnie a set of sweats and some socks. Women usually look adorable when they put on your clothes, with the sleeves all floppy, but she just looked normal in mine; they fit. She tucked the socks into the elastic of the pants. I said: 'There were a couple of calls on my answering machine. Did they come in when I was over at your house?'

She reached for the sneakers I'd brought from her house. 'One did.'

'Were you able to hear it?' She nodded. I recalled Lynne's sunny 'Hi, I love you . . .' I felt blue, for Bonnie's sake. 'So you know I have someone.'

'Yes.'

'I'm getting married.'

'Congratulations.' Direct. No bitchiness.

'Thanks. She's really a find. Teaches learning-disabled kids. Wants all the things I want, you know? Stability. A family. And she's Catholic. That's important to me.' Bonnie double-knotted her sneakers. 'Lately – I guess

322

since AA – I've been feeling this need to return to the Church. To have a place to pray. And for the ritual too, I suppose.'

I was really going on. But I wanted to tell her that the last time I'd been to church, I was eight, and the Mass had been in Latin. I was wondering what it would be like if you understood it, whether you'd wonder, This is what the big deal was all about? and lose your faith. I was a little worried about that.

And I wanted to tell her about how when my mother had married my father, she'd agreed to raise any children Catholic. She knew her obligations. She dropped me off once a week for confraternity class, but after I made my First Communion, she'd said: Steve, dear, you're a big boy. If you want to go to Queen of Whatever, you'll have to go on your bike. I would take you, but I'm on my feet all week. Sunday is *my* day of rest. I'd gone every single Sunday from that May until right after Christmas, when it began to snow. It was such a cold winter; the roads became a solid sheet of ice. After the spring thaw I never went back.

I started to smile then; I'd gotten to know Bonnie so well I could almost hear her: You're forty years old. Stop blaming your mother.

But I wanted to tell her how my mother hadn't sent Easton at all. She'd protected him from the killer Roman virus. Years later, when he was hanging out with the Southampton summer crowd, I'd heard him on the phone, going on about how his great-great-grandfather had been the Episcopal bishop of Long Island. I had no idea if my mother had told him that or if he'd made it up, but I knew it was a lie. What kind of person would lie about a God thing?

I was jabbering again. 'Listen, I know I'm going to

323

feel ridiculous when I go in and say, "Bless me, Father, for I have sinned. It's been thirty-two years since my last confession." But it's something I want to do, and Lynne's so supportive. Okay, I don't need someone to hold my hand and drag me over to the priest. But it's nice that the Church will be part of our life together.'

Bonnie turned away from me, braced herself against the wall with both hands and leaned forward to stretch out her calf muscles. I felt so dumb. I was babbling like a silly woman trying to make an impression on a man fast, before he could bolt, and I couldn't stop. 'Lynne's young for me. Twenty-four. But she's a really solid person. And great-looking. Long dark-red hair – '

'Calm down,' Bonnie said, taking one last stretch. 'I'm not going to make a pass at you.'

'I am calm,' I said, trying to sound it. 'I just thought it wouldn't hurt if you knew what the score was.'

'The score was, and is, that you're not looking for a sterile forty-five-year-old Jew. Believe me, I know I'm not a hot ticket. But since you're going back in the prayer biz, which is admirable, you might want to check out your conscience with your Big Three. Would you have told me the score if you hadn't thought there was a good chance I'd heard your machine?'

'I don't know the answer to that.'

'If I hadn't found out the score, would you have made a pass?'

'I don't know that either. I think there's still a certain attraction between us.'

'It's more than a certain attraction.'

'Okay, it is more. A lot more. All I can say is I hope I would have had the strength to fight it. But now that it's out in the open about Lynne, I feel a lot better. A lot safer, to tell you the truth. Don't you?'

Bonnie laughed, a delighted, spirited laugh. I would have loved it, except it was at my expense. She said: 'Well, I wasn't worrying about my safety. But I'm glad it's out in the open. I'm glad for you. I wish you well. And I wish myself well too,' she added. 'I want to try to get out of this mess, if that's possible. I want a future.'

'I hope you have one.'

'Well, you're the detective. What's the next step?'

'I want to check Lindsay's alibi. It sounds as if she was over in East Hampton, glued to the camera, the whole time, but I want to make sure. There's supposed to be a lot of dead time making a movie, right?' She nodded. 'Tell me how that works.'

'Whenever they change the setup to get another angle, they have to move the lights, the tracks, the camera. It depends on how complicated the shot is: If the crew hustles, it can take twenty minutes, especially if all they're doing is moving in a little for a close-up. But if they're turning around, reversing the angle completely, all the lights that were in the background need to get put into the foreground. And crew members had been standing behind where the lights and camera had been, so the grips and prop men have to get in and hang pictures, put back furniture, that sort of thing. Then the script supervisor has to check the continuity; if a chair had an afghan draped over the left arm in the last scene, it has to have the afghan draped in the exact same way again. It can take an hour. Sometimes more.'

'I want to find out if there was about forty minutes of dead time. Twenty minutes between the set and Sandy Court, twenty minutes back. Now, who would be most likely to know her whereabouts? Her agent? Ever hear of a guy named Eddie Pomerantz?'

Bonnie knew the name. 'He's probably been around since D. W. Griffith. I doubt if he'd be on the set with her. He's a businessman, a deal-maker, not a handholder. More likely it would be a manager, or a personal assistant, if she had one of her own people.'

'No. I don't think so.'

'She might have spent time with other actors.'

'No. From what I saw and from what Monteleone told me, no one could stand her. She's cold. Nasty. Like someone told her: Okay, Lindsay, you're absolved from all the normal rules of behavior that everybody else has to live by.'

'But she *is* absolved. When you're a big success in the movie business, you have license to behave badly. You know that. But even though Lindsay is a perfectly awful human being, she can act – when she wants to. She's beautiful, and she has the best breasts in the world. And the most important thing – people feel compelled to watch her. They can't take their eyes off her. She is a true star. So it makes sense that she wasn't hanging out with anyone from the cast. They're just plain actors, not stars. And Santana: even if he is her boyfriend, by late afternoon he'd be too involved in problems on the set to take care of her.'

I thought back to the reports I'd read and all the interviews I'd done. 'From what I can remember, Santana was doing whatever it is directors do the whole afternoon. There's not even an indication he took time out to go to the john; he was out there the whole time. So who else could have been with her?'

'A lot of stars get close with their makeup and hair people. Like regular ladies do with their hairdressers; it's a natural, easy intimacy. They might have been working on her.'

'The idea is to break down Lindsay's alibi, not reinforce it.'

'The idea is to find the truth. Anyway, the makeup person would at least know if Lindsay had any good friends on the set. As for off the set, if she went anywhere or needed an errand, there'd be a Teamster driver. But I can't imagine her saying, "Jack, drive me over to Sandy Court so I can knock off Sy."'

'How can I get the names of all these different crew people, fast?'

'Everybody gets a crew list. There should be one at Sy's house.'

'When Sy was killed, he was on his portable phone with Eddie Pomerantz. Do you think there's a chance that word had gotten back to Pomerantz that Sy was going to see other actresses in LA?'

'Sure.'

'How?'

'Because this is a gossipy business. More than that: a public business. *Everything* – contracts, food, cars, sex, lawsuits, flatulence – is talked about. My guess is, if Lindsay hadn't figured it out for herself, Eddie Pomerantz would know what was going on, probably from two or three different sources, and was trying to convince Sy to call off his trip.'

'He claims they were arguing about some photo approval problems.'

'To quote you,' Bonnie said, ' "bullshit".'

'Okay. I'm going out to see if I can dig anything up. I want you to stay right where you are.'

Bonnie shook her head. 'No, I have to get back.'

'You're in a hurry to get arrested?'

'No. But I can't let you ruin your career by harboring a know fugitive. I mean that.' She did.

'You may read mysteries, but you don't know shit about the law. You're not a fugitive. Not yet. You're just my houseguest. Relax. Read a book. Go to sleep.'

'I can't sleep.'

'So write a screenplay about a producer who gets killed, and figure out whodunit.' She glanced past me, out into the house, toward the front door. 'You're thinking of taking a nice little run after I go. Right, Bonnie? Maybe a nice ten-mile sprint over to Gideon's? Ask yourself: Do you want to put your best friend in the position of either protecting you or turning you in?'

'No.'

'Then stay here. Promise me. I don't want my gut in a knot, wondering where you are, what you're doing, when I'm out there.'

She reached out and took my hand. 'Will you promise me that if you decide you can't help me, you won't arrest me?'

'Jesus, give me a little credit.' She squeezed my hand, then let it go. 'If I can't help you, I'll let you know. And you'll be on your own.'

She said, 'On my word of honor: No matter how it turns out, I'll never tell anyone you did this.'

'I know.' We stood together for a minute. Finally, I said: 'I have to go now.' But then I couldn't leave. 'Bonnie?'

'What?'

'Want to kiss me goodbye?'

'I tried that once. It didn't work out so well.'

'Yes, it did.'

'No, it didn't. Anyway, you have bigger things to do besides kissing.'

'Like what?'

'Like going inside and calling your fiancée and telling her chicken breasts or roast beef. And then going out to try to save my life.'

CHAPTER 16

Easton had taken to his bed and hadn't gotten out, but at least he wasn't sleeping with his blankie pulled over his head anymore; he was lying on his side, his cheek propped up by his hand, and he was absorbed in a script. I was mature, big-brotherly. I yelled 'Boo!'

He screamed, but he was so startled it sounded more like the squawk of an oversize bird. 'Don't ever do that again!' he roared. 'Don't you dare!' Two seconds later, he calmed down enough to ask, 'What did you do, you dimwit? Sneak up the stairs so you wouldn't have to say hello to Mother?'

'Yeah. You know, I remember when you used to call her "Mom" – before you decided to be born upper-class.'

'At least I can get away with it. If you tried it . . .'

I liked it. Easton appeared to be coming out of his big sleep. Not exactly tear-assing around town – he was still in his striped pajamas – but to be fair, where did he have to go that needed a pair of pants? 'You sound a lot better. When I spoke to you on the phone, it was like listening to a Quaalude commercial.'

'I feel better. I've had some good news!'

'What?'

'I'd been planning on making a few calls, to see if I could find something resembling work. Never got around to it. Too upset. Well, a friend of Sy's whom I'd met, Philip Scholes, the director . . . He'd been renting over in Quogue in July and needed some Xeroxing done fast and called Sy to find out where to go. Sy wasn't in, but I offered to help and got it done for him in less than an hour. Well, he called me today! He's been needing an aide-de-camp, and when he heard about Sy, he started thinking about me. Bottom line is, he's paying for a round-trip ticket so I can go out to California and discuss the job with him!'

'Hey, terrific!' Easton smoothed down the top of his pajamas as if about to begin the job interview. 'I'm really glad for you. It was such a rotten break with Sy. You'd come into your own, working for him; I'd never seen you so happy.' My brother gave a fast, sad nod of assent, but I could see his allegiance was already transferring to Philip Scholes. 'You can do something for me.'

'What?'

'Get me a copy of the crew list. You have one?'

Easton got out of bed, slipped into his backless leather slippers and padded into the next room, the study, the slippers flapping against his heels. 'Why do you need it?' he asked.

'Checking out if certain people were where they claimed they were last Friday.'

'Like who?'

'Like everyone who gave a statement. Routine shit.'

But Easton shook his head, stubborn, not buying it. 'Lindsay?'

'Lindsay.'

'Steve, believe me, you're way off base.'

'East, believe me, you've got such a hard-on for her you can't see straight.'

'Well, maybe I do. But so did Sy. He never would have gotten rid of her.' He got a little petulant. 'I *told* you that.' He opened a drawer of his desk, drew out a manila folder with an orange tab, leafed through the neat stack of papers. He knew precisely what he was looking for and where. It was amazing; we were so alike in that regard. Everything had to have a place, be under control. For most of my drinking days, when I'd come off a bender, I'd find bottles and cans neatly lined up against the splashboard of the sink; in that last year before sobriety, when I started finding beer cans on the floor by my TV chair and, once, an empty bottle of wine cooler on the bathroom sink, I began to understand how lost I was.

Easton handed me the crew list. 'I know what you told me about Lindsay, but we've got a lot of evidence that says you're wrong, that Sy was getting ready to bounce her.' Easton looked unconvinced, and a little shaken by the threat to Lindsay. I tried to cheer him up. 'Look, I'm sure she was in her trailer from four to seven, with a dozen unimpeachable witnesses. It's just that we found out that there was bad blood between her and Sy. Plus she was screwing around with' – my brother drew back his head, as though somehow he could avoid hearing – 'Victor Santana.' No expression, not even surprise, crossed his face. 'And it turns out she may have known how to shoot a rifle. She had some firearms instruction for a movie she did. *Transvaal*.'

Easton smacked the folder onto the desk hard, as if swatting a big, obnoxious insect. 'But what about Sy's ex-wife? Damn it all. I thought you had her dead to rights.'

'We're having doubts. Oh, by the way, did Sy ask you to buy a computer and printer for her?'

Easton looked blank for a second. Then he stared up at the ceiling, as if searching out the answer there. I was getting a little scared. What if she was still lying? Finally, he said: 'Right. I remember now. A bargain-basement computer and printer. Sy said forget IBM; too expensive. He'd heard the Korean ones were all right, and not to go above a thousand for the whole package.'

'Did he say why he was sending it to her?'

'No. I assumed it was a consolation prize for rejecting her screenplay.'

'Do you have a copy of the screenplay? *A Sea Change.*'

'No.' He paused. 'Steve, I'm not telling you your business, but she had every reason to kill him.'

'Why?'

'He passed on her script.'

'Did you read any memos, any letters he sent her, that said "I pass"?'

'No. That sort of thing he'd dictate to his secretary in the New York office over the phone; unless she faxed it back for him to proofread, she'd have signed his name. It wouldn't have come back to the house.'

'So you don't actually know that he turned down her script.'

'He couldn't have been trying to cement a relation-ship, for God's sake. He ordered her off the set. Very harshly. She must have been humiliated.'

'Even if she was, it may not be motive for murder – unless she's crazy, and she just doesn't seem crazy.'

'So you need a suspect, and now you're going to pick on Lindsay?' My brother, Mr Moderate, wasn't acting so moderate. His neck and ears were flushed bright red.

He was really working himself up, defending his damsel in distress. 'Why? Give me one good reason why Homicide would go after her. The publicity?'

'Don't be a jerk.'

'I think what you're doing is out-and-out disgraceful!' I shrugged. Easton stomped over to the leather couch and plopped down on it. He put his face in his hands and shook his head back and forth. I was about to break in, when he looked up.

Easton's mood had changed. He was quiet, thoughtful, no longer outraged; he seemed like a man beginning to acknowledge doubt. 'I don't know; maybe I can't see straight when it comes to Lindsay – my adolescent crush. Maybe you're right.'

'Right about what?'

'About Lindsay being less than the loving . . . well, not wife. Less than the loving lover. It's possible she *could* have been stepping out. I can't swear to it. You see, no one would talk in front of me because I was Sy's boy, so to speak. But I did hear a few whispers about her and Santana.'

'Was there any chance Sy knew about the two of them?' Easton gave it a lot of thought. Too much; it was getting late. I glanced at the crew list, then at my watch. Most of the *Starry Night* company was staying at a motel in the Three Mile Harbor section of East Hampton. Maybe I could catch them; some of them might have left town for a long weekend, but I didn't think many would voluntarily walk away from what was probably the most renowned vacation spot in America for three days on West Ninety-fifth Street or in Hoboken. 'East, I've got to go.'

'Sy played it very close to the vest,' he said thoughtfully, not hearing me. 'But I remember one thing. Maybe

334

it's significant. Every Saturday, the week before, and the first two weeks of shooting, he gave Lindsay a present. Left it at her place at the table so when she came down for coffee, she'd find it. I don't mean a box of chocolates. I mean Art Deco diamond ear clips. Five-hundred-dollar cashmere shawls in a rainbow of colors: I think he gave her seven or eight of them at once. They were spilling over her chair; it was an incredible sight. A Piaget watch. Nothing he gave her cost less than two or three thousand, and the average was closer to five. But that last Saturday he was alive, all he left was a note: "In tennis tournament. See you tonight."'

'You saw the note?'

'Yes. It was just lying there. Not in an envelope, or even folded. And all right, maybe I'm not the gentleman I pretend to be. I guess you know that better than anyone. I have no qualms about reading other people's mail, especially not a note to Lindsay.'

'Was he actually playing in a tennis tournament?'

'I would seriously doubt it. He wasn't a particularly good player. Limp forehand; he would have been eliminated long before lunch. And, Steve, this is the thing: I was in the house when Lindsay came down. I saw her. She looked at her place setting. Nothing there. At her chair, under the table. Nothing. Then she read the note. And she *stormed* out of the room.'

The only time I went into a bar anymore was when I was on a case; otherwise it was a risk I figured I didn't need to take. Still, even though it was business, the first thing I did when I walked into the Harbor Room at the Summerview Motel was to grab a glass of club soda, grip it hard and sip like crazy.

The Teamster drivers, a group of six, were big-bellied

and Irish, beardless Santa Clauses who could hold their liquor. They were guys who had brothers or sons who were cops and who respected the shield. We got to be pals fast. Lindsay's driver was a two-hundred-fifty-pound, apple-cheeked guy named Pete Dooley.

'She doesn't get a chauffeured limo?' I asked.

'Uh-uh.' Classic Brooklyn. 'Maybe, you know, Stallone, somebody like that. Lindsay gets me and a station wagon.' He glanced at my glass. 'Want something stronger?'

'Can't.' He understood. 'What's she like, Pete?'

'I've had worse. She's a bitch. Big deal. Doesn't feel she has to say things like hello or please or thank you. But on the other hand, she don't snort coke, or mess herself, or cry and ask me to hook up a hose to the tail pipe.'

'She ever talk to you?'

'Uh-uh. Just says where she wants to go, what she wants.'

'What did she want on the day Sy Spencer was shot?'

'Nothing much. I picked her up at six in the morning. Didn't drive her home. Her agent came to break the bad news, and he took her back.'

'Did you see her at all during that day?'

'Just, you know, around. Before lunch, she sent a PA over to me with a note. I should pick up a package at an underwear store on Hill Street back in Southampton. Pay them, get a receipt – and make sure to count the change. What a bitch! So I waited till after lunch, did it, came back.'

'The package was already wrapped?' He nodded. 'Did it feel light like underwear, or could it have been something heavier?'

'Underwear. Four hundred sixty-three bucks and eighteen cents' worth of underwear, and this is for someone who lets 'em bounce all the time. Never wears a bra. What the hell could cost over four hundred bucks?'

'Beats me. Fancy lace shit, maybe. She gave you the money in cash, Pete?'

'Yeah. Twenties.'

I got another club soda. He and the other drivers went over the crew list with me. They said Barbara, her makeup lady, had gone back to the city for the weekend, but to try the hair guy and the costume lady. They pointed out their names and said they were probably somewhere around the motel.

Except for the fact that he had four or five super-blonde, Lindsay-color wigs in his room, on faceless Styrofoam heads, the hair guy could have passed for a cabdriver, or a steamfitter. He was about as stylish as the pizza sauce, cheese and pepperoni that had plopped down onto his shirt. He and a couple of other guys – he said they were grips – were watching one of those soft-core horny-airline-stewardess movies that motels pipe into rooms. All he could tell me was that in the party scene they'd been shooting, Lindsay trying to show how wild and carefree she was even though she was hurting inside, ran into the ocean, fully dressed. On the TV, a stewardess with no underwear in a tiny skirt was bending over to serve a passenger a drink, and the hairstylist kept turning back to watch her, like he'd never seen a bare ass before and couldn't get over how wondrous it was. Lindsay, I reminded him. We're talking about Lindsay. Right, he said.

Lindsay's own hair had been under a wig cap, and they'd put on dry wigs for when she ran and a wet wig for when she came up out of the water; he'd stood there in the surf, styling it for her. When they'd called her for a scene, she'd always been ready. Where was she when she wasn't acting? In wardrobe or her trailer. Yes, it was possible for her to have gone out and come back. Sometime late afternoon, there had been a turnaround that took over an hour. There was no big deal with the lights, but the Steadicam operator was having trouble with his harness. No one saw her during that time; she always liked her privacy. Nobody knew what she did: probably read magazines, because the trailer was filled with every magazine ever printed – she was probably looking for her name or her picture; they all did that. But maybe she slept, or meditated. Who knew? Who cared?

I thought that Lindsay would have been taking a big chance if she'd tried to slip away unnoticed, because of the time factor. Besides, as the hair guy explained, there could always be a wardrobe or script crisis that required her presence. Also, she was just too noticeable.

I asked if there were any other wigs around. Not white-blond ones. He said there were a couple of dark-brown ones in the makeup trailer, but they were for Nick Monteleone.

On the TV, one of the airline stewardesses was starting to play with another one's nipples; they were standing in the galley with their blouses off. I yawned. I was so wiped out. The grips gazed at the screen, nudged each other. I lost the hair guy's attention. I was too tired to care. I left the room.

The Summerview was standard motel, an elongated two-story rectangle with a balcony running the length of the upper floor. It was not for the socially ambitious visitor to East Hampton: no famous newspaper columnists or politicians or fashion designers would be found rubbing shoulders over the toaster waffles in the King of the Sea Coffee Shop. It was a place for normal people who wanted to sit on a perfect beach by day and get a little glamour by night: browse in shops they couldn't afford, or squint into passing Rolls-Royces to see if Steven Spielberg was inside.

The *Starry Night* production company had taken over the whole second floor of the Summerview. I walked along the balcony. From the sounds coming from room 237, either that TV was on, too, and one of the stewardesses had found a guy – or a couple was making it in a major way. I yawned again and waited about thirty seconds for them to come, but they didn't sound like that was on the agenda for a while, so I knocked, hard. About a minute later, the costume designer, Myrna Fisher, opened the chained door about two inches and peered out at me. She was a woman in her fifties, in an inside-out negligee. I showed her my shield and said I was sorry if I'd woken her, but I had some questions, and could I come in. She said she had a . . . a guest. I said I wouldn't keep them long. Just a few questions.

She unchained the door and let me in. In the bed, with the sheet pulled up to the top of his neck so just his skeleton head showed, was Gregory J. Canfield, Sy's production assistant – all one hundred and ten pounds and twenty years of him. 'Hi, Gregory,' I said.

'Hi,' he peeped.

I wanted to tell him it was okay, I wouldn't call his mother, but instead I motioned to Myrna to take a seat at the round Formica table that stood in front of the tightly closed drapes. I sat on the chair across from her. 'Tell me about Lindsay Keefe last Friday. How was she behaving? Did she see Sy Spencer when he came to the set? Anything you can think of.'

For a minute, Myrna kept feeling for the buttons of her negligee, but since it was inside out, she finally settled for holding it closed. I couldn't believe she was a costume designer; with her dumpy figure, gray hair and blotchy skin, she looked like a Suffolk County payroll clerk. 'It's the big party scene under a tent. Originally I was going to put her in a canary-yellow Scaasi – halter top, pouffy skirt – but then they changed the script and she had to run into the ocean, so she was in saffron silk pants and blouse. Cheapies: we had six of them. Elizabeth Gage jewelry. Charles Jourdan mules, but she loses them in the sand.'

Gregory chimed in from the bed. 'Mules are shoes. Backless, with heels.' I nodded thanks. Myrna beamed at him before she turned back to me.

'Sy came into the wardrobe trailer sometime around eleven. We'd just gotten Lindsay out of her wet clothes, wrapped her in a bath sheet. They said hello.'

'Did they kiss or show any signs of affection?'

Myrna considered the question. 'I think – I won't swear to it – he kissed her on the neck or shoulder. But I didn't believe it. They'd lost it.'

'Lost what?'

'Their thing for each other. Well, his thing. It was always his. I've worked on three films with her, and I don't think she *really* . . . ' She gave me a Know-what-I-mean? look; I gave her a Gotcha nod. 'But Sy Spencer was crazy for her.'

'What was the attraction, other than her looks?' I

340

liked Myrna. She was a shrewdie. 'That she was such an intellectual?'

'Sleeping with brainy men doesn't make you an intellectual. Lindsay's not really all that smart. But Sy was wild for her – and not for her mind. He was wild because she was so cold. I'd never worked on one of his projects before, but my guess is that women fell all over themselves trying to impress him. Lindsay couldn't have cared less. He wasn't one of her left-wing passion pots. He was just a rich sucker who could buy her things. She didn't care what he thought, or what he had to say. It made him *crazy* about her.'

'But that stopped.'

'Yes.'

'Why?'

'Well, I don't know what went on in their bedroom.' She snatched a quick, happy eyeful of Gregory. 'But you must have heard there was a problem with her performance. I'm sure that didn't sit well with him. And also, she's very boring. She talks about her approach to a character – for hours. Or she gives you a speech on racism or on world hunger. She acts like she's the only person in the whole world with a conscience – except her boyfriends with *Viva Zapata!* mustaches. That's ridiculous. Most of us care. Some of us are charitable. But that's not how real people talk when they're getting a seam pinned. Lindsay does, though. She can't talk about normal things, real life, because she's dead inside. And in the long run, Sy Spencer was no necrophiliac.'

'That means – ' Gregory began.

'I know what it means, Gregory.' I turned back to Myrna. She was smiling, charmed by Gregory's earnestness. 'What happened after Sy kissed her?'

'Not much. He said he was off to LA, that he hated to go and he'd miss her terribly. I didn't believe a word of it.'

'Anything else?' Then I added: 'Anything about money?'

'Yes. Right. She said she needed some cash, and he said all he had was the money he needed for the trip, but by that time she was going through his pockets – patting them, like police do – and she took out a wad of bills.'

'What did he say?'

'Nothing. He let her have it. My guess is, it had happened before.'

'And then?'

'They both said, "I love you, darling," "I'll miss you, angel," and he left.'

'Did she seem sad? Upset?'

'Actually? Angry. She held that wad of cash like it was his balls. She squeezed as hard as she could.'

I sat in the office of the Summerview. The night manager had been more than cooperative. She'd stopped just short of curtsying when I'd asked to use the phone, and she'd begged to be allowed to bring me coffee. Either she was a cop groupie or she was running numbers out of there. Probably numbers.

I called Carbone at home and told him that since I'd been in East Hampton anyway, checking out Bonnie's friends, I'd dropped over at the Summerview on a hunch; I explained how I'd gotten the catalog creep to admit he'd paid Bonnie off the books, and now I had a witness who'd seen Lindsay dredging in Sy's pocket and coming up with a bundle of cash, and another who'd taken five hundreds' worth of twenties she gave him to pay for underwear.

'The case against Bonnie is starting to look feeble,' I remarked. He didn't respond, which I took as agreement.

I asked if he'd left Robby at the office, still reading files. Carbone said no, that he'd gone into the squad room right before he'd left and Robby hadn't been there. One of the other guys had told him Robby had rushed out, as if something was up. Like what, I wanted to know. Carbone hadn't a clue, but knowing how Robby lacked stamina, maybe he'd just had to hurry and get home and hit the sack.

I hung up feeling edgy. Robby was on a rampage; he'd been enraged enough to lie about my drinking. A guy that crazed doesn't just go to sleep.

I drove west, toward Bridgehampton, then dipped south of the highway, past Bonnie's house. No sign of Robby: Thighs had just come on duty and was parked across the street from her place. He was devouring a bologna-and-American-cheese hero; the mayonnaise on his chin glistened in the moonlight. I asked, She turn up yet? He shook his head.

I had him come inside with me, up to her office. Bonnie had loads of files, but I couldn't believe it. For a writer, she had no sense of letters; it looked as though she'd never figured out how to alphabetize. Most of her papers were in folders or manila envelopes, but these were stuffed, randomly, into drawers or piled on an old-fashioned wooden in/out box. Eventually I found her *Sea Change* file. My heart started to hammer. I opened the folder as if half expecting it would blow up in my face. But there were Sy's memo and his note: 'Adore it!'

I had Thighs read over my shoulder. I told him the case against Bonnie was falling apart, and he might as well pick up a few points by helping it collapse, bringing in the file showing that although Sy hadn't written, Sure I'll make your movie, he hadn't rejected her screenplay either, not by a long shot. You're sure you don't want the points? Thighs asked. You found this. Hey, I told him, it's okay, buddy. You'll be doing me a favor. I don't need points anymore; I've gone as high as I can go in the squad. And all I've been doing lately is sabotaging the case against Bonnie. Carbone and Shea already think I'm on some crazy crusade to clear her, and since she's going to get cleared anyway, you might as well be the hero. I sensed Thighs was no great fan of Robby's, so I added: I guess you've heard Kurz is nipping at my ass on this one. He wants to nail her. I'd appreciate it if you could help me out. Thighs said, My pleasure.

Good: I wanted a witness that the memo and Sy's note really existed. I couldn't believe that if Robby came back he would actually destroy them. But I wouldn't have put it past him to lose them for a few days.

I figured any guy who could eat bologna, American cheese and mayo was my kind of guy, a human septic tank, so after I left, I stopped at the deli, got a six-pack of Yoo-Hoo and some Ring-Dings and Devil Dogs, and brought them back to Thighs. That sealed the deal. Jeez, he said, Steve, thanks a hell of a lot. Let me pay you for all this. You sure? Oh, hey.

He was mine.

Moose began to bark as I pulled into my driveway, and I had such a surge of gladness that I forgot I was stupid with fatigue. I pictured walking in to the dog's delirious tail-wagging, hand-licking greeting, then rushing into the pineapple room, sitting on the edge of the bed and having Bonnie put her arms around me, draw me close, press her cheek against mine and whisper, Please, just hold me. The homeyness of it made it such an enticing vision.

I squared my shoulders, stood up straight and braced myself. I knew from AA how fatigue can make you vulnerable; you cannot stand firm when all you want is comfort. The mood I was in, it wouldn't be the consolation of booze that would seduce me. It wouldn't be wild sex. It would be sweetness, and soft conversation.

I strolled inside, gave Moose an indifferent, platonic pat and checked my answering machine. Just Lynne: 'I guess you must be *very* busy. Good night, Steve. I love you and I'm thinking about you. Speak to you tomorrow.'

I was wiped; maybe that was why Lynne's understanding irritated the hell out of me. Why, for once, couldn't she say, You self-centered fuck, why can't you take two minutes and pick up the phone? But then I thought: No. You had to appreciate how serene she was, how adult, how truly superior. Only then, fortified, did I go in to see Bonnie.

She put the Stephen King book she'd been reading on the nightstand. She'd taken a shower, washed her hair; it was shiny and wet, pulled back tight, braided. She'd changed into the clean pink T-shirt I'd brought from her house. The plaid blanket was pulled up high, prim, almost to her neck, as if she'd decided to become the definitive old maid. Except she gave me her wonderful, welcoming beacon of a smile.

'Hi!'

'How's it going?' Hey, forewarned is forearmed. I

was on alert. I could afford to be slightly friendly.

'It's going okay,' Bonnie said. 'I had a couple of minutes of panic. I mean, I've been making jail jokes, but when I actually think about it – '

'Then take it easy on yourself. It's been a rough time. Don't think about it.'

Hearing Lynne's message had really cleared my head. Bonnie was the next couple of days; Lynne was the rest of my life. The only thing that made me edgy was sleeping in the same house with her. I'd be okay. I was so knocked out I'd probably be asleep as soon as I took off my shoes. But I was troubled by a picture of Bonnie tiptoeing through the dark house and slipping into my bed and murmuring, Please, just hold me. Any touch – her fingers grazing my chest, her legs brushing against mine – might make me lose all sense. I couldn't afford to be faced with that. My palms started to sweat. I pretended to be kneading sore muscles and wiped them on my pants. I decided I would just lock the door of my bedroom.

Then I sat, but I maneuvered the chair so it was farther from her bed. Okay, this was better. The situation was under control. 'Let me give you the Lindsay Keefe story,' I said. I told her, in detail, everything I'd learned in the course of the investigation.

She sat with her arms hugging her knees, like a kid at a campfire listening to a riveting ghost story. I waited for her to say, Wow! Good work!

Except she just shook her head and said: 'Get a good night's sleep. You need it.'

'What do you mean?'

'I mean, you'll think better in the morning.'

'Stop that patronizing crap. It irritates the hell out of me.'

'You call this a case against Lindsay?' Bonnie demanded.

'She had a motive. He was going to fire her.'

'So she'd hire a lawyer and fight it. Or hire a publicist and leak word about what a disaster *Starry Night* is and how she couldn't compromise her standards of excellence by working on such a consummate piece of schlock.'

'Come on. Word was around the movie business about what a disaster she was. If Sy fired her, it could ruin her.' Bonnie gave me a fast roll of the eyes, a supercilious you're-not-an-insider look. 'I want you to stop being so fucking condescending, Bonnie.'

'Who do you think Sy was? A 1939 mogul with a big cigar, a Louis B. Mayer who could say, "You'll never work in this town again"? No. Sy was a first-class producer, which is a good thing to be. But Lindsay's a star. One crummy performance wouldn't do her in.'

'You're the one who said her agent was probably begging Sy not to fire her.'

'That's his job. But what if Sy *had* told him to stuff it and did fire her? Lindsay would survive. Listen, she's as cold and calculating as they come. I'm sure she knew getting the ax wasn't going to help her career, but she also knew it wouldn't hurt it, not that much. Certainly not enough to kill for.'

'You're assuming she's rational,' I said.

'Do you have any evidence that she's not?'

I edged forward in the chair. I wanted to convince her, get her over to my side. 'I have to trust my gut in this business, and I'm telling you, she's flawed. Beautiful, yeah, but something major is missing. A realization that she's human. And when Sy withdrew from her, first as her number one fan, then as her boyfriend or fiancé or

347

whatever the hell he was, it was a sign she wasn't perfect. And she couldn't take it.'

'I hate to say it, but you have a better case against me.'

'You know, you can read all the stupid mysteries you want, but you're still a total ignoramus when it comes to homicide.'

'How did she get from the set in East Hampton – without being seen – to Sandy Court?'

'I'll figure it out.'

'How?'

'What are you, her goddamn defense lawyer?'

'And even assuming she knows something about a rifle, beyond holding it right so she looks like she knows how to shoot, where would she have gotten the weapon?'

'In a gun store, you jerk.'

'You have to register in New York State, don't you?'

'They have to record the sale of rifles. But she'd give a false name.'

'And the gun store owner wouldn't recognize her and be overjoyed that Lindsay Keefe had bought a .22 from him? He wouldn't tell the world? Tell the police?'

'She's an actress,' I insisted. 'Do you think she'd walk in with blonde hair and tits, or would she disguise herself – maybe in one of Nick Monteleone's wigs?'

'Where would she have hidden a rifle? Under the bed she was sharing with Sy? In Mrs Robertson's cookie jar?'

I got up. 'Anything else?'

'Don't get angry just because I don't agree with you. Listen: I used to be a pretty good shot. My dad gave me a Marlin for my twelfth birthday, and I went hunting with him and my brothers on and off for the next six years. If I had to shoot someone through the head from what . . . fifty feet?'

'Yeah.'

348

'Okay, if I decided on the spur of the moment to blast Sy, could I get him in the first round? Maybe. If I'd planned a murder, took target practice, I'd say I'd have had a good chance. But to think someone like Lindsay – who had a couple of hours of instruction with some sex-crazed white hunter she'd been sleeping with – is going to be able to fire two bullets into Sy and score bull's-eyes both times, then you should hang up that gut you trust and go into another business.'

I didn't say good night. I didn't say anything. I just stalked out of the room.

CHAPTER 17

This is why I knew I wouldn't be able to sleep:

The gallon of coffee I'd drunk during the day.

My fears about Bonnie. Fear one: The case against her was unraveling, but the sideburnless, crew-cut, pink-faced assistant DA, who looked like a cross between a pig and a Ku Klux Klan grand kleagle, might still be able to get an indictment and then a conviction. Fear two: Bonnie, knowing her own innocence (or her own guilt), would steal out of the house during the night, and none of us would ever see her again. Fear three: She'd slip into my bedroom, and I'd have to reject her. Fear four: Knowing I'd never be able to reject her, Bonnie would slip into my bedroom, keep me at it the whole night, then use her hold over me, get me to build a case against someone – anyone – else. Fear five: Bonnie Bernstein-Spencer was a killer, whose rage was surpassed only by her coolheadedness and coldbloodedness. The girl with the great smile was a criminal genius, who would always be one step ahead of the smartest cop. Fear six: Bonnie was what she seemed to be, a good and smart and thoroughly decent human being. If I did manage to prove her innocent, she would spend the rest of her life alone, without ever having had someone to love her.

Also, I couldn't sleep because of the dry tickle in the back of my throat, and I couldn't shake the memory of how an icy, malty beer could soothe it.

And I couldn't sleep because I sensed this case was crucial, a turning point in my life. Was it that the crime had been perpetrated on home ground, the South Fork? Was it the coincidence that the victim and I, two men of the world, had used (or been used by) the same woman? Was it some cockeyed sense of Brady family honor, that this case couldn't wind up in an Open Investigation file drawer; I had to come through for Sy because he had come through for my brother? Or was I wide awake simply because this would be my last homicide investigation as a free man, unencumbered by husbandly obligations? Soon I would have to be someplace at five-thirty. To choose among swatches for our upholstery. To install our energy-efficient room air conditioner—dehumidifier. To set up the barbecue for the swordfish steaks we'd serve when Sister Marie, the principal of Lynne's school, came to dinner. To umpire our Little Leaguer's Little League game.

Forget sleep. I couldn't even rest. The coffee sloshed around in my stomach, and I felt sick, disoriented, frightened, the way a kid feels in a small boat on a rough sea when he loses sight of land. I lay in bed, worrying whether I should leave my bedroom door the way it was, half open, so I could hear if Bonnie made a move to escape, or whether to close it, lock out the possibility of a silhouetted figure whispering 'Are you asleep?'

I kept flipping from my side to my back around to my other side, trying to get my stomach to calm down. But all that happened was I wound up so mummified in the sheet I had to get up and unwrap myself. Then I lay back down and stared at the dark rectangle of ceiling. I couldn't get my motor to stop racing.

Another reason for insomnia: Somewhere along the way, as I'd been following the Spencer case, had there been a signal I'd missed, a sign I should have read?'

In the stillness, I heard my breathing, shallow, rapid. God, did I feel lousy. My neck and left shoulder were horribly sore, as though I had been punched again and again. The left side of my head began to throb. I tried to recall the relaxation technique they'd taught us at South Oaks, but I forgot whether you inhaled through your nose and exhaled through your mouth, or vice versa.

A stab of pain shot down my arm. My heart raced. I put my hand against my chest; my skin was clammy. The nausea wouldn't go away. A coronary? No, exhaustion.

No, a stroke. I kneaded my upper arm. The pain was receding, but the triceps felt almost numb. God, could this actually be a stroke? I thought: By the time I get up the courage to cry out for Bonnie, it'll be too late. All I'll be able to do is dribble and make mewing-kitten noises.

Just then, instead of falling into a coma, I fell sound asleep. It was such a deep, dreamless sleep that when I woke up and it was still dark, I thought: Holy shit, I slept the clock around. But then I propped myself up on my elbow and looked at the green gleam of the clock: three forty-six.

I performed my customary back-to-sleep ritual. I turned my pillow over and puffed it up into a mountain, fluffed out the sheet, turned the clock facedown to hide its garish, Emerald City glow. No good. I was wide awake.

I knew what had woken me. I wanted Bonnie.

Moonlight slipped past the curled edges of the shades,

and the white walls of the pineapple room gleamed. I heard a rhythmic thumping, but it was only Moose's big tail slapping against the wood floor, applauding the prospect of unexpected fellowship. Bonnie stirred for a second, but the happy tail thump was obviously a familiar, comforting night sound. She curled back up, fast asleep.

I could have walked away right then. It would have been easy. Nothing to tempt me: no languorous arm draped across the narrow single bed, no naked leg or bare hip to tantalize. The only part of her not covered by the plaid blanket was her head.

But on the chair were the sweats I'd lent her, neatly folded, and dropped on the floor near the bed, less neatly, her own T-shirt. And the thin band of sheer white that was her underpants. That did it.

I sat on the edge of the bed, kissed her hair, whispered her name. She raised her head, opened her eyes. No fluttery eyelashes and pseudo-dopey where-am-I? looks. Bonnie knew.

'What do you want?'

'To visit.' I flashed what I hoped was a devil-may-care smile. Charm wasn't doing it, though. There was no smile back. I drew aside the blanket. She was naked. 'See? You knew I was coming. You got all dressed up for me.' I lay down on the bed beside her. In the moonlight, the slender strips of white where a two-piece bathing suit had prevented a tan shone with a pearly luster, like the inside of a seashell. 'A host has an obligation to entertain his guest.' I kissed her cheek, her mouth, the demarcation line between her dark chest and white breasts. I was soft and gentle, demonstrating: I'm not just out for nooky. See? I've got finesse. Style. Technique.

Bonnie didn't arch her neck, or murmur a sophisticated That feels marvelous. No, she smoothed my hair off my forehead, away from my temples. It was such a loving gesture, and so soothing, that it caught me off guard. I stopped the casual kissing. I reached for her hand, but she kept it to herself.

'Tell me,' she whispered. 'Does this visit mean something?' Direct words, forthright gaze. Give me the truth, they said. Total bullshit: I knew I could tell her whatever I wanted to tell her. She was so goddamn gullible. 'Or are you here . . . is it just for tonight?'

She made it so much harder on herself. Why couldn't she simply pretend it didn't matter to her? She all but walked through life wearing a sandwich board that said BIG MOUTH BUT COMPLETELY VULNERABLE in huge red letters. What can you say to someone like that?

'Just for tonight, Bonnie.' We lay side by side, barely apart. If either of us had taken a deep breath, skin would have grazed skin.

'Another one-night stand? That's all you want for us?'

I closed my eyes because I felt tears. 'Yeah.'

'Can't offer me anything better?'

'No.'

'Does it make any difference that I love you?'

'No, it doesn't.' Before I could tell her how sorry I was, she pressed her fingers against my lips.

'Let me cut you off at the pass,' she said. 'Don't say "I'm sorry." Not that you would. Apologizing for not being able to love me . . . Well, that would be cheap, and you're not cheap.'

'Neither are you.'

'I know.'

She shifted that fraction of an inch so we were touching. I ran my hands over the whole length of her body. She was silky, sleep-warmed. I couldn't believe the softness of her.

'Wait. Listen to me,' she said. 'Here are my one-night-stand rules. You can't say "You're beautiful." You can't say "You're a truly fine person."' She paused. 'And you can't say "I love you." Other than that, anything goes.'

She put her arms around me and guided me on top of her. Slowly, as if we had weeks, years, all the time in the world, she let her fingers drift down my back, over my ass, and then between my legs. I was so overwhelmed by finally being able to touch her again, kiss her, that I felt I was going to lose it.

I did. Suddenly tears were drenching my face.

'Stephen, are you okay?'

'Yeah. Just over-something. Overtired. Over-stimulated.' Bonnie wiped my cheeks with the sheet. It didn't help that she was so tender. I patted her hand, then pushed it away. 'I'm okay. And listen, nobody calls me Stephen.'

'You don't have to have sex with me if you don't want to, Stephen.'

'Does it feel like I don't want to?'

'No, it feels downright enthusiastic. But it and you may be two distinct entities.'

'Well, it and I want to make love to you.'

So we did.

Afterwards, I brought her into my bedroom, and before we slept, we made love again. My memory of our other night, five summers before, did not begin to do her justice. I had remembered the passion; I had forgotten the sweetness.

Except this time there were rules: Bonnie's Rules of Play for the One-Night Stand. No You're beautiful. No You're a truly fine person. No I love you. The whole time we were making love, and after, just lying there, talking softly about nothing much, I wanted more than moans, cries, animal grunts, sighs, inane sweet nothings. But all I could think of to say were the no-nos, words of love and admiration. I thought: Well, she's certainly mastered the fine points of the game; only an ace at one-night stands could anticipate the need for such rules.

I had to play fair. I didn't want her to think I was cheap. So I didn't call out, I love you. But I tried to show her.

When we finally fell asleep, my head was resting against hers on the pillow. I held both her hands tight in mine, close against my heart.

Magic hour.

Bonnie had made the bed while I took Moose for a run, but she'd folded the sheet over the top of the blanket, and there was too much sheet showing, so when she went into the shower, I fixed it. She spotted it right away. 'You remade the bed.'

'It wasn't right.'

'You're not supposed to care about order. It's not masculine.' She was sitting on the bed in her shorts and one of my undershirts. She gripped the mug of coffee the way a guy does; she didn't use the handle the way a woman is supposed to. 'Order is feminine,' she announced. 'Chaos is masculine.'

'After last night you're telling me I'm not masculine?'

'Don't you ever go to movies?' She held up her hands and positioned her thumbs at right angles to her

356

outstretched fingers, like a director framing a shot. '"CAMERA TRACKS INTO COP'S BEDROOM. Total chaos. Suspiciously gray sheet half-off mattress. CLOSE ON night table, where WE SEE gun, empty whiskey bottle, crumpled papers, remains of last week's Chinese takeout and overflowing ashtray." So how come you're neat?'

'Good cops are organized. I like things under control. The real question is: Why are you such a slob?'

'What are you talking about? I'm not a slob.'

I laughed. 'Give me a break, Bonnie. I executed a search warrant. You don't pair your socks. You just throw them into a drawer, along with your bras, which look like a pile of spaghetti. Your teaspoons and tablespoons are all mixed up. Oh, and your papers aren't in alphabetical order; they don't make any sense.'

'Neatness doesn't count. Cleanness counts.'

'You haven't thrown out a magazine or a paperback in ten years. What kind of person keeps a *TV Guide* from 1982?'

'Obviously not your kind of person.'

Well, there it was. Ever since we'd woken up, a little before six, Bonnie had been withdrawing from me. Not the injured-female bit, with cold, clipped responses to my questions. No, Bonnie was all thumbs-in-the-belt-loops, howdy-partner friendly: Gee, OJ and raisin bran would be terrific. Thanks. Of course she understood she had to stay in the bedroom once I went out, that the windows in the main room weren't covered and on the off chance someone dropped by . . . And sure she'd be glad to tell me anything more I wanted to know about Sy. Discuss the whole case? You bet!

She could have been anyone I'd put up for the night – a visiting cop, someone grateful for bed and breakfast, a cheerful, outgoing kind of guy. When she'd finished the last spoonful of milk and put the cereal bowl back on the storm window I'd used as a tray because I didn't have a tray, she'd smiled and said, real chipper: You know what's good about you? Your cereal is crisp. I can never keep things from sogging up out here. Back in Ogden, you can keep Cheerios for *decades*.

'Bonnie, let's clear the air.'

She smiled a TV weathergirl smile: much too many teeth. 'The air's clear.' She reached over and picked up my clock; it was still facedown. 'Look, it's almost seven. The night's over. The sun's shining.' Her smile faded. Her lips pursed together, serious, prim. 'It's time to work.'

But I kept at it. 'I'm not much of a bargain, you know.'

'I know.'

'Something's missing. I'm defective.' No argument, no agreement. She sat silently, with too-perfect posture. 'The thing is, with Lynne I have a chance of coming closer to having a normal life than I ever thought I could.' I waited for Bonnie to cry out: But do you love her? What about me? She said: 'Let's talk about motive.'

'It's not that I don't care about you. You know I do.'

'I'm sure every single person in the *Starry Night* crew had some grudge against Sy.'

'Bonnie, if we talk, it'll make it easier for you.'

'Sy cheated people on money, he lied to them about opening credits, he humiliated them in front of fifty people. So there are seventy, eighty people right there in East Hampton who you'd think had a motive to kill him. And another five or six hundred people he'd hurt or insulted over the years. What do you do in a case like this, where the murder victim is an SOB?'

I'd only been trying to help her. But if she wanted to work, I'd work. 'You look for real injury,' I explained.

'Was there anyone Sy really harmed, or was about to harm? Not just hurt feelings, where someone might say, 'I hope Sy Spencer dies.' I'm talking damage that could destroy someone's life. So that's the main thing; you look for serious grievances. You rule out people who are just pissed. Pissed doesn't count. With one exception. Nut jobs. Maybe Sy promised some actor star billing three movies ago and the guy wound up with his name at the tail end of the movie, next to something like best boy. A normal guy would forget it. A nut job could have spent two, three years plotting revenge.'

'How often does that happen?'

'Not often. Even nuts get bored. They find new villains. So unless we get bogged down – I'm talking completely, totally stumped – we wouldn't do anything more than a routine check on a victim's distant past. See, nuts usually don't suffer in silence. They send hate mail, make threatening phone calls. And a guy like Sy would be smart; he's seen too many celebrities hit by psychos to ignore those kind of threats. Right?'

'Definitely. If Sy had thought someone crazy was out to get him, he'd have probably gone the whole route. Hired bodyguards, even. Sy had no physical courage.'

That surprised me. He was so smooth. 'Give me a for-instance.'

Bonnie thought, rubbing her forehead to help herself along. 'Like one time, we were riding, up in the Grand Tetons. Sy got thrown. Nothing happened; he wound up with a sore behind. You couldn't blame the horse; it saw a bear and got spooked. But he wouldn't get back on that horse for anything, even when I kidded him about being a scaredy-cat – which, okay, I admit might have not been my most sensitive moment in my career as wife.

'But it didn't take an actual event to frighten him. Sy could get scared by nothing. We'd be walking in the theater district and if a couple of black guys who didn't look like they were headed for an NAACP fund-raiser at the Pierre walked by, he'd stiffen. Just a little, but you knew in the back of his mind he was seeing headlines: "Producer Castrated by Rampaging Youth Gang." What I'm getting at is, if someone from his past had been gunning for Sy, he'd have gotten protection. You'd have heard about it.'

'Good.' I went into the kitchen for another cup of coffee. When I came back I started telling her: 'You know, talk about riding, my family had a farm when I was little. We kept a horse. Prancer. I haven't ridden for years, but – '

'What do you want from me?' Bonnie asked softly.

'I don't know,' I answered, just as softly.

'Whatever we had ended an hour and a half ago. Just remember that. And no matter what happens today, what you find or don't find, I'm out of here by five o'clock. So I don't want to know that you rode horsies when you were a little boy. I don't want to hear about your first Yankee game. I don't want you to tell me how you got the monkey off your back after Vietnam.'

'I told you about that? My drug problem?'

'Your heroin problem. You told me. I don't care about it. And I don't care about your alcoholism – which obviously made you forget you told me about your heroin addiction.'

'What did I say about heroin?'

'Not much. It was when you were telling me about Vietnam.'

'I told you about Vietnam?'

Bonnie said coldly: 'It must have been one heck of a night for you, that you remember so much of it.'

'I remember enough to know it was one hell of a night.'

'Do you remember talking about why you became a cop?'

'No. I didn't think I ever really gave it much thought, much less talked about it.'

'You told me how terrified you'd been after you got back from the war. Walking down a street, if there was a crumpled-up Burger King bag on the sidewalk, you'd stop short, almost panic. Remember telling me that?' I didn't say anything, but I couldn't believe I'd told anyone about that time; my heart would bang in my chest and I'd want to scream out, Clear the area! Clear out! Watch that crumpled Burger King bag! We can all get killed! 'We were talking about how come you chose something potentially dangerous like being a cop instead of something safe, and you said, "This will show you how irrational I was – I thought of being a cop as safe, maybe because I'd be armed. I was so goddamn frightened all the time."'

'I didn't realize how I opened up to you, how I –'

Bonnie cut me off. 'Well, it doesn't matter now. I want you to understand: I don't give a damn about what you did in Vietnam, or what Vietnam did to you. I don't give a damn about your drugs or your alcohol or your recurring nightmares. I don't give a damn about *you*. And while we're at it, I don't give a damn about your fiancée's long auburn tresses or her commitment to the learning disabled. In another ten hours – unless, God forbid, I happen to wind up in court and you're a

361

witness for the prosecution – we'll never see each other again.'

I got up and walked out of the room. I remember nothing about what I thought or felt. I do remember rinsing the breakfast dishes and sticking them in the dishwasher and pouring what was left of the milk into the container. Then I went back in. Bonnie was the same; maybe even more remote.

If she had been in a movie, they'd have had some lens that would make her look as if she was moving back, farther and farther. Eventually she would become just a point of light. And then she'd vanish.

'Tell me who had a real motive to kill Sy,' she said.

'You.'

'Who else?'

'Lindsay.'

'You know what I think of that theory.'

'I don't give a flying fuck what you think,' I said. 'She's on the list.'

'Anyone else?'

'Some guy who invested in *Starry Night*, a guy from Sy's days in the meat industry.'

'Who?'

'Mikey LoTriglio.'

'Fat Mikey?' Bonnie's face got all pink and glowy; just hearing his name seemed to make her happy. She forgot to be remote. 'I love Fat Mikey!'

'You love him? He's a bad guy. Mafia.'

'I know. But for a bad guy, he was *so* wonderful. Well, wonderful to me.'

'What do you mean?'

'He knew I was a writer, so he was convinced I didn't have the foggiest notion about how the real world worked. He became very protective. Asking, "Sy treatin' you good?" I was always taking these ten-mile-long hikes through the city, and he didn't like it. Not one bit. He told Sy a husband shouldn't let a wife do things like that. But when he decided Sy couldn't stop me, he bought me a map. He marked all the neighborhoods he thought were dangerous in red. Oh, he called me Bonita. For some reason, he'd decided I was a classy dame, and he couldn't accept that I didn't have a more dignified name. When he heard we were splitting, that I wasn't asking for alimony, he called me up and gave me advice. I was so surprised to hear from him.'

'What did he say?'

'He told me he admired what I was doing but that this wasn't a movie. It was real life, "and in real life, Bonita, ladies whose husbands take a walk got to get lawyers." See, Mikey was Sy's friend. His loyalty should have been to Sy. That's the way people in his world operate. But he went out on a limb for me, tried to get me to go to a matrimonial lawyer he recommended. And the reason he did it was because he liked me a lot. And I liked him. I mean, he was a *man*. The men I met in New York, Sy's friends . . . they could get destroyed by a four-foot-two maître d' with bad breath and nose hair who sat them at a wrong table. Not Mikey. He was bad, but he was real.'

'Have you seen him or spoken to him since the divorce?'

'No.'

'Did Sy tell you he'd invested in *Starry Night*?'

'Yup.' Casual, relaxed, as if I'd asked if she wanted ketchup on her hamburger.

Except I'd asked her about Sy's investors before, and she'd given me some crap about his being edgy about 'the boys'. But she'd denied any knowledge of who they were. I blew up. 'I asked you about Sy's meat buddies before, goddamn it, and you told me – '

'Stop yelling.'

'I'm not yelling!' I banged my fist on the dresser. I hit my loose-change dish, and a dime jumped onto the floor. 'I'm talking loud.' I stopped, until I could regulate my voice. 'Tell me, Bonita, is there anything you don't lie about?'

'I didn't tell you about Mikey because he'd had a lot of trouble with the police in the past.'

'Do you think there may have been a reason for the trouble?'

'Oh, stuff it. Of course there was a reason for the trouble. He's a criminal. Just because he wears zoot suits and sounds like Sheldon Leonard in *Guys and Dolls* doesn't mean I don't know what he is. He's morally reprehensible – but he's not guilty of Sy's murder. If I'd told you about his investment it could have meant big trouble for him, and I *know* he didn't kill Sy.'

'Why? Because you did?'

'Yup.'

'Listen, honey, why don't you do Mikey a favor? Confess. Say: "Sy made me get rid of my baby, cheated on me, gave me the clap, burned out my tubes . . ."' No reaction. I could have been reciting my multiplication tables. '". . . and dropped me like a hot potato. Then he came back into my life and turned it upside down. He didn't love me, never has. He just *used* me. Over and over. And here I am: not getting any younger, lonely, broke. So I got out my .22 I brought back East from Daddy's store and shot the bastard." That would give Mikey a real alibi.'

'Stop babbling,' she ordered. 'Start thinking. Does Sy's murder sound like any kind of Mafia hit you've ever heard of?' It didn't, but all I did was shrug. 'It *couldn't* have been Mikey LoTriglio. There was no way Sy would have let things get to the point of offending Il Tubbo; he was afraid of him.'

'I thought he and Mikey were friends.'

'They were. Sort of. See, part of Sy, the cosmopolitan part, loved knowing someone who was connected, who could tell stories about how Jimmy the Nunz put Tony Tomato and his Lincoln Continental in the East River to see if they would float. And the ruthless part of Sy . . . well, having a boyhood friend like Fat Mikey was a potential business asset. But Sy's New York nervous-Nellie part was afraid of being with a man who carried a gun, someone who could order men hurt or killed. Sy was as afraid of potential violence as of real violence. He was the ultimate urban neurotic; he couldn't distinguish between a threat and an act. So no matter what it was, Sy *always* deferred to Mikey. I mean, we'd go out to dinner with Mikey and his wife or Mikey and his girlfriend, and Sy, who was the world's biggest, pickiest pain in a restaurant, would let Mikey order for him. He'd wind up eating what must have been fried goldfish or lard in marinara sauce because Mikey said, "You'll love this, Sy." So trust me on this one: If Mikey was upset that his investment was going sour, Sy would have taken out his wallet and paid Mikey back right then and there. Double.'

'We're talking a million-buck investment.'

'That wouldn't be a problem for Sy. He was probably worth ten or fifteen million.'

I shook my head. 'Forty-five big ones.' Bonnie looked astonished. 'You could have had a nice chunk.'

But she didn't seem interested in history. 'Who inherits his money?' she asked. 'His parents both died.'

'No one. He has some sort of charitable foundation set up. For the arts.'

Bonnie got up off the bed and lay facedown on the floor. She started doing push-ups, counting softly to herself. 'I don't like your list of suspects,' she said after forty-five. She wasn't at all winded.

'Why should you? You're on it.'

Maybe she and I were doing business, but I still wanted to keep my business private. Plus she'd passed sixty push-ups, which was more than I could do, and showed no signs of stopping; I figured I didn't have to be around to watch her hit a hundred.

I went into the kitchen and called Thighs, told him to track down Mikey; I had a couple more questions.

Then I woke up Germy on Beekman Place and asked him to get me the names of the cast and crew of Lindsay's rifle-toting African movie, *Transvaal*, ASAP. He told me I sounded better. I told him I was. He said he was driving out to Bridgehampton around noon, and to drop by over the weekend if I could. Bring my girl. I said I'd try. He'd just gotten a copy of a beautifully edited video about DiMaggio that hadn't been released yet. He'd bring it out.

I called Robby. According to Freckled Cleavage, he'd left for work *hours* ago. Which probably meant he'd just lifted the garage door. I called back Thighs; he said he'd been in since six-thirty and hadn't seen or heard from Robby.

Then I called Lindsay's agent, Eddie Pomerantz, who had a house in East Hampton. I told him I'd be over in an hour. He said, Today isn't good, and in fact my whole weekend is booked solid, and I said, Have your attorney call me within the next ten minutes and he said, Awright, see you in an hour.

I called Lynne. She said she'd been thinking about me, and I said I'd been thinking about her. She was going to be home most of the day, going over the psychological evaluations of her kids for next year. I said I'd try and drop over, but not to hold her breath until I got there. She said she wouldn't, but it would be lovely if I could find a few minutes.

I thought, I'll have a wife and kids. I'll be happy. And I'm going to spend the rest of my life longing for what Bonnie gave me.

When I went back into the bedroom, Bonnie was sitting on the bed again, cross-legged, seemingly communing with her feet. She didn't look up. 'Listen,' I said, 'about before. I'm sorry when I was ribbing you about killing Sy that I brought up . . .'

'My sterility.'

'Yeah. You know I go for the jugular. It was in bad taste.'

'Actually, it was beyond bad taste. It was cruel.'

'I apologize.'

'Fine,' she said to her nicely arched soles. 'Okay, let's get back to work. Any other theories? Random thoughts?'

'Like what?'

'I've been thinking about Sy. I know I told you he didn't seem worried, upset, anything like that. But on the other hand: he wasn't a hundred percent himself.' She paused. 'I feel uncomfortable talking about sex, but the last time we did it . . . he wasn't there. I mean, he was okay in the performance department, although that in itself doesn't mean a lot; Sy's equipment wasn't wired to his brain. But he wasn't concentrating on me. And that was such a critical thing for him, tuning in on precisely what a woman wanted and fulfilling that want. It was much more important than the physical act itself. But all of a sudden, it was strictly mechanical. Like he had some extra time because he'd changed his plane reservation, so he called and had me come over. But when I got there, he was an actor walking through a part that didn't interest him. He did what he had to do, but his mind was someplace else.'

'He was never preoccupied like that before?'

She shook her head. 'No. But see, it's nothing concrete. It's just a sense that a wife — or an ex-wife — gets about a man. That he wasn't really with me.'

'I don't want to hurt your feelings, but could he have been cooling down on you?'

'No, because then he wouldn't have had me come over. If he'd just wanted sex and gorgeousness, he could have spent some time with Lindsay in her trailer. Or found someone else. Don't forget; Sy was an unmarried heterosexual multimillionaire movie producer. With a hundred forty IQ and a thirty-two-inch waist. Women tend to find that attractive. But he wanted me that afternoon.'

'What for? I'm not being a shit now. I know why I would want you. Why would he want you?'

'Comfort. He could be himself with me. Well, as close to himself as Sy could ever get. I can't say he wanted me for fun, because he took himself too seriously to really let loose and laugh. But he seemed to have a good time bird-watching, walking with me; it was such a change from the rest of his life. And he loved sitting out in back — he called it his ex-yard — drinking lemonade and gossiping. And the sex was good.' I waited for her to say, Not anything approaching the way it was with you, Stephen. Ah, Stephen: what a beautiful name. She said: 'Sy and I knew how to please each other.'

'It's nice that you had that.' Tramp, I thought. I was so steamed. I went to my closet and picked out a tie, one that Easton had gotten me four or five Christmases earlier. Naturally, it was tasteful: red and blue and pale-yellow stripes.

Bonnie didn't seem to notice. 'I know you have to get going, but just think for a minute. From your professional point of view: Did anyone say anything that would back up the feeling I got of Sy's being preoccupied? Was there any kind of change in him?'

I sat on the edge of the bed and started doing my collar buttons. She did not lean over to help. 'That's not an easy call to make,' I explained. 'Sy had a talent – a genius – for being what people wanted him to be. Not just what you've told me about, in the sack. He could be tough with a Mikey, be intellectual with a film critic, be Mr Chicken Soup with an old Jewish reporter. He didn't seem to have any center. You knew him better than anyone. Who was the real Sy Spencer?'

'I don't know if there was one.'

'Right. So it's almost impossible for me to find out if Sy wasn't himself, because no one can tell me who "himself" is. Except that he always kept the lid on; I mean, his normal behavior was not screaming and kicking the crap out of production assistants and spitting on actors. And there was nothing in his behavior before his murder to show anything different. He was acting like a reasonable, rational man. No sudden blowups, no fits of melancholy.'

'So you don't see anything.'

'Shut up and let me finish.'

'Don't tell me to shut up. Ask me to please be quiet.'

'Please be quiet and go fuck yourself.'

'That's better.'

'Good. Now, two things strike me, but they're so petty they may not mean anything. But like you have a wife's sense, I have a cop's sense.'

'What are they?' She caught me staring at the inner part of her thighs again. Taut, no baggy skin. Paler than the tanned tops of her legs. She pushed herself back, so she was leaning against the headboard, stretched her legs straight out and clasped her hands over that indefinite region south of her vulva and north of her thighs. 'Come on,' she urged. 'You said two things struck you. Tell me. Function.'

'I am functioning. Okay, Sy could definitely indulge himself with material things, indulge women if he was in the mood. But basically he was a real cheapo. Always trying to get a better deal, always afraid that people were trying to cheat him. And you told me one of the reasons you didn't ask for alimony is that you wanted to stay in his good graces, and you knew he had a bug up his ass about women wanting him for his money. Am I right?'

'Yup.'

'Okay, so knowing all that, how come he paid Lindsay Keefe a half-million bucks more than her contract called for?' Bonnie looked astounded. 'Does that sound like him?'

'No. Not at all. It sounds like a schnook who never made a movie before.'

'Right. Some guy who's letting a movie star lead him around by the dick. I mean, so thrilled she's letting him in her pants, so scared she'll change her mind, that he throws in another five hundred thou.'

Bonnie brought up her clasped hands and rested her chin on them. She was intrigued. 'You're on to something. I don't know what. But Sy wouldn't let go of a nickel without a reason.'

'So what was the reason? Is it possible he made an off-the-books deal with her agent?'

She began to gnaw her knuckles while she considered the question. 'I doubt it,' she said finally. 'Lindsay and Nick were getting a million each. Normally, they're in the two-to-three-million range, but they were getting it on the back end.'

'A percentage of the profits?'

'Yup. The first-dollar gross. And Lindsay's agent ... Why would he go for an off-the-books deal? He's not going to trust an actress. He, his agency, is going to want the protection of a written contract to collect his ten percent.'

'So if a deal was struck, it would have been a private one between Sy and Lindsay.'

'It would have been. I just can't see him doing it. Except . . .'

'Except what?'

'Except she *was* living with him, had been for months. Sy took women out, had sex with them, maybe had an occasional sleep-over in Southampton for a weekend. But nobody besides me and Lindsay ever kept a toothbrush in his house; he didn't operate that way. So maybe he had fallen in love with her. Maybe he *was* going to marry her.'

'But it went sour.'

'Well, you have to ask whose fault that was. If it was hers, she was in trouble. Sy was vengeful.'

'How would he get his vengeance?'

'Just for starters, he'd stop having sex with her — but not tell her why. And he did that.'

'You don't know that for a fact.'

'I do know that's what he told me: He'd stopped sleeping with her. And I know him well enough sexually to know that you could stand on your head and whistle "Dixie" stark naked, and he still wouldn't — couldn't, probably — do it more than once a day. God, I hate getting clinical.'

'Get clinical.'

'Well, he could keep going for what seemed like forever, but once he . . . you know . . .' She got all flustered.

'Bonnie, you're forty-five years old.'

'Thank you. Well, once he came, that was it. And so if he was keeping company with me every single day, he would have had to put on a splint to do anything for her.'

'He saw you every day?'

'Every day. And he was so *angry* at her. He always got hostile during production, that quiet, nasty seething; I mean, if a fly would land on a wall, he'd want five grips with bazookas to go after it. But with Lindsay it was more. He was venomous. He called her terrible things, and that was so out of character for him.'

'Like what?'

'Well, maybe you won't think it's so terrible, because you have a filthy mouth. But Sy liked to think of himself as the epitome of refinement. And also as a clearheaded man of enlightenment. That meant buying politically correct ice cream and being pro-environment, anti-fur and ultra-pro-feminist. All of a sudden, though, he was calling her "cunt". You have no idea how out of character that was for him. Sure, he could be a miserable, heartless, vindictive rat, but always a genteel rat. He'd eat your face and tell you how profoundly he valued your friendship. So my guess is, Sy did love her. But then he turned on her. And just from his language, I'd say he'd lost control. In his mind, she'd betrayed him in some fundamental way.'

'Well, she'd betrayed him by screwing up her acting,' I suggested.

'Right. But for the first week or so, that didn't seem to stop his attraction. I mean, dailies were horrible, but you said people saw him around her on the set with steam coming out of his ears.'

'Okay. So what do we have? He was upset with her, angry with her, but he was still hot for her despite her lousy performance. But then she seeks out Santana as an ally – and Lindsay's way of forming an alliance is to fuck somebody. Then, within a day or two, Sy is looking to replace her. With other actresses for *Starry Night*. And with you for sex. So I'm asking: What's your gut? Doesn't it look like Sy knew?'

'It sure looks like it. I can't say definitely, because he had an enormous ego, and it would have been hard for him to accept that a woman would prefer anyone else to him. But on the other hand, he was very, very astute. And he *had* crossed her off his list. Now, you could call it a business decision, maybe a smart one; I don't know enough about the economics of moviemaking to say. But it was personal too. This was Lindsay's first soft, romantic role, and he was letting it leak to everyone in the business that she – his lover, girlfriend, fiancée, whatever – didn't have the versatility, the charm, the comedic talent, to handle the light stuff. He knew what the gossip would be: "If Sy has to replace Lindsay, she must be doing a *horrendous* job."'

'Was he trying to ruin her?'

'If he could have, he probably would have. But I told you: no producer today has the power to ruin a star. Still, Sy was out to do Lindsay as much damage as he could.'

'At the dailies, a few people were talking about lightning special effects. Sy said if Lindsay got hit by lightning, it would be the answer to his prayers. Obviously he was kidding about the completion guarantee business, but the impression was that for all he cared, she could be dead, and in fact, if she *had* been dead he probably would have thrown a party.'

Bonnie was doing a great job chewing her knuckles. 'Okay, Sy had fallen in love and had been cuckolded and was out to get even.'

I nodded. 'Right. Now all we've got to figure out is whether his Lindsay passion was a temporary lapse for such a dispassionate man, or if he was starting to lose his marbles.' I went and unlocked the strongbox on the top of my closet, got out my service revolver, then got my suit jacket. 'I have this feeling he was really losing his marbles.'

'Why?' She watched me putting on the holster and the jacket. I could see she didn't want me to leave. I could also see that, unlike every other woman I'd ever slept with (except for girl cops), she didn't blink or recoil or raise eyebrows or in any way show discomfort in the presence of a .38.

'Sy had this assistant or associate producer,' I said. 'A new guy he hired for *Starry Night*. A guy from around here.'

'Super WASP?'

'My brother. His name's Easton.'

'He's your *brother*? Oh. Sy told me about him.'

'What did he say?' Bonnie didn't want to tell me. 'Go on. I know what he is.'

'Sy said he was very good-looking, personable, but a little . . .'

'A loser.'

'Someone who hadn't had much success in life. But he turned out to be terrific. Sy liked him a lot. It was a perfect match. Sy needed someone who'd be on call twenty-four hours a day, who'd jump to do anything he wanted done. It sounded as though your brother was thrilled to do that. And more important, it sounded like he didn't have – forgive me, but I'm just repeating what Sy said – much ambition. Sy saw him as someone for the long haul.'

'A glorified valet.'

'Why don't we just say a lifetime retainer?'

'That's my brother. Anyway, I was over at Easton's, with Robby Kurz. Department ethics: I couldn't question my own brother. So I'm sitting there, and I pick up a script. Easton says Sy told him it was their next movie.'

'Was it mine?'

'No. Okay, now; in all fairness, I just glanced at it. And I never read a screenplay before. But I'm telling you, Bonnie, what I read was such complete, unmitigated shit I couldn't believe it. He was losing his marbles.'

'Do you remember the title?'

'Yeah. *Night of the Matador*, by – '

'Mishkin! Milton or Murray.'

'You read it?'

'Years ago. Look, Sy wasn't going to make *Night of the Matador*. Not in a million years. It was a joke. Well, the writer hadn't written it as a joke, but Sy had gotten it about a year after we were married, and it was so terrible it was funny. It was one of his Hideous Scripts collection. He treasured it. He used to give readings from it: "I kill the beast to kill the beast in my heart, Carlotta." Now, I'll grant you, Sy did get a little goofy over Lindsay. But he *never* would have gotten goofy enough to make that movie.'

'Then why would he tell my brother that was the movie they were going to do together?'

'Kidding around.'

'I don't buy that.'

'Knowing Sy, maybe he wanted to see if your brother had the guts to stand up to him, tell him it was the worst hundred and twenty pages in the world. And God forbid if he said he liked it; Sy would torture him about it for the next twenty years.'

'Easton was positive this was Sy's next project.'

'Well, it could all be a mistake. Maybe you just looked at the wrong screenplay.'

'Maybe,' I said. 'I'll give my brother a call.' I walked to the door. 'We have a deal,' I reminded her. 'You won't leave till I get back.'

'I know.'

'I said five, but if it's six, just hang on. I know it's rough on you. What can I tell you?'

'Tell me, "Bonnie, you're beautiful. You're a truly fine person. And I love you."'

'Bye,' I said.

'See you around, big boy.'

CHAPTER 18

❦

Bonnie had wanted to call Gideon to reassure him that she was all right, and I'd wanted to call him before he decided her absence had something to do with me. I could picture him gazing at his phone, wondering, Is it possible? Could this Brady be one of those congenial psychopaths, someone who smiles, chats and tortures? Slowly, he would lift the receiver, call Homicide, demand Shea, tell him I'd once slept with Bonnie and I might be obsessed. Dangerous.

But I couldn't risk a call from my house. Someone on the squad – Robby – could already have put an illegal tap on Gideon's phone, hoping she'd call him. So before I went to Pomerantz's, I stopped at one of those self-serve gas stations/snack food stores, called something like Thrif-T Gas, a place where only locals went, since to New Yorkers, concepts like fuel supplied by a company not traded on the New York Stock Exchange, thrift, and sour-cream-and-onion-flavored corn chips were too degrading to the human spirit to even consider. The place was on one of the more obscure north roads. I used the pay phone.

Gideon's boyfriend answered. He had one of those powerful, honeyed, southern Do-you-believe-in-Jesus-Christ-as-yo'-Savior? voices. When I said I was calling about Bonnie Spencer, Gideon got on right away.

'Your friend Bonnie is fine,' I said, disguising my voice so it sounded like a cross between Casey Stengel and a frog. 'She just didn't think it was time to get arrested yet.'

Gideon didn't bother to ask who I was. He knew. 'I'm concerned about her,' he said slowly. 'I would feel better if I knew – '

' – that she's okay? She said to tell you Gary Cooper was at his most beautiful in *The Westerner*.' I couldn't believe that I'd agreed to deliver such a goddamn stupid message. 'End of conversation. She'll call you tonight.'

An orange shirt, with its itsy-bitsy polo player, stretched across Eddie Pomerantz's belly, while a pair of half-glasses dangled from a darker-orange cord. The shirt hung over a pair of khaki bermuda shorts.

We were standing in his living room; the entire back wall was glass. The house itself stood on top of a bluff overlooking the bright, white-capped water and bobbing sailboats of Northwest Harbor. It was an incredible, expensive view.

'I went through this whole thing with you the night Sy got killed,' he said. 'Remember? We'd been discussing a picture of Lindsay that turned up in *USA Today* that she hadn't approved.' To show me he was keeping his temper, he filled up his cheeks with air and let it leak out. I was trying not to lose my cool, even though he was lying through his shiny false teeth. 'I had to cancel a breakfast meeting because of this,' he complained. 'I don't know what you want from me.' He looked down at the giant face of his gold-and-stainless-steel watch.

I took out my stainless-steel handcuffs and swung them before his eyes. 'I don't want anything from you, Mr Pomerantz. I'm here to arrest you. Section four ninety-two of the New York State Penal Code.' I made that up. 'Impeding a criminal investigation. And section eleven thirty-eight, Sub A: Aiding and abetting –'

I didn't have to finish. He tottered backward to a long couch and dropped onto it. He seemed mesmerized by the swinging cuffs. I put them back in my pocket. He wheezed: 'If I tell you something now that's different than what I told you last week . . .' His mouth kept working, but he couldn't finish his sentence.

I didn't want him to drop dead of a coronary. Seeing him in daylight, I realized he was well into his seventies. My guess was, if I'd caught him when he was younger, he would have been tough enough to give me a hard time. But he was old, tired, probably not in the best of health. I felt kind of bad for scaring him. 'If you cooperate, nothing will happen.'

'I'll cooperate.' The couch was covered in something like sailcloth, broad red and white stripes; his orange shirt looked particularly hideous against it.

'Tell me about the phone call,' I said. 'Did you call Sy or did he call you?'

'I called him.'

'What about?'

'He was having trouble with some aspects of Lindsay's performance.'

'I'd appreciate it if you didn't try to jerk me off, Mr Pomerantz.'

'Sy was going to California to take meetings with other actresses to discuss Lindsay's role. He seemed to be willing to throw three weeks of film into the garbage and reshoot with a new star.'

'And what were you trying to do?'

'Trying to stop him.'

'Any success?'

'I don't know. He wanted Lindsay out. He seemed to have made up his mind.' Pomerantz fiddled with his eyeglass cord. 'I was working on getting him to at least agree to call me after he met with the others, for one last talk. That's when he was shot.'

'Two shots?'

'Yes.'

'You're positive?'

'Yes. I know what a gunshot sounds like. I was in the army. Battle of the Bulge.' I nodded, respectfully. 'Wounded. You should've seen me then. A skinny kid. Three quarters of an inch lower, it would have gone straight through my heart. So I know from guns. And I heard two shots.'

'You do a lot of your business on the phone?'

'Sure. Most of it.'

'You must have a good ear.'

'A great ear.'

'If someone was having an off day, or had a sudden change of mood, you could pick that up?'

Pomerantz understood what I was saying. 'Yes. And there was nothing that made me think Sy saw anyone — with or without a rifle. Or that he felt something was wrong. But wasn't he shot from behind?'

'Yeah, but if the killer was someone he knew, he might have spotted him out of the corner of his eye, acknowledged him in some way and then turned away. What I'm looking for is a "Hi, Joe" or "Hello, Mary" that you might have picked up early in the conversation.'

'Nothing like that,' Pomerantz said.

'No pause at any point? No sudden intake of breath right before?'

'Nothing. Bang, bang, and then absolute silence.' He lifted his shirtfront and used it to clean his glasses.

'Let's talk about Lindsay. Straight talk. Did she know how bad things were with Sy, that he was getting ready to pop her?'

'Yes.'

'Did you know she was sleeping with Victor Santana?'

'Yes.' Tight lips. 'Fifty-two years in the business, and you know what I finally realize? I hate the ones who make it. Even the smartest of them are stupid. Stupid and arrogant. They think they can do anything they want, no consequences.'

'You can't do anything you want with a guy like Sy Spencer, can you?' I observed.

'No.'

'Do you think Sy had a clue that she was cheating on him?'

'Yes.'

'What makes you think so?'

'He told me. I was making my big pitch to keep her on *Starry Night*, and he said, "I can't do it, Eddie. You've seen the dailies. She's not putting out." He gave that cold laugh of his. It's like being stabbed to death with an icicle. And then he said, "Excuse me. She is putting out – in Santana's trailer."'

'In your mind, if any of those actresses in LA would have fit the bill, would it have been all over for Lindsay?'

'Bottom line?'

'Bottom line.'

'Sure it would have been all over – except for the fact that it would have cost too much. Even if Sy could have hired a not-so-hot star for less money, it still would have cost him almost three million in salary and reshooting to start from scratch. He couldn't have raised it outside; he'd already maxed out on financing. So unless it was worth it to him to ante up two-point-seven-five million of his own money to get rid of Lindsay, she would have stayed.'

'Would it have been worth it to him?'

'I think he was considering it. But I'd been doing deals with Sy for ten years. I knew him. I knew what a tightwad he was. Look, it would have gotten real ugly, but in the long run the names above the title would have been Nicholas Monteleone – and Lindsay Keefe.'

'Did Lindsay know that too?'

'I told her.'

'Did she believe you?'

'I don't know. She was scared.'

'Of what?'

'Of Sy Spencer.'

I can't say Lynne was overcome with ecstasy when she answered her door, but she did look pleased. She stood in the doorway. Her beautiful dark-red hair fell over her shoulders. She wore a crisp white blouse and a polka-dot miniskirt. It took me a minute to grasp that she was waiting for me to kiss her. I did. Then she led me inside.

The house had a Sunday hush. Judy and Maddy, her two roommates, were at work, and Lynne had spread her folders over the living room coffee table. Well, not spread. I marveled at how they were in flawlessly symmetrical piles. Her pens and colored highlighters were parallel and equidistant from each other and just the perfect distance from the curved edges of the light wood table so that, should one decide to roll, she could reach it before it fell to the floor. 'You're my kind of girl.' I smiled at her. 'In 2013, when I'm looking for my 1996 New York State tax return, you'll be able to find it in three seconds.'

'You don't think I'm compulsive?' Lynne asked. I sat down in a club chair. She squeezed in beside me. 'Judy is always saying I'm compulsive. Just because I always put away my shoes with the toes facing out. She says if I could just throw my shoes on my closet floor I'd be more creative.'

'Look at it this way. Neither of us will probably ever write *Hamlet*, but we'll never misplace a bank statement or a kid. That's reassuring.'

'It is.' She smiled. 'Tell me, how is your case going?'

'We're getting there,' I said.

'Good. There must be a lot of pressure, with all the publicity.'

'There is.' I glanced around the living room. Nothing really went with anything else. The leatherette chairs and the striped chairs, the 1950s Danish-modern coffee table, the massive brass floor lamp, the poster of a bowl of flowers from the Boston Museum of Fine Arts, were castoffs from the families of three pretty, marriageable girls in their mid-twenties, all of whom would have husbands – and nice furniture that coordinated with tasteful rugs – long before they were thirty. 'How is your class for September?'

'I think it's really going to be a challenge. I'm excited. Do you have time for me to go through the student list?'

'Can you do it in two minutes?'

Lynne snuggled against me. 'That's all you have?'

'Sorry.'

383

'Did you think about stuffed chicken breasts?'

I slipped my hand under the neckline of her blouse, around her bra. 'These aren't chicken breasts.'

'You know what I mean!'

I smiled, eased my hand out.

I had no desire for her.

'Going to the beach today?' I asked.

'Well, I'd like to, but I have to get my hair trimmed.' She seemed to think the news would upset me, so she added, 'Just a little bit off the ends.'

'The ends look all right to me.' I was so bored, and so ashamed of myself for being bored.

I thought: I could be having this same exchange with Bonnie, about chicken breasts and hair ends, and okay, it wouldn't be the world's most enthralling conversation, or the most amusing, but I'd hang on every word.

Even if I'd had two months' vacation, I wouldn't want to hear about Lynne's dyslexics and dysgraphics. And it wasn't that I couldn't get interested in that sort of stuff; it was that I couldn't get interested in Lynne.

How could someone have the perfect résumé and not be right for the job? She was precisely what I should want. Why didn't I want her? Other men did. We'd walk down the street, and heads – local guys, city guys – would turn. Turn? Spin. Half the time her phone was ringing with old boyfriends, or guys she barely knew, none of them willing to believe she could actually consider marrying someone else before she listened to their fantastic, incredible lifetime offer.

Lynne played with the veins in the back of my hand. I suddenly realized that no matter how hard I tried, I couldn't make myself love her. There was nothing more about Lynne I cared to know. Not about her job, her family, her pastimes, her feelings.

But I wanted to know every single course Bonnie had taken at the University of Utah. I wanted to know her brothers' names, who she'd voted for in 1980 and why, what her first sex experience had been like. I wanted her to tell me how a bunch of Jews wound up in Ogden, Utah. I wanted to see *Cowgirl*. I wanted to read her new screenplay and her descriptions of bathing suits for the fat-lady catalog. I wanted to meet her old man, haul him away from the new wife and the bridge games and go hunting with him. I even wanted to bird-watch with Bonnie – or at least watch her watch birds. I wanted to go running with her. Camp out. Fish for trout. Take her on a whale watch off Montauk. I wanted to tell her all about my work, my entire life. Watch the Yankees and her 1940s movies with her. Make love to her.

'You're quiet,' Lynne said.

'Yeah. I've got a lot on my mind.' I thought: Maybe all this is camouflage, and what I really want is custody of Moose.

'What are you smiling about?' Lynne demanded.

'Nothing much.'

'Tell me what else is new.'

I shifted, trying to sit up straighter, but she was wedged in so close to me I couldn't move. 'Oh, Lynne, I'm so sorry.'

She knew, but she asked, as if expecting a passionate denial: 'Is something wrong?'

'I don't know where to begin. I don't know what to say.'

'Oh, God.' She got up out of the chair, stood before me. So fabulous-looking. Such a nice person. Responsible. Solid values. Hardworking. 'What is it?' It would

385

make so much sense to marry her. 'Are you drinking again?'

'No.' I don't have to say anything at all, I thought. I can let it ride. Close the Spencer case, sort things out. It made sense to take my time. Lynne was so right for me; there must be a way it could work.

'Is there someone else?'

I should stand up, take her in my arms. Say, Someone else? With you around? Of course not! I sat, paralyzed. 'Yes,' I said at last.

'Who is she?'

'Someone I knew a few years ago.'

'Have you been seeing her?'

'No. It's nothing like that. I just ran into her again recently and realized.'

Lynne started to cry. 'Réalized what?'

'I don't know.'

'Realized *what*, Steve?'

'That I want to be with her all the time.'

At last, I was able to make myself move. I got up and put my arms around her. I wish I could say I was filled with grief. But I didn't feel anything except sadness that I was hurting her. She was such a decent person and she loved me, or at least loved the man she thought was me, and loved the idea of loving someone who needed her help in getting through life.

She pulled away and gazed up at me. Everything she did was so pretty, even her crying. Two lovely, parallel tears coursed down her cheeks. She swallowed and regained some control. 'You don't love me?' she asked.

I took her back into my arms. 'Lynne,' I said, into her glorious hair, 'you're a wonderful person. You're beautiful, kind, patient – '

'You don't love me.'

'I thought I did. I truly thought I did.'

'Are you going to marry her?'

'No. I don't know. I don't know a lot. I don't feel in control anymore, that I understand anything that's going on. It's all just happening. When I came here, I was only thinking I'd spend a few minutes with you, touch base. In my wildest dreams, it didn't occur to me that we'd be having this conversation. I wish I'd been better prepared . . .' She started to cry again. 'I wish I could have made it less painful for you.'

She pulled out of my embrace. 'My mother ordered the invitations.'

'I'm sorry.' What was I going to do? Tell her that her parents, Saint Babs and the Scourge of Godless Communism, would be breaking out the champagne, tearing the invitations into confetti, throwing it into the air in jubilation?

'Is she prettier than I am?' Lynne wiped her cheeks.

'No.'

'Younger?'

'No. Older.' Then I added: 'Older than me.' Her beautiful brown eyes grew big with disbelief, as though beholding a Medicare card in a liver-spotted hand. 'Not too much older,' I added.

'Does she have a good personality?'

'Yes.' It was gutless, but at that moment I wished more than anything that I hadn't told her there was someone else, only that it wasn't working out and the blame was all mine. I was a too-old sad case, simply not the marrying kind. But Lynne would be tolerant, compassionate, like a nurse with an invalid who has a long convalescence before him. She'd wait, helping me recuperate, helping me become a better person.

'What does she do?'

'She's a writer.'

'Is she from the city?'

'No.'

'Is she rich?'

'No.'

'What is it? Sex?' I didn't respond. 'Is that it?'

'It's a factor.'

'It was fine with us. It *was*.'

'Yes, it was.'

'You owe me an explanation, Steve.'

'I know. I know I do. Forgive me.' What the hell could I tell her? The truth. Not the whole truth, but at least no lies. 'You're everything I admire. When we first started going out, I couldn't believe you were for real, because I thought: No one can be this decent; it's some sort of an act. But it wasn't. I came to understand that you're everything any man could want in a woman.'

'Then why don't you want me?'

'Because you *are* so wonderful. Because I'm a messed-up guy and I can't live up to your high standards.'

'But I'm not telling you to be anything except what you are.'

'But see, Lynne, what I am doesn't necessarily want what you want. I can't live the life that would be right for you. I thought I could. I thought: If I have a good and beautiful wife and nice kids and a comfortable house, I'll be at peace. That's all I ever wanted. But I've got too much damage, and too many needs. Putting a white picket fence around me won't make me into a whole person.'

'What will?'

'She will.'

'Why?' Lynne asked.

388

And I finally answered: 'Because . . . we have fun.'

Carbone had me beeped three times in two minutes. I pulled off at a too-cute lobster restaurant and used the pay phone. 'What's so urgent, Ray?'

'Robby's got her nailed.'

'Her?' Lindsay. He'd say Lindsay.

'Bonnie.'

I knew I couldn't sound the way I felt: crazy with terror. I had to sound solid, sensible, the tough, experienced cop weary of Kid Robby's asshole antics. 'Jesus, is he still pulling stupid shit? I've been killing myself. I've got great stuff on Lindsay. We've got to start concentrating our resources – '

'Steve, listen to me. He went back to Sy's house late yesterday. To that area underneath the porch where we found the footprints from the thongs.'

'And?'

'He found another dark hair.'

'Stop it!'

'Like the ones on the pillow, Steve. It was caught in one of those crisscrosses of the latticework that covers the crawl space under the porch. She must have leaned against it for a minute. He drove it up to the lab in Westchester personally this morning. He's waiting for the test results, but you know and I know: It's got to be Bonnie. Now we've got her in bed with him *and* at the exact location where the shot came from.'

She lied, I thought. I stared at the phone, at its idiot instruction card for placing phone calls. That I'd believed Bonnie's explanations wasn't the worst part. The worst part was that I could go back to the house, kick furniture, throw things, pound walls, roar at her, You goddamn lying bitch, and she'd touch my arm, look me straight in the eye and say, Stephen, I wasn't there. I *swear* to you I wasn't there. Then how did your hair get there? She'd say, Someone put it there. That detective who's after me. You *said* he was out to get me, and he is. I'd say, You expect me to believe that, bitch? And she'd say, Yes, I do.

And against all reason, I would.

'Ray,' I said, 'you're not having any trouble with this?'

'What do you mean?'

'You don't think there's a chance that Robby got a little too enthusiastic?'

'Come off it. He wouldn't go that far. You know he wouldn't plant evidence. Face facts. Face what she is.' For a second it got so quiet I could hear water bubbling in the lobster tanks. 'Steve? You there?'

'I'm here.'

'What are you going to do now?'

'What do you think I should do?' I asked.

'Go find her.'

I happened to glance down toward the shelf in that dingy corner by the pay phone, with its ancient American Express application forms curled from the humidity, and the ashtray with someone's fat, ugly cigar ash. And all of a sudden, in that stinky, dreary corner, I got a gift – a flash of memory from that night five years before.

We'd finished eating and moved into the living room. It was sunset, and Bonnie left the lights off so we could see the horizon, royal blue, deep orange. Then she lit a couple of candles and we sat back in the flickering light. She told me how she'd come to love the South Fork, the vast and beautiful sky, the ocean, the marshes, the birds

– she said she was one of those creeps who clomped around with boots and binoculars – but that she missed the mountains. Not just for fishing, hiking, skiing. Growing up in Utah, she'd look out the window in school, bike to the store to pick up a quart of milk for her mother, lie in her bed staring at the stars – and the mountains were always there.

'You sound a little homesick,' I said.

'Yes.'

'You ever think of going back?'

'None of my family's there anymore. It would just be me and the mountains and the Mormons.'

'You didn't answer my question.'

'I wish I could go home,' she said, very quietly.

And I whispered: 'I'll teach you to love it here, Bonnie.'

I threw in another quarter and called my pal in the DA's office, Sally-Jo Watkins. From the name, you'd expect one of those exhausted Appalachian women with fourteen children you see on Malnutrition USA documentaries. But Sally-Jo was strictly Canarsie and unexhausted. She came from a very old but extremely undistinguished Brooklyn family. She always walked double-time and barked rather than talked. She was a career prosecutor, Chief Assistant DA for Suffolk County.

'What do you want? I'm busy. This about the Spencer case? Ralph's doing that. Talk to Ralph.'

'I have to talk to you.'

'Why? We got channels here, same as you guys. I'm drowning in a sea of motions, Brady, you stupid, insensitive mick cop moron. Whatever you want, I can't do it. Call Ralph.'

'He's too inflexible. I can't talk to him.'

'Well, I can't talk to you.'

'Sally-Jo, I saved your ass at least three times when you were in the Homicide Bureau. You fucking owe me.'

'I bought you a steak dinner. Remember? When you got sprung from the bin? I had to wait till you dried out, otherwise it would have cost me a year's salary, the way you drank.'

'Yeah, well, I put at least twenty thousand calories of cheeseburgers into you over the years, so let's say you still owe me the equivalent of one more extremely large lunch.'

'Shoot, schmuck. And shoot fast.'

'Hypothetically, say I did everything right: preserved a crime scene till after the autopsy, had my men go over everything with a fine-tooth comb. No rain, no high winds. Nothing to dirty the samples we took, nothing to make our job difficult. Ideal conditions.'

'Keep going.'

'Not much stuff except some circumstantial evidence good for making a DNA case. Hair. The victim's lover's hair in the bed where they'd been making it. Okay. Then a week later, four days after we take down the tape, I find another hair. Looks like the lover's. Let's say the lab says it is.'

'Where do you find said strand of hair?'

'Caught between two crossing slats of wood. If the lover had been firing the murder weapon, that criss-cross would be exactly where this lover of unspecified sex's head would have been. Now, as a prosecutor, would you buy this suddenly appearing new piece of evidence? Would you use it?'

'Okay. Generally, all relevant evidence is admissible at a trial. But the circumstances under which the evidence was found are admissible too. In a case like this, the defense would argue that since you did such a bang-up job under ideal conditions the first time, it's passing strange that you didn't find that extra hair when you were so busy being meticulous.'

'They'd argue it was planted.'

'Right.'

'A lawyer like Paterno would argue that.'

'A lawyer like Paterno would cream us on that. We'd claim it was an oversight. Human error. Cops are human, and what in the world would be our motive for trying to frame this lover? Because we believe with all our hearts and souls that the lover is guilty? Ridiculous!'

'If you were prosecuting a case like this, what would you do?'

'I'd spend a couple of days scaring the shit out of the cop who says he found the hair, telling him that if he's not a hundred percent sure that one of his colleagues didn't plant it – I wouldn't accuse him directly – he should forget about it because it could jeopardize our case, give the defense something to fight about. Then I'd sit back and think about it. Chances are, I wouldn't risk introducing it unless the rest of our case was very, very flimsy – but then I'd question the whole proceeding. But if our case was semi-solid, I'd still avoid using it. Look, that one hair makes the DNA testing an issue, and that would put our good evidence – the hair from the bed – into question. And who needs a lawyer like Paterno making the jury wonder how come a miracle happened after a week? From the DA's point of view, a wondering jury is a dangerous jury. Reasonable doubt is a terrible thing.'

'Thanks, Sally-Jo.'

'So, imbecile, is it your hypothesis that Bonnie Spencer shot Sy Spencer or not?'

'Not.'

'That isn't what I hear.'

It was touch and go whether Bonnie would let go of the phone or I'd break her wrist trying to get it out of her hand. She finally let go, but the next thing I knew, she was making a dash for the door, frantic to get to the cops, turn herself in.

'Stop it!' I shouted. I had her in an armlock, but it was like trying to restrain a powerful guy, and her natural strength was reinforced by hysteria. 'You didn't do it, so what the hell are you – ' She said something, but her words were swallowed up by huge, loud gasps and gulps of air. I held her, waiting for tears, followed by her fervent plea: Stephen, *please* believe me. Instead, I got an elbow to the solar plexus. It knocked the wind out of me so badly that I let her loose. I bent over, hugging myself, trying to catch my breath. Jesus, did it hurt.

At which point Bonnie asked, 'Did I hurt you? I'm sorry.' Except I couldn't speak. 'Stephen? Are you okay? Where does it hurt? Oh, God.' Actually, the shock of sudden pain – and pain inflicted by the woman you've just declared to your now ex-fiancée is the woman you love – just lasted for a second. But I didn't reassure Bonnie. I let her lead me to my bed, step by compassionate step, and ease me down. 'Take it slow,' she warned. By the time I was flat on my back, she was under control again. 'Can you breathe all right?' She peered into my eyes, maybe checking to see if the pupils were dilating. 'Stephen?'

'No,' I muttered, 'it's over.' She had to bend down to catch my words. 'You broke my rib and there's a huge splinter of bone that's piercing my heart. I'm a dead man, Bonnie. Goodbye.' I reached out, grabbed her hand and pulled her so she was sitting beside me on the bed. 'One last kiss.' She threw me a dirty look. 'All right,' I told her. 'Get hysterical again. Run. I'm not going to fight you. You're too big.'

'Listen to me. I *have* to turn myself in. That Robby – I guess it's Robby – is out to get me. If I stay here, he'll pull something else.' Her voice started to rise again. 'Let me go in now, while my lawyer still has a chance to make some sort of a decent case.'

'Get a grip on it!' She took a deep but tremulous breath. 'You can do it. I need you a little while longer. Once you're arrested, there may be a problem with bail. Second-degree murder, and your roots in the community aren't all that deep. You'll probably wind up in jail. Understand that?'

'Yes.'

'It's not a nice place. It doesn't get a fun crowd, and they don't show Bette Davis movies. You won't like it. So if I can, I want to spare you that. But even more, selfishly, I need you a little while longer for consultation. Just till five. Five o'clock, you can call your friend Gideon, have him alert Bill Paterno, and you can set the whole process in motion. But let me just warn you, if you're in the slammer, I may not be able to contact you. Your lawyer is going to say, No cops.'

'But I could explain that you're helping.'

'Bonnie, do you think a criminal lawyer is going to believe that a detective on the Homicide Squad has a soft spot for his client and will act in her best interests?'

'He might.' It disturbed me how naive she was, how

God Bless America. She wanted to turn herself in, put her faith in the System. She'd be walking into a hellhole. Jail to her was movies about exploited women with pitiful stories and one twisted prison matron. To her, ugliness was a set designer's vision. She didn't know the lunatic screams, the rage, the violence, the stink. Her crack addicts were on NBC News; she had no idea.

'Now, you told me you were going to be very busy today, solving the case. How far did you get?'

'I don't know. You tell me.'

I took her hand. She pulled it away. I'd forgotten I hadn't mentioned that I loved her, or that I wasn't marrying Lynne, so I reached out for her again. But she stood up and went over to my leather recliner. There was a pad and pen on the table next to it, and as she sat back, she picked up the pad, held it to her heart as if it were the ultimate mash note. 'I read too many mysteries, see too many detective movies,' she explained. 'When I thought about the whole case, everything you told me, I wound up suspecting Victor Santana and Mrs Robertson.'

'Why, for Christ's sake?'

'Because he was jealous of Sy and knew Sy thought he was weak – and if Lindsay was going to be fired, he'd be next.'

'And Marian Robertson?'

'Who knows? Because Sy went strolling into the kitchen once too often and lifted a lid off a pot and stuck his pinkie into her béarnaise sauce and sniffed it and put a dab on his tongue and suggested a soupçon more chervil.'

'Too bad you're over the hill. You'd be some great cop.'

'You're not impressed by my deductive powers?'

'No.'

'I didn't think you'd be. That's why I gave up looking at the big picture – because I keep trying to turn it into a movie. I decided to concentrate on Sy. Analyze my last few days with him, factor in everything you told me.'

'Go ahead.'

She pushed back so the recliner was practically horizontal. She glanced from me to the pad and back again. 'Think of Sy's behavior. What was out of character for him?'

'Not concentrating when he was humping you.'

'Let's just call it distracted behavior,' she suggested.

'Distracted behavior. Third-rate fucking. Whatever you want.'

'It was second-rate,' she said. 'With you it was third-rate.'

'No. You never had it so good. You know it. Admit it.'

'Nope. Anyway, Sy was distracted. That could have meant something big was happening – or about to happen. Now, what else?' I thought she was going to answer her own question, but she was waiting for me.

I thought about it. What in the last few days of Sy Spencer's life had in any way been atypical? Love. 'He'd fallen in love with Lindsay,' I began. 'And she hurt him. All of a sudden, the ultimate victimizer was a victim. It must have come as a real blow to him.'

'Right. And so what was going on? Under the best of circumstances, Sy was a vengeful man if someone crossed him. And here was the object of his affection or obsession, his love, cheating on him. He was going to get even.'

'But ultimately, he couldn't get even.' I told her what Eddie Pomerantz had said, that because of money, Sy would wind up keeping her on the picture.

Bonnie's eyes got huge. 'That's even better!' She jumped out of the recliner, came right over to me. 'Think!' she ordered.

'Think about what?'

'Vengeance is one thing. That's what I was concentrating on. But how could he get vengeance *and* money?'

I bolted up. 'Jesus! The completion insurance!'

Bonnie grabbed onto my jacket sleeve. 'If lightning struck Lindsay, he'd get his money, he'd get his new actress.'

'And he'd get his revenge,' I said slowly. 'Okay, but let's slow down. The theory's good, but the truth of the matter is, Lindsay *wasn't* struck by lightning. Sy was. How does that figure?'

'Stephen, ask yourself: Who was killed? Sy?'

'Of course Sy.'

'Or someone in a white, hooded bathrobe who was standing at the edge of the pool, the way Lindsay Keefe did when she came home from the set and did her laps?'

'Someone small,' I said.

And Bonnie said: 'Yup. Small, just like Sy.'

CHAPTER 19

Bonnie was all juiced up, talking too fast, bopping in a U-shaped path around the bed, stopping each time at the shaded window to bounce on the balls of her bare feet and peek out. She was not at her best, excited in a confined space. 'Okay,' she said. 'We've got to figure out if this really is a possibility, and then – '

'Stop. I'm running this show, not you. I'm the lead detective. You're zero.'

'Be quiet. I know what I'm doing.' She perched on the dresser and swung her leg back and forth fast, like a pendulum running amok.

'With all due respect, you may be semi-smart, but when it comes to police procedure you don't know your ass from a hole in the ground, and we don't have time to debate hierarchy, so I'm in charge.' She put her fingers up to her mouth, as though hiding a yawn induced by being too, too bored by such childish jockeying for position. 'Don't give me that yawn crap, Bonnie.'

'I'm not giving you yawn crap.'

'Now think; don't just shoot off your mouth. In the time you knew him, did Sy ever make threats against anyone, or wish a person dead in a way that made you fear for their lives? Beyond the "I hope he dies" we talked about.'

She swung her leg some more and finally shook her head. 'But that's not to say he wasn't spiteful. He had his hate list. If thirty years after the fact he could hurt someone who called him Peewee in junior high school, he definitely would. But he didn't think of revenge in terms of death. He didn't want to cause physical pain; he wanted to inflict maximum emotional pain on anyone who ever got in his way.'

I added another item to Bonnie's asset column, which now had about five million items: She didn't sway with each trendy breeze. The way things were looking, it would have been easy for her to portray Sy as a Man with Murderous Instincts, but she was too fair to do that.

'All right,' I said. 'So what it boils down to is that Sy was just your average, malicious guy.'

'Except his malice got more intense as he got older – or as he got more successful and powerful. Look, maybe the man I married was no cute little cuddle bunny, but the Sy I got to know again after I gave him the *Sea Change* script was much harder; he was so full of himself, so disdainful of other people. Anyone who crossed him was bad, selfish, stupid and ipso facto deserved whatever damage Sy decided to inflict. In his mind, when he got back at someone, he was only making sure justice was done.'

'All right, think about this: Did he have any morals at all?'

Bonnie gave the question some serious, leg-swinging consideration. 'He took decent political positions: apartheid is bad, rain forests are good. But no, I never saw any evidence of morals, not in a personal sense.'

'So we could call him amoral.' She nodded. 'And we can say, *maybe*, that he'd have no reservations about murder; it just was unnecessary or dangerous.'

'Or unseemly. Dartmouth men don't kill.'

'But what if Sy had gotten past unseemly? Look, he was on a nine-year roll, making good movies, big money. He could do no wrong. Is it possible he got so conceited that he finally thought everything he did was by definition seemly?'

Bonnie wriggled farther back on the dresser and sat cross-legged. She grew reflective, staring past me into space. 'Sure. It's possible. He believed his own publicity; Sy Spencer was superior, creative, refined. He could never be crass like the West Coast producers he was always going on about, screeching into their car phones or building bowling alleys in their houses. And he was so exquisitely sensitive he couldn't possibly be cruel. But forget Sy's idealized vision of Sy. I think all we've been talking about, all of what was going on in his life – thwarted love, his need for revenge, his need for money – played a part in pushing him toward the edge. What finally made him jump was that he got scared.'

'Of what?'

'Failure. The studios hadn't gone for *Starry Night*, but he believed in it and so he went out and got the financing himself. Give Sy credit. He told me *Starry* would be the best kind of American movie, where characters grow and finally come to deserve each other. But Lindsay was ruining everything. Not only making a fool out of him with Santana, really wounding him, but destroying what he really cared about most: his movie, which was his reputation, his immortality.'

'So she was costing him an extra half mil, plus future profits. And cutting off his balls and breaking his heart with Santana.'

'More than that. She was making him lose status in the business. Sy told me this much: People were starting to say, See? We were right. *Starry Night* was a dog from day one. And the way Lindsay's performance was going – so lifeless – the critics and all his fancy friends would get into the elevator after a screening and say, Was that *thing* we just saw a Sy Spencer film?'

'But you know about those old guys out in Hollywood – those Goldwyn guys,' I countered. 'They made movies the critics said were lousy, and all their so-called friends laughed at them, and they just went on.'

'But they were tough. They could take it.'

'You're telling me Sy couldn't?'

'Stephen, remember how we were talking about Sy being different things to different people, that he didn't seem to have any core? Well, it wasn't just something he chose to do when it amused him. Sy always let himself be defined by whoever he was with, and if those people were laughing at him – for being cuckolded by a fancy-pants like Victor Santana, or for making an adventure-romance that wasn't adventurous or romantic – he would allow himself to be transformed into precisely what they were laughing at: a failure, a nothing, a jackass.'

'So he wanted her dead for making him a laughing-stock. But he wouldn't have killed her himself?'

'No. I can't see him injecting strychnine into her melon balls. Sy was much too squeamish to commit a violent act. And he wouldn't have dirtied his hands in the metaphorical sense. He was a gentleman; he never did anything nasty himself.'

'Somebody was there to do it for him.'

'Always.'

'So who did he know who would do that kind of dirty work?' I asked. She knew, but she didn't want to say it. 'How about Mike LoTriglio?'

'No.'

'Why not?'

'Because if Mikey or one of his boys did it, Lindsay Keefe would be on the cover of *People* this week, with a "1957–1989" over her bazooms, and Sy would be rolling with *Starry Night* starring Nicholas Monteleone and Katherine Pourelle.'

I told her she was wrong, that La Cosa Nostra boys' invincible reputation was a myth, and in fact, half the time they were such a bunch of screwups they made the FBI look good.

She said she'd read *Wiseguy* and knew all about sociopathic Mafia morons who couldn't make it in the legitimate world, but Mikey was as clever as they come, and with a different background, he could have been CEO of Merrill Lynch.

I told her she was a fucking dunce, and she smiled at me and said she wasn't.

I had to go into the kitchen to call Thighs at Headquarters, but I didn't feel like leaving Bonnie because I liked looking at her, especially in my under-shirt, which was a washed-out cotton you could sort of see through. Also, if I left her alone she'd probably wind up lying on the floor, bench-pressing my stereo, so I picked up the phone on my nightstand. No word from Robby at the Life-codes lab up in Westchester. And no leads at all to Mikey's whereabouts: he wasn't at home in his fifteen-room Tudor in Glen Cove, in Nassau County, or at Terri Noonan's apartment in Queens, or at the Sons of Palermo social club in Little Italy. I asked, What about that bar in the meat district where he hangs out, Rosie's? Thighs said, I asked the bartender if Mikey LoTriglio was there, and he said: Mikey *who*?

'Rosie's?' Bonnie repeated when I hung up. 'I remember hearing about Rosie's.' She picked up the phone, got Manhattan information and asked for the number of Rosie's Bar and Grill on Ninth Avenue. Then she dialed and asked for Michael LoTriglio. I shook my head sadly, as in Pathetic. She was clearly hearing the same "Mikey *who*?" that Thighs had got. But she cut the guy off. 'You may not know Mr LoTriglio,' she said into the phone, 'but he comes into Rosie's every now and then.' She sounded commanding, secure, the way a good cop has to sound. 'I'd like you to do your best to get a message to him. Tell him that Bonnie Spencer – S-p-e-n-c-e-r – called and said it's urgent that she speak with him.' She gave him my number and hung up.

'Good luck,' I said.

'Thanks.'

I told her I was going to go to the set in East Hampton to try and harass Lindsay into cooperating, and tie up a few other loose ends. I started to enumerate them when the phone rang. I recognized the voice, gravelly, tough. 'Get Mrs Spencer,' it ordered. I handed it over to Bonnie.

'Mike?' Pause. 'Fine.' Pause. 'I've missed you too.' I stood beside her, tilted the receiver and put my ear right next to hers. 'Actually,' she went on, 'I'm not so fine.'

'What's the matter, Bonita?'

'I'm the major suspect in Sy's murder.'

'*What?*'

'They issued an arrest warrant for me.'

Mikey laughed. Not amused. An incredulous snort. 'That is so stupid it makes regular stupid look smart.'

'I know. But, Mike, let me tell you what happened.'

'You don't need to give me no explanations.'

'I know. But see, I was sort of keeping company with Sy again. And the police found evidence of my being at his house right before he died – and we weren't downstairs having tea. So they have this physical evidence from a bedroom, and they have this theory that Sy rejected me or my new screenplay and that I shot him. And that's another problem. They know I can handle a rifle.'

'What can I do?' Mikey asked. 'You got a blank check with me. You know that. Want me to find a nice, quiet place for you where you can not get noticed? Need money? Want me to . . . Listen, I would never talk to you this way, but what we have here is not your standard situation. So you want me to say abracadabra? Make some rabbit disappear? Name it. You're a sweet girl, a lady, and you were a good friend to my Terri.'

'Terri's a lovely woman,' Bonnie said. I couldn't believe this conversation. 'You're lucky to have each other.'

'Thanks,' Fat Mikey said. 'I tell her she's too good for me, but she don't believe it.'

'Mike, let me tell you what I'd like you to do, and please, feel free to say no. You know me. I don't live in a world where people call in IOUs.'

'I'm listenin'.'

'There's a detective on this case, Detective Brady.'

'I met him.'

'He's on my side. He's trying to help me.'

There was a long pause where Mikey contemplated the alternatives, including, if he had half the brains Bonnie credited him with, a setup. But he trusted Bonnie. He had to, because all he did was ask: 'What makes you think he's on your side?'

'He knows it's a weak case, and he thinks he can make a better one.' There was silence. 'And he's in love with me.' I stepped away from the phone and stared at her. She just continued with the conversation, so I stepped back and kept listening.

'The cop's in love with you?'

'I think so. So this is what I'd like, Mike – if you can see your way to doing it. I'd like you to talk to him. Anyplace you say. He seems to feel you might remember something now that slipped your mind during your interview.' Mikey gave another one of his laugh/snorts. 'He's sworn to me this would be off the record.' I grabbed her shoulder, shook my head, but she just kept talking. 'If you feel this would compromise you in any way, please don't do it. I know how it feels to have the police after you, and it's not something I'd want for you or Terri or your family. It's a horror.'

'Where are you now, Bonita? The truth.'

'He's hiding me, Mike. I can't tell you where.'

'Tell him to meet me at the Gold Coast restaurant on Northern Boulevard in Manhasset in an hour.' I shook my head, made a stretch-it-out signal with my hands.

'I think it will take him more than an hour to get there,' she said.

'An hour and a half, then. Tell him to meet me in the parking lot in the back. Get out of his car, walk away from it and just stand there. Got it?'

'Thank you,' Bonnie said. 'I won't say I owe you one, Mike. But I will say I appreciate this from the bottom of my heart.'

'I know you do, Bonita.'

*

'I *love* you?' I said.

'I had to say something.'

'Do you honestly think I love you?'

'Yes. Not that it means anything. You've decided you need a life with a Ford station wagon and kids with freckles and trim-a-tree parties and intercourse every Saturday, Sunday and Wednesday. It's preventive medicine, something you have to take to keep from self-destructing. I think you've convinced yourself that passion is a dark side that's too dangerous for you. Well, maybe you're right. Look at my life. Where has passion gotten me? What do I have to show for forty-five years of letting go? One movie nobody remembers and a warrant for my arrest for murder. Listen, you made the right choice. What could I offer you? Two dried-up fallopian tubes and a few laughs? So forget what I said about the love business. I get delusional under stress. Don't think twice: she's perfect. Grab her, marry her. *Mazel tov.*'

The restaurant was a block away from one of those sumptuous suburban shopping centers that attract people who need to spend eighty-five dollars for a cotton T-shirt.

Another cloudless day. Heat shimmered off the hoods of the Mercedeses, BMWs and Porsches, distorting the air, making the lot look like a slightly out-of-focus downtown Stuttgart. No Mikey. I'd been waiting for ten minutes, away from my car. All I saw was an occasional woman who had exhausted every possibility in the way of hair, makeup, nails, jewelry and clothes; one of them should have been put in a glass case in the Smithsonian just to show what we had become after eight years of Reagan.

407

I unbuttoned my jacket; all that accomplished was to allow more hot, humid air to circulate around my sweat-drenched shirt. Five minutes later, as I was loosening my tie, the door of a little red Miata convertible, top up, opened, and Mikey, with all the grace of sausage meat oozing out of its casing, somehow managed to emerge. He waddled across the blacktop. He'd obviously been watching me since I arrived. We nodded at each other. He was wearing sports clothes that looked more maternity than Mafia: white pants and a huge red, blue and purple flowered shirt.

'Nice car.' It was all I could think of to say.

'Not mine.' I wasn't sure if he meant stolen or just borrowed. 'Take off your jacket and open up your shirt.' He motioned me over to the far side of a garbage Dumpster and examined my chest and back for evidence of tape or wires. While I was buttoning my shirt back up, he checked out my holster and patted down my pants, taking out my wallet, shield and handcuffs to make sure they were what they felt like. After he finished, he rumbled: 'Wanna go inside?'

I shivered at the frigid blast of air-conditioning. Mikey chose a table and, without asking me, told the waitress to bring us two club sandwiches and two iced teas. 'You don't got to eat it. It's for looks,' he explained. He had one of those Roman noses that begin at the forehead, but his nose, like the rest of him, was fat; you wanted to squeeze it and hear it honk. 'So tell me about our mutual friend.'

'I don't think she did it.'

'No shit, Ajax.' Even his earlobes were fat.

'But unless I find out who did, there's a good chance she'll go for a long vacation.'

'What do they got?'

'Circumstantial crap: a couple of people who'll say Sy wasn't going to make a movie out of some screenplay she'd written; they have a witness that he visited her house every day and they were having an affair. Either way, the DA could make a case for a woman who's been thrown over and who wants to get even.' No wonder no one had ever been able to nail Mikey. He was too smart. He just sat there, a huge flower-shirted Buddha, but I could sense him analyzing, weighing alternatives, computing – and all the while not missing a word I was saying. 'The physical evidence is more of a problem,' I continued. 'Four of her hairs got caught in one of those wicker headboards where she was keeping Sy company no more than a half hour before he was killed. You know about the new DNA tests we do?'

'I know more than you know, Brady. Keep talking.'

'They just found another hair, right at the spot where we figure the killer stood when he fired.'

Mikey shook his head in disgust. His chins quivered. 'Who put it there?'

'It could be Bonnie's.'

'You wouldn't be here if you thought that.'

'It's not important who put it there. It's important that I get some help. She's going to have to turn herself in by five o'clock, or they're going to declare her a fugitive. That wouldn't be a plus if she has to go to trial.'

'Why are you doing this?'

'Look, I have until five o'clock. Either I sit here and talk philosophy with you – I know how you like to talk about Plato – or I try to save Bonnie Spencer's ass.'

'Don't talk about her like that. Show some respect.' A

busboy came over to pour some water. Mikey waved him off. 'What do you want to know?'

'You knew about Sy paying Lindsay an extra half million?'

'Sure. The bookkeeper told me, as I'm sure you know. It bothered her, seeing the investors fucked, so she confided in me.'

'You bribed her and probably threatened her.'

'You're tellin' me about the five o'clock deadline, so don't waste your time on cop chicken shit.'

'Did you threaten Sy when you found out about the extra payment? I'm not chicken-shitting you now. I'm trying to figure out his state of mind.'

'I didn't threaten him. I just told him what a stupid, fucking dick he was. Okay, I told him in a loud voice, and he was scared of me. I won't deny that. But I never would have killed him or had him mussed up or nothing. We went back too far, and I'm a sentimental guy.'

The sandwiches came. Giant, first-generation-rich sandwiches, showy with frilly lettuce, wasteful, so high they were held together with toothpicks the size of small swords. I ate half of mine, Mikey ate all of his and then the other half of mine. I didn't touch the iced tea because I was too jacked up from all the coffee I'd been drinking. Mikey talked and chewed simultaneously. Bits of bacon got spewed, and tomato seeds sprayed out of his mouth, but fortunately his lunch stopped just short of my plate.

'Do you think Sy was fearful of you?'

'Nervous. You know. Ever since we was kids, Sy would pee in his pants if I even made a fist. But he wasn't terrified or nothin' like that.'

'Did he say why he was giving Lindsay the extra money?'

Mikey shook his head, rolled his eyes, as if unable to believe mankind's capacity for idiocy. 'You wanna shit a brick, Brady? You ain't gonna believe this one. When I was yellin' at him, he broke down. Not cryin', but sittin' in a chair, doin' a lot of cringin' shit. He finally stopped the crap about that Lindsay got a better movie offer and needed a added financial incentive. He told me he gave it to her because she said – you ready? – "Sy, I hate men who hold back. I need a man who can give of himself."'

'*What?*'

Mikey shoved some potato chips into his mouth and said: 'I swear to God. Is that pussy-whipped, or what?'

'That's pussy-whipped,' I agreed. 'So he was really in love with her?'

'Out of his mind nuts for her. I'd never seen him so hot for anybody.'

'Not even Bonnie or his other wife?'

'The first was a stringy, ugly sourpuss wit' no tits and these big, ugly yellow teeth from some old family he married so people would think he was high-class. And Bonnie . . . I could never figure out that marriage. It was like a snake marrying a puppy dog. Probably had something to do with Sy's being all hot to get into the movie business, and she was in it then. And maybe he was tired of being a pretend WASP and got on a Jew kick, and she was a Jew but not too Jewey.'

'Do you think he would have married Lindsay?'

'Sure.'

'Then how come he took up with Bonnie?'

'Beats the hell out of me. When she called and said she'd been seeing him again, my mouth dropped open ten feet. You want my guess? The Lindsay thing knocked the shit out of him, and he was running home to Mommy.' He paused. 'You gonna eat your potato chips?' I pushed my plate over to him. He woofed down the chips and the crinkle-cut pickle slice.

'You're telling me interesting stuff but not helpful stuff.'

'You sayin' I'm holdin' back?'

'I don't know, but what you've given me isn't going to help Bonnie. Do you want to help her?'

He wiped his chin with the back of his hand. 'Don't ask dumb-fuck questions. Okay?'

'Okay.'

'I found out about the extra half mil the second week of shooting. I confronted him. He wimped out right away, apologized, like I told you. Next day he messengered over a half mil in negotiable securities to me, and if you try to use that against me, you better hire somebody to start your car every morning.'

'Mike,' I said quietly, 'no threats. I want to help Bonnie. That's all.'

'You married?' he asked.

'No.'

'Anyways, that was that. Until the Tuesday before he died. He calls me up, says he can't leave the Hamptons 'cause of the movie, but he's *got* to talk to me. He'll arrange for a private plane, or send a car and driver. I told him I don't like aer-o-planes and I don't use drivers because they got ears and mouths, but I'd drive out there because I was his friend. So I get there to his house – Jesus, that was some beautiful house. He tells me Lindsay's acting is terrible, that the movie is in deep shit. I tell him I'd heard that from my sources and so what else was new, and that if I lost my investment, I was sure he'd make good.'

'That's a great way to invest.'

'The only way. So then he tells me Lindsay is cheatin' on him. I start to say some garbage like "Too bad," but he didn't want that.'

'What did he want?'

'He wanted her removed.'

'Killed?'

'What do you think, Brady?'

'He asked you to get rid of her?' Mikey nodded. His chins, dotted with potato chip crumbs, bobbed up and down. 'Did he suggest how?'

'No, because I stopped him right there. Oh, he did say it would be easy: There could be a letter to make people think it was some crazy fan who did it. But I just told him to shut his mouth and keep it shut and don't even think about anything like that. He was an amateur, and he didn't know what the fuck he was doin'.'

'Actually, it sounds like he did.'

'I got to admit, it wasn't a bad idea. But no way I was gonna tell him that. He wanted to kill her because she was bompin' the director and because he wanted to start his movie all over again and needed the bucks. You think I'd get anywhere near somethin' like that?'

'Did he offer to pay you?'

'We didn't get that far.'

'Did he say anything else?'

'No. I got up and before I walked out I told him he didn't have what it takes, that his plan was full of holes, that if he tried to arrange something stupid with some two-bit local hood, they'd grab him in less than twenty-four hours. And then I told him to be a man. If he had to take a fall on the movie, take the fuckin' fall. And then I got the hell out of there. I gotta tell you: you know how I scared Sy?'

'Yeah.'

'Well, he scared me. I got a chill down my spine. What the hell's happenin' to this world if guys like Sy Spencer want to kill people? Tell me. What have we become?'

CHAPTER 20

❦

The tennis court of the East Hampton waterfront mansion that was *Starry Night*'s main set had everything: white wood benches, a water fountain, piles of snowy towels on a white wrought-iron stand, blue spruce and cypresses to obscure the chain-link fence. Beautiful. Except no one in their right mind would have wanted to be there. It was at least a hundred in the shade, but there was no shade. Lindsay Keefe and Nick Monteleone were volleying – if you could call it that – in about a hundred-and-ten-degree heat. There wasn't even a hint of cool air. Beyond the court, the foam on the waves made the ocean look as if it were boiling.

Every time Nick swung his racquet, he missed the ball and Victor Santana called 'Cut!' Then a sweat-removal brigade would race over to the actors. Production assistants got there first. Some of them held umbrellas over the actors' heads, others held battery-operated fans. Then the makeup and hair people went to work, while still other attendants offered bottles of water with straws so Lindsay and Nick could sip without getting drinking-glass dents around their mouths.

'One more take,' Santana promised me. His dark skin was flushed almost maroon. The color looked great against his Outfit of the Day: green jungle fatigues. All Santana needed was a scruffier haircut, an M-16 and a couple of joints of skag, and he could have passed for one of my old buddies. He went on: 'I must get enough footage of Lindsay because Nick . . . ' He sighed in weary resignation. 'This is going to cost an extra half day of long shots, with a tennis pro standing in for Nick. I simply cannot believe it; we gave him a full four weeks of tennis lessons preproduction.'

'Monteleone has zero hand-eye coordination,' I pointed out. 'He'd need an instruction manual if he wanted to scratch his balls. Now look, Mr Santana, I know making a movie is the most important thing in the world and it's not easy making a guy who doesn't know a tennis racquet from a pogo stick look like a jock. But I need more cooperation from you than I'm getting.'

'Please, just one more take for the master shot.' The brigade was walking off the court. 'I give you my word of honor.'

Lindsay was no natural athlete, but she could place a serve and look beautiful at the same time. Her dark eyes were shaded with a pink sun visor. Her pale hair, done up in some special curly ponytail, began to flutter as some guy in surfer trunks turned on a giant wind machine to the breezy setting. Santana called 'Action' one more time.

I watched the crew watching the actors. The guys were taking in the whole scene. But the women seemed to have eyes only for Lindsay. Were they contemplating what life could be like with those breasts, those legs, that perfect ponytail? Were they curious? Jealous? Raging, that such glorious gifts had not been bestowed upon them? I thought about Lindsay's competition – Bonnie.

If Mikey had, in fact, nixed killing Lindsay, could Sy have persuaded his Annie Oakley of an ex-wife to pick up a .22? I'm *aching* to make your movie next, he'd have sworn. But I need some help getting over this rough patch. Or maybe: I want to marry you, bring you to Sandy Court, back to Fifth Avenue. My life will be your life, my friends your friends, my charge cards your charge cards. Remember how it was? Bonnie, darling, it was such a ghastly mistake, our splitting, and I know how profoundly lonely you've been. Let me make it up to you. But first, help me.

Why the hell was I thinking these things? Did I believe Bonnie Spencer was capable of willfully taking the life of another human being?

No.

The compressors in the trailer air conditioners had died under the strain of the humidity, so after Santana gave everybody a twenty-minute break, Lindsay and Nick, accompanied by assistants who, probably by tradition and job description, were paid to grovel, trekked up to the mansion – a modern interpretation of the White House cross-pollinated with the Taj Mahal – and went into two upstairs bedrooms. Before he went into his, my pal Nick gave me a for-your-eyes-only, homicide-cop-to-homicide-cop one-finger salute.

I was about to walk into Lindsay's room, which seemed to be some sort of homage to mosquito netting, but one of her designated toadies tried to shut the door on me. 'She needs to recoup,' the girl whispered in hospital-corridor tones. I pushed past her, ordered everybody except Lindsay to get out and slammed the door.

Filmy stuff formed a canopy and curtains around the bed. It covered the windows from ceiling to floor. For some reason, odd pieces of it were draped over chairs. There were three chairs and one of those chaise-longues in the room, but naturally, given the choice, Lindsay stretched out on the bed. I pulled up a chair and pushed away some stuff, so I wouldn't have to interrogate her through gauze. Right away she started with the lascivious shit, running her hands slowly over her face and neck, arranging pillows so she was angled to achieve maximum tit power.

On the table next to the bed, there was a six-pack of foreign water in blue bottles. She put out a languid hand to take one but couldn't quite reach it. She waited for me to get up and hand her one. I didn't. She got one for herself and drank, not sexily, but with the loud glug-glug noises of a cartoon character.

'I feel sick from the heat,' she said. I don't think she was acting. Her whole body was red and covered in a cold sweat.

'It must be a bitch out there.'

I guessed she'd fulfilled her courtesy quotient by making a comment about the weather. She snapped: 'Well, what do you want?'

'I want you to stop lying. If you don't stop lying, you're going to find yourself under arrest.'

'You tried that tactic with my agent. He's old, losing his touch, so it worked. It won't work with me.'

'Want to bet? Fifty bucks says before I even bring you in for fingerprinting, you'll – '

'Do you honestly think you can scare me?'

'Beats me. But I do know I can interrupt your moviemaking. And when you come before the judge, I can arrange to have a lot of reporters at the courthouse. You can explain to them how I'm not scaring you – even though I've arrested you for withholding information in the matter of the death of Sy Spencer.'

'You are a low-class shit,' she said.

'Yeah, but a low-class shit with the power to arrest.'

There was a too-long moment of silence. I felt like closing my eyes, relaxing, but in the interests of projecting authority and macho intensity, I glared at her. At last, Lindsay propped herself on her elbow. 'Sometimes I like low-class shits,' she said, her voice lazy, husky. She extended her hand to me.

'Ms Keefe, let me be honest with you. As far as I can see, you're not in that much trouble that you have to fuck a cop.' She pulled away her hand. 'You just have to answer a few questions, and chances are, your answers won't get any further than me. All right?'

'Yes.' Brusque. The momentary fake desire was supplanted by her normal disdain.

'Did Sy confront you about your affair with Victor Santana?'

'Yes.'

'This isn't Twenty Questions. Tell me about it.'

She finished glugging the water and took a second bottle. 'He didn't raise his voice, not once, the whole time. He told me, very calmly, as if he were giving me the next day's weather forecast, that I was a whore. That I'd lost my ability as an actor.' She stopped. She didn't want to talk to me.

'Keep going,' I said.

Finally, reluctantly, she did. 'He wanted me off the film. He followed me around the house all that evening and the next morning, calling me Whore, as though that were my given name. 'Going up to bed so early, Whore?' He kept telling me I was ruining *Starry Night*. Always in that calm voice.'

'When did this start.'

'The week he was killed. Monday night.'

'Was he threatening to fire you?'

'No. He wanted me to quit.'

'Why?'

'*Why?*' she demanded. She gave a snort of contempt, as if I'd just asked the stupidest question of the twentieth century. 'So I'd be in violation of my contract, that's *why*. So he wouldn't have to pay me. So he could get the guarantors to pay the completion insurance and start all over again.'

'Is that possible?'

'Of course it's possible. And then the insurance company could sue me to recover their costs.'

'So you wouldn't quit.'

'Of course not. It was an insane suggestion.'

'Why would he expect you to quit if the consequences to you would be so bad?'

'Because.'

'Because why?'

'Because he was trying to make me so upset, so frightened of him, that I'd do anything he wanted.'

'What was he doing?'

'Before he told me he knew about Victor, he'd already started being cold. Very cold.'

'He stopped sleeping with you?'

She gave me a look that showed her distaste; I was getting off on her sex life. 'He wouldn't touch me,' she said. 'Do you want to know more? Of course you do. When I tried to take his hand, he pulled it away – as though I had leprosy.'

'But he wouldn't say what was wrong?'

'Not at first. Just horrible coldness.'

'Was he cold in front of other people? On the set?'

'No. That threw me off. He was delightful to me on the set.'

'And how were you to him?'

'Oh, grow up. What do you think? That I was going to let everyone know I was having terrible problems with the executive producer? He was acting very loving to me, so I acted loving to him. I thought: Well, he hasn't made anything public; maybe we can work it out. I stopped seeing Victor – in a private sense – on Wednesday.'

'You told Santana it was over.'

'No. I never burn bridges. What if I couldn't fix things with Sy? I just told him I was having a messy, painful period. *Very* bloody.'

'That's nice.'

'I know men. It works. In any case, I did everything I could to heal the breach with Sy. If not personally, then professionally. But it was so strange. And even when things got really terrible, we were still playing loving in front of everybody else.'

'Like the day he was killed, taking a wad of cash from him? Loving like that?'

'Don't make it sound like I was picking his pocket! It was a homey, wifely gesture.'

'You said things got terrible. When?'

'Thursday morning. My car came a little before six, and when I left the bedroom to go downstairs, Sy was out there in the hall, waiting.' Her face, under the sweat and layers of makeup, went rigid. Her mouth began to move mechanically, like a marionette's. She was somewhere between unsettled and petrified. 'He told me – he sounded so detached – that he had all kinds of friends. I didn't know what he was talking about, but I wanted to get away from him. He was standing right up against me. His face was less than an inch from mine. I could see each whisker where he hadn't shaved. He said some of his friends weren't very nice people, but they'd invested in *Starry Night* and they'd heard that the dailies were terrible. They were very unhappy, and they wanted me to quit. If I didn't, Sy said he couldn't be held responsible for the repercussions.'

'Did you ask what the repercussions were?'

'Yes.' Her body gave a fast, powerful involuntary shudder, almost a convulsion.

'What did he say would happen?'

'Acid in the face.'

'Jesus! What did you do?'

'I told him I was calling the police. I marched back into the bedroom and picked up the phone, but he grabbed it from me. I let him take it. The whole scene was so predictable.'

'Did he make any more threats?'

'No, of course not. He backed down. I knew he would. He actually lost his cool, the little bastard. Apologized all over himself. *Begged* me to forgive him.'

'And what did you say?'

'I told him I'd consider it.' Lindsay's lips arched into something like a smile. 'I knew how to handle Sy. I'd let him go out to LA, have his little meetings with Kat Pourelle and the other losers, and by the time he got back on Sunday night, he'd want me again. In his movie. In his bed. On a permanent basis.'

'You think he wanted marriage?'

'Oh, he would have needed a week or two to cool down over Victor, but yes. Definitely.'

'You think so?'

'I know so.'

'Would you have married him?'

'What do you think?'

'I don't know. He was a guy who threatened to

have you disfigured. Ruin your life, ruin your career.'

'He was a man eaten up inside by jealousy.'

'He was a producer who wanted you out of his life, out of his movie.'

'Only because I'd wounded him so deeply. I admit it: I made a mistake. A big one. But Sy would have come around. We were so well suited, and he knew it. I'm . . . well, what I am, and he was a brilliant, successful film producer. He cared about serious social issues. *And* he was my intellectual equal. To tell you the truth, as far as the jealousy, I *loved* it that he was finally displaying some real emotion.' Lindsay began to rub her bare legs together; she seemed to be getting aroused, not so much by her recollection of Sy's crazy behavior but by the remembrance of her power over him. 'Jealousy,' she said again, savoring the word. 'Sy was *consumed*.'

'You think he loved you?'

'Of course he loved me.'

I got up and stood behind the chair. 'The killer was fifty feet away from a small, white-robed figure about your size. At the moment the rifle was fired, Sy was supposed to have been flying somewhere over Kansas. And you were supposed to be getting ready to do your late-afternoon laps in the pool.'

'No!' The makeup didn't help. Her skin started to lose its color. It took on a waxen cast, like a corpse's.

'Yes.' I pushed aside a drooping piece of mosquito net and walked out of the room.

I called Carbone and told him I was at the *Starry Night* set on the off chance Bonnie Spencer had connected with any of the crew members, and also to check if she'd showed up again after Sy threw her off, maybe doing some kind of neurotic, obsessive number. He said that

423

Thighs, Robby and Charlie Sanchez were all out trying to get a lead on her. Casually, as if I already knew what the answer would be, I asked if the DNA results had come in on the new hair sample. It's Bonnie's, Carbone said. Still think she didn't do it?

I told him if he had nothing better to do, to check the evidence record files. Find out the number of hairs we'd picked up that first night, then go down and look in the envelope the lab had returned. He'd find a minus-one factor.

He told me I was losing my emotional equilibrium, that I was projecting something – I forget what – onto Robby Kurz, that I needed a vacation, and if I passed the fancy Italian store in East Hampton to pick him up two pounds of sausage with fennel.

I hung up. Robby *had* to have planted the hair. And for sure, he had spread the drinking rumor, the Steve luvs Bonnie 4-ever rumor. He was out to get her – and me. Sooner or later, he was going to realize that Bonnie had a protector and had gotten some help with her disappearing act. And then he would be at my house.

Gregory J. Canfield was supposed to be in a store in the village doing his job as production assistant, which, in this instance, meant picking up fresh figs, prosciutto, a semolina bread and a bottle of Dolcetto wine for Nick Monteleone since, according to a couple of people on the set, Nick had mumbled that what with the heat, he wanted a light bite, not a heavy supper, and since Lindsay's performance was still so inert, any hope of salvaging *Starry Night* seemed to rest on Nick's well-moussed head, so finally, after forty minutes of consultation between the line producer and the first assistant director (which included a call to Nick's agent in Beverly Hills), a definition of the term 'light bite' was agreed upon, and Gregory was dispatched.

But I figured he might stop in to say goodbye to his woman, Myrna the costume lady, and sure enough, they were holding hands in the costume trailer, staring into each other's eyes, giving each other sweet, delicate, pursed-lip kisses of farewell. It didn't seem to bother them that one of Myrna's assistants was no more than a foot away from them, ironing a duplicate of the tennis outfit Lindsay was wearing. And it didn't seem to bother them when I called out 'Hey, Gregory!' He gave me a slightly dopey glance, then gazed back into the depths of Myrna's eyes.

The trailer was huge, like a wildly inflated walk-in closet, with rack after rack of clothes, shelves of shoes, and drawers with scarves and underwear and fake jewelry spilling out. I walked to the back and tapped Myrna on the shoulder. 'Hello!' she said. 'How are you?'

'Fine, thanks.' She looked as messy as when I'd caught her in her inside-out negligee. This time she was wearing a long sacklike thing with a parrot design; it looked as if she'd picked it up in Woolworth's in Honolulu in 1957 and had worn it frequently since. 'Myrna, I need Gregory for a minute.'

'Is anything wrong?' she asked.

'No. Everything's fine. A couple of minor points need clarification.' She nodded, released Gregory's hands and gave him a tender nudge toward me.

I took him away from her, outside to where they had a table set up with bagels and cookies and doughnuts with melting sugar and M&Ms and nuts and raisins. There was a bowl of red grapes, but they were hot. He gave me a Coke from a cooler beneath the table. 'How's it goin', man?' he asked. A few nights with Myrna had turned him from Ultra-Geek into Mr Cool.

'It's going all right,' I told him. It wasn't. It was ten minutes to five; I wanted to get back to Bonnie, but I had nothing worth bringing her. I held the icy soda can against my forehead. 'Remember that conversation you mentioned to me that took place in dailies? The "if lightning struck" conversation.'

Gregory nodded. 'Sure, sure.' He had a thoughtful look. He was probably recalling the graininess of the film and seemed, worse, about to describe it to me. I cut him off.

'Who was there? You said it was late. Most people had gone.'

'Ummm,' he began.

'Don't "ummm." Talk.'

'Sy.'

'Good. Keep going.'

'One of the assistant producers, Sy's gofer. His name's Easton.'

'Who else?'

'Me. I think Nick Monteleone. The DP. Director of photography. That's another term for cinematographer.'

'What's his name, Gregory?'

'Alain Duvivier.'

'Is he French?'

'*Mais oui, monsieur le detective*. He was there, and his girlfriend.'

'What's her name?'

'Monica, Monique. But she's gone.'

'How come?'

'He started with the set dresser, Rachel.'

'Who else?'

Gregory shut his eyes and, for once, his mouth. He seemed to be trying to re-create the scene. 'That was it.'

'You're sure?'

'Positive.'

'Did Sy hang back to talk to anyone afterwards?'

'I don't know. He sent me out to put pink pages in his leather folder in his car. Revised pages of script. You change color with every revision. First blue, then pink, and then yellow, green, goldenrod, then buff – '

'Go get me Alain.'

'I can't. I'm supposed to be in East Hampton, and he's – '

'Get him *now*.' Now took two minutes.

One thing about movie people: none of them dressed in a normal, businesslike way. Alain Duvivier looked like a cliché of a French creative type. He was in his mid-twenties, with blond and brown hysterical hair that tumbled over his shoulders, matching heavy eyebrows and one hoop earring. He wore bubble-gum color shorts and one of those wrestler-style undershirts that have practically no sides. He was more the size of a grizzly than a man; beside him, Gregory was almost invisible.

'Hello,' I said.

'Alo,' he said, then added, with fitting somberness: 'Sy. Very, very sad.' He sounded so French you half expected him to say Ooh-la-la, but he didn't.

'Mr Duvivier, I understand you were at dailies the night a certain conversation took place.' He was concentrating too hard, so I slowed down. 'There were some remarks about lightning and a discussion – a talk – about what would happen if lightning

427

struck – hit – Lindsay Keefe. Do you recall any of that?'

'Lighting Lindsay?' he asked.

'No, light*ning*. It was a conversation about lightning.'

'Lightning?'

I turned to Gregory. 'What the hell's the word for lightning in French?'

'I took Spanish.'

I turned back to Duvivier. 'Lightning.' I pointed up to the sky and made a streaking gesture back and forth. He glanced over at Gregory a little nervously, and it didn't help when I made a thunder noise and followed it with another lightning imitation.

He blurted out: 'Rachel!'

'Rachel?' I inquired.

Gregory said: 'His girlfriends translate for him.'

'He doesn't understand English?'

'Well, technical terms. And he says "Alo, pretty girl" a lot.'

'*Au revoir*,' I said to Duvivier.

'Bye-bye,' he responded.

Smart. The sound on the TV was low enough so someone standing outside would never guess anyone was home. I found Bonnie sitting in my recliner, watching a movie. Before she zapped the remote control I saw that even though it was a black-and-white thing, it was something I would watch, with Kirk Douglas or Burt Lancaster; I always got them mixed up.

She pushed herself out of the chair. 'Ready? It's five-thirty.'

'Relax.'

'We have an agreement.' She was very subdued.

'Are you all right?'

'I'm fine.' She wasn't, but since she wasn't crying, or

sullen or angry, I couldn't get a precise reading. 'How do you want to go about this? Should I call Gideon first, or do you want to drop me off – '

'Listen, do you trust me? Trust my judgment?'

'Isn't it a little late to be asking that?'

'We've got to get out of here fast, because I have a sickening feeling that fuckface Robby is going to wind up here, looking for you.'

'Why?'

'I don't have time now. Let's get out of here. I'll explain on the way.'

'On the way home?' She sounded so quiet, thoughtful. Well, she had a right to be. Leaving my house was like picking the Go-directly-to-jail card.

'You're not going home yet.'

'You promised me.'

'I know, but there's one more shot. Will you have faith in me, give me another half hour?'

'Yes.' So hushed, proper, ladylike, even. 'I will.'

'Then let's haul ass, Bonnie.'

She looked past the mud room into the kitchen. The stove and refrigerator were older than I was, and the white porcelain table had deep black craters where it had chipped.

'Where are we?' Her voice was barely a whisper. I realized she'd seen me lift up an unplanted flowerpot and take the key that was under it. She assumed we were breaking and entering, and having gotten to know me, she did not appear to be surprised.

'My family's house.' I guided her – almost pushed her, because she didn't want to come – through the kitchen, into a hallway that led to the stairs. 'My brother was there for that "lightning" conversation. And he was always around, doing things for Sy. I want to see if he remembers what happened after those dailies, that night or maybe the next day.' Bonnie stopped so suddenly I banged into her. 'Come on.' I gave her a light shove and kept talking. 'I want to find out who Sy saw – ' She wouldn't move. ' – and who he talked to.'

And then I saw what she was staring at. A gun cabinet. Plain pine. Familiar to someone who grew up on a farm.

Or to someone who grew up in a sporting goods store, whose old man was the best shot in Ogden.

No, I thought. No. She didn't do it.

CHAPTER 21

❦

Growing up in the house of what had once been Brady Farm, I'd pretty much been able to disregard the slight stink of degeneration. That odor of decay had always been there, but it was elusive, except when I sat on the living room couch long enough. There, at the heart of the house, it could not be ignored.

But if I was just passing through – which, during the years after my father left, was how I thought of myself, a low-class transient who happened to have the last name Brady – I'd smell, instead of underlying decay, the tangy carnation scent of the room spray my mother had boosted from Saks, the stuff they used to smog dressing rooms after ladies with gamy underarms tried on Better Dresses.

On the rare occasions I visited after I'd moved out, I must have made an unconscious shift and begun breathing through my mouth, because I stopped noticing the smell. But as I led Bonnie to the staircase, I got a killer whiff of Mildew Plus.

I was embarrassed. I hoped that someday I could really unload, tell her my history, but for now I hoped she'd think well of my background. I didn't want her to notice the stink of my family's house, or the dry, blackened edges of the rips in the gray stairway runner. I wanted her to believe we were poor but nice, not that we were poor and so bitter we couldn't bestow any kindness on our surroundings.

431

When we got to the second or third step, she finally turned and faced me. 'Maybe I'd better wait downstairs.' I didn't bother to answer. What the hell could I do? Offer her a seat on the Odorama couch? That way, when I heard my mother come home from work, I'd have to run downstairs in time to say, Mom, this is Bonnie Spencer, the Jew whose ex-husband was murdered in Southampton, and my mother could say, Oh, yes, that was the old Munsey place. Paine Munsey. He's in sugar. They're up in Little Compton now. They cou'.In't bear the new element, so they sold.

I put my hand on the small of her back. 'It won't take long.' I propelled her a little harder, and she continued up the stairs. I loved the chance to touch her.

But it was more than wanting her with me. It made sense to let Bonnie hear what my brother had to say before I let her go. She was so smart; maybe she could pick up some small, free-floating fact that could be added to the equation and, finally, make it balance. Sure, Easton had been in the city the whole day of the murder, but there might be a snatch of a phone conversation, a note, a memo – some indication of hostility – he'd absorbed subliminally the day before.

Could he have picked up even a single word – like 'rifle,' 'shoot,' 'pool,' 'insurance' or 'Lindsay' – soon after the 'if lightning struck' conversation at dailies?

I thought: What if one of those words had something to do with Bonnie? All of a sudden, on the last of those shadowy steps, I felt what I'd always felt as a kid. Not a memory, or déjà vu. The feeling itself – empty, and so sad.

I knew she couldn't have done it.

But what if she had? Well, then I would be what I

432

was before. Nothing. My life offered only two compensations: baseball and work. But neither the Yankees nor the Suffolk County Police Department was set up to do the big job, save lost souls. And all the drugs I had tried – beer, pot, peyote, hash, yellows, women, 'ludes, LSD, booze, heroin, more women, more booze, Lynne – in the end had given me no peace either; they'd just taken the edge off for a little while. Only Bonnie Spencer had made me believe that, truly, I might be redeemed.

What if I was wrong about her? What could my future be? I could drink again, and die. Or I could become one of those old retired cops, clutching a felt hat in my hands, keeping busy shuffling between daily Mass at Queen of the Most Holy Rosary and AA meetings, until death came.

But I knew she didn't do it.

When I guided Bonnie into Easton's room, he wasn't the only one who was surprised. Bonnie was. Surprised, angered. Easton had stolen Sy Spencer's ties! Her hands became fists; she could have decked him. There they were – blue ties with tiny stirrups, green with minuscule anchors, red with itty-bitty French flags – laid out on the bed, ready to be packed for Easton's trip to California to meet with Philip Scholes, the director, about his new job. There was no doubt that they were Sy's: Easton could never had afforded them, plus I'd seen dozens of them on special hooks on a section of Sy's giant remote-control revolving clothes rack the night of the murder, when I did a walk-through of the house. And – Bonnie's face was so grim – there were Sy's sweaters, too, on that bed! Cotton knits and cashmeres meant to be fashionably baggy on a little guy like Sy, sweaters that would just, barely, fit Easton. Her expression declared: Arrest this man!

And Easton's expression? Furious, sure, at another of my tiptoed intrusions. He stood legs apart, arms crossed over his chest, maintaining his dignity despite the fact that all he was wearing was one of those shortie shaving robes, and a particularly hideous one. But he was also confused: I know who this woman with Steve is, but I can't place her. And embarrassed too, as all three of us stared at over a thousand bucks' worth of accessories from the wardrobe of the ultra-suave (and ultra-dead) Seymour Ira Spencer.

I suppose my expression was something less than sunny, reflecting my disgust at my brother's penny-ante thievery. I could just see him, hanging around, waiting for us to take down the crime-scene tape and go home, so he could do a search-and-destroy through Sy's closets under the guise of Setting Things in Order. My guess was that if I looked through Easton's drawers, I'd find cuff links, or one of those mini-VCRs, a pocket telephone, or maybe one of those skinny, gold-coin watches on an alligator strap.

I was just about to lighten the atmosphere with some joke about taking Easton in, when he got petulant, affronted by my drop-in with a tall woman of unknown origin in athletic shorts and grungy running shoes. 'I'd like to know what all this is about, Steve.'

'You would?'

'Yes. I would.' Just at that instant, as he was carving out a new niche in supercilious schmuckdom, he recognized Bonnie. Obviously, hers was not a calming presence. Easton began to sidle back and forth alongside the bed, doing an agitated step-together-step, as if trying to keep out of her line of sight – or block her view of her ex-husband's wardrobe. 'What is *she* doing here?' he demanded. His gracious-living voice disappeared, replaced by a troubled squeal.

'She's with me. You do know that this is Bonnie Spencer?'

'Yes.'

I steered Bonnie over to a straight-backed chair. 'Stay put,' I told her. I turned back to my brother. He stopped his sideways skedaddling. 'You saw her that day at the set, when she knocked on the door of Sy's trailer?'

'Yes.' His yeses sounded more like yaps than complete syllables. I thought: He's fucking mortified about being caught red-handed. Steal billions, everybody knows, and you're invited to the best parties; steal ties, and you're a tacky little piece of shit.

'And Sy told her to get off the set, that she didn't belong?'

'Yes.'

'Stephen, listen – ' Bonnie started to say, in her direct, you're-not-approaching-this-right voice, as though we were husband-and-wife detective partners in some 1937 movie.

'Not now!' Then I asked my brother: 'Did you know Sy was having an affair with her?'

'What?' It wasn't an assertion of amazement, as in: I don't believe it! It wasn't even a question. It was more a 'Duh' of befuddlement. Easton was on overload; he couldn't seem to get what was going on.

'Answer me,' I snapped at him.

I had to know how finely tuned in he was to Sy's private life. How much did he know? What could he guess at? After dailies that night, had Sy made any secret phone calls? When they'd gotten back to the house and

Easton was setting out Sy's papers or his pj's or pink pages for the next day, had he possibly picked up another reference to 'Lindsay'? 'Lightning'? An icy laugh? An intense 'I need your help' spoken behind a closed door? Would Easton the Refined actually eavesdrop? Would Easton *not* eavesdrop was more the question. My brother wouldn't recognize an ethic if it snuck up and bit him on the butt.

But still, as I looked at him, I knew he'd make a fantastic witness for the DA, all blue-suited and white-shirted, with one of his new ties. His fair hair would shine in the harsh light of the witness box, his low-key gentleman's voice would appeal, convince. I thought: Wouldn't it be wonderful if he actually could remember something important?

State your name, the assistant DA would command. Easton Brady. I ask you, Mr Brady, the ADA would say, did you overhear a telephone conversation between Sy Spencer and Michael LoTriglio? The defense lawyer – Fat Mikey's, maybe, although I felt a twinge of regret at the notion – would leap up and object on the grounds of no foundation. The ADA would rephrase the question and inquire, How did you know who was on the phone with Mr Spencer? Well, I answered the phone and the man said it was Mike LoTriglio and he wanted to talk to Sy *now*. I'd spoken to Mr LoTriglio before, and this sounded exactly like him, Easton would begin.

I glanced over at Bonnie. Her eyes were riveted on Easton.

I remembered her eyes in that moment when she'd stood before the gun cabinet downstairs. I thought I'd seen a fleeting shadow of pain in them, a recognition of what was behind those doors.

What was behind those doors?
My old man's twelve-gauge shotgun.
And his .22
And then I knew what Bonnie knew.

Easton seemed to understand that, at last, I knew.
He stood quietly, thumbs hooked into his pockets,
watching me.

I had to get ready for an interrogation. Oh, we Bradys
were so neat. I lifted Sy's folded sweaters from the bed
and placed them – one, two, three – gently on the
dresser. I was so painstakingly careful you could
hardly hear the rustle of the tissue paper between
the folds. Then I took my brother by the hand, and,
together, we sat side by side on the space I had
cleared.

'East,' I said.

'Yes?'

'You have something you want to tell me.'

'No.'

'Come on.'

His neck and his ears got fiery red, but he said, 'No.
Absolutely not.'

'I found the rifle.' He shook his head. It could be
taken to mean: I don't understand. Or: No, you didn't.
'I found it, East.' I prayed – neat, always put things back
where they belong – that he had returned it to the
cabinet, that he hadn't done something like take a ride
on the Shelter Island ferry to drop it into Long Island
Sound. But then I saw I was okay; Easton angled his
body away from mine and with the side of his hand was
ironing out an imperceptible wrinkle in the blue tie right
next to him. I said softly: 'It's just a question of time
before we get back the results of the ballistics tests.' He

wouldn't look at me. 'We fire the rifle and then compare the markings on the bullet with the two bullets we took from Sy.' I was afraid if I looked at Bonnie I'd lose my rhythm, but then she didn't seem to want my attention. There was no sound, no motion; if I hadn't known she was sitting in a chair five feet away, I would not have sensed she was in the room. 'The markings will match, East. You know that.'

Easton lifted his chin and breathed out sharply, giving his nostrils a scornful, Southampton flare, so Old Society. 'I can't believe you can even *think* something like this!'

'How can I *not* think it?'

'You're my brother!'

'I know. Maybe that's why it took me so long to understand.'

In the past, when a case finally came into focus, I always got a wild burst of energy, a hunger to *know*. But now I felt heavy, sluggish, incredibly weary. If Easton ran, I wouldn't have been able to go after him; I was on some other planet, with terrible gravity.

'I want both of you out of here!' he ordered. He scowled at Bonnie. 'There is nothing to discuss.'

'There's a lot to discuss,' I said.

'This is totally asinine.'

'No. This is very serious and important.'

'You have no proof of *anything*.'

'I have the murder weapon.'

'Oh, don't be melodramatic! Are there fingerprints on it? Are there?'

'There may be, even if you think you took care of that. We use laser technology now.'

He shook his head. Either he didn't believe me, he

438

wasn't impressed or he wasn't afraid. 'And what if there aren't fingerprints?' he inquired.

'Who the hell else would take Dad's .22 and shoot Sy Spencer? Mom?'

'You *would* bring her into it.'

'Relax. Who do you think she's going to blame for all this? You or me?'

I got up and walked towards Easton's closet. A regular closet, not a mahogany-and-brass state-of-the-art architectural space like Sy's. But Easton aspired. Everything was in perfect order: suits, shirts, ties – more of Sy's – slacks, blazers, shoes. Shoes in their cardboard boxes, stacked on the top shelf. The front panels of the boxes had been cut off so you could see each pair. Years of shoes: penny loafers, tassel loafers and Oxfords; white bucks, golf shoes and rubber-soled boaters; tennis sneakers, running sneakers, sandals, slippers. And thongs. Ordinary rubber thongs for the beach, the kind you can pick up anywhere. A men's size eleven, my size, my brother's size.

I covered my left hand with my handkerchief. I took out my pen with my right hand and, carefully, eased the box off the shelf and caught it in my left.

I said, 'You hated to bet when we were kids. You know why? I always won. But I'll bet you right now these thongs will match the molds we made from impressions in the grass right near Sy's house, where the shots were fired. A fancy, hot-shit lawn, East. Turf, they call it. It's a special variety of Kentucky bluegrass called Adelphi. The guy at the State Agricultural Extension said it must have cost him a fucking fortune to cover all that ground. But what the hell. The right shade of green makes a statement.' I held up the box. 'I'll bet you we find a blade or two of Adelphi right in here.'

439

It took a while before Easton could get his eyes off the shoe box. Then, in an I've-got-a-secret boyish manner that my mother would have found enchanting, he gestured me over with his index finger. Without looking at Bonnie, he whispered: 'Why is she here?'

'She's been giving me some information on the case. Some insights into Sy.'

'Oh.' He seemed hesitant about what to do next. His mouth opened, but nothing came out.

'Why don't I tell her to take a hike?' He seemed so relieved. He inclined his head; it was almost a bow.

I walked over to Bonnie and spoke softly. 'Can you drive a stick shift? Okay, you know where the nature preserve is, that swamp place, about a minute and a half north of here? Go there. Watch birds or something for an hour and a half. Then take back roads to your friend Gideon's. Don't park too close to his house. Don't call him to tell him you're coming. And make your approach from one of the houses behind his in case they're surveilling his place. Got it so far?'

She was levelheaded, serious and terse. 'Yup.'

'Explain to Gideon what's happening. Under the circumstances, he won't want you to turn yourself in. So just sit tight.'

'Do you need any help? Want me to call anyone?'

'No.'

'Promise me – '

'Yeah, I'll be careful. Now look, if for any reason they find you and scoop you up – arrest you – don't make any statements of any kind.'

'Okay.'

Her eyes darted over to Easton. I knew what she

was thinking: There was a good chance that if I didn't nail him, she'd be nailed. And maybe, in the final analysis, I couldn't nail him. Or I wouldn't be able to.

'I trust you.' That's what Bonnie said instead of goodbye. Then she held out her hand for my car keys and was gone.

'You killed Sy,' I told my brother.

'Please, Steve.'

'You killed him.'

He lowered himself on the chair Bonnie had vacated. 'I didn't mean to.' His voice had the emotional intensity of someone caught running a red light. 'I'm sorry.'

'You meant to kill Lindsay.'

'Yes. How did you figure it out? From that one conversation about lightning?'

'Just tell me what happened, Easton.'

'You know what's funny?' He kept tugging at the hem of his bathrobe like a woman with lousy legs in a too-short skirt. 'You always call me "East", and now you're saying "Easton".'

'What happened?'

My brother's bright-blue eyes filled with tears. 'I want you to know I really loved that man. There was only a sixteen-year age difference, but Sy was like a father to me.' He put his hands over his face and wept.

I sat on the edge of the bed and watched him. I wanted to be moved by his grief, but I had too many years in Homicide; I'd watched this movie, *The Crying Killer*, too many times.

People who commit murder are weird, and not just in their willingness to stick out their tongues at God, to steal His gift of life, to commit the one act that is unquestionably and universally wrong. No, what always got to me about murderers wasn't their evil, their distance from the rest of humanity, but their closeness to it. I'd watched mothers sob at the coffins of babies they'd clubbed to death; I'd heard boyfriends scream out in anguish at the funerals of the girlfriends they'd battered, strangled and, postmortem, raped. They were so vulnerable, so wounded, these killers. And I knew what would be coming next from my brother because, for me, this was the hundredth rerun of that scene. His eyes would plead: Pity me, help me, go easy on me, because I, the survivor, am also a victim of this monstrous crime. What a loss I've suffered! Look at these tears!

I played it with Easton the way I always played it. I gave him exactly what he felt he deserved: sympathy and support. 'It must be such hell,' I said.

'It is. Complete hell.' I shook my head as if I couldn't bear his – our – sadness.

What the fuck right did he have to kill? To fly off, with a new wardrobe of ties, to California, leaving Bonnie to spend the next twenty-five years paying for what he did?

I felt no sadness for my brother's stupid, wasted, empty life, and no guilt, not a goddamn twinge, about not having been a better older brother so I could have given him some values or shit like that. No, I just felt cold and very tired. 'Tell me how it happened, East,' I urged. Oh, did I sound full of compassion.

'You're calling me "East" again.'

I smiled. 'I know. Hey, you're my brother, aren't you? Come on. Let's talk. Tell me what went on. Was there any discussion about getting rid of Lindsay before that night at dailies?' Every now and then I slipped, but I knew to avoid the word 'kill' when questioning a killer.

'No. Nothing. I knew they were having troubles. Sy had turned off on her completely, went from hot to cold overnight. But I'm sure you know by now that he wasn't the confiding type.'

'But then there was that remark that if lightning struck Lindsay, if she died, the problems with *Starry Night* would be over. What happened after that?'

Easton didn't answer. He yanked at the hem of his bathrobe. It was one of those Saks uglies that my mother had bought on final, maximum markdown and saved for Christmas; it was some sort of strange, long-haired terry cloth, and grayish-brown, the color of a rag used for unpleasant chores.

'Who brought up getting Lindsay out of the picture? You or Sy?'

'I did, but it isn't the way it sounds. I just asked him some questions about the completion insurance. He said that if a star dies, the guarantors will pay to make another movie. If you're on a forty-day shooting schedule and she dies when you're fifteen days into it, the producers will get fifteen days of money. Well, minus a deductible of either a couple of hundred thousand or three days. But Sy said the coverage was quite fair.'

'But there was no suggestion he wanted you to facilitate matters?'

'No. Not then.'

My brother's face reflected a little hurt, as in why hadn't Sy leapt at his unstated offer right away. I had absolutely no doubt that Easton's questions about insurance were openings to Sy. Maybe Sy hadn't even thought about offing Lindsay before. Who knows? But all of a sudden, there it was, out in the electrified air: if lightning struck.

But Sy was no fool. He knew lightning was dangerous; only an expert could handle it. Like Mikey. Not a jerk like my brother. So he'd bypassed Easton, who was, most likely, doing everything but jumping up and down, waving his arms, calling out: Just ask me, Sy. I'm your boy. I'm your assistant producer. I'll do whatever you think needs doing. Sy, though, had gone to a pro. But the pro had been smarter than both Sy and Easton put together. He just said no.

'When did the matter come up again?'

'Wednesday night.'

I sat back on the bed, as though I were getting comfortable, all ready and eager to hear about my kid brother's first day of junior high. 'Tell me, how did he bring it up?' I asked.

'That's what amazed me, Steve! He was so unbelievably direct. He said, "We've got to terminate Lindsay." He already had the plane reservations and the appointments in LA, so he wanted it done over the weekend, when he was out there.' Easton was talking fast, freely, so I didn't stop him to ask how come he'd done it the day before the weekend. 'He didn't say, "Will you do it?" or anything. He just assumed I would.'

'Goes with the territory, right?'

'You don't have to be sarcastic.'

'Hey, East, I'm not. But I want us to talk straight, matter-of-fact. No bullshit between us. We're brothers.'

'Don't condescend to me, Steve. That's all I ask.'

'I'm not. Now, did he plan it out, or did you?'

'He had it all mapped out. He invented this imaginary

444

killer – a crazy fan. He would make believe Lindsay had gotten a letter from the fan, telling her he loved her, threatening to kill her if she didn't write back to him.'

'But she'd never gotten any letter like that?'

'Well, she *had* gotten crazy letters. All actors do. That was the beauty of it. She'd talked about them, to her agent, to some of Sy's friends at a dinner party a few weeks ago. Sy said that this murder would just seem to be a horrible extension of those letters. He'd tell the police she'd seemed a little upset about some new threatening letter, but that he'd never seen it. He'd say he kept after her to have one of the private investigation agencies who handle things for public figures look into it, and she kept saying fine, but she was busy with the movie and never bothered. And then *I* was supposed to say – but *not* volunteer it, only if the police asked me – that I'd overheard Lindsay telling him about the letter.'

'Was he going to write one for the police to find?'

'No. He said he'd given it a lot of thought, and almost did it, but it was just too chancy. Who knows what kind of scientific tests the police have these days? He didn't want to risk having it traced.'

What I couldn't get over was how clever Sy was. In the course of just a couple of days, he'd come up with a brilliant, almost foolproof scheme for getting rid of Lindsay. Except instead of convincing Mikey to carry out the plan, Sy had relied on a fool. So maybe, in the end, he wasn't such a brilliant mogul. He'd executive-produced his own death.

'Who decided on the rifle?' I asked.

'I did. He wanted me to stab her.'

'Wouldn't that be a mess?'

'Yes, but it would be very convincing,' Easton explained. 'Stab her once, to kill her, but then do it again and again, so it looked like the work of a mental case. Except I told him I didn't have the stomach for it.' I nodded with great seriousness, trying to show how much I cherished my brother's decency. 'But then I told him I'd been a pretty good shot as a kid. And he *loved* it that I already had the rifle, that we didn't have to go out and buy one. He was very edgy about leaving any kind of tracks.'

'I don't blame him. We've been checking gun dealers' records going back six months. He was a smart guy.'

'Yes, he was.' My brother got teary again. He sniffed.

'East, how did you have the balls to pick up a rifle that probably hadn't been touched for years? And then to rely on your being able to bag Lindsay with one or two shots?'

He gave me an I-thought-of-everything smile. 'Well, it did take some balls, as you say. But I did some fast planning. Although first I had to find the key to the padlock for the gun cabinet. That took me hours! You'll never guess where it was.'

'On top of the gun cabinet.'

'You *knew*?'

'Yeah. You should have given me a call. I could have saved you some time.' We both went chuckle-chuckle. 'So you just took it out, locked the cabinet and went ready, aim, fire?'

'No. I cleaned it.'

'Smart. Did you try it out?'

He inclined his head. 'I went to a range.'

446

'Which one?'

'The one up near Riverhead.'

'Right. I've been there. Where did you get the bullets?'

'At a hardware store right near there.'

'Took some target practice?'

'Yes. But I didn't need much. It's like riding a bike. You never really forget it.'

'No, you don't,' I agreed.

'And from fifty feet, it's so easy.'

'Did you and Sy plan where you'd stand?'

'Yes. It had a clear view of the whole pool, but the spot itself was sort of in shadows because of the porch. The only thing I had to worry about was to make sure no one else was around. Sy would be in LA, the cook would be off. Sy was worried Lindsay would invite some people over for drinks. Or Victor Santana for . . . you know.'

'What did he say to do if Santana was there?'

'To wait, see if he'd leave.'

'But if not? Get rid of him too?'

'Not on Saturday. If he was there, I should leave and come back on Sunday afternoon. There was a good chance he'd have left by then, to go over the next day's work. She'd be alone. But . . . You want me to be totally honest?'

'I really do, East.'

'Well, if not, get Santana too. It would look like the crazy fan saw them together and got jealous.'

I stood, walked to the open window, lifted the screen and leaned out for a minute. I pulled a couple of leaves off an overhanging branch. Then I turned back to my brother. 'It was a terrific plan.'

'It really was.'

447

'So how come it didn't work?'

Easton got real earnest. He crossed his legs, rested his elbow on his knee, braced his chin on the heel of his hand. 'That's what's so maddening. It *should* have worked. You know how impossible the traffic is Friday afternoons? I mean, the Long Island Expressway: the world's longest parking lot.' This quip hadn't been funny even in 1958, when it had probably been invented, and hadn't improved with either age or repetition. But I laughed as though hearing one of Western Civilization's Great Witticisms. 'Well,' Easton continued, apparently satisfied with my appreciation of his ability as a raconteur, 'the casting director was so crazed – she was casting another movie and two plays – that when I left, I realized she wouldn't have any idea of the time. And then I got finished at Sy's shirtmaker in about two seconds. So instead of taking the Expressway or the Northern State, I took every obscure east–west road ever built on the Island. I mean, if I'd been in your car, one of those potholes I went over would have swallowed me and the Jag whole!'

I laughed again. Such cleverness! Such superb humor! Of course, I'd done that audience appreciation bit more times than I could count. It was part of the job, not only turning a suspect into your friend but also turning yourself into the one person most able to savor his comic or tragic art. It had never bothered me before, this playacting. But now, every smile, every good-natured nod of understanding I offered, cost me too much.

A couple of times I had to fight down surges of insane vitality – like rushes of a mainlined drug – to go for him, hurt him, kick him off his chair, hold him down and smash his bland, handsome face against the floor. The killer was so civilized; the cop was so savage.

'So you pushed a little and got home earlier than you'd expected?'

'Yes, a little before four. I'd been in quite a state all day, as you can imagine. This was not going to be any ordinary weekend.'

'Doesn't sound like it,' I said.

'I said to myself: I can't wait. I have *got* to get this over with today. I cannot *stand* the tension. But I was smart. I knew I'd promised Sy to wait until Saturday or Sunday, to make sure he was safe in California. But I called MGM Grand and asked if the plane, the ten-fifteen morning flight, had taken off on time and they said yes, it had, and it had landed in LA a little after four New York time. That's how I knew' – he squared his shoulders; so proud – 'that he was there!'

'You didn't call him, just to make sure?'

The pride evaporated. Easton seemed to shrivel into a smaller, older man. 'I didn't want to seem overanxious, make Sy think I wasn't up to handling it. He said we should call each other, because that would be the normal thing to do, but not to go overboard.'

Easton was holding something back. I could tell. He had that insecure, twitchy-tentative Dan Quayle smile, the one he'd put on as a kid when my mother asked him how he was doing at school and he'd say 'Fine!' not mentioning that he'd gone through the mail, found the Failure Notice in geometry and torn it up before she got home from work. 'You're leaving something out, East,' I said good-naturedly. 'Come on. What is it?'

'Sy left a message on my machine.'

'What did it say?'

'That he was taking a helicopter and going to make the seven o'clock flight instead of the morning flight, and that he'd call when he got to the hotel. But you see, I didn't play back my messages when I got back from the city. To tell you the truth, I didn't even look at the machine to see if I had any. I can't believe I could have missed something so obvious. That's so sloppy. It's not like me to be sloppy. But I just changed out of my suit – '

'Into the thongs?'

'Yes. And a good pair of shorts and a shirt, so I'd look like I belonged.'

'Where was the rifle?'

'Oh, once I took it from the cabinet, I kept it in the trunk of my car, in one of those canvas sports duffels. Sy told me to do that, and to fill the duffel up with a bunch of clothes, so if anyone saw me, it would look like I was carrying a full weekend bag, not a rifle. He said carrying a rifle alone might call attention to the bag, make it look funny, bottom-heavy.'

'Then what?'

'I did everything Sy told me to do. Drove up to the side of the house, near the garage, to that space where there's room for three or four cars. You can't see it from the front. I opened the window, turned off the engine and sat for five minutes, by my watch.'

'He wanted you to make sure you didn't hear anyone.'

'Right. Then I got out, took the duffel and walked to that place right under the porch.'

'What time was it?'

'Sometime after four. I knew the *Starry Night* crew was doing the scene where Lindsay runs into the ocean, but I was praying she'd be very tired

450

and bitchy and they'd let her go the regular time. They'd done that the last two Fridays.'

'Because she was tired?'

'No. Because she was Sy's, and she was spoiled rotten.'

'Would they stop filming once she left?'

'No, they'd keep going till six or seven, but they were scheduled to do Nick Monteleone's reaction shots. Most actors want the actor they're playing a scene with to be there so they can have a true reaction, but believe me, Nick would have been *delighted* to have Lindsay go home. I was counting on that.'

'You weren't worried about Mrs Robertson?'

Easton clapped his hand to his forehead. 'Oh my God. That's right. It was Friday!'

'Forget about her?'

'Totally. Did she see me?'

'Come on, East. You know I can't tell you that.' I tried to make it sound as though we were kids playing a hot game of Candyland and I couldn't break any of the rules. Before he could think: This is no fucking Candyland, I pushed him further. 'So you were at that spot just under the porch. What happened?'

'Well, she was there. Standing alongside the pool, talking on the portable phone. Except it wasn't her.'

'You couldn't hear the conversation, I guess.'

'How could I? There's always the sound of the ocean, and there was classical music playing through all those speakers.'

'And his back was toward you.'

'Yes, and he had on a white robe, like the one Lindsay always wears. Well, there are robes like that all over the house, for guests, but it looked like Lindsay. It *did*, Steve.'

451

'I'm sure it did. Short, small – and with the hood up.'

My brother looked baffled. 'Why would he put the hood up?'

'He'd gone for a swim. His head was wet.'

'That was so dumb! If the hood had been down, I'd have known right away.'

'When did you know it was him?'

He swallowed hard. 'When I got home.'

'You shot him and then turned around and drove home?'

'Yes. That's what he told me to do. Drive right home, not too slow, not too fast. As if I could go fast, in that traffic! And then call him at the Bel-Air, and if he wasn't in, leave a message that I met with the casting director; that's if everything went okay. If there was any problem, I was supposed to leave a message that I was Fed Ex-ing another three copies of the script to him.' He uncrossed his legs and sat up straight. 'I can't tell you . . . those messages on my machine! First playing them back and hearing Sy's voice saying he was taking the seven o'clock flight. And then . . .' There was no doubt Easton was genuinely crying again, but overall his performance stank; he stood, walked over to the wall, rested his head against it and then pounded it with his fist, again and again. It was something Sy would have rejected in one of his movies. Overdone! Sy would have snapped at the director. Lose it! 'And then,' Easton went on, 'there was that kid, that PA saying that I "might want to know" that Sy was murdered at his house. God almighty!'

'I don't know what to say, East. What a trauma.'

He turned around and leaned against the wall for support. 'What do I do now, Steve?' He wiped his eyes with the lapel of his robe.

I ignored his question and asked one of my own. 'What about that screenplay you showed me? That *Night of the Matador* thing?'

'There were bookcases full of scripts in his house. I just grabbed one late Saturday, after the police left. You see, once I realized what I'd done, I wanted to emphasize that I had a wonderful, *continuing* relationship with Sy, that he was my mentor. I wanted all of you to think I could never kill him. Because what would I be without him?'

'Tell me about the Lindsay business,' I said. 'You were acting like you were crazy about her. You weren't, though, were you?'

'No. Of course not. I saw her for what she was.'

'But you pretended you were gone on her. Why?'

'I thought of that afterwards too,' he said, brightening a little at the recollection of his cleverness. 'If anyone remembered that talk at dailies about it being better if Lindsay was dead, and someone put two and two together . . . Well, they probably wouldn't have gotten four, but I thought if you – if the police – thought I was in love with her, I'd be counted out right away.'

'Actually, if we'd been adding and came up with Lindsay as the planned victim, you'd have been suspected right away.'

'Why?' He looked annoyed.

'Because you had an emotional tie to her.'

'That's stupid.'

'Well, that's cops for you. Stupid, unimaginative. The civil service mentality. We do it by the book.'

A barely tolerant shake of the head. 'Some book.'

'Well,' I said, 'book or no book, we got you. Didn't we, Easton?'

'No!' He rushed over and grabbed the shoulders of

my jacket. 'Steve, you're not going to do anything?' His mouth and eyes formed huge circles of astonishment. 'Steve! Are you crazy? I'm your brother.'

'I know.'

'How can you even think of doing something so terrible?'

'Get dressed,' I said. But he just stood there, right in front of me, still clutching the shoulder pads of my suit jacket. 'It's getting late. Come on.'

'*Think*. Think about what you want to do. What about Mother?'

'She's due home soon; you can explain to her what's happening. Or if she's stopping off someplace, I'll come back and sit down with her later. After I bring you in.'

He let his hands drop to his sides. He spoke softly, his voice full of gentleness and understanding. 'Steve, you have to understand. This will kill her.' The good son.

'I don't think so.'

'I know her much better than you do. She won't be able to survive a blow like this.'

'Yes, she will.'

'You think she's tough. She's not tough.'

'I know she's not. She's empty. She'll survive. Please, don't make me have to act any more like a cop than I'm already doing. Get dressed.'

Instead, he sat down in the straight-backed chair. 'What would it cost you to let me go?'

'Bonnie Spencer's life.'

'No, it wouldn't.'

'It would. There's a warrant out for her arrest.'

'Then how come she was here with you?'

'Because I was taking care of her. I didn't think she

should be arrested.' I looked outside. The light was softening, the prelude to dusk.

'Do you want me arrested? Do you want to see me go to jail?' I was still holding the two leaves in my hand. I ran my finger over a stem, up the veins. 'Steve!' Easton cried out. 'Who the hell is she? How can you want to protect her and not want to protect me?'

'I'm protecting her because she's innocent.' I spoke more to the leaves than to Easton.

'But I'm your brother.'

'You're a killer.'

Easton got up and went over to the window. I inched forward, in case he made a move to jump, but he just stared out at the muted light. 'Nothing can bring Sy back now,' he said.

'I know.'

He turned to face me. 'I don't want that woman to go to jail for me.'

'Since when?'

'Listen to me. We can work something out. I can give her an alibi.' I didn't react. 'Wait. Hold on a second. Just listen.' Easton rubbed his hands together. 'Okay, first of all, I'll tell them that Sy was very fond of her, that things with Lindsay had soured, and that he really seemed to be happy with the ex-wife again – and made no bones about it. All right. I didn't say anything earlier because I had such a crush on Lindsay I couldn't bring myself to say anything that would make her look bad. I'll admit I was terribly wrong. I'll apologize all over myself. So they won't think the ex had any reason to kill him. And I'll say . . . I know! I stopped at a pay phone on my way home from the city and called her about something. Like about her screenplay, and she was there, at home. Answered the phone and – '

'No.'

'Why not?'

'Because it's so full of holes it's a joke. Because she's decent and honorable and this fake-alibi crap would make her sick. And because she doesn't have to lie. We have our perp, Easton.'

'Is it all so black and white to you? Don't you see any grays?'

'I wish this weren't happening,' I said slowly.

'It doesn't have to.'

'What choice do I have? I'm a cop. I know there are a million shades of gray in the world. I see them. But I can only act on black and white.'

Easton came over and put his arms around me. A real hug. Except for my old man when he was soused, I don't think, until that moment, I ever had an embrace from any member of my family. 'Steve,' he said, 'I need you so much. My life has been one mistake after another. One charade after another. And now this. I don't know who I thought I was, who I was hoping to be, but I botched it. More than that. I did a terrible thing.' I stroked the back of his head. His hair was so much softer than mine. 'A wicked thing. I know that, but I'm so messed up, so weak, that I didn't have the courage to face up to it. Until now.' He let me out of his embrace and backed away. 'Just hear me out. Please?'

'Go ahead.'

'I know you think I'm useless, and you're right. I never, ever asked myself: What's really important? And even if I had, and came up with love or friendship or something like that, it probably wouldn't have mattered. You know that. I still would have gone for the razzle-dazzle. But now I really have to face the music. I can go to jail for the rest of my life. You *know* what jail is like.'

'Yes.'

'It's as bad as they say, isn't it?'

'Worse.'

'I swear to you, by all that's holy, that I'll spend the rest of my life making up for this terrible thing I've done.' He stood before me in that perfect gold and pink and blue light. 'I know we've never been close. But we are brothers. I'm not asking for special treatment, Steve, but I am asking – begging – that you give me a chance. Neither of us has ever had much of a shot at happiness, have we? I know I've lost that shot now, forever. But maybe I can have something, at least. Something from you.'

'What?'

'Forgiveness.'

I looked past him, out at the light. It was the magic hour. It comes and goes so fast. In movies, though, it returns just after dawn again, and then, once more, just before dusk. Twice a day, opportunities for wonder. But in real life, those moments that allow the possibility of grace hardly ever come at all.

If I brought my brother in, that would be the end of him. Forgiveness, he'd said. I could allow him the possibility of finding his own salvation. Because what he said was true: nothing could bring Sy back. And the beauty of it was, I wouldn't even have to stand in shamed silence and let Easton present his twisted, transparent alibi for Bonnie. I could just let him overpower me, escape, and disappear into a new life.

'Can't you forgive me, Steve? Haven't you ever done wrong?'

457

'Are you kidding? Most of my life has been wrong. That's no secret.'

'So? We're two of a kind.'

'No, East. Even when I was wrong, I knew there were laws. I knew there was a God.'

'But God forgives!'

'I know. And maybe God will forgive you, or has forgiven you. I can't know that. And maybe I, personally, can forgive you. But a life has been taken.'

'What are you saying?'

I let the leaves drop to the floor. 'I'm saying an apology won't do it.'

'You're going to send me to jail?'

'No; that's not my job. My job is much smaller. I'm just going to arrest you for the murder of Sy Spencer.'

'That's sending me to jail, damn it!'

'That's doing what I have to do.'

'I'll tell them you're setting me up to save that woman!'

'The rifle, East. The ballistics tests. Your rubber shoes with the Adelphi grass.'

'Someone else could have stolen that rifle. Or my thongs.'

'And put them back?'

'Try and prove it was me.'

'There was a man who bought bullets in a hardware store, who took target practice with an old Marlin .22 at a range near Riverhead the day before the murder. A nice-looking man in his late thirties. Don't you think witnesses will recognize his picture? Don't you think they'll be able to point him out in a lineup? In court?' I opened the door of his closet. 'Get ready, East. We have to go.'

He knew better than to try and fight me. He might

have tried to run for it, but being what he was, he just scurried around the bedroom for a few hysterical seconds. Then he got dressed. What else could he do? Rush outside on a Friday night in the height of the season, in a short, ugly, grayish-brown shaving robe? No. My brother had too much class.

CHAPTER 22

❦

In the end, I called Ray Carbone at home and asked him to please come over. I couldn't bring myself to handcuff Easton, lead him through the house and take him to Headquarters. Also, I realized that the fact the perpetrator had a brother on the Homicide Squad should be a single sentence in the last paragraph of the news story, not a nightmare headline – HOMICIDE COP ARRESTS KILLER BROTHER; MOTHER CRIES 'MY SON!'

My mother, of course, didn't cry anything of the sort. She came home around seven, a couple of minutes after Carbone arrived. She was a little tipsy from a martini or two with some rich lady with a dog name from her latest charity committee: Skip or Lolly or something. When she finally understood what was happening to Easton, she didn't scream or faint or have a heart attack.

All she did was collapse onto the couch. I got her some water. Right before he left, my brother bent down and kissed her goodbye. He aimed for her cheek but somehow missed and got her nose. He told her he was sorry, for her, not for himself. Carbone said he'd be at Headquarters all night if I needed him and then mumbled a few words to my mother about how bad he felt for her troubles.

I pulled up a footstool and sat in front of her. She was a fine-looking woman, with neat, even features, genuinely remarkable green-blue eyes, large and round, and a slender figure. After that momentary slump into the chair, her Emily Post spine straightened up. Her back was at a perfect ninety-degree angle to her lap. 'What should I do?' she asked me.

I told her Easton needed a lawyer. I went into the kitchen and looked up Bill Paterno's number in the phone book. She asked me if he was expensive, and I said yes, but he was very good, and when she called him, to tell him I'd speak to him tomorrow and work something out.

'Does that mean you'll pay for it?' she asked.

'Yeah.'

'Not "yeah".'

'Yes,' I said.

'Do you really think Easton did it?'

Yes, I told her, and explained the evidence we had against him. She asked if I thought a jury would find him guilty, and I said most likely Paterno would work out some sort of a deal with a guilty plea so there wouldn't have to be a trial, but that Easton would go to prison.

'I seem to have made a mess of things,' she said quietly.

'No. Easton did.'

Her excellent carriage became even more excellent. 'I can't understand it. He was never a troublemaker,' she said, not mentioning who had been. She looked so fine sitting there. Well, fine, but dated, like a 1952 Republican country club lady brought back in a time machine. Even now, stunned, probably anguished, all she was missing was a Rob Roy with a cherry and an Eisenhower button. 'He had no drive, but you can't fault someone for that.'

'No, you can't.'

'He didn't belong in the movie business,' she murmured. No one looked the way my mother did anymore. No one would take that amount of time to produce that strange, dated effect. She set her hair every night on fat wire rollers so it would fluff up and curl under in the chin-length pageboy she'd worn as long as I could remember. She tweezed away most of her eyebrows and redrew them into a thin, light-brown line. Her makeup was pale powder, red rouge and matching lipstick, a little smudged after her martinis. Her nails, filed short and oval, were red too. 'He should have gone into banking. Not that he could have been a bank president. I would never deceive myself. But he kept trying to be a salesman, and he couldn't sell anyone anything. And then movies, with all those people. They're so hard. He wasn't cut out to deal with them.'

'No, he wasn't.'

'I thought he liked that man, though. The one he killed.' I explained how Easton had been doing Sy's bidding, how he thought he was shooting at Lindsay. She asked: 'Why didn't he just say "I won't do it"?'

'I don't know, Mom.'

'Well, neither do I.'

I asked her if she wanted me to make her something to eat. No, she wasn't hungry, and she'd be all right. I knew that meant she wanted to be alone, but I asked if she wanted me to stay the night, or if she wanted to come over to my place. She said no thank you, and yes, she would call me if she needed me. I told her I'd be over first thing in the morning.

'It will be in all the newspapers,' she said. 'On the television too.'

'It will be a bad couple of days,' I said. 'Well, in terms of publicity. I know it will be bad for you for much longer than that.'

'Do you think they'll fire me?'

'No. You're too valuable to them. And I think most people will go out of their way to be understanding.'

'They won't understand, though. They'll just be polite. Deep down, they'll all think I did something wrong that made him turn out this way.' She stood. 'I'd like to be alone now.'

'I'm so sorry, Mom.'

And then she almost knocked me over. 'Why should you be sorry? It's not your fault. You didn't kill anyone. Your brother did.' But before I could work up a major case of filial sentiment and possibly reach for her hand, or gush, I'll always be there for you, Mom, no matter what, my mother added: 'I'd like you to leave.' So I said good night and so did she.

Ray Carbone and Thighs were getting Easton's confession on videotape, and it was being transmitted, live, in living but somewhat purplish color, on the TV monitor in Frank Shea's office. Carbone was asking, 'Did you pay cash for the bullets or charge them?' and my brother, showing how ingeniously he and Sy had planned Lindsay's murder, replied: 'Cash. Don't leave tracks: that was our motto.'

Shea started to explain to me, 'You'll see the beginning of the tape, how we read him his rights. We gave him every chance — '

I cut him off. 'A guy wants to talk, you can't muzzle him.'

'How's your mother taking it?'

'She's numb.' I didn't mention that the condition was probably congenital. But then, because Shea and I had been at each other's throats over the case and there was so much bad blood, I decided I'd better show him I was a decent guy. 'I'd be with her now, but she asked me to leave. Really wanted to be alone. I think she probably was going to fall apart and wanted to spare me.' That image of my mother going out of control and wanting to protect me had nothing much to do with reality, but it did make us sound like a normal family. Well, until you looked at that talking head on the TV screen who was telling Carbone that yes, he'd cleaned the .22 at home, but when he got to the range the lever was so stiff he could hardly move it, so one of the men there – a black man with a goatee – helped him. I said to Shea: 'Listen to him. Jesus, I can't believe we're from the same gene pool.'

He got up and walked to the TV. His gold chains clanged. 'I'll catch this later,' he said. 'Unless you really want to watch, but between you and me' – he was using his Compassionate Leader voice – 'I think you should spare yourself.'

'You can turn it off,' I agreed.

He did and then came back, stood behind my chair and put his hand on my shoulder. 'You want to take some vacation time, Steve?'

'Probably.'

'You've got it. Ray thinks you ought to see Dr Nettles, the new department shrink, get some counseling. Preventive medicine. That's up to you. Ray says she's good. I met her. She's got a face like a bulldog.' He clanged his way back to his big leather chair and sat down. 'Now listen, you've got my apology. The drinking thing. The saying you're in love with that

Spencer woman.' I started to worry. What if, finally, it had all been too much, even for Bonnie? What if, now that it was over, she wanted to leave it all behind, go back to her mountains? 'That fucking Robby Kurz,' he breathed.

'Robby's in the squad room,' I said.

'I know. Did you have it out with him?'

'No. I didn't even go in. I'm wiped. My fuse is so short I'd blow in two seconds, and I don't want to do that. There are more serious matters than him saying I'm a drunk. And they're your territory, not mine.'

'The Bonnie hair,' he said.

'Yeah, the Bonnie hair.'

He picked up his phone, pressed the intercom and said, 'I'd like to see you, Robby. No, now.' He hung up and looked me right in the eye. 'Listen, I'm sympathetic to what you're going through. A family tragedy. But I won't mince words. The Suffolk County Police Department is a paramilitary organization. You know what that means?'

'You're the captain and I'm not.'

'That's right. Sometimes you seem to have some trouble with that concept. Now, you have a personal beef against this guy, and we may have a departmental beef. Guess which gets priority tonight when he walks through –' At that instant, Robby walked through the door. 'Sit down, Robby.' It was an order, not an invitation, and Robby, after nodding at me, sat. Sitting across from Frank Shea's black-Irish, lounge-lizard good looks, Robby looked even puffier and pastier than usual; he was starting to resemble one of his crullers. 'You almost ruined Brady's career,' Shea said.

'I didn't mean to.'

'So how come you called him a drunk?'

465

'Because I thought he was.'

'Why?'

'I thought he was acting in an erratic manner, and I thought I smelled liquor on him.'

'How was I erratic, you weasel son of a bitch fucker?'

'Shut up, Brady,' Shea said. Then, remembering I was in the middle of a Major Personal Crisis, he added, 'Please.' He turned back to Robby. 'I won't call you a liar. But I question your powers of observation.'

'I know the tests say I was wrong. So I apologize.'

No one seemed to expect me to accept or decline the apology, so I just sat back and shut my eyes for a second. I wanted to call Gideon and find out how Bonnie was. I wanted to tell him my back door was open, so they could get Moose, who might need more water or a walk.

'Let's get to the Bonnie hair, Robby,' Shea was saying. 'We had *everyone* on this case. Our best people. We examine, reexamine, re-reexamine the area where the perp stood.' He paused, to indicate that out of deference to me he was not using the perp's name. 'We find zip in the hair department. And then the next week: A miracle! Crucial evidence! One of Bonnie Spencer's hairs — with a root, no less, so we can get a DNA reading on it.'

'Are you saying I planted it, Frank?' Robby asked.

'I'm saying Ray Carbone checked the plastic thing we got back from the lab and the seal looked a little funny and one hair seemed to be missing. Would you call it a plant?'

'No. Obviously the lab lost a hair. You of all people should know they're not perfect.'

I thought: What if Bonnie doesn't want me? What if she thinks I'm too unstable?

'Why would Bonnie Spencer's hair be at the exact spot the perp stood if Bonnie Spencer wasn't the perp?'

'Maybe she just passed by.' You could hardly hear Robby's voice anymore. And he was slipping lower and lower into his chair. The only part of him holding up was his sprayed hairdo.

'That's your explanation?' Shea boomed. 'She was just taking a stroll around the six acres of grounds and her hair caught on that one infinitesimal little spot?' Robby didn't reply. Shea leaned forward. 'Let me ask you something. Do you think you're any better than any of the shits we lock up?'

'I deserve a fair hearing.' It sounded like Robby had already talked to a lawyer.

'I'm sure the department will give you one.'

'Thank you.'

'But as far as Homicide goes, you know what?'

'Frank — '

'Pack up your pencils.'

As far as I know, Robby Kurz did not pack up his pencils. He certainly didn't say goodbye. He just left for good.

I took my brother's tinny excuse for a convertible, a Mustang, went back to my house and got Moose. She sat in the passenger seat, raised her snout and let the rush of air blow her hairy ears back. When we stopped at a light, she gave some Manhattan yuppies in a Volvo station wagon the patronizing glance of a glamorous dame who only travels top-down.

I pulled into Bonnie's driveway. At last the bureaucratic wheels were turning: they had discontinued the surveillance. Her Jeep was in the garage. The house was dark, and the front and back doors were locked. I rang the bell a few times, but there was no answer. I knew she had to be at Gideon's, but I was scared. I kept thinking crazy things, like what if she'd gone home, tripped on one of her stupid scatter rugs and cracked open her head and was lying inside, dead. No. Then my car would still be there. But what if she'd hit an oil patch and the Jag went out of control and she'd gone off a bridge, or gone up in flames? The only sounds came from wild ducks, and from the forced laughter over cocktails on the back deck at her neighbor's, Wendy Bubbleface.

It took me about ten minutes to get Moose back in the car. She was home and saw no reason to leave. She took a dump, chased a rabbit, then lay down on the front lawn. I made an ass of myself, clapping my hands and calling, 'Here, girl! C'mon, Moose! Oooh, let's go for a ride!' and whistling. She wouldn't budge. At last, I hefted her, all hundred pounds of her, and carried her back to the car.

It was dark when I finally found Gideon's house, one of those renovated barns set back a couple of hundred feet from the road. There was a small sign on a strip of barn siding that said 'Friedman-Sterling,' but Friedman and Sterling had planted so much fucking English ivy that I drove past it at least five times until I spotted it.

I opened the car door, but before I could get out, Moose leapt over me, then sat, waiting, tongue dangling, for me to join her. But I couldn't get out. I reknotted my tie, then loosened it, then took it off, took my jacket off, rolled up my shirt sleeves, then got dressed again.

Maybe she'd taken an overdose of sleeping pills,

thinking I was going to marry Lynne and she'd never see me again.

I wanted to hold her in my arms. I wanted to take her over to Germy's to watch the DiMaggio video and tell him, This is my girl.

I thought, I shouldn't be driving my brother's damn car, since Easton had stowed the rifle in the trunk. Now it had my prints and dog hair. The lab guys would be pissed.

My heart began to pound. She'd be in there, but she'd refuse to see me, and Gideon's boyfriend would stand at the door, his hand on his hip, and sneer: 'Bonnie's flying to the Coast tomorrow to sell her story for a CBS Movie of the Week and she's on the phone with her new agent and cannot be disturbed. Ta-ta.'

Or she wouldn't be there. She'd be on her way to the airport, to go to Utah. She'd stay with one of her brothers for a while, until her house was sold, then buy a cabin ten thousand feet high in some mountain by a trout stream. She wouldn't answer my letters or phone calls. I'd finally go out there and track her down, but she'd run out the back door up the mountains and wouldn't come back until I'd gone. The next spring, after the thaw, they'd find her. Dead. She'd frozen in February. She'd forgotten how hard winters in the mountains could be. She hadn't chopped enough wood for the stove.

I was so upset by the thought of her decomposing body that I didn't see Gideon until he was right next to the car. 'Is Bonnie here?' I demanded. 'Is she all right?'

'She's fine,' Gideon said cautiously. I guess I looked a little nuts. 'She's sleeping.' Moose, the town slut, had already transferred her allegiance to Gideon and was licking his hand.

'I guess she must be pretty tired,' I mumbled.

'Do you want to come in for a minute?'

For a barn, it was a nice place, with a vaulted ceiling and a lot of beams going to interesting places. Gideon introduced me to his friend, Jeff, who looked like a bouncer in a very rough nightclub. He stayed just long enough to shake hands, say 'Pleased to make yo' 'quaintance' and give me a thorough once-over; my guess was he could hardly wait for me to leave, so he and Gideon could launch into an exhaustive analysis.

A giant black iron chandelier hung from the main beam; it had cut-out sheep and cows and pigs all over it. Upstairs, there were closed doors off a landing that had once been the hayloft. 'Bonnie's in the middle room,' Gideon said, when he saw me looking up. I thought he would tell me not to trifle with her affections or something, but he just said how sorry he was about it being my brother. I told him my mother was calling Paterno, but that my brother had already given a videotaped confession — probably less because he wanted to make a clean breast of things than that he wanted to be thought of as pleasant company. And I told him about Easton's sick pride, that he'd planned the whole thing with Sy Spencer, big shot. Just the two of them. Sy and Easton, partners. I said I couldn't believe my brother had been so willing to let Bonnie take the fall for him. Gideon said, Take it easy. It's over now. He added that Shea had called Paterno and said they were rescinding the warrant and to tell Mrs Spencer sorry for any inconvenience.

'Do you think she'll be all right?' I asked him.

'She's strong.'

'I know.'

'But it's going to take a long time.'

'Do you mind if I go up and see her?' I asked.

'Once we knew it was officially over, after Bill Paterno called . . .' Gideon hesitated. 'Bonnie said you might drop by. She asked me to thank you for all you've done for her, but that you and she had agreed earlier that it would be best if you didn't see each other again.'

'I want to see her.'

'And I want to protect her.' We tried to stare each other down. 'It seems we're at an impasse,' he said, 'and since it's an impasse on my territory, I'm going to have to ask you to leave.' He stood.

So did I. 'I just want to tell her something.'

'I don't think that would be advisable.'

'Fuck you, Friedman.'

'Fuck *you*, Brady.'

I tried to count up to ten, to think of something else to say, but I only made it to two. 'Look, I love her.'

'You love her?' Gideon repeated. 'You must be a very loving man. You love the other one too.'

'If it's any of your goddamned business, I don't love the other one, and as a matter of fact and of law, Counselor, the other one isn't the other one anymore and the position is vacant. Now can I go up and see Bonnie?'

'Be my guest,' he said.

I could sense her waking as I opened the door. I came in and sat on the edge of the bed. 'You're beautiful,' I said.

'Sure. It's pitch black in here.' Bonnie stuck her hand out and groped for a lamp. She turned it on and squeezed her eyes shut at the light. She looked like Mr Magoo. 'Now say it.'

'You're beautiful. I love you. What was the third thing?'

'I'm a truly fine person.' The base of the lamp was a big china chicken. She turned it off.

'You're a truly fine person,' I said.

'I told Gideon not to let you up here.'

'I told him I was going to tell you I loved you, so I became his pal. Anything I want. His house is my house. His chicken lamp is my chicken lamp.' I turned it on again and pulled down the sheet a little. She'd taken off my T-shirt.

She pulled the sheet all the way up. 'Listen, I guess you'll be hearing this a lot, but I'm sorry about your brother. I'm sure it's going to be very painful for your family, and it's too bad you can't be spared that.'

'Thank you. It's too bad you couldn't have been spared your pain.'

'Thank you,' she said. 'I don't want to seem insensitive, but I'd like you to leave now.'

'Why? Are you going to cry or something?'

Bonnie gave me an angry nudge. Some nudge. It practically knocked me off the bed. 'You want to hang around and watch?'

'Yeah.'

'Well, I don't want you to. I want you to go.'

'I can't. I promised Gideon I'd ask you to marry me.'

'Well, ask me and then get out.'

'All right. Will you marry me?'

Somehow, all of a sudden, she knew. She didn't make any wisecracks about my having a previous engagement. She didn't tell me to leave. She just said 'Yes,' but then she told me I couldn't kiss her because she had sleep breath. I kissed her anyway. It was a sweet and beautiful kiss. After it was over, she asked, 'Am I *really* beautiful? Objectively.'

'No.'

'Am I *really* a truly fine person?'

'You're not bad.'

I stood up, took off my clothes and got into bed.

'Do you *really* love me?'

'More than anything in the world, Bonnie.'

'I've known that for years, Stephen.'

And together we turned off the chicken lamp, and we began our life.